MIDNIGHT'S CHILDREN

Salman Rushdie's novels include *Grimus*, *Midnight's Children*, *Shame*, *The Satanic Verses*, *Haroun and the Sea of Stories*, *The Moor's Last Sigh*, *The Ground Beneath Her Feet*, *Fury*, *Shalimar the Clown* and *The Enchantress of Florence*. He has also published one collection of short stories, entitled *East, West*, and four works of non-fiction – *The Jaguar Smile*, *Imaginary Homelands*, *Step Across This Line* and, as co-editor, *The Vintage Book of Indian Writing*.

He has received many awards for his writing, including the European Union's Aristeion Prize for Literature. He is a fellow of the Royal Society of Literature and Commandeur des Arts et des Lettres. In 2008 *Midnight's Children* was adjudged the 'Best of the Booker', the best novel to have won the Booker Prize in its forty year history.

ALSO BY SALMAN RUSHDIE

Fiction

Grimus
Shame
The Satanic Verses
Haroun and the Sea of Stories
East, West
The Moor's Last Sigh
The Ground Beneath Her Feet
Fury
Shalimar the Clown
The Enchantress of Florence

Non-fiction

The Jaguar Smile
Imaginary Homelands
Step Across This Line

Plays

Haroun and the Sea of Stories
(with Tim Supple and David Tushingham)
Midnight's Children
(with Tim Supple and Simon Reade)

Anthology

The Vintage Book of Indian Writing
(co-editor)

SALMAN RUSHDIE

Midnight's Children

VINTAGE BOOKS
London

Published by Vintage 2008

4 6 8 10 9 7 5 3

Excerpts from the Koran came from the Penguin Classics
edition, translated by N. J. Dawood, copyright © 1956, 1959,
1966, 1968, 1974. Reprinted by kind permission of
Penguin Books Ltd

First published in Great Britian in 1981 by Jonathan Cape
First published by Vintage in 1995

Vintage

www.vintage-books.co.uk

Addresses for companies within The Random House Group
Limited can be found at: www.randomhouse.co.uk/offices.htm

The Random House Group Limited Reg. No. 954009

A CIP catalogue record for this book
is available from the British Library

ISBN 9780099529781

The Random House Group Limited supports The Forest
Stewardship Council (FSC), the leading international forest
certification organisation. All our titles that are printed on
Greenpeace approved FSC certified paper carry the FSC logo.
Our paper procurement policy can be found at:
www.rbooks.co.uk/environment

Printed and bound in Great Britain by
CPI Bookmarque, Croydon CR0 4TD

For Zafar Rushdie
who, contrary to all expectations,
was born in the afternoon

Contents

Introduction

In 1975 I published my first novel, *Grimus,* and decided to use the seven-hundred-pound advance to travel in India as cheaply as possible for as long as I could make the money last, and on that journey of fifteen-hour bus rides and humble hostelries *Midnight's Children* was born. It was the year that India became a nuclear power and Margaret Thatcher was elected leader of the Conservative Party and Sheikh Mujib, the founder of Bangladesh, was murdered; when the Baader-Meinhof Gang was on trial in Stuttgart and Bill Clinton married Hillary Rodham and the last Americans were evacuated from Saigon and Generalissimo Franco died. In Cambodia it was the Khmer Rouge's bloody Year Zero. E.L. Doctorow published *Ragtime* that year, and David Mamet wrote *American Buffalo,* and Eugenio Montale won the Nobel Prize. And just after my return from India, Mrs Indira Gandhi was convicted of election fraud, and one week after my twenty-eighth birthday she declared a State of Emergency and assumed tyrannical powers. It was the beginning of a long period of darkness which would not end until 1977. I understood almost at once that Mrs G. had somehow become central to my still-tentative literary plans.

I had wanted for some time to write a novel of childhood, arising from my memories of my own childhood in Bombay. Now, having drunk deeply from the well of India, I conceived a more ambitious plan. I remembered a minor character named Saleem Sinai, born at the midnight moment of Indian independence, who had appeared in the abandoned draft of a still-born novel called *The Antagonist*. As I placed Saleem at the centre of my new scheme I understood that his time of birth would oblige me immensely to increase the size of my canvas. If he and India were to be paired, I would need to tell the story of both twins. Then Saleem, ever a striver for meaning, suggested to me that the whole of modern Indian history happened as it did because of him; that history, the life of his nation-twin, was somehow *all his fault*. With that immodest proposal the novel's characteristic tone of voice, comically assertive, unrelentingly garrulous, and with, I hope, a growing pathos in its narrator's increasingly tragic over-claiming, came into being. I even made the boy and the country identical twins. When the sadistic geography teacher Emil Zagallo, giving the boys a lesson in 'human geography,' compares Saleem's nose to the Deccan peninsula, the cruelty of his joke is also, obviously, mine.

There were many problems along the way, most of them literary, some of them urgently practical. When we returned from India I was broke. The novel in my head was clearly going to be long and strange and take quite a while to write and in the meanwhile I had no money. As a result I was forced back into the world of advertising. Before we left I had worked for a year or so as a copywriter at the London office of the Ogilvy & Mather agency, whose founder, David Ogilvy, immortally instructed us that 'the consumer is not a moron, she is your wife,' and whose creative director (and my boss) was Dan Ellerington, a man of rumoured Romanian origins with a command of English that was, let us say, eccentric, so that, according to mirthful company legend, he once had to be forcibly restrained from presenting to the Milk Marketing Board a successor campaign to the famous 'Drinka pinta milka day' which would be based on the amazing, the positively Romanian slogan, 'Milk goes down like a dose of salts'. In those less hard-nosed times Ogilvy's was prepared to employ a few oddball creative people on a part-time basis, and I managed to persuade them to re-hire me as one of that happy breed. I worked two or three days a week, essentially job-sharing with another part-timer, the writer Jonathan Gathorne-Hardy, author of *The Rise and Fall of the British Nanny*. On Friday nights I would come home to Kentish Town from the agency's offices near Waterloo Bridge, take a long hot bath, wash the week's commerce away, and emerge – or so I told myself – as a novelist. As I look back, I feel a touch of pride at my younger self's dedication to literature, which gave him the strength of mind to resist the blandishments of the enemies of promise. The sirens of ad-land sang sweetly and seductively, but I thought of Odysseus lashing himself to the mast of his ship, and somehow stayed on course.

Still, advertising taught me discipline, forcing me to learn how to get on with whatever task needed getting on with, and ever since those days I have treated my writing simply as a job to be done, refusing myself all (well, most) luxuries of artistic temperament. And it was at my desk at Ogilvy's that I remember becoming worried that I didn't know what my new novel was to be called. I took several hours off from the important work of coming up with campaigns for fresh cream cakes ('Naughty but nice'), Aero chocolate bars ('Irresistibubble'), and the *Daily Mirror* newspaper ('Look into the *Mirror* tomorrow – you'll like what you see') to solve the problem. In the end I had two titles and couldn't choose between them: *Midnight's Children* and *Children of Midnight*. I typed them out one after the other, over and over, and then all at once I understood that there was no contest, that *Children of Midnight* was a banal title and *Midnight's Children* a good one. To know the title was also to understand the book better, and after that it became easier, a little easier, to write.

I have written and spoken elsewhere about my debt to the oral narrative traditions of India; also to those great Indian novelists, Jane Austen and Charles Dickens – Austen for her portraits of brilliant women caged by the social convention of their time, women whose Indian counterparts I knew well; Dickens for his great, rotting, Bombay-like city, and his ability to root his larger-than-life characters and surrealist imagery in a sharply observed, almost hyper-realistic background, out of which the comic and fantastic elements of his work seemed to grow organically, becoming intensifications of, and not escapes from, the real world. I have probably said enough, too, about my interest in creating a literary idiolect that allowed the rhythms and thought patterns of Indian languages to blend with the idiosyncrasies of 'Hinglish' and 'Bambaiyya', the polyglot street-slang of Bombay. The novel's interest in the slippages and distortions of memory will also, I think, be evident enough to the reader. This may, however, be an appropriate moment to give thanks to the original people from whom my fictional characters sprang: my family, my *ayah* Miss Mary Menezes and my childhood friends.

My father was so angry about the character of 'Ahmed Sinai' that he refused to speak to me for many months; then he decided to 'forgive' me, which annoyed me so much that for several more months I refused to speak to *him*. I had been more worried about my mother's reaction to the book, but she immediately understood that it was 'just a story – Saleem isn't you, Amina isn't me, they're all just characters,' thus demonstrating that her level head was a lot more use to her than my father's Cambridge University education in English literature was to him. My sister Sameen, who really was called 'the brass monkey' as a girl, was also happy with the use I'd made of my raw material, even though some of that raw material was her. Of the reactions of my boyhood friends and schoolmates Arif Tayabali, Darab and Fudli Talyarkhan, Keith Stevenson and Percy Karanjia I can't be sure, but I must thank them for having contributed bits of themselves (not always the best bits) to the characters of Sonny Ibrahim, Eyeslice and Hairoil, and Fat Perce and Glandy Keith. Evie Burns was born out of an Australian girl, Beverly Burns, the first girl I ever kissed: the real Beverly was no bicycle queen, though, and I lost touch with her after she returned to Australia. Masha Miovic the champion breast-stroker owed something to the real-life Alenka Miovic, but a couple of years ago I received a letter about *Midnight's Children* from Alenka's father in Serbia, in which he mentioned a little crushingly that his daughter had no memory of ever having met me during her childhood years in Bombay. So it goes. Between the adored and the adorer falls the shadow.

And as for Mary Menezes, my second mother, who never really loved a revolutionary nursing-home employee or swapped any babies at birth, who lived to a hundred, who never married and always called me her son, she was illiterate, even though she spoke seven or eight languages, so she didn't read the book, but did tell me, one afternoon in Bombay in 1982, how proud she was of its success. If she had any objection to what I'd made her character do, she didn't mention it.

I reached the end of *Midnight's Children* in mid-1979 and sent it to my friend and editor Liz Calder at Jonathan Cape. I afterwards learned that the first reader's report had been brief and forbiddingly negative. 'The author should concentrate on short stories until he has mastered the novel form.' Liz asked for a second report, and this time I was luckier, because the second reader, Susannah Clapp, was enthusiastic; as, after her, was another eminent publishing figure, the editor Catherine Carver. Liz bought the book, and soon afterwards so did Bob Gottlieb at Alfred Knopf. I quit my part-time copywriting job. (I had moved on from Ogilvy & Mather to another agency, Ayer Barker Hegemann.) 'Oh,' the Creative Director said when I tendered my resignation, 'you want a rise?' No, I explained, I was just giving notice as required so that I could leave and be a full-time writer. 'I see,' he said. 'You want a *big* rise.' But on the night *Midnight's Children* won the Booker, he sent me a telegram of congratulations. 'One of us made it,' it read.

Liz Calder's editing saved me from making at least two bad mistakes. The manuscript as originally submitted contained a second 'audience' character, an off-stage woman journalist to whom Saleem was sending the written pages of his life story which he also read aloud to the 'mighty pickle-woman', Padma. All the book's readers at Cape agreed that this character was redundant, and I'm extremely glad I took their advice. Liz also helped me untangle a knot in the time-line. In the submitted manuscript the story jumped from the Indo-Pakistani war of 1965 to the end of the Bangladesh war, then circled back to tell the story of Saleem's rôle in that conflict, caught up with itself at the surrender of the Pakistani army, and then went on. Liz felt that there were too many temporal shifts here, and the reader's concentration was broken by them. I agreed to re-structure the story chronologically, and, again, am very relieved that I did. The rôle of the great publishing editor is often effaced by the editor's modesty. But without Liz Calder, *Midnight's Children* would have been something rather less than she helped it to become.

The novel's publication was delayed by a series of industrial strikes, but in the end it was published in London in early April 1981, and on April 6th my first wife Clarissa Luard and I threw a party at our friend Tony Stokes's little art gallery in Langley Court, Covent Garden, to celebrate it. I still have the invitation, tucked into my first-received copy of the novel, and can remember feeling, above all, relieved. When I finished the book, I suspected that I might at last have written something good, but I was not sure if anyone else would agree, and I told myself that if the book were generally disliked it would mean that I probably didn't know what a good book was, and should stop wasting my time trying to write one. So there was a lot riding on the novel's reception, and, fortunately, the reviews were good; hence the high spirits in Covent Garden that spring night.

In the West people tended to read *Midnight's Children* as a fantasy, while in India people thought of it as pretty realistic, almost a history book. ('I could have written your book,' one reader told me when I was lecturing in India in 1982. 'I know all that stuff.') But it was wonderfully well liked almost everywhere, and changed its author's life. One reader who didn't care for it, however, was Mrs Indira Gandhi, and in 1984, three years after its publication – she was Prime Minister again by this time – she brought an action against it, claiming to have been defamed by one single sentence. It appeared in the penultimate paragraph of chapter 28, 'A wedding', a paragraph in which Saleem provides a brief account of Mrs Gandhi's life. This was it: 'It has often been said that Mrs Gandhi's younger son Sanjay accused his mother of being responsible, through her neglect, for his father's death; and that this gave him an unbreakable hold over her, so that she became incapable of denying him anything.' Tame stuff, you might think, not really the kind of thing a thick-skinned politician would usually sue a novelist for mentioning, and an odd choice of *casus belli* in a book that excoriated Indira for the many crimes of the Emergency. After all, it was a thing much said in India in those days, had often been in print, and was indeed reprinted prominently in the Indian press ('The sentence Mrs Gandhi is afraid of' read one front-page headline) after she brought her action for defamation. Yet she sued nobody else.

Before the book's publication, Cape's lawyers had been worried about my criticisms of Mrs Gandhi and had asked me to write them a letter in support of the claims I was making. In this letter I justified the text to their satisfaction, except with regard to one sentence which, as I said, was hard to substantiate, as it was about three people, two of whom were dead, while the third would be the one suing us. However, I argued, as I was clearly characterizing the information as gossip, and as it had been printed before, we should be all right. The lawyers agreed; and then, three years later, this one sentence, the novel's Achilles heel, was the very sentence Mrs Gandhi tried to spear. This was not, in my view, a coincidence.

The case never came to court. The law of defamation is highly technical, and to repeat a defamatory rumour is to commit the defamation oneself, so technically we were in the wrong. Mrs Gandhi was not asking for damages, only for the sentence to be removed from future editions of the book. The only defence we had was a high-risk route: we would have had to argue that her actions during the Emergency were so heinous that she could no longer be considered a person of good character, and could therefore not be defamed. In other words, we would have had, in effect, to put her on trial for her misdeeds. But if, in the end, a British court refused to accept that the Prime Minister of India was not a woman of good character, then we would be, not to put too fine a point upon it, royally screwed. Unsurprisingly, this was not the strategy which Cape wished to follow – and when it became clear that she was also willing to accept that this was her sole complaint against the book, I agreed to settle the matter. It was after all an amazing admission she was making, considering what the Emergency chapters of *Midnight's Children* were about. Her willingness to make such an admission felt to me like an extraordinary validation of the novel's portrait of those Emergency years. The reaction to the settlement in India was not favourable to the Prime Minister. A few short weeks later, stunningly, she was dead, assassinated on October 31st, 1984, by her Sikh bodyguards. 'All of us who love India,' I wrote in a newspaper article, 'are in mourning today.' In spite of our disagreements, I meant every word.

This is by now an old story. I rehearse it here in part because I worried from the beginning that incorporating such momentarily 'hot' contemporary material in the novel was a risk – and by that I meant a *literary* risk, not a legal one. One day, I knew, the subject of Mrs Gandhi and the Emergency would cease to be current, would no longer exercise anyone overmuch, and at that point, I told myself, my novel would either get worse – because it would lose the power of topicality – or else it would get better – because once the topical had faded, the novel's literary architecture would stand alone, and even, perhaps, be better appreciated. Clearly, I hoped for the latter, but there was no way to be sure. The fact that *Midnight's Children* is still of interest twenty-five years after it first appeared is, therefore, reassuring.

In 1981, Margaret Thatcher was British Prime Minister, the American hostages in Iran were released, President Reagan was shot and wounded, there were race riots across Britain, the Pope was shot and wounded, Picasso's *Guernica* went back to Spain, and President Sadat of Egypt was assassinated. It was the year of V.S. Naipaul's *Among the Believers* and Robert Stone's *A Flag for Sunrise* and John Updike's *Rabbit is Rich*. Like all novels, *Midnight's Children* is a product of its moment in history, touched and shaped by its time in ways which its author cannot wholly know. I am very glad that it still seems like a book worth reading in this very different time. If it can pass the test of another generation or two, it may endure. I will not be around to see that. But I am happy that I saw it leap the first hurdle.

Salman Rushdie, *December 25th, 2005, London*

Book One

The perforated sheet

I was born in the city of Bombay . . . once upon a time. No, that won't do, there's no getting away from the date: I was born in Doctor Narlikar's Nursing Home on August 15th, 1947. And the time? The time matters, too. Well then: at night. No, it's important to be more . . . On the stroke of midnight, as a matter of fact. Clock-hands joined palms in respectful greeting as I came. Oh, spell it out, spell it out: at the precise instant of India's arrival at independence, I tumbled forth into the world. There were gasps. And, outside the window, fireworks and crowds. A few seconds later, my father broke his big toe; but his accident was a mere trifle when set beside what had befallen me in that benighted moment, because thanks to the occult tyrannies of those blandly saluting clocks I had been mysteriously handcuffed to history, my destinies indissolubly chained to those of my country. For the next three decades, there was to be no escape. Soothsayers had prophesied me, newspapers celebrated my arrival, politicos ratified my authenticity. I was left entirely without a say in the matter. I, Saleem Sinai, later variously called Snotnose, Stainface, Baldy, Sniffer, Buddha and even Piece-of-the-Moon, had become heavily embroiled in Fate – at the best of times a dangerous sort of involvement. And I couldn't even wipe my own nose at the time.

Now, however, time (having no further use for me) is running out. I will soon be thirty-one years old. Perhaps. If my crumbling, over-used body permits. But I have no hope of saving my life, nor can I count on having even a thousand nights and a night. I must work fast, faster than Scheherazade, if I am to end up meaning – yes, meaning – something. I admit it: above all things, I fear absurdity.

And there are so many stories to tell, too many, such an excess of intertwined lives events miracles places rumours, so dense a commingling of the improbable and the mundane! I have been a swallower of lives; and to know me, just the one of me, you'll have to swallow the lot as well. Consumed multitudes are jostling and shoving inside me; and guided only by the memory of a large white bedsheet with a roughly circular hole some seven inches in diameter cut into the centre, clutching at the dream of that holey, mutilated square of linen, which is my talisman, my open-sesame, I must commence the business of remaking my life from the point at which it really began, some thirty-two years before anything as obvious, as *present*, as my clock-ridden, crime-stained birth.

(The sheet, incidentally, is stained too, with three drops of old, faded redness. As the Quran tells us: *Recite, in the name of the Lord thy Creator, who created Man from clots of blood.*)

One Kashmiri morning in the early spring of 1915, my grandfather Aadam Aziz hit his nose against a frost-hardened tussock of earth while attempting to pray. Three drops of blood plopped out of his left nostril, hardened instantly in the brittle air and lay before his eyes on the prayer-mat, transformed into rubies. Lurching back until he knelt with his head once more upright, he found that the tears which had sprung to his eyes had solidified, too; and at that moment, as he brushed diamonds contemptuously from his lashes, he resolved never again to kiss earth for any god or man. This decision, however, made a hole in him, a vacancy in a vital inner chamber, leaving him vulnerable to women and history.

4

Unaware of this at first, despite his recently completed medical training, he stood up, rolled the prayer-mat into a thick cheroot, and holding it under his right arm surveyed the valley through clear, diamond-free eyes.

The world was new again. After a winter's gestation in its eggshell of ice, the valley had beaked its way out into the open, moist and yellow. The new grass bided its time underground; the mountains were retreating to their hill-stations for the warm season. (In the winter, when the valley shrank under the ice, the mountains closed in and snarled like angry jaws around the city on the lake.)

In those days the radio mast had not been built and the temple of Sankara Acharya, a little black blister on a khaki hill, still dominated the streets and lake of Srinagar. In those days there was no army camp at the lakeside, no endless snakes of camouflaged trucks and jeeps clogged the narrow mountain roads, no soldiers hid behind the crests of the mountains past Baramulla and Gulmarg. In those days travellers were not shot as spies if they took photographs of bridges, and apart from the Englishmen's houseboats on the lake, the valley had hardly changed since the Mughal Empire, for all its springtime renewals; but my grandfather's eyes – which were, like the rest of him, twenty-five years old – saw things differently . . . and his nose had started to itch.

To reveal the secret of my grandfather's altered vision: he had spent five years, five springs, away from home. (The tussock of earth, crucial though its presence was as it crouched under a chance wrinkle of the prayer-mat, was at bottom no more than a catalyst.) Now, returning, he saw through travelled eyes. Instead of the beauty of the tiny valley circled by giant teeth, he noticed the narrowness, the proximity of the horizon; and felt sad, to be at home and feel so utterly enclosed. He also felt – inexplicably – as though the old place resented his educated, stethoscoped return. Beneath the winter ice, it had been coldly neutral, but now there was no doubt; the years in Germany had returned him to a hostile environment. Many years later, when the hole inside him had been clogged up with hate, and he came to sacrifice himself at the shrine of the black stone god in the temple on the hill, he would try and recall his childhood springs in Paradise, the way it was before travel and tussocks and army tanks messed everything up.

On the morning when the valley, gloved in a prayer-mat, punched him on the nose, he had been trying, absurdly, to pretend that nothing had changed. So he had risen in the bitter cold of four-fifteen, washed himself in the prescribed fashion, dressed and put on his father's astrakhan cap; after which he had carried the rolled cheroot of the prayer-mat into the small lakeside garden in front of their old dark house and unrolled it over the waiting tussock. The ground felt deceptively soft under his feet and made him simultaneously uncertain and unwary. 'In the Name of God, the Compassionate, the Merciful . . .' – the exordium, spoken with hands joined before him like a book, comforted a part of him, made another, larger part feel uneasy – '. . . Praise be to Allah, Lord of the Creation . . .' – but now Heidelberg invaded his head; here was Ingrid, briefly his Ingrid, her face scorning him for this Mecca-turned parroting; here, their friends Oskar and Ilse Lubin the anarchists, mocking his prayer with their anti-ideologies – '. . . The Compassionate, the Merciful, King of the Last Judgment! . . .' – Heidelberg, in which, along with medicine and politics, he learned that India – like radium – had been 'discovered' by the Europeans; even Oskar was filled with admiration for Vasco da Gama, and this was what finally separated Aadam Aziz from his friends, this belief of theirs that he was somehow the invention of their ancestors – '. . . You alone we worship, and to You alone we pray for help . . .' – so here he was, despite their presence in his head, attempting to re-unite himself with an earlier self which ignored their influence but knew everything it ought to have known, about submission for example, about what he was doing now, as his hands, guided by old memories, fluttered upwards, thumbs pressed to ears, fingers spread, as he sank to his knees – '. . . Guide us to the straight path, The path of those whom You have favoured . . .' But it was no good, he was caught in a strange middle ground, trapped between belief and disbelief, and this was only a charade after all – '. . . Not of those who have incurred Your wrath, Nor of those who have gone astray.' My grandfather bent his forehead towards the earth. Forward he bent, and the earth, prayer-mat-covered, curved up towards him. And now it was the tussock's time. At one and the same time a rebuke from Ilse-Oskar-Ingrid-Heidelberg as well as valley-and-God, it smote him upon the point of the nose. Three drops fell. There were rubies and diamonds. And my grandfather, lurching upright, made a resolve. Stood. Rolled cheroot. Stared across the lake. And was knocked forever into that middle place, unable to worship a God in whose existence he could not wholly disbelieve. Permanent alteration: a hole.

The young, newly-qualified Doctor Aadam Aziz stood facing the springtime lake, sniffing the whiffs of change; while his back (which was extremely straight) was turned upon yet more changes. His father had had a stroke in his absence abroad, and his mother had kept it a secret. His mother's voice, whispering stoically: '. . . *Because your studies were too important, son.*' This mother, who had spent her life housebound, in purdah, had suddenly found enormous strength and gone out to run the small gemstone business (turquoises, rubies, diamonds) which had put Aadam through medical college, with the help of a scholarship; so he returned to find the seemingly immutable order of his family turned upside down, his mother going out to work while his father sat hidden behind the veil which the stroke had dropped over his brain . . . in a wooden chair, in a darkened room, he sat and made bird-noises. Thirty different species of birds visited him and sat on the sill outside his shuttered window conversing about this and that. He seemed happy enough.

(. . . And already I can see the repetitions beginning; because didn't my grandmother also find enormous . . . and the stroke, too, was not the only . . . and the Brass Monkey had her birds . . . the curse begins already, and we haven't even got to the noses yet!)

The lake was no longer frozen over. The thaw had come rapidly, as usual; many of the small boats, the shikaras, had been caught napping, which was also normal. But while these sluggards slept on, on dry land, snoring peacefully beside their owners, the oldest boat was up at the crack as old folk often are, and was therefore the first craft to move across the unfrozen lake. Tai's shikara . . . this, too, was customary.

Watch how the old boatman, Tai, makes good time through the misty water, standing stooped over at the back of his craft! How his oar, a wooden heart on a yellow stick, drives jerkily through the weeds! In these parts he's considered very odd because he rows standing up . . . among other reasons. Tai, bringing an urgent summons to Doctor Aziz, is about to set history in motion . . . while Aadam, looking down into the water, recalls what Tai taught him years ago: 'The ice is always waiting, Aadam baba, just under the water's skin.' Aadam's eyes are a clear blue, the astonishing blue of mountain sky, which has a habit of dripping into the pupils of Kashmiri men; they have not forgotten how to look. They see – there! like the skeleton of a ghost, just beneath the surface of Lake Dal! – the delicate tracery, the intricate crisscross of colourless lines, the cold waiting veins of the future. His German years, which have blurred so much else, haven't deprived him of the gift of seeing. Tai's gift. He looks up, sees the approaching V of Tai's boat, waves a greeting. Tai's arm rises – but this is a command. 'Wait!' My grandfather waits; and during this hiatus, as he experiences the last peace of his life, a muddy, ominous sort of peace, I had better get round to describing him.

Keeping out of my voice the natural envy of the ugly man for the strikingly impressive, I record that Doctor Aziz was a tall man. Pressed flat against a wall of his family home, he measured twenty-five bricks (a brick for each year of his life), or just over six foot two. A strong man also. His beard was thick and red – and annoyed his mother, who said only Hajis, men who had made the pilgrimage to Mecca, should grow red beards. His hair, however, was rather darker. His sky-eyes you know about. Ingrid had said, 'They went mad with the colours when they made your face.' But the central feature of my grandfather's anatomy was neither colour nor height, neither strength of arm nor straightness of back. There it was, reflected in the water, undulating like a mad plantain in the centre of his face . . . Aadam Aziz, waiting for Tai, watches his rippling nose. It would have dominated less dramatic faces than his easily; even on him, it is what one sees first and remembers longest. 'A cyranose,' Ilse Lubin said, and Oskar added, 'A proboscissimus.' Ingrid announced, 'You could cross a river on that nose.' (Its bridge was wide.)

My grandfather's nose: nostrils flaring, curvaceous as dancers. Between them swells the nose's triumphal arch, first up and out, then down and under, sweeping in to his upper lip with a superb and at present red-tipped flick. An easy nose to hit a tussock with. I wish to place on record my gratitude to this mighty organ – if not for it, who would ever have believed me to be truly my mother's son, my grandfather's grandson? – this colossal apparatus which was to be my birthright, too. Doctor Aziz's nose – comparable only to the trunk of the elephant-headed god Ganesh – established incontrovertibly his right to be a patriarch. It was Tai who taught him that, too. When young Aadam was barely past puberty the dilapidated boatman said, 'That's a nose to start a family on, my princeling. There'd be no mistaking whose

9

brood they were. Mughal Emperors would have given their right hands for noses like that one. There are dynasties waiting inside it,' – and here Tai lapsed into coarseness – 'like snot.'

On Aadam Aziz, the nose assumed a patriarchal aspect. On my mother, it looked noble and a little long-suffering; on my aunt Emerald, snobbish; on my aunt Alia, intellectual; on my uncle Hanif it was the organ of an unsuccessful genius; my uncle Mustapha made it a second-rater's sniffer; the Brass Monkey escaped it completely; but on me – on me, it was something else again. But I mustn't reveal all my secrets at once.

(Tai is getting nearer. He, who revealed the power of the nose, and who is now bringing my grandfather the message which will catapult him into his future, is stroking his shikara through the early morning lake . . .)

Nobody could remember when Tai had been young. He had been plying this same boat, standing in the same hunched position, across the Dal and Nageen Lakes . . . forever. As far as anyone knew. He lived somewhere in the insanitary bowels of the old wooden-house quarter and his wife grew lotus roots and other curious vegetables on one of the many 'floating gardens' lilting on the surface of the spring and summer water. Tai himself cheerily admitted he had no idea of his age. Neither did his wife – he was, she said, already leathery when they married. His face was a sculpture of wind on water: ripples made of hide. He had two golden teeth and no others. In the town, he had few friends. Few boatmen or traders invited him to share a hookah when he floated past the shikara moorings or one of the lakes' many ramshackle, waterside provision-stores and tea-shops.

The general opinion of Tai had been voiced long ago by Aadam Aziz's father the gemstone merchant: 'His brain fell out with his teeth.' (But now old Aziz sahib sat lost in bird tweets while Tai simply, grandly, continued.) It was an

10

impression the boatman fostered by his chatter, which was fantastic, grandiloquent and ceaseless, and as often as not addressed only to himself. Sound carries over water, and the lake people giggled at his monologues; but with undertones of awe, and even fear. Awe, because the old halfwit knew the lakes and hills better than any of his detractors; fear, because of his claim to an antiquity so immense it defied numbering, and moreover hung so lightly round his chicken's neck that it hadn't prevented him from winning a highly desirable wife and fathering four sons upon her . . . and a few more, the story went, on other lakeside wives. The young bucks at the shikara moorings were convinced he had a pile of money hidden away somewhere – a hoard, perhaps, of priceless golden teeth, rattling in a sack like walnuts. Years later, when Uncle Puffs tried to sell me his daughter by offering to have her teeth drawn and replaced in gold, I thought of Tai's forgotten treasure . . . and, as a child, Aadam Aziz had loved him.

He made his living as a simple ferryman, despite all the rumours of wealth, taking hay and goats and vegetables and wood across the lakes for cash; people, too. When he was running his taxi-service he erected a pavilion in the centre of the shikara, a gay affair of flowered-patterned curtains and canopy, with cushions to match; and deodorised his boat with incense. The sight of Tai's shikara approaching, curtains flying, had always been for Doctor Aziz one of the defining images of the coming of spring. Soon the English sahibs would arrive and Tai would ferry them to the Shalimar Gardens and the King's Spring, chattering and pointy and stooped. He was the living antithesis of Oskar-Ilse-Ingrid's belief in the inevitability of change . . . a quirky, enduring familiar spirit of the valley. A watery Caliban, rather too fond of cheap Kashmiri brandy.

Memory of my blue bedroom wall: on which, next to the P.M.'s letter, the Boy Raleigh hung for many years, gazing

11

rapturously at an old fisherman in what looked like a red dhoti, who sat on – what? – driftwood? – and pointed out to sea as he told his fishy tales . . . and the Boy Aadam, my grandfather-to-be, fell in love with the boatman Tai precisely because of the endless verbiage which made others think him cracked. It was magical talk, words pouring from him like fools' money, past his two gold teeth, laced with hiccups and brandy, soaring up to the most remote Himalayas of the past, then swooping shrewdly on some present detail, Aadam's nose for instance, to vivisect its meaning like a mouse. This friendship had plunged Aadam into hot water with great regularity. (Boiling water. Literally. While his mother said, 'We'll kill that boatman's bugs if it kills you.') But still the old soliloquist would dawdle in his boat at the garden's lakeside toes and Aziz would sit at his feet until voices summoned him indoors to be lectured on Tai's filthiness and warned about the pillaging armies of germs his mother envisaged leaping from that hospitably ancient body on to her son's starched white loose-pajamas. But always Aadam returned to the water's edge to scan the mists for the ragged reprobate's hunched-up frame steering its magical boat through the enchanted waters of the morning.

'But how old are you really, Taiji?' (Doctor Aziz, adult, redbearded, slanting towards the future, remembers the day he asked the unaskable question.) For an instant, silence, noisier than a waterfall. The monologue, interrupted. Slap of oar in water. He was riding in the shikara with Tai, squatting amongst goats, on a pile of straw, in full knowledge of the stick and bathtub waiting for him at home. He had come for stories – and with one question had silenced the storyteller.

'No, tell, Taiji, how old, *truly*?' And now a brandy bottle, materialising from nowhere: cheap liquor from the folds of the great warm chugha-coat. Then a shudder, a belch, a glare. Glint of gold. And – at last! – speech. 'How old? You ask how old, you little wet-head, you nosey . . .' Tai, forecasting the

12

fisherman on my wall, pointed at the mountains. 'So old, nakkoo!' Aadam, the nakkoo, the nosey one, followed his pointing finger. 'I have watched the mountains being born; I have seen Emperors die. Listen. Listen, nakkoo . . .' – the brandy bottle again, followed by brandy-voice, and words more intoxicating than booze – '. . . I saw that Isa, that Christ, when he came to Kashmir. Smile, smile, it is your history I am keeping in my head. Once it was set down in old lost books. Once I knew where there was a grave with pierced feet carved on the tombstone, which bled once a year. Even my memory is going now; but I know, although I can't read.' Illiteracy, dismissed with a flourish; literature crumbled beneath the rage of his sweeping hand. Which sweeps again to chugha-pocket, to brandy bottle, to lips chapped with cold. Tai always had woman's lips. 'Nakkoo, listen, listen. I have seen plenty. Yara, you should've seen that Isa when he came, beard down to his balls, bald as an egg on his head. He was old and fagged-out but he knew his manners. "You first, Taiji," he'd say, and "Please to sit"; always a respectful tongue, he never called me crackpot, never called me *tu* either. Always *aap*. Polite, see? And what an appetite! Such a hunger, I would catch my ears in fright. Saint or devil, I swear he could eat a whole kid in one go. And so what? I told him, eat, fill your hole, a man comes to Kashmir to enjoy life, or to end it, or both. His work was finished. He just came up here to live it up a little.' Mesmerized by this brandied portrait of a bald, gluttonous Christ, Aziz listened, later repeating every word to the consternation of his parents, who dealt in stones and had no time for 'gas'.

'Oh, you don't believe?' – licking his sore lips with a grin, knowing it to be the reverse of the truth; 'Your attention is wandering?' – again, he knew how furiously Aziz was hanging on his words. 'Maybe the straw is pricking your behind, hey? Oh, I'm so sorry, babaji, not to provide for you silk cushions with gold brocade-work – cushions such as the

Emperor Jehangir sat upon! You think of the Emperor Jehangir as a gardener only, no doubt,' Tai accused my grandfather, 'because he built Shalimar. Stupid! What do you know? His name meant Encompasser of the Earth. Is that a gardener's name? God knows what they teach you boys these days. Whereas I' . . . puffing up a little here . . . 'I knew his precise weight, to the tola! Ask me how many maunds, how many seers! When he was happy he got heavier and in Kashmir he was heaviest of all. I used to carry his litter . . . no, no, look, you don't believe again, that big cucumber in your face is waggling like the little one in your pajamas! So, come on, come on, ask me questions! Give examination! Ask how many times the leather thongs wound round the handles of the litter – the answer is thirty-one. Ask me what was the Emperor's dying word – I tell you it was "Kashmir". He had bad breath and a good heart. Who do you think I am? Some common ignorant lying pie-dog? Go, get out of the boat now, your nose makes it too heavy to row; also your father is waiting to beat my gas out of you, and your mother to boil off your skin.'

In the brandy bottle of the boatman Tai I see, foretold, my own father's possession by djinns . . . and there will be another bald foreigner . . . and Tai's gas prophesies another kind, which was the consolation of my grandmother's old age, and taught her stories, too . . . and pie-dogs aren't far away . . . Enough. I'm frightening myself.

Despite beating and boiling, Aadam Aziz floated with Tai in his shikara, again and again, amid goats hay flowers furniture lotus-roots, though never with the English sahibs, and heard again and again the miraculous answers to that single terrifying question: 'But Taiji, how old are you, *honestly*?'

From Tai, Aadam learned the secrets of the lake – where you could swim without being pulled down by weeds; the eleven varieties of water-snake; where the frogs spawned;

how to cook a lotus-root; and where the three English women had drowned a few years back. 'There is a tribe of feringhee women who come to this water to drown,' Tai said. 'Sometimes they know it, sometimes they don't, but I know the minute I smell them. They hide under the water from God knows what or who – but they can't hide from me, baba!' Tai's laugh, emerging to infect Aadam – a huge, booming laugh that seemed macabre when it crashed out of that old, withered body, but which was so natural in my giant grandfather that nobody knew, in later times, that it wasn't really his (my uncle Hanif inherited this laugh; so until he died, a piece of Tai lived in Bombay). And, also from Tai, my grandfather heard about noses.

Tai tapped his left nostril. 'You know what this is nakkoo? It's the place where the outside world meets the world inside you. If they don't get on, you feel it here. Then you rub your nose with embarrassment to make the itch go away. A nose like that, little idiot, is a great gift. I say: trust it. When it warns you, look out or you'll be finished. Follow your nose and you'll go far.' He cleared his throat; his eyes rolled away into the mountains of the past, Aziz settled back on the straw. 'I knew one officer once – in the army of that Iskandar the Great. Never mind his name. He had a vegetable just like yours hanging between his eyes. When the army halted near Gandhara, he fell in love with some local floozy. At once his nose itched like crazy. He scratched it, but that was useless. He inhaled vapours from crushed boiled eucalyptus leaves. Still no good, baba! The itching sent him wild; but the damn fool dug in his heels and stayed with his little witch when the army went home. He became – what? – a stupid thing, neither this nor that, a half-and-halfer with a nagging wife and an itch in the nose, and in the end he pushed his sword into his stomach. What do you think of that?'

. . . Doctor Aziz in 1915, whom rubies and diamonds have turned into a half-and-halfer, remembers this story as Tai

15

enters hailing distance. His nose is itching still. He scratches, shrugs, tosses his head; and then Tai shouts.

'Ohé! Doctor Sahib! Ghani the landowner's daughter is sick.'

The message, delivered curtly, shouted unceremoniously across the surface of the lake although boatman and pupil have not met for half a decade, mouthed by woman's lips that are not smiling in long-time-no-see greeting, sends time into a speeding, whirligig, blurry fluster of excitement . . .

. . . 'Just think, son,' Aadam's mother is saying as she sips fresh lime water, reclining on a takht in an attitude of resigned exhaustion, 'how life does turn out. For so many years even my ankles were a secret, and now I must be stared at by strange persons who are not even family members.'

. . . While Ghani the landowner stands beneath a large oil painting of Diana the Huntress, framed in squiggly gold. He wears thick dark glasses and his famous poisonous smile, and discussed art. 'I purchased it from an Englishman down on his luck, Doctor Sahib. Five hundred rupees only – and I did not trouble to beat him down. What are five hundred chips? You see, I am a lover of culture.'

. . . 'See, my son,' Aadam's mother is saying as he begins to examine her, 'what a mother will not do for her child. Look how I suffer. You are a doctor . . . feel these rashes, these blotchy bits, understand that my head aches morning noon and night. Refill my glass, child.'

. . . But the young Doctor has entered the throes of a most unhippocratic excitement at the boatman's cry, and shouts, 'I'm coming just now! Just let me bring my things!' The shikara's prow touches the garden's hem. Aadam is rushing indoors, prayer-mat rolled like cheroot under one arm, blue eyes blinking in the sudden interior gloom; he has placed the cheroot on a high shelf on top of stacked copies of *Vorwärts* and Lenin's *What Is To Be Done?* and other pamphlets, dusty echoes of his half-faded German life; he is pulling out, from

16

under his bed, a second-hand leather case which his mother called his 'doctori-attaché', and as he swings it and himself upwards and runs from the room, the word HEIDELBERG is briefly visible, burned into the leather on the bottom of the bag. A landowner's daughter is good news indeed to a doctor with a career to make, even if she is ill. No: *because* she is ill.

. . . While I sit like an empty pickle jar in a pool of Anglepoised light, visited by this vision of my grandfather sixty-three years ago, which demands to be recorded, filling my nostrils with the acrid stench of his mother's embarrassment which has brought her out in boils, with the vinegary force of Aadam Aziz's determination to establish a practice so successful that she'll never have to return to the gemstone-shop, with the blind mustiness of a big shadowy house in which the young Doctor stands, ill-at-ease, before a painting of a plain girl with lively eyes and a stag transfixed behind her on the horizon, speared by a dart from her bow. Most of what matters in our lives takes place in our absence: but I seem to have found from somewhere the trick of filling in the gaps in my knowledge, so that everything is in my head, down to the last detail, such as the way the mist seemed to slant across the early morning air . . . everything, and not just the few clues one stumbles across, for instance by opening an old tin trunk which should have remained cobwebby and closed.

. . . Aadam refills his mother's glass and continues, worriedly, to examine her. 'Put some cream on these rashes and blotches, Amma. For the headache, there are pills. The boils must be lanced. But maybe if you wore purdah when you sat in the store . . . so that no disrespectful eyes could . . . such complaints often begin in the mind . . .'

. . . Slap of oar in water. Plop of spittle in lake. Tai clears his throat and mutters angrily, 'A fine business. A wet-head nakkoo child goes away before he's learned one damn thing and he comes back a big doctor sahib with a big bag full of

17

foreign machines, and he's still as silly as an owl. I swear: a too bad business.'

. . . Doctor Aziz is shifting uneasily, from foot to foot, under the influence of the landowner's smile, in whose presence it is not possible to feel relaxed; and is waiting for some tic of reaction to his own extraordinary appearance. He has grown accustomed to these involuntary twitches of surprise at his size, his face of many colours, his nose . . . but Ghani makes no sign, and the young Doctor resolves, in return, not to let his uneasiness show. He stops shifting his weight. They face each other, each suppressing (or so it seems) his view of the other, establishing the basis of their future relationship. And now Ghani alters, changing from an art-lover to tough-guy. 'This is a big chance for you, young man,' he says. Aziz's eyes have strayed to Diana. Wide expanses of her blemished pink skin are visible.

. . . His mother is moaning, shaking her head. 'No, what do you know, child, you have become a big-shot doctor but the gemstone business is different. Who would buy a turquoise from a woman hidden inside a black hood? It is a question of establishing trust. So they must look at me; and I must get pains and boils. Go, go, don't worry your head about your poor mother.'

. . . 'Big shot,' Tai is spitting into the lake, 'big bag, big shot. Pah! We haven't got enough bags at home that you must bring back that thing made of a pig's skin that makes one unclean just by looking at it? And inside, God knows what all.' Doctor Aziz, seated amongst flowery curtains and the smell of incense, has his thoughts wrenched away from the patient waiting across the lake. Tai's bitter monologue breaks into his consciousness, creating a sense of dull shock, a smell like a casualty ward overpowering the incense . . . the old man is clearly furious about something, possessed by an incomprehensible rage that appears to be directed at his erstwhile acolyte, or, more precisely and oddly, at his bag. Doctor Aziz

18

attempts to make small talk . . . 'Your wife is well? Do they still talk about your bag of golden teeth?' . . . tries to remake an old friendship; but Tai is in full flight now, a stream of invective pouring out of him. The Heidelberg bag quakes under the torrent of abuse. 'Sistersleeping pigskin bag from Abroad full of foreigners' tricks. Big-shot bag. Now if a man breaks an arm that bag will not let the bone-setter bind it in leaves. Now a man must let his wife lie beside that bag and watch knives come and cut her open. A fine business, what these foreigners put in our young men's heads. I swear: it is a too-bad thing. That bag should fry in Hell with the testicles of the ungodly.'

. . . Ghani the landowner snaps his braces with his thumbs. 'A big chance, yes indeed. They are saying good things about you in town. Good medical training. Good . . . good enough . . . family. And now our own lady doctor is sick so you get your opportunity. That woman, always sick these days, too old, I am thinking, and not up in the latest developments also, what-what? I say: physician heal thyself. And I tell you this: I am wholly objective in my business relations. Feelings, love, I keep for my family only. If a person is not doing a first-class job for me, out she goes! You understand me? So: my daughter Naseem is not well. You will treat her excellently. Remember I have friends; and ill-health strikes high and low alike.'

. . . 'Do you still pickle water-snakes in brandy to give you virility, Taiji? Do you still like to eat lotus-root without any spices?' Hesitant questions, brushed aside by the torrent of Tai's fury. Doctor Aziz begins to diagnose. To the ferryman, the bag represents Abroad; it is the alien thing, the invader, progress. And yes, it has indeed taken possession of the young Doctor's mind; and yes, it contains knives, and cures for cholera and malaria and smallpox; and yes, it sits between doctor and boatman, and has made them antagonists. Doctor Aziz begins to fight, against sadness, and against Tai's anger, which is beginning to infect him, to become his own, which erupts only rarely, but comes, when it does come, unheralded in a roar from his deepest places, laying waste everything in sight; and then vanishes, leaving him wondering why everyone is so upset . . . They are approaching Ghani's house. A bearer awaits the shikara, standing with clasped hands on a little wooden jetty. Aziz fixes his mind on the job in hand.

. . . 'Has your usual doctor agreed to my visit, Ghani Sahib?' . . . Again, a hesitant question is brushed lightly aside. The landowner says, 'Oh, she will agree. Now follow me, please.'

. . . The bearer is waiting on the jetty. Holding the shikara steady as Aadam Aziz climbs out, bag in hand. And now, at last, Tai speaks directly to my grandfather. Scorn in his face, Tai asks, 'Tell me this, Doctor Sahib: have you got in that bag made of dead pigs one of those machines that foreign doctors use to smell with?' Aadam shakes his head, not understanding. Tai's voice gathers new layers of disgust. 'You know, sir, a thing like an elephant's trunk.' Aziz, seeing what he means, replies: 'A stethoscope? Naturally.' Tai pushes the shikara off from the jetty. Spits. Begins to row away. 'I knew it,' he says. 'You will use such a machine now, instead of your own big nose.'

My grandfather does not trouble to explain that a stethoscope is more like a pair of ears than a nose. He is stifling his own irritation, the resentful anger of a cast-off child; and besides, there is a patient waiting. Time settles down and concentrates on the importance of the moment.

The house was opulent but badly lit. Ghani was a widower and the servants clearly took advantage. There were cobwebs in corners and layers of dust on ledges. They walked down a long corridor; one of the doors was ajar and through it Aziz saw a room in a state of violent disorder. This glimpse, connected with a glint of light in Ghani's dark glasses, suddenly

20

informed Aziz that the landowner was blind. This aggravated his sense of unease: a blind man who claimed to appreciate European paintings? He was, also, impressed, because Ghani hadn't bumped into anything . . . they halted outside a thick teak door. Ghani said, 'Wait here two moments,' and went into the room behind the door.

In later years, Doctor Aadam Aziz swore that during those two moments of solitude in the gloomy spidery corridors of the landowner's mansion he was gripped by an almost uncontrollable desire to turn and run away as fast as his legs would carry him. Unnerved by the enigma of the blind art-lover, his insides filled with tiny scrabbling insects as a result of the insidious venom of Tai's mutterings, his nostrils itching to the point of convincing him that he had somehow contracted venereal disease, he felt his feet begin slowly, as though encased in boots of lead, to turn; felt blood pounding in his temples; and was seized by so powerful a sensation of standing upon a point of no return that he very nearly wet his German woollen trousers. He began, without knowing it, to blush furiously; and at this point his mother appeared before him, seated on the floor before a low desk, a rash spreading like a blush across her face as she held a turquoise up to the light. His mother's face had acquired all the scorn of the boatman Tai. 'Go, go, run,' she told him in Tai's voice, 'Don't worry about your poor old mother.' Doctor Aziz found himself stammering, 'What a useless son you've got, Amma; can't you see there's a hole in the middle of me the size of a melon?' His mother smiled a pained smile. 'You always were a heartless boy,' she sighed, and then turned into a lizard on the wall of the corridor and stuck her tongue out at him. Doctor Aziz stopped feeling dizzy, became unsure that he'd actually spoken aloud, wondered what he'd meant by that business about the hole, found that his feet were no longer trying to escape, and realized that he was being watched. A woman with the biceps of a wrestler was staring at him, beckoning him to follow her into the room. The state of her sari told him that she was a servant; but she was not servile. 'You look green as a fish,' she said. 'You young doctors. You come into a strange house and your liver turns to jelly. Come, Doctor Sahib, they are waiting for you.' Clutching his bag a fraction too tightly, he followed her through the dark teak door.

. . . Into a spacious bedchamber that was as ill-lit as the rest of the house; although here there were shafts of dusty sunlight seeping in through a fanlight high on one wall. These fusty rays illuminated a scene as remarkable as anything the Doctor had ever witnessed: a tableau of such surpassing strangeness that his feet began to twitch towards the door once again. Two more women, also built like professional wrestlers, stood stiffly in the light, each holding one corner of an enormous white bedsheet, their arms raised high above their heads so that the sheet hung between them like a curtain. Mr Ghani welled up out of the murk surrounding the sunlit sheet and permitted the nonplussed Aadam to stare stupidly at the peculiar tableau for perhaps half a minute, at the end of which, and before a word had been spoken, the Doctor made a discovery:

In the very centre of the sheet, a hole had been cut, a crude circle about seven inches in diameter.

'Close the door, ayah,' Ghani instructed the first of the lady wrestlers, and then, turning to Aziz, became confidential. 'This town contains many good-for-nothings who have on occasion tried to climb into my daughter's room. She needs,' he nodded at the three musclebound women, 'protectors.'

Aziz was still looking at the perforated sheet. Ghani said, 'All right, come on, you will examine my Naseem right now. *Pronto.*'

My grandfather peered around the room. 'But where is she, Ghani Sahib?' he blurted out finally. The lady wrestlers adopted supercilious expressions and, it seemed to him,

22

tightened their musculatures, just in case he intended to try something fancy.

'Ah, I see your confusion,' Ghani said, his poisonous smile broadening, 'You Europe-returned chappies forget certain things. Doctor Sahib, my daughter is a decent girl, it goes without saying. She does not flaunt her body under the noses of strange men. You will understand that you cannot be permitted to see her, no, not in any circumstances; accordingly I have required her to be positioned behind that sheet. She stands there, like a good girl.'

A frantic note had crept into Doctor Aziz's voice. 'Ghani Sahib, tell me how I am to examine her without looking at her?' Ghani smiled on.

'You will kindly specify which portion of my daughter it is necessary to inspect. I will then issue her with my instructions to place the required segment against that hole which you see there. And so, in this fashion the thing may be achieved.'

'But what, in any event, does the lady complain of?' – my grandfather, despairingly. To which Mr Ghani, his eyes rising upwards in their sockets, his smile twisting into a grimace of grief, replied: 'The poor child! She has a terrible, a too dreadful stomach-ache.'

'In that case,' Doctor Aziz said with some restraint, 'will she show me her stomach, please.'

Mercurochrome

Padma – our plump Padma – is sulking magnificently. (She can't read and, like all fish-lovers, dislikes other people knowing anything she doesn't. Padma: strong, jolly, a consolation for my last days. But definitely a bitch-in-the-manger.) She attempts to cajole me from my desk: 'Eat, na, food is spoiling.' I remain stubbornly hunched over paper. 'But what is so precious,' Padma demands, her right hand slicing the air updownup in exasperation, 'to need all this writing-shiting?' I reply: now that I've let out the details of my birth, now that the perforated sheet stands between doctor and patient, there's no going back. Padma snorts. Wrist smacks against forehead. 'Okay, starve starve, who cares two pice?' Another louder, conclusive snort . . . but I take no exception to her attitude. She stirs a bubbling vat all day for a living; something hot and vinegary has steamed her up tonight. Thick of waist, somewhat hairy of forearm, she flounces, gesticulates, exits. Poor Padma. Things are always getting her goat. Perhaps even her name: understandably enough, since her mother told her, when she was only small, that she had been named after the lotus goddess, whose most common appellation amongst village folk is 'The One Who Possesses Dung'.

In the renewed silence, I return to sheets of paper which smell just a little of turmeric, ready and willing to put out of its misery a narrative which I left yesterday hanging in mid-air – just as Scheherazade, depending for her very survival on

24

leaving Prince Shahryar eaten up by curiosity, used to do night after night! I'll begin at once: by revealing that my grandfather's premonitions in the corridor were not without foundation. In the succeeding months and years, he fell under what I can only describe as the sorcerer's spell of that enormous – and as yet unstained – perforated cloth.

'Again?' Aadam's mother said, rolling her eyes. 'I tell you, my child, that girl is so sickly from too much soft living only. Too much sweetmeats and spoiling, because of the absence of a mother's firm hand. But go, take care of your invisible patient, your mother is all right with her little nothing of a headache.'

In those years, you see, the landowner's daughter Naseem Ghani contracted a quite extraordinary number of minor illnesses, and each time a shikara wallah was despatched to summon the tall young Doctor sahib with the big nose who was making such a reputation for himself in the valley. Aadam Aziz's visits to the bedroom with the shaft of sunlight and the three lady wrestlers became weekly events; and on each occasion he was vouchsafed a glimpse, through the mutilated sheet, of a different seven-inch circle of the young woman's body. Her initial stomach-ache was succeeded by a very slightly twisted right ankle, an ingrowing toenail on the big toe of the left foot, a tiny cut on the lower left calf. 'Tetanus is a killer, Doctor Sahib,' the landowner said, 'My Naseem must not die for a scratch.') There was the matter of her stiff right knee, which the Doctor was obliged to manipulate through the hole in the sheet . . . and after a time the illnesses leapt upwards, avoiding certain unmentionable zones, and began to proliferate around her upper half. She suffered from something mysterious which her father called Finger Rot, which made the skin flake off her hands; from weakness of the wrist-bones, for which Aadam prescribed calcium tablets; and from attacks of constipation, for which he gave her a course of laxatives, since there was no question

25

of being permitted to administer an enema. She had fevers and she also had subnormal temperatures. At these times his thermometer would be placed under her armpit and he would hum and haw about the relative inefficiency of the method. In the opposite armpit she once developed a slight case of tineachloris and he dusted her with yellow powder; after this treatment – which required him to rub the powder in, gently but firmly, although the soft secret body began to shake and quiver and he heard helpless laughter coming through the sheet, because Naseem Ghani was very ticklish – the itching went away, but Naseem soon found a new set of complaints. She waxed anaemic in the summer and bronchial in the winter. ('Her tubes are most delicate,' Ghani explained, 'like little flutes.') Far away the Great War moved from crisis to crisis, while in the cobwebbed house Doctor Aziz was also engaged in a total war against his sectioned patient's inexhaustible complaints. And, in all those war years, Naseem never repeated an illness. 'Which only shows,' Ghani told him, 'that you are a good doctor. When you cure, she is cured for good. But alas!' – he struck his forehead – 'She pines for her late mother, poor baby, and her body suffers. She is a too loving child.'

So gradually Doctor Aziz came to have a picture of Naseem in his mind, a badly-fitting collage of her severally-inspected parts. This phantasm of a partitioned woman began to haunt him, and not only in his dreams. Glued together by his imagination, she accompanied him on all his rounds, she moved into the front room of his mind, so that waking and sleeping he could feel in his fingertips the softness of her ticklish skin or the perfect tiny wrists or the beauty of the ankles; he could smell her scent of lavender and chambeli; he could hear her voice and her helpless laughter of a little girl; but she was headless, because he had never seen her face.

His mother lay on her bed, spreadeagled on her stomach. 'Come, come and press me,' she said, 'my doctor son whose fingers can soothe his old mother's muscles. Press, press, my child with his expression of a constipated goose.' He kneaded her shoulders. She grunted, twitched, relaxed. 'Lower now,' she said, 'now higher. To the right. Good. My brilliant son who cannot see what that Ghani landowner is doing. So clever, my child, but he doesn't guess why that girl is forever ill with her piffling disorders. Listen, my boy: see the nose on your face for once: that Ghani thinks you are a good catch for her. Foreign-educated and all. I have worked in shops and been undressed by the eyes of strangers so that you should marry that Naseem! Of course I am right; otherwise why would he look twice at our family?' Aziz pressed his mother. 'O God, stop now, no need to kill me because I tell you the truth!'

By 1918, Aadam Aziz had come to live for his regular trips across the lake. And now his eagerness became even more intense, because it became clear that, after three years, the landowner and his daughter had become willing to lower certain barriers. Now, for the first time, Ghani said, 'A lump in the right chest. Is it worrying, Doctor? Look. Look well.' And there, framed in the hole, was a perfectly-formed and lyrically lovely . . . 'I must touch it,' Aziz said, fighting with his voice. Ghani slapped him on the back. 'Touch, touch!' he cried, 'The hands of the healer! The curing touch, eh, Doctor?' And Aziz reached out a hand . . . 'Forgive me for asking; but is it the lady's time of the month?' . . . Little secret smiles appearing on the faces of the lady wrestlers. Ghani, nodding affably: 'Yes. Don't be so embarrassed, old chap. We are family and doctor now.' And Aziz, 'Then don't worry. The lumps will go when the time ends.' . . . And the next time, 'A pulled muscle in the back of her thigh, Doctor Sahib. Such pain!' And there, in the sheet, weakening the eyes of Aadam Aziz, hung a superbly rounded and impossible buttock . . . And now Aziz: 'Is it permitted that . . .' Whereupon a word from Ghani; an obedient reply from behind the sheet; a drawstring pulled; and pajamas fall from the celestial rump, which swells wondrously through the hole. Aadam Aziz forces himself into a medical frame of mind . . . reaches out . . . feels. And swears to himself, in amazement, that he sees the bottom reddening in a shy, but compliant blush.

That evening, Aadam contemplated the blush. Did the magic of the sheet work on both sides of the hole? Excitedly, he envisaged his headless Naseem tingling beneath the scrutiny of his eyes, his thermometer, his stethoscope, his fingers, and trying to build a picture in her mind of *him*. She was at a disadvantage, of course, having seen nothing but his hands . . . Aadam began to hope with an illicit desperation for Naseem Ghani to develop a migraine or graze her unseen chin, so they could look each other in the face. He knew how unprofessional his feelings were; but did nothing to stifle them. There was not much he could do. They had acquired a life of their own. In short: my grandfather had fallen in love, and had come to think of the perforated sheet as something sacred and magical, because through it he had seen the things which had filled up the hole inside him which had been created when he had been hit on the nose by a tussock and insulted by the boatman Tai.

On the day the World War ended, Naseem developed the longed-for headache. Such historical coincidences have littered, and perhaps befouled, my family's existence in the world.

He hardly dared to look at what was framed in the hole in the sheet. Maybe she was hideous; perhaps that explained all this performance . . . he looked. And saw a soft face that was not at all ugly, a cushioned setting for her glittering, gemstone eyes, which were brown with flecks of gold: tiger's-eyes. Doctor Aziz's fall was complete. And Naseem burst out, 'But Doctor, my God, what a *nose*!' Ghani, angrily, 'Daughter, mind your . . .' But patient and doctor were laughing together, and Aziz was saying, 'Yes, yes, it is a remarkable specimen.

28

They tell me there are dynasties waiting in it . . .' And he bit his tongue because he had been about to add, '. . . like snot.'

And Ghani, who had stood blindly beside the sheet for three long years, smiling and smiling and smiling, began once again to smile his secret smile, which was mirrored in the lips of the wrestlers.

Meanwhile, the boatman, Tai, had taken his unexplained decision to give up washing. In a valley drenched in fresh-water lakes, where even the very poorest people could (and did) pride themselves on their cleanliness, Tai chose to stink. For three years now, he had neither bathed nor washed himself after answering calls of nature. He wore the same clothes, unwashed, year in, year out; his one concession to winter was to put his chugha-coat over his putrescent pajamas. The little basket of hot coals which he carried inside the chugha, in the Kashmiri fashion, to keep him warm in the bitter cold, only animated and accentuated his evil odours. He took to drifting slowly past the Aziz household, releasing the dreadful fumes of his body across the small garden and into the house. Flowers died; birds fled from the ledge outside old Father Aziz's window. Naturally, Tai lost work; the English in particular were reluctant to be ferried by a human cesspit. The story went around the lake that Tai's wife, driven to distraction by the old man's sudden filthiness, pleaded for a reason. He had answered: 'Ask our foreign-returned doctor, ask that nakkoo, that German Aziz.' Was it, then, an attempt to offend the Doctor's hyper-sensitive nostrils (in which the itch of danger had subsided somewhat under the anaesthetizing ministrations of love)? Or a gesture of unchangingness in defiance of the invasion of the doctori-attaché from Heidelberg? Once Aziz asked the ancient, straight out, what it was all for; but Tai only breathed on him and rowed away. The breath nearly felled Aziz; it was sharp as an axe.

In 1918, Doctor Aziz's father, deprived of his birds, died in his sleep; and at once his mother, who had been able to sell the gemstone business thanks to the success of Aziz's practice, and who now saw her husband's death as a merciful release for her from a life filled with responsibilities, took to her own deathbed and followed her man before the end of his own forty-day mourning period. By the time the Indian regiments returned at the end of the war, Doctor Aziz was an orphan, and a free man – except that his heart had fallen through a hole some seven inches across.

Desolating effect of Tai's behaviour: it ruined Doctor Aziz's good relations with the lake's floating population. He, who as a child had chatted freely with fishwives and flower-sellers, found himself looked at askance. 'Ask that nakkoo, that German Aziz.' Tai had branded him as an alien, and therefore a person not completely to be trusted. They didn't like the boatman, but they found the transformation which the Doctor had evidently worked upon him even more disturbing. Aziz found himself suspected, even ostracized, by the poor; and it hurt him badly. Now he understood what Tai was up to: the man was trying to chase him out of the valley.

The story of the perforated sheet got out, too. The lady wrestlers were evidently less discreet than they looked. Aziz began to notice people pointing at him. Women giggled behind their palms . . .

'I've decided to give Tai his victory,' he said. The three lady wrestlers, two holding up the sheet, the third hovering near the door, strained to hear him through the cotton wool in their ears. ('I made my father do it,' Naseem told him, 'These chatterjees won't do any more of their tittling and tattling from now on.') Naseem's eyes, hole-framed, became wider than ever.

. . . Just like his own when, a few days earlier, he had been walking the city streets, had seen the last bus of the winter arrive, painted with its colourful inscriptions – on the front,

30

GOD WILLING in green shadowed in red; on the back, blue-shadowed yellow crying THANK GOD!, and in cheeky maroon, SORRY-BYE-BYE! – and had recognized, through a web of new rings and lines on her face, Ilse Lubin as she descended . . .

Nowadays, Ghani the landowner left him alone with earplugged guardians, 'To talk a little; the doctor-patient relationship can only deepen in strictest confidentiality. I see that now, Aziz Sahib – forgive my earlier intrusions.' Nowadays, Naseem's tongue was getting freer all the time. 'What kind of talk is this? What are you – a man or a mouse? To leave home because of a stinky shikara-man!' . . .

'Oskar died,' Ilse told him, sipping fresh lime water on his mother's takht. 'Like a comedian. He went to talk to the army and tell them not to be pawns. The fool really thought the troops would fling down their guns and walk away. We watched from a window and I prayed they wouldn't just trample all over him. The regiment had learned to march in step by then, you wouldn't recognize them. As he reached the streetcorner across from the parade ground he tripped over his own shoelace and fell into the street. A staff car hit him and he died. He could never keep his laces tied, that ninny' . . . here there were diamonds freezing in her lashes . . . 'He was the type that gives anarchists a bad name.'

'All right,' Naseem conceded, 'so you've got a good chance of landing a good job. Agra University, it's a famous place, don't think I don't know. University doctor! . . . sounds good. Say you're going for that, and it's a different business.' Eyelashes drooped in the hole. 'I will miss you, naturally . . .'

'I'm in love,' Aadam Aziz said to Ilse Lubin. And later, '. . . So I've only seen her through a hole in a sheet, one part at a time; and I swear her bottom blushes.'

'They must be putting something in the air up here,' Ilse said.

31

'Naseem, I've got the job,' Aadam said excitedly. 'The letter came today. With effect from April 1919. Your father says he can find a buyer for my house and the gemstone shop also.'

'Wonderful,' Naseem pouted. 'So now I must find a new doctor. Or maybe I'll get that old hag again who didn't know two things about anything.'

'Because I am an orphan,' Doctor Aziz said, 'I must come myself in place of my family members. But I have come nevertheless, Ghani Sahib, for the first time without being sent for. This is not a professional visit.'

'Dear boy!' Ghani, clapping Aadam on the back. 'Of course you must marry her. With an A-1 fine dowry! No expense spared! It will be the wedding of the year, oh most certainly, yes!'

'I cannot leave you behind when I go,' Aziz said to Naseem. Ghani said, 'Enough of this tamasha! No more need for this sheet tomfoolery! Drop it down, you women, these are young lovers now!'

'At last,' said Aadam Aziz, 'I see you whole at last. But I must go now. My rounds . . . and an old friend is staying with me, I must tell her, she will be very happy for us both. A dear friend from Germany.'

'No, Aadam baba,' his bearer said, 'since the morning I have not seen Ilse Begum. She hired that old Tai to go for a shikara ride.'

'What can be said, sir?' Tai mumbled meekly. 'I am honoured indeed to be summoned into the home of a so-great personage as yourself. Sir, the lady hired me for a trip to the Mughal Gardens, to do it before the lake freezes. A quiet lady, Doctor Sahib, not one word out of her all the time. So I was thinking my own unworthy private thoughts as old fools will and suddenly when I look she is not in her seat. Sahib, on my wife's head I swear it, it is not possible to see over the back of the seat, how was I to tell? Believe a poor old boatman who was your friend when you were young . . .'

'Aadam baba,' the old bearer interrupted, 'excuse me but just now I have found this paper on her table.'

'I know where she is,' Doctor Aziz stared at Tai. 'I don't know how you keep getting mixed up in my life; but you showed me the place once. You said: certain foreign women come here to drown.'

'I, Sahib?' Tai shocked, malodorous, innocent. 'But grief is making your head play trick! How can I know these things?'

And after the body, bloated, wrapped in weeds, had been dredged up by a group of blank-faced boatmen, Tai visited the shikara halt and told the men there, as they recoiled from his breath of a bullock with dysentery, 'He blames me, only imagine! Brings his loose Europeans here and tells me it is my fault when they jump into the lake! . . . I ask, how did he know just where to look? Yes, ask him that, ask that nakkoo Aziz!'

She had left a note. It read: 'I didn't mean it.'

I make no comment; these events, which have tumbled from my lips any old how, garbled by haste and emotion, are for others to judge. Let me be direct now, and say that during the long, hard winter of 1918–19, Tai fell ill, contracting a violent skin disease, akin to that European curse called the King's Evil; but he refused to see Doctor Aziz, and was treated by a local homeopath. And in March, when the lake thawed, a marriage took place in a large marquee in the grounds of Ghani the landowner's house. The wedding contract assured Aadam Aziz of a respectable sum of money, which would help buy a house in Agra, and the dowry included, at Doctor Aziz's especial request, a certain mutilated bedsheet. The young couple sat on a dais, garlanded and cold, while the guests filed past dropping rupees into their laps. That night my grandfather placed the perforated sheet beneath his bride and himself and in the morning it was adorned by three drops of blood, which formed a small triangle. In the morning, the sheet was displayed, and after the consummation ceremony a limousine hired by the landowner arrived to drive my grandparents to Amritsar, where they would catch the Frontier Mail. Mountains crowded round and stared as my grandfather left his home for the last time. (He would return, once, but not to leave.) Aziz thought he saw an ancient boatman standing on land to watch them pass – but it was probably a mistake, since Tai was ill. The blister of a temple atop Sankara Acharya, which Muslims had taken to calling the Takht-e-Sulaiman, or Seat of Solomon, paid them no attention. Winter-bare poplars and snow-covered fields of saffron undulated around them as the car drove south, with an old leather bag containing, amongst other things, a stethoscope and a bedsheet, packed in the boot. Doctor Aziz felt, in the pit of his stomach, a sensation akin to weightlessness.

Or falling.

(. . . And now I am cast as a ghost. I am nine years old and the whole family, my father, my mother, the Brass Monkey and myself, are staying at my grandparents' house in Agra, and the grandchildren – myself among them – are staging the customary New Year's play; and I have been cast as a ghost. Accordingly – and surreptitiously so as to preserve the secrets of the forthcoming theatricals – I am ransacking the house for a spectral disguise. My grandfather is out and about his rounds. I am in his room. And here on top of this cupboard is an old trunk, covered in dust and spiders, but unlocked. And here, inside it, is the answer to my prayers. Not just a sheet, but one with a hole already cut in it! Here it is, inside this leather bag inside this trunk, right beneath an old stethoscope and a tube of mildewed Vick's Inhaler . . . the sheet's appearance in our show was nothing less than a sensation. My grandfather took one look at it and rose roaring to his feet. He strode up on stage and unghosted me right in front of everyone. My grandmother's lips were so tightly pursed they seemed to disappear. Between them, the one booming at me in the voice of a forgotten boatman, the other conveying her fury through vanished lips, they reduced the awesome ghost to a weeping wreck. I fled, took to my heels and ran into the little cornfield, not knowing what had happened. I sat there – perhaps on the very spot on which Nadir Khan had sat! – for several hours, swearing over and over that I would never again open a forbidden trunk, and feeling vaguely resentful that it had not been locked in the first place. But I knew, from their rage, that the sheet was somehow very important indeed.)

I have been interrupted by Padma, who brought me my dinner and then withheld it, blackmailing me: 'So if you're going to spend all your time wrecking your eyes with that scribbling, at least you must read it to me.' I have been singing for my supper – but perhaps our Padma will be useful, because it's impossible to stop her being a critic. She is particularly angry with my remarks about her name. 'What do you know, city boy?' she cried – hand slicing the air. 'In my village there is no shame in being named for the Dung Goddess. Write at once that you are wrong, completely.' In accordance with my lotus's wishes, I insert, forthwith, a brief paean to Dung.

Dung, that fertilizes and causes the crops to grow! Dung, which is patted into thin chapati-like cakes when still fresh and moist, and is sold to the village builders, who use it to secure and strengthen the walls of kachcha buildings made of mud! Dung, whose arrival from the nether end of cattle goes a long way towards explaining their divine and sacred status! Oh, yes, I was wrong, I admit I was prejudiced, no doubt because its unfortunate odours do have a way of offending my sensitive nose – how wonderful, how ineffably lovely it must be to be named for the Purveyor of Dung!

. . . On April 6th, 1919, the holy city of Amritsar smelled (gloriously, Padma, celestially!) of excrement. And perhaps the (beauteous!) reek did not offend the Nose on my grandfather's face – after all, Kashmiri peasants used it, as described above, for a kind of plaster. Even in Srinagar, hawkers with barrows of round dung-cakes were not an uncommon sight. But then the stuff was drying, muted, useful. Amritsar dung was fresh and (worse) redundant. Nor was it all bovine. It issued from the rumps of the horses between the shafts of the city's many tongas, ikkas and gharries; and mules and men and dogs attended nature's calls, mingling in a brotherhood of shit. But there were cows, too: sacred kine roaming the dusty streets, each patrolling its own territory, staking its claims in excrement. And flies! Public Enemy Number One, buzzing gaily from turd to steaming turd, celebrated and cross-pollinated these freely-given offerings. The city swarmed about, too, mirroring the motion of the flies. Doctor Aziz looked down from his hotel window on to this scene as a Jain in a face-mask walked past, brushing the pavement before him with a twig-broom, to avoid stepping on an ant, or even a fly. Spicy sweet fumes rose from a street-snack barrow. 'Hot pakoras, pakoras hot!' A white woman was buying silks from a shop across the street and men in turbans were ogling her. Naseem – now Naseem Aziz – had a sharp headache; it was the first time she'd ever repeated an illness, but life outside her quiet valley had come as something of a shock to her. There was a jug of fresh lime water by her bed, emptying rapidly. Aziz stood at the window, inhaling the city. The spire of the Golden Temple gleamed in the sun. But his nose itched: something was not right here.

Close-up of my grandfather's right hand: nails knuckles fingers all somehow bigger than you'd expect. Clumps of red hair on the outside edges. Thumb and forefinger pressed together, separated only by a thickness of paper. In short: my grandfather was holding a pamphlet. It had been inserted into his hand (we cut to a long-shot – nobody from Bombay should be without a basic film vocabulary) as he entered the hotel foyer. Scurrying of urchin through revolving door, leaflets falling in his wake, as the chaprassi gives chase. Mad revolutions in the doorway, roundandround; until chaprassi-hand demands a close-up, too, because it is pressing thumb to forefinger, the two separated only by the thickness of urchin-ear. Ejection of juvenile disseminator of gutter-tracts; but still my grandfather retained the message. Now, looking out of his, window, he sees it echoed on a wall opposite; and there, on the minaret of a mosque; and in the large black type of newsprint under a hawker's arm. Leaflet newspaper mosque and wall are crying: *Hartal!* Which is to say, literally speaking, a day of mourning, of stillness, of silence. But this is India in the heyday of the Mahatma, when even language obeys the instructions of Gandhiji, and the word has acquired, under his influence, new resonances. *Hartal – April 7*, agree mosque newspaper wall and pamphlet, because Gandhi has decreed that the whole of India shall, on that day, come to a halt. To mourn, in peace, the continuing presence of the British.

'I do not understand this hartal when nobody is dead,' Naseem is crying softly. 'Why will the train not run? How long are we stuck for?'

Doctor Aziz notices a soldierly young man in the street, and thinks – the Indians have fought for the British; so many of them have seen the world by now, and been tainted by Abroad. They will not easily go back to the old world. The British are wrong to try and turn back the clock. 'It was a mistake to pass the Rowlatt Act,' he murmurs.

'What rowlatt?' wails Naseem. 'This is nonsense where I'm concerned!'

'Against political agitation,' Aziz explains, and returns to his thoughts. Tai once said: 'Kashmiris are different.

37

Cowards, for instance. Put a gun in a Kashmiri's hand and it will have to go off by itself – he'll never dare to pull the trigger. We are not like Indians, always making battles.' Aziz, with Tai in his head, does not feel Indian, Kashmir, after all, is not strictly speaking a part of the Empire, but an independent princely state. He is not sure if the hartal of pamphlet mosque wall newspaper is his fight, even though he is in occupied territory now. He turns from the window . . .

. . . To see Naseem weeping into a pillow. She has been weeping ever since he asked her, on their second night, to move a little. 'Move where?' she asked. 'Move how?' He became awkward and said, 'Only move, I mean, like a woman . . .' She shrieked in horror. 'My God, what have I married? I know you Europe-returned men. You find terrible women and then you try to make us girls be like them! Listen, Doctor Sahib, husband or no husband, I am not any . . . bad word woman.' This was a battle my grandfather never won; and it set the tone for their marriage, which rapidly developed into a place of frequent and devastating warfare, under whose depredations the young girl behind the sheet and the gauche young Doctor turned rapidly into different, stranger beings . . . 'What now, wife?' Aziz asks. Naseem buries her face in the pillow. 'What else?' she says in muffled tones. 'You, or what? You want me to walk naked in front of strange men.' (He has told her to come out of purdah.)

He says, 'Your shirt covers you from neck to wrist to knee. Your loose pajamas hide you down to and including your ankles. What we have left are your feet and face. Wife, are your face and feet obscene?' But she wails, 'They will see more than that! They will see my deep-deep shame!'

And now an accident, which launches us into the world of Mercurochrome . . . Aziz, finding his temper slipping from him, drags all his wife's purdah-veils from her suitcase, flings them into a wastepaper basket made of tin with a painting of Guru Nanak on the side, and sets fire to them. Flames leap up, taking him by surprise, licking at curtains. Aadam rushes to the door and yells for help as the cheap curtains begin to blaze . . . and bearers guests washerwomen stream into the room and flap at the burning fabric with dusters towels and other people's laundry. Buckets are brought; the fire goes out; and Naseem cowers on the bed as about thirty-five Sikhs, Hindus and untouchables throng in the smoke-filled room. Finally they leave, and Naseem unleashes two sentences before clamping her lips obstinately shut.

'You are a mad man. I want more lime water.'

My grandfather opens the windows, turns to his bride. 'The smoke will take time to go; I will take a walk. Are you coming?'

Lips clamped; eyes squeezed; a single violent No from the head; and my grandfather goes into the streets alone. His parting shot: 'Forget about being a good Kashmiri girl. Start thinking about being a modern Indian woman.'

. . . While in the Cantonment area, at British Army H.Q., one Brigadier R. E. Dyer is waxing his moustache.

It is April 7th, 1919, and in Amritsar the Mahatma's grand design is being distorted. The shops have shut; the railway station is closed; but now rioting mobs are breaking them up. Doctor Aziz, leather bag in hand, is out in the streets, giving help wherever possible. Trampled bodies have been left where they fell. He is bandaging wounds, daubing them liberally with Mercurochrome, which makes them look bloodier than ever, but at least disinfects them. Finally he returns to his hotel room, his clothes soaked in red stains, and Naseem commences a panic. 'Let me help, let me help, Allah what a man I've married, who goes into gullies to fight with goondas!' She is all over him with water on wads of cotton wool. 'I don't know why can't you be a respectable doctor like ordinary people are just cure important illnesses and all? O God you've got blood everywhere! Sit, sit now, let me wash you at least!'

'It isn't blood, wife.'

'You think I can't see for myself with my own eyes? Why must you make a fool of me even when you're hurt? Must your wife not look after you, even?'

'It's Mercurochrome, Naseem. Red medicine.'

Naseem – who had become a whirlwind of activity, seizing clothes, running taps – freezes. 'You do it on purpose,' she says, 'to make me look stupid. I am not stupid. I have read several books.'

It is April 13th, and they are still in Amritsar. 'This affair isn't finished,' Aadam Aziz told Naseem. 'We can't go, you see: they may need doctors again.'

'So we must sit here and wait until the end of the world?'

He rubbed his nose. 'No, not so long, I am afraid.'

That afternoon, the streets are suddenly full of people, all moving in the same direction, defying Dyer's new Martial Law regulations. Aadam tells Naseem, 'There must be a meeting planned – there will be trouble from the military. They have banned meetings.'

'Why do you have to go? Why not wait to be called?'

. . . A compound can be anything from a wasteland to a park. The largest compound in Amritsar is called Jallianwala Bagh. It is not grassy. Stones cans glass and other things are everywhere. To get into it, you must walk down a very narrow alleyway between two buildings. On April 13th, many thousands of Indians are crowding through this alleyway. 'It is peaceful protest,' someone tells Doctor Aziz. Swept along by the crowds, he arrives at the mouth of the alley. A bag from Heidelberg is in his right hand. (No close-up is necessary.) He is, I know, feeling very scared, because his nose is itching worse than it ever has; but he is a trained doctor, he puts it out of his mind, he enters the compound. Somebody is making a passionate speech. Hawkers move through the crowd selling channa and sweetmeats. The air is filled with dust. There do not seem to be any goondas, any troublemakers, as far as my grandfather can see. A group of Sikhs has spread a cloth on the ground and is eating, seated around it. There is still a smell of ordure in the air. Aziz penetrates the heart of the crowd, as Brigadier R. E. Dyer arrives at the entrance to the alleyway, followed by fifty crack troops. He is the Martial Law Commander of Amritsar – an important man, after all; the waxed tips of his moustache are rigid with importance. As the fifty-one men march down the alleyway a tickle replaces the itch in my grandfather's nose. The fifty-one men enter the compound and take up positions, twenty-five to Dyer's right and twenty-five to his left; and Aadam Aziz ceases to concentrate on the events around him as the tickle mounts to unbearable intensities. As Brigadier Dyer issues a command the sneeze hits my grandfather full in the face. 'Yaaaakh-*thoooo*!' he sneezes and falls forward, losing 'his balance, following his nose and thereby saving his life. His 'doctori-attaché' flies open; bottles, liniment and syringes scatter in the dust. He is scrabbling furiously at people's feet, trying to save his equipment before it is crushed. There is a noise like teeth chattering in winter and someone falls on him. Red stuff stains his shirt. There are screams now and sobs and the strange chattering continues. More and more people seem to have stumbled and fallen on top of my grandfather. He becomes afraid for his back. The clasp of his bag is digging into his chest, inflicting upon it a bruise so severe and mysterious that it will not fade until after his death, years later, on the hill of Sankara Acharya or Takht-e-Sulaiman. His nose is jammed against a bottle of red pills. The chattering stops and is replaced by the noises of people and birds. There seems to be no traffic noise whatsoever. Brigadier Dyer's fifty men put down their machine-guns and go away. They have fired a total of one thousand six hundred and fifty rounds into the unarmed crowd. Of these, one thousand five hundred and sixteen have found their mark, killing or wounding some person. 'Good shooting,' Dyer tells his men, 'We have done a jolly good thing.'

When my grandfather got home that night, my grandmother was trying hard to be a modern woman, to please him, and so she did not turn a hair at his appearance. 'I see you've been spilling the Mercurochrome again, clumsy,' she said, appeasingly.

'It's blood,' he replied, and she fainted. When he brought her round with the help of a little sal volatile, she said, 'Are you hurt?'

'No,' he said.

'But *where* have you *been*, my *God*?'

'Nowhere on earth,' he said, and began to shake in her arms.

My own hand, I confess, has begun to wobble; not entirely because of its theme, but because I have noticed a thin crack, like a hair, appearing in my wrist, beneath the skin . . . No matter. We all owe death a life. So let me conclude with the uncorroborated rumour that the boatman Tai, who recovered from his scrofulous infection soon after my grandfather left Kashmir, did not die until 1947, when (the story goes) he was infuriated by India and Pakistan's struggle over his valley, and walked to Chhamb with the express purpose of standing between the opposing forces and giving them a piece of his mind. Kashmiri for the Kashmiris: that was his line. Naturally, they shot him. Oskar Lubin would probably have approved of his rhetorical gesture; R. E. Dyer might have commended his murderers' rifle skills.

I must go to bed. Padma is waiting; and I need a little warmth.

Hit-the-spittoon

Please believe that I am falling apart.

I am not speaking metaphorically; nor is this the opening gambit of some melodramatic, riddling, grubby appeal for pity. I mean quite simply that I have begun to crack all over like an old jug – that my poor body, singular, unlovely, buffeted by too much history, subjected to drainage above and drainage below, mutilated by doors, brained by spittoons, has started coming apart at the seams. In short, I am literally disintegrating, slowly for the moment, although there are signs of acceleration. I ask you only to accept (as I have accepted) that I shall eventually crumble into (approximately) six hundred and thirty million particles of anonymous, and necessarily oblivious dust. This is why I have resolved to confide in paper, before I forget. (We are a nation of forgetters.)

There are moments of terror, but they go away. Panic like a bubbling sea-beast comes up for air, boils on the surface, but eventually returns to the deep. It is important for me to remain calm. I chew betel-nut and expectorate in the direction of a cheap brassy bowl, playing the ancient game of hit-the-spittoon: Nadir Khan's game, which he learned from the old men in Agra . . . and these days you can buy 'rocket paans' in which, as well as the gum-reddening paste of the betel, the comfort of cocaine lies folded in a leaf. But that would be cheating.

. . . Rising from my pages comes the unmistakable whiff of chutney. So let me obfuscate no further: I, Saleem Sinai, possessor of the most delicately-gifted olfactory organ in history, have dedicated my latter days to the large-scale preparation of condiments. But now, 'A cook?' you gasp in horror, 'A khansama merely? How is it possible?' And, I grant, such mastery of the multiple gifts of cookery and language is rare indeed; yet I possess it. You are amazed; but then I am not, you see, one of your 200-rupees-a-month cookery johnnies, but my own master, working beneath the saffron and green winking of my personal neon goddess. And my chutneys and kasaundies are, after all, connected to my nocturnal scribblings – by day amongst the pickle-vats, by night within these sheets, I spend my time at the great work of preserving. Memory, as well as fruit, is being saved from the corruption of the clocks.

But here is Padma at my elbow, bullying me back into the world of linear narrative, the universe of what-happened-next: 'At this rate,' Padma complains, 'you'll be two hundred years old before you manage to tell about your birth.' She is affecting nonchalance, jutting a careless hip in my general direction, but doesn't fool me. I know now that she is, despite all her protestations, hooked. No doubt about it: my story has her by the throat, so that all at once she's stopped nagging me to go home, to take more baths, to change my vinegar-stained clothes, to abandon even for a moment this darkling pickle-factory where the smells of spices are forever frothing in the air . . . now my dung goddess simply makes up a cot in the corner of this office and prepares my food on two blackened gas-rings, only interrupting my Anglepoise-lit writing to expostulate, 'You better get a move on or you'll die before you get yourself born.' Fighting down the proper pride of the successful storyteller, I attempt to educate her. 'Things – even people – have a way of leaking into each other,' I explain, 'like flavours when you cook. Ilse Lubin's suicide, for example, leaked into old Aadam and sat there in a puddle until he saw God. Likewise,' I intone earnestly, 'the past has dripped into me . . . so we can't ignore it . . .' Her shrug, which does pleasantly wavy things to her chest, cuts me off. 'To me it's a crazy way of telling your life story,' she cries, 'if you can't even get to where your father met your mother.'

. . . And certainly Padma is leaking into me. As history pours out of my fissured body, my lotus is quietly dripping in, with her down-to-earthery, and her paradoxical superstition, her contradictory love of the fabulous – so it's appropriate that I'm about to tell the story of the death of Mian Abdullah. The doomed Hummingbird: a legend of our times.

. . . And Padma is a generous woman, because she stays by me in these last days, although I can't do much for her. That's right – and once again, it's a fitting thing to mention before I launch into the tale of Nadir Khan – I am unmanned. Despite Padma's many and varied gifts and ministrations, I can't leak into her, not even when she puts her left foot on my right, winds her right leg around my waist, inclines her head up toward mine and makes cooing noises; not even when she whispers in my ear, 'So now that the writery is done, let's see if we can make your other pencil work!'; despite everything she tries, I cannot hit her spittoon.

Enough confessions. Bowing to the ineluctable Padma-pressures of what-happened-nextism, and remembering the finite quantity of time at my disposal, I leap forwards from Mercurochrome and land in 1942. (I'm keen to get my parents together, too.)

It seems that in the late summer of that year my grand-father, Doctor Aadam Aziz, contracted a highly dangerous form of optimism. Bicycling around Agra, he whistled piercingly, badly, but very happily. He was by no means alone, because, despite strenuous efforts by the authorities to stamp it out, this virulent disease had been breaking out all over India that year, and drastic steps were to be taken before it was brought under control. The old men at the paan-shop at the top of Cornwallis Road chewed betel and suspected a trick. 'I have lived twice as long as I should have,' the oldest one said, his voice crackling like an old radio because decades were rubbing up against each other around his vocal cords, 'and I've never seen so many people so cheerful in such a bad time. It is the devil's work.' It was, indeed, a resilient virus – the weather alone should have discouraged such germs from breeding, since it had become clear that the rains had failed. The earth was cracking. Dust ate the edges of roads, and on some days huge gaping fissures appeared in the midst of macadamed intersections. The betel-chewers at the paan-shop had begun to talk about omens; calming themselves with their game of hit-the-spittoon, they speculated upon the numberless nameless Godknowswhats that might now issue from the fissuring earth. Apparently a Sikh from the bicycle-repair shop had had his turban pushed off his head in the heat of one afternoon, when his hair, without any reason, had suddenly stood on end. And, more prosaically, the water shortage had reached the point where milkmen could no longer find clean water with which to adulterate the milk . . . Far away, there was a World War in progress once again. In Agra, the heat mounted. But still my grandfather whistled. The old men at the paan-shop found his whistling in rather poor taste, given the circumstances.

(And I, like them, expectorate and rise above fissures.)

Astride his bicycle, leather attaché attached to carrier, my grandfather whistled. Despite irritations of the nose, his lips pursed. Despite a bruise on his chest which had refused to fade for twenty-three years, his good humour was unimpaired. Air passed his lips and was transmuted into sound. He whistled an old German tune: *Tannenbaum*.

The optimism epidemic had been caused by one single human being, whose name, Mian Abdullah, was only used by newspapermen. To everyone else, he was the Hummingbird, a creature which would be impossible if it did not exist. 'Magician turned conjurer,' the newspapermen wrote, 'Mian

46

Abdullah rose from the famous magicians' ghetto in Delhi to become the hope of India's hundred million Muslims.' The Hummingbird was the founder, chairman, unifier and moving spirit of the Free Islam Convocation; and in 1942, marquees and rostrums were being erected on the Agra maidan, where the Convocation's second annual assembly was about to take place. My grandfather, fifty-two years old, his hair turned white by the years and other afflictions, had begun whistling as he passed the maidan. Now he leaned round corners on his bicycle, taking them at a jaunty angle, threading his way between cowpats and children . . . and, in another time and place, told his friend the Rani of Cooch Naheen: 'I started off as a Kashmiri and not much of a Muslim. Then I got a bruise on the chest that turned me into an Indian. I'm still not much of a Muslim, but I'm all for Abdullah. He's fighting my fight.' His eyes were still the blue of Kashmiri sky . . . he arrived home, and although his eyes retained a glimmer of contentment, the whistling stopped; because waiting for him in the courtyard filled with malevolent geese were the disapproving features of my grandmama, Naseem Aziz, whom he had made the mistake of loving in fragments, and who was now unified and transmuted into the formidable figure she would always remain, and who was always known by the curious title of Reverend Mother.

She had become a prematurely old, wide woman, with two enormous moles like witch's nipples on her face; and she lived within an invisible fortress of her own making, an ironclad citadel of traditions and certainties. Earlier that year Aadam Aziz had commissioned life-size blow-up photographs of his family to hang on the living-room wall; the three girls and two boys had posed dutifully enough, but Reverend Mother had rebelled when her turn came. Eventually, the photographer had tried to catch her unawares, but she seized his camera and broke it over his skull. Fortunately, he lived; but there are no photographs of my grandmother anywhere on the earth. She was not one to be trapped in anyone's little black box. It was enough for her that she must live in unveiled, barefaced shamelessness – there was no question of allowing the fact to be recorded.

It was perhaps the obligation of facial nudity, coupled with Aziz's constant requests for her to move beneath him, that had driven her to the barricades; and the domestic rules she established were a system of self-defence so impregnable that Aziz, after many fruitless attempts, had more or less given up trying to storm her many ravelins and bastions, leaving her, like a large smug spider, to rule her chosen domain. (Perhaps, too, it wasn't a system of self-defence at all, but a means of defence against her self.)

Among the things to which she denied entry were all political matters. When Doctor Aziz wished to talk about such things, he visited his friend the Rani, and Reverend Mother sulked; but not very hard, because she knew his visits represented a victory for her.

The twin hearts of her kingdom were her kitchen and her pantry. I never entered the former, but remembered staring through the pantry's locked screen-doors at the enigmatic world within, a world of hanging wire baskets covered with linen cloths to keep out the flies, of tins which I knew to be full of gur and other sweets, of locked chests with neat square labels, of nuts and turnips and sacks of grain, of goose-eggs and wooden brooms. Pantry and kitchen were her inalienable territory; and she defended them ferociously. When she was carrying her last child, my aunt Emerald, her husband offered to relieve her of the chore of supervising the cook. She did not reply; but the next day, when Aziz approached the kitchen, she emerged from it with a metal pot in her hands and barred the doorway. She was fat and also pregnant, so there was not much room left in the doorway. Aadam Aziz frowned. 'What is this, wife?' To which my grandmother answered, 'This, whatsitsname, is a very heavy pot; and if just once I catch you in here, whatsitsname, I'll push your head into it, add some dahi, and make, whatsitsname, a korma.' I don't know how my grandmother came to adopt the term *whatsitsname* as her leitmotif, but as the years passed it invaded her sentences more and more often. I like to think of it as an unconscious cry for help . . . as a seriously-meant question. Reverend Mother was giving us a hint that, for all her presence and bulk, she was adrift in the universe. She didn't know, you see, what it was called.

. . . And at the dinner-table, imperiously, she continued to rule. No food was set upon the table, no plates were laid. Curry and crockery were marshalled upon a low side-table by her right hand, and Aziz and the children ate what she dished out. It is a sign of the power of this custom that, even when her husband was afflicted by constipation, she never once permitted him to choose his food, and listened to no requests or words of advice. A fortress may not move. Not even when its dependants' movements become irregular.

During the long concealment of Nadir Khan, during the visits to the house on Cornwallis Road of young Zulfikar who fell in love with Emerald and of the prosperous reccine-and-leathercloth merchant named Ahmed Sinai who hurt my aunt Alia so badly that she bore a grudge for twenty-five years before discharging it cruelly upon my mother, Reverend Mother's iron grip upon her household never faltered; and even before Nadir's arrival precipitated the great silence, Aadam Aziz had tried to break this grip, and been obliged to go to war with his wife. (All this helps to show how remarkable his affliction by optimism actually was.)

. . . In 1932, ten years earlier, he had taken control of his children's education. Reverend Mother was dismayed; but it was a father's traditional role, so she could not object. Alia was eleven; the second daughter, Mumtaz, was almost nine. The two boys, Hanif and Mustapha, were eight and six, and young Emerald was not yet five. Reverend Mother took to confiding her fears to the family cook, Daoud. 'He fills their heads with I don't know what foreign languages, whatsitsname, and other rubbish also, no doubt.' Daoud stirred pots and Reverend Mother cried, 'Do you wonder, whatsitsname, that the little one calls herself Emerald? In English, whatsitsname? That man will ruin my children for me. Put less cumin in that, whatsitsname, you should pay more attention to your cooking and less to minding other people's business.'

She made only one educational stipulation: religious instruction. Unlike Aziz, who was racked by ambiguity, she had remained devout. 'You have your Hummingbird,' she told him, 'but I, whatsitsname, have the Call of God. A better noise, whatsitsname, than that man's hum.' It was one of her rare political comments . . . and then the day arrived when Aziz threw out the religious tutor. Thumb and forefinger closed around the maulvi's ear. Naseem Aziz saw her husband leading the stragglebearded wretch to the door in the garden wall; gasped; then cried out as her husband's foot was applied to the divine's fleshy parts. Unleashing thunderbolts, Reverend Mother sailed into battle.

'Man without dignity!' she cursed her husband, and, 'Man without, whatsitsname, *shame*!' Children watched from the safety of the back verandah. And Aziz, 'Do you know what that man was teaching your children?' And Reverend Mother hurling question against question, 'What will you not do to bring disaster, whatsitsname, on our heads?' – But now Aziz, 'You think it was Nastaliq script? Eh?' – to which his wife, warming up: 'Would you eat pig? Whatsitsname? Would you spit on the Quran?' And, voice rising, the doctor ripostes, 'Or was it some verses of "The Cow"? You think that?' . . . Paying no attention, Reverend Mother arrives at her climax: 'Would you marry your daughters to Germans!?' And pauses, fighting for breath, letting my grandfather reveal, 'He was teaching them to hate, wife. He tells them to hate Hindus and

Buddhists and Jains and Sikhs and who knows what other vegetarians. Will you have hateful children, woman?'

'Will you have godless ones?' Reverend Mother envisages the legions of the Archangel Gabriel descending at night to carry her heathen brood to hell. She has vivid pictures of hell. It is as hot as Rajputana in June and everyone is made to learn seven foreign languages ... 'I take this oath, whatsitsname,' my grandmother said, 'I swear no food will come from my kitchen to your lips! No, not one chapati, until you bring the maulvi sahib back and kiss his, whatsitsname, feet!'

The war of starvation which began that day very nearly became a duel to the death. True to her word, Reverend Mother did not hand her husband, at mealtimes, so much as an empty plate. Doctor Aziz took immediate reprisals, by refusing to feed himself when he was out. Day by day the five children watched their father disappearing, while their mother grimly guarded the dishes of food. 'Will you be able to vanish completely?' Emerald asked with interest, adding solicitously, 'Don't do it unless you know how to come back again.' Aziz's face acquired craters; even his nose appeared to be getting thinner. His body had become a battlefield and each day a piece of it was blasted away. He told Alia, his eldest, the wise child: 'In any war, the field of battle suffers worse devastation than either army. This is natural.' He began to take rickshaws when he did his rounds. Hamdard the rickshaw-wallah began to worry about him.

The Rani of Cooch Naheen sent emissaries to plead with Reverend Mother. 'India isn't full enough of starving people?' the emissaries asked Naseem, and she unleashed a basilisk glare which was already becoming a legend. Hands clasped in her lap, a muslin dupatta wound miser-tight around her head, she pierced her visitors with lidless eyes and stared them down. Their voices turned to stone; their hearts froze; and alone in a room with strange men, my grandmother sat in triumph, surrounded by downcast eyes. 'Full enough, whatsitsname?' she crowed. 'Well, perhaps. But also, perhaps not.'

But the truth was that Naseem Aziz was very anxious; because while Aziz's death by starvation would be a clear demonstration of the superiority of her idea of the world over his, she was unwilling to be widowed for a mere principle; yet she could see no way out of the situation which did not involve her in backing down and losing face, and having learned to bare her face, my grandmother was most reluctant to lose any of it.

'Fall ill, why don't you?' – Alia, the wise child, found the solution. Reverend Mother beat a tactical retreat, announced a pain, a killing pain absolutely, whatsitsname, and took to her bed. In her absence Alia extended the olive branch to her father, in the shape of a bowl of chicken soup. Two days later, Reverend Mother rose (having refused to be examined by her husband for the first time in her life), reassumed her powers, and with a shrug of acquiescence in her daughter's decision, passed Aziz his food as though it were a mere trifle of a business.

That was ten years earlier; but still, in 1942, the old men at the paan-shop are stirred by the sight of the whistling doctor into giggling memories of the time when his wife had nearly made him do a disappearing trick, even though he didn't know how to come back. Late into the evening they nudge each other with, 'Do you remember when –' and 'Dried up like a skeleton on a washing line! He couldn't even ride his –' and '– I tell you, baba, that woman could do terrible things. I heard she could even dream her daughters' dreams, just to know what they were getting up to!' But as evening settles in the nudges die away, because it is time for the contest. Rhythmically, in silence, their jaws move; then all of a sudden there is a pursing of lips, but what emerges is not air-made-sound. No whistle, but instead a long red jet of betel-juice passes decrepit lips, and moves in unerring accuracy towards an old brass spittoon. There is much slapping of thighs and self-admiring utterance of 'Wah, wah, sir!' and, 'Absolute master shot!' . . . Around the oldsters, the town fades into desultory evening pastimes. Children play hoop and kabaddi and draw beards on posters of Mian Abdullah. And now the old men place the spittoon in the street, further and further from their squatting-place, and aim longer and longer jets at it. Still the fluid flies true. 'Oh too good, yara!' The street urchins make a game of dodging in and out between the red streams, superimposing this game of chicken upon the serious art of hit-the-spittoon . . . But here is an army staff car, scattering urchins as it comes . . . here, Brigadier Dodson, the town's military commander, stifling with heat . . . and here, his A.D.C., Major Zulfikar, passing him a towel. Dodson mops his face; urchins scatter; the car knocks over the spittoon. A dark red fluid with clots in it like blood congeals like a red hand in the dust of the street and points accusingly at the retreating power of the Raj.

Memory of a mildewing photograph (perhaps the work of the same poor brained photographer whose life-size blow-ups so nearly cost him his life): Aadam Aziz, aglow with optimism-fever, shakes hands with a man of sixty or so, an impatient, sprightly type with a lock of white hair falling across his brow like a kindly scar. It is Mian Abdullah, the Hummingbird. ('You see, Doctor Sahib, I keep myself fit. You wish to hit me in the stomach? Try, try. I'm in tiptop shape.' . . . In the photograph, folds of a loose white shirt conceal the stomach, and my grandfather's fist is not clenched, but swallowed up by the hand of the ex-conjurer.) And behind them, looking benignly on, the Rani of Cooch Naheen, who was going white in blotches, a disease which leaked into history and erupted on an enormous scale shortly after Independence . . . 'I am the victim,' the Rani whispers, through photographed lips that never move, 'the hapless victim of my cross-cultural concerns. My skin is the outward expression of the internationalism of my spirit.' Yes, there is a conversation going on in this photograph, as like expert ventriloquists the optimists meet their leader. Beside the Rani – listen carefully now; history and ancestry are about to meet! – stands a peculiar fellow, soft and paunchy, his eyes like stagnant ponds, his hair long like a poet's. Nadir Khan, the Hummingbird's personal secretary. His feet, if they were not frozen by the snapshot, would be shuffling in embarrassment. He mouths through his foolish, rigid smile, 'It's true; I have written verses . . .' Whereupon Mian Abdullah interrupts, booming through his open mouth with glints of pointy teeth: 'But what verses! Not one rhyme in page after page! . . .' And the Rani, gently: 'A modernist, then?' And Nadir, shyly: 'Yes.' What tensions there are now in the still, immobile scene! What edgy banter, as the Hummingbird speaks: 'Never mind about that; art should uplift; it should remind us of our glorious literary heritage!' . . . And is that a shadow, or a frown on his secretary's brow? . . . Nadir's voice, issuing lowaslow from the fading picture: 'I do not believe in high art, Mian Sahib. Now art must be beyond categories; my poetry and – oh – the game of hit-the-spittoon are equals.' . . . So now the Rani, kind woman that she is, jokes, 'Well, I shall set aside a room, perhaps; for paan-eating and spittoon-hittery. I have a superb silver spittoon, inlaid with lapis lazuli, and you must all come and practise. Let the walls be splashed with our inaccurate expectorating! They will be honest stains, at least.' And now the photograph has run out of words; now I notice, with my mind's eye, that all the while the Hummingbird has been staring towards the door, which is past my grandfather's shoulder at the very edge of the picture. Beyond the door, history calls. The Hummingbird is impatient to get away . . . but he has been with us, and his presence has brought us two threads which will pursue me through all my days: the thread that leads to the ghetto of the magicians; and the thread that tells the story of Nadir the rhymeless, verbless poet and a priceless silver spittoon.

'What nonsense,' our Padma says. 'How can a picture talk? Stop now; you must be too tired to think.' But when I say to her that Mian Abdullah had the strange trait of humming without pause, humming in a strange way, neither musical nor unmusical, but somehow mechanical, the hum of an engine or dynamo, she swallows it easily enough, saying judiciously, 'Well, if he was such an energetic man, it's no surprise to me.' She's all ears again; so I warm to my theme and report that Mian Abdullah's hum rose and fell in direct relationship to his work rate. It was a hum that could fall low enough to give you toothache, and when it rose to its highest, most feverish pitch, it had the ability of inducing erections in anyone within its vicinity. ('Arré baap,' Padma laughs, 'no wonder he was so popular with the men!') Nadir Khan, as his secretary, was attacked constantly by his master's vibratory quirk, and his ears jaw penis were forever behaving according to the dictates of the Hummingbird. Why, then, did Nadir stay, despite erections which embarrassed him in the company of strangers, despite aching molars and a work schedule which often occupied twenty-two hours in every twenty-four? Not – I believe – because he saw it as his poetic duty to get close to the centre of events and transmute them into literature. Nor because he wanted fame for himself. No: but Nadir had one thing in common with my grandfather, and it was enough. He, too, suffered from the optimism disease.

Like Aadam Aziz, like the Rani of Cooch Naheen, Nadir Khan loathed the Muslim League ('That bunch of toadies!' the Rani cried in her silvery voice, swooping around the octaves like a skier. 'Landowners with vested interests to protect! What do they have to do with Muslims? They go like toads to the British and form governments for them, now that the Congress refuses to do it!' It was the year of the 'Quit India' resolution. 'And what's more,' the Rani said with finality, 'they are mad. Otherwise why would they want to partition India?')

Mian Abdullah, the Hummingbird, had created the Free Islam Convocation almost single-handedly. He invited the leaders of the dozens of Muslim splinter groups to form a loosely federated alternative to the dogmatism and vested interests of the Leaguers. It had been a great conjuring trick, because they had all come. That was the first Convocation, in Lahore; Agra would see the second. The marquees would be filled with members of agrarian movements, urban labourers' syndicates, religious divines and regional groupings. It would see confirmed what the first assembly had intimated: that the League, with its demand for a partitioned India, spoke on nobody's behalf but its own. 'They have turned their backs on us,' said the Convocation's posters, 'and now they claim we're standing behind them!' Mian Abdullah opposed the partition.

In the throes of the optimism epidemic, the Hummingbird's patron, the Rani of Cooch Naheen, never mentioned the clouds on the horizon. She never pointed out that Agra was a Muslim League stronghold, saying only, 'Aadam my boy, if the Hummingbird wants to hold Convocation here, I'm not about to suggest he goes to Allahabad.' She was bearing the entire expense of the event without complaint or interference; not, let it be said, without making enemies in the town. The Rani did not live like other Indian princes. Instead of teetar-hunts, she endowed scholarships. Instead of hotel scandals, she had politics. And so the rumours began. 'These scholars of hers, man, everyone knows they have to perform extra-curricular duties. They go to her bedroom in the dark, and she never lets them see her blotchy face, but bewitches them into bed with her voice of a singing witch!' Aadam Aziz had never believed in witches. He enjoyed her brilliant circle of friends who were as much at home in Persian as they were in German. But Naseem Aziz, who half-believed the stories about the Rani, never accompanied him to the princess's house. 'If God meant people to speak many tongues,' she argued, 'why did he put only one in our heads?'

And so it was that none of the Hummingbird's optimists were prepared for what happened. They played hit-the-spittoon, and ignored the cracks in the earth.

Sometimes legends make reality, and become more useful than the facts. According to legend, then – according to the polished gossip of the ancients at the paan-shop – Mian Abdullah owed his downfall to his purchase, at Agra railway station, of a peacock-feather fan, despite Nadir Khan's warning about bad luck. What is more, on that night of crescent moons, Abdullah had been working with Nadir, so that when the new moon rose they both saw it through glass. 'These things matter,' the betel-chewers say. 'We have been alive too long, and we know.' (Padma is nodding her head in agreement.)

The Convocation offices were on the ground floor of the historical faculty building at the University campus. Abdullah and Nadir were coming to the end of their night's work; the Hummingbird's hum was low-pitched and Nadir's teeth were on edge. There was a poster on the office wall, expressing Abdullah's favourite anti-Partition sentiment, a quote from the poet Iqbal: 'Where can we find a land that is foreign to God?' And now the assassins reached the campus.

Facts: Abdullah had plenty of enemies. The British attitude to him was always ambiguous. Brigadier Dodson hadn't wanted him in town. There was a knock on the door and Nadir answered it. Six new moons came into the room, six crescent knives held by men dressed all in black, with covered faces. Two men held Nadir while the others moved towards the Hummingbird.

'At this point,' the betel-chewers say, 'the Hummingbird's hum became higher. Higher and higher, yara, and the assassins' eyes became wide as their members made tents under their robes. Then – Allah, then! – the knives began to sing and Abdullah sang louder, humming high-high like he'd never hummed before. His body was hard and the long curved blades had trouble killing him; one broke on a rib, but the others quickly became stained with red. But now – listen! – Abdullah's humming rose out of the range of our human ears, and was heard by the dogs of the town. In Agra there are maybe eight thousand four hundred and twenty pie-dogs. On that night, it is certain that some were eating, others dying; there were some who fornicated and others who did not hear the call. Say about two thousand of these; that left six thousand four hundred and twenty of the curs, and all of these turned and ran for the University, many of them rushing across the railway tracks from the wrong side of town. It is well known that this is true. Everyone in town saw it, except those who were asleep. They went noisily, like an army, and afterwards their trail was littered with bones and dung and bits of hair . . . and all the time Abdullahji was humming, humming-humming, and the knives were singing. And know this: suddenly one of the killers' eyes cracked and fell out of its socket. Afterwards the pieces of glass were found, ground into the carpet!'

They say, 'When the dogs came Abdullah was nearly dead and the knives were blunt . . . they came like wild things, leaping through the window, which had no glass because Abdullah's hum had shattered it . . . they thudded against the door until the wood broke . . . and then they were every-where, baba! . . . some without legs, others lacking hair, but most of them had some teeth at least, and some of these were sharp . . . And now see this: the assassins cannot have feared interruption, because they had posted no guards; so the dogs got them by surprise . . . the two men holding Nadir Khan, that spineless one, fell beneath the weight of the beasts, with maybe sixty-eight dogs on their necks . . . afterwards the killers were so badly damaged that nobody could say who they were.'

'At some point,' they say, 'Nadir dived out of the window and ran. The dogs and assassins were too busy to follow him.'

Dogs? Assassins? . . . If you don't believe me, check. Find out about Mian Abdullah and his Convocations. Discover how we've swept his story under the carpet . . . then let me tell how Nadir Khan, his lieutenant, spent three years under my family's rugs.

As a young man he had shared a room with a painter whose paintings had grown larger and larger as he tried to get the whole of life into his art. 'Look at me,' he said before he killed himself, 'I wanted to be a miniaturist and I've got elephantiasis instead!' The swollen events of the night of the crescent knives reminded Nadir Khan of his room-mate, because life had once again, perversely, refused to remain life-sized. It had turned melodramatic: and that embarrassed him.

How did Nadir Khan run across the night town without being noticed? I put it down to his being a bad poet, and as such, a born survivor. As he ran, there was a self-consciousness about him, his body appearing to apologize for behaving as if it were in a cheap thriller, of the sort hawkers sell on railway stations, or give away free with bottles of green medicine that can cure colds, typhoid, impotence, homesickness and poverty . . . On Cornwallis Road, it was a warm night. A coal-brazier stood empty by the deserted rickshaw rank. The paan-shop was closed and the old men were asleep on the roof, dreaming of tomorrow's game. An insomniac cow, idly chewing a Red and White cigarette packet, strolled by a bundled street-sleeper, which meant he would wake in the morning, because a cow will ignore a sleeping man unless he's about to die. Then it nuzzles at him thoughtfully. Sacred cows eat anything.

My grandfather's large old stone house, bought from the proceeds of the gemstone shops and blind Ghani's dowry settlement, stood in the darkness, set back a dignified distance from the road. There was a walled-in garden at the rear and by the garden door was the low outhouse rented cheaply to the family of old Hamdard and his son Rashid the rickshaw boy. In front of the outhouse was the well with its cow-driven waterwheel, from which irrigation channels ran down to the small cornfield which lined the house all way to the gate in the perimeter wall along Cornwallis Road. Between house and field ran a small gully for pedestrians and rickshaws. In Agra the cycle-rickshaw had recently replaced the kind where a man stood between wooden shafts. There was still trade for the horse-drawn tongas, but it was dwindling . . . Nadir Khan ducked in through the gate, squatted for a moment with his back to the perimeter wall, reddening as he passed his water. Then, seemingly upset by the vulgarity of his decision, he fled to the cornfield and plunged in. Partially concealed by the sun-withered stalks, he lay down in the foetal position.

Rashid the rickshaw boy was seventeen and on his way home from the cinema. That morning he'd seen two men pushing a low trolley on which were mounted two enormous hand-painted posters, back-to-back, advertising the new film *Gai-Wellah,* starring Rashid's favourite actor Dev. FRESH FROM FIFTY FIERCE WEEKS IN DELHI! STRAIGHT FROM SIXTY-THREE SHARPSHOOTER WEEKS IN BOMBAY! the posters cried, SECOND RIP-ROARIOUS YEAR! The film was an eastern Western. Its hero, Dev, who was not slim, rode the range alone. It looked very like the Indo-Gangetic plain. Gai-Wallah means cow-fellow and Dev played a sort of one-man vigilante force for the protection of cows, SINGLE-HANDED! and DOUBLE-BARRELLED!, he stalked the many herds of cattle which were being driven across the range to the slaughterhouse, vanquished the cattlemen and liberated the sacred beasts. (The film was made for Hindu audiences; in Delhi it had caused riots. Muslim Leaguers had driven cows past cinemas to the slaughter, and had been mobbed.) The songs and dances were good and there was a beautiful nautch girl who would have looked more graceful if they hadn't made her dance in a ten-gallon cowboy hat. Rashid sat on a bench in the front stalls and joined in the whistles and cheers. He ate two samosas, spending too much money; his mother would be hurt but he'd had a fine time. As he pedalled his rickshaw home he practised some of the fancy riding he'd seen in the film, hanging down low on one side, freewheeling down a slight slope, using the rickshaw the way Gai-Wallah used his horse to conceal him from his enemies. Eventually he reached up, turned the handlebars and to his delight the rickshaw moved sweetly through the gate and down the gully by the cornfield. Gai-Wallah had used this trick to steal up on a gang of cattlemen as they sat in the brush, drinking and gambling. Rashid applied the brakes and flung himself into the cornfield, running – FULL-TILT! – at the unsuspecting cattlemen, his guns cocked and ready. As he neared their camp-fire he released his 'yell of hate' to frighten them, YAAAAAAAA! Obviously he did not really shout so close to the Doctor Sahib's house, but he distended his mouth as he ran, screaming silently, BLAMM! BLAMM! Nadir Khan had been finding sleep hard to come by and now he opened his eyes. He saw – EEEYAAAH! – a wild stringy figure coming at him like a mail-train, yelling at the top of his voice – but maybe he had gone deaf, because there wasn't any *noise*! – and he was rising to his feet, the shriek was just passing his over-plump lips, when Rashid saw him and found voice as well. Hooting in terrified unison, they both turned tail and ran. Then they stopped, each having noted the other's flight, and peered at one another through the shrivelling corn. Rashid recognized Nadir Khan, saw his torn clothes and was deeply troubled.

'I am a friend,' Nadir said foolishly. 'I must see Doctor Aziz.'

'But the Doctor is asleep, and is not in the cornfield.' Pull yourself together, Rashid told himself, stop talking nonsense! This is Mian Abdullah's friend! . . . But Nadir didn't seem to have noticed; his face was working furiously, trying to get out some words which had stuck like shreds of chicken between his teeth . . . 'My life,' he managed it at last, 'is in danger.'

And now Rashid, still full of the spirit of Gai-Wallah, came to the rescue. He led Nadir to a door in the side of the house. It was bolted and locked; but Rashid pulled, and the lock came away in his hand. 'Indian-made,' he whispered, as if that explained everything. And, as Nadir stepped inside, Rashid hissed, 'Count on me completely, sahib. Mum's the word! I swear on my mother's grey hairs.'

He replaced the lock on the outside. To have actually saved the Hummingbird's right-hand man! . . . But from what? Whom? . . . Well, real life was better than the pictures, sometimes.

'Is that him?' Padma asks, in some confusion. 'That fat soft cowardly plumpie? Is he going to be your father?'

Under the carpet

That was the end of the optimism epidemic. In the morning a sweeper-woman entered the offices of the Free Islam Convocation and found the Hummingbird, silenced, on the floor, surrounded by paw-prints and the shreds of his murderers. She screamed; but later, when the authorities had been and gone, she was told to clean up the room. After clearing away innumerable dog-hairs, swatting countless fleas and extracting from the carpet the remnants of a shattered glass eye, she protested to the University's comptroller of works that, if this sort of thing was going to keep happening, she deserved a small pay rise. She was possibly the last victim of the optimism bug, and in her case the illness didn't last long, because the comptroller was a hard man, and gave her the boot.

The assassins were never identified, nor were their paymasters named. My grandfather was called to the campus by Major Zulfikar, Brigadier Dodson's A.D.C., to write his friend's death certificate. Major Zulfikar promised to call on Doctor Aziz to tie up a few loose ends; my grandfather blew his nose and left. At the maidan, tents were coming down like punctured hopes; the Convocation would never be held again. The Rani of Cooch Naheen took to her bed. After a lifetime of making light of her illnesses she allowed them to claim her, and lay still for years, watching herself turn the colour of her bedsheets. Meanwhile, in the old house on Cornwallis Road, the days were full of potential mothers and possible fathers. You see, Padma: you're going to find out now.

Using my nose (because, although it has lost the powers which enabled it, so recently, to make history, it has acquired other, compensatory gifts) – turning it inwards, I've been sniffing out the atmosphere in my grandfather's house in those days after the death of India's humming hope; and wafting down to me through the years comes a curious mélange of odours, filled with unease, the whiff of things concealed mingling with the odours of burgeoning romance and the sharp stink of my grandmother's curiosity and strength . . . while the Muslim League rejoiced, secretly of course, at the fall of its opponent, my grandfather could be found (my nose finds him) seated every morning on what he called his 'thunder box', tears standing in his eyes. But these are not tears of grief; Aadam Aziz has simply paid the price of being Indianized, and suffers terribly from constipation. Balefully, he eyes the enema contraption hanging on the toilet wall.

Why have I invaded my grandfather's privacy? Why, when I might have described how, after Mian Abdullah's death, Aadam buried himself in his work, taking upon himself the care of the sick in the shanty-towns by the railway tracks – rescuing them from quacks who injected them with pepperwater and thought that fried spiders could cure blindness – while continuing to fulfil his duties as university physician; when I might have elaborated on the great love that had begun to grow between my grandfather and his second daughter, Mumtaz, whose dark skin stood between her and the affections of her mother, but whose gifts of gentleness, care and fragility endeared her to her father with his inner torments which cried out for her form of unquestioning tenderness; why, when I might have chosen to describe the by-now-constant itch in his nose, do I choose to wallow in excrement? Because this is where Aadam Aziz was, on the afternoon after his signing of a death certificate, when all of a sudden a voice – soft, cowardly, embarrassed, the voice of a rhymeless poet – spoke to him from the depths of the large old laundry-chest standing in the corner of the room, giving him a shock so profound that it proved laxative, and the enema contraption did not have to be unhooked from its perch. Rashid the rickshaw boy had let Nadir Khan into the thunderbox-room by way of the sweeper's entrance, and he had taken refuge in the washing-chest. While my grandfather's astonished sphincter relaxed, his ears heard a request for sanctuary, a request muffled by linen, dirty underwear, old shirts and the embarrassment of the speaker. And so it was that Aadam Aziz resolved to hide Nadir Khan.

Now comes the scent of a quarrel, because Reverend Mother Naseem is thinking about her daughters, twenty-one-year-old Alia, black Mumtaz, who is nineteen, and pretty, flighty Emerald, who isn't fifteen yet but has a look in her eyes that's older than anything her sisters possess. In the town, among spittoon-hitters and rickshaw-wallahs, among film-poster-trolley pushers and college students alike, the three sisters are known as the 'Teen Batti', the three bright lights . . . and how can Reverend Mother permit a strange man to dwell in the same house as Alia's gravity, Mumtaz's black, luminous skin and Emerald's eyes? . . . 'You are out of your mind, husband; that death has hurt your brain.' But Aziz, determinedly: 'He is staying.' In the cellars . . . because concealment has always been a crucial architectural consideration in India, so that Aziz's house has extensive underground chambers, which can be reached only through trap-doors in the floors, which are covered by carpets and mats . . . Nadir Khan hears the dull rumble of the quarrel and fears for his fate. My God (I sniff the thoughts of the clammy-palmed poet), the world is gone insane . . . are we men in this country? Are we beasts? And if I must go, when will the knives come for me? . . . And through his mind pass images of peacock-feather fans and the new moon seen through glass and transformed into a stabbing, red-stained blade . . . Upstairs, Reverend Mother says, 'The house is full of young unmarried girls, whatsitsname; is this how you show your daughters respect?' And now the aroma of a temper lost; the great destroying rage of Aadam Aziz is unleashed, and instead of pointing out that Nadir Khan will be under ground, swept under the carpet where he will scarcely be able to defile daughters; instead of paying due testimony to the verbless bard's sense of propriety, which is so advanced that he could not even dream of making improper advances without blushing in his sleep; instead of these avenues of reason, my grandfather bellows, 'Be silent, woman! The man needs our shelter; he will stay.' Whereupon an implacable perfume, a hard cloud of determination settles upon my grandmother, who says, 'Very well. You ask me, whatsitsname, for silence. So not one word, whatsitsname, will pass my lips from now on.' And Aziz, groaning, 'Oh, damnation, woman, spare us your crazy oaths!'

But Reverend Mother's lips were sealed, and silence descended. The smell of silence, like a rotting goose-egg, fills my nostrils; overpowering everything else, it possesses the earth . . . While Nadir Khan hid in his half-lit underworld, his hostess hid, too, behind a deafening wall of soundlessness. At first my grandfather probed the wall, looking for chinks; he found none. At last he gave up, and waited for her sentences to offer up their glimpses of her self, just as once he had lusted after the brief fragments of her body he had seen through a perforated sheet; and the silence filled the house, from wall to wall, from floor to ceiling, so that the flies seemed to give up buzzing, and mosquitoes refrained from humming before they bit; silence stilling the hissing of geese in the courtyard. The children spoke in whispers at first, and then fell quiet: while in the cornfield, Rashid the rickshaw boy yelled his silent 'yell of hate', and kept his own vow of silence, which he had sworn upon his mother's hairs.

Into this bog of muteness there came, one evening, a short man whose head was as flat as the cap upon it; whose legs were as bowed as reeds in the wind; whose nose nearly touched his up-curving chin; and whose voice, as a result, was thin and sharp – it had to be, to squeeze through the narrow gap between his breathing apparatus and his jaw . . . a man whose short sight obliged him to take life one step at a time, which gained him a reputation for thoroughness and dullness, and endeared him to his superiors by enabling them to feel well-served without feeling threatened; a man whose starched, pressed uniform reeked of Blanco and rectitude, and about whom, despite his appearance of a character out of a puppet-show, there hung the unmistakable scent of success: Major Zulfikar, a man with a future, came to call, as he had promised, to tie up a few loose ends. Abdullah's murder, and Nadir Khan's suspicious disappearance, were much on his mind, and since he knew about Aadam Aziz's infection by the optimism bug, he mistook the silence in the house for a hush of mourning, and did not stay for long. (In the cellar, Nadir huddled with cockroaches.) Sitting quietly in the drawing-room with the five children, his hat and stick beside him on the Telefunken radiogram, the life-size images of the young Azizes staring at him from the walls, Major Zulfikar fell in love. He was short-sighted, but he wasn't blind, and in the impossibly adult gaze of young Emerald, the brightest of the 'three bright lights', he saw that she had understood his future, and forgiven him, because of it, for his appearance; and before he left, he had decided to marry her after a decent interval. ('Her?' Padma guesses. 'That hussy is your mother?' But there are other mothers-to-be, other future fathers, wafting in and out through the silence.)

In that marshy time without words the emotional life of grave Alia, the eldest, was also developing; and Reverend Mother, locked up in the pantry and kitchen, sealed behind her lips, was incapable – because of her vow – of expressing her distrust of the young merchant in reccine and leathercloth who came to visit her daughter. (Aadam Aziz had always insisted that his daughters be permitted to have male friends.) Ahmed Sinai – 'Ahaa!' yells Padma in triumphant recognition – had met Alia at the University, and seemed intelligent enough for the bookish, brainy girl on whose face my grandfather's nose had acquired an air of overweight wisdom; but Naseem Aziz felt uneasy about him, because he had been divorced at twenty. ('Anyone can make one mistake,' Aadam had told her, and that nearly began a fight, because she thought for a moment that there had been something overly personal in his tone of voice. But then Aadam had added, 'Just let this divorce of his fade away for a year or two; then we'll give this house its first wedding, with a big marquee in the garden, and singers and sweetmeats and all.' Which, despite everything, was an idea that appealed to Naseem.) Now, wandering through the walled-in gardens of silence, Ahmed Sinai and Alia communed without speech; but although everyone expected him to propose, the silence seemed to have got through to him, too, and the question remained unasked. Alia's face acquired a weightiness at this time, a jowly pessimistic quality which she was never entirely to lose. ('Now then,' Padma reproves me, 'that's no way to describe your respected motherji.')

One more thing: Alia had inherited her mother's tendency to put on fat. She would balloon outwards with the passing years.

And Mumtaz, who had come out of her mother's womb black as midnight? Mumtaz was never brilliant; not as beautiful as Emerald; but she was good, and dutiful, and alone. She spent more time with her father than any of her sisters, fortifying him against the bad temper which was being exaggerated nowadays by the constant itch in his nose; and she took upon herself the duties of caring for the needs of Nadir Khan, descending daily into his underworld bearing trays of food, and brooms, and even emptying his personal thunderbox, so that not even a latrine cleaner could guess at his presence. When she descended, he lowered his eyes; and no words, in that dumb house, were exchanged between them.

What was it the spittoon hitters said about Naseem Aziz? 'She eavesdropped on her daughters' dreams, just to know what they were up to.' Yes, there's no other explanation, stranger things have been known to happen in this country of ours, just pick up any newspaper and see the daily titbits recounting miracles in this village or that – Reverend Mother began to dream her daughters' dreams. (Padma accepts this without blinking; but what others will swallow as effortlessly as a laddoo, Padma may just as easily reject. No audience is without its idiosyncrasies of belief.) So, then: asleep in her bed at night, Reverend Mother visited Emerald's dreams, and found another dream within them – Major Zulfikar's private fantasy, of owning a large modern house with a bath beside his bed. This was the zenith of the Major's ambitions; and in this way Reverend Mother discovered, not only that her daughter had been meeting her Zulfy in secret, in places where speech was possible, but also that Emerald's ambitions were greater than her man's. And (why not?) in Aadam Aziz's dreams she saw her husband walking mournfully up a mountain in Kashmir with a hole in his stomach the size of a fist, and guessed that he was falling out of love with her, and also foresaw his death; so that years later, when she heard, she said only. 'Oh, I knew it, after all.'

. . . It could not be long now, Reverend Mother thought, before our Emerald tells her Major about the guest in the cellar; and then I shall be able to speak again. But then, one night, she entered the dreams of her daughter Mumtaz, the blackie whom she had never been able to love because of her skin of a South Indian fisherwoman, and realized the trouble would not stop there; because Mumtaz Aziz –

69

like her admirer under the carpets – was also falling in love.

There was no proof. The invasion of dreams – or a mother's knowledge, or a woman's intuition, call it what you like – is not something that will stand up in court, and Reverend Mother knew that it was a serious business to accuse a daughter of getting up to hanky-panky under her father's roof. In addition to which, something steely had entered Reverend Mother; and she resolved to do nothing, to keep her silence intact, and let Aadam Aziz discover just how badly his modern ideas were ruining his children – let him find out for himself, after his lifetime of telling her to be quiet with her decent old-fashioned notions. 'A bitter woman,' Padma says; and I agree.

'Well?' Padma demands. 'Was it true?'

Yes: after a fashion: true.

'There was hankying and pankying? In the cellars? Without even chaperones?'

Consider the circumstances – extenuating, if ever circumstances were. Things seem permissible underground that would seem absurd or even wrong in the clear light of day.

'That fat poet did it to the poor blackie? He *did*?'

He was down there a long time, too – long enough to start talking to flying cockroaches and fearing that one day someone would ask him to leave and dreaming of crescent knives and howling dogs and wishing and wishing that the Hummingbird were alive to tell him what to do and to discover that you could not write poetry underground; and then this girl comes with food and she doesn't mind cleaning away your pots and you lower your eyes but you see an ankle that seems to glow with graciousness, a black ankle like the black of the underground nights . . .

'I'd never have thought he was up to it.' Padma sounds admiring. 'The fat old good-for-nothing!'

And eventually in that house where everyone, even the fugitive hiding in the cellar from his faceless enemies, finds his tongue cleaving dryly to the roof of his mouth, where even the sons of the house have to go into the cornfield with the rickshaw boy to joke about whores and compare the length of their members and whisper furtively about dreams of being film directors (Hanif's dream, which horrifies his dream-invading mother, who believes the cinema to be an extension of the brothel business), where life has been transmuted into grotesquery by the irruption into it of history, eventually in the murkiness of the underworld he cannot help himself, he finds his eyes straying upwards, up along delicate sandals and baggy pajamas and past loose kurta and above the dupatta, the cloth of modesty, until eyes meet eyes, and then

'And then? Come on, baba, what then?'

Shyly, she smiles at him.

'What?'

And after that, there are smiles in the underworld, and something has begun.

'Oh, so what? You're telling me that's *all*?'

That's all: until the day Nadir Khan asked to see my grandfather – his sentences barely audible in the fog of silence – and asked for his daughter's hand in marriage.

'Poor girl,' Padma concludes, 'Kashmiri girls are normally fair like mountain snow, but she turned out black. Well, well, her skin would have stopped her making a good match, probably; and that Nadir's no fool. Now they'll have to let him stay, and get fed, and get a roof over his head, and all he has to do is hide like a fat earthworm under the ground. Yes, maybe he's not such a fool.'

My grandfather tried hard to persuade Nadir Khan that he was no longer in danger; the assassins were dead, and Mian Abdullah had been their real target; but Nadir Khan still dreamed about the singing knives, and begged, 'Not yet,

Doctor Sahib; please, some more time.' So that one night in the late summer of 1943 – the rains had failed again – my grandfather, his voice sounding distant and eerie in that house in which so few words were spoken, assembled his children in the drawing-room where their portraits hung. When they entered they discovered that their mother was absent, having chosen to remain immured in her room with her web of silence; but present were a lawyer and (despite Aziz's reluctance, he had complied with Mumtaz's wishes) a mullah, both provided by the ailing Rani of Cooch Naheen, both 'utterly discreet'. And their sister Mumtaz was there in bridal finery, and beside her in a chair set in front of the radiogram was the lank-haired, overweight, embarrassed figure of Nadir Khan. So it was that the first wedding in the house was one at which there were no tents, no singers, no sweetmeats and only a minimum of guests; and after the rites were over and Nadir Khan lifted his bride's veil – giving Aziz a sudden shock, making him young for a moment, and in Kashmir again, sitting on a dais while people put rupees in his lap – my grandfather made them all swear an oath not to reveal the presence in their cellar of their new brother-in-law. Emerald, reluctantly, gave her promise last of all.

After that Aadam Aziz made his sons help him carry all manner of furnishings down through the trap-door in the drawing-room floor: draperies and cushions and lamps and a big comfortable bed. And at last Nadir and Mumtaz stepped down into the vaults; the trap-door was shut and the carpet rolled into place and Nadir Khan, who loved his wife as delicately as a man ever had, had taken her into his underworld.

Mumtaz Aziz began to lead a double life. By day she was a single girl, living chastely with her parents, studying mediocrely at the university, cultivating those gifts of assiduity, nobility and forbearance which were to be her hallmarks throughout her life, up to and including the time

72

when she was assailed by the talking washing-chests of her past and then squashed flat as a rice pancake; but at night, descending through a trap-door, she entered a lamplit, secluded marriage chamber which her secret husband had taken to calling the Taj Mahal, because Taj Bibi was the name by which people had called an earlier Mumtaz – Mumtaz Mahal, wife of Emperor Shah Jehan, whose name meant 'king of the world'. When she died he built her that mausoleum which has been immortalized on postcards and chocolate boxes and whose outdoor corridors stink of urine and whose walls are covered in graffiti and whose echoes are tested for visitors by guides although there are signs in three languages pleading for silence. Like Shah Jehan and his Mumtaz, Nadir and his dark lady lay side by side, and lapis lazuli inlay work was their companion because the bedridden, dying Rani of Cooch Naheen had sent them, as a wedding gift, a wondrously-carved, lapis-inlaid, gemstone-crusted silver spittoon. In their comfortable lamplit seclusion, husband and wife played the old men's game.

Mumtaz made the paans for Nadir but did not like the taste herself. She spat streams of nibu-pani. His jets were red and hers were lime. It was the happiest time of her life. And she said afterwards, at the ending of the long silence, 'We would have had children in the end; only then it wasn't right, that's all.' Mumtaz Aziz loved children all her life.

Meanwhile, Reverend Mother moved sluggishly through the months in the grip of a silence which had become so absolute that even the servants received their instructions in sign language, and once the cook Daoud had been staring at her, trying to understand her somnolently frantic signalling, and as a result had not been looking in the direction of the boiling pot of gravy which fell upon his foot and fried it like a five-toed egg; he opened his mouth to scream but no sound emerged, and after that he became convinced that the old hag had the power of witchery, and became too scared to leave her service. He stayed until his death, hobbling around the courtyard and being attacked by the geese.

They were not easy years. The drought led to rationing, and what with the proliferation of meatless days and riceless days it was hard to feed an extra, hidden mouth. Reverend Mother was forced to dig deep into her pantry, which thickened her rage like heat under a sauce. Hairs began to grow out of the moles on her face. Mumtaz noticed with concern that her mother was swelling, month by month. The unspoken words inside her were blowing her up . . . Mumtaz had the impression that her mother's skin was becoming dangerously stretched.

And Doctor Aziz spent his days out of the house, away from the deadening silence, so Mumtaz, who spent her nights underground, saw very little in those days of the father whom she loved; and Emerald kept her promise, telling the Major nothing about the family secret; but conversely, she told her family nothing about her relationship with him, which was fair, she thought; and in the cornfield Mustapha and Hanif and Rashid the rickshaw boy became infected with the listlessness of the times; and finally the house on Cornwallis Road drifted as far as August 9th, 1945, and things changed.

Family history, of course, has its proper dietary laws. One is supposed to swallow and digest only the permitted parts of it, the halal portions of the past, drained of their redness, their blood. Unfortunately, this makes the stories less juicy; so I am about to become the first and only member of my family to flout the laws of halal. Letting no blood escape from the body of the tale, I arrive at the unspeakable part; and, undaunted, press on.

What happened in August 1945? The Rani of Cooch Naheen died, but that's not what I'm after, although when she went she had become so sheetly-white that it was difficult to see her against the bed-clothes; having fulfilled her function by bequeathing my story a silver spittoon, she had the grace to exit quickly . . . also in 1945, the monsoons did not fail. In the Burmese jungle, Orde Wingate and his Chindits, as well as the army of Subhas Chandra Bose, which was fighting on the Japanese side, were drenched by the returning rains. Satyagraha demonstrators in Jullundur, lying non-violently across railway lines, were soaked to the skin. The cracks in the long-parched earth began to close; there were towels wedged against the doors and windows of the house on Cornwallis Road, and they had to be wrung out and replaced constantly. Mosquitoes sprouted in the pools of water standing by every roadside. And the cellar – Mumtaz's Taj Mahal grew damp, until at last she fell ill. For some days she told nobody, but when her eyes became red-rimmed and she began to shake with fever, Nadir, fearing pneumonia, begged her to go to her father for treatment. She spent the next many weeks back in her maiden's bed, and Aadam Aziz sat by his daughter's bedside, putting cooling flannels on her forehead while she shook. On August 6th the illness broke. On the morning of the 9th Mumtaz was well enough to take a little solid food.

And now my grandfather fetched an old leather bag with the word HEIDELBERG burned into the leather at the base, because he had decided that, as she was very run-down, he had better give her a thorough physical check-up. As he unclasped the bag, his daughter began to cry.

(And now we're here. Padma: this is it.)

Ten minutes later the long time of silence was ended for ever as my grandfather emerged roaring from the sick-room. He bellowed for his wife, his daughters, his sons. His lungs were strong and the noise reached Nadir Khan in the cellar. It would not have been difficult for him to guess what the fuss was about.

The family assembled in the drawing-room around the radiogram, beneath the ageless photographs. Aziz carried

Mumtaz into the room and set her down on a couch. His face looked terrible. Can you imagine how the insides of his nose must have felt? Because he had this bombshell to drop: that, after two years of marriage, his daughter was still a virgin.

It had been three years since Reverend Mother had spoken. 'Daughter, is this thing true?' The silence, which had been hanging in the corners of the house like a torn cobweb, was finally blown away; but Mumtaz just nodded: Yes. True.

Then she spoke. She said she loved her husband and the other thing would come right in the end. He was a good man and when it was possible to have children he would surely find it possible to do the thing. She said a marriage should not depend on the thing, she had thought, so she had not liked to mention it, and her father was not right to tell everyone out loud like he had. She would have said more; but now Reverend Mother burst.

Three years of words poured out of her (but her body, stretched by the exigencies of storing them, did not diminish). My grandfather stood very still by the Telefunken as the storm broke over him. Whose idea had it been? Whose crazy fool scheme, whatsitsname, to let this coward who wasn't even a man into the house? To stay here, whatsitsname, free as a bird, food and shelter for three years, what did you care about meatless days, whatsitsname, what did you know about the cost of rice? Who was the weakling, whatsitsname, yes, the white-haired weakling who had permitted this iniquitous marriage? Who had put his daughter into that scoundrel's, whatsitsname, *bed*? Whose head was full of every damn fool incomprehensible thing, whatsitsname, whose brain was so softened by fancy foreign ideas that he could send his child into such an unnatural marriage? Who had spent his life offending God, whatsitsname, and on whose head was this a judgment? Who had brought disaster down upon his house . . . she spoke against my grandfather for an hour and nineteen minutes and by the time she had finished the clouds had run out of water and the house was full of puddles. And, before she ended, her youngest daughter Emerald did a very curious thing.

Emerald's hands rose up beside her face, bunched into fists, but with index fingers extended. Index fingers entered earholes and seemed to lift Emerald out of her chair until she was running, fingers plugging ears, running – FULL-TILT! – without her dupatta on, out into the street, through the puddles of water, past the rickshaw-stand, past the paan-shop where the old men were just emerging cautiously into the clean fresh air of after-the-rain, and her speed amazed the urchins who were on their marks, waiting to begin their game of dodging in and out between the betel-jets, because nobody was used to seeing a young lady, much less one of the Teen Batti, running alone and distraught through the rain-soaked streets with her fingers in her ears and no dupatta around her shoulders. Nowadays, the cities are full of modern, fashionable, dupatta-less misses; but back then the old men clicked their tongues in sorrow, because a woman without a dupatta was a woman without honour, and why had Emerald Bibi chosen to leave her honour at home? The old ones were baffled, but Emerald knew. She saw, clearly, freshly in the after-rain air, that the fountain-head of her family's troubles was that cowardly plumpie (yes, Padma) who lived underground. If she could get rid of him everyone would be happy again . . . Emerald ran without pausing to the Cantonment district. The Cantt, where the army was based; where Major Zulfikar would be! Breaking her oath, my aunt arrived at his office.

Zulfikar is a famous name amongst Muslims. It was the name of the two-pronged sword carried by Ali, the nephew of the prophet Muhammad. It was a weapon such as the world had never seen.

Oh, yes: something else was happening in the world that day. A weapon such as the world had never seen was being dropped on yellow people in Japan. But in Agra, Emerald was using a secret weapon of her own. It was bandylegged, short, flat-headed; its nose almost touched its chin; it dreamed of a big modern house with a plumbed-in bath right beside the bed.

Major Zulfikar had never been absolutely sure whether or not he believed Nadir Khan to have been behind the Hummingbird's murder; but he itched for the chance to find out. When Emerald told him about Agra's subterranean Taj, he became so excited that he forgot to be angry, and rushed to Cornwallis Road with a force of fifteen men. They arrived in the drawing-room with Emerald at their head. My aunt: treason with a beautiful face, no dupatta and pink loose-pajamas. Aziz watched dumbly as the soldiers rolled back the drawing-room carpet and opened the big trap-door as my grandmother attempted to console Mumtaz. 'Women must marry men,' she said. 'Not mice, whatsitsname! There is no shame in leaving that, whatsitsname, worm.' But her daughter continued to cry.

Absence of Nadir in his underworld! Warned by Aziz's first roar, overcome by the embarrassment which flooded over him more easily than monsoon rain, he vanished. A trap-door flung open in one of the toilets – yes, the very one, why not, in which he had spoken to Doctor Aziz from the sanctuary of a washing-chest. A wooden 'thunderbox' – a 'throne' – lay on one side, empty enamel pot rolling on coir matting. The toilet had an outside door giving out on to the gully by the cornfield; the door was open. It had been locked from the outside, but only with an Indian-made lock, so it had been easy to force . . . and in the soft lamplit seclusion of the Taj Mahal, a shining spittoon, and a note, addressed to Mumtaz, signed by her husband, three words long, six syllables, three exclamation marks:

Talaaq! Talaaq! Talaaq!

The English lacks the thunderclap sound of the Urdu, and

anyway you know what it means. I divorce thee. I divorce thee. I divorce thee.

Nadir Khan had done the decent thing.

O awesome rage of Major Zulfy when he found the bird had flown! This was the colour he saw: red. O anger fully comparable to my grandfather's fury, though expressed in petty gestures! Major Zulfy, at first, hopped up and down in helpless fits of temper; controlled himself at last; and rushed out through bathroom, past throne, alongside cornfield, through perimeter gate. No sign of a running, plump, longhair, rhymeless poet. Looking left: nothing. And right: zero. Enraged Zulfy made his choice, pelted past the cycle-rickshaw rank. Old men were playing hit-the-spittoon and the spittoon was out in the street. Urchins, dodging in and out of the streams of betel-juice. Major Zulfy ran, ononon. Between the old men and their target, but he lacked the urchins' skill. What an unfortunate moment: a low hard jet of red fluid caught him squarely in the crotch. A stain like a hand clutched at the groin of his battledress; squeezed; arrested his progress. Major Zulfy stopped in almighty wrath. O even more unfortunate; because a second player, assuming the mad soldier would keep on running, had unleashed a second jet. A second red hand clasped the first and completed Major Zulfy's day . . . slowly, with deliberation, he went to the spittoon and kicked it over, into the dust. He jumped on it – once! twice! again! – flattening it, and refusing to show that it had hurt his foot. Then, with some dignity, he limped away, back to the car parked outside my grandfather's house. The old ones retrieved their brutalized receptacle and began to knock it back into shape.

'Now that I'm getting married,' Emerald told Mumtaz, 'it'll be very rude of you if you don't even try to have a good time. And you should be giving me advice and everything.' At the time, although Mumtaz smiled at her younger sister, she had thought it a great cheek on Emerald's part to say this; and, unintentionally perhaps, had increased the pressure of the pencil with which she was applying henna tracery to the soles of her sister's feet. 'Hey!' Emerald squealed, 'No need to get mad! I just thought we should try to be friends.'

Relations between the sisters had been somewhat strained since Nadir Khan's disappearance; and Mumtaz hadn't liked it when Major Zulfikar (who had chosen not to charge my grandfather with harbouring a wanted man, and squared it with Brigadier Dodson) asked for, and received, permission to marry Emerald. 'It's like blackmail,' she thought. 'And anyway, what about Alia? The eldest shouldn't be married last, and look how patient she's been with her merchant fellow.' But she said nothing, and smiled her forbearing smile, and devoted her gift of assiduity to the wedding preparations, and agreed to try and have a good time; while Alia went on waiting for Ahmed Sinai. ('She'll wait forever,' Padma guesses: correctly.)

January 1946. Marquees, sweetmeats, guests, songs, fainting bride, stiff-at-attention groom: a beautiful wedding . . . at which the leather-cloth merchant, Ahmed Sinai, found himself deep in conversation with the newly-divorced Mumtaz. 'You love-children? – what a coincidence, so do I . . .' 'And you didn't have any, poor girl? Well, matter of fact, my wife couldn't . . .' 'Oh, no; how sad for you; and she must have been bad-tempered like anything!' '. . . Oh, like hell . . . excuse me. Strength of emotions carried me away.' '– Quite all right; don't think about it. Did she throw dishes and all?' 'Did she throw? In one month we had to eat out of newspaper!' 'No, my goodness, what whoppers you tell!' 'Oh, it's no good, you're too clever for me. But she did throw dishes all the same.' 'You poor, poor man.' 'No – you. Poor, poor you.' And thinking: 'Such a charming chap, with Alia he always looked so bored . . .' And, '. . . This girl, I never looked at her, but my goodness me . . .' And, '. . . You can tell he loves children; and for that I could . . .' And, '. . . Well, never mind about the skin . . .' It was noticeable that, when it was time to sing, Mumtaz found the spirit to join in all the songs, but Alia remained silent. She had been bruised even more badly than her father in Jallianwala Bagh; and you couldn't see a mark on her.

'So, gloomy sis, you managed to enjoy yourself after all.'

In June that year, Mumtaz re-married. Her sister – taking her cue from their mother – would not speak to her until, just before they both died, she saw her chance of revenge. Aadam Aziz and Reverend Mother tried, unsuccessfully, to persuade Alia that these things happen, it was better to find out now than later, and Mumtaz had been badly hurt and needed a man to help her recover . . . besides. Alia had brains, she would be all right.

'But, but,' Alia said, 'nobody ever married a book.'

'Change your name,' Ahmed Sinai said. 'Time for a fresh start. Throw Mumtaz and her Nadir Khan out of the window, I'll choose you a new name. Amina. Amina Sinai; you'd like that?'

'Whatever you say, husband,' my mother said.

'Anyway,' Alia, the wise child, wrote in her diary, 'who wants to get landed with this marrying business? Not me; never; no.'

Mian Abdullah was a false start for a lot of optimistic people; his assistant (whose name could not be spoken in my father's house) was my mother's wrong turning. But those were the years of the drought; many crops planted at that time ended up by coming to nothing.

'What happened to the plumpie?' Padma asks, crossly. 'You don't mean you aren't going to *tell*?'

A public announcement

There followed an illusionist January, a time so still on its surface that 1947 seemed not to have begun at all. (While, of course, in fact . . .) In which the Cabinet Mission – old Pethick-Lawrence, clever Cripps, military A. V. Alexander – saw their scheme for the transfer of power fail. (But of course, in fact it would only be six months until . . .) in which the viceroy, Wavell, understood that be was finished, washed-up, or in our own expressive word, funtoosh. (Which, of course, in fact only speeded things up, because it let in the last of the viceroys, who . . .) In which Mr Attlee seemed too busy deciding the future of Burma with Mr Aung Sam. (While, of course, in fact he was briefing the last viceroy, before announcing his appointment; the last-viceroy-to-be was visiting the King and being granted plenipotentiary powers; so that soon, soon . . .) In which the Constituent Assembly stood self-adjourned, without having settled on a Constitution. (But, of course, in fact Earl Mountbatten, the last viceroy, would be with us any day, with his inexorable ticktock, his soldier's knife that could cut subcontinents in three, and his wife who ate chicken breasts secretly behind a locked lavatory door.) And in the midst of the mirror-like stillness through which it was impossible to see the great machineries grinding, my mother, the brand-new Amina Sinai, who also looked still and unchanging although great things were happening beneath her skin, woke up one morning with a head buzzing with insomnia and a tongue thickly coated with unslept sleep and found herself saying aloud, without meaning to at all, 'What's the sun doing here, Allah? It's come up in the wrong place.'

. . . I must interrupt myself. I wasn't going to today, because Padma has started getting irritated whenever my narration becomes self-conscious, whenever, like an incompetent puppeteer, I reveal the hands holding the strings; but I simply must register a protest. So, breaking into a chapter which, by a happy chance, I have named 'A public announcement', I issue (in the strongest possible terms) the following general medical alert: 'A certain Doctor N. Q. Baligga,' I wish to proclaim – from the rooftops! Through the loudhailers of minarets! – 'is a quack. Ought to be locked up, struck off, defenestrated. Or worse: subjected to his own quackery, brought out in leprous boils by a mis-prescribed pill. Damn fool,' I underline my point, 'can't see what's under his nose!'

Having let off steam, I must leave my mother to worry for a further moment about the curious behaviour of the sun, to explain that our Padma, alarmed by my references to cracking up, has confided covertly in this Baligga – this ju-ju man! this green-medicine wallah! – and as a result, the charlatan, whom I will not deign to glorify with a description, came to call. I, in all innocence and for Padma's sake, permitted him to examine me. I should have feared the worst; the worst is what he did. Believe this if you can: the fraud has pronounced me whole! 'I see no cracks,' he intoned mournfully, differing from Nelson at Copenhagen in that he possessed no good eye, his blindness not the choice of stubborn genius but the inevitable curse of his folly! Blindly, he impugned my state of mind, cast doubts on my reliability as a witness, and Godknowswhatelse: 'I see no cracks.'

In the end it was Padma who shooed him away. 'Never mind, Doctor Sahib,' Padma said, 'we will look after him ourselves.' On her face I saw a kind of recognition of her own dull guilt . . . exit Baligga, never to return to these pages. But good God! Has the medical profession – the calling of Aadam Aziz – sunk so low? To this cess-pool of Baliggas? In the end, if this be true, everyone will do without doctors . . . which brings me back to the reason why Amina Sinai awoke one morning with the sun on her lips.

'It's come up in the wrong place!' she yelped, by accident; and then, through the fading buzzing of her bad night's sleep, understood how in this month of illusion she had fallen victim to a trick, because all that had happened was that she had woken up in Delhi, in the home of her new husband, which faced east towards the sun; so the truth of the matter was that the sun was in the right place, and it was her position which had changed . . . but even after she grasped this elementary thought, and stored it away with the many similar mistakes she had made since coming here (because her confusion about the sun had been a regular occurrence, as if her mind were refusing to accept the alteration in her circumstances, the new, above-ground position of her bed), something of its jumbling influence remained with her and prevented her from feeling entirely at ease.

'In the end, everyone can do without fathers,' Doctor Aziz told his daughter when he said goodbye; and Reverend Mother added, 'Another orphan in the family, whatsitsname, but never mind, Muhammad was an orphan too; and you can say this for your Ahmed Sinai, whatsitsname, at least he is half Kashmiri.' Then, with his own hands, Doctor Aziz had passed a green tin trunk into the railway compartment where Ahmed Sinai awaited his bride. 'The dowry is neither small nor vast as these things go,' my grandfather said. 'We are not crorepatis, you understand. But we have given you enough; Amina will give you more.' Inside the green tin trunk: silver samovars, brocade saris, gold coins given to Doctor Aziz by grateful patients, a museum in which the exhibits represented illnesses cured and lives saved. And now Aadam Aziz lifted his daughter (with his own arms), passing her up after the dowry into the care of this man who had renamed and so re-invented her, thus becoming in a sense her father as well as her new husband . . . he walked (with his own feet) along the platform as the train began to move. A relay runner at the end of his lap, he stood wreathed in smoke and comic-book vendors and the confusion of peacock-feather fans and hot snacks and the whole lethargic hullabaloo of squatting porters and plaster animals on trolleys as the train picked up speed and headed for the capital city, accelerating into the next lap of the race. In the compartment the new Amina Sinai sat (in mint condition) with her feet on the green tin trunk which had been an inch too high to fit under the seat. With her sandals bearing down on the locked museum of her father's achievements she sped away into her new life, leaving Aadam Aziz behind to dedicate himself to an attempt to fuse the skills of Western and hakimi medicine, an attempt which would gradually wear him down, convincing him that the hegemony of superstition, mumbo-jumbo and all things magical would never be broken in India, because the hakims refused to co-operate; and as he aged and the world became less real he began to doubt his own beliefs, so that by the time he saw the God in whom he had never been able to believe or disbelieve he was probably expecting to do so.

As the train pulled out of the station Ahmed Sinai jumped up and bolted the compartment door and pulled down the shutters, much to Amina's amazement; but then suddenly there were thumps outside and hands moving the doorknobs and voices saying 'Let us in, maharaj! Maharajin, are you there, ask your husband to open.' And always, in all the trains in this story, there were these voices and these fists banging and pleading; in the Frontier Mail to Bombay and in all the expresses of the years; and it was always frightening, until at last I was the one on the outside, hanging on for dear life, and begging, 'Hey, maharaj! Let me in, great sir.'

'Fare dodgers,' Ahmed Sinai said, but they were more than that. They were a prophecy. There were to be others soon.

. . . And now the sun was in the wrong place. She, my mother, lay in bed and felt ill-at-ease; but also excited by the thing that had happened inside her and which, for the moment, was her secret. At her side, Ahmed Sinai snored richly. No insomnia for him; none, despite the troubles which had made him bring a grey bag full of money and hide it under his bed when he thought Amina wasn't looking. My father slept soundly, wrapped in the soothing envelope of my mother's greatest gift, which turned out to be worth a good deal more than the contents of the green tin trunk: Amina Sinai gave Ahmed the gift of her inexhaustible assiduity.

Nobody ever took pains the way Amina did. Dark of skin, glowing of eye, my mother was by nature the most meticulous person on earth. Assiduously, she arranged flowers in the corridors and rooms of the Old Delhi house; carpets were selected with infinite care. She could spend twenty-five minutes worrying at the positioning of a chair. By the time she'd finished with her home-making, adding tiny touches here, making fractional alterations there, Ahmed Sinai found his orphan's dwelling transformed into something gentle and loving. Amina would rise before he did, her assiduity driving her to dust everything, even the cane chick-blinds (until he agreed to employ a hamal for the purpose); but what Ahmed never knew was that his wife's talents were most dedicatedly, most determinedly applied not to the externals of their lives, but to the matter of Ahmed Sinai himself.

Why had she married him? – For solace, for children. But at first the insomnia coating her brain got in the way of her first aim; and children don't always come at once. So Amina had found herself dreaming about an undreamable poet's face and waking with an unspeakable name on her lips. You ask: what did she do about it? I answer: she gritted her teeth and set about putting herself straight. This is what she told herself: 'You big ungrateful goof, can't you see who is your husband now? Don't you know what a husband deserves?' To avoid fruitless controversy about the correct answers to these questions, let me say that, in my mother's opinion, a husband deserved unquestioning loyalty, and unreserved, full-hearted love. But there was a difficulty: Amina, her mind clogged up with Nadir Khan and insomnia, found she couldn't naturally provide Ahmed Sinai with these things. And so, bringing her gift of assiduity to bear, she began to train herself to love him. To do this she divided him, mentally, into every single one of his component parts, physical as well as behavioural, compartmentalizing him into lips and verbal tics and prejudices and likes . . . in short, she fell under the spell of the perforated sheet of her own parents, because she resolved to fall in love with her husband bit by bit.

Each day she selected one fragment of Ahmed Sinai, and concentrated her entire being upon it until it became wholly familiar; until she felt fondness rising up within her and becoming affection and, finally, love. In this way she came to adore his over-loud voice and the way it assaulted her eardrums and made her tremble; and his peculiarity of always being in a good mood until after he had shaved – after which, each morning, his manner became stern, gruff, businesslike and distant; and his vulture-hooded eyes which concealed what she was sure was his inner goodness behind a bleakly ambiguous gaze; and the way his lower lip jutted out beyond his upper one; and his shortness which led him to forbid her ever to wear high heels . . . 'My God,' she told herself, 'it seems that there are a million different things to love about every man!' But she was undismayed. 'Who, after all,' she reasoned privately, 'ever truly knows another human being completely?' and continued to learn to love and admire his appetite for fried foods, his ability to quote Persian poetry, the furrow of anger between his eyebrows . . . 'At this rate,' she thought, 'there will always be something fresh about him to love; so our marriage just can't go stale.' In this way, assiduously, my mother settled down to life in the old city. The tin trunk sat unopened in an old almirah.

And Ahmed, without knowing or suspecting, found himself and his life worked upon by his wife until, little by little, he came to resemble – and to live in a place that resembled – a man he had never known and an underground chamber he had never seen. Under the influence of a painstaking magic so obscure that Amina was probably unaware of working it, Ahmed Sinai found his hair thinning, and what was left becoming lank and greasy; he discovered that he was willing to let it grow until it began to worm over the tops of his ears. Also, his stomach began to spread, until it became the yielding, squashy belly in which I would so often be smothered and which none of us, consciously at any rate, compared to the pudginess of Nadir Khan. His distant cousin Zohra told him, coquettishly, 'You must diet, cousinji, or we won't be able to reach you to kiss!' But it did no good . . . and little by little Amina constructed in Old Delhi a world of soft cushions and draperies over the windows which let in as little light as possible . . . she lined the chick-blinds with black cloths; and all these minute transformations helped her in her Herculean task, the task of accepting, bit by bit, that she must love a new man. (But she remained susceptible to the forbidden dream-images of . . . and was always drawn to men with soft stomachs and longish, lankish hair.)

You could not see the new city from the old one. In the new city, a race of pink conquerors had built palaces in pink stone; but the houses in the narrow lanes of the old city leaned over, jostled, shuffled, blocked each other's view of the roseate edifices of power. Not that anyone ever looked in that direction, anyway. In the Muslim muhallas or neighbourhoods which clustered around Chandni Chowk, people were content to look inwards into the screened-off courtyards of their lives; to roll chick-blinds down over their windows and verandahs. In the narrow lanes, young loafers held hands and linked arms and kissed when they met and stood in hip-jutting circles, facing inwards. There was no greenery and the cows kept away, knowing they weren't sacred here. Bicycle bells rang constantly. And above their cacophony sounded the cries of itinerant fruit-sellers: *Come all you greats-O, eat a few dates-O!*

To all of which was added, on that January morning when my mother and father were each concealing secrets from the other, the nervous clatter of the footsteps of Mr Mustapha Kemal and Mr S. P. Butt; and also the insistent rattle of Lifafa Das's dugdugee drum.

When the clattering footsteps were first heard in the gullies of the muhalla, Lifafa Das and his peepshow and drum were still some distance away. Clatter-feet descended from a taxi and rushed into the narrow lanes; meanwhile, in their corner house, my mother stood in her kitchen stirring khichri for breakfast overhearing my father conversing with his distant cousin Zohra. Feet clacked past fruit salesmen and hand-holding loafers; my mother overheard: '. . . You newlyweds, I can't stop coming to see, *cho chweet* I can't tell you!' While feet approached, my father actually coloured. In those days he was in the high summer of his charm; his lower lip really didn't jut so much, the line between his eyebrows was still only faint . . . and Amina, stirring khichri, heard Zohra squeal, 'Oh look, pink! But then you are so fair, cousinji! . . .' And he was letting her listen to All-India Radio at the table, which Amina was not allowed to do; Lata Mangeshkar was singing a waily love-song as 'Just like me, don'tyouthink,' Zohra went on. 'Lovely pink babies we'll have, a perfect match, no, cousinji, pretty white couples?' And the feet clattering and the pan being stirred while 'How awful to be black, cousinji, to wake every morning and see it staring at you, in the mirror to be shown proof of your inferiority! Of course they know; even blackies know white is nicer, don'tyouthinkso?' The feet very close now and Amina stamping into the dining-room pot in hand, concentrating hard at restraining herself, thinking Why must she come today when I have news to tell and also I'll have to ask for money in front of her. Ahmed Sinai liked to be asked nicely for money, to have it wheedled out of him with caresses and sweet words until his table napkin began to rise in his lap as something moved in his pajamas; and she didn't mind, with her assiduity she learned to love this also, and when she needed money there were strokes and 'Janum, my life, please . . .' and '. . . Just a little so that I can make nice food and pay the bills . . .' and 'Such a generous man, give me what you like, I know it will be enough' . . . the techniques of street beggars and she'd have to do it in front of that one with her saucer eyes and giggly voice and loud chat about blackies. Feet at the door almost and Amina in the dining-room with hot khichri at the ready, so very near to Zohra's silly head, whereupon Zohra cries, 'Oh, present company excluded, *of course*!' just in case, not being sure whether she's been overheard or not, and 'Oh, Ahmed, cousinji, you are really too dreadful to think I meant our lovely Amina who really isn't so black but only like a white lady standing in the shade!' While Amina with her pot in hand looks at the pretty head and thinks Should I? And, Do I dare? And calms herself down with: 'It's a big day for me; and at least she raised the subject of children; so now it'll be easy for me to . . .' But it's too late, the wailing of Lata on the radio has drowned the sound of the doorbell so they haven't heard old Musa the bearer going to answer the door; Lata has obscured the sound of anxious feet clattering upstairs; but all of a sudden here they are, the feet of Mr Mustapha Kemal and Mr S. P. Butt, coming to a shuffling halt.

'The rapscallions have perpetrated an outrage!' Mr Kemal, who is the thinnest man Amina Sinai has ever seen, sets off with his curiously archaic phraseology (derived from his fondness for litigation, as a result of which he has become infected with the cadences of the lawcourts) a kind of chain reaction of farcical panic, to which little, squeaky, spineless S. P. Butt, who has something wild dancing like a monkey in the eyes, adds considerably, by getting out these three words: 'Yes, the firebugs!' And now Zohra in an odd reflex action clutches the radio to her bosom, muffling Lata between her breasts, screaming, 'O God, O God, what firebugs, where? This house? O God I can feel the heat!' Amina stands frozen khichri-in-hand staring at the two men in their business suits as her husband, secrecy thrown to the winds now, rises shaven but as-yet-unsuited to his feet and asks, 'The godown?'

Godown, gudam, warehouse, call it what you like; but no sooner had Ahmed Sinai asked his question than a hush fell upon the room, except of course that Lata Mangeshkar's voice still issued from Zohra's cleavage; because these three men shared one such large edifice, located on the industrial estate at the outskirts of the city. 'Not the godown, God forfend,' Amina prayed silently, because the reccine and leathercloth business was doing well – through Major Zulfikar, who was now an aide at Military G.H.Q, in Delhi, Ahmed Sinai had landed a contract to supply leathercloth jackets and waterproof table coverings to the Army itself – and large stocks of the material on which their lives depended were stored in that warehouse. 'But who would do such a thing?' Zohra wailed in harmony with her singing breasts, 'What mad people are loose in the world these days?' . . . and that was how Amina heard, for the first time, the name which her husband had hidden from her, and which was, in those times, striking terror into many hearts. 'It is Ravana,' said S. P. Butt . . . but Ravana is the name of a many-headed demon; are demons, then, abroad in the land? 'What rubbish is this?' Amina, speaking with her father's hatred of superstition, demanded an answer; and Mr Kemal provided it. 'It is the name of a dastardly crew, Madam; a band of incendiary rogues. These are troubled days; troubled days.'

In the godown, roll upon roll of leathercloth; and the commodities dealt in by Mr Kemal, rice tea lentils – he hoards them all over the country in vast quantities, as a form of protection against the many-headed many-mouthed rapacious monster that is the public, which, if given its heads, would force prices so low in a time of abundance that godfearing entrepreneurs would starve while the monster grew fat . . . 'Economics is scarcity,' Mr Kemal argues, 'therefore my hoards not only keep prices at a decent level but underpin the very structure of the economy.' – And then there is, in the godown, Mr Butt's stockpile, boxed in cartons bearing the words AAG BRAND. I do not need to tell you that aag means fire. S. P. Butt was a manufacturer of matches.

'Our informations,' Mr Kemal says, 'reveal only the fact of a fire at the estate. The precise godown is not specified.'

'But why should it be ours?' Ahmed Sinai asks. 'Why, since we still have time to pay?'

'Pay?' Amina interrupts. 'Pay whom? Pay what? Husband, janum, life of mine, what is happening here?' . . . But 'We must go,' S. P. Butt says, and Ahmed Sinai is leaving, crumpled night-pajamas and all, rushing clatterfooted out of the house with the thin one and the spineless one, leaving behind him uneaten khichri, wide-eyed women, muffled Lata, and hanging in the air the name of Ravana . . . 'a gang of ne'er-do-wells, Madam; unscrupulous cut-throats and bounders to a man!'

And S. P. Butt's last quavering words: 'Damnfool Hindu firebugs, Begum Sahiba. But what can we Muslims do?'

What is known about the Ravana gang? That it posed as a fanatical anti-Muslim movement, which, in those days before the Partition riots, in those days when pigs' heads could be left with impunity in the courtyards of Friday mosques, was nothing unusual. That it sent men out, at dead of night, to paint slogans on the walls of both old and new cities: NO PARTITION OR ELSE PERDITION! MUSLIMS ARE THE JEWS OF ASIA! and so forth. And that it burned down Muslim-owned factories, shops, godowns. But there's more, and this is not commonly known: behind this façade of racial hatred, the Ravana gang was a brilliantly-conceived commercial enterprise. Anonymous phone calls, letters written with words cut out of newspapers were issued to Muslim business-men, who were offered the choice between paying a single, once-only cash sum and having their world burned down. Interestingly, the gang proved itself to be ethical. There were no second demands. And they meant business: in the absence of grey bags full of pay-off money, fire would lick at shop-fronts factories warehouses. Most people paid, preferring that to the risky alternative of trusting to the police. The police, in 1947, were not to be relied upon by Muslims. And it is said (though I can't be sure of this) that when the blackmail letters arrived, they contained a list of 'satisfied customers' who had paid up and stayed in business. The Ravana gang – like all professionals – gave references.

Two men in business suits, one in pajamas, ran through the narrow gullies of the Muslim muhalla to the taxi waiting on Chandni Chowk. They attracted curious glances: not only because of their varied attire, but because they were trying not to run. 'Don't show panic,' Mr Kemal said, 'Look calm.' But their feet kept getting out of control and rushing on. Jerkily, in little rushes of speed followed by a few badly-disciplined steps at walking pace, they left the muhalla; and passed, on their way, a young man with a black metal peepshow box on wheels, a man holding a dugdugee drum: Lifafa Das, on his way to the scene of the important annunciation which gives this episode its name. Lifafa Das was rattling his drum and calling: 'Come see everything, come see everything, come see! Come see Delhi, come see India, come see! Come see, come see!'

But Ahmed Sinai had other things to look at.

The children of the muhalla had their own names for most of the local inhabitants. One group of three neighbours was known as the 'fighting-cock people', because they comprised one Sindhi and one Bengali householder whose homes were separated by one of the muhalla's few Hindu residences. The Sindhi and the Bengali had very little in common – they didn't speak the same language or cook the same food; but they were both Muslims, and they both detested the interposed Hindu. They dropped garbage on his house from their rooftops. They hurled multilingual abuse at him from their windows. They flung scraps of meat at his door . . . while he, in turn, paid urchins to throw stones at their windows, stones with messages wrapped round them: 'Wait,' the messages said, 'Your turn will come' . . . the children of the muhalla did not call my father by his right name. They knew him as 'the man who can't follow his nose'.

Ahmed Sinai was the possessor of a sense of direction so inept that, left to his own devices, he could even get lost in the winding gullies of his own neighbourhood. Many times the street-arabs in the lanes had come across him, wandering forlornly, and been offered a four-anna chavanni piece to escort him home. I mention this because I believe that my father's gift for taking wrong turnings did not simply afflict him throughout his life; it was also a reason for his attraction to Amina Sinai (because thanks to Nadir Khan, she had shown that she could take wrong turnings, too); and, what's more, his inability to follow his own nose dripped into me, to some extent clouding the nasal inheritance I received from other places, and making me, for year after year, incapable of sniffing out true road . . . But that's enough for now, because I've given the three businessmen enough time to get to the industrial estate. I shall add only that (in my opinion as a direct consequence of his lack of a sense of direction) my father was a man over whom, even in his moments of triumph, there hung the stink of future failure, the odour of a wrong turning that was just around the corner, an aroma which could not be washed away by his frequent baths. Mr Kemal, who smelled it, would say privately to S. P. Butt, 'These Kashmiri types, old boy: well-known fact they never wash.' This slander connects my father to the boatman Tai . . . to Tai in the grip of the self-destructive rage which made him give up being clean.

At the industrial estate, night-watchmen were sleeping peacefully through the noise of the fire-engines. Why? How? Because they had made a deal with the Ravana mob, and, when tipped off about the gang's impending arrival, would take sleeping draughts and pull their charpoy beds away from the buildings of the estate. In this way the gang avoided violence, and the nightwatchmen augmented their meagre wages. It was an amicable and not unintelligent arrangement.

Amid sleeping night-watchmen, Mr Kemal, my father and S. P. Butt watched cremated bicycles rise up into the sky in thick black clouds. Butt father Kemal stood alongside fire engines, as relief flooded through them, because it was the Arjuna Indiabike godown that was burning – the Arjuna brand-name, taken from a hero of Hindu mythology, had failed to disguise the fact that the company was Muslim-owned. Washed by relief, father Kemal Butt breathed air filled with incendiarized bicycles, coughing and spluttering as the fumes of incinerated wheels, the vaporized ghosts of chains bells saddlebags handlebars, the transubstantiated frames of Arjuna Indiabikes moved in and out of their lungs. A crude cardboard mask had been nailed to a telegraph pole in front of the flaming godown – a mask of many faces – a devil's mask of snarling faces with broad curling lips and bright red nostrils. The faces of the many-headed monster,

Ravana the demon king, looking angrily down at the bodies of the night-watchmen who were sleeping so soundly that no one, neither the firemen, nor Kemal, nor Butt, nor my father, had the heart to disturb them; while the ashes of pedals and inner tubes fell upon them from the skies.

'Damn bad business,' Mr Kemal said. He was not being sympathetic. He was criticizing the owners of the Arjuna Indiabike Company.

Look: the cloud of the disaster (which is also a relief) rises and gathers like a ball in the discoloured morning sky. See how it thrusts itself westward into the heart of the old city; how it is pointing, good lord, like a finger, pointing down at the Muslim muhalla near Chandni Chowk! . . . Where, right now, Lifafa Das is crying his wares in the Sinais' very own gully.

'Come see everything, see the whole world, come see!'

It's almost time for the public announcement. I won't deny I'm excited: I've been hanging around in the background of my own story for too long, and although it's still a little while before I can take over, it's nice to get a look in. So, with a sense of high expectation, I follow the pointing finger in the sky and look down on my parents' neighbourhood, upon bicycles, upon street-vendors touting roasted gram in twists of paper, upon the hip-jutting, hand-holding street loafers, upon flying scraps of paper and little clustered whirlwinds of flies around the sweetmeat stalls . . . all of it foreshortened by my high-in-the-sky point of view. And there are children, swarms of them, too, attracted into the street by the magical rattle of Lifafa Das's dugdugee drum and his voice, 'Dunya dekho', see the whole world! Boys without shorts on, girls without vests, and other, smarter infants in school whites, their shorts held up by elasticated belts with S-shaped snake-buckles, fat little boys with podgy fingers; all flocking to the black box on wheels, including this one particular girl, a girl with one long hairy continuous eyebrow shading both eyes, the eight-year-old daughter of that same discourteous Sindhi who is even now raising the flag of the still-fictional country of Pakistan on his roof, who is even now hurling abuse at his neighbour, while his daughter rushes into the street with her chavanni in her hand, her expression of a midget queen, and murder lurking just behind her lips. What's her name? I don't know; but I know those eyebrows.

Lifafa Das: who has by an unfortunate chance set up his black peepshow against a wall on which someone has daubed a swastika (in those days you saw them everywhere; the extremist R.S.S.S. party got them on every wall; not the Nazi swastika which was the wrong way round, but the ancient Hindu symbol of power. Svasti is Sanskrit for good) . . . this Lifafa Das whose arrival I've been trumpeting was a young fellow who was invisible until he smiled, when he became beautiful, or rattled his drum, whereupon he became irresistible to children. Dugdugee-men: all over India, they shout, 'Dilli dekho', 'come see Delhi!' But this was Delhi, and Lifafa Das had altered his cry accordingly. 'See the whole world, come see everything!' The hyperbolic formula began, after a time, to, prey upon his mind; more and more picture postcards went into his peepshow as he tried, desperately, to deliver what he promised, to put every thing into his box. (I am suddenly reminded of Nadir Khan's friend the painter: is this an Indian disease, this urge to encapsulate the whole of reality? Worse: am I infected, too?)

Inside the peepshow of Lifafa Das were pictures of the Taj Mahal, and Meenakshi Temple, and the holy Ganges; but as well as these famous sights the peepshow-man had felt the urge to include more contemporary images – Stafford Cripps leaving Nehru's residence; untouchables being touched; educated persons sleeping in large numbers on railway lines; a publicity still of a European actress with a mountain of fruit on her head – Lifafa called her Carmen Verandah; even a newspaper photograph, mounted on card, of a fire at the industrial estate. Lifafa Das did not believe in shielding his audiences from the not-always-pleasant features of the age . . . and often, when he came into these gullies, grown-ups as well as children came to see what was new inside his box on wheels, and among his most frequent customers was Begum Amina Sinai.

But today there is something hysterical in the air; something brittle and menacing has settled on the muhalla as the cloud of cremated Indiabikes hangs overhead . . . and now it slips its leash, as this girl with her one continuous eyebrow squeals, her voice lisping with an innocence it does not possess, 'Me firtht! Out of my way . . . let me thee! I can't *thee*!' Because there are already eyes at the holes in the box, there are already children absorbed in the progression of postcards, and Lifafa Das says (without pausing in his work – he goes right on turning the knob which keeps the postcards moving inside the box), 'A few minutes, bibi; everyone will have his turn; wait only.' To which the one-eyebrowed midget queen replies, 'No! No! I want to be firtht!' Lifafa stops smiling – becomes invisible – shrugs. Unbridled fury appears on the face of the midget queen. And now an insult rises; a deadly barb trembles on her lips. 'You've got a *nerve*, coming into thith muhalla! I know you: my father knows you: everyone knows you're a Hindu!!'

Lifafa Das stands silently, turning the handles of his box; but now the ponytailed one-eyebrowed valkyrie is chanting, pointing with pudgy fingers, and the boys in their school whites and snake-buckles are joining in, 'Hindu! Hindu! Hindu!' And chick-blinds are flying up; and from his window the girl's father leans out and joins in, hurling abuse at a new target, and the Bengali joins in in Bengali . . . 'Mother raper! Violator of our daughters!' . . . and remember the papers have been talking of assaults on Muslim children, so suddenly a voice screams out – a woman's voice, maybe even silly

98

Zohra's, 'Rapist! Arré my God they found the badmaash! There he *is*!' And now the insanity of the cloud like a pointing finger and the whole disjointed unreality of the times seizes the muhalla, and the screams are echoing from every window, and the schoolboys have begun to chant, 'Ra-pist! Ra-pist! Ray-ray-ray-*pist*!' without really knowing what they're saying; the children have edged away from Lifafa Das and he's moved, too, dragging his box on wheels, trying to get away, but now he is surrounded by voices filled with blood, and the street loafers are moving towards him, men are getting off bicycles, a pot flies through the air and shatters on a wall beside him; he has his back against a doorway as a fellow with a quiff of oily hair grins sweetly at him and says, 'So, mister: it is you? Mister Hindu, who defiles our daughters? Mister idolater, who sleeps with his sister?' And Lifafa Das, 'No, for the love of . . .', smiling like a fool . . . and then the door behind him opens and he falls backwards, landing in a dark cool corridor beside my mother Amina Sinai.

She had spent the morning alone with giggling Zohra and the echoes of the name Ravana, not knowing what was happening out there at the industrial estate, letting her mind linger upon the way the whole world seemed to be going mad; and when the screaming started and Zohra – before she could be stopped – joined in, something hardened inside her, some realization that she was her father's daughter, some ghost-memory of Nadir Khan hiding from crescent knives in a cornfield, some irritation of her nasal passages, and she went downstairs to the rescue, although Zohra screeched, 'What you doing, sisterji, that mad beast, for God, don't let him in here, have your brains gone raw?' . . . My mother opened the door and Lifafa Das fell in.

Picture her that morning, a dark shadow between the mob and its prey, her womb bursting with its invisible untold secret: 'Wah, wah,' she applauded the crowd. 'What heroes! Heroes, I swear, absolutely! Only fifty of you against this terrible monster of a fellow! Allah, you make my eyes shine with pride.'

. . . And Zohra, 'Come back, sisterji!' And the oily quiff, 'Why speak for this goonda, Begum Sahiba? This is not right acting.' And Amina, 'I know this man. He is a decent type. Go, get out, none of you have anything to do? In a Muslim muhalla you would tear a man to pieces? Go, remove yourselves.' But the mob has stopped being surprised, and is moving forward again . . . and now. Now it comes.

'Listen,' my mother shouted, *'Listen well. I am with child. I am a mother who will have a child, and I am giving this man my shelter. Come on now, if you want to kill, kill a mother also and show the world what men you are!'*

That was how it came about that my arrival – the coming of Saleem Sinai – was announced to the assembled masses of the people before my father had heard about it. From the moment of my conception, it seems, I have been public property.

But although my mother was right when she made her public announcement, she was also wrong. This is why: the baby she was carrying did not turn out to be her son.

My mother came to Delhi; worked assiduously at loving her husband; was prevented by Zohra and khichri and clattering feet from telling her husband her news; heard screams; made a public announcement. And it worked. My annunciation saved a life.

After the crowd dispersed, old Musa the bearer went into the street and rescued Lifafa Das's peepshow, while Amina gave the young man with the beautiful smile glass after glass of fresh lime water. It seemed that his experience had drained him not only of liquid but also sweetness, because he put four spoonfuls of raw sugar into every glass, while Zohra cowered

100

in pretty terror on a sofa. And, at length, Lifafa Das (rehydrated by lime water, sweetened by sugar) said: 'Begum Sahiba, you are a great lady. If you allow, I bless your house; also your unborn child. But also – please permit – I will do one thing more for you.'

'Thank you,' my mother said, 'but you must do nothing at all.'

But he continued (the sweetness of sugar coating his tongue). 'My cousin, Shri Ramram Seth, is a great seer, Begum Sahiba. Palmist, astrologer, fortune-teller. You will please come to him, and he will reveal to you the future of your son.'

Soothsayers prophesied me . . . in January 1947, my mother Amina Sinai was offered the gift of a prophecy in return for her gift of a life. And despite Zohra's 'It is madness to go with this one, Amina sister, do not even think of it for one sec, these are times to be careful'; despite her memories of her father's scepticism and of his thumbandforefinger closing around a maulvi's ear, the offer touched my mother in a place which answered Yes. Caught up in the illogical wonderment of her brand-new motherhood of which she had only just become certain, 'Yes,' she said, 'Lifafa Das, you will please meet me after some days at the gate to the Red Fort. Then you will take me to your cousin.'

'I shall be waiting every day,' he joined his palms; and left.

Zohra was so stunned that, when Ahmed Sinai came home, she could only shake her head and say, 'You newlyweds; crazy as owls; I must leave you to each other!'

Musa, the old bearer, kept his mouth shut, too. He kept himself in the background of our lives, always, except twice . . . once when he left us; once when he returned to destroy the world by accident.

Many-headed monsters

Unless, of course, there's no such thing as chance; in which case Musa – for all his age and servility – was nothing less than a time-bomb, ticking softly away until his appointed time; in which case, we should either – optimistically – get up and cheer, because if everything is planned in advance, then we all have a meaning, and are spared the terror of knowing ourselves to be random, without a *why;* or else, of course, we might – as pessimists – give up right here and now, understanding the futility of thought decision action, since nothing we think makes any difference anyway; things will be as they will. Where, then, is optimism? In fate or in chaos? Was my father being opti- or pessimistic when my mother told him her news (after everyone in the neighbourhood had heard it), and he replied with, 'I told you so; it was only a matter of time'? My mother's pregnancy, it seems, was fated; my birth, however, owed a good deal to accident.

'It was only a matter of time,' my father said, with every appearance of pleasure; but time has been an unsteady affair, in my experience, not a thing to be relied upon. It could even be partitioned: the clocks in Pakistan would run half an hour ahead of their Indian counterparts . . . Mr Kemal, who wanted nothing to do with Partition, was fond of saying, 'Here's proof of the folly of the scheme! Those Leaguers plan to abscond with a whole thirty minutes! Time Without Partitions,' Mr Kemal cried, 'That's the ticket!' And S. P. Butt said, 'If they can change the time just like that, what's real any more? I ask you? What's true?'

It seems like a day for big questions. I reply across the unreliable years to S. P. Butt, who got his throat slit in the Partition riots and lost interest in time: 'What's real and what's true aren't necessarily the same.' *True*, for me, was from my earliest days something hidden inside the stories Mary Pereira told me: Mary my ayah who was both more and less than a mother; Mary who knew everything about all of us. *True* was a thing concealed just over the horizon towards which the fisherman's finger pointed in the picture on my wall, while the young Raleigh listened to his tales. Now, writing this in my Anglepoised pool of light, I measure truth against those early things: Is this how Mary would have told it? I ask. Is this what that fisherman would have said? . . . And by those standards it is undeniably true that, one day in January 1947, my mother heard all about me six months before I turned up, while my father came up against a demon king.

Amina Sinai had been waiting for a suitable moment to accept Lifafa Das's offer; but for two days after the burning of the India bike factory Ahmed Sinai stayed at home, never visiting his office at Connaught Place, as if he were steeling himself for some unpleasant encounter. For two days the grey moneybag lay supposedly secret in its place under his side of their bed. My father showed no desire to talk about the reasons for the grey bag's presence; so Amina said to herself, 'Let him be like that; who cares?' because she had her secret, too, waiting patiently for her by the gates of the Red Fort at the top of Chandni Chowk. Pouting in secret petulance, my mother kept Lifafa Das to herself. 'Unless-and-until he tells me what he's up to, why should I tell him?' she argued.

And then a cold January evening, on which 'I've got to go out tonight' said Ahmed Sinai; and despite her pleas of 'It's cold – you'll get sick . . .' he put on his business suit and coat under which the mysterious grey bag made a ridiculously obvious lump; so finally she said, 'Wrap up warm,' and sent him off wherever he was going, asking, 'Will you be late?' To which he replied, 'Yes, certainly.' Five minutes after he left, Amina Sinai set off for the Red Fort, into the heart of her adventure.

One journey began at a fort; one should have ended at a fort, and did not. One foretold the future; the other settled its geographical location. During one journey, monkeys danced entertainingly; while, in the other place, a monkey was also dancing, but with disastrous results. In both adventures, a part was played by vultures. And many-headed monsters lurked at the end of both roads.

One at a time, then . . . and here is Amina Sinai beneath the high walls of the Red Fort, where Mughals ruled, from whose heights the new nation will be proclaimed . . . neither monarch nor herald, my mother is nevertheless greeted with warmth (despite the weather). In the last light of the day, Lifafa Das exclaims, 'Begum Sahiba! Oh, that is excellent that you came!' Dark-skinned in a white sari, she beckons him towards the taxi; he reaches for the back door; but the driver snaps, 'What do you think? Who do you think you are? Come on now, get in the front seat damn smart, leave the lady to sit in the back!' So Amina shares her seat with a black peepshow on wheels, while Lifafa Das apologizes: 'Sorry, hey, Begum Sahiba? Good intents are no offence.'

But here, refusing to wait its turn, is another taxi, pausing outside another fort unloading its cargo of three men in business suits, each carrying a bulky grey bag under his coat . . . one man long as a life and thin as a lie, a second who seems to lack a spine, and a third whose lower lip juts, whose belly tends to squashiness, whose hair is thinning and greasy and worming over the tops of his ears, and between whose eyebrows is the telltale furrow that will, as he ages, deepen into the scar of a bitter, angry man. The taxi-driver is ebullient despite the cold. 'Purana Qila!' he calls out, 'Everybody out, please! Old Fort, here we are!' . . . There have been many, many cities of Delhi, and the Old Fort, that blackened ruin, is a Delhi so ancient that beside it our own Old City is merely a babe in arms. It is to this ruin of an impossibly antique time that Kemal, Butt and Ahmed Sinai have been brought by an anonymous telephone call which ordered, 'Tonight. Old Fort. Just after sunset. But no police . . . or godown funtoosh!' Clutching their grey bags, they move into the ancient, crumbling world.

. . . Clutching at her handbag, my mother sits beside a peepshow, while Lifafa Das rides in front with the puzzled, irascible driver, and directs the cab into the streets on the wrong side of the General Post Office; and as she enters these causeways where poverty eats away at the tarmac like a drought, where people lead their invisible lives (because they share Lifafa Das's curse of invisibility, and not all of them have beautiful smiles), something new begins to assail her. Under the pressure of these streets which are growing narrower by the minute, more crowded by the inch, she has lost her 'city eyes'. When you have city eyes you cannot see the invisible people, the men with elephantiasis of the balls and the beggars in boxcars don't impinge on you, and the concrete sections of future drainpipes don't look like dormitories. My mother lost her city eyes and the newness of what she was seeing made her flush, newness like a hailstorm pricking her cheeks. Look, my God, those beautiful children have black teeth! Would you believe . . . girl children baring their nipples! How terrible, truly! And, Allah-tobah, heaven forfend, sweeper women with – no! – how *dreadful*! – collapsed spines, and bunches of twigs, and no caste marks; untouchables, sweet Allah! . . . and cripples everywhere, mutilated by loving parents to ensure them of a lifelong income from begging . . . yes, beggars in boxcars, grown men with babies' legs, in crates on wheels, made out of discarded roller-skates and old mango boxes; my mother cries out, 'Lifafa Das, turn back!' . . . but he is smiling his beautiful smile, and says, 'We must walk from here.' Seeing that there is no going back, she tells the taxi to wait, and the bad-tempered driver says, 'Yes, of course, for a great lady what is there to do but wait, and when you come I must drive my car in reverse all the way back to main-road, because here is no room to turn!' . . . Children tugging at the pallu of her sari, heads everywhere staring at my mother, who thinks, It's like being surrounded by some terrible monster, a creature with heads and heads and heads; but she corrects herself, no, of course not a monster, these poor poor people – what then? A power of some sort, a force which does not know its strength, which has perhaps decayed into impotence through never having been used . . . No, these are not decayed people, despite everything. 'I'm frightened,' my mother finds herself thinking, just as a hand touches her arm. Turning, she finds herself looking into the face of – impossible! – a white man, who stretches out a raggedy hand and says in a voice like a high foreign song, 'Give something, Begum Sahiba . . .' and repeats and repeats like a stuck record while she looks with embarrassment into a white face with long eyelashes and a curved patrician nose – embarrassment, because he was white, and begging was not for white people. '. . . All the way from Calcutta, on foot,' he was saying, 'and covered in ashes, as you see, Begum Sahiba, because of my shame at having been there for the Killing – last August you remember, Begum Sahiba, thousands knifed in four days of screaming . . .' Lifafa Das is standing helplessly by, not knowing how to behave with a white man, even a beggar, and '. . . Did you hear about the European?' the beggar asks, '. . . Yes, among the killers, Begum Sahiba, walking through the town at night with blood on his shirt, a white man deranged by the coming futility of his kind; did you hear?' . . . And now a pause in that perplexing song of a voice, and then: 'He was my husband.' Only now did my mother see the stifled breasts beneath the rags . . . 'Give something for my shame.' Tugging at her arm. Lifafa Das tugging at the other, whispering Hijra, transvestite, come away, Begum Sahiba; and Amina standing still as she is tugged in opposite directions wants to say Wait, white woman, just let me finish my business, I will take you home, feed you clothe you, send you back into your own world; but just then the woman shrugs and walks off empty-handed down the narrowing street, shrinking to a point until she vanishes – now! – into the distant meanness of the lane. And now Lifafa Das, with a curious expression on his face, says, 'They're funtoosh! All finished! Soon they will all go; and then we'll be free to kill each other.' Touching her belly with one light hand, she follows him into a darkened doorway while her face bursts into flames.

 . . . While at the Old Fort, Ahmed Sinai waits for Ravana. My father in the sunset: standing in the darkened doorway of what was once a room in the ruined walls of the fort, lower lip protruding fleshily, hands clasped behind his back, head full of money worries. He was never a happy man. He smelled faintly of future failure; he mistreated servants; perhaps he wished that, instead of following his late father into the leathercloth business, he had had the strength to pursue his original ambition, the re-arrangement of the Quran in accurately chronological order. (He once told me: 'When Muhammed prophesied, people wrote down what he said on palm leaves, which were kept any old how in a box. After he died, Abubakr and the others tried to remember the correct sequence; but they didn't have very good memories.' Another wrong turning: instead of rewriting a sacred book, my father lurked in a ruin, awaiting demons. It's no wonder he wasn't happy; and I would be no help. When I was born, I broke his big toe.) . . . My unhappy father, I repeat, thinks bad-temperedly about cash. About his wife, who wheedles rupees out of him and picks his pockets at night. And his ex-wife (who eventually died in an accident, when she argued with a camel-cart driver and was bitten in the neck by the camel), who writes him endless begging letters, despite the divorce settlement. And his distant cousin Zohra, who needs dowry money from him, so that she can raise children to marry his and so get her hooks into even more of his cash. And then there are Major Zulfikar's promises of money (at this stage, Major Zulfy and my father got on very well). The Major had been writing letters saying, 'You must decide for Pakistan when it comes, as it surely will. It's certain to be a goldmine for men like us. Please let me introduce you to M. A. J. himself . . .' but Ahmed Sinai distrusted Muhammad Ali Jinnah, and never accepted Zulfy's offer; so when Jinnah became President of Pakistan, there would be another wrong turning to think about. And, finally, there were letters from my father's old friend, the gynaecologist Doctor Narlikar, in Bombay. 'The British are leaving in droves, Sinai bhai. Property is dirt cheap! Sell up; come here; buy; live the rest of your life in luxury!' Verses of the Quran had no place in a head so full of cash . . . and, in the meantime, here he is, alongside S. P. Butt who will die in a train to Pakistan, and Mustapha Kemal who will be murdered by goondas in his grand Flagstaff Road house and have the words 'mother-sleeping hoarder' written on his chest in his own blood . . . alongside these two doomed men, waiting in the secret shadow of a ruin to spy on a blackmailer coming for his money. 'South-west corner,' the phone call said, 'Turret. Stone staircase inside. Climb. Topmost landing. Leave money there. Go. Understood?' Defying orders, they hide in the ruined room; somewhere above them, on the topmost landing of the turret tower, three grey bags wait in the gathering dark.

. . . In the gathering dark of an airless stairwell, Amina Sinai is climbing towards a prophecy. Lifafa Das is comforting her; because now that she has come by taxi into the narrow bottle of his mercy, he has sensed an alteration in her, a regret at her decision; he reassures her as they climb. The darkened stairwell is full of eyes, eyes glinting through shuttered doors at the spectacle of the climbing dark lady, eyes lapping her up like bright rough cats' tongues; and as Lifafa talks, soothingly, my mother feels her will ebbing away, What will be, will be, her strength of mind and her hold on the world seeping out of her into the dark sponge of the staircase air. Sluggishly her feet follow his, up into the upper reaches of the huge gloomy chawl, the broken-down tenement building in which Lifafa Das and his cousins have a small corner, at the very top . . . here, near the top, she sees dark light filtering down on to the heads of queueing cripples. 'My number two cousin,' Lifafa Das says, 'is bone-setter.' She climbs past men with broken arms, women with feet twisted backwards at impossible angles, past fallen window-cleaners and splintered bricklayers, a doctor's daughter entering a world older then syringes and hospitals; until, at last, Lifafa Das says, 'Here we are, Begum,' and leads her through a room in which the bone-setter is fastening twigs and leaves to shattered limbs, wrapping cracked heads in palm-fronds, until his patients begin to resemble artificial trees, sprouting vegetation from their injuries . . . then out on to a flat expanse of cemented roof. Amina, blinking in the dark at the brightness of lanterns, makes out insane shapes on the roof: monkeys dancing; mongeese leaping; snakes swaying in baskets; and on the parapet, the silhouettes of large birds, whose bodies are as hooked and cruel as their beaks: vultures.

'Arré baap,' she cries, 'where are you bringing me?'

'Nothing to worry, Begum, please,' Lifafa Das says. 'These are my cousins here. My number-three-and-four cousins. That one is monkey-dancer . . .'

'Just practising, Begum!' a voice calls. 'See: monkey goes to war and dies for his country!'

'. . . and there, snake-and-mongoose man.'

'See mongoose jump, Sahiba! See cobra dance!'

'. . . But the birds? . . .'

'Nothing, Madam: only there is Parsee Tower of Silence just near here; and when there are no dead ones there, the vultures come. Now they are asleep; in the days, I think, they like to watch my cousins practising.'

A small room, on the far side of the roof. Light streams through the door as Amina enters . . . to find, inside, a man the same age as her husband, a heavy man with several chins, wearing white stained trousers and a red check shirt and no shoes, munching aniseed and drinking from a bottle of Vimto, sitting cross-legged in a room on whose walls are pictures of Vishnu in each of his avatars, and notices reading, WRITING TAUGHT, and SPITTING DURING VISIT IS QUITE A BAD HABIT. There is no furniture . . . and Shri Ramram Seth is sitting cross-legged, six inches above the ground.

I must admit it: to her shame, my mother screamed . . .

. . . While, at the Old Fort, monkeys scream among ramparts. The ruined city, having been deserted by people, is now the abode of langoors. Long-tailed and black-faced, the monkeys are possessed of an overriding sense of mission. Upupup they clamber, leaping to the topmost heights of the ruin, staking out territories, and thereafter dedicating themselves to the dismemberment, stone by stone, of the entire fortress. Padma, it's true: you've never been there, never stood in the twilight watching straining, resolute, furry creatures working at the stones, pulling and rocking, rocking and pulling, working the stones loose one at a time . . . every day the monkeys send stones rolling down the walls, bouncing off angles and outcrops, crashing down into the ditches below. One day there will be no Old Fort; in the end, nothing but a pile of rubble surmounted by monkeys screaming in triumph . . . and here is one monkey, scurrying along the ramparts – I shall call him Hanuman, after the monkey god who helped Prince Rama defeat the original

Ravana, Hanuman of the flying chariots ... Watch him now as he arrives at this turret – his territory; as he hops chatters runs from corner to corner of his kingdom, rubbing his rear on the stones; and then pauses, sniffs something that should not be here ... Hanuman races to the alcove here, on the topmost landing, in which the three men have left three soft grey alien things. And, while monkeys dance on a roof behind the post office, Hanuman the monkey dances with rage. Pounces on the grey things. Yes, they are loose enough, won't take much rocking and pulling, pulling and rocking ... watch Hanuman now, dragging the soft grey stones to the edge of the long drop of the outside wall of the Fort. See him tear at them: rip! rap! rop! ... Look how deftly he scoops paper from the insides of the grey things, sending it down like floating rain to bathe the fallen stones in the ditch! ... Paper falling with lazy, reluctant grace, sinking like a beautiful memory into the maw of the darkness; and now, kick! thump! and again kick! the three soft grey stones go over the edge, downdown into the dark, and at last there comes a soft disconsolate plop. Hanuman, his work done, loses interest, scurries away to some distant pinnacle of his kingdom, begins to rock on a stone.

... While, down below, my father has seen a grotesque figure emerging from the gloom. Not knowing a thing about the disaster which has taken place above, he observes the monster from the shadow of his ruined room: a ragged-pajama'd creature in the head-dress of a demon, a papier-mâché devil-top which has faces grinning on every side of it ... the appointed representative of the Ravana gang. The collector. Hearts thumping, the three businessmen watch this spectre out of a peasant's nightmare vanish into the stairwell leading to the landing; and after a moment, in the stillness of the empty night, hear the devil's perfectly human oaths. 'Mother-sleepers! Eunuchs from somewhere!' ... Uncomprehending, they see their bizarre tormentor emerge, rush away into the darkness, vanish. His imprecations . . . 'Sodomizers of asses! Sons of pigs! Eaters of their own excrement!' . . . linger on the breeze. And up they go now, confusion addling their spirits; Butt finds a torn fragment of grey cloth; Mustapha Kemal stoops over a crumpled rupee; and maybe, yes, why not, my father sees a dark flurry of monkey out of the corner of an eye . . . and they guess.

And now their groans and Mr Butt's shrill curses, which are echoes of the devil's oaths; and there's a battle raging, unspoken, in all their heads: money or godown or godown or money? Businessmen ponder, in mute panic, this central riddle – but then, even if they abandon the cash to the depredations of scavenging dogs and humans, how to stop the fire-raisers? – and at last, without a word having been spoken, the inexorable law of cash-in-hand wins them over; they rush down stone stairs, along grassed lawns, through ruined gates, and arrive – PELL-MELL! – at the ditch, to begin scooping rupees into their pockets, shovelling grabbing scrabbling, ignoring pools of urine and rotting fruit, trusting against all likelihood that tonight – by the grace of – just tonight for once, the gang will fail to wreak its promised revenge. But, of course . . .

. . . But, of course, Ramram the seer was not really floating in mid-air, six inches above the ground. My mother's scream faded; her eyes focused; and she noticed the little shelf, protruding from the wall. 'Cheap trick,' she told herself, and, 'What am I doing here in this godforsaken place of sleeping vultures and monkey-dancers, waiting to be told who knows what foolishness by a guru who levitates by sitting on a shelf?'

What Amina Sinai did not know was that, for the second time in history, I was about to make my presence felt. (No: not that fraudulent tadpole in her stomach: I mean myself, in my historical role, of which prime ministers have written '. . . it is, in a sense, the mirror of us all.' Great forces were working that night; and all present were about to feel their power, and be afraid.)

Cousins – one to four – gathering in the doorway through which the dark lady has passed, drawn like moths to the candle of her screech . . . watching her quietly as she advanced, guided by Lifafa Das, towards the unlikely sooth-sayer, were bone-setter cobra-wallah and monkey-man. Whispers of encouragement now (and were there also giggles behind rough hands?): 'O such a too fine fortune he will tell, Sahiba!' and, 'Come, cousinji, lady is waiting!' . . . But what was this Ramram? A huckster, a two-chip palmist, a giver of cute forecasts to silly women – or the genuine article, the holder of the keys? And Lifafa Das: did he see, in my mother, a woman who could be satisfied by a two-rupee fake, or did he see deeper, into the underground heart of her weakness? – And when the prophecy came, were cousins astonished too? – And the frothing at the mouth? What of that? And was it true that my mother, under the dislocating influence of that hysterical evening, relinquished her hold on her habitual self – which she had felt slipping away from her into the absorbing sponge of the lightless air in the stairwell – and entered a state of mind in which anything might happen and be believed? And there is another, more horrible possibility, too; but before I voice my suspicion, I must describe, as nearly as possible in spite of this filmy curtain of ambiguities, what actually happened: I must describe my mother, her palm slanted outwards towards the advancing palmist, her eyes wide and unblinking as a pomfret's – and the cousins (giggling?), 'What a reading you are coming to get, Sahiba!' and, 'Tell, cousinji, tell!' – but the curtain descends again, so I cannot be sure – did he begin like a cheap circus-tent man and go through the banal conjugations of life-line heart-line and children who would be multi-millionaires, while cousins cheered, 'Wah wah!' and, 'Absolute master reading, yara!' – and then, did he change? – did Ramram become stiff – eyes rolling upwards until they were white as eggs – did he, in a voice as strange as a mirror, ask, 'You permit, Madam, that I touch the place?' – while cousins fell as silent as sleeping vultures – and did my mother, just as strangely, reply, 'Yes, I permit,' so that the seer became only the third man to touch her in her life, apart from her family members? – and was it then, at that instant, that a brief sharp jolt of electricity passed between pudgy fingers and maternal skin? And my mother's face, rabbit-startled, watching the prophet in the check shirt as he began to circle, his eyes still egg-like in the softness of his face; and suddenly a shudder passing through him and again that strange high voice as the words issued through his lips (I must describe those lips, too – but later, because now . . .) 'A son.'

Silent cousins – monkeys on leashes, ceasing their chatter – cobras coiled in baskets – and the circling fortune-teller, finding history speaking through his lips. (Was that how?) Beginning, 'A son . . . such a son!' And then it comes, 'A son, Sahiba, who will never be older than his motherland – neither older nor younger.' And now, real fear amongst snake-charmer mongoose-dancer bone-setter and peepshow-wallah, because they have never heard Ramram like this, as he continues, singsong, high-pitched: 'There will be two heads – but you shall see only one – there will be knees and a nose, a nose and knees.' Nose and knees and knees and nose . . . listen carefully, Padma; the fellow got nothing wrong! 'Newspaper praises him, two mothers raise him! Bicyclists love him – but, crowds will shove him! Sisters will weep; cobra will creep . . .' Ramram, circling fasterfaster, while four cousins murmur, 'What is this, baba?' and, 'Deo, Shiva, guard us!' While Ramram, 'Washing will hide him – voices will guide him! Friends mutilate him – blood will betray him!' And Amina Sinai, 'What does he mean? I don't understand – Lifafa Das – what has got into him?' But, inexorably, whirling egg-eyed around her statue-still presence, goes Ramram Seth:

114

'Spittoons will brain him – doctors will drain him – jungle will claim him – wizards reclaim him! Soldiers will try him – tyrants will fry him . . .' While Amina begs for explanations and the cousins fall into a hand-flapping frenzy of helpless alarm because something has taken over and nobody dares touch Ramram Seth as he whirls to his climax: 'He will have sons without having sons! He will be old before he is old! *And he will die . . . before he is dead.*'

Is that how it was? Is that when Ramram Seth, annihilated by the passage through him of a power greater than his own, fell suddenly to the floor and frothed at the mouth? Was mongoose-man's stick inserted between his twitching teeth? Did Lifafa Das say, 'Begum Sahiba, you must leave, please: our cousinji has become sick'?

And finally the cobra-wallah – or monkey-man, or bone-setter, or even Lifafa Das of the peepshow on wheels – saying, 'Too much prophecy, man. Our Ramram made too much damn prophecy tonight.'

Many years later, at the time of her premature dotage, when all kinds of ghosts welled out of her past to dance before her eyes, my mother saw once again the peepshow man whom she saved by announcing my coming and who repaid her by leading her to too much prophecy, and spoke to him evenly, without rancour. 'So you're back,' she said, 'Well, let me tell you this: I wish I'd understood what your cousinji meant – about blood, about knees and nose. Because who knows? I might have had a different son.'

Like my grandfather at the beginning, in a webbed corridor in a blind man's house, and again at the end; like Mary Pereira after she lost her Joseph, and like me, my mother was good at seeing ghosts.

. . . But now, because there are yet more questions and ambiguities, I am obliged to voice certain suspicions. Suspicion, too, is a monster with too many heads; why, then, can't I stop myself unleashing it at my own mother? . . . What,

I ask, would be a fair description of the seer's stomach? And memory – my new, all-knowing memory, which encompasses most of the lives of mother father grandfather grandmother and everyone else – answers: soft; squashy as cornflour pudding. Again, reluctantly, I ask: What was the condition of his lips? And the inevitable response: full; overfleshed; poetic. A third time I interrogate this memory of mine: what of his hair? The reply: thinning; dark; lank; worming over his ears. And now my unreasonable suspicions ask the ultimate question . . . did Amina, pure-as-pure, actually . . . because of her weakness for men who resembled Nadir Khan, could she have . . . in her odd frame of mind, and moved by the seer's illness, might she not . . . 'No!' Padma shouts, furiously. 'How dare you suggest? About that good woman – your own mother? That she would? You do not know one thing and still you say it?' And, of course, she is right, as always. If she knew, she would say I was only getting my revenge, for what I certainly did see Amina doing, years later, through the grimy windows of the Pioneer Café; and maybe that's where my irrational notion was born, to grow illogically backwards in time, and arrive fully mature at this earlier – and yes, almost certainly innocent – adventure. Yes, that must be it. But the monster won't lie down . . . 'Ah,' it says, 'but what about the matter of her tantrum – the one she threw the day Ahmed announced they were moving to Bombay?' Now it mimics her: 'You – always you decide. What about me? Suppose I don't want . . . I've only now got this house straight and already . . . !' So, Padma: was that housewifely zeal – or a masquerade?

Yes – a doubt lingers. The monster asks, 'Why did she fail, somehow or other, to tell her husband about her visit?' Reply of the accused (voiced by our Padma in my mother's absence): 'But think how angry he'd've got, my God! Even if there hadn't been all that firebug business to worry him! Strange men; a woman on her own; he'd've gone wild! Wild, completely!'

116

Unworthy suspicions . . . I must dismiss them; must save my strictures for later, when, in the absence of ambiguity, without the clouding curtain, she gave me hard, clear, irrefutable proofs.

. . . But, of course, when my father came home late that night, with a ditchy smell on him which overpowered his customary reek of future failure, his eyes and cheeks were streaked with ashy tears; there was sulphur in his nostrils and the grey dust of smoked leathercloth on his head . . . because of course they had burned the godown.

'But the night-watchmen?' – asleep, Padma, asleep. Warned in advance to take their sleeping draughts just in case . . . Those brave lalas, warrior Pathans who, city-born, had never seen the Khyber, unwrapped little paper packets, poured rust-coloured powders into their bubbling cauldron of tea. They pulled their charpoys well away from my father's godown to avoid falling beams and showering sparks; and lying on their rope-beds they sipped their tea and entered the bittersweet declensions of the drug. At first they became raucous, shouting the praises of their favourite whores in Pushtu; then they fell into wild giggling as the soft fluttering fingers of the drug tickled their ribs . . . until the giggling gave way to dreams and they roamed in the frontier passes of the drug, riding the horses of the drug, and finally reached a dreamless oblivion from which nothing on earth could awaken them until the drug had run its course.

Ahmed, Butt and Kemal arrived by taxi – the taxi-driver, unnerved by the three men who clutched wads of crumpled banknotes which smelled worse than hell on account of the unpleasant substances they had encountered in the ditch, would not have waited, except that they refused to pay him. 'Let me go, big sirs,' he pleaded, 'I am a little man; do not keep me here . . .' but by then their backs were moving away from him, towards the fire. He watched them as they ran, clutching their rupees that were stained by tomatoes and dogshit; open-mouthed he stared at the burning godown, at the clouds in the night sky, and like everyone else on the scene he was obliged to breathe air filled with leathercloth and matchsticks and burning rice. With his hands over his eyes, watching through his fingers, the little taxi-driver with his incompetent moustache saw Mr Kemal, thin as a demented pencil, lashing and kicking at the sleeping bodies of night-watchmen; and he almost gave up his fare and drove off in terror at the instant when my father shouted, 'Look out!' ... but, staying despite it all, he saw the godown as it burst apart under the force of the licking red tongues, he saw pouring out of the godown an improbable lava flow of molten rice lentils chick-peas waterproof jackets matchboxes and pickle, he saw the hot red flowers of the fire bursting skywards as the contents of the warehouse spilled on to the hard yellow ground like a black charred hand of despair. Yes, of course the godown was burned, it fell on their heads from the sky in cinders, it plunged into the open mouths of the bruised, but still snoring, watchmen ... 'God save us,' said Mr Butt, but Mustapha Kemal, more pragmatically, answered: 'Thank God we are well insured.'

'It was right then,' Ahmed Sinai told his wife later, 'right at that moment that I decided to get out of the leathercloth business. Sell the office, the goodwill, and forget everything I know about the reccine trade. Then – not before, not afterwards – I made up my mind, also, to think no more about this Pakistan claptrap of your Emerald's Zulfy. In the heat of that fire,' my father revealed – unleashing a wifely tantrum – 'I decided to go to Bombay, and enter the property business. Property is dirt cheap there now,' he told her before her protests could begin, 'Narlikar knows.'

(But in time, he would call Narlikar a traitor.)

In my family, we always go when we're pushed – the freeze of '48 being the only exception to this rule. The boatman Tai drove my grandfather from Kashmir; Mercurochrome chased him out of Amritsar; the collapse of her life under the carpets led directly to my mother's departure from Agra; and many-headed monsters sent my father to Bombay, so that I could be born there. At the end of that January, history had finally, by a series of shoves, brought itself to the point at which it was almost ready for me to make my entrance. There were mysteries that could not be cleared up until I stepped on to the scene . . . the mystery, for example, of Shri Ramram's most enigmatic remark: 'There will be a nose and knees: knees, and a nose.' The insurance money came; January ended; and in the time it took to close down their affairs in Delhi and move to the city in which – as Dr Narlikar the gynaecologist knew – property was temporarily as cheap as dirt, my mother concentrated on her segmented scheme for learning to love her husband. She came to feel a deep affection for the question marks of his ears; for the remarkable depth of his navel, into which her finger could go right up to the first joint, without even pushing; she grew to love the knobbliness of his knees; but, try as she might (and as I'm giving her the benefit of my doubts I shall offer no possible reasons here), there was one part of him which she never managed to love, although it was the one thing he possessed, in full working order, which Nadir Khan had certainly lacked; on those nights when he heaved himself up on top of her – when the baby in her womb was no bigger than a frog – it was just no good at all.

. . . 'No, not so quick, janum, my life, a little longer, please,' she is saying; and Ahmed, to spin things out, tries to think back to the fire, to the last thing that happened on that blazing night, when just as he was turning to go he heard a dirty screech in the sky, and, looking up, had time to register that a vulture – at night! – a vulture from the Towers of Silence was flying overhead, and that it had dropped a barely-chewed Parsee hand, a right hand, the same hand which – now! – slapped him full in the face as it fell; while Amina, beneath him in bed, ticks herself off: Why can't you enjoy, you stupid woman, from now on you must really *try*.

On June 4th, my ill-matched parents left for Bombay by Frontier Mail. (There were hangings, voices hanging on for dear life, fists crying out, 'Maharaj! Open, for one tick only! Ohé, from the milk of your kindness, great sir, do us favour!' And there was also – hidden beneath dowry in a green tin trunk – a forbidden, lapis-lazuli-encrusted, delicately-wrought silver spittoon.) On the same day, Earl Mountbatten of Burma held a press conference at which he announced the Partition of India, and hung his countdown calendar on the wall: seventy days to go to the transfer of power . . . sixty-nine . . . sixty-eight . . . tick, tock.

Methwold

The fishermen were here first. Before Mountbatten's ticktock, before monsters and public announcements; when underworld marriages were still unimagined and spittoons were unknown; earlier than Mercurochrome; longer ago than lady wrestlers who held up perforated sheets; and back and back, beyond Dalhousie and Elphinstone, before the East India Company built its Fort, before the first William Methwold; at the dawn of time, when Bombay was a dumb-bell-shaped island tapering, at the centre, to a narrow shining strand beyond which could be seen the finest and largest natural harbour in Asia, when Mazagaon and Worli, Matunga and Mahirn, Salsette and Colaba were islands, too – in short, before reclamation, before tetrapods and sunken piles turned the Seven Isles into a long peninsula like an outstretched, grasping hand, reaching westward into the Arabian Sea; in this primeval world before clocktowers, the fishermen – who were called Kolis – sailed in Arab dhows, spreading red sails against the setting sun. They caught pomfret and crabs, and made fish-lovers of us all. (Or most of us. Padma has succumbed to their piscine sorceries; but in our house, we were infected with the alienness of Kashmiri blood, with the icy reserve of Kashmiri sky, and remained meateaters to a man.)

There were also coconuts and rice. And, above it all, the benign presiding influence of the goddess Mumbadevi, whose name – Mumbadevi, Mumbabai, Mumbai – may well have become the city's. But then, the Portuguese named the place Bom Bahia for its harbour, and not for the goddess of the pomfret folk . . . the Portuguese were the first invaders, using the harbour to shelter their merchant ships and their men-of-war; but then, one day in 1633, and East India Company Officer named Methwold saw a vision. This vision – a dream of a British Bombay, fortified, defending India's West against all comers – was a notion of such force that it set time in motion. History churned ahead; Methwold died; and in 1660, Charles II of England was betrothed to Catharine of the Portuguese House of Braganza – that same Catharine who would, all her life, play second fiddle to orange-selling Nell. But she has this consolation – that it was her marriage dowry which brought Bombay into British hands, perhaps in a green tin trunk, and brought Methwold's vision a step closer to reality. After that, it wasn't long until September 21st, 1668, when the Company at last got its hands on the island . . . and then off they went, with their Fort and land-reclamation, and before you could blink there was a city here, Bombay, of which the old tune sang:

> Prima in Indis,
> Gateway to India,
> Star of the East
> With her face to the West.

Our Bombay, Padma! It was very different then, there were no night-clubs or pickle factories or Oberoi-Sheraton Hotels or movie studios; but the city grew at breakneck speed, acquiring a cathedral and an equestrian statue of the Mahratta warrior-king Sivaji which (we used to think) came to life at night and galloped awesomely through the city streets – right along Marine Drive! On Chowpatty sands! Past the great houses on Malabar Hill, round Kemp's Corner, giddily along the sea to Scandal Point! And yes, why not, on and on, down my very own Warden Road, right alongside the segregated swimming pools of Breach Candy, right up to huge Mahalaxmi Temple and the old Willingdon Club . . . Throughout my childhood, whenever bad times came to Bombay, some insomniac nightwalker would report that he had seen the statue moving; disasters, in the city of my youth, danced to the occult music of a horse's grey, stone hooves.

And where are they now, the first inhabitants? Coconuts have done best of all. Coconuts are still beheaded daily on Chowpatty beach; while on Juhu beach, under the languid gaze of film stars at the Sun'n'Sand hotel, small boys still shin up coconut palms and bring down the bearded fruit. Coconuts even have their own festival, Coconut Day, which was celebrated a few days before my synchronistic birth. You may feel reassured about coconuts. Rice has not been so lucky; rice-paddies lie under concrete now; tenements tower where once rice wallowed within sight of the sea. But still, in the city, we are great rice-eaters. Patna rice, Basmati, Kashmiri rice travels to the metropolis daily; so the original, ur-rice has left its mark upon us all, and cannot be said to have died in vain. As for Mumbadevi – she's not so popular these days, having been replaced by elephant-headed Ganesh in the people's affections. The calendar of festivals reveals her decline: Ganesh – 'Ganpati Baba' – has his day of Ganesh Chaturthi, when huge processions are 'taken out' and march to Chowpatty bearing plaster effigies of the god, which they hurl into the sea. Ganesh's day is a rain-making ceremony, it makes the monsoon possible, and it, too, was celebrated in the days before my arrival at the end of the ticktock countdown – but where is Mumbadevi's day? It is not on the calendar. Where the prayers of pomfret folk, the devotions of crab-catchers? . . . Of all the first inhabitants, the Koli fishermen have come off worst of all. Squashed now into a tiny village in the thumb of the handlike peninsula, they have admittedly given their name to a district – Colaba. But follow

Colaba Causeway to its tip – past cheap clothes shops and Irani restaurants and the second-rate flats of teachers, journalists and clerks – and you'll find them, trapped between the naval base and the sea. And sometimes Koli women, their hands stinking of pomfret guts and crabmeat, jostle arrogantly to the head of a Colaba bus-queue, with their crimson (or purple) saris hitched brazenly up between their legs, and a smarting glint of old defeats and dispossessions in their bulging and somewhat fishy eyes. A fort, and afterwards a city, took their land; pile-drivers stole (tetrapods would steal) pieces of their sea. But there are still Arab dhows, every evening, spreading their sails against the sunset . . . in August 1947, the British, having ended the dominion of fishing-nets, coconuts, rice and Mumbadevi, were about to depart themselves; no dominion is everlasting.

And on June 19th, two weeks after their arrival by Frontier Mail, my parents entered into a curious bargain with one such departing Englishman. His name was William Methwold.

The road to Methwold's Estate (we are entering my kingdom now, coming into the heart of my childhood; a little lump has appeared in my throat) turns off Warden Road between a bus-stop and a little row of shops. Chimalker's Toyshop; Reader's Paradise; the Chimanbhoy Fatbhoy jewellery store; and, above all, Bombelli's the Confectioners, with their Marquis cake, their One Yard of Chocolates! Names to conjure with; but there's no time now. Past the saluting cardboard bellboy of the Band Box Laundry, the road leads us home. In those days the pink skyscraper of the Narlikar women (hideous echo of Srinagar's radio mast!) had not even been thought of; the road mounted a low hillock, no higher than a two-storey building; it curved round to face the sea, to look down on Breach Candy Swimming Club, where pink people could swim in a pool the shape of British India without fear of rubbing up against a black skin; and there, arranged nobly around a little roundabout, were the palaces of William Methwold, on which hung signs that would – thanks to me – reappear many years later, signs bearing two words; just two, but they lured my unwitting parents into Methwold's peculiar game: FOR SALE.

Methwold's Estate: four identical houses built in a style befitting their original residents (conquerors' houses! Roman mansions; three-storey homes of gods standing on a two-storey Olympus, a stunted Kailash!) – large, durable mansions with red gabled roofs and turret towers in each corner, ivory-white corner towers wearing pointy red-tiled hats (towers, fit to lock princesses in!) – houses with verandahs, with servants' quarters reached by spiral iron staircases hidden at the back – houses which their owner, William Methwold, had named majestically after the palaces of Europe: Versailles Villa, Buckingham Villa, Escorital Villa and Sans Souci. Bougainvillaea crept across them; goldfish swam in pale blue pools; cacti grew in rock-gardens; tiny touch-me-not plants huddled beneath tamarind trees; there were butterflies and roses and cane chairs on the lawns. And on that day in the middle of June, Mr Methwold sold his empty palaces for ridiculously little – but there were conditions. So now, without more ado, I present him to you, complete with the centre-parting in his hair . . . a six-foot Titan, this Methwold, his face the pink of roses and eternal youth. He had a head of thick black brilliantined hair, parted in the centre. We shall speak again of this centre-parting, whose ramrod precision made Methwold irresistible to women, who felt unable to prevent themselves wanting to rumple it up . . . Methwold's hair, parted in the middle, has a lot to do with my beginnings. It was one of those hairlines along which history and sexuality moved. Like tightrope-walkers. (But despite everything, not even I, who never saw him, never laid eyes on languid gleaming teeth or

125

devastatingly combed hair, am incapable of bearing him any grudge.)

And his nose? What did that look like? Prominent? Yes, it must have been, the legacy of a patrician French grandmother – from Bergerac! – whose blood ran aquamarinely in his veins and darkened his courtly charm with something crueller, some sweet murderous shade of absinthe.

Methwold's Estate was sold on two conditions: that the houses be bought complete with every last thing in them, that the entire contents be retained by the new owners; and that the actual transfer should not take place until midnight on August 15th.

'Everything?' Amina Sinai asked. 'I can't even throw away a spoon? Allah, that lampshade . . . I can't get rid of one *comb*?'

'Lock, stock and barrel,' Methwold said, 'Those are my terms. A whim, Mr Sinai . . . you'll permit a departing colonial his little game? We don't have much left to do, we British, except to play our games.'

'Listen now, listen, Amina,' Ahmed is saying later on, 'You want to stay in this hotel room for ever? It's a fantastic price; fantastic, absolutely. And what can he do after he's transferred the deeds? Then you can throw out any lampshade you like. It's less than two months . . .'

'You'll take a cocktail in the garden?' Methwold is saying, 'Six o'clock every evening. Cocktail hour. Never varied in twenty years.'

'But my God, the paint . . . and the cupboards are full of old clothes, janum . . . we'll have to live out of suitcases, there's nowhere to put one suit!'

'Bad business, Mr Sinai,' Methwold sips his Scotch amid cacti and roses, 'Never seen the like. Hundreds of years of decent government, then suddenly, up and off. You'll admit we weren't all bad: built your roads. Schools, railway trains, parliamentary system, all worthwhile things. Taj Mahal was falling down until an Englishman bothered to see to it. And now, suddenly, independence. Seventy days to get out. I'm dead against it myself, but what's to be done?'

'. . . And look at the stains on the carpets, janum; for two months we must live like those Britishers? You've looked in the bathrooms? No water near the pot. I never believed, but it's true, my God, they wipe their bottoms with paper only! . . .'

'Tell me, Mr Methwold,' Ahmed Sinai's voice has changed, in the presence of an Englishman it has become a hideous mockery of an Oxford drawl, 'why insist on the delay? Quick sale is best business, after all. Get the thing buttoned up.'

'. . . And pictures of old Englishwomen everywhere, baba! No place to hang my own father's photo on the wall! . . .'

'It seems, Mr Sinai,' Mr Methwold is refilling the glasses as the sun dives towards the Arabian Sea behind the Breach Candy pool, 'that beneath this stiff English exterior lurks a mind with a very Indian lust for allegory.'

'And drinking so much, janum . . . that's not good.'

'I'm not sure – Mr Methwold, ah – what exactly you mean by . . .'

'. . . Oh, you know: after a. fashion, I'm transferring power, too. Got a sort of itch to do it at the same time the Raj does. As I said: a game. Humour me, won't you, Sinai? After all: the price, you've admitted, isn't bad.'

'Has his brain gone raw, janum? What do you think: is it safe to do bargains if he's loony?'

'Now listen, wife,' Ahmed Sinai is saying, 'this has gone on long enough. Mr Methwold is a fine man; a person of breeding; a man of honour; I will not have his name . . . And besides, the other purchasers aren't making so much noise, I'm sure . . . Anyway, I have told him yes, so there's an end to it.'

'Have a cracker,' Mr Methwold is saying, proffering a plate, 'Go on, Mr S., do. Yes, a curious affair. Never seen anything like it. My old tenants – old India hands, the lot – suddenly, up and off. Bad show. Lost their stomachs for India. Overnight. Puzzling to a simple fellow like me. Seemed like they washed their hands – didn't want to take a scrap with them. "Let it go," they said. Fresh start back home. Not short of a shilling, none of them, you understand, but still, Rum. Leaving me holding the baby. Then I had my notion.'

'. . . Yes, decide, decide,' Amina is saying spiritedly, 'I am sitting here like a lump with a baby, what have I to do with it? I must live in a stranger's house with this child growing, so what? . . . Oh, what things you make me do . . .'

'Don't cry,' Ahmed is saying now, flapping about the hotel room, 'It's a good house. You know you like the house. And two months . . . less than two . . . what, is it kicking? Let me feel . . . Where? Here?'

'There,' Amina says, wiping her nose, 'Such a good big kick.'

'My notion,' Mr Methwold explains, staring at the setting sun, 'is to stage my own transfer of assets. Leave behind everything you see? Select suitable persons – such as yourself, Mr Sinai! – hand everything over absolutely intact: in tiptop working order. Look around you: everything's in fine fettle, don't you agree? Tickety-boo, we used to say. Or, as you say in Hindustani: Sabkuch ticktock hai. Everything's just fine.'

'Nice people are buying the houses,' Ahmed offers Amina his handkerchief, 'nice new neighbours . . . that Mr Homi Catrack in Versailles Villa, Parsee chap, but a racehorse-owner. Produces films and all. And the Ibrahims in Sans Souci, Nussie Ibrahim is having a baby, too, you can be friends . . . and the old man Ibrahim, with so-big sisal farms in Africa. Good family.'

'. . . And afterwards I can do what I like with the house . . . ?'

'Yes, afterwards, naturally, he'll be gone . . .'

'. . . It's all worked out excellently,' William Methwold says. 'Did you know my ancestor was the chap who had the

128

idea of building this whole city? Sort of Raffles of Bombay. As his descendant, at this important juncture, I feel the, I don't know, need to play my part. Yes, excellently . . . when d'you move in? Say the word and I'll move off to the Taj Hotel. Tomorrow? Excellent. Sabkuch ticktock hai.'

These were the people amongst whom I spent my childhood: Mr Homi Catrack, film magnate and racehorse-owner, with his idiot daughter Toxy who had to be locked up with her nurse, Bi-Appah, the most fearsome woman I ever knew; also the Ibrahims in Sans Souci, old man Ibrahim Ibrahim with his goatee and sisal, his sons Ismail and Ishaq, and Ismail's tiny flustery hapless wife Nussie, whom we always called Nussie-the-duck on account of her waddling gait, and in whose womb my friend Sonny was growing, even now, getting closer and closer to his misadventure with a pair of gynae-cological forceps . . . Escorial Villa was divided into flats. On the ground floor lived the Dubashes, he a physicist who would become a leading light at the Trombay nuclear research base, she a cipher beneath whose blankness a true religious fanaticism lay concealed – but I'll let it lie, mentioning only that they were the parents of Cyrus (who would not be conceived for a few months yet), my first mentor, who played girls' parts in school plays and was known as Cyrus-the-great. Above them was my father's friend Dr Narlikar, who had bought a flat here too . . . he was as black as my mother; had the ability of glowing brightly whenever he became excited or aroused; hated children, even though he brought us into the world; and would unleash upon the city, when he died, that tribe of women who could do anything and in whose path no obstacle could stand. And, finally, on the top floor, were Commander Sabarmati and Lila – Sabarmati who was one of the highest flyers in the Navy, and his wife with her expensive tastes; he hadn't been able to believe his luck in getting her a home so cheaply. They had two sons, aged eighteen months and four months, who would grow up to be slow and boisterous and to be nicknamed Eyeslice and Hairoil; and they didn't know (how could they?) that I would destroy their lives . . . Selected by William Methwold, these people who would form the centre of my world moved into the Estate and tolerated the curious whims of the Englishman – because the price, after all, was right.

. . . There are thirty days to go to the transfer of power and Lila Sabarmati is on the telephone, 'How can you stand it, Nussie? In every room here there are talking budgies, and in the almirahs I find moth-eaten dresses and used brassières!' . . . And Nussie is telling Amina, 'Goldfish, Allah, I can't stand the creatures, but Methwold sahib comes himself to feed . . . and there are half-empty pots of Bovril he says I can't throw . . . it's mad, Amina sister, what are we doing like this?' . . . And old man Ibrahim is refusing to switch on the ceiling fan in his bedroom, muttering, 'That machine will fall – it will slice my head off in the night – how long can something so heavy stick on a ceiling?' . . . and Homi Catrack who is something of an ascetic is obliged to lie on a large soft mattress, he is suffering from backache and sleeplessness and the dark rings of inbreeding around his eyes are being circled by the whorls of insomnia, and his bearer tells him, 'No wonder the foreign sahibs have all gone away, sahib, they must by dying to get some sleep.' But they are all sticking it out; and there are advantages as well as problems. Listen to Lila Sabarmati ('That one – too beautiful to be good,' my mother said) . . . 'A pianola, Amina sister! And it works! All day I'm sitting sitting, playing God knows what-all! "Pale Hands I Loved Beside The Shalimar" . . . such fun, too much, you just push the pedals!' . . . And Ahmed Sinai finds a cocktail cabinet in Buckingham Villa (which was Methwold's own house before it was ours); he is discovering the delights of fine Scotch whisky and cries, 'So what? Mr Methwold is a little eccentric, that's all – can we not humour him? With our ancient civilization, can we not be as civilized as he?' . . . and he drains his glass at one go. Advantages and disadvantages: 'All these dogs to look after, Nussie sister,' Lila Sabarmati complains. 'I hate dogs, completely. And my little choochie cat, *cho chweet* she is I swear, terrified absolutely!' . . . And Dr Narlikar, glowing with pique, 'Above my bed! Pictures of children, Sinai brother! I am telling you: fat! Pink! Three! Is that fair?' . . . But now there are twenty days to go, things are settling down, the sharp edges of things are getting blurred, so they have all failed to notice what is happening: the Estate, Methwold's Estate, is changing them. Every evening at six they are out in their gardens, celebrating the cocktail hour, and when William Methwold comes to call they slip effortlessly into their imitation Oxford drawls; and they are learning, about ceiling fans and gas cookers and the correct diet for budgerigars, and Methwold, supervising their transformation, is mumbling under his breath. Listen carefully: what's he saying? Yes, that's it. 'Sabkuch ticktock hai,' mumbles William Methwold. All is well.

When the Bombay edition of the *Times of India,* searching for a catchy human-interest angle to the forthcoming Independence celebrations, announced that it would award a prize to any Bombay mother who could arrange to give birth to a child at the precise instant of the birth of the new nation, Amina Sinai, who had just awoken from a mysterious dream of flypaper, became glued to newsprint. Newsprint was thrust beneath Ahmed Sinai's nose; and Amina's finger, jabbing triumphantly at the page, punctuated the utter certainty of her voice.

'See, janum?' Amina announced. 'That's going to be me.'

There rose, before their eyes, a vision of bold headlines declaring 'A Charming Pose of Baby Sinai – the Child of this Glorious Hour!' – a vision of A-1 top-quality front-page jumbo-sized baby-snaps; but Ahmed began to argue, 'Think of the odds against it, Begum,' until she set her mouth into a clamp of obstinacy and reiterated, 'But me no buts; it's me all right; I just know it for sure. Don't ask me how.'

And although Ahmed repeated his wife's prophecy to William Methwold, as a cocktail-hour joke, Amina remained unshaken, even when Methwold laughed, 'Woman's intuition – splendid thing, Mrs S.! But really, you can scarcely expect us to . . .' Even under the pressure of the peeved gaze of her neighbour Nussie-the-duck, who was also pregnant, and had also read the *Times of India,* Amina stuck to her guns, because Ramram's prediction had sunk deep into her heart.

To tell the truth, as Amina's pregnancy progressed, she had found the words of the fortune-teller pressing more and more heavily down upon her shoulders, her head, her swelling balloon, so that as she became trapped in a web of worries about giving birth to a child with two heads she somehow escaped the subtle magic of Methwold's Estate, remaining uninfected by cocktail-hours, budgerigars, pianolas and English accents . . . At first, then, there was something equivocal about her certainty that she would win the *Times*'s prize, because she had convinced herself that if this part of the fortune-teller's prognostications were fulfilled, it proved that the rest would be just as accurate, whatever their meaning might be. So it was not in tones of unadulterated pride and anticipation that my mother said, 'Never mind intuition, Mr Methwold. This is guaranteed fact.'

To herself she added: 'And this, too: I'm going to have a son. But he'll need plenty of looking after, or else.'

It seems to me that, running deep in the veins of my mother, perhaps deeper than she knew, the supernatural conceits of Naseem Aziz had begun to influence her thoughts and behaviour – those conceits which persuaded Reverend Mother that aeroplanes were inventions of the devil, and that cameras could steal your soul, and that ghosts were as obvious a part of reality as Paradise, and that it was nothing less than a sin to place certain sanctified ears between one's thumb and forefinger, were now whispering in her daughter's darkling head. 'Even if we're sitting in the middle of all this English garbage,' my mother was beginning to think, 'this is still India, and people like Ramram Seth know what they know.' In this way the scepticism of her beloved father was replaced by the credulity of my grandmother; and, at the same time, the adventurous spark which Amina had inherited from Doctor Aziz was being snuffed out by another, and equally heavy, weight.

By the time the rains came at the end of June, the foetus was fully formed inside her womb. Knees and nose were present; and as many heads as would grow were already in position. What had been (at the beginning) no bigger than a full stop had expanded into a comma, a word, a sentence, a paragraph, a chapter; now it was bursting into more complex developments, becoming, one might say, a book – perhaps an encyclopaedia – even a whole language . . . which is to say that the lump in the middle of my mother grew so large, and became so heavy, that while Warden Road at the foot of our two-storey hillock became flooded with dirty yellow rain-water and stranded buses began to rust and children swam in the liquid road and newspapers sank soggily beneath the surface, Amina found herself in a circular first-floor tower room, scarcely able to move beneath the weight of her leaden balloon.

Endless rain. Water seeping in under windows in which stained-glass tulips danced along leaded panes. Towels, jammed against window-frames, soaked up water until they became heavy, saturated, useless. The sea: grey and ponderous and stretching out to meet the rainclouds at a narrowed horizon. Rain drumming against my mother's ears, adding to the confusion of fortune-teller and maternal credulity and the dislocating presence of strangers' possessions, making her imagine all manner of strange things. Trapped beneath her growing child, Amina pictured herself as a convicted murderer in Mughal times, when death by crushing beneath a boulder had been a common punishment . . . and in the years to come, whenever she looked back at that time which was the end of the time before she became a mother, that time in which the ticktock of countdown calendars was rushing everyone towards August 15th, she would say: 'I don't know about any of that. To me, it was like time had come to a complete stop. The baby in my stomach stopped the clocks. I'm sure of that. Don't laugh: you remember the clocktower at the end of the hill? I'm telling you, after that monsoon it never worked again.'

. . . And Musa, my father's old servant, who had accompanied the couple to Bombay, went off to tell the other servants, in the kitchens of the red-tiled palaces, in the servants' quarters at the backs of Versailles and Escorial and Sans Souci: 'It's going to be a real ten-rupee baby; yes, sir! A whopper of a ten-chip pomfret, wait and see!' The servants were pleased; because a birth is a fine thing and a good big baby is best of all . . .

. . . And Amina whose belly had stopped the clocks sat immobilized in a room in a tower and told her husband, 'Put your hand there and feel him . . . there, did you feel? . . . such a big strong boy; our little piece-of-the-moon.'

Not until the rains ended, and Amina became so heavy that two manservants had to make a chair with their hands to lift her, did Wee Willie Winkie return to sing in the circus-ring between the four houses; and only then did Amina realize that she had not one, but two serious rivals (two that she knew of) for the *Times of India's* prize, and that, prophecy or no prophecy, it was going to be a very close-run finish.

*

'Wee Willie Winkie is my name; to sing for my supper is my fame!'

Ex-conjurers and peepshow-men and singers . . . even before I was born, the mould was set. Entertainers would orchestrate my life.

'I hope you are com-for-table! . . . Or are you come-for-tea? Oh, joke-joke, ladies and ladahs, let me see you laugh now!'

Talldarkhandsome, a clown with an accordion, he stood in the circus-ring. In the gardens of Buckingham Villa, my father's big toe strolled (with its nine colleagues) beside and beneath the centre-parting of William Methwold . . . sandalled, bulbous, a toe unaware of its coming doom. And Wee Willie Winkie (whose real name we never knew) cracked jokes and sang. From a first-floor verandah, Amina watched and listened; and from the neighbouring verandah, felt the prick of the envious competitive gaze of Nussie-the-duck.

. . . While I, at my desk, feel the sting of Padma's impatience. (I wish, at times, for a more discerning audience, someone who would understand the need for rhythm, pacing, the subtle introduction of minor chords which will later rise, swell, seize the melody; who would know, for instance, that although baby-weight and monsoons have silenced the clock on the Estate clocktower, the steady beat of Mountbatten's ticktock is still there, soft but inexorable, and that it's only a matter of time before it fills our ears with its metronomic, drumming music.) Padma says: 'I don't want to know about this Winkie now; days and nights I've waited and still you won't get to being born!' But I counsel patience; everything in its proper place, I admonish my dung-lotus, because Winkie, too, has his purpose and his place, here he is now teasing the pregnant ladies on their verandahs, pausing from singing to say, 'You've heard about the prize, ladies? Me, too. My Vanita will have her time soon, soon-soon; maybe she and not you will have her picture in the paper!' . . . and Amina is frowning, and Methwold is smiling (is that a forced smile?

Why?) beneath his centre-parting, and my father's lip is jutting judiciously as his big toe strolls and he says, 'That's a cheeky fellow; he goes too far.' But now Methwold in what looks very like embarrassment – even guilt! – reproves Ahmed Sinai, 'Nonsense, old chap. The tradition of the fool, you know. Licensed to provoke and tease. Important social safety-valve.' And my father, shrugging, 'Hm.' But he's a clever type, this Winkie, because he's pouring oil on the waters now, saying, 'A birth is a fine thing; two births are two fine! Too fine, madams, joke, you see?' And a switch of mood as he introduces a dramatic notion, an overpowering, crucial thought: 'Ladies, gentlemen, how can you feel comfortable here, in the middle of Mr Methwold sahib's long past? I tell you: it must be strange; not real; but now it is a new place here, ladies, ladahs, and no new place is real until it has seen a birth. The first birth will make you feel at home.' After which, a song: 'Daisy, Daisy . . .' And Mr Methwold, joining in, but still there's something dark staining his brow . . .

. . . And here's the point: yes, it is guilt, because our Winkie may be clever and funny but he's not clever enough, and now it's time to reveal the first secret of the centre-parting of William Methwold, because it has dripped down to stain his face: one day, long before ticktock and lockstockandbarrel sales, Mr Methwold invited Winkie and his Vanita to sing for him, privately, in what is now my parents' main reception room; and after a while he said, 'Look here, Wee Willie, do me a favour, man: I need this prescription filling, terrible headaches, take it to Kemp's Corner and get the chemist to give you the pills, the servants are all down with colds.' Winkie, being a poor man, said Yes sahib at once sahib and left; and then Vanita was alone with the centre-parting, feeling it exert a pull on her fingers that was impossible to resist, and as Methwold sat immobile in a cane chair, wearing a lightweight cream suit with a single rose in the lapel, she found herself approaching him, fingers outstretched, felt fingers touching hair; found centre-parting; and began to rumple it up.

So that now, nine months later, Wee Willie Winkie joked about his wife's imminent baby and a stain appeared on an Englishman's forehead.

'So?' Padma says. 'So what do I care about this Winkie and his wife whom you haven't even told me about?'

Some people are never satisfied; but Padma will be, soon.

And now she's about to get even more frustrated; because, pulling away in a long rising spiral from the events at Methwold's Estate – away from goldfish and dogs and baby contests and centre-partings, away from big toes and tiled roofs – I am flying across the city which is fresh and clean in the aftermath of the rains; leaving Ahmed and Amina to the songs of Wee Willie Winkie, I'm winging towards the Old Fort district, past Flora Fountain, and arriving at a large building filled with dim fustian light and the perfume of swinging censers . . . because here, in St Thomas's Cathedral, Miss Mary Pereira is learning about the colour of God.

'Blue,' the young priest said earnestly. 'All available evidence, my daughter, suggests that Our Lord Christ Jesus was the most beauteous, crystal shade of pale sky blue.'

The little woman behind the wooden latticed window of the confessional fell silent for a moment. An anxious, cogitating silence. Then: 'But how, Father? People are not *blue*. No people are blue in the whole big world!'

Bewilderment of little woman, matched by perplexity of the priest . . . because this is not how she's supposed to react. The Bishop had said, 'Problems with recent converts . . . when they ask about colour they're almost always that . . . important to build bridges, my son. Remember,' thus spake the Bishop, 'God is love; and the Hindu love-god, Krishna, is always depicted with blue skin. Tell them blue; it will be a sort of bridge between the faiths; gently does it, you follow;

137

and besides blue is a neutral sort of colour, avoids the usual colour problems, gets you away from black and white: yes, on the whole I'm sure it's the one to choose.' Even bishops can be wrong, the young father is thinking, but meanwhile he's in quite a spot, because the little woman is clearly getting into a state, has begun issuing a severe reprimand through the wooden grille: 'What type of answer is blue, Father, how to believe such a thing? You should write to Holy Father Pope in Rome, he will surely put you straight; but one does not have to be Pope to know that the mens are not ever blue!' The young father closes his eyes; breathes deeply; counter-attacks. 'Skins have been dyed blue,' he stumbles. 'The Picts; the blue Arab nomads; with the benefits of education, my daughter, you would see . . .' But now a violent snort echoes in the confessional. 'What, Father? You are comparing Our Lord to *junglee* wild men? O Lord, I must catch my ears for shame!' . . . And there is more, much more, while the young father whose stomach is giving him hell suddenly has the inspiration that there is something more important lurking behind this blue business, and asks the question; whereupon tirade gives way to tears, and the young father says panickily, 'Come, come, surely the Divine Radiance of Our Lord is not a matter of mere pigment?' . . . And a voice through the flooding salt water: 'Yes, Father, you're not so bad after all; I told him just that, exactly that very thing only, but he said many rude words and would not listen . . .' So there it is, *him* has entered the story, and now it all tumbles out, and Miss Mary Pereira, tiny virginal distraught, makes a confession which gives us a crucial clue about her motives when, on the night of my birth, she made the last and most important contribution to the entire history of twentieth-century India from the time of my grandfather's nose-bump until the time of my adulthood.

Mary Pereira's confession: like every Mary she had her Joseph. Joseph D'Costa, an orderly at a Pedder Road clinic called Dr Narlikar's Nursing Home ('Oho!' Padma sees a connection at last), where she worked as a midwife. Things had been very good at first; he had taken her for cups of tea or lassi or falooda and told her sweet things. He had eyes like road-drills, hard and full of ratatat, but he spoke softly and well. Mary, tiny, plump, virginal, had revelled in his attentions; but now everything had changed.

'Suddenly suddenly he's sniffing the air all the time. In a funny way, nose high up. I ask, "You got a cold or what, Joe?" But he says no; no, he says, he's sniffing the wind from the north. But I tell him, Joe, in Bombay the wind comes off the sea, from the west, Joe . . .' In a fragile voice Mary Pereira describes the ensuing rage of Joseph D'Costa, who told her, 'You don't know nothing, Mary, the air comes from the north now, and it's full of dying. This independence is for the rich only; the poor are being made to kill each other like flies. In Punjab, in Bengal. Riots riots, poor against poor. It's in the wind.'

And Mary: 'You talking crazy, Joe, why you worrying with those so-bad things? We can live quietly still, no?'

'Never mind, you don't know one thing.'

'But Joseph, even if it's true about the killing, they're Hindu and Muslim people only; why get good Christian folk mixed up in their fight? Those ones have killed each other for ever and ever.'

'You and your Christ. You can't get it into your head that that's the white people's religion? Leave white gods for white men. Just now our own people are dying. We got to fight back; show the people who to fight instead of each other, you see?'

And Mary, 'That's why I asked about colour, Father . . . and I told Joseph, I told and told, fighting is bad, leave off these wild ideas; but then he stops talking with me, and starts hanging about with dangerous types, and there are rumours starting up about him, Father, how he's throwing bricks at big cars apparently, and burning bottles also, he's going crazy, Father, they say he helps to burn buses and blow up trams, and I don't know what. What to do, Father, I tell my sister about it all. My sister Alice, a good girl really, Father. I said: "That Joe, he lives near a slaughterhouse, maybe that's the smell that got into his nose and muddled him all up." So Alice went to find him, "I will talk for you," she says; but then, O God what is happening to the world . . . I tell you truly, Father . . . O baba . . .' And the floods are drowning her words, her secrets are leaking saltily out of her eyes, because Alice came back to say that in her opinion Mary was the one to blame, for haranguing Joseph until he wanted no more of her, instead of giving him support in his patriotic cause of awakening the people. Alice was younger than Mary; and prettier; and after that there were more rumours, Alice-and-Joseph stories, and Mary came to her wits' end.

'That one,' Mary said, 'What does she know about this politics-politics? Only to get her nails into my Joseph she will repeat any rubbish he talks, like one stupid mynah bird. I swear, Father . . .'

'Careful, daughter. You are close to blasphemy . . .'

'No, Father, I swear to God, I don't know what I won't do to get me back that man. Yes: in spite of . . . never mind what he . . . ai-o-ai-ooo!'

Salt water washes the confessional floor . . . and now, is there a new dilemma for the young father? Is he, despite the agonies of an unsettled stomach, weighing in invisible scales the sanctity of the confessional against the danger to civilized society of a man like Joseph D'Costa? Will he, in fact, ask Mary for her Joseph's address, and then reveal . . . In short, would this bishop-ridden, stomach-churned young father have behaved like, or unlike, Montgomery Clift in *I Confess*? (Watching it some years ago at the New Empire cinema, I couldn't decide.) – But no; once again, I must stifle my baseless suspicions. What happened to Joseph would probably have happened anyway. And in all likelihood the young father's only relevance to my history is that he was the first outsider to hear about Joseph D'Costa's virulent hatred of the rich, and of Mary Pereira's desperate grief.

Tomorrow I'll have a bath and shave; I am going to put on a brand new kurta, shining and starched, and pajamas to match. I'll wear mirrorworked slippers curling up at the toes, my hair will be neatly brushed (though not parted in the centre), my teeth gleaming . . . in a phrase, I'll look my best. ('Thank God' from pouting Padma.)

Tomorrow, at last, there will be an end to stories which I (not having been present at their birth) have to drag out of the whirling recesses of my mind; because the metronome music of Mountbatten's countdown calendar can be ignored no longer. At Methwold's Estate, old Musa is still ticking like a time-bomb; but he can't be heard, because another sound is swelling now, deafening, insistent; the sound of seconds passing, of an approaching, inevitable midnight.

Tick, tock

Padma can hear it: there's nothing like a countdown for building suspense. I watched my dung-flower at work today, stirring vats like a whirlwind, as if that would make the time go faster. (And perhaps it did; time, in my experience, has been as variable and inconstant as Bombay's electric power supply. Just telephone the speaking clock if you don't believe me – tied to electricity, it's usually a few hours wrong. Unless we're the ones who are wrong . . . no people whose word for 'yesterday' is the same as their word for 'tomorrow' can be said to have a firm grip on the time.)

But today, Padma heard Mountbatten's ticktock . . . English-made, it beats with relentless accuracy. And now the factory is empty; fumes linger, but the vats are still; and I've kept my word. Dressed up to the nines, I greet Padma as she rushes to my desk, flounces down on the floor beside me, commands: 'Begin.' I give a little satisfied smile; feel the children of midnight queueing up in my head, pushing and jostling like Koli fishwives; I tell them to wait, it won't be long now; I clear my throat, give my pen a little shake; and start.

Thirty-two years before the transfer of power, my grandfather bumped his nose against Kashmiri earth. There were rubies and diamonds. There was the ice of the future, waiting beneath the water's skin. There was an oath: not to bow down before god or man. The oath created a hole, which would temporarily be filled by a woman behind a perforated sheet. A boatman who had once prophesied dynasties lurking in my grandfather's nose ferried him angrily across a lake. There were blind landowners and lady wrestlers. And there was a sheet in a gloomy room. On that day, my inheritance began to form – the blue of Kashmiri sky which dripped into my grandfather's eyes; the long sufferings of my great-grandmother which would become the forebearance of my own mother and the late steeliness of Naseem Aziz; my great-grandfather's gift of conversing with birds which would descend through meandering bloodlines into the veins of my sister the Brass Monkey; the conflict between grandpaternal scepticism and grandmaternal credulity; and above all the ghostly essence of that perforated sheet, which doomed my mother to learn to love a man in segments, and which condemned me to see my own life – its meanings, its structures – in fragments also; so that by the time I understood it, it was far too late.

Years ticking away – and my inheritance grows, because now I have the mythical golden teeth of the boatman Tai, and his brandy bottle which foretold my father's alcoholic djinns; I have Ilse Lubin for suicide and pickled snakes for virility; I have Tai-for-changelessness opposed to Aadam-for-progress; and I have, too, the odours of the unwashed boatman which drove my grandparents south, and made Bombay a possibility.

. . . And now, driven by Padma and ticktock, I move on, acquiring Mahatma Gandhi and his hartal, ingesting thumb-and-forefinger, swallowing the moment at which Aadam Aziz did not know whether he was Kashmiri or Indian; now I'm drinking Mercurochrome and stains the shape of hands which will recur in spilt betel-juice, and I'm gulping down Dyer, moustache and all; my grandfather is saved by his nose and a bruise appears on his chest, never to fade, so that he and I find in its ceaseless throbbing the answer to the question, Indian or Kashmiri? Stained by the bruise of a Heidelberg bag's clasp, we throw our lot in with India; but the alienness of blue eyes remains. Tai dies, but his magic hangs over us still, and makes us men apart.

. . . Hurtling on, I pause to pick up the game of hit-the-spittoon. Five years before the birth of a nation, my inheritance grows, to include an optimism disease which would flare up again in my own time, and cracks in the earth which will-be-have-been reborn in my skin, and ex-conjurer Hummingbirds who began the long line of street-entertainers which has run in parallel with my life, and my grandmother's moles like witchnipples and hatred of photographs, and whatsitsname, and wars of starvation and silence, and the wisdom of my aunt Alia which turned into spinsterhood and bitterness and finally burst out in deadly revenge, and the love of Emerald and Zulfikar which would enable me to start a revolution, and crescent knives, fatal moons echoed by my mother's love-name for me, her innocent chand-ka-tukra, her affectionate piece-of-the- . . . growing larger now, floating in the amniotic fluid of the past, I feed on a hum that rose higherhigher until dogs came to the rescue, on an escape into a cornfield and a rescue by Rashid the rickshaw-wallah with his Gai-Wallah antics as he ran – FULL-TILT! – screaming silently, as he revealed the secrets of locks made in India and brought Nadir Khan into a toilet containing a washing-chest; yes, I'm getting heavier by the second, fattening up on washing-chests and the under-the-carpet love of Mumtaz and the rhymeless bard, plumping out as I swallow Zulfikar's dream of a bath by his bedside and an underground Taj Mahal and a silver spittoon encrusted with lapis lazuli; a marriage disintegrates, and feeds me; an aunt runs traitor-ously through Agra streets, without her honour, and that feeds me too; and now false starts are over, and Amina has stopped being Mumtaz, and Ahmed Sinai has become, in a sense, her father as well as her husband . . . my inheritance includes this gift, the gift of inventing new parents for myself whenever necessary. The power of giving birth to fathers and mothers: which Ahmed wanted and never had.

Through my umbilical cord, I'm taking in fare dodgers and the dangers of purchasing peacock-feather fans; Amina's assiduity seeps into me, and more ominous things – clattering footsteps, my mother's need to plead for money until the napkin in my father's lap began to quiver and make a little tent – and the cremated ashes of Arjuna Indiabikes, and a peepshow into which Lifafa Das tried to put everything in the world, and rapscallions perpetrating outrages; many-headed monsters swell inside me – masked Ravanas, eight-year-old girls with lisps and one continuous eyebrow, mobs crying Rapist. Public announcements nurture me as I grow towards my time, and there are only seven months left to go.

How many things people notions we bring with us into the world, how many possibilities and also restrictions of possibility! – Because all of these were the parents of the child born that midnight, and for every one of the midnight children there were as many more. Among the parents of midnight: the failure of the Cabinet Mission scheme; the determination of M. A. Jinnah, who was dying and wanted to see Pakistan formed in his lifetime, and would have done anything to ensure it – that same Jinnah whom my father, missing a turn as usual, refused to meet; and Mountbatten with his extraordinary haste and his chicken-breast-eater of a wife; and more and more – Red Fort and Old Fort, monkeys and vultures dropping hands, and white transvestites, and bone-setters and mongoose-trainers and Shri Ramram Seth who made too much prophecy. And my father's dream of rearranging the Quran has its place; and the burning of a godown which turned him into a man of property and not leathercloth; and the piece of Ahmed which Amina could not love. To understand just one life, you have to swallow the world. I told you that.

And fishermen, and Catharine of Braganza, and Mumbadevi coconuts rice; Sivaji's statue and Methwold's

Estate; a swimming pool in the shape of British India and a two-storey hillock; a centre-parting and a nose from Bergerac; an inoperative clocktower and a little circus-ring; an Englishman's lust for an Indian allegory and the seduction of an accordionist's wife. Budgerigars, ceiling fans, the *Times of India* are all part of the luggage I brought into the world . . . do you wonder, then, that I was a heavy child? Blue Jesus leaked into me; and Mary's desperation, and Joseph's revolutionary wildness, and the flightiness of Alice Pereira . . . all these made me, too.

If I seem a little bizarre, remember the wild profusion of my inheritance . . . perhaps, if one wishes to remain an individual in the midst of the teeming multitudes, one must make oneself grotesque.

'At last,' Padma says with satisfaction, 'you've learned how to tell things really fast.'

August 13th, 1947: discontent in the heavens. Jupiter, Saturn and Venus are in quarrelsome vein; moreover, the three crossed stars are moving into the most ill-favoured house of all. Benarsi astrologers name it fearfully: 'Karamstan! They enter Karamstan!'

While astrologers make frantic representations to Congress Party bosses, my mother lies down for her afternoon nap. While Earl Mountbatten deplores the lack of trained occultists on his General Staff, the slowly turning shadows of a ceiling fan caress Amina into sleep. While M. A. Jinnah, secure in the knowledge that his Pakistan will be born in just eleven hours, a full day before independent India, for which there are still thirty-five hours to go, is scoffing at the protestations of horoscope-mongers, shaking his head in amusement, Amina's head, too, is moving from side to side.

But she is asleep. And in these days of her boulder-like pregnancy, an enigmatic dream of flypaper has been plaguing her sleeping hours . . . in which she wanders now, as before, in a crystal sphere filled with dangling strips of the sticky brown material, which adhere to her clothing and rip it off as she stumbles through the impenetrable papery forest; and now she struggles, tears at paper, but it grabs at her, until she is naked, with the baby kicking inside her, and long tendrils of flypaper stream out to seize her by her undulating womb, paper glues itself to her hair nose teeth breasts thighs, and as she opens her mouth to shout a brown adhesive gag falls across her parting lips . . .

'Amina Begum!' Musa is saying. 'Wake up! Bad dream, Begum Sahiba!'

Incidents of those last few hours – the last dregs of my inheritance: when there were thirty-five hours to go, my mother dreamed of being glued to brown paper like a fly. And at the cocktail hour (thirty hours to go) William Methwold visited my father in the garden of Buckingham Villa. Centre-parting strolling beside and above big toe, Mr Methwold reminisced. Tales of the first Methwold, who had dreamed the city into existence, filled the evening air in that penultimate sunset. And my father – apeing Oxford drawl, anxious to impress the departing Englishman – responded with, 'Actually, old chap, ours is a pretty distinguished family, too.' Methwold listening: head cocked, red rose in cream lapel, wide-brimmed hat concealing parted hair, a veiled hint of amusement in his eyes . . . Ahmed Sinai, lubricated by whisky, driven on by self-importance, warms to his theme. 'Mughal blood, as a matter of fact.' To which Methwold, 'No! Really? You're pulling my leg.' And Ahmed, beyond the point of no return, is obliged to press on. 'Wrong side of the blanket, of course; but Mughal, certainly.'

That was how, thirty hours before my birth, my father demonstrated that he, too, longed for fictional ancestors . . . how he came to invent a family pedigree that, in later years, when whisky had blurred the edges of his memory and djinn-bottles came to confuse him, would obliterate all traces of reality . . . and how, to hammer his point home, he introduced into our lives the idea of the family curse.

'Oh yes,' my father said as Methwold cocked a grave unsmiling head, 'many old families possessed such curses. In our line, it is handed down from eldest son to eldest son – in writing only, because merely to speak it is to unleash its power, you know.' Now Methwold: 'Amazing! And you know the words?' My father nods, lip jutting, toe still as he taps his forehead for emphasis. 'All in here; all memorized. Hasn't been used since an ancestor quarrelled with the Emperor Babar and put the curse on his son Humayun . . . terrible story, that – every schoolboy knows.'

And the time would come when my father, in the throes of his utter retreat from reality, would lock himself in a blue room and try to remember a curse which he had dreamed up one evening in the gardens of his house while he stood tapping his temple beside the descendant of William Methwold.

Saddled now with flypaper-dreams and imaginary ancestors, I am still over a day away from being born . . . but now the remorseless ticktock reasserts itself: twenty-nine hours to go, twenty-eight, twenty-seven . . .

What other dreams were dreamed on that last night? Was it then – yes, why not – that Dr Narlikar, ignorant of the drama that was about to unfold at his Nursing Home, first dreamed of tetrapods? Was it on that last night – while Pakistan was being born to the north and west of Bombay – that my uncle Hanif, who had come (like his sister) to Bombay, and who had fallen in love with an actress, the divine Pia ('Her face is her fortune!' the *Illustrated Weekly* once said), first imagined the cinematic device which would soon give him the first of his three hit pictures? . . . It seems likely; myths, nightmares, fantasies were in the air. This much is certain: on that last night, my grandfather Aadam Aziz, alone now in the big old house in Cornwallis Road – except for a wife whose strength of will seemed to increase as Aziz was ground down by age, and for a daughter, Alia, whose embittered virginity would last until a bomb split her in two over eighteen years later – was suddenly imprisoned by great metal hoops of nostalgia, and lay awake as they pressed down upon his chest; until finally, at five o'clock in the morning of August 14th – nineteen hours to go – he was pushed out of bed by an invisible force and drawn towards an old tin trunk. Opening it, he found: old copies of German magazines; Lenin's *What Is To Be Done?*; a folded prayer-mat; and at last the thing which he had felt an irresistible urge to see once more – white and folded and glowing faintly in the dawn – my grandfather drew out, from the tin trunk of his past, a stained and perforated sheet, and discovered that the hole had grown; that there were other, smaller holes in the surrounding fabric; and in the grip of a wild nostalgic rage he shook his wife awake and astounded her by yelling, as he waved her history under her nose:

'Moth-eaten! Look, Begum: moth-eaten! You forgot to put in any naphthalene balls!'

But now the countdown will not be denied . . . eighteen hours; seventeen; sixteen . . . and already, at Dr Narlikar's Nursing Home, it is possible to hear the shrieks of a woman in labour. Wee Willie Winkie is here; and his wife Vanita; she has been in a protracted, unproductive labour for eight hours now. The first pangs hit her just as, hundreds of miles away, M. A. Jinnah announced the midnight birth of a Muslim nation . . . but still she writhes on a bed in the Narlikar Home's 'charity ward' (reserved for the babies of the poor) . . . her eyes are standing halfway out of her head; her body glistens with sweat, but the baby shows no signs of coming, nor is its father present; it is eight o'clock in the morning, but there is still the possibility that, given the circumstances, the baby could be waiting for midnight.

Rumours in the city: 'The statue galloped last night!' . . . 'And the stars are unfavourable!' . . . But despite these signs of ill-omen, the city was poised, with a new myth glinting in the corners of its eyes. August in Bombay: a month of festivals, the month of Krishna's birthday and Coconut Day; and this year – fourteen hours to go, thirteen, twelve – there was an extra festival on the calendar, a new myth to celebrate, because a nation which had never previously existed was about to win its freedom, catapulting us into a world which, although it had five thousand years of history, although it had invented the game of chess and traded with Middle Kingdom Egypt, was nevertheless quite imaginary; into a mythical land, a country which would never exist except by the efforts of a phenomenal collective will – except in a dream we all agreed to dream; it was a mass fantasy shared in varying degrees by Bengali and Punjabi, Madrasi and Jat, and would periodically need the sanctification and renewal which can only be provided by rituals of blood. India, the new myth – a collective fiction in which anything was possible, a fable rivalled only by the two other mighty fantasies: money and God.

I have been, in my time, the living proof of the fabulous nature of this collective dream; but for the moment, I shall turn away from these generalized, macrocosmic notions to concentrate upon a more private ritual; I shall not describe the mass blood-letting in progress on the frontiers of the divided Punjab (where the partitioned nations are washing themselves in one another's blood, and a certain punchinello-faced Major Zulfikar is buying refugee property at absurdly low prices, laying the foundations of a fortune that will rival the Nizam of Hyderabad's); I shall avert my eyes from the violence in Bengal and the long pacifying walk of Mahatma Gandhi. Selfish? Narrow-minded? Well, perhaps; but excusably so, in my opinion. After all, one is not born every day.

Twelve hours to go. Amina Sinai, having awakened from her flypaper nightmare, will not sleep again until after . . . Ramram Seth is filling her head, she is adrift in a turbulent sea

150

in which waves of excitement alternate with deep, giddying, dark, watery hollows of fear. But something else is in operation, too, Watch her hands – as, without any conscious instructions, they press down, hard, upon her womb; watch her lips, muttering without her knowledge: 'Come on, slowpoke, you don't want to be late for the newspapers!'

Eight hours to go . . . at four o'clock that afternoon, William Methwold drives up the two-storey hillock in his black 1946 Rover. He parks in the circus-ring between the four noble villas; but today he visits neither goldfish-pond nor cactus-garden; he does not greet Lila Sabarmati with his customary, 'How goes the pianola? Everything tickety-boo?' – nor does he salute old man Ibrahim who sits in the shade of a ground-floor verandah, rocking in a rocking-chair and musing about sisal; looking neither towards Catrack nor Sinai, he takes up his position in the exact centre of the circus-ring. Rose in lapel, cream hat held stiffly against his chest, centre-parting glinting in afternoon light, William Methwold stares straight ahead, past clock-tower and Warden Road, beyond Breach Candy's map-shaped pool, across the golden four o'clock waves, and salutes; while out there, above the horizon, the sun begins its long dive towards the sea.

Six hours to go. The cocktail hour. The successors of William Methwold are in their gardens – except that Amina sits in her tower-room, avoiding the mildly competitive glances being flung in her direction by Nussie-next-door, who is also, perhaps, urging her Sonny down and out between her legs; curiously they watch the Englishman, who stands as still and stiff as the ramrod to which we have previously compared his centre-parting; until they are distracted by a new arrival. A long, stringy man, wearing three rows of beads around his neck, and a belt of chicken-bones around his waist; his dark skin stained with ashes, his hair loose and long – naked except for beads and ashes, the sadhu strides up amongst the red-tiled mansions. Musa, the old bearer,

151

descends upon him to shoo him away; but hangs back, not knowing how to command a holy man. Cleaving through the veils of Musa's indecision, the sadhu enters the garden of Buckingham Villa; walks straight past my astonished father; seats himself, cross-legged, beneath the dripping garden tap.

'What do you want here, sadhuji?' – Musa, unable to avoid deference; to which the sadhu, calm as a lake: 'I have come to await the coming of the One. The Mubarak – He who is Blessed. It will happen very soon.'

Believe it or not: I was prophesied twice! And on that day on which everything was so remarkably well-timed, my mother's sense of timing did not fail her; no sooner had the sadhu's last word left his lips than there issued, from a first-floor tower-room with glass tulips dancing in the windows, a piercing yell, a cocktail containing equal proportions of panic, excitement and triumph . . . 'Arré Ahmed!' Amina Sinai yelled, 'Janum, the baby! It's coming – bang on time!'

Ripples of electricity through Methwold's Estate . . . and here comes Homi Catrack, at a brisk emaciated sunken-eyed trot, offering: 'My Studebaker is at your disposal, Sinai Sahib; take it now – go at once!' . . . and when there are still five hours and thirty minutes left, the Sinais, husband and wife, drive away down the two-storey hillock in the borrowed car; there is my father's big toe pressing down on the accelerator; there are my mother's hands pressing down on her moon-belly; and they are out of sight now, around the bend, past Band Box Laundry and Reader's Paradise, past Fatbhoy jewels and Chimalker toys, past One Yard of Chocolates and Breach Candy gates, driving towards Dr Narlikar's Nursing Home where, in a charity ward, Wee Willie's Vanita still heaves and strains, spine curving, eyes popping, and a midwife called Mary Pereira is waiting for her time, too . . . so that neither Ahmed of the jutting lip and squashy belly and fictional ancestors, nor dark-skinned prophecy-ridden Amina were present when the sun finally set over Methwold's Estate, and at the precise instant of its last disappearance – five hours and two minutes to go – William Methwold raised a long white arm above his head. White hand dangled above brilliantined black hair; long tapering white fingers twitched towards centre-parting, and the second and final secret was revealed, because fingers curled, and seized hair; drawing away from his head, they failed to release their prey; and in the moment after the disappearance of the sun Mr Methwold stood in the afterglow of his Estate with his hairpiece in his hand.

'A baldie!' Padma exclaims. 'That slicked-up hair of his . . . I knew it; too good to be true!'

Bald, bald; shiny-pated! Revealed: the deception which had tricked an accordionist's wife. Samson-like, William Methwold's power had resided in his hair; but now, bald patch glowing in the dusk, he flings his thatch through the window of his motor-car; distributes, with what looks like carelessness, the signed title-deeds to his palaces; and drives away. Nobody at Methwold's Estate ever saw him again; but I, who never saw him once, find him impossible to forget.

Suddenly everything is saffron and green. Amina Sinai in a room with saffron walls and green woodwork. In a neighbouring room, Wee Willie Winkie's Vanita, green-skinned, the whites of her eyes shot with saffron, the baby finally beginning its descent through inner passages that are also, no doubt, similarly colourful. Saffron minutes and green seconds tick away on the clocks on the walls. Outside Dr Narlikar's Nursing Home, there are fireworks and crowds, also conforming to the colours of the night – saffron rockets, green sparkling rain; the men in shirts of zafaran hue, the women in saris of lime. On a saffron-and-green carpet, Dr Narlikar talks to Ahmed Sinai. 'I shall see to your Begum personally,' he says, in gentle tones the colour of the evening, 'Nothing to worry about. You wait here; plenty of room to pace.' Dr

Narlikar, who dislikes babies, is nevertheless an expert gynaecologist. In his spare time he lectures writes pamphlets berates the nation on the subject of contraception. 'Birth Control,' he says, 'is Public Priority Number One. The day will come when I get that through people's thick heads, and then I'll be out of a job.' Ahmed Sinai smiles, awkward, nervous. 'Just for tonight,' my father says, 'forget lectures – deliver my child.'

It is twenty-nine minutes to midnight. Dr Narlikar's Nursing Home is running on a skeleton staff; there are many absentees, many employees who have preferred to celebrate the imminent birth of the nation, and will not assist tonight at the births of children. Saffron-shirted, green-skirted, they throng in the illuminated streets, beneath the infinite balconies of the city on which little dia-lamps of earthenware have been filled with mysterious oils; wicks float in the lamps which line every balcony and rooftop, and these wicks, too, conform to our two-tone colour scheme: half the lamps burn saffron, the others flame with green.

Threading its way through the many-headed monster of the crowd is a police car, the yellow and blue of its occupants' uniforms transformed by the unearthly lamplight into saffron and green. (We are on Colaba Causeway now, just for a moment, to reveal that at twenty-seven minutes to midnight, the police are hunting for a dangerous criminal. His name: Joseph D'Costa. The orderly is absent, has been absent for several days, from his work at the Nursing Home, from his room near the slaughterhouse, and from the life of a distraught virginal Mary.)

Twenty minutes pass, with aaahs from Amina Sinai, coming harder and faster by the minute, and weak tiring aaahs from Vanita in the next room. The monster in the streets has already begun to celebrate; the new myth courses through its veins, replacing its blood with corpuscles of saffron and green. And in Delhi, a wiry serious man sits in the

Assembly Hall and prepares to make a speech. At Methwold's Estate goldfish hang stilly in ponds while the residents go from house to house bearing pistachio sweetmeats, embracing and kissing one another – green pistachio is eaten, and saffron laddoo-balls. Two children move down secret passages while in Agra an ageing doctor sits with his wife, who has two moles on her face like witchnipples, and in the midst of sleeping geese and moth-eaten memories they are somehow struck silent, and can find nothing to say. And in all the cities all the towns all the villages the little dia-lamps burn on window-sills porches verandahs, while trains burn in the Punjab, with the green flames of blistering paint and the glaring saffron of fired fuel, like the biggest dias in the world.

And the city of Lahore, too, is burning.

The wiry serious man is getting to his feet. Anointed with holy water from the Tanjore River, he rises; his forehead smeared with sanctified ash, he clears his throat. Without written speech in hand, without having memorized any prepared words, Jawaharlal Nehru begins: '. . . Long years ago we made a tryst with destiny; and now the time comes when we shall redeem our pledge – not wholly or in full measure, but very substantially . . .'

It is two minutes to twelve. At Dr Narlikar's Nursing Home, the dark glowing doctor, accompanied by a midwife called Flory, a thin kind lady of no importance, encourages Amina Sinai: 'Push! Harder! . . . I can see the head! . . .' while in the neighbouring room one Dr Bose – with Miss Mary Pereira by his side – presides over the terminal stages of Vanita's twenty-four-hour labour . . . 'Yes; now; just one last try, come on; at last, and then it will be over! . . .' Women wail and shriek while in another room men are silent. Wee Willie Winkie – incapable of song – squats in a corner, rocking back and forth, back and forth . . . and Ahmed Sinai is looking for a chair. But there are no chairs in this room; it is a room designated for pacing; so Ahmed Sinai opens a door, finds a chair at a deserted receptionist's desk, lifts it, carries it back into the pacing room, where Wee Willie Winkie rocks, rocks, his eyes as empty as a blind man's . . . will she live? won't she? . . . and now, at last, it is midnight.

The monster in the streets has begun to roar, while in Delhi a wiry man is saying, '. . . At the stroke of the midnight hour, while the world sleeps, India awakens to life and freedom . . .' And beneath the roar of the monster there are two more yells, cries, bellows, the howls of children arriving in the world, their unavailing protests mingling with the din of independence which hangs saffron-and-green in the night sky – 'A moment comes, which comes but rarely in history, when we step out from the old to the new; when an age ends; and when the soul of a nation long suppressed finds utterance . . .' while in a room with saffron-and-green carpet Ahmed Sinai is still clutching a chair when Dr Narlikar enters to inform him: 'On the stroke of midnight, Sinai brother, your Begum Sahiba gave birth to a large, healthy child: a son!' Now my father began to think about me (not knowing . . .); with the image of my face filling his thoughts he forgot about the chair; possessed by the love of me (even though . . .), filled with it from top of head to fingertips, he let the chair fall.

Yes, it was my fault (despite everything) . . . it was the power of my face, mine and nobody else's, which caused Ahmed Sinai's hands to release the chair; which caused the chair to drop, accelerating at thirty-two feet per second, and as Jawaharlal Nehru told the Assembly Hall, 'We end today a period of ill-fortune,' as conch-shells blared out the news of freedom, it was on my account that my father cried out too, because the falling chair shattered his toe.

And now we come to it: the noise brought everyone running; my father and his injury grabbed a brief moment of limelight from the two aching mothers, the two, synchronous midnight births – because Vanita had finally been delivered of a baby of remarkable size: 'You wouldn't have believed it,' Dr

156

Bose said, 'It just kept on coming, more and more of the boy forcing its way out, it's a real ten-chip whopper all right!' And Narlikar, washing himself: 'Mine, too.' But that was a little later – just now Narlikar and Bose were tending to Ahmed Sinai's toe; midwives had been instructed to wash and swaddle the new-born pair; and now Miss Mary Pereira made her contribution.

'Go, go,' she said to poor Flory, 'see if you can help. I can do all right here.'

And when she was alone – two babies in her hands – two lives in her power – she did it for Joseph, her own private revolutionary act, thinking *He will certainly love me for this*, as she changed name-tags on the two huge infants, giving the poor baby a life of privilege and condemning the rich-born child to accordions and poverty . . . 'Love me, Joseph!' was in Mary Pereira's mind, and then it was done. On the ankle of a ten-chip whopper with eyes as blue as Kashmiri sky – which were also eyes as blue as Methwold's – and a nose as dramatic as a Kashmiri grandfather's – which was also the nose of a grandmother from France – she placed this name: *Sinai*.

Saffron swaddled me as, thanks to the crime of Mary Pereira, I became the chosen child of midnight, whose parents were not his parents, whose son would not be his own . . . Mary took the child of my mother's womb, who was not to be her son, another ten-chip pomfret, but with eyes which were already turning brown, and knees as knobbly as Ahmed Sinai's, wrapped it in green, and brought it to Wee Willie Winkie – who was staring at her blind-eyed, who hardly saw his new son, who never knew about centre-partings . . . Wee Willie Winkie, who had just learned that Vanita had not managed to survive her childbearing. At three minutes past midnight, while doctors fussed over broken toe, Vanita had haemorrhaged and died.

So I was brought to my mother; and she never doubted my authenticity for an instant. Ahmed Sinai, toe in splint, sat on her bed as she said: 'Look, janum, the poor fellow, he's got his grandfather's nose.' He watched mystified as she made sure there was only one head; and then she relaxed completely, understanding that even fortune-tellers have only limited gifts.

'Janum,' my mother said excitedly, 'you must call the papers. Call them at the *Times of India*. What did I tell you? I won.'

'. . . This is no time for petty or destructive criticism,' Jawaharlal Nehru told the Assembly. 'No time for ill-will. We have to build the noble mansion of free India, where all her children may dwell.' A flag unfurls: it is saffron, white and green.

'An Anglo?' Padma exclaims in horror. 'What are you telling me? You are an Anglo-Indian? Your name is not your own?'

'I am Saleem Sinai,' I told her, 'Snotnose, Stainface, Sniffer, Baldy, Piece-of-the-Moon. Whatever do you mean – not my own?'

'All the time,' Padma wails angrily, 'you tricked me. Your mother, you called her; your father, your grandfather, your aunts. What thing are you that you don't even care to tell the truth about who your parents were? You don't care that your mother died giving you life? That your father is maybe still alive somewhere, penniless, poor? You are a monster or what?'

No: I'm no monster. Nor have I been guilty of trickery. I provided clues . . . but there's something more important than that. It's this: when we eventually discovered the crime of Mary Pereira, we all found that it *made no difference*! I was still their son: they remained my parents. In a kind of collective failure of imagination, we learned that we simply could not think our way out of our pasts . . . if you had asked my father (even him, despite all that happened!) who his son was, nothing on earth would have induced him to point in the direction of the accordionist's knock-kneed, unwashed boy. Even though he would grow up, this Shiva, to be something of a hero.

So: there were knees and a nose, a nose and knees. In fact, all over the new India, the dream we all shared, children were being born who were only partially the offspring of their parents – the children of midnight were also the children *of the time*: fathered, you understand, by history. It can happen. Especially in a country which is itself a sort of dream.

'Enough,' Padma sulks. 'I don't want to listen.' Expecting one type of two-headed child, she is peeved at being offered another. Nevertheless, whether she is listening or not, I have things to record.

Three days after my birth, Mary Pereira was consumed by remorse. Joseph D'Costa, on the run from the searching police cars, had clearly abandoned her sister Alice as well as Mary; and the little plump woman – unable, in her fright, to confess her crime – realized that she had been a fool. 'Donkey from somewhere!' she cursed herself; but she kept her secret. She decided, however, to make amends of a kind. She gave up her job at the Nursing Home and approached Amina Sinai with, 'Madam, I saw your baby just one time and fell in love. Are you needing an ayah?' And Amina, her eyes shining with motherhood, 'Yes.' Mary Pereira ('You might as well call *her* your mother,' Padma interjects, proving she is still interested, 'She made you, you know'), from that moment on, devoted her life to bringing me up, thus binding the rest of her days to the memory of her crime.

On August 20th, Nussie Ibrahim followed my mother into the Pedder Road clinic, and little Sonny followed me into the world – but he was reluctant to emerge; forceps were obliged to reach in and extract him; Dr Bose, in the heat of the moment, pressed a little too hard, and Sonny arrived with little dents beside each of his temples, shallow forcep-hollows which would make him as irresistibly attractive as the hairpiece of William Methwold had made the Englishman. Girls (Evie, the Brass Monkey, others) reached out to stroke his little valleys . . . it would lead to difficulties between us.

But I've saved the most interesting snippet for the last. So let me reveal now that, on the day after I was born, my mother and I were visited in a saffron and green bedroom by two persons from the *Times of India* (Bombay edition). I lay in a green crib, swaddled in saffron, and looked up at them. There was a reporter, who spent his time interviewing my mother; and a tall, aquiline photographer who devoted his attentions to me. The next day, words as well as pictures appeared in newsprint . . .

Quite recently, I visited a cactus-garden where once, many years back, I buried a toy tin globe, which was badly dented and stuck together with Scotch Tape; and extracted from its insides the things I had placed there all those years ago. Holding them in my left hand now, as I write, I can still see – despite yellowing and mildew – that one is a letter, a personal letter to myself, signed by the Prime Minister of India; but the other is a newspaper cutting.

It has a headline: MIDNIGHT'S CHILD.

And a text: 'A charming pose of Baby Saleem Sinai, who was born last night at the exact moment of our Nation's independence – the happy Child of that glorious Hour!'

And a large photograph: an A-1 top-quality front-page jumbo-sized baby-snap, in which it is still possible to make out a child with birthmarks staining his cheeks and a runny and glistening nose. (The picture is captioned: *Photo by Kalidas Gupta.*)

Despite headline, text and photograph, I must accuse our visitors of the crime of trivialization; mere journalists, looking no further than the next day's paper, they had no idea of the importance of the event they were covering. To them, it was no more than a human-interest drama.

How do I know this? Because, at the end of the interview, the photographer presented my mother with a cheque – for one hundred rupees.

One hundred rupees! Is it possible to imagine a more piffling, derisory sum? It is a sum by which one could, were one of a mind to do so, feel insulted. I shall, however, merely thank them for celebrating my arrival, and forgive them for their lack of a genuine historical sense.

'Don't be vain,' Padma says grumpily. 'One hundred rupees is not so little; after all, everybody gets born, it's not such a big big thing.'

Book Two

The fisherman's pointing finger

Is it possible to be jealous of written words? To resent nocturnal scribblings as though they were the very flesh and blood of a sexual rival? I can think of no other reason for Padma's bizarre behaviour; and this explanation at least has the merit of being as outlandish as the rage into which she fell when, tonight, I made the error of writing (and reading aloud) a word which should not have been spoken . . . ever since the episode of the quack doctor's visit, I have sniffed out a strange discontent in Padma, exuding its enigmatic spoor from her eccrine (or apocrine) glands. Distressed, perhaps, by the futility of her midnight attempts at resuscitating my 'other pencil', the useless cucumber hidden in my pants, she has been waxing grouchy. (And then there was her ill-tempered reaction, last night, to my revelation of the secrets of my birth, and her irritation at my low opinion of the sum of one hundred rupees.) I blame myself: immersed in my autobiographical enterprise, I failed to consider her feelings, and began tonight on the most unfortunate of false notes.

'Condemned by a perforated sheet to a life of fragments,' I wrote and read aloud, 'I have nevertheless done better than my grandfather; because while Aadam Aziz remained the sheet's victim, I have become its master – and Padma is the one who is now under its spell. Sitting in my enchanted shadows, I vouchsafe daily glimpses of myself – while she, my squatting glimpser, is captivated, helpless as a mongoose frozen into immobility by the swaying, blinkless eyes of a hooded snake, paralysed – yes! – by love.'

That was the word: love. Written-and-spoken, it raised her voice to an unusually shrill pitch; it unleashed from her lips a violence which would have wounded me, were I still vulnerable to words. 'Love *you*?' our Padma piped scornfully, 'What for, my God? What use are you, little princeling,' – and now came her attempted *coup de grâce* – 'as a *lover*?' Arm extended, its hairs glowing in the lamplight, she jabbed a contemptuous index finger in the direction of my admittedly nonfunctional loins; a long, thick digit, rigid with jealousy, which unfortunately served only to remind me of another, long-lost finger . . . so that she, seeing her arrow miss its mark, shrieked, 'Madman from somewhere! That doctor was right!' and rushed distractedly from the room. I heard footsteps clattering down the metal stairs to the factory floor; feet rushing between the dark-shrouded pickle vats; and a door, first unbolted and then slammed.

Thus abandoned, I have returned, having no option, to my work.

The fisherman's pointing finger: unforgettable focal point of the picture which hung on a sky-blue wall in Buckingham Villa, directly above the sky-blue crib in which, as Baby Saleem, midnight's child, I spent my earliest days. The young Raleigh – and who else? – sat, framed in teak, at the feet of an old, gnarled, net-mending sailor – did he have a walrus moustache? – whose right arm, fully extended, stretched out towards a watery horizon, while his liquid tales rippled around the fascinated ears of Raleigh – and who else? Because there was certainly another boy in the picture, sitting cross-legged in frilly collar and button-down tunic . . . and now a memory comes back to me: of a birthday party in which a proud mother and an equally proud ayah dressed a child with a gargantuan nose in just such a collar, just such a tunic. A tailor sat in a sky-blue room, beneath the pointing finger, and copied the attire of the English milords . . . 'Look, how *chweet*!' Lila Sabarmati exclaimed to my eternal mortification, 'It's like he's just stepped out of the *picture*!'

In a picture hanging on a bedroom wall, I sat beside Walter Raleigh and followed a fisherman's pointing finger with my eyes; eyes straining at the horizon, beyond which lay – what? – my future, perhaps; my special doom, of which I was aware from the beginning, as a shimmering grey presence in that sky-blue room, indistinct at first, but impossible to ignore . . . because the finger pointed even further than that shimmering horizon, it pointed beyond teak frame, across a brief expanse of sky-blue wall, driving my eyes towards another frame, in which my inescapable destiny hung, forever fixed under glass: here was a jumbo-sized baby-snap with its prophetic captions, and here, beside it, a letter on high-quality vellum, embossed with the seal of state – the lions of Sarnath stood above the dharma-chakra on the Prime Minister's missive, which arrived, via Vishwanath the post-boy, one week after my photograph appeared on the front page of the *Times of India*.

Newspapers celebrated me; politicians ratified my position. Jawaharlal Nehru wrote: 'Dear Baby Saleem, My belated congratulations on the happy accident of your moment of birth! You are the newest bearer of that ancient face of India which is also eternally young. We shall be watching over your life with the closest attention; it will be, in a sense, the mirror of our own.'

And Mary Pereira, awestruck, 'The Government, Madam? It will be keeping one eye on the boy? But why, Madam? What's wrong with him?' – And Amina, not understanding the note of panic in her ayah's voice: 'It's just a way of putting things, Mary; it doesn't really mean what it says.' But Mary does not relax; and always, whenever she enters the baby's room, her eyes flick wildly towards the letter in its frame; her eyes look around her, trying to see whether the Government is watching; wondering eyes: what do they know? Did somebody see? . . . As for me, as I grew up, I didn't quite accept my mother's explanation, either; but it lulled me into a sense of false security; so that, even though something of Mary's suspicions had leaked into me, I was still taken by surprise when . . .

Perhaps the fisherman's finger was not pointing at the letter in the frame; because if one followed it even further, it led one out through the window, down the two-storey hillock, across Warden Road, beyond Breach Candy Pools, and out to another sea which was not the sea in the picture; a sea on which the sails of Koli dhows glowed scarlet in the setting sun . . . an accusing finger, then, which obliged us to look at the city's dispossessed.

Or maybe – and this idea makes me feel a little shivery despite the heat – it was a finger of warning, its purpose to draw attention to *itself*; yes, it could have been, why not, a prophecy of another finger, a finger not dissimilar from itself, whose entry into my story would release the dreadful logic of Alpha and Omega . . . my God, what a notion! How much of my future hung above my crib, just waiting for me to understand it? How many warnings was I given – how many did I ignore? . . . But no. I will not be a 'madman from somewhere', to use Padma's eloquent phrase. I will not succumb to cracked digressions; not while I have the strength to resist the cracks.

When Amina Sinai and Baby Saleem arrived home in a borrowed Studebaker, Ahmed Sinai brought a manilla envelope along for the ride. Inside the envelope: a pickle-jar, emptied of lime kasaundy, washed, boiled, purified – and now, refilled. A well-sealed jar, with a rubber diaphragm stretched over its tin lid and held in place by a twisted rubber band. What was sealed beneath rubber, preserved in glass, concealed in manilla? This: travelling home with father, mother and baby was a quantity of briny water in which, floating gently, hung an umbilical cord. (But was it mine or the Other's? That's something I can't tell you.) While the newly-hired ayah, Mary Pereira, made her way to Methwold's Estate by bus, an umbilical cord travelled in state in the glove compartment of a film magnate's Studey. While Baby Saleem grew towards manhood, umbilical tissue hung unchanging in bottled brine, at the back of a teak almirah. And when, years later, our family entered its exile in the Land of the Pure, when I was struggling towards purity, umbilical cords would briefly have their day.

Nothing was thrown away; baby and afterbirth were both retained; both arrived at Methwold's Estate; both awaited their time.

I was not a beautiful baby. Baby-snaps reveal that my large moon-face was too large; too perfectly round. Something lacking in the region of the chin. Fair skin curved across my features – but birthmarks disfigured it; dark stains spread down my western hairline, a dark patch coloured my eastern ear. And my temples: too prominent: bulbous Byzantine domes. (Sonny Ibrahim and I were born to be friends – when we bumped our foreheads, Sonny's forcep-hollows permitted my bulby temples to nestle within them, as snugly as carpenter's joints.) Amina Sinai, immeasurably relieved by my single head, gazed upon it with redoubled maternal fondness, seeing it through a beautifying mist, ignoring the ice-like eccentricity of my sky-blue eyes, the temples like stunted horns, even the rampant cucumber of the nose.

Baby Saleem's nose: it was monstrous; and it ran.

Intriguing features of my early life: large and unbeautiful as I was, it appears I was not content. From my very first days I embarked upon an heroic programme of self-enlargement. (As though I knew that, to carry the burdens of my future life, I'd need to be pretty big.) By mid-September I had drained my mother's not inconsiderable breasts of milk. A wet-nurse was briefly employed but she retreated, dried-out as a desert after only a fortnight, accusing Baby Saleem of trying to bite off her nipples with his toothless gums. I moved on to the bottle and downed vast quantities of compound: the bottle's nipples suffered, too, vindicating the complaining wet-nurse. Baby-book records were meticulously kept; they reveal that I expanded almost visibly, enlarging day by day; but unfortunately no nasal measurements were taken so I cannot say whether my breathing apparatus grew in strict proportion, or faster than the rest. I must say that I had a healthy metabolism. Waste matter was evacuated copiously from the appropriate orifices; from my nose there flowed a shining cascade of goo. Armies of handkerchiefs, regiments of nappies found their way into the large washing-chest in my mother's bathroom . . . shedding rubbish from various apertures, I kept my eyes quite dry. 'Such a good baby, Madam,' Mary Pereira said, 'Never takes out one tear.'

Good baby Saleem was a quiet child; I laughed often, but soundlessly. (Like my own son, I began by taking stock, listening before I rushed into gurgles and, later, into speech.) For a time Amina and Mary became afraid that the boy was dumb; but, just when they were on the verge of telling his father (from whom they had kept their worries secret – no father wants a damaged child), he burst into sound, and became, in that respect at any rate, utterly normal, 'It's as if,' Amina whispered to Mary, 'he's decided to put our minds at rest.'

There was one more serious problem. Amina and Mary took a few days to notice it. Busy with the mighty, complex processes of turning themselves into a two-headed mother, their vision clouded by a fog of stenchy underwear, they failed to notice the immobility of my eyelids. Amina, remembering how, during her pregnancy, the weight of her unborn child had held time as still as a dead green pond, began to wonder whether the reverse might not be taking place now –

whether the baby had some magical power over all the time in his immediate vicinity, and was speeding it up, so that mother-and-ayah never had enough time to do everything that needed doing, so that the baby could grow at an apparently fantastic rate; lost in such chronological day-dreams, she didn't notice my problem. Only when she shrugged the idea off, and told herself I was just a good strapping hoy with a big appetite, an early developer, did the veils of maternal love part sufficiently for her and Mary to yelp, in unison: 'Look, baap-re-baap! Look, Madam! See, Mary! The little chap never blinks!'

The eyes were too blue: Kashmiri-blue, changeling-blue, blue with the weight of unspilled tears, too blue to blink. When I was fed, my eyes did not flutter; when virginal Mary set me across her shoulder, crying, 'Oof, so heavy, sweet Jesus!' I burped without nictating. When Ahmed Sinai limped splint-toed to my crib, I yielded to jutting lips with keen and batless gaze . . . 'Maybe a mistake, Madam,' Mary suggested. 'Maybe the little sahib is copying us – blinking when we blink.' And Amina: 'We'll blink in turn and watch.' Their eyelids opening-and-closing alternately, they observed my icy blueness; but there was not the slightest tremor; until Amina took matters into her own hands and reached into the cradle to stroke my eyelids downwards. They closed: my breathing altered, instantly, to the contented rhythms of sleep. After that, for several months, mother and ayah took it in turns to open and close my lids. 'He'll learn, Madam,' Mary comforted Amina, 'He is a good obedient child and he will get the hang of it for sure.' I learned: the first lesson of my life: nobody can face the world with his eyes open all the time.

Now, looking back through baby eyes, I can see it all perfectly – it's amazing how much you can remember when you try. What I can see: the city, basking like a bloodsucker lizard in the summer heat. Our Bombay: it looks like a hand but it's really a mouth, always open, always hungry, swallowing food and talent from everywhere else in India. A glamorous leech, producing nothing except films bush-shirts fish . . . in the aftermath of Partition, I see Vishwanath the postboy bicycling towards our two-storey hillock, vellum envelope in his saddlebag, riding his aged Arjuna Indiabike past a rotting bus – abandoned although it isn't the monsoon season, because its driver suddenly decided to leave for Pakistan, switched off the engine and departed, leaving a full busload of stranded passengers, hanging off the windows, clinging to the roof-rack, bulging through the doorway . . . I can hear their oaths, son-of-a-pig, brother-of-a-jackass; but they will cling to their hard-won places for two hours before they leave the bus to its fate. And, and: here is India's first swimmer of the English Channel, Mr Pushpa Roy, arriving at the gates of the Breach Candy Pools. Saffron bathing-cap on his head, green trunks wrapped in flag-hued towel, this Pushpa has declared war on the whites-only policy of the baths. He holds a cake of Mysore sandalwood soap; draws himself up; marches through the gate . . . whereupon hired Pathans seize him, Indians save Europeans from an Indian mutiny as usual, and out he goes, struggling valiantly, frogmarched into Warden Road and flung into the dust. Channel swimmer dives into the street, narrowly missing camels taxis bicycles (Vishwanath swerves to avoid his cake of soap) . . . but he is not deterred; picks himself up; dusts himself down; and promises to be back tomorrow. Throughout my childhood years, the days were punctuated by the sight of Pushpa the swimmer, in saffron cap and flag-tinted towel, diving unwillingly into Warden Road. And in the end his indomitable campaign won a victory, because today the Pools permit certain Indians – 'the better sort' – to step into their map-shaped waters. But Pushpa does not belong to the better sort; old now and forgotten, he watches the Pools from afar . . . and now more and more of the multitudes are flooding into me – such as Bano Devi, the famous lady wrestler of those days, who would only wrestle men and threatened to marry anyone who beat her, as a result of which vow she never lost a bout; and (closer to home now) the sadhu under our garden tap, whose name was Purushottam and whom we (Sonny, Eyeslice, Hairoil, Cyrus and I) would always call Puru-the-guru – believing me to be the Mubarak, the Blessed One, he devoted his life to keeping an eye on me, and filled his days teaching my father palmistry and witching away my mother's verrucas; and then there is the rivalry of the old bearer Musa and the new ayah Mary, which will grow until it explodes; in short, at the end of 1947, life in Bombay was as teeming, as manifold, as multitudinously shapeless as ever . . . except that I had arrived; I was already beginning to take my place at the centre of the universe; and by the time I had finished, I would give meaning to it all. You don't believe me? Listen: at my cradle-side, Mary Pereira is singing a little song:

> Anything you want to be, you can be:
> You can be just what-all you want.

By the time of my circumcision by a barber with a cleft palate from the Royal Barber House on Gowalia Tank Road (I was just over two months old), I was already much in demand at Methwold's Estate. (Incidentally, on the subject of the circumcision: I still swear that I can remember the grinning barber, who held me by the foreskin while my member waggled frantically like a slithering snake; and the razor descending, and the pain; but I'm told that, at the time, I didn't even blink.)

Yes, I was a popular little fellow: my two mothers, Amina and Mary, couldn't get enough of me. In all practical matters, they were the most intimate of allies. After my circumcision, they bathed me together; and giggled together as my mutilated organ waggled angrily in the bathwater. 'We better watch this boy, Madam,' Mary said naughtily, 'His thing has a life of its own!' And Amina, 'Tch, tch, Mary, you're terrible, really . . .' But then amid sobs of helpless laughter, 'Just see, Madam, his poor little soo-soo!' Because it was wiggling again, thrashing about, like a chicken with a slitted gullet . . . Together, they cared for me beautifully; but in the matter of emotion, they were deadly rivals. Once, when they took me for a pram-ride through the Hanging Gardens on Malabar Hill, Amina overheard Mary telling the other ayahs, 'Look: here's my own big son' – and felt oddly threatened. Baby Saleem became, after that, the battleground of their loves; they strove to outdo one another in demonstrations of affection; while he, blinking by now, gurgling aloud, fed on their emotions, using it to accelerate his growth, expanding and swallowing infinite hugs kisses chucks-under-the-chin, charging towards the moment when he would acquire the essential characteristic of human beings: every day, and only in those rare moments when I was left alone with the fisherman's pointing finger, I tried to heave myself erect in my cot.

(And while I made unavailing efforts to get to my feet, Amina, too, was in the grip of a useless resolve – she was trying to expel from her mind the dream of her unnameable husband, which had replaced the dream of flypaper on the night after I was born; a dream of such overwhelming reality that it stayed with her throughout her waking hours. In it, Nadir Khan came to her bed and impregnated her; such was the mischievous perversity of the dream that it confused Amina about the parentage of her child, and provided me, the child of midnight, with a fourth father to set beside Winkie and Methwold and Ahmed Sinai. Agitated but helpless in the clutches of the dream, my mother Amina began at that time to form the fog of guilt which would, in later years, surround her head like a dark black wreath.)

*

I never heard Wee Willie Winkie in his prime. After his blind-eyed bereavement, his sight gradually returned; but something harsh and bitter crept into his voice. He told us it was asthma, and continued to arrive at Methwold's Estate once a week to sing songs which were, like himself, relics of the Methwold era. 'Good Night, Ladies,' he sang; and, keeping up to date, added 'The Clouds Will Soon Roll By' to his repertoire, and, a little later, 'How Much Is That Doggie In The Window?' Placing a sizeable infant with menacingly knocking knees on a small mat beside him in the circus-ring, he sang songs filled with nostalgia, and nobody had the heart to turn him away. Winkie and the fisherman's finger were two of the few survivals of the days of William Methwold, because after the Englishman's disappearance his successors emptied his palaces of their abandoned contents. Lila Sabarmati preserved her pianola; Ahmed Sinai kept his whisky-cabinet; old man Ibrahim came to terms with ceiling-fans; but the goldfish died, some from starvation, others as a result of being so colossally overfed that they exploded in little clouds of scales and undigested fish-food; the dogs ran wild, and eventually ceased to roam the Estate; and the fading clothes in the old almirahs were distributed amongst the sweeper-women and other servants on the Estate, so that for years afterwards the heirs of William Methwold were cared for by men and women wearing the increasingly ragged shirts and cotton print dresses of their erstwhile masters. But Winkie and the picture on my wall survived; singer and fisherman became institutions of our lives, like the cocktail hour, which was already a habit too powerful to be broken. 'Each little tear and sorrow,' Winkie sang, 'only brings you closer to me . . .' And his voice grew worse and worse, until it sounded like a sitar whose resonating drum, made out of lacquered pumpkin, had been eaten away by mice; 'It's asthma,' he insisted stubbornly. Before he died he lost his voice completely; doctors revised his diagnosis to throat cancer; but they were wrong, too, because Winkie died of no disease but of the bitterness of losing a wife whose infidelity he never suspected. His son, named Shiva after the god of procreation and destruction, sat at his feet in those early days, silently bearing the burden of being the cause (or so he thought) of his father's slow decline; and gradually, down the years, we watched his eyes filling with an anger which could not be spoken; we watched his fists close around pebbles and hurl them, ineffectually at first, more dangerously as he grew, into the surrounding emptiness. When Lila Sabarmati's elder son was eight, he took it upon himself to tease young Shiva about his surliness, his unstarched shorts, his knobbly knees; whereupon the boy whom Mary's crime had doomed to poverty and accordions hurled a sharp flat stone, with a cutting edge like a razor, and blinded his tormentor in the right eye. After Eyeslice's accident, Wee Willie Winkie came to Methwold's Estate alone, leaving his son to enter the dark labyrinths from which only a war would save him.

Why Methwold's Estate continued to tolerate Wee Willie Winkie despite the decay of his voice and the violence of his son: he had, once, given them an important clue about their lives. 'The first birth,' he had said, 'will make you real.'

As a direct result of Winkie's clue, I was, in my early days, highly in demand. Amina and Mary vied for my attention; but in every house on the Estate, there were people who wanted to know me; and eventually Amina, allowing her pride in my popularity to overcome her reluctance to let me out of her sight, agreed to lend me, on a kind of rota basis, to the various families on the hill. Pushed by Mary Pereira in a sky-blue pram, I began a triumphal progress around the red-tiled palaces, gracing each in turn with my presence, and making them seem real to their owners. And so, looking back now through the eyes of Baby Saleem, I can reveal most of the secrets of my neighbourhood, because the grown-ups lived their lives in my presence without fear of being observed, not

176

knowing that, years later, someone would look back through baby-eyes and decide to let the cats out of their bags.

So here is old man Ibrahim, dying with worry because, back in Africa, governments are nationalizing his sisal plantations; here is his elder son Ishaq fretting over his hotel business, which is running into debt, so that he is obliged to borrow money from local gangsters; here are Ishaq's eyes, coveting his brother's wife, though why Nussie-the-duck should have aroused sexual interest in anyone is a mystery to me; and here is Nussie's husband, Ismail the lawyer, who has learned an important lesson from his son's forcep-birth: 'Nothing comes out right in life,' he tells his duck of a wife, 'unless it's forced out.' Applying this philosophy to his legal career, he embarks on a career of bribing judges and fixing juries; all children have the power to change their parents, and Sonny turned his father into a highly successful crook. And, moving across to Versailles Villa, here is Mrs Dubash with her shrine to the god Ganesh, stuck in the corner of an apartment of such supernatural untidiness that, in our house, the word 'dubash' became a verb meaning 'to make a mess' ... 'Oh, Saleem, you've dubashed your room again, you black man!' Mary would cry. And now the cause of the mess, leaning over the hood of my pram to chuck me under the chin: Adi Dubash, the physicist, genius of atoms and litter. His wife, who is already carrying Cyrus-the-great within her, hangs back, growing her child, with something fanatical gleaming in the inner corners of her eyes, biding its time; it will not emerge until Mr Dubash, whose daily life was spent working with the most dangerous substances in the world, dies by choking on an orange from which his wife forgot to remove the pips. I was never invited into the flat of Dr Narlikar, the child-hating gynaecologist; but in the homes of Lila Sabarmati and Homi Catrack I became a voyeur, a tiny party to Lila's thousand and one infidelities, and eventually a witness to the beginnings of the liaison between the naval officer's wife and the film-magnate-and-racehorse-owner; which, all in good time, would serve me well when I planned a certain act of revenge.

Even a baby is faced with the problem of defining itself; and I'm bound to say that my early popularity had its problematic aspects, because I was bombarded with a confusing multiplicity of views on the subject, being a Blessed One to a guru under a tap, a voyeur to Lila Sabarmati; in the eyes of Nussie-the-duck I was a rival, and a more successful rival, to her own Sonny (although, to her credit, she never showed her resentment, and asked to borrow me just like everyone else); to my two-headed mother I was all kinds of babyish things – they called me joonoo-moonoo, and putch-putch, and little-piece-of-the-moon.

But what, after all, can a baby do except swallow all of it and hope to make sense of it later? Patiently, dry-eyed, I imbibed Nehru-letter and Winkie's prophecy; but the deepest impression of all was made on the day when Homi Catrack's idiot daughter sent her thoughts across the circus-ring and into my infant head.

Toxy Catrack, of the outsize head and dribbling mouth; Toxy, who stood at a barred top-floor window, stark naked, masturbating with motions of consummate self-disgust; who spat hard and often through her bars, and sometimes hit us on the head . . . she was twenty-one years old, a gibbering half-wit, the product of years of inbreeding; but inside my head she was beautiful, because she had not lost the gifts with which every baby is born and which life proceeds to erode. I can't remember anything Toxy said when she sent her thoughts to whisper to me; probably nothing except gurgles and spittings; but she gave a door in my mind a little nudge, so that when an accident took place in a washing-chest it was probably Toxy who made it possible.

That's enough for the moment, about the first days of Baby Saleem – already my very presence is having an effect on history; already Baby Saleem is working changes on the people around him; and, in the case of my father, I am convinced that it was I who pushed him into the excesses which led, perhaps inevitably, to the terrifying time of the freeze.

Ahmed Sinai never forgave his son for breaking his toe. Even after the splint was removed, a tiny limp remained. My father leaned over my crib and said, 'So, my son: you're starting as you mean to go on. Already you've started bashing your poor old father!' In my opinion, this was only half a joke. Because, with my birth, everything changed for Ahmed Sinai. His position in the household was undermined by my coming. Suddenly Amina's assiduity had acquired different goals; she never wheedled money out of him any more, and the napkin in his lap at the breakfast-table felt sad pangs of nostalgia for the old days. Now it was, 'Your son needs so-and-so,' or 'Janum, you must give money for such-and-such.' Bad show, Ahmed Sinai thought. My father was a self-important man.

And so it was my doing that Ahmed Sinai fell, in those days after my birth, into the twin fantasies which were to be his undoing, into the unreal worlds of the djinns and of the land beneath the sea.

A memory of my father in a cool-season evening, sitting on my bed (I was seven years old) and telling me, in a slightly thickened voice, the story of the fisherman who found the djinn in a bottle washed up on the beach . . . 'Never believe in a djinn's promises, my son! Let them out of the bottle and they'll eat you up!' And I, timidly – because I could smell danger on my father's breath: 'But, Abba, can a djinn really live inside a bottle?' Whereupon my father, in a mercurial change of mood, roared with laughter and left the room, returning with a dark green bottle with a white label. 'Look,' he said sonorously, 'Do you want to see the djinn in here?' 'No!' I squealed in fright; but 'Yes!' yelled my sister the Brass

179

Monkey from the neighbouring bed . . . and cowering together in excited terror we watched him unscrew the cap and dramatically cover the bottleneck with the palm of his hand; and now, in the other hand, a cigarette-lighter materialized. 'So perish all evil djinns!' my father cried; and, removing his palm, applied the flame to the neck of the bottle. Awestruck, the Monkey and I watched an eerie flame, blue-green-yellow, move in a slow circle down the interior walls of the bottle; until, reaching the bottom, it flared briefly and died. The next day I provoked gales of laughter when I told Sonny, Eyeslice and Hairoil, 'My father fights with djinns; he beats them; it's true!' . . . And it was true. Ahmed Sinai, deprived of wheedles and attention, began, soon after my birth, a life-long struggle with djinn-bottles. But I was mistaken about one thing: he didn't win.

Cocktail-cabinets had whetted his appetite; but it was my arrival that drove him to it . . . In those days, Bombay had been declared a dry state. The only way to get a drink was to get yourself certified as an alcoholic; and so a new breed of doctors sprang up, djinn-doctors, one of whom, Dr Sharabi, was introduced to my father by Homi Catrack next door. After that, on the first of every month, my father and Mr Catrack and many of the city's most respectable men queued up outside Dr Sharabi's mottled-glass surgery door, went in, and emerged with the little pink chitties of alcoholism. But the permitted ration was too small for my father's needs; and so he began to send his servants along, too, and gardeners, bearers, drivers (we had a motor-car now, a 1946 Rover with running-boards, just like William Methwold's), even old Musa and Mary Pereira, brought my father back more and more pink chitties, which he took to Vijay Stores opposite the circumcising barbershop in Gowalia Tank Road and exchanged for the brown paper bags of alcoholism, inside which were the chinking green bottles, full of djinn. And whisky, too: Ahmed Sinai blurred the edges of himself by drinking the green bottles and red labels of his servants. The poor, having little else to peddle, sold their identities on little pieces of pink paper; and my father turned them into liquid and drank them down.

At six o'clock every evening, Ahmed Sinai entered the world of the djinns; and every morning, his eyes red, his head throbbing with the fatigue of his night-long battle, he came unshaven to the breakfast table; and with the passage of the years, the good mood of the time before he shaved was replaced by the irritable exhaustion of his war with the bottled spirits.

After breakfast, he went downstairs. He had set aside two rooms on the ground floor for his office, because his sense of direction was as bad as ever, and he didn't relish the notion of getting lost in Bombay on the way to work; even he could find his way down a flight of stairs. Blurred at the edges, my father did his property deals; and his growing anger at my mother's preoccupation with her child found a new outlet behind his office door – Ahmed Sinai began to flirt with his secretaries. After nights in which his quarrel with bottles would sometimes erupt in harsh language – 'What a wife I found! I should have bought myself a son and hired a nurse – what difference?' And then tears, and Amina, 'Oh, janum – don't torture me!' which, in turn, provoked, 'Torture my foot! You think it's torture for a man to ask his wife for attention? God save me from stupid women!' – my father limped downstairs to make googly eyes at Colaba girls. And after a while Amina began to notice how his secretaries never lasted long, how they left suddenly, flouncing down our drive without any notice; and you must judge whether she chose to be blind, or whether she took it as a punishment, but she did nothing about it, continuing to devote her time to me; her only act of recognition was to give the girls a collective name. 'Those Anglos,' she said to Mary, revealing a touch of snobbery, 'with their funny names, Fernanda and Alonso and all, and surnames, my God! Sulaca and Colaco and I don't know what. What should I care about them? Cheap type females. I call them all his Coca-Cola girls – that's what they all sound like.'

While Ahmed pinched bottoms, Amina became long-suffering; but he might have been glad if she had appeared to care.

Mary Pereira said, 'They aren't so funny names, Madam; beg your pardon, but they are good Christian words.' And Amina remembered Ahmed's cousin Zohra making fun of dark skin – and, falling over herself to apologize, tumbled into Zohra's mistake: 'Oh, not *you*, Mary, how could you think I was making fun of you?'

Horn-templed, cucumber-nosed, I lay in my crib and listened; and everything that happened, happened because of me . . . One day in January 1948, at five in the afternoon, my father was visited by Dr Narlikar. There were embraces as usual, and slaps on the back. 'A little chess?' my father asked, ritually, because these visits were getting to be a habit. They would play chess in the old Indian way, the game of shatranj, and, freed by the simplicities of the chess-board from the convolutions of his life, Ahmed would daydream for an hour about the re-shaping of the Quran; and then it would be six o'clock, cocktail hour, time for the djinns . . . but this evening Narlikar said, 'No.' And Ahmed, 'No? What's this *no*? Come, sit, play, gossip . . .' Narlikar, interrupting: 'Tonight, brother Sinai, there is something I must show you.' They are in a 1946 Rover now, Narlikar working the crankshaft and jumping in; they are driving north along Warden Road, past Mahalaxmi Temple on the left and Willingdon Club golf-course on the right, leaving the race-track behind them, cruising along Hornby Vellard beside the sea wall; Vallabhbhai Patel Stadium is in sight, with its giant cardboard cut-outs of wrestlers, Bano Devi the Invincible Woman and Dara Singh, mightiest of all . . . there are channa-vendors and dog-walkers promenading by the sea. 'Stop,' Narlikar commands, and they get out. They stand facing the sea; sea-breeze cools their faces; and out there, at the end of a narrow cement path in the midst of the waves, is the island on which stands the tomb of Haji Ali the mystic. Pilgrims are strolling between Vellard and tomb.

'There,' Narlikar points, 'What do you see?' And Ahmed, mystified, 'Nothing. The tomb. People. What's this about, old chap?' And Narlikar, 'None of that. *There*!' And now Ahmed sees that Narlikar's pointing finger is aimed at the cement path . . . 'The promenade?' he asks, 'What's that to you? In some minutes the tide will come and cover it up; everybody knows . . .' Narlikar, his skin glowing like a beacon, becomes philosophical. 'Just so, brother Ahmed; just so. Land and sea; sea and land; the eternal struggle, not so?' Ahmed, puzzled, remains silent. 'Once there were seven islands,' Narlikar reminds him, 'Worli, Mahim, Salsette, Matunga, Colaba, Mazagaon, Bombay. The British joined them up. Sea, brother Ahmed, became land. Land arose, and did not sink beneath the tides!' Ahmed is anxious for his whisky; his lip begins to jut while pilgrims scurry off the narrowing path. 'The point,' he demands. And Narlikar, dazzling with effulgence: 'The point, Ahmed bhai, is *this*!'

It comes out of his pocket: a little plaster-of-paris model two inches high: the tetrapod! Like a three-dimensional Mercedes-Benz sign, three legs standing on his palm, a fourth rearing lingam-fashion into the evening air, it transfixes my father. 'What is it?' he asks; and now Narlikar tells him: 'This is the baby that will make us richer than Hyderabad, bhai! The little gimmick that will make you, you and me, the masters of *that*!' He points outwards to where sea is rushing over deserted cement pathway . . . 'The land beneath the sea, my friend! We must manufacture these by the thousand – by tens of thousands! We must tender for reclamation contracts; a fortune is waiting; don't miss it, brother, this is the chance of a lifetime!'

Why did my father agree to dream a gynaecologist's entrepreneurial dream? Why, little by little, did the vision of full-sized concrete tetrapods marching over sea walls, four-legged conquerors triumphing over the sea, capture him as surely as it had the gleaming doctor? Why, in the following years, did Ahmed dedicate himself to the fantasy of every island-dweller – the myth of conquering the waves? Perhaps because he was afraid of missing yet another turning; perhaps for the fellowship of games of shatranj; or maybe it was Narlikar's plausibility – 'Your capital and my contacts, Ahmed bhai, what problem can there be? Every great man in this city has a son brought into the world by me; no doors will close. You manufacture; I will get the contract! Fifty-fifty; fair is fair!' But, in my view, there is a simpler explanation. My father, deprived of wifely attention, supplanted by his son, blurred by whisky and djinn, was trying to restore his position in the world; and the dream of tetrapods offered him the chance. Whole-heartedly, he threw himself into the great folly; letters were written, doors knocked upon, black money changed hands; all of which served to make Ahmed Sinai a name known in the corridors of the Sachivalaya – in the passageways of the State Secretariat they got the whiff of a Muslim who was throwing his rupees around like water. And Ahmed Sinai, drinking himself to sleep, was unaware of the danger he was in.

Our lives, at this period, were shaped by correspondence. The Prime Minister wrote to me when I was just seven days old – before I could even wipe my own nose I was receiving fan letters from *Times of India* readers; and one morning in January Ahmed Sinai, too, received a letter he would never forget.

Red eyes at breakfast were followed by the shaven chin of the working day; footsteps down the stairs; alarmed giggles of Coca-Cola girl. The squeak of a chair drawn up to a desk topped with green leathercloth. Metallic noise of a metal paper-cutter being lifted, colliding momentarily with telephone. The brief rasp of metal slicing envelope; and one minute later, Ahmed was running back up the stairs, yelling for my mother, shouting:

'Amina! Come here, wife! The bastards have shoved my balls in an ice-bucket!'

In the days after Ahmed received the formal letter informing him of the freezing of all his assets, the whole world was talking at once ... 'For pity's sake, janum, such language!' Amina is saying – and is it my imagination, or does a baby blush in a sky-blue crib?

And Narlikar, arriving in a lather of perspiration, 'I blame myself entirely; we made ourselves too public. These are bad times, Sinai bhai – freeze a Muslim's assets, they say, and you make him run to Pakistan, leaving all his wealth behind him. Catch the lizard's tail and he'll snap it off! This so-called secular state gets some damn clever ideas.'

'Everything,' Ahmed Sinai is saying, 'bank account; savings bonds; the rents from the Kurla properties – all blocked, frozen. By order, the letter says. By order they will not let me have four annas, wife – not a chavanni to see the peepshow!'

'It's those photos in the paper,' Amina decides. 'Otherwise how could those jumped-up clever dicks know whom to prosecute? My God, janum, it's my fault ...'

'Not ten pice for a twist of channa,' Ahmed Sinai adds, 'not one anna to give alms to a beggar. Frozen – like in the fridge!'

'It's my fault,' Ismail Ibrahim is saying, 'I should have warned you, Sinai bhai. I have heard about these freezings – only well-off Muslims are selected, naturally. You must fight ...'

'... Tooth and nail!' Homi Catrack insists, 'Like a lion! Like Aurangzeb – your ancestor, isn't it? – like the Rani of Jhansi! Then let's see what kind of country we've ended up in!'

'There are law courts in this State,' Ismail Ibrahim adds; Nussie-the-duck smiles a bovine smile as she suckles Sonny; her fingers move, absently stroking his hollows, up and around, down and about, in a steady, unchanging rhythm . . . 'You must accept my legal services,' Ismail tells Ahmed, 'Absolutely free, my good friend. No, no I won't hear of it. How can it be? We are neighbours.'

'Broke,' Ahmed is saying, 'Frozen, like water.'

'Come on now,' Amina interrupts him; her dedication rising to new heights, she leads him towards her bedroom . . . 'Janum, you need to lie for some time.' And Ahmed: 'What's this, wife? A time like this – cleaned out; finished; crushed like ice – and you think about . . .' But she has closed the door; slippers have been kicked off; arms are reaching towards him; and some moments later her hands are stretching down down down; and then, 'Oh my goodness, janum, I thought you were just talking dirty but it's true! So cold, Allah, so coooold, like little round cubes of ice!'

Such things happen; after the State froze my father's assets, my mother began to feel them growing colder and colder. On the first day, the Brass Monkey was conceived – just in time, because after that, although Amina lay every night with her husband to warm him, although she snuggled up tightly when she felt him shiver as the icy fingers of rage and powerlessness spread upwards from his loins, she could no longer bear to stretch out her hand and touch because his little cubes of ice had become too frigid to hold.

They – we – should have known something bad would happen. That January, Chowpatty Beach, and Juhu and Trombay, too, were littered with the ominous corpses of dead pomfret, which floated, without the ghost of an explanation, belly-side-up, like scaly fingers in to shore.

186

Snakes and ladders

And other omens: comets were seen exploding above the Back Bay; it was reported that flowers had been seen bleeding real blood; and in February the snakes escaped from the Schaapsteker Institute. The rumour spread that a mad Bengali snake-charmer, a Tubriwallah, was travelling the country, charming reptiles from captivity, leading them out of snake farms (such as the Schaapsteker, where snake venom's medicinal functions were studied, and antivenenes devised) by the Pied Piper fascination of his flute, in retribution for the partition of his beloved Golden Bengal. After a while the rumours added that the Tubriwallah was seven feet tall, with bright blue skin. He was Krishna come to chastise his people; he was the sky-hued Jesus of the missionaries.

It seems that, in the aftermath of my changeling birth, while I enlarged myself at breakneck speed, everything that could possibly go wrong began to do so. In the snake winter of early 1948, and in the succeeding hot and rainy seasons, events piled upon events, so that by the time the Brass Monkey was born in September we were all exhausted, and ready for a few years' rest.

Escaped cobras vanished into the sewers of the city; banded kraits were seen on buses. Religious leaders described the snake escape as a warning – the god Naga had been unleashed, they intoned, as a punishment for the nation's official renunciation of its deities. ('We are a secular State,' Nehru announced, and Morarji and Patel and Menon all agreed; but still Ahmed Sinai shivered under the influence of the freeze.) And one day, when Mary had been asking, 'How are we going to live now, Madam?' Homi Catrack introduced us to Dr Schaapsteker himself. He was eighty-one years old; his tongue flicked constantly in and out between his papery lips; and he was prepared to pay cash rent for a top-floor apartment overlooking the Arabian Sea. Ahmed Sinai, in those days, had taken to his bed; the icy cold of the freeze impregnated his bedsheets; he downed vast quantities of whisky for medicinal purposes, but it failed to warm him up . . . so it was Amina who agreed to let the upper storey of Buckingham Villa to the old snake-doctor. At the end of February, snake poison entered our lives.

Dr Schaapsteker was a man who engendered wild stories. The more superstitious orderlies at his Institute swore that he had the capacity of dreaming every night about being bitten by snakes, and thus remained immune to their bites. Others whispered that he was half-snake himself, the child of an unnatural union between a woman and a cobra. His obsession with the venom of the banded krait – *bungarus fasciatus* – was becoming legendary. There is no known antivenene to the bite of *bungarus:* but Schaapsteker had devoted his life to finding one. Buying broken-down horses from the Catrack stables (among others) he injected them with small doses of poison; but the horses, unhelpfully, failed to develop antibodies, frothed at the mouth, died standing up and had to be transformed into glue. It was said that Dr Schaapsteker – 'Sharpsticker sahib' – had now acquired the power of killing horses simply by approaching them with a hypodermic syringe . . . but Amina paid no attention to these tall stories. 'He is an old gentleman,' she told Mary Pereira; 'What should we care about people who black-tongue him? He pays his rent, and permits us to live.' Amina was grateful to the European snake-doctor, particularly in those days of the freeze when Ahmed did not seem to have the nerve to fight.

'My beloved father and mother,' Amina wrote, 'By my eyes and head I swear I do not know why such things are happening to us . . . Ahmed is a good man, but this business has hit him hard. If you have advice for your daughter, she is greatly in need of it.' Three days after they received this letter, Aadam Aziz and Reverend Mother arrived at Bombay Central Station by Frontier Mail; and Amina, driving them home in our 1946 Rover, looked out of a side window and saw the Mahalaxmi Racecourse; and had the first germ of her reckless idea.

'This modern decoration is all right for you young people, whatsitsname,' Reverend Mother said. 'But give me one old-fashioned takht to sit on. These chairs are so soft, whatsitsname, they make me feel like I'm falling.'

'Is he ill?' Aadam Aziz asked. 'Should I examine him and prescribe medicines?'

'This is no time to hide in bed,' Reverend Mother pronounced. 'Now he must be a man, whatsitsname, and do a man's business.'

'How well you both look, my parents,' Amina cried, thinking that her father was turning into an old man who seemed to be getting shorter with the passing years; while Reverend Mother had grown so wide that armchairs, though soft, groaned beneath her weight . . . and sometimes, through a trick-of the light, Amina thought she saw, in the centre of her father's body, a dark shadow like a hole.

'What is left in this India?' Reverend Mother asked, hand slicing air. 'Go, leave it all, go to Pakistan. See how well that Zulfikar is doing – he will give you a start. Be a man, my son – get up and start again!'

'He doesn't want to speak now,' Amina said, 'he must rest.'

'Rest?' Aadam Aziz roared. 'The man is a jelly!'

'Even Alia, whatsitsname,' Reverend Mother said, 'all on her own, gone to Pakistan – even she is making a decent life, teaching in a fine school. They say she will be headmistress soon.'

'Shhh, mother, he wants to sleep . . . let's go next door . . .'

'There is a time to sleep, whatsitsname, and a time to wake! Listen: Mustapha is making many hundreds of rupees a month, whatsitsname, in the Civil Service. What is your husband? Too good to work?'

'Mother, he is upset. His temperature is so low . . .'

'What food are you giving? From today, whatsitsname, I will run your kitchen. Young people today – like babies, whatsitsname!'

'Just as you like, mother.'

'I tell you whatsitsname, it's those photos in the paper. I wrote – didn't I write? – no good would come of that. Photos take away pieces of you. My God, whatsitsname, when I saw your picture, you had become so transparent I could see the writing from the other side coming right through your face!'

'But that's only . . .'

'Don't tell me your stories, whatsitsname! I give thanks to God you have recovered from that photography!'

After that day, Amina was freed from the exigencies of running her home. Reverend Mother sat at the head of the dining-table, doling out food (Amina took plates to Ahmed, who stayed in bed, moaning from time to time, 'Smashed, wife! Snapped – like an icicle!'); while, in the kitchens, Mary Pereira took the time to prepare, for the benefit of their visitors, some of the finest and most delicate mango pickles, lime chutneys and cucumber kasaundies in the world. And now, restored to the status of daughter in her own home, Amina began to feel the emotions of other people's food seeping into her – because Reverend Mother doled out the curries and meatballs of intransigence, dishes imbued with the personality of their creator; Amina ate the fish salans of stubbornness and the birianis of determination. And, although Mary's pickles had a partially counteractive effect – since she had stirred into them the guilt of her heart, and the fear of discovery, so that, good as they tasted, they had the

190

power of making those who ate them subject to nameless uncertainties and dreams of accusing fingers – the diet provided by Reverend Mother filled Amina with a kind of rage, and even produced slight signs of improvement in her defeated husband. So that finally the day came when Amina, who had been watching me play incompetently with toy horses of sandalwood in the bath, inhaling the sweet odours of sandalwood which the bathwater released, suddenly rediscovered within herself the adventurous streak which was her inheritance from her fading father, the streak which had brought Aadam Aziz down from his mountain valley; Amina turned to Mary Pereira and said, 'I'm fed up. If nobody in this house is going to put things right, then it's just going to be up to me!'

Toy horses galloped behind Amina's eyes as she left Mary to dry me and marched into her bedroom. Remembered glimpses of Mahalaxmi Racecourse cantered in her head as she pushed aside saris and petticoats. The fever of a reckless scheme flushed her cheeks as she opened the lid of an old tin trunk . . . filling her purse with the coins and rupee notes of grateful patients and wedding-guests, my mother went to the races.

With the Brass Monkey growing inside her, my mother stalked the paddocks of the racecourse named after the goddess of wealth; braving early-morning sickness and varicose veins, she stood in line at the Tote window, putting money on three-horse accumulators and long-odds outsiders. Ignorant of the first thing about horses, she backed mares known not to be stayers to win long races; she put her money on jockeys because she liked their smiles. Clutching a purse full of the dowry which had lain untouched in its trunk since her own mother had packed it away, she took wild flutters on stallions who looked fit for the Schaapsteker Institute . . . and won, and won, and won.

'Good news,' Ismail Ibrahim is saying, 'I always thought

191

you should fight the bastards. I'll begin proceedings at once
. . . but it will take cash, Amina. Have you got cash?'

'The money will be there.'

'Not for myself,' Ismail explains, 'My services are, as I said,
free, gratis absolutely. But, forgive me, you must know how
things are, one must give little presents to people to smooth
one's way . . .'

'Here,' Amina hands him an envelope, 'Will this do for
now?'

'My God,' Ismail Ibrahim drops the packet in surprise and
rupee notes in large denominations scatter all over his sitting-
room floor, 'Where did you lay your hands on . . .' And
Amina, 'Better you don't ask – and I won't ask how you
spend it.'

Schaapsteker money paid for our food bills; but horses
fought our war. The streak of luck of my mother at the race-
track was so long, a seam so rich, that if it hadn't happened
it wouldn't have been credible . . . for month after month, she
put her money on a jockey's nice tidy hair-style or a horse's
pretty piebald colouring; and she never left the track without
a large envelope stuffed with notes.

'Things are going well,' Ismail Ibrahim told her, 'But
Amina sister, God knows what you are up to. Is it decent? Is
it legal?' And Amina: 'Don't worry your head. What can't be
cured must be endured. I am doing what must be done.'

Never once in all that time did my mother take pleasure in
her mighty victories; because she was weighed down by more
than a baby – eating Reverend Mother's curries filled with
ancient prejudices, she had become convinced that gambling
was the next worst thing on earth, next to alcohol; so,
although she was not a criminal, she felt consumed by sin.

Verrucas plagued her feet, although Purushottam the
sadhu, who sat under our garden tap until dripping water
created a bald patch amid the luxuriantly matted hair on his
head, was a marvel at charming them away; but throughout

the snake winter and the hot season, my mother fought her husband's fight.

You ask: how is it possible? How could a housewife, however assiduous, however determined, win fortunes on the horses, day after racing day, month after month? You think to yourself: aha, that Homi Catrack, he's a horse-owner; and everyone knows that most of the races are fixed; Amina was asking her neighbour for hot tips! A plausible notion; but Mr Catrack himself lost as often as he won; he saw my mother at the race-track and was astounded by her success. ('Please,' Amina asked him, 'Catrack Sahib, let this be our secret. Gambling is a terrible thing; it would be so shaming if my mother found out.' And Catrack, nodding dazedly, said, 'Just as you wish.') So it was not the Parsee who was behind it – but perhaps I can offer another explanation. Here it is, in a sky-blue crib in a sky-blue room with a fisherman's pointing finger on the wall: here, whenever his mother goes away clutching a purse full of secrets, is Baby Saleem, who has acquired an expression of the most intense concentration, whose eyes have been seized by a singleness of purpose of such enormous power that it has darkened them to deep navy blue, and whose nose is twitching strangely while he appears to be watching some distant event, to be guiding it from a distance, just as the moon controls the tides.

'Coming to court very soon,' Ismail Ibrahim said, 'I think you can be fairly confident . . . my God, Amina, have you found King Solomon's Mines?'

The moment I was old enough to play board games, I fell in love with Snakes and Ladders. O perfect balance of rewards and penalties! O seemingly random choices made by tumbling dice! Clambering up ladders, slithering down snakes, I spent some of the happiest days of my life. When, in my time of trial, my father challenged me to master the game of shatranj, I infuriated him by preferring to invite him, instead, to chance his fortune among the ladders and nibbling snakes.

All games have morals; and the game of Snakes and Ladders captures, as no other activity can hope to do, the eternal truth that for every ladder you climb, a snake is waiting just around the corner; and for every snake, a ladder will compensate. But it's more than that; no mere carrot-and-stick affair; because implicit in the game is the unchanging twoness of things, the duality of up against down, good against evil; the solid rationality of ladders balances the occult sinuosities of the serpent; in the opposition of staircase and cobra we can see, metaphorically, all conceivable oppositions, Alpha against Omega, father against mother; here is the war of Mary and Musa, and the polarities of knees and nose . . . but I found, very early in my life, that the game lacked one crucial dimension, that of ambiguity – because, as events are about to show, it is also possible to slither down a ladder and climb to triumph on the venom of a snake . . . Keeping things simple for the moment, however, I record that no sooner had my mother discovered the ladder to victory represented by her racecourse luck than she was reminded that the gutters of the country were still teeming with snakes.

Amina's brother Hanif had not gone to Pakistan. Following the childhood dream which he had whispered to Rashid the rickshaw-boy in an Agra cornfield, he had arrived in Bombay and sought employment in the great film studios. Precociously confident, he had not only succeeded in becoming the youngest man ever to be given a film to direct in the history of the Indian cinema; he had also wooed and married one of the brightest stars of that celluloid heaven, the divine Pia, whose face was her fortune, and whose saris were made of fabrics whose designers had clearly set out to prove that it was possible to incorporate every colour known to man in a single pattern. Reverend Mother did not approve of the

194

divine Pia, but Hanif of all my family was the one who was free of her confining influence; a jolly, burly man with the booming laugh of the boatman Tai and the explosive, innocent anger of his father Aadam Aziz, he took her to live simply in a small, un-filmi apartment on Marine Drive, telling her, 'Plenty of time to live like Emperors after I've made my name.' She acquiesced; she starred in his first feature, which was partly financed by Homi Catrack and partly by D. W. Rama Studios (Pvt.) Ltd – it was called *The Lovers of Kashmir,* and one evening in the midst of her racing days Amina Sinai went to the première. Her parents did not come, thanks to Reverend Mother's loathing of the cinema, against which Aadam Aziz no longer had the strength to struggle – just as he, who had fought with Mian Abdullah against Pakistan, no longer argued with her when she praised the country, retaining just enough strength to dig in his heels and refuse to emigrate; but Ahmed Sinai, revived by his mother-in-law's cookery, but resentful of her continued presence, got to his feet and accompanied his wife. They took their seats, next to Hanif and Pia and the male star of the film, one of India's most successful 'lover-boys', I. S. Nayyar. And, although they didn't know it, a serpent waited in the wings . . . but in the meanwhile, let us permit Hanif Aziz to have his moment; because *The Lovers of Kashmir* contained a notion which was to provide my uncle with a spectacular, though brief, period of triumph. In those days it was not permitted for lover-boys and their leading ladies to touch one another on screen, for fear that their osculations might corrupt the nation's youth . . . but thirty-three minutes after the beginning of *The Lovers* the première audience began to give off a low buzz of shock, because Pia and Nayyar had begun to kiss – not one another – but *things.*

Pia kissed an apple, sensuously, with all the rich fullness of her painted lips; then passed it to Nayyar; who planted, upon its opposite face, a virilely passionate mouth. This was the birth of what came to be known as the indirect kiss – and how much more sophisticated a notion it was than anything in our current cinema; how pregnant with longing and eroticism! The cinema audience (which would, nowadays, cheer raucously at the sight of a young couple diving behind a bush, which would then begin to shake ridiculously – so low have we sunk in our ability to suggest) watched, riveted to the screen, as the love of Pia and Nayyar, against a background of Dal Lake and ice-blue Kashmiri sky, expressed itself in kisses applied to cups of pink Kashmiri tea; by the fountains of Shalimar they pressed their lips to a sword . . . but now, at the height of Hanif Aziz's triumph, the serpent refused to wait; under its influence, the house-lights came up. Against the larger-than-life figures of Pia and Nayyar, kissing mangoes as they mouthed to playback music, the figure of a timorous, inadequately bearded man was seen, marching on to the stage beneath the screen, microphone in hand. The Serpent can take most unexpected forms; now, in the guise of this ineffectual house-manager, it unleashed its venom. Pia and Nayyar faded and died; and the amplified voice of the bearded man said: 'Ladies and gents, your pardon; but there is terrible news.' His voice broke – a sob from the Serpent, to lend power to its teeth! – and then continued, 'This afternoon, at Birla House in Delhi, our beloved Mahatma was killed. Some madman shot him in the stomach, ladies and gentlemen – our Bapu is gone!'

The audience had begun to scream before he finished; the poison of his words entered their veins – there were grown men rolling in the aisles clutching their bellies, not laughing but crying, *Hai Ram! Hai Ram!* – and women tearing their hair: the city's finest coiffures tumbling around the ears of the poisoned ladies – there were film-stars yelling like fishwives and something terrible to smell in the air – and Hanif whispered, 'Get out of here, big sister – if a Muslim did this thing there will be hell to pay.'

For every ladder, there is a snake . . . and for forty-eight hours after the abortive end of *The Lovers of Kashmir,* our family remained within the walls of Buckingham Villa ('Put furniture against the doors, whatsitsname!' Reverend Mother ordered. 'If there are Hindu servants, let them go home!'); and Amina did not dare to visit the racetrack.

But for every snake, there is a ladder: and finally the radio gave us a name. Nathuram Godse. 'Thank God,' Amina burst out, 'It's not a Muslim name!'

And Aadam, upon whom the news of Gandhi's death had placed a new burden of age: 'This Godse is nothing to be grateful for!'

Amina, however, was full of the light-headedness of relief, she was rushing dizzily up the long ladder of relief . . . 'Why not, after all? By being Godse he has saved our lives!'

Ahmed Sinai, after rising from his supposed sickbed, continued to behave like an invalid. In a voice like cloudy glass he told Amina, 'So, you have told Ismail to go to court; very well, good; but we will lose. In these courts you have to buy judges . . .' And Amina, rushing to Ismail, 'Never – never under any circumstances – must you tell Ahmed about the money. A man must keep his pride.' And, later on, 'No, janum, I'm not going anywhere; no, the baby is not being tiring at all; you rest, I must just go to shop – maybe I will visit Hanif – we women, you know, must fill up our days!'

And coming home with envelopes brimming with rupee-notes . . . 'Take, Ismail, now that he's up we have to be quick and careful!' And sitting dutifully beside her mother in the evenings, 'Yes, of course you're right, and Ahmed will be getting so rich soon, you'll just see!'

And endless delays in court; and envelopes, emptying; and the growing baby, nearing the point at which Amina will not be able to insert herself behind the driving-wheel of the 1946

Rover; and can her luck hold?; and Musa and Mary, quarrelling like aged tigers.

What starts fights?

What remnants of guilt fear shame, pickled by time in Mary's intestines, led her willingly? unwillingly? to provoke the aged bearer in a dozen different ways – by a tilt of the nose to indicate her superior status; by aggressive counting of rosary beads under the nose of the devout Muslim; by acceptance of the title mausi, little mother, bestowed upon her by the other Estate servants, which Musa saw as a threat to his status; by excessive familiarity with the Begum Sahiba – little giggled whispers in corners, just loud enough for formal, stiff, correct Musa to hear and feel somehow cheated?

What tiny grain of grit, in the sea of old age now washing over the old bearer, lodged between his lips to fatten into the dark pearl of hatred – into what unaccustomed torpors did Musa fall, becoming leaden of hand and foot, so that vases were broken, ashtrays spilled, and a veiled hint of forthcoming dismissal – from Mary's conscious or unconscious lips? – grew into an obsessive fear, which rebounded upon the person who started it off?

And (not to omit social factors) what was the brutalizing effect of servant status, of a servants' room behind a blackstoved kitchen, in which Musa was obliged to sleep along with gardener, odd-job boy, and hamal – while Mary slept in style on a rush mat beside a new-born child?

And was Mary blameless or not? Did her inability to go to church – because in churches you found confessionals, and in confessionals secrets could not be kept – turn sour inside her and make her a little sharp, a little hurtful?

Or must we look beyond psychology – seeking our answer in statements such as, there was a snake lying in wait for Mary, and Musa was doomed to learn about the ambiguity of ladders? Or further still, beyond snake-and-ladder, should we see the Hand of Fate in the quarrel – and say, in order for

198

Musa to return as explosive ghost, in order for him to adopt the role of Bomb-in-Bombay, it was necessary to engineer a departure . . . or, descending from such sublimities to the ridiculous, could it be that Ahmed Sinai – whom whisky provoked, whom djinns goaded into excesses of rudeness – had so incensed the aged bearer that his crime, with which he equalled Mary's record, was committed out of the injured pride of an abused old servitor – and was nothing to do with Mary at all?

Ending questions, I confine myself to facts: Musa and Mary were perpetually at daggers drawn. And yes: Ahmed insulted him, and Amina's pacifying efforts may not have been successful; and yes: the fuddling shadows of age had convinced him he would be dismissed, without warning, at any moment; and so it was that Amina came to discover, one August morning, that the house had been burgled.

The police came. Amina reported what was missing: a silver spittoon encrusted with lapis lazuli; gold coins; bejewelled samovars and silver tea-services; the contents of a green tin trunk. Servants were lined up in the hall and subjected to the threats of Inspector Johnny Vakeel. 'Come on, own up now' – lathi-stick tapping against his leg – 'or you'll see what we can't do to you. You want to stand on one leg all day and night? You want water thrown over you, sometimes boiling hot, sometimes freezing cold? We have many methods in the Police Force . . .' And now a cacophony of noise from servants, Not me, Inspector Sahib, I am honest boy; for pity's sake, search my things, sahib! And Amina: 'This is too much, sir, you go too far. My Mary I know, anyway, is innocent. I will not have her questioned.' Suppressed irritation of police officer. A search of belongings is instituted – 'Just in case, Madam. These fellows have limited intelligence – and maybe you discovered the theft too soon for the felon to abscond with the booty!'

The search succeeds. In the bedroll of Musa the old bearer:

a silver spittoon. Wrapped in his puny bundle of clothes: gold coins, a silver samovar. Secreted under his charpoy bed: a missing tea-service. And now Musa has thrown himself at Ahmed Sinai's feet; Musa is begging, 'Forgive, sahib! I was mad; I thought you were going to throw me into the street!' but Ahmed Sinai will not listen; the freeze is upon him; 'I feel so weak,' he says, and leaves the room; and Amina, aghast, asks: 'But, Musa, why did you make that terrible oath?'

. . . Because, in the interim between line-up in passageway and discoveries in servants' quarters, Musa had said to his master: 'It was not me, sahib. If I have robbed you, may I be turned into a leper! May my old skin run with sores!'

Amina, with horror on her face, awaits Musa's reply. The bearer's old face twists into a mask of anger; words are spat out. 'Begum Sahiba, I only took your precious possessions, but you, and your sahib, and his father, have taken my whole life; and in my old age you have humiliated me with Christian ayahs.'

There is silence in Buckingham Villa – Amina has refused to press charges, but Musa is leaving. Bedroll on his back, he descends a spiral iron staircase, discovering that ladders can go down as well as up; he walks away down hillock, leaving a curse upon the house.

And (was it the curse that did it?) Mary Pereira is about to discover that even when you win a battle; even when staircases operate in your favour, you can't avoid a snake.

Amina says, 'I can't get you any more money, Ismail; have you had enough?' And Ismail, 'I hope so – but you never know – is there any chance of . . . ?' But Amina: 'The trouble is, I've got so big and all, I can't get in the car any more. It will just have to do.'

. . . Time is slowing down for Amina once more; once again, her eyes look through leaded glass, in which red tulips, green-stemmed, dance in unison; for a second time, her gaze lingers on a clocktower which has not worked since the rains of 1947; once again, it is raining. The racing season is over.

A pale blue clocktower: squat, peeling, inoperational. It stood on black-tarred concrete at the end of the circus-ring – the flat roof of the upper storey of the buildings along Warden Road, which abutted our two-storey hillock, so that if you climbed over Buckingham Villa's boundary wall, flat black tar would be under your feet. And beneath black tar, Breach Candy Kindergarten School, from which, every afternoon during term, there rose the tinkling music of Miss Harrison's piano playing the unchanging tunes of childhood; and below that, the shops, Reader's Paradise, Fatbhoy Jewellery, Chimalker's Toys and Bombelli's, with its windows filled with One Yards of Chocolates. The door to the clocktower was supposed to be locked, but it was a cheap lock of a kind Nadir Khan would have recognized: made in India. And on three successive evenings immediately before my first birthday, Mary Pereira, standing by my window at night, noticed a shadowy figure floating across the roof, his hands full of shapeless objects, a shadow which filled her with an unidentifiable dread. After the third night, she told my mother; the police were summoned; and Inspector Vakeel returned to Methwold's Estate, accompanied by a special squad of crack officers – 'all deadeye shots, Begum Sahiba; just you leave it all to us!' – who, disguised as sweepers, with guns concealed under their rags, kept the clocktower under surveillance while sweeping up the dust in the circus-ring.

Night fell. Behind curtains and chick-blinds, the inhabitants of Methwold's Estate peered fearfully in the direction of the clocktower. Sweepers, absurdly, went about their duties in the dark. Johnny Vakeel took up a position on our verandah, rifle just out of sight . . . and, at midnight, a shadow came over the side wall of the Breach Candy school and made its way towards the tower, with a sack slung over one shoulder . . . 'He must enter,' Vakeel had told Amina;

'Must be sure we get the proper johnny.' The johnny, padding across flat tarred roof, arrived at the tower; entered.

'Inspector Sahib, what are you waiting for?'

'Shhh, Begum, this is police business; please go inside some way. We shall take him when he comes out; you mark my words. Caught,' Vakeel said with satisfaction, 'like a rat in a trap.'

'But who is he?'

'Who knows?' Vakeel shrugged. 'Some badmaash for sure. There are bad eggs everywhere these days.'

. . . And then the silence of the night is split like milk by a single, sawn-off shriek; somebody lurches against the inside of the clocktower door; it is wrenched open; there is a crash; and something streaks out on to black tarmac. Inspector Vakeel leaps into action, swinging up his rifle, shooting from the hip like John Wayne; sweepers extract marksmen's weapons from their brushes and blaze away . . . shrieks of excited women, yells of servants . . . silence.

What lies, brown and black, banded and serpentine on the black tarmac? What, leaking black blood, provokes Dr Schaapsteker to screech from his top-floor vantage-point: 'You complete fools! Brothers of cockroaches! Sons of transvestites!' . . . what, flick-tongued, dies while Vakeel races on to tarred roof?

And inside the clocktower door? What weight, falling, created such an almighty crash? Whose hand wrenched a door open; in whose heel are visible the two red, flowing holes, filled with a venom for which there is no known antivenene, a poison which has killed stablefuls of worn-out horses? Whose body is carried out of the tower by plain-clothes men, in a dead march, coffinless, with imitation sweepers for pallbearers? Why, when the moonlight falls upon the dead face, does Mary Pereira fall like a sack of potatoes to the floor, eyes rolling upwards in their sockets, in a sudden and dramatic faint?

And lining the interior walls of the clocktower: what are these strange mechanisms, attached to cheap time-pieces – why are there so many bottles with rags stuffed into their necks?

'Damn lucky you called my boys out, Begum Sahiba,' Inspector Vakeel is saying. 'That was Joseph D'Costa – on our Most Wanted list. Been after him for a year or thereabouts. Absolute black-hearted badmaash. You should see the walls inside that clocktower! Shelves, filled from floor to ceiling with home-made bombs. Enough explosive power to blow this hill into the sea!'

Melodrama piling upon melodrama; life acquiring the colouring of a Bombay talkie; snakes following ladders, ladders succeeding snakes; in the midst of too much incident, Baby Saleem fell ill. As if incapable of assimilating so many goings-on, he closed his eyes and became red and flushed. While Amina awaited the results of Ismail's case against the State authorities; while the Brass Monkey grew in her womb; while Mary entered a state of shock from which she would fully emerge only when Joseph's ghost returned to haunt her; while umbilical cord hung in pickle-jar and Mary's chutneys filled our dreams with pointing fingers; while Reverend Mother ran the kitchens, my grandfather examined me and said, 'I'm afraid there is no doubt; the poor lad has typhoid.'

'O God in heaven,' Reverend Mother cried out, 'What dark devil has come, whatsitsname, to sit upon this house?'

This is how I have heard the story of the illness which nearly stopped me before I'd started: day and night, at the end of August 1948, mother and grandfather looked after me; Mary dragged herself out of her guilt and pressed cold flannels to my forehead; Reverend Mother sang lullabies and spooned food into my mouth; even my father, forgetting momentarily his own disorders, stood flapping helplessly in the doorway. But the night came when Doctor Aziz, looking as broken as an old horse, said, 'There is nothing more I can do. He will be dead by morning.' And in the midst of wailing women and the incipient labour of my mother who had been pushed into it by grief and the tearing of Mary Pereira's hair there was a knock; a servant announced Dr Schaapsteker; who handed my grandfather a little bottle and said, 'I make no bones about it: this is kill or cure. Two drops exactly; then wait and see.'

My grandfather, sitting head in hands in the rubble of his medical learning, asked, 'What is it?' And Dr Schaapsteker, nearly eighty-two, tongue flicking at the corners of his mouth: 'Diluted venene of the king cobra. It has been known to work.'

Snakes can lead to triumph, just as ladders can be descended: my grandfather, knowing I would die anyway, administered the cobra poison. The family stood and watched while poison spread through the child's body . . . and six hours later, my temperature had returned to normal. After that, my growth-rate lost its phenomenal aspects; but something was given in exchange for what was lost: life, and an early awareness of the ambiguity of snakes.

While my temperature came down, my sister was being born at Narlikar's Nursing Home. It was September 1st; and the birth was so uneventful, so effortless that it passed virtually unnoticed on Methwold's Estate; because on the same day Ismail Ibrahim visited my parents at the clinic and announced that the case had been won . . . While Ismail celebrated, I was grabbing the bars of my cot; while he cried, 'So much for freezes! Your assets are your own again! By order of the High Court!', I was heaving red-faced against gravity; and while Ismail announced, with a straight face, 'Sinai bhai, the rule of law has won a famous victory,' and avoided my mother's delighted, triumphant eyes, I, Baby Saleem, aged exactly one year, two weeks and one day, hauled myself upright in my cot.

The effects of the events of that day were twofold: I grew

up with legs that were irretrievably bowed, because I had got to my feet too early; and the Brass Monkey (so called because of her thick thatch of red-gold hair, which would not darken until she was nine) learned that, if she was going to get any attention in her life, she would have to make plenty of noise.

Accident in a washing-chest

It has been two whole days since Padma stormed out of my life. For two days, her place at the vat of mango kasaundy has been taken by another woman – also thick of waist, also hairy of forearm; but, in my eyes, no replacement at all! – while my own dung-lotus has vanished into I don't know where. A balance has been upset; I feel cracks widening down the length of my body; because suddenly I am alone, without my necessary ear, and it isn't enough. I am seized by a sudden fist of anger: why should I be so unreasonably treated by my one disciple? Other men have recited stories before me; other men were not so impetuously abandoned. When Valmiki, the author of the *Ramayana*, dictated his masterpiece to elephant-headed Ganesh, did the god walk out on him halfway? He certainly did not. (Note that, despite my Muslim background, I'm enough of a Bombayite to be well up in Hindu stories, and actually I'm very fond of the image of trunk-nosed, flap-eared Ganesh solemnly taking dictation!)

How to dispense with Padma? How give up her ignorance and superstition, necessary counterweights to my miracle-laden omniscience? How to do without her paradoxical earthiness of spirit, which keeps – kept? – my feet on the ground? I have become, it seems to me, the apex of an isosceles triangle, supported equally by twin deities, the wild god of memory and the lotus-goddess of the present . . . but must I now become reconciled to the narrow one-dimensionality of a straight line?

I am, perhaps, hiding behind all these questions. Yes, perhaps that's right. I should speak plainly, without the cloak of a question-mark: our Padma has gone, and I miss her. Yes, that's it.

But there is still work to be done: for instance:

In the summer of 1956, when most things in the world were still larger than myself, my sister the Brass Monkey developed the curious habit of setting fire to shoes. While Nasser sank ships at Suez, thus slowing down the movements of the world by obliging it to travel around the Cape of Good Hope, my sister was also trying to impede our progress. Obliged to fight for attention, possessed by her need to place herself at the centre of events, even of unpleasant ones (she was my sister, after all; but no prime minister wrote letters to her, no sadhus watched her from their places under garden taps; unprophesied, un-photographed, her life was a struggle from the start), she carried her war into the world of footwear, hoping, perhaps, that by burning our shoes she would make us stand still long enough to notice that she was there . . . she made no attempt at concealing her crimes. When my father entered his room to find a pair of black Oxfords on fire, the Brass Monkey was standing over them, match in hand. His nostrils were assailed by the unprecedented odour of ignited boot-leather, mingled with Cherry Blossom boot-polish and a little Three-In-One oil . . . 'Look, Abba!' the Monkey said charmingly, 'Look how pretty – just the exact colour of my hair!'

Despite all precautions, the merry red flowers of my sister's obsession blossomed all over the Estate that summer, blooming in the sandals of Nussie-the-duck and the film-magnate footwear of Homi Catrack; hair-coloured flames licked at Mr Dubash's down-at-heel suedes and at Lila Sabarmati's stiletto heels. Despite the concealment of matches and the vigilance of servants, the Brass Monkey found her ways, undeterred by punishment and threats. For one year, on and off, Methwold's Estate was assailed by the fumes of incendiarized shoes; until her hair darkened into anonymous brown, and she seemed to lose interest in matches.

Amina Sinai, abhorring the idea of beating her children, temperamentally incapable of raising her voice, came close to her wits' end; and the Monkey was sentenced, for day after day, to silence. This was my mother's chosen disciplinary method: unable to strike us, she ordered us to seal our lips. Some echo, no doubt, of the great silence with which her own mother had tormented Aadam Aziz lingered in her ears – because silence, too, has an echo, hollower and longer-lasting than the reverberations of any sound – and with an emphatic '*Chup!*' she would place a finger across her lips and command our tongues to be still. It was a punishment which never failed to cow me into submission; the Brass Monkey, however, was made of less pliant stuff. Soundlessly, behind lips clamped tight as her grandmother's, she plotted the incineration of leather – just as once, long ago, another monkey in another city had performed the act which made inevitable the burning of a leathercloth godown . . .

She was as beautiful (if somewhat scrawny) as I was ugly; but she was from the first, mischievous as a whirlwind and noisy as a crowd. Count the windows and vases, broken accidentally-on-purpose; number, if you can, the meals that somehow flew off her treacherous dinner-plates, to stain valuable Persian rugs! Silence was, indeed, the worst punishment she could have been given; but she bore it cheerfully, standing innocently amid the ruins of broken chairs and shattered ornaments.

Mary Pereira said, 'That one! That Monkey! Should have been born with four legs!' But Amina, in whose mind the memory of her narrow escape from giving birth to a two-headed son had obstinately refused to fade, cried, 'Mary! What are you saying? Don't even think such things!' . . .

Despite my mother's protestations, it was true that the Brass Monkey was as much animal as human; and, as all the servants and children on Methwold's Estate knew, she had the gift of talking to birds, and to cats. Dogs, too: but after she was bitten, at the age of six, by a supposedly rabid stray, and had to be dragged kicking and screaming to Breach Candy Hospital, every afternoon for three weeks, to be given an injection in the stomach, it seems she either forgot their language or else refused to have any further dealings with them. From birds she learned how to sing; from cats she learned a form of dangerous independence. The Brass Monkey was never so furious as when anyone spoke to her in words of love; desperate for affection, deprived of it by my overpowering shadow, she had a tendency to turn upon anyone who gave her what she wanted, as if she were defending herself against the possibility of being tricked.

. . . Such as the time when Sonny Ibrahim plucked up his courage to tell her, 'Hey, listen, Saleem's sister – you're a solid type. I'm, um, you know, damn keen on you . . .' And at once she marched across to where his father and mother were sipping lassi in the gardens of Sans Souci to say, 'Nussie auntie, I don't know what your Sonny's been getting up to. Only just now I saw him and Cyrus behind a bush, doing such funny rubbing things with their soo-soos!' . . .

The Brass Monkey had bad table manners; she trampled flowerbeds; she acquired the tag of problem-child; but she and I were close-as-close, in spite of framed letters from Delhi and sadhu-under-the-tap. From the beginning, I decided to treat her as an ally, not a competitor; and, as a result, she never once blamed me for my preeminence in our household, saying, 'What's to blame? Is it your fault if they think you're so great?' (But when, years later, I made the same mistake as Sonny, she treated me just the same.)

And it was Monkey who, by answering a certain wrong-number telephone call, began the process of events which led

209

to my accident in a white washing-chest made of slatted wood.

Already, at the age of nearlynine, I knew this much: everybody was waiting for me. Midnight and baby-snaps, prophets and prime ministers had created around me a glowing and inescapable mist of expectancy . . . in which my father pulled me into his squashy belly in the cool of the cocktail hour to say, 'Great things! My son: what is not in store for you? Great deeds, a great life!' While I, wriggling between jutting lip and big toe, wetting his shirt with my eternally leaking nose-goo, turned scarlet and squealed, 'Let me go, Abba! Everyone will *see*!' And he, embarrassing me beyond belief, bellowed, 'Let them look! Let the whole world see how I love my son!' . . . and my grandmother, visiting us one winter, gave me advice, too: 'Just pull up your socks, whatsitsname, and you'll be better than anyone in the whole wide world!' . . . Adrift in this haze of anticipation, I had already felt within myself the first movings of that shapeless animal which still, on these Padmaless nights, champs and scratches in my stomach: cursed by a multitude of hopes and nicknames (I had already acquired Sniffer and Snotnose), I became afraid that everyone was wrong – that my much-trumpeted existence might turn out to be utterly useless, void, and without the shred of a purpose. And it was to escape from this beast that I took to hiding myself, from an early age, in my mother's large white washing-chest; because although the creature was inside me, the comforting presence of enveloping soiled linen seemed to lull it into sleep.

Outside the washing-chest, surrounded by people who seemed to possess a devastatingly clear sense of purpose, I buried myself in fairy-tales. Hatim Tai and Batman, Superman and Sinbad helped to get me through the nearlynine years. When I went shopping with Mary Pereira – overawed by her ability to tell a chicken's age by looking at

210

its neck, by the sheer determination with which she stared dead pomfrets in the eyes – I became Aladdin, voyaging in a fabulous cave; watching servants dusting vases with a dedication as majestic as it was obscure, I imagined Ali Baba's forty thieves hiding in the dusted urns; in the garden, staring at Purushottam the sadhu being eroded by water, I turned into the genie of the lamp, and thus avoided, for the most part, the terrible notion that I, alone in the universe, had no idea what I should be, or how I should behave. Purpose: it crept up behind me when I stood staring down from my window at European girls cavorting in the map-shaped pool beside the sea. 'Where do you get it?' I yelped aloud; the Brass Monkey, who shared my sky-blue room, jumped half-way out of her skin. I was then nearlyeight; she was almostseven. It was a very early age at which to be perplexed by meaning.

But servants are excluded from washing-chests; school buses, too, are absent. In my nearlyninth year I had begun to attend the Cathedral and John Connon Boys' High School on Outram Road in the old Fort district; washed and brushed every morning, I stood at the foot of our two-storey hillock, white-shorted, wearing a blue-striped elastic belt with a snake-buckle, satchel over my shoulder, my mighty cucumber of a nose dripping as usual; Eyeslice and Hairoil, Sonny Ibrahim and precocious Cyrus-the-great waited too. And on the bus, amid rattling seats and the nostalgic cracks of the window-panes, what certainties! What nearlynine-year-old certitudes about the future! A boast from Sonny: 'I'm going to be a bullfighter; Spain! Chiquitas! Hey, toro, toro!' His satchel held before him like the muleta of Manolete, he enacted his future while the bus rattled around Kemp's Corner, past Thomas Kemp and Co. (Chemists), beneath the Air-India rajah's poster ('See you later, alligator! I'm off to London on Air-India!') and the other hoarding, on which, throughout my childhood, the Kolynos Kid, a gleamtoothed pixie in a green, elfin, chlorophyll hat proclaimed the virtues of Kolynos

Toothpaste: 'Keep Teeth Kleen and Keep Teeth Brite! Keep Teeth Kolynos *Super* White!' The kid on his hoarding, the children in the bus: one-dimensional, flattened by certitude, they knew what they were for. Here is Glandy Keith Colaco, a thyroid balloon of a child with hair already sprouting tuftily on his lip: 'I'm going to run my father's cinemas; you bastards want to watch movies, you'll have to come an' beg me for seats!' . . . And Fat Perce Fishwala, whose obesity is due to nothing but overeating, and who, along with Glandy Keith, occupies the privileged position of class bully: 'Bah! That's nothing! I'll have diamonds and emeralds and moonstones! Pearls as big as my balls!' Fat Perce's father runs the city's other jewellery business; his great enemy is the son of Mr Fatbhoy, who, being small and intellectual, comes off badly in the war of the pearl-testicled children . . . And Eyeslice, announcing his future as a Test cricketer, with a fine disregard for his one empty socket; and Hairoil, who is as slicked-down and neat as his brother is curly-topped and dishevelled, says, 'What selfish bums you are! I shall follow my father into the Navy; I shall defend my country!' Whereupon he is pelted with rulers, compasses, inky pellets . . . in the school bus, as it clattered past Chowpatty Beach, as it turned left off Marine Drive beside the apartment of my favourite uncle Hanif and headed past Victoria Terminus towards Flora Fountain, past Churchgate Station and Crawford Market, I held my peace; I was mild-mannered Clark Kent protecting my secret identity; but what on earth was that? 'Hey, Snotnose!' Glandy Keith yelled, 'Hey, whaddya suppose our Sniffer'll grow up to be?' And the answering yell from Fat Perce Fishwala, 'Pinocchio!' And the rest, joining in, sing a raucous chorus of 'There are no strings on me!' . . . while Cyrus-the-great sits quiet as genius and plans the future of the nation's leading nuclear research establishment.

And, at home, there was the Brass Monkey with her shoe-burning; and my father, who had emerged from the depths of his collapse to fall, once more, into the folly of tetrapods . . . 'Where do you find it?' I pleaded at my window; the fisherman's finger pointed, misleadingly, out to sea.

Banned from washing-chests: cries of 'Pinocchio! Cucumber-nose! Goo-face!' Concealed in my hiding-place, I was safe from the memory of Miss Kapadia, the teacher at Breach Candy Kindergarten, who had, on my first day at school, turned from her blackboard to greet me, seen my nose, and dropped her duster in alarm, smashing the nail on her big toe, in a screechy but minor echo of my father's famous mishap; buried amongst soiled hankies and crumpled pajamas, I could forget, for a time, my ugliness.

Typhoid attacked me; krait-poison cured me; and my early, overheated growth-rate cooled off. By the time I was nearlynine, Sonny Ibrahim was an inch and a half taller than I. But one piece of Baby Saleem seemed immune to disease and extract-of-snakes. Between my eyes, it mushroomed outwards and downwards, as if all my expansionist forces, driven out of the rest of my body, had decided to concentrate on this single incomparable thrust . . . between my eyes and above my lips, my nose bloomed like a prize marrow. (But then, I was spared wisdom teeth; one should try to count one's blessings.)

What's in a nose? The usual answer: 'That's simple. A breathing apparatus; olfactory organs; hairs.' But in my case, the answer was simpler still, although, I'm bound to admit, somewhat repellent: what was in my nose was snot. With apologies, I must unfortunately insist on details: nasal congestion obliged me to breathe through my mouth, giving me the air of a gasping goldfish; perennial blockages doomed me to a childhood without perfumes, to days which ignored the odours of musk and chambeli and mango kasaundy and home-made ice-cream: and dirty washing, too. A disability in the world outside washing-chests can be a positive advantage once you're in. But only for the duration of your stay.

Purpose-obsessed, I worried about my nose. Dressed in the bitter garments which arrived regularly from my headmistress aunt Alia, I went to school, played French cricket, fought, entered fairy-tales . . . and worried. (In those days, my aunt Alia had begun to send us an unending stream of children's clothes, into whose seams she had sewn her old maid's bile; the Brass Monkey and I were clothed in her gifts, wearing at first the baby-things of bitterness, then the rompers of resentment; I grew up in white shorts starched with the starch of jealousy, while the Monkey wore the pretty flowered frocks of Alia's undimmed envy . . . unaware that our wardrobe was binding us in the webs of her revenge, we led our well-dressed lives.) My nose: elephantine as the trunk of Ganesh, it should, I thought, have been a superlative breather; a smeller without an answer, as we say; instead, it was permanently bunged-up, and as useless as a wooden sikh-kabab.

Enough. I sat in the washing-chest and forgot my nose; forgot about the climbing of Mount Everest in 1953 – when grubby Eyeslice giggled, 'Hey, men! You think that Tenzing could climb up Sniffer's face?' – and about the quarrels between my parents over my nose, for which Ahmed Sinai never tired of blaming Amina's father: 'Never before in my family has there been a nose like it! We have excellent noses; proud noses; royal noses, wife!' Ahmed Sinai had already begun, at that time, to believe in the fictional ancestry he had created for the benefit of William Methwold; djinn-sodden, he saw Mughal blood running in his veins . . . Forgotten, too, the night when I was eight and a half, and my father, djinns on his breath, came into my bedroom to rip the sheets off me and demand: 'What are you up to? Pig! Pig from somewhere?' I looked sleepy; innocent; puzzled. He roared on. '*Chhi-chhi!* Filthy! God punishes boys who do that! Already he's made your nose as big as poplars. He'll stunt your growth; he'll make your soo-soo shrivel up!' And my mother, arriving nightdressed in the startled room, 'Janum, for pity's sake; the boy was only sleeping.' The djinn roared through my father's lips, possessing him completely: 'Look on his face! Whoever got a nose like that from sleeping?'

There are no mirrors in a washing-chest; rude jokes do not enter it, nor pointing fingers. The rage of fathers is muffled by used sheets and discarded brassières. A washing-chest is a hole in the world, a place which civilization has put outside itself, beyond the pale; this makes it the finest of hiding-places. In the washing-chest, I was like Nadir Khan in his underworld, safe from all pressures, concealed from the demands of parents and history . . .

. . . My father, pulling me into his squashy belly, speaking in a voice choked with instant emotion: 'All right, all right, there, there, you're a good boy; you can be anything you want; you just have to want it enough! Sleep now . . .' And Mary Pereira, echoing him in her little rhyme: 'Anything you want to be, you can be; You can be just what-all you want!' It had already occurred to me that our family believed implicitly in good business principles; they expected a handsome return for their investment in me. Children get food shelter pocket-money longholidays and love, all of it apparently free gratis, and most of the little fools think it's a sort of compensation for having been born. 'There are no strings on me!' they sing; but I, Pinocchio, saw the strings. Parents are impelled by the profit motive – nothing more, nothing less. For their attentions, they expected, from me, the immense dividend of greatness. Don't misunderstand me. I didn't mind. I was, at that time, a dutiful child. I longed to give them what they wanted, what soothsayers and framed letters had promised them; I simply did not know how. Where did greatness come from? How did you get some? *When?* . . . When I was seven years old, Aadam Aziz and Reverend Mother came to visit us. On my seventh birthday, dutifully, I permitted myself to be dressed up like the boys in the fisherman picture; hot and constricted in the outlandish garb, I smiled and smiled. 'See, my little piece-of-the-moon!' Amina cried cutting a cake covered with candied farmyard animals, 'So *chweet*! Never takes out one tear!' Sandbagging down the floods of tears lurking just beneath my eyes, the tears of heat discomfort and the absence of One Yard Of Chocolates in my pile of presents, I took a slice of cake to Reverend Mother, who was ill in bed. I had been given a doctor's stethoscope; it was around my neck. She gave me permission to examine her; I prescribed more exercise. 'You must walk across the room, to the almirah and back, once a day. You may lean on me; I am the doctor.' Stethoscoped English milord guided witchmoled grandmother across the room; hobblingly, creakingly, she obeyed. After three months of this treatment, she made a full recovery. The neighbours came to celebrate, bearing rasgullas and gulab-jamans and other sweets. Reverend Mother, seated regally on a takht in the living-room, announced: 'See my grandson? He cured me, whatsitsname. Genius! Genius, whatsitsname: it is a gift from God.' Was that it, then? Should I stop worrying? Was genius something utterly unconnected with wanting, or learning how, or knowing about, or being able to? Something which, at the appointed hour, would float down around my shoulders like an immaculate, delicately worked pashmina shawl? Greatness as a falling mantle: which never needed to be sent to the dhobi. One does not beat genius upon a stone . . . That one clue, my grandmother's one chance sentence, was my only hope; and, as it turned out, she wasn't very far wrong. (The accident is almost upon me; and the children of midnight are waiting.)

Years later, in Pakistan, on the very night when the roof was to fall in on her head and squash her flatter than a rice-pancake, Amina Sinai saw the old washing-chest in a vision. When it popped up inside her eyelids, she greeted it like a not-particularly-welcome cousin. 'So it's you again,' she told it, 'Well, why not? Things keep coming back to me these days.

Seems you just can't leave anything behind.' She had grown prematurely old like all the women in our family; the chest reminded her of the year in which old age had first begun creeping up on her. The great heat of 1956 – which Mary Pereira told me was caused by little blazing invisible insects – buzzed in her ears once again. 'My corns began killing me then,' she said aloud, and the Civil Defence official who had called to enforce the blackout smiled sadly to himself and thought, Old people shroud themselves in the past during a war; that way they're ready to die whenever required. He crept away past the mountains of defective terry towels which filled most of the house, and left Amina to discuss her dirty laundry in private . . . Nussie Ibrahim – Nussie-the-duck – used to admire Amina: 'Such *posture,* my dear, that you've got! Such *tone*! I swear it's a wonder to me: you glide about like you're on an invisible *trolley*!' But in the summer of the heat insects, my elegant mother finally lost her battle against verrucas, because the sadhu Purushottam suddenly lost his magic. Water had worn a bald patch in his hair; the steady dripping of the years had worn him down. Was he disillusioned with his blessed child, his Mubarak? Was it my fault that his mantras lost their power? With an air of great trouble, he told my mother, 'Never mind; wait only; I'll fix your feet for sure.' But Amina's corns grew worse; she went to doctors who froze them with carbon dioxide at absolute zero; but that only brought them back with redoubled vigour, so that she began to hobble, her gliding days done for ever; and she recognized the unmistakable greeting of old age. (Chock-full of fantasy, I transformed her into a silkie – 'Amma, maybe you're a mermaid really, taking human form for the love of a man – so every step is like walking on razor blades'.' My mother smiled, but did not laugh.)

1956, Ahmed Sinai and Dr Narlikar played chess and argued – my father was a bitter opponent of Nasser, while Narlikar admired him openly. 'The man is bad for business,'

Ahmed said; 'But he's got style,' Narlikar responded, glowing passionately, 'Nobody pushes him around.' At the same time, Jawaharlal Nehru was consulting astrologers about the country's Five Year Plan, in order to avoid another Karamstan; and while the world combined aggression and the occult, I lay concealed in a washing-chest which wasn't really big enough for comfort any more; and Amina Sinai became filled with guilt.

She was already trying to put out of her mind her adventure at the race-track; but the sense of sin which her mother's cooking had given her could not be escaped; so it was not difficult for her to think of the verrucas as a punishment . . . not only for the years-ago escapade at Mahalaxmi, but for failing to save her husband from the pink chitties of alcoholism; for the Brass Monkey's untamed, unfeminine ways; and for the size of her only son's nose. Looking back at her now, it seems to me that a fog of guilt had begun to form around her head – her black skin exuding black cloud which hung before her eyes. (Padma would believe it; Padma would know what I mean!) And as her guilt grew, the fog thickened – yes, why not? – there were days when you could hardly see her head above her neck! . . . Amina had become one of those rare people who take the burdens of the world upon their own backs; she began to exude the magnetism of the willingly guilty; and from then on everyone who came into contact with her felt the most powerful of urges to confess their own, private guilts. When they succumbed to my mother's powers, she would smile at them with a sweet sad foggy smile and they would go away, lightened, leaving their burdens on her shoulders; and the fog guilt thickened. Amina heard about servants being beaten and officials being bribed; when my uncle Hanif and his wife the divine Pia came to call they related their quarrels in minute detail; Lila Sabarmati confided her infidelities to my mother's graceful, inclined, long-suffering ear; and Mary Pereira had to fight constantly against the almost-irresistible temptation to confess her crime.

Faced with the guilts of the world, my mother smiled foggily and shut her eyes tight; and by the time the roof fell in on her head her eyesight was badly impaired; but she could still see the washing-chest.

What was really at the bottom of my mother's guilt? I mean really, beneath verrucas and djinns and confessions? It was an unspeakable malaise, an affliction which could not even be named, and which no longer confined itself to dreams of an underworld husband . . . my mother had fallen (as my father would soon fall) under the spell of the telephone.

In the afternoons of that summer, afternoons as hot as towels, the telephone would ring. When Ahmed Sinai was asleep in his room, with his keys under his pillow and umbilical cords in his almirah, telephonic shrilling penetrated the buzzing of the heat insects; and my mother, verruca-hobbled, came into the hall to answer. And now, what expression is this, staining her face the colour of drying blood? . . . Not knowing that she's being observed, what fish-like flutterings of lips are these, what strangulated mouthings? . . . And why, after listening for a full five minutes, does my mother say, in a voice like broken glass, 'Sorry: wrong number'? Why are diamonds glistening on her eyelids? . . . The Brass Monkey whispered to me, 'Next time it rings, let's find out.'

Five days later. Once more it is afternoon; but today Amina is away, visiting Nussie-the-duck, when the telephone demands attention. 'Quick! Quick or it'll wake him!' The Monkey, agile as her name, picks up the receiver before Ahmed Sinai has even changed the pattern of his snoring . . . 'Hullo? Yaas? This is seven zero five six one; hullo?' We listen, every nerve on edge; but for a moment there is nothing at all. Then, when we're about to give up, the voice comes. '. . . Oh . . . yes . . . hullo . . .' And the Monkey, shouting almost, 'Hullo? Who is it, please?' Silence again; the voice, which has not been able to prevent itself from speaking, considers its answer; and then, '. . . Hullo . . . This is Shanti Prasad Truck Hire Company, please? . . .' And the Monkey, quick as a flash: 'Yes, what d'you want?' Another pause; the voice, sounding embarrassed, apologetic almost, says, 'I want to rent a truck.'

O feeble excuse of telephonic voice! O transparent flummery of ghosts! The voice on the phone was no truck-renter's voice; it was soft, a little fleshy, the voice of a poet . . . but after that, the telephone rang regularly; sometimes my mother answered it, listened in silence while her mouth made fish-motions, and finally, much too late, said, 'Sorry, wrong number'; at other times the Monkey and I clustered around it, two ears to earpiece, while the Monkey took orders for trucks. I wondered: 'Hey, Monkey, what d'you think? Doesn't the guy ever wonder why the trucks don't *arrive*?' And she, wide-eyed, flutter-voiced: 'Man, do you suppose . . . maybe they *do*!'

But I couldn't see how; and a tiny seed of suspicion was planted in me, a tiny glimmering of a notion that our mother might have a secret – our Amma! Who always said, 'Keep secrets and they'll go bad inside you; don't tell things and they'll give you stomach-ache!' – a minute spark which my experience in the washing-chest would fan into a forest fire. (Because this time, you see, she gave me proof.)

And now, at last, it is time for dirty laundry. Mary Pereira was fond of telling me, 'If you want to be a big man, baba, you must be very clean. Change clothes,' she advised, 'take regular baths. Go, baba, or I'll send you to the washerman, and he'll wallop you on his stone.' She also threatened me with bugs: 'All right, stay filthy, you will be nobody's darling except the flies'. They will sit on you while you sleep; eggs they'll lay under your skin!' In part, my choice of hiding-place was an act of defiance. Braving dhobis and houseflies, I concealed myself in the unclean place; I drew strength and comfort from sheets and towels; my nose ran freely into the stone-doomed linens; and always, when I emerged into the world from my wooden whale, the sad mature wisdom of dirty washing lingered with me, teaching me its philosophy of coolness and dignity-despite-everything and the terrible inevitability of soap.

One afternoon in June, I tiptoed down the corridors of the sleeping house towards my chosen refuge; sneaked past my sleeping mother into the white-tiled silence of her bathroom; lifted the lid off my goal; and plunged into its soft continuum of (predominantly white) textiles, whose only memories were of my earlier visits. Sighing softly, I pulled down the lid, and allowed pants and vests to massage away the pains of being alive, purposeless and nearly nine years old.

Electricity in the air. Heat, buzzing like bees. A mantle, hanging somewhere in the sky, waiting to fall gently around my shoulders . . . somewhere, a finger reaches towards a dial; a dial whirs around and around, electrical pulses dart along cable, seven, zero, five, six, one. The telephone rings. Muffled shrilling of a bell penetrates the washing-chest, in which a nearlynineyearold boy lies uncomfortably concealed . . . I, Saleem, became stiff with the fear of discovery, because now more noises entered the chest: squeak of bedsprings; soft clatter of slippers along corridor; the telephone, silenced in mid-shrill; and – or is this imagination? Was her voice too soft to hear? – the words, spoken too late as usual: 'Sorry. Wrong number.'

And now, hobbling footsteps returning to the bedroom; and the worst fears of the hiding boy are fulfilled. Door-knobs, turning, scream warnings at him; razor-sharp steps cut him deeply as they move across cool white tiles. He stays frozen as ice, still as a stick; his nose drips silently into dirty clothes. A pajama-cord – snake-like harbinger of doom! – inserts itself into his left nostril. To sniff would be to die: he refuses to think about it.

. . . Clamped tight in the grip of terror, he finds his eye looking through a chink in dirty washing . . . and sees a woman crying in a bathroom. Rain dropping from a thick black cloud. And now more sound, more motion: his mother's voice has begun to speak, two syllables, over and over again; and her hands have begun to move. Ears muffled by underwear strain to catch the sounds – that one: *dir? Bir? Dil?* – and the other: *Ha? Ra?* No – Na. Ha and Ra are banished; Dil and Bir vanish forever; and the boy hears, in his ears, a name which has not been spoken since Mumtaz Aziz became Amina Sinai: Nadir. Nadir. Na. Dir. Na.

And her hands are moving. Lost in their memory of other days, of what happened after games of hit-the-spittoon in an Agra cellar, they flutter gladly at her cheeks; they hold her bosom tighter than any brassières; and now they caress her bare midriff, they stray below decks . . . yes, this is what we used to do, my love, it was enough, enough for me, even though my father made us, and you ran, and now the telephone, Nadirnadirnadirnadirnadirnadir . . . hands which held telephone now hold flesh, while in another place what does another hand do? To what, after replacing receiver, is another hand getting up? . . . No matter; because here, in her spied-out privacy, Amina Sinai repeats an ancient name, again and again, until finally she bursts out with, 'Arré Nadir Khan, where have you come from now?'

Secrets. A man's name. Never-before-glimpsed motions of the hands. A boy's mind filled with thoughts which have no shape, tormented by ideas which refuse to settle into words; and in a left nostril, a pajama-cord is snaking up up up, refusing to be ignored . . .

And now – O shameless mother! Revealer of duplicity, of emotions which have no place in family life; and more: O brazen unveiler of Black Mango! – Amina Sinai, drying her eyes, is summoned by a more trivial necessity; and as her son's right eye peers out through the wooden slats at the top

222

of the washing-chest, my mother unwinds her sari! While I, silently in the washing-chest: 'Don't do it don't do it don't do!' . . . but I cannot close my eye. Unblinking pupil takes in upside-down image of sari falling to the floor, an image which is, as usual, inverted by the mind; through ice-blue eyes I see a slip follow the sari; and then – O horrible! – my mother, framed in laundry and slatted wood, bends over to pick up her clothes! And there it is, searing my retina – the vision of my mother's rump, black as night, rounded and curved, resembling nothing on earth so much as a gigantic, black Alfonso mango! In the washing-chest, unnerved by the vision, I wrestle with myself . . . self-control becomes simultaneously imperative and impossible . . . under the thunderclap influence of the Black Mango, my nerve cracks; pajama-cord wins its victory; and while Amina Sinai seats herself on a commode, I . . . what? Not sneeze; it was less than a sneeze. Not a twitch, either; it was more than that. It's time to talk plainly: shattered by two-syllabic voice and fluttering hands, devastated by Black Mango, the nose of Saleem Sinai, responding to the evidence of maternal duplicity, quivering at the presence of maternal rump, gave way to a pajama-cord, and was possessed by a cataclysmic – a world-altering – an irreversible *sniff*. Pajama-cord rises painfully half an inch further up the nostril. But other things are rising, too: hauled by that feverish inhalation, nasal liquids are being sucked relentlessly up up up, nose-goo flowing upwards, against gravity, against nature. Sinuses are subjected to unbearable pressure . . . until, inside the nearlynineyearold head, something bursts. Snot rockets through a breached dam into dark new channels. Mucus, rising higher than mucus was ever intended to rise. Waste fluid, reaching as far, perhaps, as the frontiers of the brain . . . there is a shock. Something electrical has been moistened.

Pain.

223

And then noise, deafening manytongued terrifying, *inside his head*! . . . Inside a white wooden washing-chest, within the darkened auditorium of my skull, my nose began to sing.

But just now there isn't time to listen; because one voice is very close indeed. Amina Sinai has opened the lower door of the washing-chest; I am tumbling downdown with laundry wrapped around my head like a caul. Pajama-cord jerks out of my nose; and now there is lightning flashing through the dark clouds around my mother – and a refuge has been lost forever.

'I didn't look!' I squealed up through socks and sheets. 'I didn't see one thing, Ammi, I swear!!'

And years later, in a cane chair among reject towels and a radio announcing exaggerated war victories, Amina would remember how with thumb and forefinger around the ear of her lying son she led him to Mary Pereira, who was sleeping as usual on a cane mat in a sky-blue room; how she said, 'This young donkey; this good-for-nothing from nowhere is not to speak for one whole day.' . . . And, just before the roof fell in on her, she said aloud: 'It was my fault. I brought him up too badly.' As the explosion of the bomb ripped through the air, she added, mildly but firmly, addressing her last words on earth to the ghost of a washing-chest: 'Go away now, I've seen enough of you.'

On Mount Sinai, the prophet Musa or Moses heard disembodied commandments; on Mount Hira, the prophet Muhammad (also known as Mohammed, Mahomet, the Last-But-One, and Mahound) spoke to the Archangel. (Gabriel or Jibreel, as you please.) And on the stage of the Cathedral and John Connon Boys' High School, run 'under the auspices' of the Anglo-Scottish Education Society, my friend Cyrus-the-great, playing a female part as usual, heard the voices of St Joan speaking the sentences of Bernard Shaw. But Cyrus is the odd one out: unlike Joan, whose voices were heard in a field, but like Musa or Moses, like Muhammad the Penultimate, I heard voices on a hill.

Muhammad (on whose name be peace, let me add; I don't want to offend anyone) heard a voice saying, 'Recite!' and thought he was going mad; I heard, at first, a headful of gabbling tongues, like an untuned radio; and with lips sealed by maternal command, I was unable to ask for comfort. Muhammad, at forty, sought and received reassurance from wife and friends: 'Verily,' they told him, 'you are the Messenger of God'; I, suffering my punishment at nearlynine, could neither seek Brass Monkey's assistance nor solicit softening words from Mary Pereira. Muted for an evening and a night and a morning, I struggled, alone, to understand what had happened to me; until at last I saw the shawl of genius fluttering down, like an embroidered butterfly, the mantle of greatness settling upon my shoulders.

In the heat of that silent night (I was silent; outside me, the sea rustled like distant paper; crows squawked in the throes of their feathery nightmares; the puttering noises of tardy taxi-cabs wafted up from Warden Road; the Brass Monkey, before she fell asleep with her face frozen into a mask of curiosity, begged, 'Come on, Saleem; nobody's listening; what did you do? Tell tell tell!' . . . while, inside me, the voices rebounded against the walls of my skull) I was gripped by hot fingers of excitement – the agitated insects of excitement danced in my stomach – because finally, in some way I did not then fully understand, the door which Toxy Catrack had once nudged in my head had been forced open; and through it I could glimpse – shadowy still, undefined, enigmatic – my reason for having been born.

Gabriel or Jibreel told Muhammad: 'Recite!' And then began The Recitation, known in Arabic as Al-Quran: 'Recite: In the Name of the Lord thy Creator, who created Man from clots of blood . . .' That was on Mount Hira outside Mecca Sharif; on a two-storey hillock opposite Breach Candy Pools, voices also instructed me to recite: Tomorrow!' I thought excitedly. 'Tomorrow!'

By sunrise, I had discovered that the voices could be controlled – I was a radio receiver, and could turn the volume down or up; I could select individual voices; I could even, by an effort of will, switch off my newly-discovered inner ear. It was astonishing how soon fear left me; by morning, I was thinking, 'Man, this is better than All-India Radio, man; better than Radio Ceylon!'

To demonstrate the loyalty of sisters: when the twenty-four hours were up, on the dot, the Brass Monkey ran into my mother's bedroom. (It was, I think, a Sunday: no school. Or perhaps not – that was the summer of the language marches, and the schools were often shut, because of the danger of violence on the bus-routes.)

'The time's up!' she exclaimed, shaking my mother out of sleep. 'Amma, wake up: it's time: can he talk now?'

'All right,' my mother said, coming into a sky-blue room to embrace me, 'you're forgiven now. But never hide in there again . . .'

'Amma,' I said eagerly, 'my Ammi, please listen. I must tell you something. Something big. But please, please first of all, wake Abba.'

And after a period of 'What?' 'Why?' and 'Certainly not,' my mother saw something extraordinary sitting in my eyes and went to wake Ahmed Sinai anxiously, with 'Janum, please come. I don't know what's got into Saleem.'

Family and ayah assembled in the sitting-room. Amid cut-glass vases and plump cushions, standing on a Persian rug beneath the swirling shadows of ceiling-fans, I smiled into their anxious eyes and prepared my revelation. This was it; the beginning of the repayment of their investment; my first dividend – first, I was sure, of many . . . my black mother, lip-jutting father, Monkey of a sister and crime-concealing ayah waited in hot confusion.

Get it out. Straight, without frills. 'You should be the first to know,' I said, trying to give my speech the cadences of adulthood. And then I told them. 'I heard voices yesterday. Voices are speaking to me inside my head. I think – Ammi, Abboo, I really think – that Archangels have started to talk to me.'

There! I thought. There! It's said! Now there will be pats on the back, sweetmeats, public announcements, maybe more photographs; now their chests will puff up with pride. O blind innocence of childhood! For my honesty – for my open-hearted desperation to please – I was set upon from all sides. Even the Monkey: 'O *God*, Saleem, all this tamasha, all this performance, for one of your stupid *cracks*?' And worse than the Monkey was Mary Pereira: 'Christ Jesus! Save us, Lord! Holy Father in Rome, such blasphemy I've heard today!' And worse than Mary Pereira was my mother Amina Sinai: Black Mango concealed now, her own unnameable names still warm upon her lips, she cried, 'Heaven forfend! The child will bring down the roof upon our heads!' (Was that my fault, too?) And Amina continued: 'You black man! Goonda! O Saleem, has your brain gone raw? What has happened to my darling baby boy – are you growing into a madman – a *torturer*!?' And worse than Amina's shrieking was my father's silence; worse than her fear was the wild anger sitting on his forehead; and worst of all was my father's hand, which stretched out suddenly, thick-fingered, heavy-jointed, strong-as-an-ox, to fetch me a mighty blow on the side of my head, so that I could never hear properly in my left ear after that day; so that I fell sideways across the startled room through the scandalized air and shattered a green tabletop of opaque glass; so that, having been certain of myself for the first time in my life, I was plunged into a green, glass-cloudy world filled with cutting edges, a world in which I could no longer tell the people who mattered most about the goings-on inside my head; green shards lacerated my hands as I entered that swirling universe in which I was doomed, until it was far too late, to be plagued by constant doubts about what I was *for*.

In a white-tiled bathroom beside a washing-chest, my mother daubed me with Mercurochrome; gauze veiled my cuts, while through the door my father's voice commanded, 'Wife, let nobody give him food today. You hear me? Let him enjoy his joke on an empty stomach!'

That night, Amina Sinai would dream of Ramram Seth, who was floating six inches above the ground, his eye-sockets filled with egg-whites, intoning: 'Washing will hide him . . . voices will guide him' . . . but when, after several days in which the dream sat upon her shoulders wherever she went, she plucked up the courage to ask her disgraced son a little more about his outrageous claim, he replied in a voice as restrained as the unwept tears of his childhood: 'It was just fooling, Amma. A stupid joke, like you said.'

She died, nine years later, without discovering the truth.

All-India radio

Reality is a question of perspective; the further you get from the past, the more concrete and plausible it seems – but as you approach the present, it inevitably seems more and more incredible. Suppose yourself in a large cinema, sitting at first in the back row, and gradually moving up, row by row, until your nose is almost pressed against the screen. Gradually the stars' faces dissolve into dancing grain; tiny details assume grotesque proportions; the illusion dissolves or rather, it becomes clear that the illusion itself *is* reality . . . we have come from 1915 to 1956, so we're a good deal closer to the screen . . . abandoning my metaphor, then, I reiterate, entirely without a sense of shame, my unbelievable claim: after a curious accident in a washing-chest, I became a sort of radio.

. . . But today, I feel confused. Padma has not returned – should I alert the police? Is she a Missing Person? – and in her absence, my certainties are falling apart. Even my nose has been playing tricks on me – by day, as I stroll between the pickle-vats tended by our army of strong, hairy-armed, formidably competent women, I have found myself failing to distinguish lemon-odours from lime. The workforce giggles behind its hands: the poor sahib has been crossed in – what? – surely not *love*? . . . Padma, and the cracks spreading all over me, radiating like a spider's web from my navel; and the heat . . . a little confusion is surely permissible in these circumstances. Re-reading my work, I have discovered an error in chronology. The assassination of Mahatma Gandhi occurs, in these pages, on the wrong date. But I cannot say, now, what the actual sequence of events might have been; in my India, Gandhi will continue to die at the wrong time.

Does one error invalidate the entire fabric? Am I so far gone, in my desperate need for meaning, that I'm prepared to distort everything – to re-write the whole history of my times purely in order to place myself in a central role? Today, in my confusion, I can't judge. I'll have to leave it to others. For me, there can be no going back; I must finish what I've started, even if, inevitably, what I finish turns out not to be what I began . . .

Yé Akaskvani hai. This is All-India Radio.

Having gone out into the boiling streets for a quick meal at a nearby Irani café, I have returned to sit in my nocturnal pool of Anglepoised light with only a cheap transistor for company. A hot night; bubbling air filled with the lingering scents of the silenced pickle-vats; voices in the dark. Pickle-fumes, heavily oppressive in the heat, stimulate the juices of memory, accentuating similarities and differences between now and then . . . it was hot then; it is (unseasonably) hot now. Then as now, someone was awake in the dark, hearing disembodied tongues. Then as now, the one deafened ear. And fear, thriving in the heat . . . it was not the voices (then or now) which were frightening. He, young-Saleem-then, was afraid of an idea – the idea that his parents' outrage might lead to a withdrawal of their love; that even if they began to believe him, they would see his gift as a kind of shameful deformity . . . while I, now, Padma-less, send these words into the darkness and am afraid of being disbelieved. He and I, I and he . . . I no longer have his gift; he never had mine. There are times when he seems a stranger, almost . . . he had no cracks. No spiders' webs spread through him in the heat.

Padma would believe me; but there is no Padma. Then as now, there is hunger. But of a different kind: not, now, the then-hunger of being denied my dinner, but that of having lost my cook.

And another, more obvious difference: then, the voices did not arrive through the oscillating valves of a transistor (which will never cease, in our part of the world, to symbolize impotence – ever since the notorious free-transistor sterilization bribe, the squawking machine has represented what men could do before scissors snipped and knots were tied) . . . then, the nearlynineyearold in his midnight bed had no need of machines.

Different and similar, we are joined by heat. A shimmering heat-haze, then and now, blurs his then-time into mine . . . my confusion, travelling across the heat-waves, is also his.

What grows best in the heat: cane-sugar; the coconut palm; certain millets such as bajra, ragi and jowar; linseed, and (given water) tea and rice. Our hot land is also the world's second largest producer of cotton – at least, it was when I learned geography under the mad eye of Mr Emil Zagallo, and the steelier gaze of a framed Spanish conquistador. But the tropical summer grows stranger fruit as well: the exotic flowers of the imagination blossom, to fill the close perspiring nights with odours as heavy as musk, which give men dark dreams of discontent . . . then as now, unease was in the air. Language marchers demanded the partition of the state of Bombay along linguistic boundaries – the dream of Maharashtra was at the head of some processions, the mirage of Gujarat led the others forward. Heat, gnawing at the mind's divisions between fantasy and reality, made anything seem possible; the half-waking chaos of afternoon siestas fogged men's brains, and the air was filled with the stickiness of aroused desires.

What grows best in the heat: fantasy; unreason; lust.

In 1956, then, languages marched militantly through the daytime streets; by night, they rioted in my head. *We shall be watching your life with the closest attention; it will be, in a sense, the mirror of our own.*

It's time to talk about the voices.

But if only our Padma were here . . .

I was wrong about the Archangels, of course. My father's hand – walloping my ear in (conscious? unintentional?) imitation of another, bodiless hand, which once hit him full in the face – at least had one salutary effect: it obliged me to reconsider and finally to abandon my original, Prophet-apeing position. In bed that very night of my disgrace, I withdrew deep inside myself, despite the Brass Monkey, who filled our blue room with her pesterings: 'But what did you do it *for,* Saleem? You who're always too good and all?' . . . until she fell into dissatisfied sleep with her mouth still working silently, and I was alone with the echoes of my father's violence, which buzzed in my left ear, which whispered, 'Neither Michael nor Anael; not Gabriel; forget Cassiel, Sachiel and Samael! Archangels no longer speak to mortals; the Recitation was completed in Arabia long ago; the last prophet will come only to announce the End.' That night, understanding that the voices in my head far outnumbered the ranks of the angels, I decided, not without relief, that I had not after all been chosen to preside over the end of the world. My voices, far from being scared, turned out to be as profane, and as multitudinous, as dust.

Telepathy, then; the kind of thing you're always reading about in the sensational magazines. But I ask for patience – wait. Only wait. It was telepathy; but also more than telepathy. Don't write me off too easily.

Telepathy, then: the inner monologues of all the so-called teeming millions, of masses and classes alike, jostled for space within my head. In the beginning, when I was content to be an audience – before I began to *act* – there was a language problem. The voices babbled in everything from Malayalam to Naga dialects, from the purity of Lucknow Urdu to the Southern slurrings of Tamil. I understood only a fraction of the things being said within the walls of my skull. Only later, when I began to probe, did I learn that below the surface transmissions – the front-of-mind stuff which is what I'd originally been picking up – language faded away, and was replaced by universally intelligible thought-forms which far transcended words . . . but that was after I heard, beneath the polyglot frenzy in my head, those other precious signals, utterly different from everything else, most of them faint and distant, like far-off drums whose insistent pulsing eventually broke through the fish-market cacophony of my voices . . . those secret, nocturnal calls, like calling out to like . . . the unconscious beacons of the children of midnight, signalling nothing more than their existence, transmitting simply: 'I.' From far to the North, 'I.' And the South East West: 'I.' 'I.' 'And I.'

But I mustn't get ahead of myself. In the beginning, before I broke through to more-than-telepathy, I contented myself with listening; and soon I was able to 'tune' my inner ear to those voices which I could understand; nor was it long before I picked out, from the throng, the voices of my own family; and of Mary Pereira; and of friends, classmates, teachers. In the street, I learned how to identify the mind-stream of passing strangers – the laws of Doppler shift continued to operate in these paranormal realms, and the voices grew and diminished as the strangers passed.

All of which I somehow kept to myself. Reminded daily (by the buzzing in my left, or sinister, ear) of my father's wrath, and anxious to keep my right ear in good working order, I sealed my lips. For a nine-year-old boy, the difficulties of concealing knowledge are almost insurmountable; but fortunately, my nearest and dearest were as anxious to forget my outburst as I was to conceal the truth.

'O, you Saleem! Such things you talked yesterday! Shame on you, boy: you better go wash out your mouth with soap!' . . . The morning after my disgrace, Mary Pereira, shaking with indignation like one of her jellies, suggested the perfect means of my rehabilitation. Bowing my head contritely, I went, without a word, into the bathroom, and there, beneath the amazed gaze of ayah and Monkey, scrubbed teeth tongue roofofmouth gums with a toothbrush covered in the sharp foul lather of Coal Tar Soap. The news of my dramatic atonement rushed rapidly around the house, borne by Mary and Monkey; and my mother embraced me, 'There, good boy; we'll say no more about it,' and Ahmed Sinai nodded gruffly at the breakfast table, 'At least the boy has the grace to admit when he's gone too far.'

As my glass-inflicted cuts faded, it was as though my announcement was also erased; and by the time of my ninth birthday, nobody besides myself remembered anything about the day when I had taken the name of Archangels in vain. The taste of detergent lingered on my tongue for many weeks, reminding me of the need for secrecy.

Even the Brass Monkey was satisfied by my show of contrition – in her eyes, I had returned to form, and was once more the goody-two-shoes of the family. To demonstrate her willingness to re-establish the old order, she set fire to my mother's favourite slippers, and regained her rightful place in the family doghouse. Amongst outsiders, what's more – displaying a conservatism you'd never have suspected in such a tomboy – she closed ranks with my parents, and kept my one aberration a secret from her friends and mine.

In a country where any physical or mental peculiarity in a child is a source of deep family shame, my parents, who had become accustomed to facial birthmarks, cucumber-nose and bandy legs, simply refused to see any more embarrassing things in me; for my part, I did not once mention the buzzings in my ear, the occasional ringing bells of deafness, the intermittent pain. I had learned that secrets were not always a bad thing.

*

But imagine the confusion inside my head! Where, behind the hideous face, above the tongue tasting of soap, hard by the perforated eardrum, lurked a not-very-tidy mind, as full of bric-à-brac as nine-year-old pockets . . . imagine yourself inside me somehow, looking out through my eyes, hearing the noise, the voices, and now the obligation of not letting people know, the hardest part was acting surprised, such as when my mother said Hey Saleem guess what we're going for a picnic to the Aarey Milk Colony and I had to go Ooo, exciting!, when I had known all along because I had heard her unspoken inner voice And on my birthday seeing all the presents in the donors' minds before they were even unwrapped And the treasure hunt ruined because there in my father's head was the location of each clue every prize And much harder things such as going to see my father in his ground-floor office, here we are, and the moment I'm in there my head is full of godknowswhat rot because he's thinking about his secretary, Alice or Fernanda, his latest Coca-Cola girl, he's undressing her slowly in his head and it's in my head too, she's sitting stark naked on a cane-bottomed chair and now getting up, crisscross marks all across her rump, that's my father thinking, MY FATHER, now he's looking at me all funny What's the matter son don't you feel well Yes fine Abba fine, must go now GOT TO GET AWAY homework to do, Abba, and out, run away before he sees the clue on your face (my father always said that when I was lying there was a red light flashing on my forehead) . . . You see how hard it is, my uncle Hanif comes to take me to the wrestling, and even before we've arrived at Vallabhbai Patel Stadium on Hornby Vellard I'm feeling sad We're walking with the crowds past giant cardboard cut-outs of Dara Singh and Tagra Baba and the rest and his sadness, my favourite uncle's sadness is pouring into me, it lives like a lizard just beneath the hedge of his jollity, concealed by his booming laugh which was once the laugh of the boatman Tai, we're sitting in excellent seats as floodlights dance on the backs of the interlocked wrestlers and I am caught in the unbreakable grip of my uncle's grief, the grief of his failing film career, flop after flop, he'll probably never get a film again But I mustn't let the sadness leak out of my eyes He's butting into my thoughts, hey phaelwan, hey little wrestler, what's dragging your face down, it looks longer than a bad movie, you want channa? pakoras? what? And me shaking my head, No, nothing, Hanif mamu, so that he relaxes, turns away, starts yelling Ohé come on Dara, that's the ticket, give him hell, Dara *yara*! And back home my mother squatting in the corridor with the ice-cream tub, saying with her real outside-voice, You want to help me make it, son, your favourite pistachio flavour, and I'm turning the handle, but her inside-voice is bouncing against the inside of my head, I can see how she's trying to fill up every nook and cranny of her thoughts with everyday things, the price of pomfret, the roster of household chores, must call in the electrician to mend the ceiling-fan in the dining-room, how she's desperately concentrating on parts of her husband to love, but the unmentionable word keeps finding room, the two syllables which leaked out of her in the bathroom that day, Na Dir Na Dir Na, she's finding it harder and harder to put down the telephone when the wrong numbers come MY MOTHER I tell you when a boy gets inside grown-up thoughts they can really mess him up completely And even at night, no respite, I wake up at the stroke of midnight with Mary Pereira's dreams inside my head Night after night Always at my personal witching-hour, which also has meaning for her Her dreams are plagued by the image of a man who has been dead for years, Joseph D'Costa, the dream tells me the name, it is coated with a guilt I cannot understand, the same guilt which seeps into us all every time we eat her chutneys, there is a mystery here but because the secret is not in the front of her mind I can't find it out, and meanwhile Joseph is there, each night, sometimes in human form, but not always, sometimes he's a wolf, or a snail, once a broomstick, but we (she-dreaming, I-looking in) know it's him, baleful implacable accusative, cursing her in the language of his incarnations, howling at her when he's wolf-Joseph, covering her in the slime-trails of Joseph-the-snail, beating her with the business end of his broomstick incarnation . . . and in the morning when she's telling me to bathe clean up get ready for school I have to bite back the questions, I am nine years old and lost in the confusion of other people's lives which are blurring together in the heat.

To end this account of the early days of my transformed life, I must add one painful confession: it occurred to me that I could improve my parents' opinion of me by using my new faculty to help out with my schoolwork – in short, I began to cheat in class. That is to say, I tuned in to the inner voices of my schoolteachers and also of my cleverer classmates, and picked information out of their minds. I found that very few of my masters could set a test without rehearsing the ideal answers in their minds – and I knew, too, that on those rare occasions when the teacher was preoccupied by other things, his private love-life or financial difficulties, the solutions could always be found in the precocious, prodigious mind of our class genius, Cyrus-the-great. My marks began to improve dramatically – but not overly so, because I took care to make my versions different from their stolen originals; even when I telepathically cribbed an entire English essay from Cyrus, I added a number of mediocre touches of my own. My purpose was to avoid suspicion; I did not, but I escaped discovery. Under Emil Zagallo's furious, interrogating eyes I remained innocently seraphic; beneath the bemused, head-shaking perplexity of Mr Tandon the English master I worked my treachery in silence – knowing that they would not believe the truth even if, by chance or folly, I spilled the beans.

Let me sum up: at a crucial point in the history of our child-nation, at a time when Five Year Plans were being drawn up and elections were approaching and language marchers were fighting over Bombay, a nine-year-old boy named Saleem Sinai acquired a miraculous gift. Despite the many vital uses to which his abilities could have been put by his impoverished, underdeveloped country, he chose to conceal his talents, frittering them away on inconsequential voyeurism and petty cheating. This behaviour – not, I confess, the behaviour of a hero – was the direct result of a confusion in his mind, which invariably muddled up morality – the desire to do what is right – and popularity – the rather more dubious desire to do what is approved of. Fearing parental ostracism, he suppressed the news of his transformation; seeking parental congratulations, he abused his talents at school. This flaw in his character can partially be excused on the grounds of his tender years; but only partially. Confused thinking was to bedevil much of his career.

I can be quite tough in my self-judgements when I choose.

What stood on the flat roof of the Breach Candy Kindergarten – a roof, you will recall, which could be reached from the garden of Buckingham Villa, simply by climbing over a boundary wall? What, no longer capable of performing the function for which it was designed, watched over us that year when even the winter forgot to cool down – what observed Sonny Ibrahim, Eyeslice, Hairoil, and myself, as we played kabaddi, and French Cricket, and seven-tiles, with the occasional participation of Cyrus-the-great and of other, visiting friends: Fat Perce Fishwala and Glandy Keith Colaco? What was present on the frequent occasions when Toxy Catrack's nurse Bi-Appah yelled down from the top floor of Homi's home: 'Brats! Rackety good-for-nothings! Shut your noise!' . . . so that we all ran away, returning (when she vanished from our sight) to make mute faces at the window at which she'd stood? In short, what was it, tall and blue and flaking, which oversaw our lives, which seemed, for a while, to be marking time, waiting not only for the nearby time when we would put on long trousers, but also, perhaps, for the coming of Evie Burns? Perhaps you'd like clues: what had once hidden bombs? In what had Joseph D'Costa died of snake-bite? . . . When, after some months of inner torment, I at last sought refuge from grown-up voices, I found it in an old clocktower, which nobody bothered to lock; and here, in the solitude of rusting time, I paradoxically took my first tentative steps towards that involvement with mighty events and public lives from which I would never again be free . . . never, until the Widow . . .

Banned from washing-chests, I began, whenever possible, to creep unobserved into the tower of crippled hours. When the circus-ring was emptied by heat or chance or prying eyes; when Ahmed and Amina went off to the Willingdon Club for canasta evenings; when the Brass Monkey was away, hanging around her newly-acquired heroines, the Walsingham School for Girls' swimming and diving team . . . that is to say, when circumstances permitted, I entered my secret hideout, stretched out on the straw mat I'd stolen from the servants' quarters, closed my eyes, and let my newly-awakened inner ear (connected, like all ears, to my nose) rove freely around the city – and further, north and south, east and west – listening in to all manner of things. To escape the intolerable pressures of eavesdropping on people I knew, I practised my art upon strangers. Thus my entry into public affairs of India occurred for entirely ignoble reasons – upset by too much intimacy, I used the world outside our hillock for light relief.

The world as discovered from a broken-down clocktower: at first, I was no more than a tourist, a child peeping through the miraculous peepholes of a private 'Dilli-dekho' machine. Dugdugee-drums rattled in my left (damaged) ear as I gained my first glimpse of the Taj Mahal through the eyes of a fat Englishwoman suffering from the tummy-runs; after which, to balance south against north, I hopped down to Madurai's

Meenakshi temple and nestled amongst the woolly, mystical perceptions of a chanting priest. I toured Connaught Place in New Delhi in the guise of an auto-rickshaw driver, complaining bitterly to my fares about the rising price of gasoline; in Calcutta I slept rough in a section of drainpipe. By now thoroughly bitten by the travel bug, I zipped down to Cape Comorin and became a fisherwoman whose sari was as tight as her morals were loose . . . standing on red sands washed by three seas, I flirted with Dravidian beachcombers in a language I couldn't understand; then up into the Himalayas, into the neanderthal moss-covered hut of a Goojar tribal, beneath the glory of a completely circular rainbow and the tumbling moraine of the Kolahoi glacier. At the golden fortress of Jaisalmer I sampled the inner life of a woman making mirrorwork dresses and at Khajuraho I was an adolescent village boy, deeply embarrassed by the erotic, Tantric carvings on the Chandela temples standing in the fields, but unable to tear away my eyes . . . in the exotic simplicities of travel I was able to find a modicum of peace. But, in the end, tourism ceased to satisfy; curiosity began to niggle; 'Let's find out,' I told myself, 'what really goes on around here.'

With the eclectic spirit of my nine years spurring me on, I leaped into the heads of film stars and cricketers – I learned the truth behind the *Filmfare* gossip about the dancer Vyjayantimala, and I was at the crease with Polly Umrigar at the Brabourne Stadium; I was Lata Mangeshkar the playback singer and Bubu the clown at the circus behind Civil Lines . . . and inevitably, through the random processes of my mind-hopping, I discovered politics.

At one time I was a landlord in Uttar Pradesh, my belly roiling over my pajama-cord as I ordered serfs to set my surplus grain on fire . . . at another moment I was starving to death in Orissa, where there was a food shortage as usual: I was two months old and my mother had run out of breast-milk. I occupied, briefly, the mind of a Congress Party worker, bribing a village schoolteacher to throw his weight behind the party of Gandhi and Nehru in the coming election campaign; also the thoughts of a Keralan peasant who had decided to vote Communist. My daring grew: one afternoon I deliberately invaded the head of our own State Chief Minister, which was how I discovered, over twenty years before it became a national joke, that Morarji Desai 'took his own water' daily . . . I was inside him, tasting the warmth as he gurgled down a frothing glass of urine. And finally I hit my highest point: I became Jawaharlal Nehru, Prime Minister and author of framed letters: I sat with the great man amongst a bunch of gaptoothed, stragglebeard astrologers and adjusted the Five Year Plan to bring it into harmonic alignment with the music of the spheres . . . the high life is a heady thing. 'Look at me!' I exulted silently. 'I can go any place I want!' In that tower which had once been filled choc-à-bloc with the explosive devices of Joseph D'Costa's hatred, this phrase (accompanied by appropriate ticktock sound effects) plopped fully-formed into my thoughts: 'I am the tomb in Bombay . . . watch me explode!'

Because the feeling had come upon me that I was somehow creating a world; that the thoughts I jumped inside were *mine*, that the bodies I occupied acted at my command; that, as current affairs, arts, sports, the whole rich variety of a first-class radio station poured into me, I was somehow *making them happen* . . . which is to say, I had entered into the illusion of the artist, and thought of the multitudinous realities of the land as the raw unshaped material of my gift. 'I can find out any damn thing!' I triumphed, 'There isn't a thing I cannot know!'

Today, with the hindsight of the lost, spent years, I can say that the spirit of self-aggrandizement which seized me then was a reflex, born of an instinct for self-preservation. If I had not believed myself in control of the flooding multitudes, their massed identities would have annihilated mine . . . but there in my clocktower, filled with the cockiness of my glee, I became Sin, the ancient moon-god (no, not Indian: I've imported him from Hadhramaut of old), capable of acting-at-a-distance and shifting the tides of the world.

But death, when it visited Methwold's Estate, still managed to take me by surprise.

Even though the freezing of his assets had ended many years ago, the zone below Ahmed Sinai's waist had remained as cold as ice. Ever since the day he had cried out, 'The bastards are shoving my balls in an ice-bucket!', and Amina had taken them in her hands to warm them so that her fingers got glued to them by the cold, his sex had lain dormant, a woolly elephant in an iceberg, like the one they found in Russia in '56. My mother Amina, who had married for children, felt the uncreated lives rotting in her womb and blamed herself for becoming unattractive to him, what with her corns and all. She discussed her unhappiness with Mary Pereira, but the ayah only told her that there was no happiness to be gained from 'the mens'; they made pickles together as they talked, and Amina stirred her disappointments into a hot lime chutney which never failed to bring tears to the eyes.

Although Ahmed Sinai's office hours were filled with fantasies of secretaries taking dictation in the nude, visions of his Fernandas or Poppys strolling around the room in their birthday suits with crisscross cane-marks on their rumps, his apparatus refused to respond; and one day, when the real Fernanda or Poppy had gone home, he was playing chess with Dr Narlikar, his tongue (as well as his game) made somewhat loose by djinns, and he confided awkwardly, 'Narlikar, I seem to have lost interest in you-know-what.'

A gleam of pleasure radiated from the luminous gynae-cologist; the birth-control fanatic in the dark, glowing doctor leaped out through his eyes and made the following speech:

'Bravo!' Dr Narlikar cried, 'Brother Sinai, *damn good show*! You – and, may I add, myself – yes, you and I, Sinai bhai, are persons of rare spiritual worth! Not for us the panting humiliations of the flesh – is it not a finer thing, I ask you, to eschew procreation – to avoid adding one more miserable human life to the vast multitudes which are presently beggaring our country – and, instead, to bend our energies to the task of giving them *more land to stand on*? I tell you, my friend: you and I and our tetrapods: from the very oceans we shall bring forth soil!' To consecrate this oration, Ahmed Sinai poured drinks; my father and Dr Narlikar drank a toast to their four-legged concrete dream.

'Land, yes! Love, no!' Dr Narlikar said, a little unsteadily; my father refilled his glass.

By the last days of 1956, the dream of reclaiming land from the sea with the aid of thousands upon thousands of large concrete tetrapods – that same dream which had been the cause of the freeze – and which was now, for my father, a sort of surrogate for the sexual activity which the aftermath of the freeze denied him – actually seemed to be coming close to fruition. This time, however, Ahmed Sinai was spending his money cautiously; this time he remained hidden in the background, and his name appeared on no documents; this time, he had learned the lessons of the freeze and was determined to draw as little attention to himself as possible; so that when Dr Narlikar betrayed him by dying, leaving behind him no record of my father's involvement in the tetrapod scheme, Ahmed Sinai (who was prone, as we have seen, to react badly in the face of disaster) was swallowed up by the mouth of a long, snaking decline from which he would not emerge until, at the very end of his days, he at last fell in love with his wife.

This is the story that got back to Methwold's Estate: Dr Narlikar had been visiting friends near Marine Drive; at the

243

end of the visit, he had resolved to stroll down to Chowpatty Beach and buy himself some bhel-puri and a little coconut milk. As he strolled briskly along the pavement by the sea-wall, he overtook the tail-end of a language march, which moved slowly along, chanting peacefully. Dr Narlikar neared the place where, with the Municipal Corporation's permission, he had arranged for a single, symbolic tetrapod to be placed upon the sea-wall, as a kind of icon pointing the way to the future; and here he noticed a thing which made him lose his reason. A group of beggar-women had clustered around the tetrapod and were performing the rite of puja. They had lighted oil-lamps at the base of the object; one of them had painted the OM-symbol on its upraised tip; they were chanting prayers as they gave the tetrapod a thorough and worshipful wash. Technological miracle had been transformed into Shiva-lingam; Doctor Narlikar, the opponent of fertility, was driven wild at this vision, in which it seemed to him that all the old dark priapic forces of ancient, procreative India had been unleashed upon the beauty of sterile twentieth-century concrete . . . sprinting along, he shouted his abuse at the worshipping women, gleaming fiercely in his rage; reaching them, he kicked away their little dia-lamps; it is said he even tried to push the women. And he was seen by the eyes of the language marchers.

The ears of the language marchers heard the roughness of his tongue; the marchers' feet paused, their voices rose in rebuke. Fists were shaken; oaths were oathed. Whereupon the good doctor, made incautious by anger, turned upon the crowd and denigrated its cause, its breeding and its sisters. A silence fell and exerted its powers. Silence guided marcher-feet towards the gleaming gynaecologist, who stood between the tetrapod and the wailing women. In silence the marchers' hands reached out towards Narlikar and in a deep hush he clung to four-legged concrete as they attempted to pull him towards them. In absolute soundlessness, fear gave Dr

Narlikar the strength of limpets; his arms stuck to the tetrapod and would not be detached. The marchers applied themselves to the tetrapod . . . silently they began to rock it; mutely the force of their numbers overcame its weight. In an evening seized by a demonic quietness the tetrapod tilted, preparing to become the first of its kind to enter the waters and begin the great work of land reclamation. Dr Suresh Narlikar, his mouth opening in a voiceless A, clung to it like a phosphorescent mollusc . . . man and four-legged concrete fell without a sound. The splash of the waters broke the spell.

It was said that when Dr Narlikar fell and was crushed into death by the weight of his beloved obsession, nobody had any trouble locating the body because it sent light glowing upwards through the waters like a fire.

'Do you know what's happening?' 'Hey, man, what gives?' – children, myself included, clustered around the garden hedge of Escorial Villa, in which was Dr Narlikar's bachelor apartment; and a hamal of Lila Sabarmati's, taking on an air of grave dignity, informed us, 'They have brought his death home, wrapped in silk.'

I was not allowed to see the death of Dr Narlikar as it lay wreathed in saffron flowers on his hard, single bed; but I got to know all about it anyway, because the news of it spread far beyond the confines of his room. Mostly, I heard about it from the Estate servants, who found it quite natural to speak openly of a death, but rarely said much about life, because in life everything was obvious. From Dr Narlikar's own bearer I learned that the death had, by swallowing large quantities of the sea, taken on the qualities of water: it had become a fluid thing, and looked happy, sad or indifferent according to how the light hit it. Homi Catrack's gardener interjected: 'It is dangerous to look too long at death; otherwise you come away with a little of it inside you, and there are effects.' We asked: effects? what effects? which effects? how? And

Purushottam the sadhu, who had left his place under the Buckingham Villa garden tap for the first time in years, said: 'A death makes the living see themselves too clearly; after they have been in its presence, they become exaggerated.' This extraordinary claim was, in fact, borne out by events, because afterwards Toxy Catrack's nurse Bi-Appah, who had helped to clean up the body, became shriller, more shrewish, more terrifying than ever; and it seemed that everyone who saw the death of Dr Narlikar as it lay in state was affected, Nussie Ibrahim became even sillier and more of a duck, and Lila Sabarmati, who lived upstairs from the death and had helped to arrange its room, afterwards gave in to a promiscuity which had always been lurking within her, and set herself on a road at whose end there would be bullets, and her husband Commander Sabarmati conducting the Colaba traffic with a most unusual baton . . .

Our family, however, stayed away from the death. My father refused to go and pay his respects, and would never refer to his late friend by name, calling him simply: 'that traitor'.

Two days later, when the news had been in the papers, Dr Narlikar suddenly acquired an enormous family of female relations. Having been a bachelor and misogynist all his life, he was engulfed, in death, by a sea of giant, noisy, omnicompetent women, who came crawling out from strange corners of the city, from milking jobs at Amul Dairies and from the box-offices of cinemas, from street-side soda-fountains and unhappy marriages; in a year of processions the Narlikar women formed their own parade, an enormous stream of outsize womanhood flowing up our two-storey hillock to fill Dr Narlikar's apartment so full that from the road below you could see their elbows sticking out of the windows and their behinds overflowing on to the verandah. For a week nobody got any sleep because the wailing of the Narlikar women filled the air; but beneath their howls the women were proving as competent as they looked. They took over the running of the Nursing Home; they investigated all of Narlikar's business deals; and they cut my father out of the tetrapod deal just as coolly as you please. After all those years my father was left with nothing but a hole in his pocket, while the women took Narlikar's body to Benares to have it cremated, and the Estate servants whispered to me that they had heard how the Doctor's ashes were sprinkled on the waters of Holy Ganga at Manikarnika-ghat at dusk, and they did not sink, but floated on the surface of the water like tiny glowing firebugs, and were washed out to sea where their strange luminosity must have frightened the captains of ships.

As for Ahmed Sinai: I swear that it was after Narlikar's death and the arrival of the women that he began, literally, to fade . . . gradually his skin paled, his hair lost its colour, until within a few months he had become entirely white except for the darkness of his eyes. (Mary Pereira told Amina: 'That man is cold in the blood; so now his skin has made ice, white ice like a fridge.') I should say, in all honesty, that although he pretended to be worried by his transformation into a white man, and went to see doctors and so forth, he was secretly rather pleased when they failed to explain the problem or prescribe a cure, because he had long envied Europeans their pigmentation. One day, when it was permissible to make jokes again (a decent interval had been allowed to elapse after Dr Narlikar's death), he told Lila Sabarmati at the cocktail hour: 'All the best people are white under the skin; I have merely given up pretending.' His neighbours, all of whom were darker than he, laughed politely and felt curiously ashamed.

Circumstantial evidence indicates that the shock of Narlikar's death was responsible for giving me a snow-white father to set beside my ebony mother; but (although I don't know how much you're prepared to swallow) I shall risk giving an alternative explanation, a theory developed in the abstract privacy of my clocktower . . . because during my frequent psychic travels, I discovered something rather odd: during the first nine years after Independence, a similar pigmentation disorder (whose first recorded victim may well have been the Rani of Cooch Naheen) afflicted large numbers of the nation's business community. All over India, I stumbled across good Indian businessmen, their fortunes thriving thanks to the first Five Year Plan, which had concentrated on building up commerce . . . businessmen who had become or were becoming very, very pale indeed! It seems that the gargantuan (even heroic) efforts involved in taking over from the British and becoming masters of their own destinies had drained the colour from their cheeks . . . in which case, perhaps my father was a late victim of a widespread, though generally unremarked phenomenon. The businessmen of India were turning white.

That's enough to chew on for one day. But Evelyn Lilith Burns is coming; the Pioneer Café is getting painfully close; and – more vitally – midnight's other children, including my alter ego Shiva, he of the deadly knees, are pressing extremely hard. Soon the cracks will be wide enough for them to escape . . .

By the way: some time around the end of 1956, in all probability, the singer and cuckold Wee Willie Winkie also met his death.

Love in Bombay

During Ramzàn, the month of fasting, we went to the movies as often as we could. After being shaken awake at five a.m. by my mother's assiduous hand; after pre-dawn breakfasts of melon and sugared lime-water, and especially on Sunday mornings, the Brass Monkey and I took it in turns (or sometimes called out in unison) to remind Amina: 'The ten-thirty-in-the-morning show! It's Metro Cub Club day, Amma, pleeeese!' Then the drive in the Rover to the cinema where we would taste neither Coca-Cola nor potato crisps, neither Kwality ice-cream nor samosas in greasy paper; but at least there was air-conditioning, and Cub Club badges pinned to our clothes, and competitions, and birthday-announcements made by a compère with an inadequate moustache; and finally, the film, after the trailers with their introductory titles, 'Next Attraction' and 'Coming Soon', and the cartoon ('In A Moment, The Big Film; But First . . .!'): *Quentin Durward*, perhaps, or *Scaramouche*. 'Swashbuckling!' we'd say to one another afterwards, playing movie critic; and, 'A rumbustious, bawdy romp!' – although we were ignorant of swashbuckles and bawdiness. There was not much praying in our family (except on Eid-ul-Fitr, when my father took me to the Friday mosque to celebrate the holiday by tying a handkerchief around my head and pressing my forehead to the ground) . . . but we were always willing to fast, because we liked the cinema.

Evie Burns and I agreed: the world's greatest movie star was Robert Taylor. I also liked Jay Silverheels as Tonto; but his kemo-sabay, Clayton Moore, was too fat for the Lone Ranger, in my view.

Evelyn Lilith Burns arrived on New Year's Day, 1957, to take up residence with her widower father in an apartment in one of the two squat, ugly concrete blocks which had grown up, almost without our noticing them, on the lower reaches of our hillock, and which were oddly segregated: Americans and other foreigners lived (like Evie) in Noor Ville; arriviste Indian success-stories ended up in Laxmi Vilas. From the heights of Methwold's Estate, we looked down on them all, on white and brown alike; but nobody ever looked down on Evie Burns – except once. Only once did anyone get on top of her.

Before I climbed into my first pair of long pants, I fell in love with Evie; but love was a curious, chain-reactive thing that year. To save time, I shall place all of us in the same row at the Metro cinema; Robert Taylor is mirrored in our eyes as we sit in flickering trances – and also in symbolic sequence: Saleem Sinai is sitting-next-to-and-in-love-with Evie Burns who is sitting-next-to-and-in-love-with Sonny Ibrahim who is sitting-next-to-and-in-love-with the Brass Monkey who is sitting next to the aisle and feeling starving hungry . . . I loved Evie for perhaps six months of my life; two years later, she was back in America, knifing an old woman and being sent to reform school.

A brief expression of my gratitude is in order at this point: if Evie had not come to live amongst us, my story might never have progressed beyond tourism-in-a-clocktower and cheating in class . . . and then there would have been no climax in a widows' hostel, no clear proof of my meaning, no coda in a fuming factory over which there presides the winking, saffron-and-green dancing figure of the neon goddess Mumbadevi. But Evie Burns (was she snake or ladder? The answer's obvious: *both)* did come, complete with the silver bicycle which enabled me not only to discover the midnight children, but also to ensure the partition of the state of Bombay.

To begin at the beginning: her hair was made of scarecrow straw, her skin was peppered with freckles and her teeth lived in a metal cage. These teeth were, it seemed, the only things on earth over which she was powerless – they grew wild, in malicious crazy-paving overlaps, and stung her dreadfully when she ate ice-cream. (I permit myself this one generalization: Americans have mastered the universe, but have no dominion over their mouths; whereas India is impotent, but her children tend to have excellent teeth.)

Racked by toothaches, my Evie rose magnificently above the pain. Refusing to be ruled by bone and gums, she ate cake and drank Coke whenever they were going; and never complained. A tough kid, Evie Burns: her conquest of suffering confirmed her sovereignty over us all. It has been observed that all Americans need a frontier: pain was hers, and she was determined to push it out.

Once, I shyly gave her a necklace of flowers (queen-of-the-night for my lily-of-the-eve), bought with my own pocket-money from a hawker-woman at Scandal Point. 'I don't wear flowers,' Evelyn Lilith said, and tossed the unwanted chain into the air, spearing it before it fell with a pellet from her unerring Daisy air-pistol. Destroying flowers with a Daisy, she served notice that she was not to be manacled, not even by a necklace: she was our capricious, whirligig Lill-of-the-Hill. And also Eve. The Adam's-apple of my eye.

How she arrived: Sonny Ibrahim, Eyeslice and Hairoil Sabarmati, Cyrus Dubash, the Monkey and I were playing French cricket in the circus-ring between Methwold's four palaces. A New Year's Day game: Toxy clapping at her barred window; even Bi-Appah was in good humour and not, for once, abusing us. Cricket – even French cricket, and even when played by children – is a quiet game: peace anointed in linseed oil. The kissing of leather and willow; sprinkled applause; the occasional cry – 'Shot! Shot, sir!' – 'Ow*zatt*??' but Evie on her bicycle was having none of that.

'Hey, you! Alla you! Hey, whassamatter? You all deaf or what?'

I was batting (elegantly as Ranji, powerfully as Vinoo Mankad) when she charged up the hill on her two-wheeler, straw hair flying, freckles ablaze, mouth-metal flashing semaphore messages in the sunlight, a scarecrow astride a silver bullet . . . 'Hey, you widda leaky nose! Stop watching the schoopid ball, ya crumb! I'll showya something worth watching!'

Impossible to picture Evie Burns without also conjuring up a bicycle; and not just any two-wheeler, but one of the last of the great old-timers, an Arjuna Indiabike in mint condition, with drop-handlebars wrapped in masking tape and five gears and a seat made of reccine cheetah-skin. And a silver frame (the colour, I don't need to tell you, of the Lone Ranger's horse) . . . slobby Eyeslice and neat Hairoil, Cyrus the genius and the Monkey, and Sonny Ibrahim and myself – the best of friends, the true sons of the Estate, its heirs by right of birth – Sonny with the slow innocence he had had ever since the forceps dented his brain and me with my dangerous secret knowledge – yes, all of us, future bullfighters and Navy chiefs and all, stood frozen in open-mouthed attitudes as Evie Burns began to ride her bike, fasterfasterfaster, around and around the edges of the circus-ring. 'Lookit me now: watch me go, ya dummies!'

On and off the cheetah-seat, Evie performed. One foot on the seat, one leg stretched out behind her, she whirled around us; she built up speed and then did a headstand on the seat! She could straddle the front wheel, facing the rear, and work the pedals the wrong way round . . . gravity was her slave, speed her element, and we knew that a power had come among us, a witch on wheels, and the flowers of the hedgerows threw her petals, the dust of the circus-ring stood up in clouds of ovation, because the circus-ring had found its mistress, too: it was the canvas beneath the brush of her whirling wheels.

Now we noticed that our heroine packed a Daisy air-pistol on her right hip . . . 'More to come, ya zeroes!' she yelled, and drew the weapon. Her pellets gave stones the gift of flight; we threw annas into the air and she gunned them down, stone-dead. 'Targets! More targets!' – and Eyeslice surrendered his beloved pack of rummy cards without a murmur, so that she could shoot the heads off the kings. Annie Oakley in tooth-braces – nobody dared question her sharp-shooting, except once, and that was the end of her reign, during the great cat invasion; and there were extenuating circumstances.

Flushed, sweating, Evie Burns dismounted and announced: 'From now on, there's a new big chief around here. Okay, Indians? Any arguments?'

No arguments; I knew then that I had fallen in love.

At Juhu Beach with Evie: she won the camel-races, could drink more coconut milk than any of us, could open her eyes under the sharp salt water of the Arabian Sea.

Did six months make such a difference? (Evie was half a year older than me.) Did it entitle you to talk to grown-ups as an equal? Evie was seen gossiping with old man Ibrahim Ibrahim; she claimed Lila Sabarmati was teaching her to put on make-up; she visited Homi Catrack to gossip about guns. (It was the tragic irony of Homi Catrack's life that he, at whom a gun would one day be pointed, was a true *aficionado* of firearms . . . in Evie he found a fellow-creature, a mother-less child who was, unlike his own Toxy, as sharp as a knife and as bright as a bottle. Incidentally, Evie Burns wasted no sympathy on poor Toxy Catrack. 'Wrong inna head,' she opined carelessly to us all, 'Oughta be put down like rats.' But Evie: rats are not weak! There was more that was rodent-like in your face than in the whole body of your despised Tox.)

That was Evelyn Lilith; and within weeks of her arrival, I had set off the chain reaction from whose effects I would never fully recover.

It began with Sonny Ibrahim, Sonny-next-door, Sonny of the forcep-hollows, who has been sitting patiently in the wings of my story, awaiting his cue. In those days, Sonny was a badly bruised fellow: more than forceps had dented him. To love the Brass Monkey (even in the nine-year-old sense of the word) was no easy thing to do.

As I've said, my sister, born second and unheralded, had begun to react violently to any declarations of affection. Although she was believed to speak the languages of birds and cats, the soft words of lovers roused in her an almost animal rage; but Sonny was too simple to be warned off. For months now, he had been pestering her with statements such as, 'Saleem's sister, you're a pretty solid type!' or, 'Listen, you want to be my girl? We could go to the pictures with your ayah, maybe . . .' And for an equal number of months, she had been making him suffer for his love – telling tales to his mother; pushing him into mud-puddles accidentally-on-purpose; once even assaulting him physically, leaving him with long raking claw-marks down his face and an expression of sad-dog injury in his eyes; but he would not learn. And so, at last, she had planned her most terrible revenge.

The Monkey attended Walsingham School for Girls on Nepean Sea Road; a school full of tall, superbly muscled Europeans, who swam like fish and dived like submarines. In their spare time, they could be seen from our bedroom window, cavorting in the map-shaped pool of the Breach Candy Club, from which we were, of course, barred . . . and when I discovered that the Monkey had somehow attached herself to these segregated swimmers, as a sort of mascot, I felt genuinely aggrieved with her for perhaps the first time . . . but there was no arguing with her; she went her own way. Beefy fifteen-year-old white girls let her sit with them on the

Walsingham school bus. Three such females would wait with her every morning at the same place where Sonny, Eyeslice, Hairoil, Cyrus-the-great and I awaited the bus from the Cathedral School.

One morning, for some forgotten reason, Sonny and I were the only boys at the stop. Maybe there was a bug going round or something. The Monkey waited until Mary Pereira had left us alone, in the care of the beefy swimmers; and then suddenly the truth of what she was planning flashed into my head as, for no particular reason, I tuned into her thoughts; and I yelled 'Hey!' – but too late. The Monkey screeched, 'You keep out of this!' and then she and the three beefy swimmers had jumped upon Sonny Ibrahim, street-sleepers and beggars and bicycling clerks were watching with open amusement, because they were ripping every scrap of clothing off his body . . . 'Damn it man, are you going just to stand and watch?' – Sonny yelling for help, but I was immobilized, how could I take sides between my sister and my best friend, and he, 'I'll tell my daddy on you!', tearful now, while the Monkey, 'That'll teach you to talk shit – and that'll teach you', his shoes, off; no shirt any more; his vest, dragged off by a high-board diver, 'And that'll teach you to write your sissy love letters', no socks now, and plenty of tears, and 'There!' yelled the Monkey; the Walsingham bus arrived and the assailants and my sister jumped in and sped away, 'Ta-ta-ba-ta, lover-boy!' they yelled, and Sonny was left in the street, on the pavement opposite Chimalker's and Reader's Paradise, naked as the day he was born; his forcep-hollows glistened like rock-pools, because Vaseline had dripped into them from his hair; and his eyes were wet as well, as he, 'Why's she do it, man? Why, when I only told her I liked . . .'

'Search me,' I said, not knowing where to look, 'She does things, that's all.' Not knowing, either, that the time would come when she did something worse to me.

But that was nine years later . . . meanwhile, early in 1957, election campaigns had begun: the Jan Sangh was campaigning for rest homes for aged sacred cows; in Kerala, E. M. S. Namboodiripad was promising that Communism would give everyone food and jobs; in Madras, the Anna-D.M.K. party of C. N. Annadurai fanned the flames of regionalism; the Congress fought back with reforms such as the Hindu Succession Act, which gave Hindu women equal rights of inheritance . . . in short, everybody was busy pleading his own cause; I, however, found myself tongue-tied in the face of Evie Burns, and approached Sonny Ibrahim to ask him to plead on my behalf.

In India, we've always been vulnerable to Europeans . . . Evie had only been with us a matter of weeks, and already I was being sucked into a grotesque mimicry of European literature. (We had done *Cyrano*, in a simplified version, at school; I had also read the *Classics Illustrated* comic book.) Perhaps it would be fair to say that Europe repeats itself, in India, as farce . . . Evie was American. Same thing.

'But hey, man, that's no-fair man, why don't you do it yourself?'

'Listen, Sonny,' I pleaded, 'you're my friend, right?'

'Yeah, but you didn't even help . . .'

'That was my sister, Sonny, so how could I?'

'No, so you have to do your own dirty . . .'

'Hey, Sonny, man, think. Think only. These girls need careful handling, man. Look how the Monkey flies off the handle! You've got the experience, yaar, you've been through it. You'll know how to go gently this time. What do I know, man? Maybe she doesn't like me even. You want me to have my clothes torn off, too? That would make you feel better?'

And innocent, good-natured Sonny, '. . . Well, no . . .'

'Okay, then. You go. Sing my praises a little. Say never mind about my nose. Character is what counts. You can do that?'

'. . . Weeeelll . . . I . . . okay, but you talk to your sis also, yah?' 'I'll talk, Sonny. What can I promise? You know what she's like. But I'll talk to her for sure.'

You can lay your strategies as carefully as you like, but women will undo them at a stroke. For every victorious election campaign, there are twice as many that fail . . . from the verandah of Buckingham Villa, through the slats of the chick-blind, I spied on Sonny Ibrahim as he canvassed my chosen constituency . . . and heard the voice of the electorate, the rising nasality of Evie Burns, splitting the air with scorn: 'Who? *Him?* Whynt'cha tell him to jus' go blow his nose? That sniffer? He can't even ride a *bike*!'

Which was true.

And there was worse to come; because now (although a chick-blind divided the scene into narrow slits) did I not see the expression on Evie's face begin to soften and change? – did Evie's hand (sliced lengthways by the chick) not reach out towards my electoral agent? – and weren't those Evie's fingers (the nails bitten down to the quick) touching Sonny's temple-hollows, the fingertips getting covered in dribbled Vaseline? – and did Evie say or did she not; 'Now you, f'r instance: you're *cute*'? Let me sadly affirm that I did; it did; they were; she did.

Saleem Sinai loves Evie Burns; Evie loves Sonny Ibrahim; Sonny is potty about the Brass Monkey; but what does the Monkey say?

'Don't make me sick, Allah,' my sister said when I tried – rather nobly, considering how he'd failed me – to argue Sonny's case. The voters had given the thumbs-down to us both.

I wasn't giving in just yet. The siren temptations of Evie Burns – who never cared about me, I'm bound to admit – led me inexorably towards my fall. (But I hold nothing against her; because my fall led to a rise.)

Privately, in my clocktower, I took time off my trans-subcontinental rambles to consider the wooing of my freckled Eve. 'Forget middlemen,' I advised myself, 'You'll have to do this personally.' Finally, I formed my scheme: I would have to share her interests, to make her passions mine . . . guns have never appealed to me. I resolved to learn how to ride a bike.

Evie, in those days, had given in to the many demands of the hillock-top children that she teach them her bicycle-arts; so it was a simple matter for me to join the queue for lessons. We assembled in the circus-ring; Evie, ring-mistress supreme, stood in the centre of five wobbly, furiously concentrating cyclists . . . while I stood beside her, bikeless. Until Evie's coming I'd shown no interest in wheels, so I'd never been given any . . . humbly, I suffered the lash of Evie's tongue.

'Where've you been *living*, fat nose? I suppose you wanna borrow mine?'

'No,' I lied penitently, and she relented. 'Okay, okay,' Evie shrugged, 'Get in the saddle and lessee whatchou're made of.'

Let me reveal at once that, as I climbed on to the silver Arjuna Indiabike, I was filled with the purest elation; that, as Evie walked roundandround, holding the bike by the handle-bars, exclaiming, 'Gotcha balance yet? *No?* Geez, nobody's got all year!' – as Evie and I perambulated, I felt . . . what's the word? . . . happy.

Roundandroundand . . . Finally, to please her, I stammered, 'Okay . . . I think I'm . . . let me,' and instantly I was on my own, she had given me a farewell shove, and the silver creature flew gleaming and uncontrollable across the circus-ring . . . I heard her shouting: 'The brake! Use the goddamn brake, ya dummy!' – but my hands couldn't move, I had gone rigid as a plank, and there LOOK OUT in front of me was the blue two-wheeler of Sonny Ibrahim, collision course, OUTA THE WAY YA CRAZY, Sonny in the saddle, trying to swerve and miss, but still blue streaked towards silver, Sonny swung right but I went the same way EEYAH MY

258

BIKE and silver wheel touched blue, frame kissed frame, I was flying up and over handlebars towards Sonny who had embarked on an identical parabola towards me CRASH bicycles fell to earth beneath us, locked in an intimate embrace CRASH suspended in mid-air Sonny and I met each other, Sonny's head greeted mine . . . Over nine years ago I had been born with bulging temples, and Sonny had been given hollows by forceps; everything is for a reason, it seems, because now my bulging temples found their way into Sonny's hollows. A perfect fit. Heads fitting together, we began our descent to earth, falling clear of the bikes, fortunately, WHUMMP and for a moment the world went away.

Then Evie with her freckles on fire, 'O ya little creep, ya pile of snot, ya wrecked my . . .' But I wasn't listening, because circus-ring accident had completed what washing-chest calamity had begun, and they were there in my head, in the front now, no longer a muffled background noise I'd never noticed, all of them, sending their here-I-am signals, from north south east west . . . the other children born during that midnight hour, calling 'I,' 'I,' 'I' and 'I.'

'Hey! Hey, snothead! You okay? . . . Hey, where's his *mother*?'

Interruptions, nothing but interruptions! The different parts of my somewhat complicated life refuse, with a wholly unreasonable obstinacy, to stay neatly in their separate compartments. Voices spill out of their clocktower to invade the circus-ring, which is supposed to be Evie's domain . . . and now, at the very moment when I should be describing the fabulous children of ticktock, I'm being whisked away by Frontier Mail – spirited off *to* the decaying world of my grandparents, so that Aadam Aziz is getting in the way of the natural unfolding of my tale. Ah well. *What can't be cured must be endured.*

That January, during my convalescence from the severe concussion I received in my bicycling accident, my parents took us off to Agra for a family reunion that turned out worse than the notorious (and arguably fictional) Black Hole of Calcutta. For two weeks we were obliged to listen to Emerald and Zulfikar (who was now a Major-General and insisted on being called a General) dropping names, and also hints of their fabulous wealth, which had by now grown into the seventh largest private fortune in Pakistan; their son Zafar tried (but only once!) to pull the Monkey's fading red pig-tails. And we were obliged to watch in silent horror while my Civil Servant uncle Mustapha and his half-Irani wife Sonia beat and bludgeoned their litter of nameless, genderless brats into utter anonymity; and the bitter aroma of Alia's spinsterhood filled the air and ruined our food; and my father would retire early to begin his secret nightly war against the djinns; and worse, and worse, and worse.

One night I awoke on the stroke of twelve to find my grandfather's dream inside my head, and was therefore unable to avoid seeing him as he saw himself – as a crumbling old man in whose centre, when the light was right, it was possible to discern a gigantic shadow. As the convictions which had given strength to his youth withered away under the combined influence of old age, Reverend Mother and the absence of like-minded friends, an old hole was reappearing in the middle of his body, turning him into just another shrivelled, empty old man, over whom the God (and other superstitions) against which he'd fought for so long was beginning to reassert His dominion . . . meanwhile, Reverend Mother spent the entire fortnight finding little ways of insulting my uncle Hanif's despised film-actress wife. And that was also the time when I was cast as a ghost in a children's play, and found, in an old leather attaché-case on top of my grandfather's almirah, a sheet which had been chewed by moths, but whose largest hole was man-made: for which discovery I was repaid (you will recall) in roars of grandparental rage.

But there was one achievement. I was befriended by Rashid the rickshaw-wallah (the same fellow who had, in his youth, screamed silently in a cornfield and helped Nadir Khan into Aadam Aziz's toilet) : taking me under his wing – and without telling my parents, who would have forbidden it so soon after my accident – he taught me how to ride a bicycle. By the time we left, I had this secret tucked away with all my others: only I didn't intend this one to stay secret for very long.

. . . And on the train home, there were voices hanging on to the outside of the compartment: 'Ohé, maharaj! Open up, great sir!' – fare-dodgers' voices fighting with the ones I wanted to listen to, the new ones inside my head – and then back to Bombay Central Station, and the drive home past racecourse and temple, and now Evelyn Lilith Burns is demanding that I finish her part first before concentrating on higher things.

'Home again!' the Monkey shouts. 'Hurray . . . Back-to-Bom!' (She is in disgrace. In Agra, she incinerated the General's boots.)

It is a matter of record that the States Reorganization Committee had submitted its report to Mr Nehru as long ago as October 1955; a year later, its recommendations had been implemented. India had been divided anew, into fourteen states and six centrally-administered 'territories'. But the boundaries of these states were not formed by rivers, or mountains, or any natural features of the terrain; they were, instead, walls of words. Language divided us: Kerala was for speakers of Malayalam, the only palindromically-named tongue on earth; in Karnataka you were supposed to speak Kanarese; and the amputated state of Madras – known today as Tamil Nadu – enclosed the *aficionados* of Tamil. Owing to some oversight, however, nothing was done with the state

261

of Bombay; and in the city of Mumbadevi, the language marches grew longer and noisier and finally metamorphosed into political parties, the Samyukta Maharashtra Samiti ('United Maharashtra Party') which stood for the Marathi language and demanded the creation of the Deccan state of Maharashtra, and the Maha Gujarat Parishad ('Great Gujarat Party') which marched beneath the banner of the Gujarati language and dreamed of a state to the north of Bombay City, stretching all the way to the Kathiawar peninsula and the Rann of Kutch . . . I am warming over all this cold history, these old dead struggles between the barren angularity of Marathi which was born in the arid heat of the Deccan and Gujarati's boggy, Kathiawari softness, to explain why, on the day in February 1957 immediately following our return from Agra, Methwold's Estate was cut off from the city by a stream of chanting humanity which flooded Warden Road more completely than monsoon water, a parade so long that it took two days to pass, and of which it was said that the statue of Sivaji had come to life to ride stonily at its head. The demonstrators carried black flags; many of them were shopkeepers on hartal; many were striking textile-workers from Mazagaon and Matunga; but on our hillock, we knew nothing about their jobs; to us children, the endless ant-trail of language in Warden Road seemed as magnetically fascinating as a light-bulb to a moth. It was a demonstration so immense, so intense in its passions, that it made all previous marches vanish from the mind as if they had never occurred – and we had all been banned from going down the hill for even the tiniest of looks. So who was the boldest of us all? Who urged us to creep at least half-way down, to the point where the hillock-road swung round to face Warden Road in a steep U-bend? Who said, 'What's to be scared of? We're only going half-way for a *peek*'? . . . Wide-eyed, disobedient Indians followed their freckled American chief. ('They killed Dr Narlikar – marchers did,'

Hairoil warned us in a shivery voice. Evie spat on his shoes.)

But I, Saleem Sinai, had other fish to fry. 'Evie,' I said with quiet offhandedness, 'how'd you like to see me bicycling?' No response. Evie was immersed in the-spectacle . . . and was that her fingerprint in Sonny Ibrahim's left forcep-hollow, embedded in Vaseline for all the world to see? A second time, and with slightly more emphasis, I said, 'I can do it, Evie. I'll do it on the Monkey's cycle. You want to watch?' And now Evie, cruelly, 'I'm watching this. This is good. Why'd I wanna watch *you*?' And me, a little snivelly now, 'But I *learned*, Evie, you've *got* to . . .' Roars from Warden Road below us drown my words. Her back is to me; and Sonny's back, the backs of Eyeslice and Hairoil, the intellectual rear of Cyrus-the-great . . . my sister, who has seen the fingerprint too, and looks displeased, eggs me on: 'Go on. Go on, show her. Who's she think she is?' And up on her bike . . . 'I'm doing it, Evie, look!' Bicycling in circles, round and round the little cluster of children, 'See? You *see*?' A moment of exultation; and then Evie, deflating impatient couldn't-care-less; 'Willya get outa my way, fer Petesake? I wanna see *that*!' Finger, chewed-off nail and all, jabs down in the direction of the language march; I am dismissed in favour of the parade of the Samyukta Maharashtra Samiti! And despite the Monkey, who loyally, 'That's not fair! He's doing it really *good*!' – and in spite of the exhilaration of the thing-in-itself – something goes haywire inside me; and I'm riding round Evie, fasterfasterfaster, crying sniffing out of control, 'So what is it with you, anyway? What do I have to do to . . .' And then something else takes over, because I realize I don't have to ask her, I can just get inside that freckled mouth-metalled head and find out, for once I can really get to know what's going on . . . and in I go, still bicycling, but the front of her mind is all full up with Marathi language-marchers, there are American pop songs stuck in the corners of her thoughts, but nothing I'm interested in; and now, only now, now for the very first time, now driven on by the tears of unrequited love, I begin to probe . . . I find myself pushing, diving, forcing my way behind her defences . . . into the secret place where there's a picture of her mother who wears a pink smock and holds up a tiny fish by the tail, and I'm ferreting deeperdeeperdeeper, where is it, what makes her tick, when she gives a sort of jerk and swings round to stare at me as I bicycle roundandroundandroundandroundand . . .

'Get out!' screams Evie Burns. Hands lifted to forehead. I bicycling, wet-eyed, diving ininin: to where Evie stands in the doorway of a clapboard bedroom holding a, holding a something sharp and glinty with red dripping off it, in the doorway of a, my God and on the bed a woman, who, in a pink, my God, and Evie with the, and red staining the pink, and a man coming, my God, and no no no no no . . .

'GET OUT GET OUT GET OUT!' Bewildered children watch as Evie screams, language march forgotten, but suddenly remembered again, because Evie has grabbed the back of the Monkey's bike WHAT'RE YOU DOING EVIE as she pushes it THERE GET OUT YA BUM THERE GET OUT TO HELL! – She's pushed me hard-as-hard, and I losing control hurtling down the slope round the end of the U-bend downdown, MY GOD THE MARCH past Band Box laundry, past Noor Ville and Laxmi Vilas, AAAAA and down into the mouth of the march, heads feet bodies, the waves of the march parting as I arrive, yelling blue murder, crashing into history on a runaway, young-girl's bike.

Hands grabbing handlebars as I slow down in the impassioned throng. Smiles filled with good teeth surround me. They are not friendly smiles. 'Look look, a little laad-sahib comes down to join us from the big rich hill!' In Marathi which I hardly understand, it's my worst subject at school, and the smiles asking, 'You want to join S.M.S., little princeling?' And I, just about knowing what's being said, but dazed into telling the truth, shake my head No. And the smiles, 'Oho! The young nawab does not like our tongue! What does he like?' And another smile, 'Maybe Gujarati! You speak Gujarati, my lord?' But my Gujarati was as bad as my Marathi; I only knew one thing in the marshy tongue of Kathiawar; and the smiles, urging, and the fingers, prodding, 'Speak, little master! Speak some Gujarati!' – so I told them what I knew, a rhyme I'd learned from Glandy Keith Colaco at school, which he used when he was bullying Gujarati boys, a rhyme designed to make fun of the speech rhythms of the language:

> Soo ché? Saru ché!
> Danda lé ké maru ché!

How are you? – I am well! – I'll take a stick and thrash you to hell! A nonsense; a nothing; nine words of emptiness . . . but when I'd recited them, the smiles began to laugh; and then voices near me and then further and further away began to take up my chant, HOW ARE YOU? I AM WELL!, and they lost interest in me, 'Go go with your bicycle, masterji,' they scoffed, I'LL TAKE A STICK AND THRASH YOU TO HELL, I fled away up the hillock as my chant rushed forward and back, up to the front and down to the back of the two-day-long procession, becoming, as it went, a song of war.

That afternoon, the head of the procession of the Samyukta Maharashtra Samiti collided at Kemp's Corner, with the head of a Maha Gujarat Parishad demonstration; S.M.S. voices chanted 'Soo ché? Saru ché!' and M.G.P. throats were opened in fury; under the posters of the Air-India rajah and of the Kolynos Kid, the two parties fell upon one another with no little zeal, and to the tune of my little rhyme the first of the language riots got under way, fifteen killed, over three hundred wounded.

In this way I became directly responsible for triggering off the violence which ended with the partition of the state of Bombay, as a result of which the city became the capital of Maharashtra – so at least I was on the winning side.

What was it in Evie's head? Crime or dream? I never found out; but I had learned something else: when you go deep inside someone's head, *they can feel you in there*.

Evelyn Lilith Burns didn't want much to do with me after that day; but, strangely enough, I was cured of her. (Women have always been the ones to change my life: Mary Pereira, Evie Burns, Jamila Singer, Parvati-the-witch must answer for who I am; and the Widow, who I'm keeping for the end; and after the end, Padma, my goddess of dung. Women have fixed me all right, but perhaps they were never central – perhaps the place which they should have filled, the hole in the centre of me which was my inheritance from my grandfather Aadam Aziz, was occupied for too long by my voices. Or perhaps – one must consider all possibilities – they always made me a little afraid.)

266

My tenth birthday

'Oh mister, what to say? Everything is my own poor fault!'

Padma is back. And, now that I have recovered from the poison and am at my desk again, is too overwrought to be silent. Over and over, my returned lotus castigates herself, beats her heavy breasts, wails at the top of her voice. (In my fragile condition, this is fairly distressing; but I don't blame her for anything.)

'Only believe, mister, how much I have your well-being at heart! What creatures we are, we women, never for one moment at peace when our men lie sick and low . . . I am so happy you are well, you don't know!'

Padma's story (given in her own words, and read back to her for eye-rolling, high-wailing, mammary-thumping confirmation): 'It was my own foolish pride and vanity, Saleem baba, from which cause I did run from you, although the job here is good, and you so much needing a looker-after! But in a short time only I was dying to return.

'So then I thought, how to go back to this man who will not love me and only does some foolish writery? (Forgive, Saleem baba, but I must tell it truly. And love, to us women, is the greatest thing of all.)

'So I have been to a holy man, who taught me what I must do. Then with my few pice I have taken a bus into the country to dig for herbs, with which your manhood could be awakened from its sleep . . . imagine, mister, I have spoken magic with these words: "Herb thou hast been uprooted by Bulls!" Then I have ground herbs in water and milk and said, "Thou potent and lusty herb! Plant which Varuna had dug up for him by Gandharva! Give my Mr Saleem thy power. Give heat like that of Fire of Indra. Like the male antelope, O herb, thou hast all the force that Is, thou hast powers of Indra, and the lusty force of beasts."

'With this preparation I returned to find you alone as always and as always with your nose in paper. But jealousy, I swear, I have put behind me; it sits on the face and makes it old. O God forgive me, quietly I put the preparation in your food! . . . And then, hai-hai, may Heaven forgive me, but I am a simple woman, if holy men tell me, how should I argue? . . . But now at least you are better, thanks be to God, and maybe you will not be angry.'

Under the influence of Padma's potion, I became delirious for a week. My dung-lotus swears (through much-gnashed teeth) that I was stiff as a board, with bubbles around my mouth. There was also a fever. In my delirium I babbled about snakes; but I know that Padma is no serpent, and never meant me harm.

'This love, mister,' Padma is wailing, 'It will drive a woman to craziness.'

I repeat: I don't blame Padma. At the feet of the Western Ghats, she searched for the herbs of virility, *mucuna pruritus* and the root of *feronia elephantum*; who knows what she found? Who knows what, mashed with milk and mingled with my food, flung my innards into that state of 'churning' from which, as all students of Hindu cosmology will know, Indra created matter, by stirring the primal soup in his own great milk-churn? Never mind. It was a noble attempt; but I am beyond regeneration. – the Widow has done for me. Not even the real *mucuna* could have put an end to my incapacity; *feronia* would never have engendered in me the 'lusty force of beasts'.

268

Still, I am at my table once again; once again Padma sits at my feet, urging me on. I am balanced once more – the base of my isosceles triangle is secure. I hover at the apex, above present and past, and feel fluency returning to my pen.

A kind of magic has been worked, then; and Padma's excursion in search of love-potions has connected me briefly with that world of ancient learning and sorcerers' lore so despised by most of us nowadays; but (despite stomach-cramps and fever and frothings at the mouth) I'm glad of its irruption into my last days, because to contemplate it is to regain a little, lost sense of proportion.

Think of this: history, in my version, entered a new phase on August 15th, 1947 – but in another version, that inescapable date is no more than one fleeting instant in the Age of Darkness, Kali-Yuga, in which the cow of morality has been reduced to standing, teeteringly, on a single leg! Kali-Yuga – the losing throw in our national dice-game; the worst of everything; the age when property gives a man rank, when wealth is equated with virtue, when passion becomes the sole bond between men and women, when falsehood brings success (is it any wonder, in such a time, that I too have been confused about good and evil?) . . . began on Friday, February 18th, 3102 B.C.; and will last a mere 432,000 years! Already feeling somewhat dwarfed, I should add nevertheless that the Age of Darkness is only the fourth phase of the present Maha-Yuga cycle which is, in total, ten times as long; and when you consider that it takes a thousand Maha-Yugas to make just one Day of Brahma, you'll see what I mean about proportion.

A little humility at this point (when I'm trembling on the brink of introducing the Children) does not, I feel, come amiss.

Padma shifts her weight, embarrassed. 'What are you talking?' she asks, reddening a little. 'That is brahmin's talk; what's it to do with me?'

269

. . . Born and raised in the Muslim tradition, I find myself overwhelmed all of a sudden by an older learning; while here beside me is my Padma, whose return I had so earnestly desired . . . my Padma! The Lotus Goddess; the One Who Possesses Dung; who is Honey-Like, and Made of Gold; whose sons are Moisture and Mud . . .

'You must be fevered still,' she expostulates, giggling. 'How made of gold, mister? And you know I have no chil . . .'

. . . Padma, who along with the yaksa genii, who represent the sacred treasure of the earth, and the sacred rivers, Ganga Yamuna Sarasvati, and the tree goddesses, is one of the Guardians of Life, beguiling and comforting mortal men while they pass through the dream-web of Maya . . . Padma, the Lotus calyx, which grew out of Vishnu's navel, and from which Brahma himself was born; Padma the Source, the mother of Time! . . .

'Hey,' she is sounding worried now, 'let me feel your forehead!'

. . . And where, in this scheme of things, am I? Am I (beguiled and comforted by her return) merely mortal – or something more? Such as – yes, why not – mammoth-trunked, Ganesh-nosed as I am – perhaps, the Elephant. Who, like Sin the moon, controls the waters, bringing the gift of rain . . . whose mother was Ira, queen consort of Kashyap, the Old Tortoise Man, lord and progenitor of all creatures on the earth . . . the Elephant who is also the rainbow, and lightning, and whose symbolic value, it must be added, is highly problematic and unclear.

Well, then: elusive as rainbows, unpredictable as lightning, garrulous as Ganesh, it seems I have my own place in the ancient wisdom, after all.

'My God.' Padma is rushing for a towel to wet in cold water, 'your forehead is on fire! Better you lie down now; too soon for all this writing! The sickness is talking; not you.'

But I've already lost a week; so, fever or no fever, I must press on; because, having (for the moment) exhausted this strain of old-time fabulism, I am coming to the fantastic heart of my own story, and must write in plain unveiled fashion, about the midnight children.

Understand what I'm saying: during the first hour of August 15th, 1947 – between midnight and one a.m. – no less than one thousand and one children were born within the frontiers of the infant sovereign state of India. In itself, that is not an unusual fact (although the resonances of the number are strangely literary) – at the time, births in our part of the world exceeded deaths by approximately six hundred and eighty-seven an hour. What made the event noteworthy (note-worthy! There's a dispassionate word, if you like!) was the nature of these children, every one of whom was, through some freak of biology, or perhaps owing to some preter-natural power of the moment, or just conceivably by sheer coincidence (although synchronicity on such a scale would stagger even C. G. Jung), endowed with features, talents or faculties which can only be described as miraculous. It was as though – if you will permit me one moment of fancy in what will otherwise be, I promise, the most, sober account I can manage – as though history, arriving at a point of the highest significance and promise, had chosen to sow, in that instant, the seeds of a future which would genuinely differ from anything the world had seen up to that time.

If a similar miracle was worked across the border, in the newly-partitioned-off Pakistan, I have no knowledge of it; my perceptions were, while they lasted, bounded by the Arabian Sea, the Bay of Bengal, the Himalaya mountains, but also by the artificial frontiers which pierced Punjab and Bengal.

Inevitably, a number of these children failed to survive. Malnutrition, disease and the misfortunes of everyday life had accounted for no less than four hundred and twenty of

271

them by the time I became conscious of their existence; although it is possible to hypothesize that these deaths, too, had their purpose, since 420 has been, since time immemorial, the number associated with fraud, deception and trickery. Can it be, then, that the missing infants were eliminated because they had turned out to be somehow inadequate, and were not the true children of that midnight hour? Well, in the first place, that's another excursion into fantasy; in the second, it depends on a view of life which is both excessively theological and barbarically cruel. It is also an unanswerable question; any further examination of it is therefore profitless.

By 1957, the surviving five hundred and eighty-one children were all nearing their tenth birthdays, wholly ignorant, for the most part, of one another's existence – although there were certainly exceptions. In the town of Baud, on the Mahanadi river in Orissa, there was a pair of twin sisters who were already a legend in the region, because despite their impressive plainness they both possessed the ability of making every man who saw them fall hopelessly and often suicidally in love with them, so that their bemused parents were endlessly pestered by a stream of men offering their hands in marriage to either or even both of the bewildering children; old men who had forsaken the wisdom of their beards and youths who ought to have been becoming besotted with the actresses in the travelling picture-show which visited Baud once a month; and there was another, more disturbing procession of bereaved families cursing the twin girls for having bewitched their sons into committing acts of violence against themselves, fatal mutilations and scourgings and even (in one case) self-immolation. With the exception of such rare instances, however, the children of midnight had grown up quite unaware of their true siblings, their fellow-chosen-ones across the length and breadth of India's rough and badly-proportioned diamond.

And then, as a result of a jolt received in a bicycle-accident, I, Saleem Sinai, became aware of them all.

To anyone whose personal cast of mind is too inflexible to accept these facts, I have this to say: That's how it was; there can be no retreat from the truth. I shall just have to shoulder the burden of the doubter's disbelief. But no literate person in this India of ours can be wholly immune from the type of information I am in the process of unveiling – no reader of our national press can have failed to come across a series of – admittedly lesser – magic children and assorted freaks. Only last week there was that Bengali boy who announced himself as the reincarnation of Rabindranath Tagore and began to extemporize verses of remarkable quality, to the amazement of his parents; and I can myself remember children with two heads (sometimes one human, one animal), and other curious features such as bullock's horns.

I should say at once that not all the children's gifts were desirable, or even desired by the children themselves; and, in some cases, the children had survived but been deprived of their midnight-given qualities. For example (as a companion piece to the story of the Baudi twins) let me mention a Delhi beggar-girl called Sundari, who was born in a street behind the General Post Office, not far from the rooftop on which Amina Sinai had listened to Ramram Seth, and whose beauty was so intense that within moments of her birth it succeeded in blinding her mother and the neighbouring women who had been assisting at her delivery; her father, rushing into the room when he heard the women's screams, had been warned by them just in time; but his one fleeting glimpse of his daughter so badly impaired his vision that he was unable, afterwards, to distinguish between Indians and foreign tourists, a handicap which greatly affected his earning power as a beggar. For some time after that Sundari was obliged to have a rag placed across her face; until an old and ruthless great-aunt took her into her bony arms and slashed her face nine times with a kitchen knife. At the time when I became aware of her, Sundari was earning a healthy living, because nobody who looked at her could fail to pity a girl who had clearly once been too beautiful to look at and was now so cruelly disfigured; she received more alms than any other member of her family.

Because none of the children suspected that their time of birth had anything to do with what they were, it took me a while to find it out. At first, after the bicycle accident (and particularly once language marchers had purged me of Evie Burns), I contented myself with discovering, one by one, the secrets of the fabulous beings who had suddenly arrived in my mental field of vision, collecting them ravenously, the way some boys collect insects, and others spot railway trains; losing interest in autograph books and all other manifestations of the gathering instinct, I plunged whenever possible into the separate, and altogether brighter reality of the five hundred and eighty-one. (Two hundred and sixty-six of us were boys; and we were outnumbered by our female counterparts – three hundred and fifteen of them, including Parvati. Parvati-the-witch.)

Midnight's children! . . . From Kerala, a boy who had the ability of stepping into mirrors and re-emerging through any reflective surface in the land – through lakes and (with greater difficulty) the polished metal bodies of automobiles . . . and a Goanese girl with the gift of multiplying fish . . . and children with powers of transformation: a werewolf from the Nilgiri Hills, and from the great watershed of the Vindhyas, a boy who could increase or reduce his size at will, and had already (mischievously) been the cause of wild panic and rumours of the return of Giants . . . from Kashmir, there was a blue-eyed child of whose original sex I was never certain, since by immersing herself in water he (or she) could alter it as she (or he) pleased. Some of us called this child Narada, others Markandaya, depending on which old fairy story of sexual

274

change we had heard . . . near Jalna in the heart of the parched Deccan I found a water-divining youth, and at Budge-Budge outside Calcutta a sharp-tongued girl whose words already had the power of inflicting physical wounds, so that after a few adults had found themselves bleeding freely as a result of some barb flung casually from her lips, they had decided to lock her in a bamboo cage and float her off down the Ganges to the Sundarbans jungles (which are the rightful home of monsters and phantasms); but nobody dared approach her, and she moved through the town surrounded by a vacuum of fear; nobody had the courage to deny her food. There was a boy who could eat metal and a girl whose fingers were so green that she could grow prize aubergines in the Thar desert; and more and more and more . . . overwhelmed by their numbers, and by the exotic multiplicity of their gifts, I paid little attention, in those early days, to their ordinary selves; but inevitably our problems, when they arose, were the everyday, human problems which arise from character-and-environment; in our quarrels, we were just a bunch of kids.

One remarkable fact: the closer to midnight our birth-times were, the greater were our gifts. Those children born in the last seconds of the hour were (to be frank) little more than circus freaks: bearded girls, a boy with the fully-operative gills of a freshwater mahaseer trout, Siamese twins with two bodies dangling off a single head and neck – the head could speak in two voices, one male, one female, and every language and dialect spoken in the subcontinent; but for all their marvellousness, these were the unfortunates, the living casualties of that numinous hour. Towards the half-hour came more interesting and useful faculties – in the Gir Forest lived a witch-girl with the power of healing by the laying-on of hands, and there was a wealthy tea-planter's son in Shillong who had the blessing (or possibly the curse) of being incapable of forgetting anything he ever saw or heard. But the children born in the first minute of all – for these children the hour had reserved the highest talents of which men had ever dreamed. If you, Padma, happened to possess a register of births in which times were noted down to the exact second, you, too, would know what scion of a great Lucknow family (born at twenty-one seconds past midnight) had completely mastered, by the age of ten, the lost arts of alchemy, with which he regenerated the fortunes of his ancient but dissipated house; and which dhobi's daughter from Madras (seventeen seconds past) could fly higher than any bird simply by closing her eyes; and to which Benarsi silversmith's son (twelve seconds after midnight) was given the gift of travelling in time and thus prophesying the future as well as clarifying the past . . . a gift which, children that we were, we trusted implicitly when it dealt with things gone and forgotten, but derided when he warned us of our own ends . . . fortunately, no such records exist; and, for my part, I shall not reveal – or else, in appearing to reveal, shall falsify – their names and even their locations; because, although such evidence would provide absolute proof of my claims, still the children of midnight deserve, now, after everything, to be left alone; perhaps to forget; but I hope (against hope) to remember . . .

Parvati-the-witch was born in Old Delhi in a slum which clustered around the steps of the Friday mosque. No ordinary slum, this, although the huts built out of old packing cases and pieces of corrugated tin and shreds of jute sacking which stood higgledy-piggledy in the shadow of the mosque looked no different from any other shanty-town . . . because this was the ghetto of the magicians, yes, the very same place which had once spawned a Hummingbird whom knives had pierced and pie-dogs had failed to save . . . the conjurers' slum, to which the greatest fakirs and prestidigitators and illusionists in the land continually flocked, to seek their fortune in the capital city. They found tin huts, and police harassment, and rats . . . Parvati's father had once been the greatest conjurer in Oudh; she had grown up amid ventriloquists who could make stones tell jokes and contortionists who could swallow their own legs and fire-eaters who exhaled flames from their arseholes and tragic clowns who could extract glass tears from the corners of their eyes; she had stood mildly amid gasping crowds while her father drove spikes through her neck; and all the time she had guarded her own secret, which was greater than any of the illusionist flummeries surrounding her; because to Parvati-the-witch, born a mere seven seconds after midnight on August 15th, had been given the powers of the true adept, the illuminatus, the genuine gifts of conjuration and sorcery, the art which required no artifice.

So among the midnight children were infants with powers of transmutation, flight, prophecy and wizardry . . . but two of us were born on the stroke of midnight. Saleem and Shiva, Shiva and Saleem, nose and knees and knees and nose . . . to Shiva, the hour had given the gifts of war (of Rama, who could draw the undrawable bow; of Arjuna and Bhima; the ancient prowess of Kurus and Pandavas united, unstoppably, in him!) . . . and to me, the greatest talent of all – the ability to look into the hearts and minds of men.

But it is Kali-Yuga; the children of the hour of darkness were born, I'm afraid, in the midst of the age of darkness; so that although we found it easy to be brilliant, we were always confused about being good.

There; now I've said it. That is who I was – who we were.

Padma is looking as if her mother had died – her face, with its opening-shutting mouth, is the face of a beached pomfret. 'O baba!' she says at last. 'O baba! You are sick; what have you said?'

No, that would be too easy. I refuse to take refuge in illness. Don't make the mistake of dismissing what I've unveiled as mere delirium; or even as the insanely exaggerated fantasies of a lonely, ugly child. I have stated before that I am not speaking metaphorically; what I have just written (and read aloud to stunned Padma) is nothing less than the literal, by-the-hairs-of-my-mother's-head truth.

Reality can have metaphorical content; that does not make it less real. A thousand and one children were born; there were a thousand and one possibilities which had never been present in one place at one time before; and there were a thousand and one dead ends. Midnight's children can be made to represent many things, according to your point of view; they can be seen as the last throw of everything antiquated and retrogressive in our myth-ridden nation, whose defeat was entirely desirable in the context of a modernizing, twentieth-century economy; or as the true hope of freedom, which is now forever extinguished; but what they must not become is the bizarre creation of a rambling, diseased mind. No: illness is neither here nor there.

'All right, all right, baba,' Padma attempts to placate me. 'Why become so cross? Rest now, rest some while, that is all I am asking.'

Certainly it was a hallucinatory time in the days leading up to my tenth birthday; but the hallucinations were not in my head. My father, Ahmed Sinai, driven by the traitorous death of Dr Narlikar and by the increasingly powerful effect of djinns-and-tonics, had taken flight into a dream-world of disturbing unreality; and the most insidious aspect of his slow decline was that, for a very long time, people mistook it for the very opposite of what it was . . . Here is Sonny's mother, Nussie-the-duck, telling Amina one evening in our garden: 'What great days for you all, Amina sister, now that your Ahmed is in his prime! Such a fine man, and so much he is prospering for his family's sake!' She says it loud enough for him to hear; and although he pretends to be telling the gardener what to do about the ailing bougainvillaea, although he assumes an expression of humble self-deprecation, it's utterly unconvincing, because his bloated body has begun, without his knowing it, to puff up and strut about. Even Purushottam, the dejected sadhu under the garden tap, looks embarrassed.

My fading father . . . for almost ten years he had always been in a good mood at the breakfast table, before he shaved his chin; but as his facial hairs whitened along with his fading skin, this fixed point of happiness ceased to be a certainty; and the day came when he lost his temper at breakfast for the first time. That was the day on which taxes were raised and tax thresholds simultaneously lowered; my father flung down the *Times of India* with a violent gesture and glared around him with the red eyes I knew he only wore in his tempers. 'It's like going to the bathroom!' he exploded, cryptically; egg toast tea shuddered in the blast of his wrath. 'You raise your shirt and lower your trousers! Wife, this government is going to the bathroom all over us!' And my mother, blushing pink through the black, 'Janum, the children, please,' but he had stomped off, leaving me with a clear understanding of what people meant when they said the country was going to pot.

In the following weeks my father's morning chin continued to fade, and something more than the peace of the breakfast table was lost: he began to forget what sort of man he'd been in the old days before Narlikar's treason. The rituals of our home life began to decay. He began to stay away from the breakfast table, so that Amina could not wheedle money out of him; but, to compensate, he became careless with his cash, and his discarded clothes were full of rupee notes and coins, so that by picking his pockets she could make ends meet. But a more depressing indication of his withdrawal from family life was that he rarely told us bedtime stories any more, and when he did we didn't enjoy them, because they had become ill-imagined and unconvincing. Their subject-matter was still the same, princes goblins flying horses and adventures in magic lands, but in

279

his perfunctory voice we could hear the creaks and groans of a rustling, decayed imagination.

My father had succumbed to abstraction. It seems that Narlikar's death and the end of his tetrapod dream had shown Ahmed Sinai the unreliable nature of human relationships; he had decided to divest himself of all such ties. He took to rising before dawn and locking himself with his current Fernanda or Flory in his downstairs office, outside whose windows the two evergreen trees he planted to commemorate my birth and the Monkey's had already grown tall enough to keep out most of the daylight when it arrived. Since we hardly ever dared disturb him, my father entered a deep solitude, a condition so unusual in our overcrowded country as to border on abnormality; he began to refuse food from our kitchen and to live on cheap rubbish brought daily by his girl in a tiffin-carrier, lukewarm parathas and soggy vegetable samosas and bottles of fizzy drinks. A strange perfume wafted out from under his office door; Amina took it for the odour of stale air and second-rate food; but it's my belief that an old scent had returned in a stronger form, the old aroma of failure which had hung about him from the earliest days.

He sold off the many tenements or chawls which he'd bought cheaply on his arrival in Bombay, and on which our family's fortunes had been based. Freeing himself from all business connections with human beings – even his anonymous tenants in Kurla and Worli, in Matunga and Mazagaon and Mahim – he liquefied his assets, and entered the rarefied and abstract air of financial speculation. Locked in his office, in those days, his one contact with the outside world (apart from his poor Fernandas) was his telephone. He spent his day deep in conference with this instrument, as it put his money into such-andsuch shares or soandso stocks, as it invested in government bonds or bear market equities, selling long or short as he commanded . . . and invariably getting the best price of the day. In a streak of good fortune comparable only to my mother's success on the horses all those years previously, my father and his telephone took the stock exchange by storm, a feat made more remarkable by Ahmed Sinai's constantly-worsening drinking habits. Djinn-sodden, he nevertheless managed to ride high on the abstract undulations of the money market, reacting to its emotional, unpredictable shifts and changes the way a lover does to his beloved's slightest whim . . . he could sense when a share would rise, when the peak would come; and he always got out before the fall. This was how his plunge into the abstract solitude of his telephonic days was disguised, how his financial coups obscured his steady divorce from reality; but under cover of his growing riches, his condition was getting steadily worse.

Eventually the last of his calico-skirted secretaries quit, being unable to tolerate life in an atmosphere so thin and abstract as to make breathing difficult; and now my father sent for Mary Pereira and coaxed her with, 'We're friends, Mary, aren't we, you and I?', to which the poor woman replied, 'Yes, sahib, I know; you will look after me when I'm old,' and promised to find him a replacement. The next day she brought him her sister, Alice Pereira, who had worked for all kinds of bosses and had an almost infinite tolerance of men. Alice and Mary had long since made up their quarrel over Joe D'Costa; the younger woman was often upstairs with us at the end of the day, bringing her qualities of sparkle and sauciness into the somewhat oppressive air of our home. I was fond of her, and it was through her that we learned of my father's greatest excesses, whose victims were a budgerigar and a mongrel dog.

By July Ahmed Sinai had entered an almost permanent state of intoxication; one day, Alice reported, he had suddenly gone off for a drive, making her fear for his life, and returned somehow or other with a shrouded bird-cage in which, he said, was his new acquisition, a bulbul or Indian nightingale. 'For God knows how long,' Alice confided, 'he tells me all about bulbuls; all fairy stories of its singing and what-all; how this Calipha was captivated by its song, how the singing could make longer the beauty of the night; God knows what the poor man was babbling, quoting Persian and Arabic, I couldn't make top or bottom of it. But then he took off the cover, and in the cage is nothing but a talking budgie, some crook in Chor Bazaar must have painted the feathers! Now how could I tell the poor man, him so excited with his bird and all, sitting there calling out, "Sing, little bulbul! Sing!" . . . and it's so funny, just before it died from the paint it just repeated his line back at him, straight out like that – not squawky like a bird, you know, but in his own self-same voice: *Sing! Little bulbul, sing!*'

But there was worse on the way. A few days later I was sitting with Alice on the servants' spiral iron staircase when she said, 'Baba, I don't know what got into your daddy now. All day sitting down there cursing curses at the dog!'

The mongrel bitch we named Sherri had strolled up to the two-storey hillock earlier that year and simply adopted us, not knowing that life was a dangerous business for animals on Methwold's Estate; and in his cups Ahmed Sinai made her the guinea-pig for his experiments with the family curse.

This was that same fictional curse which he'd dreamed up to impress William Methwold, but now in the liquescent chambers of his mind the djinns persuaded him that it was no fiction, that he'd just forgotten the words; so he spent long hours in his insanely solitary office experimenting with formulae . . . 'Such things he is cursing the poor creature with!' Alice said, 'I wonder she don't drop down dead straight off!'

But Sherri just sat there in a corner and grinned stupidly back at him, refusing to turn purple or break out in boils, until one evening he erupted from his office and ordered

Amina to drive us all to Hornby Vellard. Sherri came too. We promenaded, wearing puzzled expressions, up and down the Vellard, and then he said, 'Get in the car, all of you.' Only he wouldn't let Sherri in . . . as the Rover accelerated away with my father at the wheel she began to chase after us, while the Monkey yelled Daddydaddy and Amina pleaded Janumplease and I sat in mute horror, we had to drive for miles, almost all the way to Santa Cruz airport, before he had his revenge on the bitch for refusing to succumb to his sorceries . . . she burst an artery as she ran and died spouting blood from her mouth and her behind, under the gaze of a hungry cow.

The Brass Monkey (who didn't even like dogs) cried for a week; my mother became worried about dehydration and made her drink gallons of water, pouring it into her as if she were a lawn, Mary said; but I liked the new puppy my father bought me for my tenth birthday, out of some flicker of guilt perhaps: her name was the Baroness Simki von der Heiden, and she had a pedigree chock-full of champion Alsatians, although in time my mother discovered that that was as false as the mock-bulbul, as imaginary as my father's forgotten curse and Mughal ancestry; and after six months she died of venereal disease. We had no pets after that.

My father was not the only one to approach my tenth birthday with his head lost in the clouds of his private dreams; because here is Mary Pereira, indulging in her fondness for making chutneys, kasaundies and pickles of all descriptions, and despite the cheery presence of her sister Alice there is something haunted in her face.

'Hullo, Mary!' Padma – who seems to have developed a soft spot for my criminal ayah – greets her return to centre-stage. 'So what's eating *her*?'

This, Padma: plagued by her nightmares of assaults by Joseph D'Costa, Mary was finding it harder and harder to get sleep. Knowing what dreams had in store for her, she forced herself to stay awake; dark rings appeared under her eyes, which were covered in a thin, filmy glaze; and gradually the blurriness of her perceptions merged waking and dreaming into something very like each other . . . a dangerous condition to get into, Padma. Not only does your work suffer but things start escaping from your dreams . . . Joseph D'Costa had, in fact, managed to cross the blurred frontier, and now appeared in Buckingham Villa not as a nightmare, but as a full-fledged ghost. Visible (at this time) only to Mary Pereira, he began haunting her in all the rooms of our home, which, to her horror and shame, he treated as casually as if it were his own. She saw him in the drawing-room amongst cut-glass vases and Dresden figurines and the rotating shadows of ceiling fans, lounging in soft armchairs with his long raggedy legs sprawling over the arms; his eyes were filled up with egg-whites and there were holes in his feet where the snake had bitten him. Once she saw him in Amina Begum's bed in the afternoon, lying down cool as cucumber right next to my sleeping mother, and she burst out, 'Hey, you! Go on out from there! What do you think, you're some sort of lord?' – but she only succeeded in awaking my puzzled mother. Joseph's ghost plagued Mary wordlessly; and the worst of it was that she found herself growing accustomed to him, she found forgotten sensations of fondness nudging at her insides, and although she told herself it was a crazy thing to do she began to be filled with a kind of nostalgic love for the spirit of the dead hospital porter.

But the love was not returned; Joseph's egg-white eyes remained expressionless; his lips remained set in an accusing, sardonic grin; and at last she realized that this new manifestation was no different from her old dream-Joseph (although it never assaulted her), and that if she was ever to be free of him she would have to do the unthinkable thing and confess her crime to the world. But she didn't confess, which was probably my fault – because Mary loved me like her own unconceived and inconceivable son, and to make her confession would have hurt me badly, so for my sake she suffered the ghost of her conscience and stood haunted in the kitchen (my father had sacked the cook one djinn-soaked evening) cooking our dinner and becoming, accidentally, the embodiment of the opening line of my Latin textbook, *Ora Maritima;* 'By the side of the sea, the ayah cooked the meal.' *Ora maritima, ancilla cenam parat.* Look into the eyes of a cooking ayah, and you will see more than textbooks ever know.

On my tenth birthday, many chickens were coming home to roost.

On my tenth birthday, it was clear that the freak weather – storms, floods, hailstones from a cloudless sky – which had succeeded the intolerable heat of 1956, had managed to wreck the second Five Year Plan. The government had been forced – although the elections were just around the corner – to announce to the world that it could accept no more development loans unless the lenders were willing to wait indefinitely for repayment. (But let me not overstate the case: although the production of finished steel reached only 2.4 million tons by the Plan's end in 1961, and although, during those five years, the number of landless and unemployed masses actually increased, so that it was greater than it had ever been under the British Raj, there were also substantial gains. The production of iron ore was almost doubled; power capacity did double; coal production leaped from thirty-eight million to fifty-four million tons. Five billion yards of cotton textiles were produced each year. Also large numbers of bicycles, machine tools, diesel engines, power pumps and ceiling fans. But I can't help ending on a downbeat: illiteracy survived unscathed; the population continued to mushroom.)

On my tenth birthday, we were visited by my uncle Hanif, who made himself excessively unpopular at Methwold's Estate by booming cheerily, 'Elections coming! Watch out for the Communists!'

On my tenth birthday, when my uncle Hanif made his gaffe, my mother (who had begun disappearing on mysterious 'shopping trips') dramatically and unaccountably blushed.

On my tenth birthday, I was given an Alsatian puppy with a false pedigree who would shortly die of syphilis.

On my tenth birthday, everyone at Methwold's Estate tried hard to be cheerful, but beneath this thin veneer everyone was possessed by the same thought: 'Ten years, my God! Where have they gone? What have we done?'

On my tenth birthday, old man Ibrahim announced his support for the Maha Gujarat Parishad; as far as possession of the city of Bombay was concerned, he nailed his colours to the losing side.

On my tenth birthday, my suspicions aroused by a blush, I spied on my mother's thoughts; and what I saw there led to my beginning to follow her, to my becoming a private eye as daring as Bombay's legendary Dom Minto, and to important discoveries at and in the vicinity of the Pioneer Café.

On my tenth birthday, I had a party, which was attended by my family, which had forgotten how to be gay, by classmates from the Cathedral School, who had been sent by their parents, and by a number of mildly bored girl swimmers from the Breach Candy Pools, who permitted the Brass Monkey to fool around with them and pinch their bulging musculatures; as for adults, there were Mary and Alice Pereira, and the Ibrahims and Homi Catrack and Uncle Hanif and Pia Aunty, and Lila Sabarmati to whom the eyes of every schoolboy (and also Homi Catrack) remained firmly glued, to the considerable irritation of Pia. But the only member of the hilltop gang to attend was loyal Sonny Ibrahim, who had

286

defied an embargo placed upon the festivities by an embittered Evie Burns. He gave me a message: 'Evie says to tell you you're out of the gang.'

On my tenth birthday, Evie, Eyeslice, Hairoil and even Cyrus-the-great stormed my private hiding-place; they occupied the clocktower, and deprived me of its shelter.

On my tenth birthday, Sonny looked upset, and the Brass Monkey detached herself from her swimmers and became utterly furious with Evie Burns. 'I'll teach her,' she told me. 'Don't you worry, big brother; I'll show that one, all right.'

On my tenth birthday, abandoned by one set of children, I learned that five hundred and eighty-one others were celebrating their birthdays, too; which was how I understood the secret of my original hour of birth; and, having been expelled from one gang, I decided to form my own, a gang which was spread over the length and breadth of the country, and whose headquarters were behind my eyebrows.

And on my tenth birthday, I stole the initials of the Metro Cub Club – which were also the initials of the touring English cricket team – and gave them to the new Midnight Children's Conference, my very own M.C.C.

That's how it was when I was ten: nothing but trouble outside my head, nothing but miracles inside it.

At the Pioneer Café

No colours except green and black the walls are green the sky is black (there is no roof) the stars are green the Widow is green but her hair is black as black. The Widow sits on a high high chair the chair is green the seat is black the Widow's hair has a centre-parting it is green on the left and on the right black. High as the sky the chair is green the seat is black the Widow's arm is long as death its skin is green the fingernails are long and sharp and black. Between the walls the children green the walls are green the Widow's arm comes snaking down the snake is green the children scream the fingernails are black they scratch the Widow's arm is hunting see the children run and scream the Widow's hand curls round them green and black. Now one by one the children mmff are stifled quiet the Widow's hand is lifting one by one the children green their blood is black unloosed by cutting fingernails it splashes black on walls (of green) as one by one the curling hand lifts children high as sky the sky is black there are no stars the Widow laughs her tongue is green but her teeth are black. And children torn in two in Widow hands which rolling rolling halves of children roll them into little balls the balls are green the night is black. And little balls fly into night between the walls the children shriek as one by one the Widow's hand. And in a corner the Monkey and I (the walls are green the shadows black) cowering crawling wide high walls green fading into black there is no roof and Widow's hand comes onebyone the children scream and

288

mmff and little balls and hand and scream and mmff and splashing stains of black. Now only she and I and no more screams the Widow's hand comes hunting hunting the skin is green the nails are black towards the corner hunting hunting while we shrink closer into the corner our skin is green our fear is black and now the Hand comes reaching reaching and she my sister pushes me out out of the corner while she stays cowering staring the hand the nails are curling scream and mmff and splash of black and up into the high as sky and laughing Widow tearing I am rolling into little balls the balls are green and out into the night the night is black . . .

The fever broke today. For two days (I'm told) Padma has been sitting up all night, placing cold wet flannels on my forehead, holding me through my shivers and dreams of Widow's hands; for two days she has been blaming herself for her potion of unknown herbs. 'But,' I reassure her, 'this time, it wasn't anything to do with that.' I recognize this fever; it's come up from inside me and from nowhere else; like a bad stink, it's oozed through my cracks. I caught exactly such a fever on my tenth birthday, and spent two days in bed; now, as my memories return to leak out of me, this old fever has come back, too. 'Don't worry,' I say, 'I caught these germs almost twenty-one years ago.'

We are not alone. It is morning at the pickle-factory; they have brought my son to see me. Someone (never mind who) stands beside Padma at my bedside, holding him in her arms. 'Baba, thank God you are better, you don't know what you were talking in your sickness.' Someone speaks anxiously, trying to force her way into my story ahead of time; but it won't work . . . someone, who founded this pickle-factory and its ancillary bottling works, who has been looking after my impenetrable child, just as once . . . wait on! She nearly wormed it out of me then, but fortunately I've still got my wits about me, fever or no fever! Someone will just have to step back and remain cloaked in anonymity until it's her turn;

and that won't be until the very end. I turn my eyes away from her to look at Padma. 'Do not think,' I admonish her, 'that because I had a fever, the things I told you were not completely true. Everything happened just as I described.'

'O God, you and your stories,' she cries, 'all day, all night – you have made yourself sick! Stop some time, na, what will it hurt?' I set my lips obstinately; and now she, with a sudden change of mood: 'So, tell me now, mister: is there anything you want?'

'Green chutney,' I request, 'Bright green – green as grasshoppers.' And someone who cannot be named remembers and tells Padma (speaking in the soft voice which is only used at sickbeds and funerals), 'I know what he means.'

... Why, at this crucial instant, when all manner of things were waiting to be described – when the Pioneer Café was so close, and the rivalry of knees and nose – did I introduce a mere condiment into the conversation? (Why do I waste time, in this account, on a humble preserve, when I could be describing the elections of 1957 – when all India is waiting, twenty-one years ago, to vote?) Because I sniffed the air; and scented, behind the solicitous expressions of my visitors, a sharp whiff of danger. I intended to defend myself; but I required the assistance of chutney ...

I have not shown you the factory in daylight until now. This is what has remained undescribed: through green-tinged glass windows, my room looks out on to an iron catwalk and then down to the cooking-floor, where copper vats bubble and seethe, where strong-armed women stand atop wooden steps, working long-handled ladles through the knife-tang of pickle fumes; while (looking the other way, through a green-tinged window on the world) railway tracks shine dully in morning sun, bridged over at regular intervals by the messy gantries of the electrification system. In daylight, our saffron-and-green neon goddess does not dance above the factory doors; we switch her off to save power. But electric trains are using power: yellow-and-brown local trains clatter south towards Churchgate Station from Dadar and Sorivli, from Kurla and Bassein Road. Human flies hang in thick white-trousered clusters from the trains; I do not deny that, within the factory walls, you may also see some flies. But there are also compensating lizards, hanging stilly upside-down on the ceiling, their jowls reminiscent of the Kathiawar peninsula . . . sounds, too, have been waiting to be heard: bubbling of vats, loud singing, coarse imprecations, bawdy humour of fuzz-armed women; the sharp-nosed, thin-lipped admonitions of overseers; the all-pervasive clank of pickle-jars from the adjacent bottling-works; and rush of trains, and the buzzing (infrequent, but inevitable) of flies . . . while grasshopper-green chutney is being extracted from its vat, to be brought on a wiped-clean plate with saffron and green stripes around the rim, along with another plate piled high with snacks from the local Irani shop; while what-has-now-been-shown goes on as usual, and what-can-now-be-heard fills the air (to say nothing of what can be smelled), I, alone in bed in my office realize with a start of alarm that outings are being suggested.

'. . . When you are stronger,' someone who cannot be named is saying, 'a day at Elephanta, why not, a nice ride in a motor-launch, and all those caves with so-beautiful carvings; or Juhu Beach, for swimming and coconut-milk and camel-races; or Aarey Milk Colony, even! . . .' And Padma: 'Fresh air, yes, and the little one will like to be with his father.' And someone, patting my son on his head: 'There, of course, we will all go. Nice picnic; nice day out. Baba, it will do you good . . .'

As chutney arrives, bearer-borne, in my room, I hasten to put a stop to these suggestions. 'No,' I refuse. 'I have work to do.' And I see a look pass between Padma and someone; and I see that I've been right to be suspicious. Because I've been tricked by offers of picnics once before! Once before, false smiles and offers of Aarey Milk Colony have fooled me into going out of doors and into a motor car; and then before I knew it there were hands seizing me, there were hospital corridors and doctors and nurses holding me in place while over my nose a mask poured anaesthetic over me and a voice said, Count now, count to ten . . . I know what they are planning. 'Listen,' I tell them, 'I don't need doctors.'

And Padma, 'Doctors? Who is talking about . . .' But she is fooling nobody; and with a little smile I say, 'Here: everybody: take some chutney. I must tell you some important things.'

And while chutney – the same chutney which, back in 1957, my ayah Mary Pereira had made so perfectly; the grasshopper-green chutney which is forever associated with those days – carried them back into the world of my past, while chutney mellowed them and made them receptive, I spoke to them, gently, persuasively, and by a mixture of condiment and oratory kept myself out of the hands of the pernicious green-medicine men. I said: 'My son will understand. As much as for any living being, I'm telling my story for him, so that afterwards, when I've lost my struggle against cracks, he will know. Morality, judgment, character . . . it all starts with memory . . . and I am keeping carbons.'

Green chutney on chilli-pakoras, disappearing down someone's gullet; grasshopper-green on tepid chapatis, vanishing behind Padma's lips. I see them begin to weaken, and press on. 'I told you the truth,' I say yet again, 'Memory's truth, because memory has its own special kind. It selects, eliminates, alters, exaggerates, minimizes, glorifies, and vilifies also; but in the end it creates its own reality, its heterogeneous but usually coherent version of events; and no sane human being ever trusts someone else's version more than his own.'

Yes: I said 'sane'. I knew what they were thinking: 'Plenty of children invent imaginary friends; but one thousand and one! That's just crazy!' The midnight children shook even

292

Padma's faith in my narrative; but I brought her round, and now there's no more talk of outings.

How I persuaded them: by talking about my son, who needed to know my story; by shedding light on the workings of memory; and by other devices, some naively honest, others wily as foxes. 'Even Muhammad,' I said, 'at first believed himself insane: do you think the notion never crossed my mind? But the Prophet had his Khadija, his Abu-Bakr, to reassure him of the genuineness of his Calling; nobody betrayed him into the hands of asylum-doctors.' By now, the green chutney was filling them with thoughts of years ago; I saw guilt appear on their faces, and shame. 'What is truth?' I waxed rhetorical, 'What is sanity? Did Jesus rise up from the grave? Do Hindus not accept – Padma – that the world is a kind of dream; that Brahma dreamed, is dreaming the universe; that we only see dimly through that dream-web, which is Maya. Maya,' I adopted a haughty, lecturing tone, 'may be defined as all that is illusory; as trickery, artifice and deceit. Apparitions, phantasms, mirages, sleight-of-hand, the seeming form of things: all these are parts of Maya. If I say that certain things took place which you, lost in Brahma's dream, find hard to believe, then which of us is right? Have some more chutney,' I added graciously, taking a generous helping myself. 'It tastes very good.'

Padma began to cry. 'I never said I didn't believe,' she wept. 'Of course, every man must tell his story in his own true way; but . . .'

'But,' I interrupted conclusively, 'you also – don't you – want to know what happens? About the hands that danced without touching, and the knees? And later, the curious baton of Commander Sabarmati, and of course the Widow? And the Children – what became of them?'

And Padma nodded. So much for doctors and asylums; I have been left to write. (Alone, except for Padma at my feet.) Chutney and oratory, theology and curiosity: these are the things that saved me. And one more – call it education, or class-origins; Mary Pereira would have called it my 'brought-up'. By my show of erudition and by the purity of my accents, I shamed them into feeling unworthy of judging me; not a very noble deed, but when the ambulance is waiting round the corner, all's fair. (It was: I smelled it.) Still – I've had a valuable warning. It's a dangerous business to try and impose one's view of things on others.

Padma: if you're a little uncertain of my reliability, well, a little uncertainty is no bad thing. Cocksure men do terrible deeds. Women, too.

Meanwhile, I am ten years old, and working out how to hide in the boot of my mother's car.

That was the month when Purushottam the sadhu (whom I had never told about my inner life) finally despaired of his stationary existence and contracted the suicidal hiccups which assailed him for an entire year, frequently lifting him bodily several inches off the ground so that his water-balded head cracked alarmingly against the garden tap, and finally killed him, so that one evening at the cocktail hour he toppled sideways with his legs still locked in the lotus position, leaving my mother's verrucas without any hope of salvation; when I would often stand in the garden of Buckingham Villa in the evenings, watching the Sputniks cross the sky, and feeling as simultaneously exalted and isolated as little Laika, the first and still the only dog to be shot into space (the Baroness Simki von der Heiden, shortly to contract syphilis, sat beside me following the bright pinprick of Sputnik II with her Alsatian eyes – it was a time of great canine interest in the space race); when Evie Burns and her gang occupied my clocktower, and washing-chests had been both forbidden and outgrown, so that for the sake of secrecy and sanity I was obliged to limit my visits to the midnight children to our private, silent hour – I communed with them every midnight, and only at midnight, during that hour which is reserved for

294

miracles, which is somehow outside time; and when – to get to the point – I resolved to prove, with the evidence of my own eyes, the terrible thing I had glimpsed sitting in the front of my mother's thoughts. Ever since I lay hidden in a washing-chest and heard two scandalous syllables, I had been suspecting my mother of secrets; my incursions into her thought processes confirmed my suspicions; so it was with a hard glint in my eye, and a steely determination, that I visited Sonny Ibrahim one afternoon after school, with the intention of enlisting his help.

I found Sonny in his room, surrounded by posters of Spanish bullfights, morosely playing Indoor Cricket by himself. When he saw me he cried unhappily, 'Hey man I'm damn sorry about Evie man she won't listen to anyone man what the hell'd you do to her anyway?' . . . But I held up a dignified hand, commanding and being accorded silence.

'No time for that now, man,' I said. 'The thing is, I need to know how to open locks without keys.'

A true fact about Sonny Ibrahim: despite all his bullfighting dreams, his genius lay in the realm of mechanical things. For some time now, he had taken on the job of maintaining all the bikes on Methwold's Estate in return for gifts of comic-books and a free supply of fizzy drinks. Even Evelyn Lilith Burns gave her beloved Indiabike into his care. All machines, it seemed, were won over by the innocent delight with which he caressed their moving parts; no contraption could resist his ministrations. To put it another way: Sonny Ibrahim had become (out of a spirit of pure inquiry) an expert at picking locks.

Now offered a chance of demonstrating his loyalty to me, his eyes brightened. 'Jus' show me the lock, man! Lead me to the thing!'

When we were sure we were unobserved, we crept along the driveway between Buckingham Villa and Sonny's Sans Souci; we stood behind my family's old Rover; and I pointed at the boot. 'That's the one,' I stated. 'I need to be able to open it from the outside, and the inside also.'

Sonny's eyes widened. 'Hey, what're you up to, man? You running away from home secretly and all?'

Finger to lips, I adopted a mysterious expression. 'Can't explain, Sonny,' I said solemnly, 'Top-drawer classified information.'

'Wow, man,' Sonny said, and showed me in thirty seconds how to open the boot with the aid of a strip of thin pink plastic. 'Take it, man,' said Sonny Ibrahim, 'You need it more than me.'

Once upon a time there was a mother who, in order to become a mother, had agreed to change her name; who set herself the task of falling in love with her husband bit-by-bit, but who could never manage to love one part, the part, curiously enough, which made possible her motherhood; whose feet were hobbled by verrucas and whose shoulders were stooped beneath the accumulating guilts of the world; whose husband's unlovable organ failed to recover from the effects of a freeze; and who, like her husband, finally succumbed to the mysteries of telephones, spending long minutes listening to the words of wrong-number callers . . . shortly after my tenth birthday (when I had recovered from the fever which has recently returned to plague me after an interval of nearly twenty-one years), Amina Sinai resumed her recent practice of leaving suddenly, and always immediately after a wrong number, on urgent shopping trips. But now, hidden in the boot of the Rover, there travelled with her a stowaway, who lay hidden and protected by stolen cushions, clutching a thin strip of pink plastic in his hand.

O, the suffering one undergoes in the name of righteousness! The bruising and the bumps! The breathing-in of rubbery boot-air through jolted teeth! And constantly, the fear of discovery . . . 'Suppose she really does go shopping?

Will the boot suddenly fly open? Will live chickens be flung in, feet tied together, wings clipped, fluttery pecky birds invading my hidey-hole? Will she see, my God, I'll have to be silent for a week!' My knees drawn in beneath my chin – which was protected-against knee-bumps by an old faded cushion – I voyaged into the unknown in the vehicle of maternal perfidy. My mother was a cautious driver; she went slowly, and turned corners with care; but afterwards I was bruised black and blue and Mary Pereira berated me soundly for getting into fights: 'Arré God what a thing it's a wonder they didn't smash you to pieces completely my God what will you grow up into you bad black boy you haddi-phaelwan you skin-and-bone wrestler!'

To take my mind off the jolting darkness I entered, with extreme caution, that part of my mother's mind which was in charge of driving operations, and as a result was able to follow our route. (And, also, to discern in my mother's habitually tidy mind an alarming degree of disorder. I was already beginning, in those days, to classify people by their degree of internal tidiness, and to discover that I preferred the messier type, whose thoughts, spilling constantly into one another so that anticipatory images of food interfered with the serious business of earning a living and sexual fantasies were superimposed upon their political musings, bore a closer relationship to my own pell-mell tumble of a brain, in which everything ran into everything else and the white dot of consciousness jumped about like a wild flea from one thing to the next . . . Amina Sinai, whose assiduous ordering-instincts had provided her with a brain of almost abnormal neatness, was a curious recruit to the ranks of confusion.)

We headed north, past Breach Candy Hospital and Mahalaxmi Temple, north along Hornby Vellard past Vallabhbhai Patel Stadium and Haji Ali's island tomb, north off what had once been (before the dream of the first William Methwold became a reality) the island of Bombay. We were heading towards the anonymous mass of tenements and fishing-villages and textile-plants and film-studios that the city became in these northern zones (not far from here! Not at all far from where I sit within view of local trains!) . . . an area which was, in those days, utterly unknown to me; I rapidly became disoriented and was then obliged to admit to myself that I was lost. At last, down an unprepossessing side-street full of drainpipe-sleepers and bicycle-repair shops and tattered men and boys, we stopped. Clusters of children assailed my mother as she descended; she, who could never shoo away a fly, handed out small coins, thus enlarging the crowd enormously. Eventually, she struggled away from them and headed down the street; there was a boy pleading, 'Gib the car poliss, Begum? Number one A-class poliss, Begum? I watch car until you come, Begum? I very fine watchman, ask anyone!' . . . In some panic, I listened in for her reply. How could I get out of this boot under the eyes of a guardian-urchin? There was the embarrassment of it; and besides, my emergence would have created a sensation in the street . . . my mother said, 'No.' She was disappearing down the street; the would-be polisher and watchman gave up eventually; there was a moment when all eyes turned to watch the passing of a second car, just in case it, too, stopped to disgorge a lady who gave away coins as if they were nuts; and in that instant (I had been looking through several pairs of eyes to help me choose my moment) I performed my trick with the pink plastic and was out in the street beside a closed car-boot in a flash. Setting my lips grimly, and ignoring all outstretched palms, I set off in the direction my mother had taken, a pocket-sized sleuth with the nose of a bloodhound and a loud drum pounding in the place where my heart should have been . . . and arrived, a few minutes later, at the Pioneer Café.

Dirty glass in the window; dirty glasses on the tables – the Pioneer Café was not much when compared to the Gaylords and Kwalitys of the city's more glamorous parts; a real rutputty joint, with painted boards proclaiming LOVELY LASSI and FUNTABULOUS FALOODA and BHEL-PURI BOMBAY FASHION, with filmi playback music blaring out from a cheap radio by the cash-till, a long narrow greeny room lit by flickering neon, a forbidding world in which broken-toothed men sat at reccine-covered tables with crumpled cards and expressionless eyes. But for all its grimy decrepitude, the Pioneer Café was a repository of many dreams. Early each morning, it would be full of the best-looking ne'er-do-wells in the city, all the goondas and taxi-drivers and petty smugglers and racecourse tipsters who had once, long ago, arrived in the city dreaming of film stardom, of grotesquely vulgar homes and black money payments; because every morning at six, the major studios would send minor functionaries to the Pioneer Café to rope in extras for the day's shooting. For half an hour each morning, when D. W. Rama Studios and Filmistan Talkies and R K Films were taking their pick, the Pioneer was the focus of all the city's ambitions and hopes; then the studio scouts left, accompanied by the day's lucky ones, and the Café emptied into its habitual, neon-lit torpor. Around lunchtime, a different set of dreams walked into the Café, to spend the afternoon hunched over cards and Lovely Lassi and rough biris – different men with different hopes: I didn't know it then, but the afternoon Pioneer was a notorious Communist Party hangout.

It was afternoon; I saw my mother enter the Pioneer Café; not daring to follow her, I stayed in the street, pressing my nose against a spider-webbed corner of the grubby window-pane; ignoring the curious glances I got – because my whites, although boot-stained, were nevertheless starched; my hair, although boot-rumpled, was well-oiled; my shoes, scuffed as they were, were still the plimsolls of a prosperous child – I followed her with my eyes as she went hesitantly and verruca-hobbled past rickety tables and hard-eyed men; I saw my mother sit down at a shadowed table at the far end of the narrow cavern; and then I saw the man who rose to greet her.

The skin on his face hung in folds which revealed that he had once been overweight; his teeth were stained with paan. He wore a clean white kurta with Lucknow-work around the buttonholes. He had long hair, poetically long, hanging lankly over his ears; but the top of his head was bald and shiny. Forbidden syllables echoed in my ears: Na. Dir. Nadir. I realized that I wished desperately that I'd never resolved to come.

Once upon a time there was an underground husband who fled, leaving loving messages of divorce; a poet whose verses didn't even rhyme, whose life was saved by pie-dogs. After a lost decade he emerged from goodness-knows-where, his skin hanging loose in memory of his erstwhile plumpness; and, like his once-upon-a-time wife, he had acquired a new name . . . Nadir Khan was now Qasim Khan, official candidate of the official Communist Party of India. Lal Qasim. Qasim the Red. Nothing is without meaning: not without reason are blushes red. My uncle Hanif said, 'Watch out for the Communists!' and my mother turned scarlet; politics and emotions were united in her cheeks . . . through the dirty, square, glassy cinema-screen of the Pioneer Café's window, I watched Amina Sinai and the no-longer-Nadir play out their love scene; they performed with the ineptitude of genuine amateurs.

On the reccine-topped table, a packet of cigarettes: State Express 555. Numbers, too, have significance: 420, the name given to frauds; 1001, the number of night, of magic, of alternative realities – a number beloved of poets and detested by politicians, for whom all alternative versions of the world are threats; and 555, which for years I believed to be the most sinister of numbers, the cipher of the Devil, the Great Beast, Shaitan himself! (Cyrus-the-great told me so, and I didn't contemplate the possibility of his being wrong. But he was: the true daemonic number is not 555, but 666: yet, in my mind, a dark aura hangs around the three fives to this day.) . . . But I am getting carried away. Suffice to say that Nadir-Qasim's preferred brand was the aforesaid State Express; that the figure five was repeated three times on the packet; and that its manufacturers were W.D. & H.O. Wills. Unable to look into my mother's face, I concentrated on the cigarette-packet, cutting from two-shot of lovers to this extreme close-up of nicotine.

But now hands enter the frame – first the hands of Nadir-Qasim, their poetic softness somewhat calloused these days; hands flickering like candle-flames, creeping forward across reccine, then jerking back; next a woman's hands, black as jet, inching forwards like elegant spiders; hands lifting up, off reccine tabletop, hands hovering above three fives, beginning the strangest of dances, rising, falling, circling one another, weaving in and out between each other, hands longing for touch, hands outstretching tensing quivering demanding to be – but always at last jerking back, fingertips avoiding fingertips, because what I'm watching here on my dirty glass cinema-screen is, after all, an Indian movie, in which physical contact is forbidden lest it corrupt the watching flower of Indian youth; and there are feet beneath the table and faces above it, feet advancing towards feet, faces tumbling softly towards faces, but jerking away all of a sudden in a cruel censor's cut . . . two strangers, each bearing a screen-name which is not the name of their birth, act out their half-unwanted roles. I left the movie before the end, to slip back into the boot of the unpolished unwatched Rover, wishing I hadn't gone to see it, unable to resist wanting to watch it all over again.

What I saw at the very end: my mother's hands raising a half-empty glass of Lovely Lassi; my mother's lips pressing gently, nostalgically against the mottled glass; my mother's

301

hands handing the glass to her Nadir-Qasim; who also applied, to the opposite side of the glass, his own, poetic mouth. So it was that life imitated bad art, and my uncle Hanif's sister brought the eroticism of the indirect kiss into the green neon dinginess of the Pioneer Café.

To sum up: in the high summer of 1957, at the peak of an election campaign, Amina Sinai blushed inexplicably at a chance mention of the Communist Party of India. Her son – in whose turbulent thoughts there was still room for one more obsession, because a ten-year-old brain can accommodate any number of fixations – followed her into the north of the city, and spied on a pain-filled scene of impotent love. (Now that Ahmed Sinai was frozen up, Nadir-Qasim didn't even have a sexual disadvantage; torn between a husband who locked himself in an office and cursed mongrels, and an ex-husband who had once, lovingly, played games of hit-the-spittoon, Amina Sinai was reduced to glass-kissery and hand-dances.)

Questions: did I ever, after that time, employ the services of pink plastic? Did I return to the café of extras and Marxists? Did I confront my mother with the heinous nature of her offence – because what mother has any business to – never mind about what once-upon-a-time – in full view of her only son, how could she how could she how could she? Answers: I did not; I did not; I did not.

What I did: when she went on 'shopping trips', I lodged myself in her thoughts. No longer anxious to gain the evidence of my own eyes, I rode in my mother's head, up to the north of the city; in this unlikely incognito, I sat in the Pioneer Café and heard conversations about the electoral prospects of Qasim the Red; disembodied but wholly present, I trailed my mother as she accompanied Qasim on his rounds, up and down the tenements of the district (were they the same chawls which my father had recently sold, abandoning his tenants to their fate?), as she helped him to get water-taps

302

fixed and pestered landlords to initiate repairs and dis-infections. Amina Sinai moved amongst the destitute on behalf of the Communist Party – a fact which never failed to leave her amazed. Perhaps she did it because of the growing impoverishment of her own life; but at the age of ten I wasn't disposed to be sympathetic; and in my own way, I began to dream dreams of revenge.

The legendary Caliph, Haroun al-Rashid, is said to have enjoyed moving incognito amongst the people of Baghdad; I, Saleem Sinai, have also travelled in secret through the byways of my city, but I can't say I had much fun.

Matter of fact descriptions of the outré and bizarre, and their reverse, namely heightened, stylized versions of the everyday – these techniques, which are also attitudes of mind, I have lifted – or perhaps absorbed – from the most formidable of the midnight children, my rival, my fellow-changeling, the supposed son of Wee Willie Winkie: Shiva-of-the-knees. They were techniques which, in his case, were applied entirely without conscious thought, and their effect was to create a picture of the world of startling uniformity, in which one could mention casually, in passing as it were, the dreadful murders of prostitutes which began to fill the gutter-press in those days (while the bodies filled the gutters), while lingering passionately on the intricate details of a particular hand of cards. Death, and defeat at rummy were all of a piece to Shiva; hence his terrifying, nonchalant violence, which in the end . . . but to begin with beginnings:

Although, admittedly, it's my own fault, I'm bound to say that if you think of me purely as a radio, you'll only be grasping half the truth. Thought is as often pictorial or purely emblematic as verbal; and anyway, in order to communicate with, and understand, my colleagues in the Midnight Children's Conference, it was necessary for me quickly to advance beyond the verbal stage. Arriving in their infinitely various minds, I was obliged to get beneath the surface veneer of front-of-mind thoughts in incomprehensible tongues, with the obvious (and previously demonstrated) effect that they became aware of my presence. Remembering the dramatic effect such an awareness had had on Evie Burns, I went to some pains to alleviate the shock of my entry. In all cases, my standard first transmission was an image of my face, smiling in what I trusted was a soothing, friendly, confident and leader-like fashion, and of a hand stretched out in friendship. There were, however, teething troubles.

It took me a little while to realize that my picture of myself was heavily distorted by my own self-consciousness about my appearance; so that the portrait I sent across the thought-waves of the nation, grinning like a Cheshire cat, was about as hideous as a portrait could be, featuring a wondrously enlarged nose, a completely non-existent chin and giant stains on each temple. It's no wonder that I was often greeted by yelps of mental alarm. I, too, was often similarly frightened by the self-images of my ten-year-old fellows. When we discovered what was happening, I encouraged the member-ship of the Conference, one by one, to go and look into a mirror, or a patch of still water; and then we did manage to find out what we really looked like. The only problems were that our Keralan member (who could, you remember, travel through mirrors) accidentally ended up emerging through a restaurant mirror in the smarter part of New Delhi, and had to make a hurried retreat; while the blue-eyed member for Kashmir fell into a lake and accidentally changed sex, entering as a girl and emerging as a beautiful boy.

When I first introduced myself to Shiva, I saw in his mind the terrifying image of a short, rat-faced youth with filed-down teeth and two of the biggest knees the world has ever seen.

Faced with a picture of such grotesque proportions, I allowed the smile on my own beaming image to wither a little;

my outstretched hand began to falter and twitch. And Shiva, feeling my presence, reacted at first with utter rage; great boiling waves of anger scalded the inside of my head; but then, 'Hey – look – I know you! You're the rich kid from Methwold's Estate, isn't it?' And I, equally astonished, 'Winkie's son – the one who blinded Eyeslice!' His self-image puffed up with pride. 'Yah, yaar, that's me. Nobody messes with me, man!' Recognition reduced me to banalities: 'So! How's your father, anyway? He doesn't come round . . .' And he, with what felt very like relief: 'Him, man? My father's dead.'

A momentary pause; then puzzlement – no anger now – and Shiva, 'Lissen, yaar, this is damn good – how you doin' it?' I launched into my standard explanation, but after a few instants he interrupted, 'So! Lissen, my father said I got born at exactly midnight also – so don't you see, that makes us joint bosses of this gang of yours! Midnight is best, agreed? So – those other kids gotta do like we tell them!' There rose before my eyes the image of a second, and more potent, Evelyn Lilith Burns . . . dismissing this unkind notion, I explained, 'That wasn't exactly my idea for the Conference; I had in mind something more like a, you know, sort of loose federation of equals, all points of view given free expression . . .' Something resembling a violent snort echoed around the walls of my head. 'That, man, that's only rubbish. What we ever goin' to do with a gang like that? Gangs gotta have gang bosses. You take me –' (the puff of pride again) 'I been running a gang up here in Matunga for two years now. Since I was eight. Older kids and all. What d'you think of that?' And I, without meaning to, 'What's it do, your gang – does it have rules and all?' Shiva-laughter in my ears . . . 'Yah, little rich boy: one rule. Everybody does what I say or I squeeze the shit outa them with my knees!' Desperately, I continued to try and win Shiva round to my point of view: 'The thing is, we must be here for a *purpose*, don't you think? I mean, there has

305

to be a *reason*, you must agree? So what I thought, we should try and work out what it is, and then, you know, sort of dedicate our lives to . . .' 'Rich kid,' Shiva yelled, 'you don't know one damn thing! What *purpose*, man? What thing in the whole sister-sleeping world got *reason*, yara? For what reason you're rich and I'm poor? Where's the reason in starving, man? God knows how many millions of damn fools living in this country, man, and you think there's a purpose! Man, I'll tell you – you got to get what you can, do what you can with it, and then you got to die. That's reason, rich – boy. Everything else is only mother-sleeping *wind*!'

And now I, in my midnight bed, begin to shake . . . 'But history,' I say, 'and the Prime Minister wrote me a letter . . . and don't you even believe in . . . who knows what we might . . .' He, my alter ego, Shiva, butted in: 'Lissen, little boy – you're so full of crazy stuff, I can see I'm going to have to take this thing over. You tell that to all these other freak kids!'

Nose and knees and knees and nose . . . the rivalry that began that night would never be ended, until two knives slashed, downdowndown . . . whether the spirits of Mian Abdullah, whom knives killed years before, had leaked into me, imbuing me with the notion of loose federalism and making me vulnerable to knives, I cannot say; but at that point I found a measure of courage and told Shiva, 'You can't run the Conference; without me, they won't even be able to listen to you!'

And he, confirming the declaration of war: 'Rich kid, they'll want to know about me; you just try and stop me!'

'Yes,' I told him, 'I'll try.'

Shiva, the god of destruction, who is also most potent of deities; Shiva, greatest of dancers; who rides on a bull; whom no force can resist . . . the boy Shiva, he told us, had to fight for survival from his earliest days. And when his father had, about a year previously, completely lost his singing voice, Shiva had had to defend himself against Wee Willie Winkie's parental zeal. 'He blindfolded me, man! He wrapped a rag around my eyes an' took me to the roof of the chawl, man! You know what was in his hand? A sister-sleeping hammer, man! A hammer! Bastard was going to smash my legs up, man – it happens, you know, rich boy, they do it to kids so they can always earn money begging – you get more if you're all broken up, man! So I'm pushed over till I'm lying down on the roof, man; and then –' And then hammer swinging down towards knees larger and knobblier than any policeman's, an easy target, but now the knees went into action, faster than lightning the knees parted – felt the breath of the down-rushing hammer and spread wide apart; and then hammer plunging between knees, still held in his father's hand; and then, the knees rushing together like fists. The hammer, clattering harmlessly on concrete. The wrist of Wee Willie Winkie, clamped between the knees of his blindfolded son. Hoarse breaths escaping from the lips of the anguished father. And still the knees, closing ininin, tighter and tighter, until there is a snap. 'Broke his goddamn wrist, man! That showed him – damn fine, no? I swear!'

Shiva and I were born under Capricorn rising; the constellation left me alone, but it gave Shiva its gift. Capricorn, as any astrologer will tell you, is the heavenly body with power over the knees.

On election day, 1957, the All-India Congress was badly shocked. Although it won the election, twelve million votes made the Communists the largest single opposition party; and in Bombay, despite the efforts of Boss Patil, large numbers of electors failed to place their crosses against the Congress symbol of sacred-cow-and-suckling-calf, preferring the less emotive pictograms of the Samyukta Maharashtra Samiti and Maha Gujarat Parishad. When the Communist peril was discussed on our hillock, my mother continued to blush; and we resigned ourselves to the partition of the state of Bombay.

One member of the Midnight Children's Conference played a minor role in the elections. Winkie's supposed son Shiva was recruited by – well, perhaps I will not name the party; but only one party had really large sums to spend – and on polling day, he and his gang, who called themselves Cowboys, were to be seen standing outside a polling station in the north of the city, some holding long stout sticks, others juggling with stones, still others picking their teeth with knives, all of them encouraging the electorate to use its vote with wisdom and care . . . and after the polls closed, were seals broken on ballot-boxes? Did ballot-stuffing occur? At any rate, when the votes were counted, it was discovered that Qasim the Red had narrowly failed to win the seat; and my rival's paymasters were well pleased.

. . . But now Padma says, mildly, 'What date was it?' And, without thinking, I answer: 'Some time in the spring.' And then it occurs to me that I have made another error – that the election of 1957 took place before, and not after, my tenth birthday; but although I have racked my brains, my memory refuses, stubbornly, to alter the sequence of events. This is worrying. I don't know what's gone wrong.

She says, trying uselessly to console me: 'What are you so long for in your face? Everybody forgets some small things, all the time!'

But if small things go, will large things be close behind?

Alpha and Omega

There was turmoil in Bombay in the months after the election; there is turmoil in my thoughts as I recall those days. My error has upset me badly; so now, to regain my equilibrium, I shall place myself firmly on the familiar ground of Methwold's Estate; leaving the history of the Midnight Children's Conference to one side, and the pain of the Pioneer Café to another, I shall tell you about the fall of Evie Burns.

I have titled this episode somewhat oddly. 'Alpha and Omega' stares back at me from the page, demanding to be explained – a curious heading for what will be my story's half-way point, one that reeks of beginnings and ends, when you could say it should be more concerned with middles; but, unrepentantly, I have no intention of changing it, although there are many alternative titles, for instance 'From Monkey to Rhesus', or 'Finger Redux', or – in a more allusive style – 'The Gander', a reference, obviously, to the mythical bird, the hamsa or parahamsa, symbol of the ability to live in two worlds, the physical and the spiritual, the world of land-and-water and the world of air, of flight. But 'Alpha and Omega' it is; 'Alpha and Omega' it remains. Because there are beginnings here, and all manner of ends; but you'll soon see what I mean.

Padma clicks her tongue in exasperation. 'You're talking funny again,' she criticizes, 'Are you going to tell about Evie or not?'

. . . After the general election, the Central Government continued to shilly-shally about the future of Bombay. The

State was to be partitioned; then not to be partitioned; then partition reared its head again. And as for the city itself – it was to be the capital of Maharashtra; or of both Maharashtra and Gujarat; or an independent state of its own . . . while the government tried to work out what on earth to do, the city's inhabitants decided to encourage it to be quick. Riots proliferated (and you could still hear the old battle-song of the Mahrattas – *How are you? I am well! I'll take a stick and thrash you to hell!* – rising above the fray); and to make things worse, the weather joined in the mêlée. There was a severe drought; roads cracked; in the villages, peasants were being forced to kill their cows; and on Christmas Day (of whose significance no boy who attended a mission school and was attended upon by a Catholic ayah could fail to be aware) there was a series of loud explosions at the Walkeshwar Reservoir and the main fresh-water pipes which were the city's lifelines began to blow fountains into the air like giant steel whales. The newspapers were full of talk of saboteurs; speculation over the criminals' identities and political affiliation jostled for space against reports of the continuing wave of whore-murders. (I was particularly interested to learn that the murderer had his own curious 'signature'. The corpses of the ladies of the night were all strangled to death; there were bruises on their necks, bruises too large to be thumbprints, but wholly consistent with the marks which would be left by a pair of giant, preternaturally powerful knees.)

But I digress. What, Padma's frown demands, does all this have to do with Evelyn Lilith Burns? Instantly, leaping to attention, as it were, I provide the answer: in the days after the destruction of the city's fresh-water supply, the stray cats of Bombay began to congregate in those areas of the city where water was still relatively plentiful; that is to say, the better-off areas, in which each house owned its own overhead or underground water-tank. And, as a result, the two-storey

310

hillock of Methwold's Estate was invaded by an army of thirsting felines; cats swarming all over the circus-ring, cats climbing bougainvillaea creepers and leaping into sitting-rooms, cats knocking over flower-vases to drink the plant-stale water, cats bivouacked in bathrooms, slurping liquid out of water-closets, cats rampant in the kitchens of the palaces of William Methwold. The Estate's servants were vanquished in their attempts to repel the great cat invasion; the ladies of the Estate were reduced to helpless exclamations of horror. Hard dry worms of cat-excrement were everywhere; gardens were ruined by sheer feline force of numbers: and at night sleep became an impossibility as the army found voice, and sang its thirst at the moon. (The Baroness Simki von der Heiden refused to fight the cats; she was already showing signs of the disease which would shortly lead to her extermination.)

Nussie Ibrahim rang my mother to announce, 'Amina sister, it is the end of the world.'

She was wrong; because on the third day after the great cat invasion, Evelyn Lilith Burns visited each Estate household in turn, carrying her Daisy air-gun casually in one hand, and offered, in return for bounty money, to end the plague of pussies double-quick.

All that day, Methwold's Estate echoed with the sounds of Evie's air-gun and the agonized wauls of the cats, as Evie stalked the entire army one by one and made herself rich. But (as history so often demonstrates) the moment of one's greatest triumph also contains the seeds of one's final downfall; and so it proved, because Evie's persecution of the cats was, as far as the Brass Monkey was concerned, absolutely the last straw.

'Brother,' the Monkey told me grimly, 'I told you I'd get that girl; now, right now, the time has come.'

Unanswerable questions: was it true that my sister had acquired the languages of cats as well as birds? Was it her

fondness for feline life which pushed her over the brink? . . .
by the time of the great cat invasion, the Monkey's hair had
faded into brown; she had broken her habit of burning shoes;
but still, and for whatever reason, there was a fierceness in her
which none of the rest of is ever possessed; and she went
down into the circus-ring and yelled at the top of her voice:
'Evie! Evie Burns! You come out here, this minute, wherever
you are!'

Surrounded by fleeing cats, the Monkey awaited Evelyn
Burns. I went out on to the first-floor verandah to watch;
from their verandahs, Sonny and Eyeslice and Hairoil and
Cyrus were watching too. We saw Evie Burns appear from
the direction of the Versailles Villa kitchens; she was blowing
the smoke away from the barrel of her gun.

'You Indians c'n thank your stars you got me around,' Evie
declared, 'or you'd just've got eaten by these cats!'

We saw Evie fall silent as she saw the thing sitting tensely
in the Monkey's eyes; and then like a blur the Monkey
descended on Evie and a battle began which lasted for what
seemed like several hours (but it can only have been a few
minutes). Shrouded in the dust of the circus-ring they rolled
kicked scratched bit, small tufts of hair flew out of the dust-
cloud and there were elbows and feet in dirtied white socks
and knees and fragments of frock flying out of the cloud;
grownups came running, servants couldn't pull them apart,
and in the end Homi Catrack's gardener turned his hose on
them to separate them . . . the Brass Monkey stood up a little
crookedly and shook the sodden hem of her dress, ignoring
the cries of retribution proceeding from the lips of Amina
Sinai and Mary Pereira; because there in the hose-wet dirt of
the circus-ring lay Evie Burns, her tooth-braces broken, her
hair matted with dust and spittle, her spirit and her dominion
over us broken for once and for all.

A few weeks later her father sent her home for good, 'To
get a decent education away from these savages,' he was

heard to remark; I only heard from her once, six months later, when right out of the blue she wrote me the letter which informed me that she had knifed an old lady who had objected to her assault on a cat. 'I gave it to her all right,' Evie wrote, 'Tell your sister she just got lucky.' I salute that unknown old woman: she paid the Monkey's bill.

More interesting than Evie's last message is a thought which occurs to me now, as I look back down the tunnel of time. Holding before my eyes the image of Monkey and Evie rolling in the dirt, I seem to discern the driving force behind their battle to the death, a motive far deeper than the mere persecution of cats: they were fighting over me. Evie and my sister (who were, in many ways, not at all dissimilar) kicked and scratched, ostensibly over the fate of a few thirsty strays; but perhaps Evie's kicks were aimed at me, perhaps they were the violence of her anger at my invasion of her head; and then maybe the strength of the Monkey was the strength of sibling-loyalty, and her act of war was actually an act of love.

Blood, then, was spilled in the circus-ring. Another rejected title for these pages – you may as well know – was 'Thicker Than Water'. In those days of water shortages, something thicker than water ran down the face of Evie Burns; the loyalties of blood motivated the Brass Monkey; and in the streets of the city, rioters spilled each other's blood. There were bloody murders, and perhaps it is not appropriate to end this sanguinary catalogue by mentioning, once again, the rushes of blood to my mother's cheeks. Twelve million votes were coloured red that year, and red is the colour of blood. More blood will flow soon: the types of blood, A and O, Alpha and Omega – and another, a third possibility – must be kept in mind. Also other factors: zygosity, and Kell antibodies, and that most mysterious of sanguinary attributes, known as rhesus, which is also a type of monkey.

313

Everything has shape, if you look for it. There is no escape from form.

But before blood has its day, I shall take wing (like the parahamsa gander who can soar out of one element into another) and return, briefly, to the affairs of my inner world; because although the fall of Evie Burns ended my ostracism by the hilltop children, still I found it difficult to forgive; and for a time, holding myself solitary and aloof, I immersed myself in the events inside my head, in the early history of the association of the midnight children.

To be honest: I didn't like Shiva. I disliked the roughness of his tongue, the crudity of his ideas; and I was beginning to suspect him of a string of terrible crimes – although I found it impossible to find any evidence in his thoughts, because he, alone of the children of midnight, could close off from me any part of his thoughts he chose to keep to himself – which, in itself, increased my growing dislike and suspicion of the rat-faced fellow. However, I was nothing if not fair; and it would not have been fair to have kept him apart from the other members of the Conference.

I should explain that as my mental facility increased, I found that it was possible not only to pick up the children's transmissions; not only to broadcast my own messages; but also (since I seem to be stuck with this radio metaphor) to act as a sort of national network, so that by opening my transformed mind to all the children I could turn it into a kind of forum in which they could talk to one another, through me. So, in the early days of 1958, the five hundred and eighty-one children would assemble, for one hour, between midnight and one a.m., in the lok sabha or parliament of my brain.

We were as motley, as raucous, as undisciplined as any bunch of five hundred and eighty-one ten year olds; and on top of our natural exuberance, there was the excitement of our discovery of each other. After one hour of top-volume yelling jabbering arguing giggling, I would fall exhausted into a sleep too deep for nightmares, and still wake up with a headache; but I didn't mind. Awake I was obliged to face the multiple miseries of maternal perfidy and paternal decline, of the fickleness of friendship and the varied tyrannies of school; asleep, I was at the centre of the most exciting world any child had ever discovered. Despite Shiva, it was nicer to be asleep.

Shiva's conviction that he (or he-and-I) was the natural leader of our group by dint of his (and my) birth on the stroke of midnight had, I was bound to admit, one strong argument in its favour. It seemed to me then – it seems to me now – that the midnight miracle had indeed been remarkably hier-archical in nature, that the children's abilities declined dramatically on the basis of the distance of their time of birth from midnight; but even this was a point of view which was hotly contested . . . 'Whatdoyoumeanhowcanyousaythat,' they chorused, the boy from the Gir forest whose face was absolutely blank and featureless (except for eyes noseholes spaceformouth) and could take on any features he chose, and Harilal who could run at the speed of the wind, and God knows how many others . . . 'Who says it's better to do one thing or another?' And, 'Can you fly? I can *fly*!' And, 'Yah, and me, can you turn one fish into fifty?' And, 'Today I went to visit tomorrow. You can do that? Well then –' . . . in the face of such a storm of protest, even Shiva changed his tune; but he was to find a new one, which would be much more dangerous – dangerous for the Children, and for me.

Because I had found that I was not immune to the lure of leadership. Who found the Children, anyway? Who formed the Conference? Who gave them their meeting-place? Was I not the joint-eldest, and should I not receive the respect and obeisances merited by my seniority? And didn't the one who provided the club-house run the club? . . . To which Shiva, 'Forget all that, man. That club-shub stuff is only for you rich boys!' But – for a time – he was overruled, Parvati-the-witch, the conjurer's daughter from Delhi, took my part (just as, years later, she would save my life), and announced, 'No, listen now, everybody: without Saleem we are nowhere, we can't talk or anything, he is right. Let him be the chief!' And I, 'No, never mind *chief*, just think of me as a . . . a big brother, maybe. Yes; we're a family, of a kind. I'm just the oldest, me.' To which Shiva replied, scornful, but unable to argue: 'Okay, big brother: so now tell us what we do?'

At this point I introduced the Conference to the notions which plagued me all this time: the notions of purpose, and meaning. 'We must think,' I said, 'what we are for.'

I record, faithfully, the views of a typical selection of the Conference members (excepting the circus-freaks, and the ones who, like Sundari the beggar-girl with the knife-scars, had lost their powers, and tended to remain silent in our debates, like poor relations at a feast): among the philosophies and aims suggested were collectivism – 'We should all get together and live somewhere, no? What would we need from anyone else?' – and individualism – 'You say we; but we together are unimportant; what matters is that each of us has a gift to use for his or her own good' – filial duty – 'However we can help our father-mother, that is what it is for us to do' – and infant revolution – 'Now at last we must show all kids that it is possible to get rid of parents!' – capitalism – 'Just think what businesses we could do! How rich, Allah, we could be!' – and altruism – 'Our country needs gifted people; we must ask the government how it wishes to use our skills' – science – 'We must allow ourselves to be studied' – and religion – 'Let us declare ourselves to the world, so that all may glory in God' – courage – 'We should invade Pakistan!' – and cowardice – 'O heavens, we must stay secret, just think what they will do to us, stone us for witches or what-all'; there were declarations of women's rights and pleas for the improvement of the lot of untouchables; landless children dreamed of land and tribals from the hills, of Jeeps;

and there were, also, fantasies of power. 'They can't stop us, man! We can bewitch, and fly, and read minds, and turn them into frogs, and make gold and fishes, and they will fall in love with us, and we can vanish through mirrors and change our sex . . . how will they be able to fight?'

I won't deny I was disappointed. I shouldn't have been; there was nothing unusual about the children except for their gifts; their heads were full of all the usual things, fathers mothers money food land possessions fame power God. Nowhere, in the thoughts of the Conference, could I find anything as new as ourselves . . . but then I was on the wrong track, too; I could not see any more clearly than anyone else; and even when Soumitra the time-traveller said, 'I'm telling you – all this is pointless – they'll finish us before we start!' we all ignored him; with the optimism of youth – which is a more virulent form of the same disease that once infected my grandfather Aadam Aziz – we refused to look on the dark side, and not a single one of us suggested that the purpose of Midnight's Children might be annihilation; that we would have no meaning until we were destroyed.

For the sake of their privacy, I am refusing to distinguish the voices from one another; and for other reasons. For one thing, my narrative could not cope with five hundred and eighty-one fully-rounded personalities; for another, the children, despite their wondrously discrete and varied gifts, remained, to my mind, a sort of many-headed monster, speaking in the myriad tongues of Babel; they were the very essence of multiplicity, and I see no point in dividing them now. (But there were exceptions. In particular, there was Shiva; and there was Parvati-the-witch.)

. . . Destiny, historical role, numen: these were mouthfuls too large for ten-year-old gullets. Even, perhaps, for mine; despite the ever-present admonitions of the fisherman's pointing finger and the Prime Minister's letter, I was constantly distracted from my sniff-given marvels by the tiny occurrences of everyday life, by feeling hungry or sleepy, by monkeying around with the Monkey, or going to the cinema to see *Cobra Woman* or *Vera Cruz,* by my growing longing for long trousers and by the inexplicable below-the-belt heat engendered by the approaching School Social at which we, the boys of the Cathedral and John Connon Boys' High School, would be permitted to dance the box-step and the Mexican Hat Dance with the girls from our sister institution – such as Masha Miovic the champion breast-stroker ('Hee hee,' said Glandy Keith Colaco) and Elizabeth Purkiss and Janey Jackson – European girls, my God, with loose skirts and kissing ways! – in short, my attention was continually seized by the painful, engrossing torture of growing up.

Even a symbolic gander must come down, at last, to earth; so it isn't nearly enough for me now (as it was not then) to confine my story to its miraculous aspects; I must return (as I used to return) to the quotidian; I must permit blood to spill.

The first mutilation of Saleem Sinai, which was rapidly followed by the second, took place one Wednesday early in 1958 – the Wednesday of the much-anticipated Social – under the auspices of the Anglo-Scottish Education Society. That is, it happened at school.

Saleem's assailant: handsome, frenetic, with a barbarian's shaggy moustache: I present the leaping, hair-tearing figure of Mr Emil Zagallo, who taught us geography and gymnastics, and who, that morning, unintentionally precipitated the crisis of my life. Zagallo claimed to be Peruvian, and was fond of catling us jungle-Indians, bead-lovers; he hung a print of a stern, sweaty soldier in a pointy tin hat and metal pantaloons above his blackboard and had a way of stabbing a finger at it in times of stress and shouting, 'You see heem, you savages? Thees man eez civilization! You show heem respect: he's got a *sword*!' And he'd swish his cane through the stonewalled

318

air. We called him Pagal-Zagal, crazy Zagallo, because for all his talk of llamas and conquistadores and the Pacific Ocean we knew, with the absolute certainty of rumour, that he'd been born in a Mazagaon tenement and his Goanese mother had been abandoned by a decamped shipping agent; so he was not only an 'Anglo' but probably a bastard as well. Knowing this, we understood why Zagallo affected his Latin accent, and also why he was always in a fury, why he beat his fists against the stone walls of the classroom; but the knowledge didn't stop us being afraid. And this Wednesday morning, we knew we were in for trouble, because Optional Cathedral had been cancelled.

The Wednesday morning double period was Zagallo's geography class; but only idiots and boys with bigoted parents attended it, because it was also the time when we could choose to troop off to St Thomas's Cathedral in crocodile formation, a long line of boys of every conceivable religious denomination, escaping from school into the bosom of the Christians' considerately optional God. It drove Zagallo wild, but he was helpless; today, however, there was a dark glint in his eye, because the Croaker (that is to say, Mr Crusoe the headmaster) had announced at morning Assembly that Cathedral was cancelled. In a bare, scraped voice emerging from his face of an anaesthetized frog, he sentenced us to double geography and Pagal-Zagal, taking us all by surprise, because we hadn't realized that God was permitted to exercise an option, too. Glumly we trooped into Zagallo's lair; one of the poor idiots whose parents never allowed them to go to Cathedral whispered viciously into my ear, 'You jus' wait: he'll really get you guys today.'

Padma: he really did.

Seated gloomily in class: Glandy Keith Colaco, Fat Perce Fishwala, Jimmy Kapadia the scholarship boy whose father was a taxi-driver, Hairoil Sabarmati, Sonny Ibrahim, Cyrus-the-great and I. Others, too, but there's no time now, because with eyes narrowing in delight, crazy Zagallo is calling us to order.

'Human geography,' Zagallo announces. 'Thees ees *what*? Kapadia?'

'Please sir don't know sir.' Hands fly into the air – five belong to church-banned idiots, the sixth inevitably to Cyrus-the-great. But Zagallo is out for blood today: the godly are going to suffer. 'Feelth from the jongle,' he buffets Jimmy Kapadia, then begins to twist an ear casually, 'Stay in class sometimes and find out!'

'Ow ow ow yes sir sorry sir . . .' Six hands are waving but Jimmy's ear is in danger of coming off. Heroism gets the better of me . . . 'Sir please stop sir he has a heart condition sir!' Which is true; but the truth is dangerous, because now Zagallo is rounding on me: 'So, a leetle arguer, ees eet?' And I am being led by my hair to the front of the class. Under the relieved eyes of my fellow-pupils – *thank God it's him not us* – I writhe in agony beneath imprisoned tufts.

'So answer the question. You know what ees human geography?'

Pain fills my head, obliterating all notions of telepathic cheatery: 'Aiee sir no sir ouch!'

. . . And now it is possible to observe a joke descending on Zagallo, a joke pulling his face apart into the simulacrum of a smile; it is possible to watch his hand darting forward, thumb-and-forefinger extended; to note how thumb-and-forefinger close around the tip of my nose and pull downwards . . . where the nose leads, the head must follow, and finally the nose is hanging down and my eyes are obliged to stare damply at Zagallo's sandalled feet with their dirty toenails while Zagallo unleashes his wit.

'See, boys – you see what we have here? Regard, please, the heedeous face of thees primitive creature. It reminds you of?'

And the eager responses: 'Sir the devil sir.' 'Please sir one cousin of mine!' 'No sir a vegetable sir I don't know which.'

Until Zagallo, shouting above the tumult, 'Silence! Sons of baboons! Thees object here' – a tug on my nose – '*thees* is human geography!'

'How sir where sir what sir?'

Zagallo is laughing now. 'You don't see?' he guffaws. 'In the face of thees ugly ape you don't see the whole map of *India*?'

'Yes sir no sir you show us sir!'

'See here – the Deccan peninsula hanging down!' Again ouchmynose.

'Sir sir if that's the map of India what are the stains sir?' It is Glandy Keith Colaco feeling bold. Sniggers, titters from my fellows. And Zagallo, taking the question in his stride: 'These stains,' he cries, 'are Pakistan! Thees birthmark on the right ear is the East Wing; and thees horrible stained left cheek, the West! Remember, stupid boys: Pakistan ees a stain on the face of India!'

'Ho ho,' the class laughs, 'Absolute master joke, sir!'

But now my nose has had enough; staging its own, unprompted revolt against the grasping thumb-and-forefinger, it unleashes a weapon of its own . . . a large blob of shining goo emerges from the left nostril, to plop into Mr Zagallo's palm. Fat Perce Fishwala yells, 'Lookit that, sir! The drip from his nose, sir! Is that supposed to be *Ceylon*?'

His palm smeared with goo, Zagallo loses his jokey mood. 'Animal,' he curses me, 'You see what you do?' Zagallo's hand releases my nose; returns to hair. Nasal refuse is wiped into my neatly-parted locks. And now, once again, my hair is seized; once again, the hand is pulling . . . but upwards now, and my head has jerked upright, my feet are moving on to tiptoe, and Zagallo, 'What are you? Tell me what you are!'

'Sir an animal sir!'

The hand pulls harder higher. 'Again.' Standing on my toenails now, I yelp: 'Aiee sir an animal an animal: please sir aiee!'

And still harder and still higher . . . 'Once more!' But suddenly it ends; my feet are flat on the ground again; and the class has fallen into a deathly hush.

'Sir,' Sonny Ibrahim is saying, 'you pulled his hair out, sir.'

And now the cacophony: 'Look sir, blood.' 'He's bleeding sir.' 'Please sir shall I take him to the nurse?'

Mr Zagallo stood like a statue with a clump of my hair in his fist. While I – too shocked to feel any pain – felt the patch on my head where Mr Zagallo had created a monkish tonsure, a circle where hair would never grow again, and realized that the curse of my birth, which connected me to my country, had managed to find yet one more unexpected expression of itself.

Two days later, Croaker Crusoe announced that, unfortunately, Mr Emil Zagallo was leaving the staff for personal reasons; but I knew what the reasons were. My uprooted hairs had stuck to his hands, like bloodstains that wouldn't wash out, and nobody wants a teacher with hair on his palms, 'The first sign of madness,' as Glandy Keith was fond of saying, 'and the second sign is looking for them.'

Zagallo's legacy: a monk's tonsure; and, worse than that, a whole set of new taunts, which my classmates flung at me while we waited for school buses to take us home to get dressed for the Social: 'Snot-nose is a bal-die!' and, 'Sniffer's got a map-face!' When Cyrus arrived in the bus-queue, I tried to turn the crowd against him, by attempting to set up a chant of 'Cyrus-the-great, Born on a plate, In nineteen hundred and forty-eight,' but nobody took up the offer.

So we come to the events of the Cathedral School Social. At which bullies became instruments of destiny, and fingers were transmuted into fountains, and Masha Miovic, the legendary breast-stroker, fell into a dead faint . . . I arrived at the Social with the nurse's bandage still on my head. I was late, because it hadn't been easy to persuade my mother to let me come; so by the time I stepped into the Assembly Hall, beneath streamers and balloons and the professionally suspicious gazes of bony female chaperones, all the best girls were already box-stepping and Mexican-Hatting with absurdly smug partners. Naturally, the prefects had the pick of the ladies; I watched them with passionate envy, Guzder and Joshi and Stevenson and Rushdie and Talyarkhan and Tayabali and Jussawalla and Waglé and King; I tried butting in on them during excuse-mes but when they saw my bandage and my cucumber of a nose and the stains on my face they just laughed and turned their backs . . . hatred burgeoning in my bosom, I ate potato chips and drank Bubble-Up and Vimto and told myself, 'Those jerks; if they knew who I was they'd get out of my way pretty damn quick!' But still the fear of revealing my true nature was stronger than my somewhat abstract desire for the whirling European girls.

'Hey, Saleem, isn't it? Hey, man, what happened to you?' I was dragged out of my bitter, solitary reverie (even Sonny had someone to dance with; but then, he had his forcep-hollows, and he didn't wear underpants – there were reasons for his attractiveness) by a voice behind my left shoulder, a low, throaty voice, full of promises – but also of menace. A girl's voice. I turned with a sort of jump and found myself staring at a vision with golden hair and a prominent and famous chest . . . my God, she was fourteen years old, why was she talking to me? . . . 'My name is Masha Miovic,' the vision said, 'I've met your sister.'

Of course! The Monkey's heroines, the swimmers from Walsingham School, would certainly know the School's champion breast-stroker! . . . 'I know . . .' I stuttered, 'I know your name.'

'And I know yours,' she straightened my tie, 'so that's fair.' Over her shoulder, I saw Glandy Keith and Fat Perce watching us in drooling paroxysms of envy. I straightened my back and pushed out my shoulders. Masha Miovic asked

323

again about my bandage. 'It's nothing,' I said in what I hoped was a deep voice, 'A sporting accident.' And then, working feverishly to hold my voice steady, 'Would you like to . . . to dance?'

'Okay,' said Masha Miovic, 'But don't try any smooching.'

Saleem takes the floor with Masha Miovic, swearing not to smooch. Saleem and Masha, doing the Mexican Hat; Masha and Saleem, box-stepping with the best of them! I allow my face to adopt a superior expression; you see, you don't have to be a prefect to get a girl! . . . The dance ended; and, still on top of my wave of elation, I said, 'Would you care for a stroll, you know, in the quad?'

Masha Miovic smiling privately. 'Well, yah, just for a sec; but hands off, okay?'

Hands off, Saleem swears. Saleem and Masha, taking the air . . . man, this is fine. This is the life. Goodbye Evie, hello breast-stroke . . . Glandy Keith Colaco and Fat Perce Fishwala step out of the shadows of the quadrangle. They are giggling: 'Hee hee.' Masha Miovic looks puzzled as they block our path. 'Hoo hoo,' Fat Perce says, 'Masha, hoo hoo. Some date you got there.' And I, 'Shut up, you.' Whereupon Glandy Keith, 'You wanna know how he got his war-wound, Mashy?' And Fat Perce, 'Hee hoo ha.' Masha says, 'Don't be *crude*; he got it in a sporting accident!' Fat Perce and Glandy Keith are almost falling over with mirth; then Fishwala reveals all. 'Zagallo pulled his hair out in class!' Hee hoo. And Keith, 'Snotnose is a bal-die!' And both together, 'Sniffer's got a map-face!' There is puzzlement on Masha Miovic's face. And something more, some budding spirit of sexual mischief . . . 'Saleem, they're being so rude about you!'

'Yes,' I say, 'ignore them.' I try to edge her away. But she goes on, 'You aren't going to let them get away with it?' There are beads of excitement on her upper lip; her tongue is in the corner of her mouth; the eyes of Masha Miovic say, *What are you? A man or a mouse?* . . . and under the spell of the champion breast-stroker, something else floats into my head: the image of two irresistible knees; and now I am rushing at Colaco and Fishwala; while they are distracted by giggles, my knee drives into Glandy's groin; before he's dropped, a similar genuflection has laid Fat Perce low. I turn to my mistress; she applauds, softly. 'Hey man, pretty good.'

But now my moment has passed; and Fat Perce is picking himself up, and Glandy Keith is already moving towards me . . . abandoning all pretence of manhood, I turn and run. And the two bullies are after me and behind them comes Masha Miovic calling, 'Where are you running, little hero?' But there's no time for her now, mustn't let them get me, into the nearest classroom and try and shut the door, but Fat Perce's foot is in the way and now the two of them are inside too and I dash at the door, I grab it with my right hand, trying to force it open, *get out if you can*, they are pushing the door shut, but I'm pulling with the strength of my fear, I have it open a few inches, my hand curls around it, and now Fat Perce slams all his weight against the door and it shuts too fast for me to get my hand out of the way and it's shut. A thud. And outside, Masha Miovic arrives and looks down at the floor; and sees the top third of my middle finger lying there like a lump of well-chewed bubble-gum. This was the point at which she fainted.

No pain. Everything very far away. Fat Perce and Glandy Keith fleeing, to get help or to hide. I look at my hand out of pure curiosity. My finger has become a fountain: red liquid spurts out to the rhythm of my heart-beat. Never knew a finger held so much blood. Pretty. Now here's nurse, don't worry, nurse. Only a scratch. *Your parents are being phoned; Mr Crusoe is getting his car keys*. Nurse is putting a great wad of cotton-wool over the stump. Filling up like red candyfloss. And now Crusoe. Get in the car, Saleem, your mother is going straight to the hospital. Yes sir. And the bit, has anybody got the *bit*? Yes headmaster here it is. Thank you nurse. Probably

no use but you never know. Hold this while I drive, Saleem
. . . and holding up my severed finger-tip in my unmutilated
left hand, I am driven to the Breach Candy Hospital through
the echoing streets of night.

At the hospital: white walls stretchers everyone talking at
once. Words pour around me like fountains. 'O God preserve
us, my little piece-of-the-moon, what have they done to you?'
To which old Crusoe, 'Heh heh. Mrs Sinai. Accidents will
happen. Boys will be.' But my mother, enraged, 'What kind
of school? Mr Caruso? I'm here with my son's finger in pieces
and you tell me. Not good enough. No, sir.' And now, while
Crusoe, 'Actually the name's – like Robinson, you know –
heh heh,' the doctor is approaching and a question is being
asked, whose answer will change the world.

'Mrs Sinai, your blood group, please? The boy has lost
blood. A transfusion may be necessary.' And Amina: 'I am A;
but my husband, O.' And now she is crying, breaking down,
and still the doctor, 'Ah; in that case, are you aware of your
son's . . .' But she, the doctor's daughter, must admit she
cannot answer the question: Alpha or Omega? 'Well in that
case a very quick test; but on the subject of rhesus?' My
mother, through her tears: 'Both my husband and I, rhesus
positive.' And the doctor, 'Well, good, that at least.'

But when I am on the operating table – 'Just sit there, son,
I'll give you a local anaesthetic, no, madam, he's in shock,
total anaesthesia would be impossible, all right son, just hold
your finger up and still, help him nurse, and it'll be over in a
jiffy' – while the surgeon is sewing up the stump and
performing the miracle of transplanting the roots of the nail,
all of a sudden there's a fluster in the background, a million
miles away, and 'Have you got a second Mrs Sinai' and I can't
hear properly . . . words float across the infinite distance . . .
Mrs Sinai, you are sure? O and A? A and O? And rhesus
negative, both of you? Heterozygous or homozygous? No,
there must be some mistake, how can he be . . . I'm sorry,

absolutely clear . . . positive . . . and neither A nor . . . excuse me, Madam, but is he your . . . not adopted or . . . The hospital nurse interposes herself between me and miles-away chatter, but it's no good, because now my mother is shrieking, 'But of course you must believe me, doctor; my God, *of course he is our son*!'

Neither A nor O. And the rhesus factor: impossibly negative. And zygosity offers no clues. And present in the blood, rare Kell antibodies. And my mother, crying, crying-crying, crying . . . 'I don't understand. A doctor's daughter, and I don't understand.'

Have Alpha and Omega unmasked me? Is rhesus pointing its unanswerable finger? And will Mary Pereira be obliged to . . . I wake up in a cool, white, Venetian-blinded room with All-India Radio for company. Tony Brent is singing: 'Red Sails In The Sunset'.

Ahmed Sinai, his face ravaged by whisky and now by something worse, stands beside the Venetian blind. Amina, speaking in whispers. Again, snatches across the million miles of distance. Janumplease. Ibegyou. No, what are you saying. Of course it was. Of course you are the. How could you think I would. Who could it have. O God don't just stand and look. I swear Iswearonmymother'shead. Now shh he is . . .

A new song from Tony Brent, whose repertoire today is uncannily similar to Wee Willie Winkie's: 'How Much Is That Doggie In The Window?' hangs in the air, floating on radio waves. My father advances on my bed, towers over me, I've never seen him look like this before. 'Abba . . .' And he, 'I should have known. Just look, where am I in that face. That nose, I should have . . .' He turns on his heel and leaves the room; my mother follows him, too distraught to whisper now: 'No, janum, I won't let you believe such things about me! I'll kill myself! I'll,' and the door swings shut behind them. There is a noise outside: like a clap. Or a slap. Most of what matters in your life takes place in your absence.

Tony Brent begins crooning his latest hit into my good ear: and assures me, melodiously, that 'The Clouds Will Soon Roll By'.

. . . And now I, Saleem Sinai, intend briefly to endow myself-then with the benefits of hindsight; destroying the unities and conventions of fine writing, I make him cognizant of what was to come, purely so that he can be permitted to think the following thoughts: 'O eternal opposition of inside and outside! Because a human being, inside himself, is anything but a whole, anything but homogeneous; all kinds of everywhichthing are jumbled up inside him, and he is one person one minute and another the next. The body, on the other hand, is homogeneous as anything. Indivisible, a one-piece suit, a sacred temple, if you will. It is important to preserve this wholeness. But the loss of my finger (which was conceivably foretold by the pointing digit of Raleigh's fisherman), not to mention the removal of certain hairs from my head, has undone all that. Thus we enter into a state of affairs which is nothing short of revolutionary; and its effect on history is bound to be pretty damn startling. Uncork the body, and God knows what you permit to come tumbling out. Suddenly you are forever other than you were; and the world becomes such that parents can cease to be parents, and love can turn to hate. And these, mark you, are only the effects on private life. The consequences for the sphere of public action, as will be shown, are – were – will be no less profound.'

Finally, withdrawing my gift of foreknowledge, I leave you with the image of a ten-year-old boy with a bandaged finger, sitting in a hospital bed, musing about blood and noises-like-claps and the expression on his father's face; zooming out slowly into long-shot, I allow the sound-track music to drown my words, because Tony Brent is reaching the end of his medley, and his finale, too, is the same as Winkie's: 'Good Night, Ladies' is the name of the song. Merrily it rolls along, rolls along, rolls along . . .

(Fade-out.)

The Kolynos Kid

From ayah to Widow, I've been the sort of person *to whom things have been done*; but Saleem Sinai, perennial victim, persists in seeing himself as protagonist. Despite Mary's crime; setting aside typhoid and snake-venom; dismissing two accidents, in washing-chest and circus-ring (when Sonny Ibrahim, master lock-breaker, permitted my budding horns of temples to invade his forcep-hollows, and through this combination unlocked the door to the midnight children); disregarding the effects of Evie's push and my mother's infidelity; in spite of losing my hair to the bitter violence of Emil Zagallo and my finger to the lip-licking goads of Masha Miovic; setting my face against all indications to the contrary, I shall now amplify, in the manner and with the proper solemnity of a man of science, my claim to a place at the centre of things.

'. . . Your life, which will be, in a sense, the mirror of our own,' the Prime Minister wrote, obliging me scientifically to face the question: *In what sense?* How, in what terms, may the career of a single individual be said to impinge on the fate of a nation? I must answer in adverbs and hyphens: I was linked to history both literally and metaphorically, both actively and passively, in what our (admirably modern) scientists might term 'modes of connection' composed of 'dualistically-combined configurations' of the two pairs of opposed adverbs given above. This is why hyphens are necessary: actively-literally, passively-metaphorically, actively-metaphorically and passively-literally, I was inextricably entwined with my world.

Sensing Padma's unscientific bewilderment, I revert to the inexactitudes of common speech: By the combination of 'active' and 'literal' I mean, of course, all actions of mine which directly – *literally* – affected, or altered the course of, seminal historical events, for instance the manner in which I provided the language marchers with their battle-cry. The union of 'passive' and 'metaphorical' encompasses all socio-political trends and events which, merely by existing, affected me metaphorically – for example, by reading between the lines of the episode entitled 'The Fisherman's Pointing Finger', you will perceive *the* unavoidable connection between the infant state's attempts at rushing towards full-sized adulthood and my own early, explosive efforts at growth . . . Next, 'passive' and 'literal', when hyphenated, cover all moments at which national events had a direct bearing upon the lives of myself and my family – under this heading you should file the freezing of my father's assets, and also the explosion at Walkeshwar Reservoir, which unleased the great cat invasion. And finally there is the 'mode' of the 'active-metaphorical', which groups together those occasions on which things done by or to me were mirrored in the macrocosm of public affairs, and my private existence was shown to be symbolically at one with history. The mutilation of my middle finger was a case in point, because when I was detached from my fingertip and blood (neither Alpha nor Omega) rushed out in fountains, a similar thing happened to history, and all sorts of everywhichthing began pouring out all over us; but because history operates on a grander scale than any individual, it took a good deal longer to stitch it back together and mop up the mess.

'Passive-metaphorical', 'passive-literal', 'active-metaphorical': the Midnight Children's Conference was all three; but it never became what I most wanted it to be; we never operated in the

331

first, most significant of the 'modes of connection'. The 'active-literal' passed us by.

Transformation without end: nine-fingered Saleem has been brought to the doorway of the Breach Candy Hospital by a squat blonde nurse whose face is frozen into a smile of terrifying insincerity. He is blinking in the hot glare of the outside world, trying to focus on two swimming shadow-shapes coming towards him out of the sun; 'See?' the nurse coos, 'See who's come to get you, then?' And Saleem realizes that something terrible has gone wrong with the world, because his mother and father, who should have come to collect him, have apparently been transformed *en route* into his ayah Mary Pereira and his Uncle Hanif.

Hanif Aziz boomed like the horns of ships in the harbour and smelled like an old tobacco factory. I loved him dearly, for his laughter, his unshaven chin, his air of having been put together rather loosely, his lack of co-ordination which made his every movement fraught with risk. (When he visited Buckingham Villa my mother hid the cut-glass vases.) Adults never trusted him to behave with proper decorum ('Watch out for the Communists!' he bellowed, and they blushed), which was a bond between himself and all children – other people's children, since he and Pia were childless. Uncle Hanif who would one day, without warning, take a walk off the roof of his home.

. . . He wallops me in the back, toppling me forwards into Mary's arms. 'Hey, little wrestler! You look fine!' But Mary, hastily, 'But so thin, Jesus! They haven't been feeding you properly? You want cornflour pudding? Banana mashed with milk? Did they give you chips?' . . . while Saleem is looking round at this new world in which everything seems to be going too fast; his voice, when it comes, sounds high-pitched, as though somebody had speeded it up: 'Amma-Abba?' he asks. 'The Monkey?' And Hanif booms, 'Yes, tickety-boo!

The boy is really ship-shape! Come on phaelwan: a ride in my Packard, okay?' And talking at the same time is Mary Pereira, 'Chocolate cake,' she is promising, 'laddoos, pista-ki-lauz, meat samosas, kulfi. So thin you got, baba, the wind will blow you away.' The Packard is driving away; it is failing to turn off Warden Road, up the two-storey hillock; and Saleem, 'Hanif mamu, where are we . . .' No time to get it out; Hanif roars, 'Your Pia aunty is waiting! My God, you see if we don't have a number one good time!' His voice drops conspiratorially: 'Lots,' he says darkly, 'of *fun*.' And Mary: 'Arré baba yes! Such steak! And green chutney!' . . .

'Not the dark one,' I say, captured at last; relief appears on the cheeks of my captors. 'No no no,' Mary babbles, 'light green, baba. Just like you like.' And, '*Pale* green!' Hanif is bellowing, 'My God, green like grasshoppers!'

All too fast . . . we are at Kemp's Corner now, cars rushing around like bullets . . . but one thing is unchanged. On his billboard, the Kolynos Kid is grinning, the eternal pixie grin of the boy in the green chlorophyll cap, the lunatic grin of the timeless Kid, who endlessly squeezes an inexhaustible tube of toothpaste on to a bright green brush: *Keep Teeth Kleen And Keep Teeth Brite, Keep Teeth Kolynos Super White!* . . . and you may wish to think of me, too, as an involuntary Kolynos Kid, squeezing crises and transformations out of a bottomless tube, extruding time on to my metaphorical toothbrush; clean, white time with green chlorophyll in the stripes.

This, then, was the beginning of my first exile. (There will be a second, and a third.) I bore it uncomplainingly. I had guessed, of course, that there was one question I must never ask; that I had been loaned out, like a comic-book from the Scandal Point Second Hand Library, for some indefinite period; and that when my parents wanted me back, they would send for me. When, or even if: because I blamed myself not a little for my banishment. Had I not inflicted upon myself one more deformity to add to bandylegs cucumbernose horn-temples staincheeks? Was it not possible that my mutilated finger had been (as my announcement of my voices had nearly been), for my long-suffering parents, the last straw? That I was no longer a good business risk, no longer worth the investment of their love and protection? . . . I decided to reward my uncle and aunt for their kindness in taking in so wretched a creature as myself, to play the model nephew and await events. There were times when I wished that the Monkey would come and see me, or even call me on the phone; but dwelling on such matters only punctured the balloon of my equanimity, so I did my best to put them out of my mind. Besides, living with Hanif and Pia Aziz turned out to be exactly what my uncle had promised: lots of fun.

They made all the fuss of me that children expect, and accept graciously, from childless adults. Their flat overlooking Marine Drive wasn't large, but there was a balcony from which I could drop monkey-nut shells on to the heads of passing pedestrians; there was no spare bedroom, but I was offered a deliriously soft white sofa with green stripes (an early proof of my transformation into the Kolynos Kid); ayah Mary, who had apparently followed me into exile, slept on the floor by my side. By day, she filled my stomach with the promised cakes and sweetmeats (paid for, I now believe, by my mother); I should have grown immensely fat, except that I had begun once again to grow in other directions, and at the end of the year of accelerated history (when I was only eleven and a half) I had actually attained my full adult height, as if someone had grasped me by the folds of my puppy-fat and squeezed them harder than any toothpaste-tube, so that inches shot out of me under the pressure. Saved from obesity by the Kolynos effect, I basked in my uncle and aunt's delight at having a child around the house. When I spilt 7-Up on the carpet or sneezed into my dinner, the worst my uncle would say was 'Hai-yo! Black man!' in his booming steamship's voice, spoiling the effect by grinning hugely. Meanwhile, my aunty Pia was becoming the next in the long series of women who have bewitched and finally undone me good and proper.

(I should mention that, while I stayed in the Marine Drive apartment, my testicles, forsaking the protection of pelvic bone, decided prematurely and without warning to drop into their little sacs. This event, too, played its part in what followed.)

My mumani – my aunt – the divine Pia Aziz: to live with her was to exist in the hot sticky heart of a Bombay talkie. In those days, my uncle's career in the cinema had entered a dizzy decline, and, for such is the way of the world, Pia's star had gone into decline along with his. In her presence, however, thoughts of failure were impossible. Deprived of film roles, Pia had turned her life into a feature picture, in which I was cast in an increasing number of bit-parts. I was the Faithful Body-Servant: Pia in petticoats, soft hips rounding towards my desperately-averted eyes, giggling while her eyes, bright with antimony, flashed imperiously – 'Come on, boy, what are you shy for, holds these pleats in my sari while I fold.' I was her Trusted Confidant, too. While my uncle sat on chlorophyll-striped sofa pounding out scripts which nobody would ever film, I listened to the nostalgic soliloquy of my aunt, trying to keep my eyes away from two impossible orbs, spherical as melons, golden as mangoes: I refer, you will have guessed, to the adorable breasts of Pia mumani. While she, sitting on her bed, one arm flung across her brow, declaimed: 'Boy, you know, I am great actress; I have interpreted several major roles! But look, what fate will do! Once, boy, goodness knows who would beg absolutely to come to this flat; once the reporters of *Filmfare* and *Screen Goddess* would pay black-money to get inside! Yes, and dancing, and I was well-known at Venice restaurant – all of those great jazzmen came to sit at my feet, yes, even that Braz. Boy, after *Lovers of Kashmir*, who was a bigger star? Not Poppy; not Vyjayantimala; not one person!' And I, nodding emphatically, no-naturally-nobody, while her wondrous skin-wrapped melons heaved and . . . With a dramatic cry, she went on: 'But even then, in the time of our world-beating fame, every picture a golden jubilee movie, this uncle of yours wants to live in a two-room flat like a clerk! So I make no fuss; I am not like some of your cheap-type actresses; I live simply and ask for no Cadillacs or air-conditioners or Dunlopillo beds from England; no swimming pools shaped like bikinis like that Roxy Vishwanatham's! Here, like a wife of the masses, I have stayed; here, now, I am rotting! Rotting, absolutely. But I know this: my face is my fortune; after that, what riches do I need?' And I, anxiously agreeing: 'Mumani, none; none at all.' She shrieked wildly; even my slap-deafened ear was penetrated. 'Yes, of course, you also want me to be poor! All the world wants Pia to be in rags! Even that one, your uncle, writing his boring-boring scripts! O my God, I tell him, put in dances, or exotic locations! Make your villains villainous, why not, make heroes like men! But he says, no, all that is rubbish, he sees that now – although once he was not so proud! Now he must write about ordinary people and social problems! And I say, yes, Hanif, do that, that is good; but put in a little comedy routine, a little dance for your Pia to do, and tragedy and drama also; that is what the Public is wanting!' Her eyes were brimming with tears. 'So you know what he is writing now? About . . .' she looked as if her heart would break '. . . the Ordinary Life of a Pickle Factory!'

'Shh, mumani, shh,' I beg, 'Hanif mamu will hear!'

'Let him hear!' she stormed, weeping copiously now; 'Let his mother hear also, in Agra; they will make me die for shame!'

Reverend Mother had never liked her actress daughter-in-law. I overheard her once telling my mother: 'To marry an actress, whatsitsname, my son has made his bed in the gutter, soon, whatsitsname, she will be making him drink alcohol and also eat some pig.' Eventually, she accepted the inevitability of the match with bad grace; but she took to writing improving epistles to Pia. 'Listen, daughter,' she wrote, 'don't do this actressy thing. Why to do such shameless behaviour? Work, yes, you girls have modern ideas, but to dance naked on the screen! When for a small sum only you could acquire the concession on a good petrol pump. From my own pocket I would get it for you in two minutes. Sit in an office, hire attendants; that is proper work.' None of us ever knew whence Reverend Mother acquired her dream of petrol pumps, which would be the growing obsession of her old age; but she bombarded Pia with it, to the actress's disgust.

'Why that woman doesn't ask me to be shorthand typist?' Pia wailed to Hanif and Mary and me at breakfast. 'Why not taxi-driver, or handloom weaver? I tell you, this pumpery-shumpery makes me wild.'

My uncle quivered (for once in his life) on the edge of anger. 'There is a child present,' he said, 'and she is your mother; show her respect.'

'Respect she can have,' Pia flounced from the room, 'but she wants *gas*.'

. . . And my most-treasured bit-part of all was played out when during Pia and Hanif's regular card-games with friends, I was promoted to occupy the sacred place of the son she never had. (Child of an unknown union, I have had more mothers than most mothers have children; giving birth to parents has been one of my stranger talents – a form of reverse fertility beyond the control of contraception, and even of the Widow herself.) In the company of visitors, Pia Aziz would cry: 'Look, friends, here's my own crown prince! The jewel in my ring! The pearl in my necklace!' And she would draw me towards her, cradling my head so that my nose was pushed down against her chest and nestled wonderfully between the soft pillows of her indescribable . . . unable to cope with such delights, I pulled my head away.

337

But I was her slave; and I know now why she permitted herself such familiarity with me. Prematurely testicled, growing rapidly, I nevertheless wore (fraudulently) the badge of sexual innocence: Saleem Sinai, during his sojourn at his uncle's home, was still in shorts. Bare knees proved my childishness to Pia; deceived by ankle-socks, she held my face against her breasts while her sitar-perfect voice whispered in my good ear: 'Child, child, don't fear; your clouds will soon roll by.'

For my uncle, as well as my histrionic aunt, I acted out (with growing polish) the part of the surrogate son. Hanif Aziz was to be found during the day on the striped sofa, pencil and exercise book in hand, writing his pickle epic. He wore his usual lungi wound loosely around his waist and fastened with an enormous safety-pin; his legs protruded hairily from its folds. His fingernails bore the stains of a lifetime of Gold Flakes; his toenails seemed similarly discoloured. I imagined him smoking cigarettes with his toes. Highly impressed by the vision, I asked him if he could, in fact, perform this feat; and without a word, he inserted Gold Flake between big toe and its sidekick and wound himself into bizarre contortions. I clapped wildly, but he seemed to be in some pain for the rest of the day.

I ministered to his needs as a good son should, emptying ashtrays, sharpening pencils, bringing water to drink; while he, who after his fabulist beginnings had remembered that he was his father's son and dedicated himself against everything which smacked of the unreal, scribbled out his ill-fated screenplay.

'Sonny Jim,' he informed me, 'this damn country has been dreaming for five thousand years. It's about time it started waking up.' Hanif was fond of railing against princes and demons, gods and heroes, against, in fact, the entire iconography of the Bombay film; in the temple of illusions, he had become the high priest of reality; while I, conscious of my miraculous nature, which involved me beyond all mitigation in the (Hanif-despised) myth-life of India, bit my lip and didn't know where to look.

Hanif Aziz, the only realistic writer working in the Bombay film industry, was writing the story of a pickle-factory created, run and worked in entirely by women. There were long scenes describing the formation of a trade union; there were detailed descriptions of the pickling process. He would quiz Mary Pereira about recipes; they would discuss, for hours, the perfect blend of lemon, lime and garam masala. It is ironic that this arch-disciple of naturalism should have been so skilful (if unconscious) a prophet of his own family's fortunes; in the indirect kisses of the *Lovers of Kashmir* he foretold my mother and her Nadir-Qasim's meetings at the Pioneer Café; and in his unfilmed chutney scenario, too, there lurked a prophecy of deadly accuracy.

He besieged Homi Catrack with scripts. Catrack produced none of them; they sat in the small Marine Drive apartment, covering every available surface, so that you had to pick them off the toilet seat before you could lift it; but Catrack (out of charity? Or for another, soon-to-be-revealed reason?) paid my uncle a studio salary. That was how they survived, Hanif and Pia, on the largesse of the man who would, in time, become the second human being to be murdered by mushrooming Saleem.

Homi Catrack begged him, 'Maybe just one love scene?' And Pia, 'What do you think, village people are going to give their rupees to see women pickling Alfonsos?' But Hanif, obdurately: 'This is a film about work, not kissing. And nobody pickles Alfonsos. You must use mangoes with bigger stones.'

The ghost of Joe D'Costa did not, so far as I know, follow Mary Pereira into exile; however, his absence only served to increase her anxiety. She began, in these Marine Drive days, to fear that he would become visible to others besides herself, and reveal, during her absence, the awful secrets of what happened at Dr Narlikar's Nursing Home on Independence night. So each morning she left the apartment in a state of jelly-like worry, arriving at Buckingham Villa in near-collapse; only when she found that Joe had remained both invisible and silent did she relax. But after she returned to Marine Drive, laden with samosas and cakes and chutneys, her anxiety began to mount once again . . . but as I had resolved (having troubles enough of my own) to keep out of all heads except the Children's, I did not understand why.

Panic attracts panic; on her journeys, sitting in jam-packed buses (the trams had just been discontinued), Mary heard all sorts of rumours and tittle-tattle, which she relayed to me as matters of absolute fact. According to Mary, the country was in the grip of a sort of supernatural invasion. 'Yes, baba, they say in Kurukshetra an old Sikh woman woke up in her hut and saw the old-time war of the Kurus and Pandavas happening right outside! It was in the papers and all, she pointed to the place where she saw the chariots of Arjun and Kama, and there were truly wheel-marks in the mud! Baap-re-baap, such so-bad things: at Gwalior they have seen the ghost of the Rani of Jhansi; rakshasas have been seen many-headed like Ravana, doing things to women and pulling down trees with one finger. I am good Christian woman, baba; but it gives me fright when they tell that the tomb of Lord Jesus is found in Kashmir. On the tombstones are carved two pierced feet and a local fisherwoman has sworn she saw them bleeding – real blood, God save us! – on Good Friday . . . what is happening, baba, why these old things can't stay dead and not plague honest folk?' And I, wide-eyed, listening; and although my uncle Hanif roared with laughter, I remain, today, half-convinced that in that time of accelerated events and diseased hours the past of India rose up to confound her present; the new-born, secular state was

340

being given an awesome reminder of its fabulous antiquity, in which democracy and votes for women were irrelevant . . . so that people were seized by atavistic longings, and forgetting the new myth of freedom reverted to their old ways, their old regionalist loyalties and prejudices, and the body politic began to crack. As I said: lop off just one finger-tip and you never know what fountains of confusion you will unleash.

'And cows, baba, have been vanishing into thin air; poof! and in the villages, the peasants must starve.'

It was at this time that I, too, was possessed by a strange demon; but in order that you may understand me properly, I must begin my account of the episode on an innocent evening, when Hanif and Pia Aziz had a group of friends round for cards.

My aunty was prone to exaggerate; because although *Filmfare* and *Screen Goddess* were absent, my uncle's house was a popular place. On card-evenings, it would burst at the seams with jazzmen gossiping about quarrels and reviews in American magazines, and singers who carried throat-sprays in their handbags, and members of the Uday Shankar dance-troupe, which was trying to form a new style of dance by fusing Western ballet with bharatanatyam; there were musicians who had been signed up to perform in the All-India Radio music festival, the Sangeet Sammelan; there were painters who argued violently amongst each other. The air was thick with political, and other, chatter. 'As a matter of fact, I am the only artist in India who paints with a genuine sense of ideological commitment!' – 'O, it's too bad about Ferdy, he'll never get another band after this' – 'Menon? Don't talk to me about Krishna. I knew him when he had principles. I, myself, have never abandoned . . .' '. . . Ohé, Hanif yaar, why we don't see Lal Qasim here these days?' And my uncle, looking anxiously towards me: 'Shh . . . what Qasim? I don't know any person by that name.'

. . . And mingling with the hubbub in the apartment, there

was the evening colour and noise of Marine Drive: promenaders with dogs, buying chambeli and channa from hawkers; the cries of beggars and bhel-puri vendors; and the lights coming on in a great arcing necklace, round and up to Malabar Hill . . . I stood on the balcony with Mary Pereira, turning my bad ear to her whispered rumours, the city at my back and the crowding, chatting card-schools before my eyes. And one day, amongst the card-players, I recognized the sunken-eyed, ascetic form of Mr Homi Catrack. Who greeted me with embarrassed heartiness: 'Hi there, young chap! Doing fine? Of course, of course you are!'

My uncle Hanif played rummy dedicatedly; but he was in the thrall of a curious obsession – namely, that he was determined never to lay down a hand until he completed a thirteen-card sequence in hearts. Always hearts; all the hearts, and nothing but the hearts would do. In his quest for this unattainable perfection, my uncle would discard perfectly good threes-of-a-kind, and whole sequences of spades clubs diamonds, to the raucous amusement of his friends. I heard the renowned shehnai-player Ustad Changez Khan (who dyed his hair, so that on hot evenings the tops of his ears were discoloured by running black fluid) tell my uncle: 'Come on, mister; leave this heart business, and just play like the rest of us fellows.' My uncle confronted temptation; then boomed above the din, 'No, dammit, go to the devil and leave me to my game!' He played cards like a fool; but I, who had never seen such singleness of purpose, felt like clapping.

One of the regulars at Hanif Aziz's legendary card-evenings was a *Times of India* staff photographer, who was full of sharp tales and scurrilous stories. My uncle introduced me to him: 'Here's the fellow who put you on the front page, Saleem. Here is Kalidas Gupta. A terrible photographer; a really badmaash type. Don't talk to him too long; he'll make your head spin with scandal!' Kalidas had a head of silver hair and a nose like an eagle. I thought he was wonderful. 'Do you really know scandals?' I asked him; but all he said was, 'Son, if I told, they would make your ears burn.' But he never found out that the evil genius, the *éminence grise* behind the greatest scandal the city had ever known was none other than Saleem Snotnose . . . I mustn't race ahead. The affair of the curious baton of Commander Sabarmati must be recounted in its proper place. Effects must not (despite the tergiversatory nature of time in 1958) be permitted to precede causes.

I was alone on the balcony. Mary Pereira was in the kitchen helping Pia to prepare sandwiches and cheese-pakoras; Hanif Aziz was immersed in his search for the thirteen hearts; and now Mr Homi Catrack came out to stand beside me. 'Breath of fresh air,' he said. 'Yes, sir,' I replied. 'So,' he exhaled deeply. 'So, so. Life is treating you good? Excellent little fellow. Let me shake you by the hand.' Ten-year-old hand is swallowed up by film magnate's fist (the left hand; the mutilated right hand hangs innocently by my side) . . . and now a shock. Left palm feels paper being thrust into it – sinister paper, inserted by dexterous fist! Catrack's grip tightens; his voice becomes low, but also cobra-like, sibilant; inaudible in the room with the green-striped sofa, his words penetrate my one good ear: 'Give this to your aunty. Secretly secretly. Can do? And keep mum; or I'll send the police to cut your tongue out.' And now, loud and cheery. 'Good! Glad to see you in such high spirits!' Homi Catrack is patting me on the head; and moving back to his game.

Threatened by policemen, I have remained silent for two decades; but no longer. Now, everything has to come out.

The card-school broke up early: 'The boy has to sleep,' Pia was whispering, 'Tomorrow he goes to school again.' I found no opportunity of being alone with my aunt; I was tucked up on my sofa with the note still clutched in my left fist. Mary was asleep on the floor . . . I decided to feign a nightmare, (Deviousness did not come unnaturally to me.) Unfortunately, however, I was so tired that I fell asleep; and, in the event, there was no need to pretend: because I dreamed the murder of my classmate Jimmy Kapadia.

. . . We are playing football in the main stairwell at school, on red tiles, slipping sliding. A black cross set in the blood-red tiles. Mr Crusoe at the head of the stairs: 'Mustn't slide down the banisters boys that cross is where one boy fell.' Jimmy plays football on the cross. 'The cross is lies,' Jimmy says, 'They tell you lies to spoil your fun.' His mother calls up on the telephone. 'Don't play Jimmy your bad heart.' The bell. The telephone, replaced, and now the bell . . . Ink-pellets stain the classroom air. Fat Perce and Glandy Keith have fun. Jimmy wants a pencil, prods me in the ribs. 'Hey man, you got a pencil, give. Two ticks, man.' I give. Zagallo enters. Zagallo's hand is up for silence: look at my hair growing on his palm! Zagallo in pointy tin-soldier hat . . . I must have my pencil back. Stretching out my finger giving Jimmy a poke. 'Sir, please look sir, Jimmy fell!' 'Sir I saw sir Snotnose poked!' 'Snotnose shot Kapadia, sir!' 'Don't play Jimmy your bad heart!' 'You be quiet,' Zagallo cries, 'Jongle feelth, shut up.'

Jimmy in a bundle on the floor. 'Sir sir please sir will they put up a cross?' He borrowed a pencil, I poked, he fell. His father is a taxi-driver. Now the taxi drives into class; a dhobi-bundle is put on the back seat, out goes Jimmy. Ding, a bell. Jimmy's father puts down the taxi flag. Jimmy's father looks at me: 'Snotnose, you'll have to pay the fare.' 'But please sir haven't got the money sir.' And Zagallo: 'We'll put it on your bill.' See my hair on Zagallo's hand. Flames are pouring from Zagallo's eyes. 'Five hundred meelion, what's one death?' Jimmy is dead; five hundred million still alive. I start counting: one two three. Numbers march over Jimmy's grave. One million two million three million four. Who cares if anyone, anyone dies. One hundred million and one two three. Numbers march through the classroom now. Crushing pounding two hundred million three four five. Five hundred million still alive. And only one of me . . .

. . . In the dark of the night, I awoke from the dream of Jimmy Kapadia's death which became the dream of annihilation-by-numbers, yelling howling screaming, but still with the paper in my fist; and a door flew open, to reveal my uncle Hanif and aunt Pia. Mary Pereira tried to comfort me, but Pia was imperious, she was a divine swirl of petticoats and dupatta, she cradled me in her arms: 'Never mind! My diamond, never mind now!' And Uncle Hanif, sleepily: 'Hey, phaelwan! It's okay now; come on, you come with us; bring the boy, Pia!' And now I'm safely in Pia's arms; 'Just for tonight, my pearl, you can sleep with us!' – and there I am, nestling between aunt and uncle, huddling against my mumani's perfumed curves.

Imagine, if you can, my sudden joy; imagine with what speed the nightmare fled from my thoughts, as I nestled against my extraordinary aunt's petticoats! As she re-arranged herself, to get comfortable, and one golden melon caressed my cheek! As Pia's hand sought out mine and grasped it firmly . . . now I discharged my duty. When my aunt's hand wrapped itself around mine, paper passed from palm to palm. I felt her stiffen, silently; then, although I snuggled up closer closer closer, she was lost to me; she was reading in the dark, and the stiffness of her body was increasing; and then suddenly I knew that I had been tricked, that Catrack was my enemy; and only the threat of policemen prevented me from telling my uncle.

(At school, the next day, I was told of Jimmy Kapadia's tragic death, suddenly at home, of a heart seizure. Is it possible to kill a human being by dreaming his death? My mother always said so; and, in that case, Jimmy Kapadia was my first murder victim. Homi Catrack was to be the next.)

When I returned from my first day back at school, having basked in the unusual sheepishness of Fat Perce and Glandy

Keith ('Lissen, yaar, how did we know your finger was in the
... hey, man, we got free tickets for a picture tomorrow, you
want to come?') and my equally unexpected popularity ('No
more Zagallo! Solid, man! You really lost your hair for
something good!'), aunty Pia was out. I sat quietly with uncle
Hanif while, in the kitchen, Mary Pereira prepared dinner. It
was a peaceful little family scene; but the peace was shattered,
abruptly, by the crash of a slamming door. Hanif dropped his
pencil as Pia, having slammed the front door, flung open the
living-room door with equal force. Then he boomed
cheerfully, 'So, wife: what's the drama?' ... But Pia was not
to be defused. 'Scribble,' she said, her hand slicing air, 'Allah,
don't stop for me! So much talent, a person cannot go to the
pot in this house without finding your genius. Are you happy,
husband? We are making much money? God is good to you?'
Still Hanif remained cheerful. 'Come Pia, our little guest is
here. Sit, have tea . . .' Actress Pia froze in an attitude of
disbelief. 'O God! Such a family I have come to! My life is in
ruins, and you offer tea; your mother offers petrol! All is
madness . . .' And uncle Hanif, frowning now: 'Pia, the
boy . . .' A shriek. 'Ahaaa! The boy – but the boy has suffered;
he is suffering now; he knows what it is to lose, to feel
forlorn! I, too, have been abandoned: I am great actress, and
here I sit surrounded by tales of bicycle-postmen and donkey-
cart drivers! What do you know of a woman's grief? Sit, sit,
let some fat rich Parsee film-producer give you charity, never
mind that your wife wears paste jewels and no new saris for
two years; a woman's back is broad, but, beloved husband,
you have made my days into deserts! Go, ignore me now, just
leave me in peace to jump from the window! I will go into the
bedroom now,' she concluded, 'and if you hear no more from
me it is because my heart is broken and I am dead.' More
doors slammed: it was a terrific exit.

Uncle Hanif broke a pencil, absent-mindedly, into two
halves. He shook his head wonderingly: 'What's got into

her?' But I knew . . . I, bearer of secrets, threatened by policemen, I knew and bit my lip. Because, trapped as I was in the crisis of the marriage of my uncle and aunt, I had broken my recently-made rule and entered Pia's head; I had seen her visit to Homi Catrack and knew that, for years now, she had been his fancy-woman; I had heard him telling her that he had tired of her charms, and there was somebody else now; and I, who would have hated him enough just for seducing my beloved aunt, found myself hating him twice as passionately for doing her the dishonour of discarding her.

'Go to her,' my uncle was saying, 'Maybe you can cheer her up.'

The boy Saleem moves through repeatedly-slammed doors to the sanctum of his tragic aunt; and enters, to find her loveliest of bodies splayed out in wondrous abandon across the marital bed – where, only last night, bodies nestled against bodies – where paper passed from hand to hand . . . a hand flutters at her heart; her chest heaves; and the boy Saleem stammers, 'Aunt, O aunt, I'm sorry.'

A banshee-wail from the bed. Tragedienne's arms, flying outwards towards me. 'Hai! Hai, hai! *Ai*-hai-hai!' Needing no further invitation, I fly towards those arms; I fling myself between them, to lie atop my mourning aunt. The arms close around me, tightertighter, nails digging through my school-white shirt, but I don't care! – Because something has started twitching below my S-buckled belt. Aunty Pia thrashes about beneath me in her despair and I thrash with her, remembering to keep my right hand clear of the action. I hold it stiffly out above the fray. One-handed, I begin to caress her, not knowing what I'm doing, I'm only ten years old and still in shorts, but I'm crying because she's crying, and the room is full of the noise – and on the bed as two bodies thrash, two bodies begin to acquire a kind of rhythm, unnameable unthinkable, hips pushing up towards me, while she yells, 'O! O God, O God, O!' And maybe I am yelling too, I can't say, something is taking over from grief here, while my uncle snaps pencils on a striped sofa, something getting stronger, as she writhes and twists beneath me, and at last in the grip of a strength greater than my strength I am bringing down my right hand, I have forgotten my finger, and when it touches her breast, wound presses against skin . . .

'Yaaaouuuu!' I scream with the pain; and my aunt, snapping out of the macabre spell of those few moments, pushes me off her and delivers a resounding wallop to my face. Fortunately, it is the left cheek; there is no danger of damage to my remaining good ear. '*Badmaash*!' my aunty screams, 'A family of maniacs and perverts, woe is me, what woman ever suffered so badly?'

There is a cough in the doorway. I am standing up now, shivering with pain. Pia is standing, too, her hair dripping off her head like tears. Mary Pereira is in the doorway, coughing, scarlet confusion all over her skin, holding a brown paper parcel in her hands.

'See, baba, what I have forgotten,' she finally manages to say, 'You are a big man now: look, your mother has sent you two pairs of nice, white long trousers.'

After I got so indiscreetly carried away while trying to cheer up my aunt, it became difficult for me to remain in the apartment on Marine Drive. Long intense telephone calls were made regularly during the next few days; Hanif persuading someone, while Pia gesticulated, that perhaps now, after five weeks . . . and one evening after I got back from school, my mother picked me up in our old Rover, and my first exile came to an end.

Neither during our drive home, nor at any other time, was I given any explanation for my exile. I decided, therefore, that I would not make it my business to ask. I was wearing long pants now; I was, therefore, a man, and must bear my troubles accordingly. I told my mother: 'The finger is not so

348

bad. Hanif mamu has taught me to hold the pen differently, so I can write okay.' She seemed to be concentrating very hard on the road. 'It was a nice holiday,' I added, politely. 'Thank you for sending me.'

'O child,' she burst out, 'with your face like the sun coming out, what can I tell you? Be good with your father; he is not happy these days.' I said I would try to be good; she seemed to lose control of the wheel and we passed dangerously near a bus. 'What a world,' she said after a time, 'Terrible things happen and you don't know how.'

'I know,' I agreed, 'Ayah has been telling me.' My mother looked at me fearfully, then glared at Mary in the back seat. 'You black woman,' she cried, 'what have you been saying?' I explained about Mary's stories of miraculous events, but the dire rumours seemed to calm my mother down. 'What do you know,' she sighed, 'You are only a child.'

What do I know, Amma? I know about the Pioneer Café! Suddenly, as we drove home, I was filled once again with my recent lust for revenge upon my perfidious mother, a lust which had faded in the brilliant glare of my exile, but which now returned and was united with my new-born loathing of Homi Catrack. This two-headed lust was the demon which possessed me, and drove me into doing the worst thing I ever did . . . 'Everything will be all right,' my mother was saying, 'You just wait and see.'

Yes, mother.

It occurs to me that I have said nothing, in this entire piece, about the Midnight Children's Conference; but then, to tell the truth, they didn't seem very important to me in those days. I had other things on my mind.

Commander Sabarmati's baton

A few months later, when Mary Pereira finally confessed her crime, and revealed the secrets of her eleven-year-long haunting by the ghost of Joseph D'Costa, we learned that, after her return from exile, she was badly shocked by the condition into which the ghost had fallen in her absence. It had begun to decay, so that now bits of it were missing: an ear, several toes on each foot, most of its teeth; and there was a hole in its stomach larger than an egg. Distressed by this crumbling spectre, she asked it (when she was sure nobody else was within earshot): 'O God, Joe, what you been doing to yourself?' He replied that the responsibility of her crime had been placed squarely on his shoulders until she confessed, and it was playing hell with his system. From that moment it became inevitable that she would confess; but each time she looked at me she found herself prevented from doing so. Still, it was only a matter of time.

In the meanwhile, and utterly ignorant of how close I was to being exposed as a fraud, I was attempting to come to terms with a Methwold's Estate in which, too, a number of transformations had occurred. In the first place, my father seemed to want nothing more to do with me, an attitude of mind which I found hurtful but (considering my mutilated body) entirely understandable. In the second place, there was the remarkable change in the fortunes of the Brass Monkey. 'My position in this household,' I was obliged to admit to myself, 'has been usurped.' Because now it was the Monkey whom my father admitted into the abstract sanctum of his office, the Monkey whom he smothered in his squashy belly, and who was obliged to bear the burdens of his dreams about the future. I even heard Mary Pereira singing to the Monkey the little ditty which had been my theme-song all my days: 'Anything you want to be,' Mary sang, 'you can be; You can be just what-all you want!' Even my mother seemed to have caught the mood; and now it was my sister who always got the biggest helping of chips at the dinner-table, and the extra nargisi kofta, and the choicest pasanda. While I – whenever anyone in the house chanced to look at me – was conscious of a deepening furrow between their eyebrows, and an atmosphere of confusion and distrust. But how could I complain? The Monkey had tolerated my special position for years. With the possible exception of the time I fell out of a tree in our garden after she nudged me (which could have been an accident, after all), she had accepted my primacy with excellent grace and even loyalty. Now it was my turn; long-trousered, I was required to be adult about my demotion. 'This growing up,' I told myself, 'is harder than I expected.'

The Monkey, it must be said, was no less astonished than I at her elevation to the role of favoured child. She did her best to fall from grace, but it seemed she could do no wrong. These were the days of her flirtation with Christianity, which was partly due to the influence of her European school-friends and partly to the rosary-fingering presence of Mary Pereira (who, unable to go to church because of her fear of the confessional, would regale us instead with Bible stories); mostly, however, I believe it was an attempt by the Monkey to regain her old, comfortable position in the family dog-house (and, speaking of dogs, the Baroness Simki had been put to sleep during my absence, killed by promiscuity).

My sister spoke highly of gentle Jesus meek and mild; my mother smiled vaguely and patted her on the head. She went around the house humming hymns; my mother took up the tunes and sang along. She requested a nun's outfit to replace her favourite nurse's dress; it was given to her. She threaded chick-peas on a string and used them as a rosary, muttering Hail-Mary-full-of-grace, and my parents praised her skill with her hands. Tormented by her failure to be punished, she mounted to extremes of religious fervour, reciting the Our Father morning and night, fasting in the weeks of Lent instead of during Ramzàn, revealing an unsuspected streak of fanaticism which would, later, begin to dominate her personality; and still, it appeared, she was tolerated. Finally she discussed the matter with me. 'Well, brother,' she said, 'looks like from now on I'll just have to be the good guy, and you can have all the fun.'

She was probably right; my parents' apparent loss of interest in me should have given me a greater measure of freedom; but I was mesmerized by the transformations which were taking place in every aspect of my life, and fun, in such circumstances, seemed hard to have. I was altering physically; too early, soft fuzz was appearing on my chin and my voice swooped, out of control, up and down the vocal register. I had a strong sense of absurdity: my lengthening limbs were making me clumsy, and I must have cut a clownish figure, as I outgrew shirts and trousers and stuck gawkily and too far out of the ends of my clothes. I felt somehow conspired against, by these garments which flapped comically around my ankles and wrists; and even when I turned inwards to my secret Children, I found change, and didn't like it.

The gradual disintegration of the Midnight Children's Conference – which finally fell apart on the day the Chinese armies came down over the Himalayas to humiliate the Indian fauj – was already well under way. When novelty wears off, boredom, and then dissension, must inevitably ensue. Or (to put it another way) when a finger is mutilated, and fountains of blood flow out, all manner of vilenesses become possible . . . whether or not the cracks in the Conference were the (active-metaphorical) result of my finger-loss, they were certainly widening. Up in Kashmir, Narada-Markandaya was falling into the solipsistic dreams of the true narcissist, concerned only with the erotic pleasures of constant sexual alterations; while Soumitra the time-traveller, wounded by our refusal to listen to his descriptions of a future in which (he said) the country would be governed by a urine-drinking dotard who refused to die, and people would forget everything they had ever learned, and Pakistan would split like an amoeba, and the prime ministers of each half would be assassinated by their successors, both of whom – he swore despite our disbelief – would be called by the same name . . . wounded Soumitra became a regular absentee from our nightly meetings, disappearing for long periods into the spidery labyrinths of Time. And the sisters from Baud were content with their ability to bewitch fools young and old. 'What can this Conference help?' they inquired. 'We already have too many lovers.' And our alchemist member was busying himself in a laboratory built for him by his father (to whom he had revealed his secret); pre-occupied with the Philosopher's Stone, he had very little time for us. We had lost him to the lure of gold.

And there were other factors at work as well. Children, however magical, are not immune to their parents; and as the prejudices and world-views of adults began to take over their minds, I found children from Maharashtra loathing Gujaratis, and fair-skinned northerners reviling Dravidian 'blackies'; there were religious rivalries; and class entered our councils. The rich children turned up their noses at being in such lowly company; Brahmins began to feel uneasy at permitting even their thoughts to touch the thoughts of untouchables; while, among the low-born, the pressures of poverty and Communism were becoming evident . . . and, on top of all this, there were clashes of personality, and the hundred squalling rows which are unavoidable in a parliament composed entirely of half-grown brats.

In this way the Midnight Children's Conference fulfilled the prophecy of the Prime Minister and became, in truth, a mirror of the nation; the passive-literal mode was at work, although I railed against it, with increasing desperation, and finally with growing resignation . . . 'Brothers, sisters!' I broadcast, with a mental voice as uncontrollable as its physical counterpart, 'Do not let this happen! Do not permit the endless duality of masses-and-classes, capital-and-labour, them-and-us to come between us! We,' I cried passionately, 'must be a third principle, we must be the force which drives between the horns of the dilemma; for only by being other, by being new, can we fulfil the promise of our birth!' I had supporters, and none greater than Parvati-the-witch; but I felt them slipping away from me, each distracted by his or her own life . . . just as, in truth, I was being distracted by mine. It was as though our glorious congress was turning out to be more than another of the toys of childhood, as though long trousers were destroying what midnight had created . . . 'We must decide on a programme,' I pleaded, 'our own Five Year Plan, why not?' But I could hear, behind my anxious broadcast, the amused laughter of my greatest rival; and there was Shiva in all our heads, saying scornfully, 'No, little rich boy; there is no third principle; there is only money-and-poverty, and have-and-lack, and right-and-left; there is only me-against-the-world! The world is not ideas, rich boy; the world is no place for dreamers or their dreams; the world, little Snotnose, is things. Things and their makers rule the world; look at Birla, and Tata, and all the powerful: they make things. For things, the country is run. Not for people. For things, America and Russia send aid; but five hundred million stay hungry. When you have things, then there is time to dream; when you don't, you fight.' The Children, listening fascinatedly as we fought . . . or perhaps not, perhaps even

354

our dialogue failed to hold their interest. And now I: 'But people are not things; if we come together, if we love each other, if we show that this, just this, this people-together, this Conference, this children-sticking-together-through-thick-and-thin, can be that third way . . .' But Shiva, snorting: 'Little rich boy, that's all just wind. All that importance-of-the-individual. All that possibility-of-humanity. Today, what people are is just another kind of thing.' And I, Saleem, crumbling: 'But . . . free will . . . hope . . . the great soul, otherwise known as *mahatma*, of mankind . . . and what of poetry, and art, and . . .' Whereupon Shiva seized his victory: 'You see? I knew you'd turn out to be like that. Mushy, like overcooked rice. Sentimental as a grandmother. Go, who wants your rubbish? We all have lives to live. Hell's bells, cucumber-nose, I'm fed up with your Conference. It's got nothing to do with one single thing.'

You ask: there are ten-year-olds? I reply: Yes, but. You say: did ten-year-olds, or even almost-elevens, discuss the role of the individual in society? And the rivalry of capital and labour? Were the internal stresses of agrarian and industrialized zones made explicit? And conflicts in socio-cultural heritages? Did children of less than four thousand days discuss identity, and the inherent conflicts of capitalism? Having got through fewer than one hundred thousand hours, did they contrast Gandhi and Marxlenin, power and impotence? Was collectivity opposed to singularity? Was God killed by children? Even allowing for the truth of the supposed miracles, can we now believe that urchins spoke like old men with beards?

I say: maybe not in these words; maybe not in words at all, but in the purer language of thought; but yes, certainly, this is what was at the bottom of it all; because children are the vessels into which adults pour their poison, and it was the poison of grown-ups which did for us. Poison, and after a gap of many years, a Widow with a knife.

In short: after my return to Buckingham Villa, even the salt of the midnight children lost its savour; there were nights, now, when I did not even bother to set up my nationwide network; and the demon lurking inside me (it had two heads) was free to get on with its devilment. (I never knew about Shiva's guilt or innocence of whore-murders; but such was the influence of Kali-Yuga that I, the good guy and natural victim, was certainly responsible for two deaths. First came Jimmy Kapadia; and second was Homi Catrack.)

If there is a third principle, its name is childhood. But it dies; or rather, it is murdered.

We all had our troubles in those days. Homi Catrack had his idiot Toxy, and the Ibrahims had other worries: Sonny's father Ismail, after years of bribing judges and juries, was in danger of being investigated by the Bar Commission; and Sonny's uncle Ishaq, who ran the second-rate Embassy Hotel near Flora Fountain, was reputedly deep in debt to local gangsters, and worried constantly about being 'bumped off' (in those days, assassinations were becoming as quotidian as the heat) . . . so perhaps it isn't surprising that we had all forgotten about the existence of Professor Schaapsteker. (Indians grow larger and more powerful as they age; but Schaapsteker was a European, and his kind unfortunately fade away with the years, and often completely disappear.)

But now, driven, perhaps, by my demon, my feet led me upstairs to the top floor of Buckingham Villa, where I found a mad old man, incredibly tiny and shrunken, whose narrow tongue darted constantly in and out between his lips – flicking, licking: the former searcher after antivenenes, assassin of horses, Sharpsticker sahib, now ninety-two and no longer of his eponymous Institute, but retired into a dark top-floor apartment filled with tropical vegetation and serpents pickled in brine. Age, failing to draw his teeth and poison-sacs, had turned him instead into the incarnation of snakehood; like other Europeans who stay too long, the ancient insanities of India had pickled his brains, so that he had come to believe the superstitions of the Institute orderlies, according to whom he was the last of a line which began when a king cobra mated with a woman who gave birth to a human (but serpentine) child . . . it seems that all my life I've only had to turn a corner to tumble into yet another new and fabulously transmogrified world. Climb a ladder (or even a staircase) and you find a snake awaiting you.

The curtains were always drawn; in Schaapsteker's rooms, the sun neither rose nor set, and no clocks ticked. Was it the demon, or our mutual sense of isolation which drew us together? . . . Because, in those days of the Monkey's ascendancy and the Conference's decline, I began to ascend the stairs whenever possible, and listen to the ravings of the crazy, sibilant old man.

His first greeting to me, when I stumbled into his unlocked lair, was: 'So, child – you have recovered from the typhoid.' The sentence stirred time like a sluggish dust-cloud and rejoined me to my one-year-old self; I remembered the story of how Schaapsteker had saved my life with snake-poison. And afterwards, for several weeks, I sat at his feet, and he revealed to me the cobra which lay coiled within myself.

Who listed, for my benefit, the occult powers of snakes? (Their shadows kill cows; if they enter a man's dreams, his wife conceives; if they are killed, the murderer's family is denied male issue for twenty generations.) And who described to me – with the aid of books and stuffed corpses – the cobra's constant foes? 'Study your enemies, child,' he hissed, 'or they will surely kill you.' . . . At Schaapsteker's feet, I studied the mongoose and the boar, the dagger-billed adjutant bird and the barasinha deer, which crushes snakes' heads under its feet; and the Egyptian ichneumon, and ibis; the four-feet-high secretary bird, fearless and hook-beaked, whose appearance and name made me think suspicious thoughts about my father's Alice Pereira; and the jackal buzzard, the stink cat, the honey ratel from the hills; the road runner, the peccary, and the formidable cangamba bird. Schaapsteker, from the depths of his senility, instructed me in life. 'Be wise, child. Imitate the action of the snake. Be secret; strike from the cover of a bush.'

Once he said: 'You must think of me as another father. Did I not give you your life when it was lost?' With this statement he proved that he was as much under my spell as I under his; he had accepted that he, too, was one of that endless series of parents to whom I alone had the power of giving birth. And although, after a time, I found the air in his chambers too oppressive, and left him once more to the isolation from which he would never again be disturbed, he had shown me how to proceed. Consumed by the two-headed demon of revenge, I used my telepathic powers (for the first time) as a weapon; and in this way I discovered the details of the relationship between Homi Catrack and Lila Sabarmati. Lila and Pia were always rivals in beauty; it was the wife of the heir-apparent to the title of Admiral of the Fleet who had become the film magnate's new fancy-woman. While Commander Sabarmati was at sea on manoeuvres, Lila and Homi were performing certain manoeuvres of their own; while the lion of the seas awaited the death of the then-Admiral, Homi and Lila, too, were making an appointment with the Reaper. (With my help.)

'Be secret,' said Sharpsticker sahib; secretly, I spied on my enemy Homi, and on the promiscuous mother of Eyeslice and Hairoil (who were very full of themselves of late, ever since, in fact, the papers announced that Commander Sabarmati's promotion was a mere formality. *Only a matter of time . . .*). 'Loose woman,' the demon within me whispered silently, 'Perpetrator of the worst of maternal perfidies! We shall turn you into an awful example; through you we shall demonstrate the fate which awaits the lascivious. O unobservant adulteress! Did you not see what sleeping around did to the illustrious Baroness Simki von der Heiden? – who was, not to put too fine a point upon it, a bitch, just like yourself.'

My view of Lila Sabarmati has mellowed with age; after all, she and I had one thing in common – her nose, like mine, possessed tremendous powers. Hers, however, was a purely worldly magic: a wrinkle of nasal skin could charm the steeliest of Admirals; a tiny flare of the nostrils ignited strange fires in the hearts of film magnates. I am a little regretful about betraying that nose; it was a little like stabbing a cousin in the back.

What I discovered: every Sunday morning at ten a.m., Lila Sabarmati drove Eyeslice and Hairoil to the Metro cinema for the weekly meetings of the Metro Cub Club. (She volunteered to take the rest of us, too; Sonny and Cyrus, the Monkey and I piled into her Indian-made Hindustan car.) And while we drove towards Lana Turner or Robert Taylor or Sandra Dee, Mr Homi Catrack was also preparing himself for a weekly rendezvous. While Lila's Hindustan puttered along beside railway-lines, Homi was knotting a cream silk scarf around his throat; while she halted at red lights, he donned a Technicolored bush-coat; when she was ushering us into the darkness of the auditorium, he was putting on gold-rimmed sunglasses; and when she left us to watch our film, he, too, was abandoning a child. Toxy Catrack never failed to react to his departures by wailing kicking thrashing-of-legs; she knew what was going on, and not even Bi-Appah could restrain her.

Once upon a time there were Radha and Krishna, and Rama and Sita, and Laila and Majnu; also (because we are not unaffected by the West) Romeo and Juliet, and Spencer Tracy and Katharine Hepburn. The world is full of love stories, and all lovers are in a sense the avatars of their predecessors. When Lila drove her Hindustan to an address off Colaba Causeway, she was Juliet coming out on to her balcony; when cream-scarfed, gold-shaded Homi sped off to meet her (in the same

Studebaker in which my mother had once been rushed to Dr Narlikar's Nursing Home), he was Leander swimming the Hellespont towards Hero's burning candle. As for my part in the business – I will not give it a name.

I confess: what I did was no act of heroism. I did not battle Homi on horseback, with fiery eyes and flaming sword; instead, imitating the action of the snake, I began to cut pieces out of newspapers. From GOAN LIBERATION COMMITTEE LAUNCHES SATYAGRAHA CAMPAIGN I extracted the letters 'COM'; SPEAKER OF E-PAK ASSEMBLY DECLARED MANIAC gave me my second syllable, 'MAN'. I found 'DER' concealed in NEHRU CONSIDERS RESIGNATION AT CONGRESS ASSEMBLY; into my second word now, I excised 'SAB' from RIOTS, MASS ARRESTS IN RED-RUN KERALA: SABOTEURS RUN AMOK: GHOSH ACCUSES CONGRESS GOONDAS, and got 'ARM' from CHINESE ARMED FORCES' BORDER ACTIVITIES SPURN BANDUNG PRINCIPLES. To complete the name, I snipped the letters 'ATI' from DULLES FOREIGN POLICY IS INCONSISTENT, ERRATIC, P.M. AVERS. Cutting up history to suit my nefarious purposes, I seized on WHY INDIRA GANDHI IS CONGRESS PRESIDENT NOW and kept the 'WHY'; but I refused to be tied exclusively to politics, and turned to advertising for the 'DOES YOUR' in DOES YOUR CHEWING GUM LOSE ITS FLAVOUR? BUT P.K. KEEPS ITS SAVOUR! A sporting human-interest story, MOHUN BAGAN CENTRE-FORWARD TAKES WIFE, gave me its last word, and 'GO TO' I took from the tragic MASSES GO TO ABUL KALAM AZAD'S FUNERAL. Now I was obliged to find my words in little pieces once again: DEATH ON SOUTH COL: SHERPA PLUNGES provided me with a much-needed 'COL', but 'ABA' was hard to find, turning up at last in a cinema advertisement: ALI-BABA, SEVENTEENTH SUPERCOLOSSAL WEEK – PLANS FILLING UP FAST! . . . Those were the days when Sheikh Abdullah, the Lion of Kashmir, was campaigning for a plebiscite in his state to determine its future; his courage gave me the syllable 'CAUSE', because it led to this headline: ABDULLAH 'INCITEMENT' CAUSE OF HIS RE-ARREST — GOVT SPOKESMAN. Then, too, Acharya Vinobha Bhave, who had spent ten years persuading landowners to donate plots to the poor in his bhoodan campaign, announced that donations had passed the million-acre mark, and launched two new campaigns, asking for the donations of whole villages ('gramdan') and of individual lives ('jivandan'). When J. P. Narayan announced the dedication of his life to Bhave's work, the headline NARAYAN WALKS IN BHAVE'S WAY gave me *my* much-sought 'WAY', I had nearly finished now; plucking an 'ON' from PAKISTAN ON COURSE FOR POLITICAL CHAOS: FACTION STRIFE BEDEVILS PUBLIC AFFAIRS, and a 'SUNDAY' from the masthead of the *Sunday Blitz,* I found myself just one word short. Events in East Pakistan provided me with my finale, FURNITURE HURLING SLAYS DEPUTY E-PAK SPEAKER: MOURNING PERIOD DECLARED gave me 'MOURNING', from which, deftly and deliberately, I excised the letter 'u'. I needed a terminal question-mark, and found it at the end of the perennial query of those strange days: AFTER NEHRU, WHO?

In the secrecy of a bathroom, I glued my completed note – my first attempt at rearranging history – on to a sheet of paper; snake-like, I inserted the document in my pocket, like poison in a sac. Subtly, I arranged to spend an evening with Eyeslice and Hairoil. We played a game: 'Murder in the Dark' . . . During a game of murder, I slipped inside Commander Sabarmati's almirah and inserted my lethal missive into the inside pocket of his spare uniform. At that moment (no point hiding it) I felt the delight of the snake who hits its target, and feels its fangs pierce its victim's heel . . .

COMMANDER SABARMATI (my note read)
WHY DOES YOUR WIFE GO TO COLABA
CAUSEWAY ON SUNDAY MORNING?

No, I am no longer proud of what I did; but remember that my demon of revenge had two heads. By unmasking the perfidy of Lila Sabarmati, I hoped also to administer a salutary shock to my own mother. Two birds with one stone; there were to be two punished women, one impaled on each fang of my forked snake's tongue. It is not untrue to say that what came to be known as the Sabarmati affair had its real beginnings at a dingy café in the north of the city, when a stowaway watched a ballet of circling hands.

I was secret; I struck from the cover of a bush. What drove me? Hands at the Pioneer Café; wrong-number telephone calls; notes slipped to me on balconies, and passed under cover of bedsheets; my mother's hypocrisy and Pia's inconsolable grief: 'Hai! *Ai*-hai! Ai-hai-*hai*!' . . . Mine was a slow poison; but three weeks later, it had its effect.

It emerged, afterwards, that after receiving my anonymous note Commander Sabarmati had engaged the services of the illustrious Dom Minto, Bombay's best-known private detective. (Minto, old and almost lame, had lowered his rates by then.) He waited until he received Minto's report. And then:

That Sunday morning, six children sat in a row at the Metro Cub Club, watching *Francis The Talking Mule And The Haunted House*. You see, I had my alibi; I was nowhere near the scene of the crime. Like Sin, the crescent moon, I acted from a distance upon the tides of the world . . . while a mule talked on a screen, Commander Sabarmati visited the naval arsenal. He signed out a good, long-nosed revolver; also ammunition. He held, in his left hand, a piece of paper on which an address had been written in a private detective's tidy hand; in his right hand, he grasped the unholstered gun. By taxi, the Commander arrived at Colaba Causeway. He paid off the cab, walked gun-in-hand down a narrow gully past shirt-stalls and toyshops, and ascended the staircase of an apartment block set back from the gully at the rear of a concrete courtyard. He rang the doorbell of apartment 18c; it was heard in 18B by an Anglo-Indian teacher giving private Latin tuition. When Commander Sabarmati's wife Lila answered the door, he shot her twice in the stomach at point-blank range. She fell backwards; he marched past her, and found Mr Homi Catrack rising from the toilet, his bottom unwiped, pulling frantically at his trousers. Commander Vinoo Sabarmati shot him once in the genitals, once in the heart and once through the right eye. The gun was not silenced; but when it had finished speaking, there was an enormous silence in the apartment. Mr Catrack sat down on the toilet after he was shot and seemed to be smiling.

Commander Sabarmati walked out of the apartment block with the smoking gun in his hand (he was seen, through the crack of a door, by a terrified Latin tutor); he strolled along Colaba Causeway until he saw a traffic policeman on his little podium. Commander Sabarmati told the policeman, 'I have only now killed my wife and her lover with this gun; I surrender myself into your . . .' But he had been waving the gun under the policeman's nose; the officer was so scared that he dropped his traffic-conducting baton and fled. Commander Sabarmati, left alone on the policeman's pedestal amid the sudden confusion of the traffic, began to direct the cars, using the smoking gun as a baton. This is how he was found by the posse of twelve policemen who arrived ten minutes later, who sprang courageously upon him and seized him hand and foot, and who removed from him the unusual baton with which, for ten minutes, he had expertly conducted the traffic.

A newspaper said of the Sabarmati affair: 'It is a theatre in which India will discover who she was, what she is, and what she might become.' . . . But Commander Sabarmati was only a puppet; I was the puppet-master, and the nation performed my play – only I hadn't meant it! I didn't think he'd . . . I only wanted to . . . a scandal, yes, a scare, a lesson to all unfaithful wives and mothers, but not that, never, no.

Aghast at the result of my actions, I rode the turbulent thought-waves of the city . . . at the Parsee General Hospital, a doctor said, 'Begum Sabarmati will live; but she will have to watch what she eats.' . . . But Homi Catrack was dead . . . And who was engaged as the lawyer for the defence? – Who said, 'I will defend him free gratis and for nothing'? – Who, once the victor of the Freeze Case, was now the Commander's champion? Sonny Ibrahim said, 'My father will get him off if anyone can.'

Commander Sabarmati was the most popular murderer in the history of Indian jurisprudence. Husbands acclaimed his punishment of an errant wife; faithful women felt justified in their fidelity. Inside Lila's own sons, I found these thoughts: 'We knew she was like that. We knew a Navy man wouldn't stand for it.' A columnist in the *Illustrated Weekly of India*, writing a pen-portrait to go alongside the 'Personality of the Week' full-colour caricature of the Commander, said: 'In the Sabarmati Case, the noble sentiments of the Ramayana combine with the cheap melodrama of the Bombay talkie; but as for the chief protagonist, all agree on his upstandingness; and he is undeniably an attractive chap.'

My revenge on my mother and Homi Catrack had precipitated a national crisis . . . because Naval regulations decreed that no man who had been in a civil jail could aspire to the rank of Admiral of the Fleet. So Admirals, and city politicians, and of course Ismail Ibrahim, demanded: 'Commander Sabarmati must stay in a Navy jail. He is innocent until proven guilty. His career must not be ruined if it can possibly be avoided.' And the authorities: 'Yes.' And Commander Sabarmati, safe in the Navy's own lock-up, discovered the penalties of fame – deluged with telegrams of support, he awaited trial; flowers filled his cell, and although he asked to be placed on an ascetic's diet of rice and water, well-wishers inundated him with tiffin-carriers filled with birianis and pista-ki-lauz and other rich foods. And, jumping the queue in the Criminal Court, the case began in double-quick time . . . The prosecution said, 'The charge is murder in the first degree.'

Stern-jawed, strong-eyed, Commander Sabarmati replied: 'Not guilty.'

My mother said, 'O my God, the poor man, so sad, isn't it?'

I said, 'But an unfaithful wife is a terrible thing, Amma . . .' and she turned away her head.

The prosecution said, 'Here is an open and shut case. Here is motive, opportunity, confession, corpse and premeditation: the gun signed out, the children sent to the cinema, the detective's report. What else to say? The state rests.'

And public opinion: 'Such a good man, Allah!'

Ismail Ibrahim said: 'This is a case of attempted suicide.'

To which, public opinion: '?????????'

Ismail Ibrahim expounded: 'When the Commander received Dom Minto's report, he wanted to see for himself if it was true; and if so, to kill himself. He signed out the gun; it was for himself. He went to the Colaba address in a spirit of despair only; not as killer, but as dead man! But there – seeing his wife there, jury members! – seeing her half-clothed with her shameless lover! – jury members, this good man, this great man saw red. Red, absolutely, and while seeing red he did his deeds. Thus there is no premeditation, and so no murder in the first degree. Killing yes, but not cold-blooded. Jury members, you must find him not guilty as charged.'

And buzzing around the city was, 'No, too much . . . Ismail Ibrahim has gone too far this time . . . but, but . . . he has got a jury composed mostly of women . . . and not rich ones . . . therefore doubly susceptible, to the Commander's charm and the lawyer's wallet . . . who knows? Who can tell?'

The jury said, 'Not guilty.'

My mother cried, 'Oh wonderful! . . . But, but: is it *justice*?' And the judge, answering her: 'Using the powers vested in me, I reverse this absurd verdict. Guilty as charged.'

O, the wild furor of those days! When Naval dignitaries and bishops and other politicians demanded, 'Sabarmati must stay in the Navy jail pending High Court appeal. The bigotry of one judge must not ruin this great man!' And police authorities, capitulating, 'Very well.' The Sabarmati Case goes rushing upwards, hurtling towards High Court hearing at unprecedented speed . . . and the Commander tells his lawyer, 'I feel as though destiny is no longer in my control; as though something has taken over . . . let us call it Fate.'

I say: 'Call it Saleem, or Snotnose, or Sniffer, or Stainface; call it little-piece-of-the-moon.'

The High Court verdict: 'Guilty as charged.' The press headlines: SABARMATI FOR CIVIL JAIL AT LAST? Ismail Ibrahim's statement: 'We are going all the way! To the Supreme Court!' And now, the bombshell. A pronouncement from the State Chief Minister himself: 'It is a heavy thing to make an exception to the law; but in view of Commander Sabarmati's service to his country, I am permitting him to remain in Naval confinement pending the Supreme Court decision.'

And more press headlines, stinging as mosquitoes: STATE GOVERNMENT FLOUTS LAW! SABARMATI SCANDAL NOW A PUBLIC DISGRACE! . . . When I realized that the press had turned against the Commander, I knew he was done for.

The Supreme Court verdict: 'Guilty.'

Ismail Ibrahim said: 'Pardon! We appeal for pardon to the President of India!'

And now great matters are to be weighed in Rashtrapati Bhavan – behind the gates of President House, a man must decide if any man can be set above the law; whether the assassination of a wife's fancy-man should be set aside for the sake of a Naval career; and still higher things – is India to give

366

her approval to the rule of law, or to the ancient principle of the overriding primacy of heroes? If Rama himself were alive, would we send him to prison for slaying the abductor of Sita? Great matters; my vengeful irruption into the history of my age was certainly no trivial affair.

The President of India said, 'I shall not pardon this man.'

Nussie Ibrahim (whose husband had lost his biggest case) wailed, 'Hai! Ai-hai!' And repeated an earlier observation: 'Amina sister, that good man going to prison – I tell you, it is the end of the world!'

A confession, trembling just beyond my lips: 'It was all my doing, Amma; I wanted to teach you a lesson. Amma, do not go to see other men, with Lucknow-work on their shirt; enough, my mother, of teacup-kissery! I am in long trousers now, and may speak to you as a man.' But it never spilled out of me; there was no need, because I heard my mother answering a wrong-number telephone call – and with a strange, subdued voice, speak into the mouthpiece as follows: 'No; nobody by that name here; please believe what I am telling you, and never call me again.'

Yes, I had taught my mother a lesson; and after the Sabarmati affair she never saw her Nadir-Qasim in the flesh, never again, not as long as she lived; but, deprived of him, she fell victim to the fate of all women in our family, namely the curse of growing old before her time; she began to shrink, and her hobble became more pronounced, and there was the emptiness of age in her eyes.

My revenge brought in its wake a number of unlooked-for developments; perhaps the most dramatic of these was the appearance in the gardens of Methwold's Estate of curious flowers, made out of wood and tin, and hand-painted with bright red lettering . . . the fatal signboards erected in all the gardens except our own, evidence that my powers exceeded even my own understanding, and that, having once been

367

exiled from my two-storey hillock, I had now managed to send everyone else away instead.

Signboards in the gardens of Versailles Villa, Escorial Villa and Sans Souci; signboards nodding to each other in the sea-breeze of the cocktail hour. On each signboard could be discerned the same seven letters, all bright red, all twelve inches high: FOR SALE. That was the signboards' message.

FOR SALE – Versailles Villa, its owner dead on a toilet seat; the sale was handled by the ferocious nurse Bi-Appah on behalf of poor idiot Toxy; once the sale was complete, nurse and nursed vanished forever, and Bi-Appah held, on her lap, a bulging suitcase filled with banknotes . . . I don't know what happened to Toxy, but considering the avarice of her nurse, I'm sure it was nothing good . . . FOR SALE, the Sabarmati apartment in Escorial Villa; Lila Sabarmati was denied custody of her children and faded out of our lives, while Eyeslice and Hairoil packed their bags and departed into the care of the Indian Navy, which had placed itself *in loco parentis* until their father completed his thirty years in jail . . . FOR SALE, too, the Ibrahims' Sans Souci, because Ishaq Ibrahim's Embassy Hotel had been burned down by gangsters on the day of Commander Sabarmati's final defeat, as though the criminal classes of the city were punishing the lawyer's family for his failure; and then Ismail Ibrahim was suspended from practice, *owing to certain proofs of professional misconduct* (to quote the Bombay Bar Commission's report); financially 'embarrassed', the Ibrahims also passed out of our lives; and, finally FOR SALE, the apartment of Cyrus Dubash and his mother, because during the hue and cry of the Sabarmati affair, and almost entirely unnoticed, the nuclear physicist had died his orange-pip-choking death, thus unleashing upon Cyrus the religious fanaticism of his mother and setting in motion the wheels of the period of revelations which will be the subject of my next little piece.

The signboards nodded in the gardens, which were losing their memories of goldfish and cocktail-hours and invading cats; and who took them down? Who were the heirs of the heirs of William Methwold? . . . They came swarming out of what had once been the residence of Dr Narlikar: fat-bellied and grossly competent women, grown fatter and more competent than ever on their tetrapod-given wealth (because those were the years of the great land reclamations). The Narlikar women – from the Navy they bought Commander Sabarmati's flat, and from the departing Mrs Dubash her Cyrus's home; they paid Bi-Appah in used banknotes, and the Ibrahims' creditors were appeased by Narlikar cash.

My father, alone of all the residents, refused to sell; they offered him vast sums, but he shook his head. They explained their dream – a dream of razing the buildings to the ground and erecting on the two-storey hillock a mansion which would soar thirty stories into the skies, a triumphant pink obelisk, a signpost of their future; Ahmed Sinai, lost in abstractions, would have none of it. They told him, 'When you're surrounded by rubble you'll have to sell for a song'; he (remembering their tetrapodal perfidy) was unmoved.

Nussie-the-duck said, as she left, 'I told you so, Amina sister – the end! The end of the world!' This time she was right and wrong; after August 1958, the world continued to spin; but the world of my childhood had, indeed, come to an end.

Padma – did you have, when you were little, a world of your own? A tin orb, on which were imprinted the continents and oceans and polar ice? Two cheap metal hemispheres, clamped together by a plastic stand? No, of course not; but I did. It was a world full of labels: *Atlantic Ocean* and *Amazon* and *Tropic of Capricorn*. And, at the North Pole, it bore the legend: MADE AS ENGLAND. By the August of the nodding signboards and the rapaciousness of the Narlikar women, this tin world had lost its stand; I found Scotch Tape and stuck the earth together at the Equator, and then, my urge for play overcoming my respect, began to use it as a football. In the aftermath of the Sabarmati affair, when the air was filled with the repentance of my mother and the private tragedies of Methwold's heirs, I clanked my tin sphere around the Estate, secure in the knowledge that the world was still in one piece (although held together by adhesive tape) and also at my feet . . . until, on the day of Nussie-the-duck's last eschatological lament – on the day Sonny Ibrahim ceased to be Sonny-next-door – my sister the Brass Monkey descended on me in an inexplicable rage, yelling, 'O God, stop your kicking, brother; you don't feel even a little *bad* today?' And jumping high in the air, she landed with both feet on the North Pole, and crushed the world into the dust of our driveway under her furious heels.

It seems the departure of Sonny Ibrahim, her reviled adorer, whom she had stripped naked in the middle of the road, had affected the Brass Monkey, after all, despite her lifelong denial of the possibility of love.

Revelations

Om Hare Khusro Hare Khusrovand Om

Know, O unbleivers, that in the dark Midnights of CELESTIAL SPACE in a time before Time lay the sphere of Blessed KHUSROVAND!!! Even MODERN SCIENTISTS now affirm that for *generations* they have LIED to conceal from the People whose *right it is to know* of the Unquestionabel TRUE existance of this HOLY HOME OF TRUTH!!! Leading Intellectuals the World Over, also in America, speak of the ANTI-RELIGIOUS CONSPIRACY of reds, JEWS, etc., to hide these VITAL NEWS! The Veil lifts now. Blessed LORD KHUSRO comes with Irrefutable Proofs. Read and believe!

Know that in TRUE-EXISTING Khusrovand lived Saints whose Spiritual Purity-Advancement was such that they had, through MEDITATION &c., gained powers FOR THE GOOD OF ALL, powers Beyond Imagining! They SAW THROUGH steel, and could BEND GIRDERS with TEETH!!!

*   *   *   NOW!   *   *   *
For 1st Time, such powers may be used
in Your Service! LORD   KHUSRO   is
*   *   *   HERE!   *   *   *

Hear of the Fall of Khusrovand: how the RED DEVIL *Bhimutha* (BLACK be his name) unleashed a fearsome Hail of Meteorites (which has been well chronicled by WORLD

OBSERVATORIES, but not Explained) . . . so horrible a RAIN OF STONE, that Fair Khusrovand was RUINED & its Saints DESTROYD.

But noble *Juraell* and beauteous *Khalila* were wise, SACRIFICING THEMSELVES in an ecstasy of Kundalini Art, they saved the SOUL of their unborn son LORD KHUSRO. Entering True Oneness in a Supreme Yogic Trance (whose powers are now ACCEPTED in WHOLE WORLD!) they transformed their Noble Spirits into a Flashing *Beam* of KUNDALINI LIFE FORCE ENERGY LIGHT, of which today's wellknown LASER is a common imitation & *Copy*. Along this BEAM, Soul of unborn Khusro flew, traversing the BOTTOMLESS DEEPS of Celestial Space-Eternity, until by OUR LUCK! it came to our own Duniya (World) & lodged in Womb of a humble Parsee matron of Good Family.

So the Child was born & was of true Goodness & Unparalleled BRAIN (giving the LIE to that LIE, that we are all Born Equal! Is a Crook the equal of Saint? OF COURSE NOT!!) But for some Time his true nature lay Hidden, until while portraying and Earth-Saint in a DRAMA production (of which LEADING CRITICS have said, The Purity of His Performance Defied The Blief), he CAME AWAKE & knew WHO he WAS. Now has he taken up his True Name,

LORD
KHUSRO
KHUSROVANI
* BHAGWAN *

& is Set Forth humbly with Ash on his Ascetic's Brow to heal Disease and End Droughts & FIGHT the Legions of *Bhimutha* wherever they may Come. For BE AFRAID! *Bhimutha's* RAIN OF STONE will come to us ALSO! Do not heed LIES of politicos poets Reds &cetera. PUT YOUR TRUST in Only True Lord

& send Donations to PO Box 555, Head Post Office,
Bombay-1.
BLESSINGS!   BEAUTY!!   TRUTH!!!
Om Hare Khusro Hare Khusrovand Om

Cyrus-the-great had a nuclear physicist for a father and, for a
mother, a religious fanatic whose faith had gone sour inside
her as a result of so many years of being suppressed by the
domineering rationality of her Dubash; and when Cyrus's
father choked on an orange from which his mother had
forgotten to remove the pips, Mrs Dubash applied herself to
the task of erasing her late husband from the personality of
her son – of remaking Cyrus in her own strange image, *Cyrus-
the-great, Born on a plate, In nineteen hundred and forty-
eight* – Cyrus the school prodigy – Cyrus as Saint Joan in
Shaw's play – all these Cyruses, to whom we had grown
accustomed, with whom we had grown up, now disappeared;
in their place there emerged the overblown, almost bovinely
placid figure of Lord Khusro Khusrovand. At the age of ten,
Cyrus vanished from the Cathedral School and the meteoric
rise of India's richest guru began. (There are as many versions
of India as Indians; and, when set beside Cyrus's India, my
own version seems almost mundane.)

Why did he let it happen? Why did posters cover the city,
and advertisements fill the newspapers, without a peep out of
the child genius? . . . Because Cyrus (although he used to
lecture us, not unmischievously, on the Parts of a Wooman's
Body) was simply the most malleable of boys, and would not
have dreamed of crossing his mother. For his mother, he put
on a sort of brocade skirt and a turban; for the sake of filial
duty, he permitted millions of devotees to kiss his little finger.

In the name of maternal love, he truly became Lord Khusro, the most successful holy child in history; in no time at all he was being hailed by crowds half a million strong, and credited with miracles; American guitarists came to sit at his feet, and they all brought their cheque-books along. Lord Khusrovand acquired accountants, and tax havens, and a luxury liner called the *Khusrovand Starship,* and an aircraft – *Lord Khusro's Astral Plane.* And somewhere inside the faintly-smiling, benediction-scattering boy . . . in a place which was forever hidden by his mother's frighteningly efficient shadow (she had, after all, lived in the same house as the Narlikar women; how well did she know them? How much of their awesome competence leaked into her?), there lurked the ghost of a boy who had been my friend.

'That Lord Khusro?' Padma asks, amazed. 'You mean that same mahaguru who drowned at sea last year?' Yes, Padma; he could not walk on water; and very few people who have come into contact with me have been vouchsafed a natural death . . . let me confess that I was somewhat resentful of Cyrus's apotheosis. 'It should have been me,' I even thought, 'I am the magic child; not only my primacy at home, but even my true innermost nature, has now been purloined.'

Padma: I never became a 'mahaguru'; millions have never seated themselves at my feet; and it was my own fault, because one day, many years ago, I had gone to hear Cyrus's lecture on the Parts of a Wooman's Body.

'What?' Padma shakes her head, puzzled. 'What's this now?'

The nuclear physicist Dubash possessed a beautiful marble statuette – a female nude – and with the help of this figurine, his son would give expert lectures on female anatomy to an audience of sniggering boys. Not free; Cyrus-the-great charged a fee. In exchange for anatomy, he demanded comic-books – and I, in all innocence, gave him a copy of that most precious of *Superman* comics, the one containing the frame-story, about the explosion of the planet Krypton and the rocket-ship in which Jor-El his father despatched him through space, to land on earth and be adopted by the good, mild Kents . . . did nobody else see it? In all those years, did no person understand that what Mrs Dubash had done was to rework and reinvent the most potent of all modern myths – the legend of the coming of the superman? I saw the hoardings trumpeting the coming of Lord Khusro Khusrovand Bhagwan; and found myself obliged, yet again, to accept responsibility for the events of my turbulent, fabulous world.

How I admire the leg-muscles of my solicitous Padma! There she squats, a few feet from my table, her sari hitched up in fisherwoman-fashion. Calf-muscles show no sign of strain; thigh-muscles, rippling through sari-folds, display their commendable stamina. Strong enough to squat forever, simultaneously defying gravity and cramp, my Padma listens unhurriedly to my lengthy tale; O mighty pickle-woman! What reassuring solidity, how comforting an air of permanence, in her biceps and triceps . . . for my admiration extends also to her arms, which could wrestle mine down in a trice, and from which, when they enfold me nightly in futile embraces, there is no escape. Past our crisis now, we exist in perfect harmony: I recount, she is recounted to; she ministers, and I accept her ministrations with grace. I am, in fact, entirely content with the uncomplaining thews of Padma Mangroli, who is, unaccountably, more interested in me than my tales.

Why I have chosen to expound on Padma's musculature: these days, it's to those muscles, much as to anything or -one (for instance, my son, who hasn't even learned to read as yet), that I'm telling my story. Because I am rushing ahead at breakneck speed; errors are possible, and overstatements, and jarring alterations in tone; I'm racing the cracks, but I remain conscious that errors have already been made, and that, as my decay accelerates (my writing speed is having trouble keeping up), the risk of unreliability grows . . . in this condition, I am learning to use Padma's muscles as my guides. When she's bored, I can detect in her fibres the ripples of uninterest; when she's unconvinced, there is a tic which gets going in her cheek. The dance of her musculature helps to keep me on the rails; because in autobiography, as in all literature, what actually happened is less important than what the author can manage to persuade his audience to believe . . . Padma, having accepted the story of Cyrus-the-great, gives me the courage to speed on, into the worst time of my eleven-year-old life (there is, was, worse to come) – into the August-and-September when revelations flowed faster than blood.

Nodding signboards had scarcely been taken down when the demolition crews of the Narlikar women moved in; Buckingham Villa was enveloped in the tumultuous dust of the dying palaces of William Methwold. Concealed by dust from Warden Road below, we were nevertheless still vulnerable to telephones; and it was the telephone which informed us, in the tremulous voice of my aunt Pia, of the suicide of my beloved uncle Hanif. Deprived of the income he had received from Homi Catrack, my uncle had taken his booming voice and his obsessions with hearts and reality up to the roof of his Marine Drive apartment block; he had stepped out into the evening sea-breeze, frightening the beggars so much (when he fell) that they gave up pretending to be blind and ran away yelling . . . in death as in life, Hanif Aziz espoused the cause of truth and put illusion to flight. He was nearly thirty-four years old. Murder breeds death; by killing Homi Catrack, I had killed my uncle, too. It was my fault; and the dying wasn't over yet.

The family gathered at Buckingham Villa: from Agra, Aadam Aziz and Reverend Mother; from Delhi, my uncle Mustapha, the Civil Servant who had polished the art of agreeing with his superiors to the point at which they had stopped hearing him, which is why he never got promoted; and his half-Irani wife Sonia and their children who had been so thoroughly beaten into insignificance that I can't even remember how many of them there were; and from Pakistan, bitter Alia, and even General Zulfikar and my aunt Emerald, who brought twenty-seven pieces of luggage and two servants, and never stopped looking at their watches and inquiring about the date. Their son Zafar also came. And, to complete the circle, my mother brought Pia to stay in our house, 'at least for the forty-day mourning period, my sister"

For forty days, we were besieged by the dust; dust creeping under the wet towels we placed around all the windows, dust slyly following in each mourning arrival, dust filtering through the very walls to hang like a shapeless wraith in the air, dust deadening the sounds of formal ululation and also the deadly sniping of grieving kinsfolk; the remnants of Methwold's Estate settled on my grandmother and goaded her towards a great fury; they irritated the pinched nostrils of Punchinello-faced General Zulfikar and forced him to sneeze on to his chin. In the ghost-haze of the dust it sometimes seemed we could discern the shapes of the past, the mirage of Lila Sabarmati's pulverized pianola or the prison bars at the window of Toxy Catrack's cell; Dubash's nude statuette danced in dust-form through our chambers, and Sonny Ibrahim's bullfight-posters visited us as clouds. The Narlikar women had moved away while bulldozers did their work; we were alone inside the dust-storm, which gave us all the appearance of neglected furniture, as if we were chairs and tables which had been abandoned for decades without covering-sheets; we looked like the ghosts of ourselves. We were a dynasty born out of a nose, the aquiline monster on the face of Aadam Aziz, and the dust, entering our nostrils in our time of grief, broke down our reserve, eroded the barriers which permit families to survive; in the dust storm of the dying palaces things were said and seen and done from which none of us ever recovered.

It was started by Reverend Mother, perhaps because the years had filled her out until she resembled the Sankara Acharya mountain in her native Srinagar, so that she presented the dust with the largest surface area to attack. Rumbling up from her mountainous body came a noise like an avalanche, which, when it turned into words, became a fierce attack on aunt Pia, the bereaved widow. We had all noticed that my mumani was behaving unusually. There was an unspoken feeling that an actress of her standing should have risen to the challenge of widowhood in high style; we had unconsciously been eager to see her grieving, looking forward to watching an accomplished tragedienne orchestrate her own calamity, anticipating a forty-day raga in which bravura and gentleness, howling pain and soft despond would all be blended in the exact proportions of art; but Pia remained still, dry-eyed, and anticlimactically composed. Amina Sinai and Emerald Zulfikar wept and rent their hair, trying to spark off Pia's talents; but finally, when it seemed nothing would move Pia, Reverend Mother lost patience. The dust entered her disappointed fury and increased its bitterness. 'That woman, whatsitsname,' Reverend Mother rumbled, 'didn't I tell you about her? My son, Allah, he could have been anything, but no, whatsitsname, she must make him ruin his life; he must jump off a roof, whatsitsname, to be free of her.'

It was said; could not be unsaid. Pia sat like stone; my insides shook like cornflour pudding. Reverend Mother went grimly on; she swore an oath upon the hairs of her dead son's head. 'Until that woman shows my son's memory some respect, whatsitsname, until she takes out a wife's true tears, no food will pass my lips. It is shame and scandal, whatsitsname, how she sits with antimony instead of tears in her eyes!' The house resounded with this echo of her old wars with Aadam Aziz. And until the twentieth day of the forty, we were all afraid that my grandmother would die of starvation and the forty days would have to start all over again. She lay dustily on her bed; we waited and feared.

I broke the stalemate between grandmother and aunt; so at least I can legitimately claim to have saved one life. On the twentieth day, I sought out Pia Aziz who sat in her ground-floor room like a blind woman; as an excuse for my visit, I apologized clumsily for my indiscretions in the Marine Drive apartment. Pia spoke, after a distant silence: 'Always melodrama,' she said, flatly, 'In his family members, in his work. He died for his hate of melodrama; it is why I would not cry.' At the time I did not understand; now I'm sure that Pia Aziz was exactly right. Deprived of a livelihood by spurning the cheap-thrill style of the Bombay cinema, my uncle strolled off the edge of a roof; melodrama inspired (and perhaps tainted) his final dive to earth. Pia's refusal to weep was in honour of his memory . . . but the effort of admitting it breached the walls of her self-control. Dust made her sneeze; the sneeze brought tears to her eyes; and now the tears would not stop, and we all witnessed our hoped-for performance after all, because once they fell they fell like Flora Fountain, and she was unable to resist her own talent; she shaped the flood like the performer she was, introducing dominant themes and subsidiary motifs, beating her astonishing breasts in a manner genuinely painful to observe, now squeezing, now pummelling . . . she tore her garments and her hair. It was an exaltation of tears, and it persuaded Reverend Mother to eat. Dal and pistachio-nuts poured into my grandmother while salt water flooded from my aunt. Now Naseem Aziz descended upon Pia, embracing her, turning the solo into a duet, mingling the music of reconciliation with the unbearably beautiful tunes of grief. Our palms itched with inexpressible applause. And the best was still to come, because Pia, the artiste, brought her epic efforts to a superlative close. Laying her head in her mother-in-law's lap, she said in a voice filled with submission and emptiness, 'Ma, let your unworthy daughter listen to you at last; tell me what to do, I will do.' And Reverend Mother, tearfully: 'Daughter, your father Aziz and I will go to Rawalpindi soon; in our old age we will live near our youngest daughter, our Emerald. You will also come, and a petrol pump will be purchased.' And so it was that Reverend Mother's dream began to come true, and Pia Aziz agreed to relinquish the world of films for that of fuel. My uncle Hanif, I thought, would probably have approved.

The dust affected us all during those forty days; it made Ahmed Sinai churlish and raucous, so that he refused to sit in the company of his in-laws and made Alice Pereira relay messages to the mourners, messages which he also yelled out from his office: 'Keep the racket down! I am working in the middle of this hullaballoo!' It made General Zulfikar and Emerald look constantly at calendars and airline timetables, while their son Zafar began to boast to the Brass Monkey that he was getting his father to arrange a marriage between them. 'You should think you're lucky,' this cocky cousin told my sister, 'My father is a big man in Pakistan.' But although Zafar had inherited his father's looks, the dust had clogged up the Monkey's spirits, and she didn't have the heart to fight him. Meanwhile my aunt Alia spread her ancient, dusty disappointment through the air and my most absurd relatives, the family of my uncle Mustapha, sat sullenly in corners and were forgotten, as usual; Mustapha Aziz's moustache, proudly waxed and upturned at the tips when he arrived, had long since sagged under the depressive influence of the dust.

And then, on the twenty-second day of the mourning period, my grandfather, Aadam Aziz, saw God.

He was sixty-eight that year – still a decade older than the century. But sixteen years without optimism had taken a

380

heavy toll; his eyes were still blue, but his back was bent. Shuffling around Buckingham Villa in embroidered skull-cap and full-length chugha-coat – coated, too, in a thin film of dust – he munched aimlessly on raw carrots and sent thin streaks of spittle down the grizzled white contours of his chin. And as he declined, Reverend Mother grew larger and stronger; she, who had once wailed pitifully at the sight of Mercurochrome, now appeared to thrive on his weakness, as though their marriage had been one of those mythical unions in which succubi appear to men as innocent damsels, and, after luring them into the matrimonial bed, regain their true, awful aspect and begin to swallow their souls . . . my grandmother, in those days, had acquired a moustache almost as luxuriant as the dustily-sagging hair on the upper lip of her one surviving son. She sat cross-legged on her bed, smearing her lip with a mysterious fluid which set hard around the hairs and was then ripped off by a sharp, violent hand; but the remedy only served to exacerbate the ailment.

'He has become like a child again, whatsitsname,' Reverend Mother told my grandfather's children, 'and Hanif has finished him off.' She warned us that he had begun to see things. 'He talks to people who are not there,' she whispered loudly while he wandered through the room sucking his teeth, 'How he calls out, whatsitsname! In the middle of the night!' And she mimicked him: 'Ho, Tai? Is it you?' She told us children about the boatman, and the Hummingbird, and the Rani of Cooch Naheen. 'Poor man has lived too long, whatsitsname; no father should see his son die first.' . . . And Amina, listening, shook her head in sympathy, not knowing that Aadam Aziz would leave her this legacy – that she, too, in her last days, would be visited by things which had no business to return.

We could not use the ceiling-fans for the dust; perspiration ran down the face of my stricken grandfather and left streaks of mud on his cheeks. Sometimes he would grab anyone who was near him and speak with utter lucidity: 'These Nehrus will not be happy until they have made themselves hereditary kings!' Or, dribbling into the face of a squirming General Zulfikar: 'Ah, unhappy Pakistan! How ill-served by her rulers!' But at other times he seemed to imagine himself in a gemstone store, and muttered, '. . . Yes: there were emeralds and rubies . . .' The Monkey whispered to me, 'Is grandpa going to die?'

What leaked into me from Aadam Aziz: a certain vulnerability to women, but also its cause, the hole at the centre of himself caused by his (which is also my) failure to believe or disbelieve in God. And something else as well – something which, at the age of eleven, I saw before anyone else noticed. My grandfather had begun to crack.

'In the head?' Padma asks, 'You mean in the upper storey?'

The boatman Tai said: 'The ice is always waiting, Aadam baba, just under the water's skin.' I saw the cracks in his eyes – a delicate tracery of colourless lines against the blue; I saw a network of fissures spreading beneath his leathery skin; and I answered the Monkey's question: 'I think he is.' Before the end of the forty-day mourning period, my grandfather's skin had begun to split and flake and peel; he could hardly open his mouth to eat because of the cuts in the corners of his lips; and his teeth began to drop like Flitted flies. But a crack-death can be slow; and it was a long time before we knew about the other cracks, about the disease which was nibbling at his bones, so that finally his skeleton disintegrated into powder inside the weatherbeaten sack of his skin.

Padma is looking suddenly panicky. 'What are you saying? You, mister: are you telling that you also . . . what nameless thing can eat up any man's *bones?* Is it . . .'

No time to pause now; no time for sympathy or panic; I have already gone further than I should. Retreating a little in time, I must mention that something also leaked into Aadam Aziz from me; because on the twenty-third day of the

382

mourning period, he asked the entire family to assemble in the same room of glass vases (no need to hide them from my uncle now) and cushions and immobilized fans, the same room in which I had announced visions of my own . . . Reverend Mother had said, 'He has become like a child again'; like a child, my grandfather announced that, three weeks after he had heard of the death of a son whom he had believed to be alive and well, he had seen with his own eyes the God in whose death he had tried all his life to believe. And, like a child, he was not believed. Except by one person . . . 'Yes, listen,' my grandfather said, his voice a weak imitation of his old booming tones, 'Yes, Rani? You are here? And Abdullah? Come, sit, Nadir, this is news – where is Ahmed? Alia will want him here . . . God, my children; God, whom I fought all my life, Oskar? Ilse? – No, of course I know they are dead. You think I'm old, maybe foolish; but I have seen God.' And the story, slowly, despite rambles and diversions, comes inching out: at midnight, my grandfather awoke in his darkened room. Someone else present – someone who was not his wife. Reverend Mother, snoring in her bed. But someone. Someone with shining dust on him, lit by the setting moon. And Aadam Aziz, 'Ho, Tai? Is it you?' And Reverend Mother, mumbling in her sleep, 'O, sleep, husband, forget this . . .' But the someone, the something, cries in a loud startling (and startled?) voice, 'Jesus Christ Almighty!' (Amid the cut-glass vases, my grandfather laughs apologetically heh-heh, for mentioning the infidel name.) 'Jesus Christ Almighty!' and my grandfather looking, and seeing, yes, there are holes in hands, perforations in the feet as there once were in a . . . But he is rubbing his eyes, shaking his head, saying: 'Who? What name? What did you say?' And the apparition, startling-startled, 'God! God!' And, after a pause, 'I didn't think you could see me.'

'But I saw Him,' my grandfather says beneath motionless fans. 'Yes, I can't deny it, I surely did.' . . . And the apparition:

'You're the one whose son died'; and my grandfather, with a pain in his chest: 'Why? Why did that happen?' To which the creature, made visible only by dust: 'God has his reasons, old man; life's like that, right?'

Reverend Mother dismissed us all. 'Old man doesn't know what he means, whatsitsname. Such a thing, that grey hairs should make a man blaspheme!' But Mary Pereira left with her face pale as bedsheets; Mary knew whom Aadam Aziz had seen – who, decayed by his responsibility for her crime, had holes in hands and feet; whose heel had been penetrated by a snake; who died in a nearby clocktower, and had been mistaken for God.

I may as well finish my grandfather's story here and now; I've gone this far, and the opportunity may not present itself later on . . . somewhere in the depths of my grandfather's senility, which inevitably reminded me of the craziness of Professor Schaapsteker upstairs, the bitter idea took root that God, by his off-hand attitude to Hanif's suicide, had proved his own culpability in the affair; Aadam grabbed General Zulfikar by his military lapels and whispered to him: 'Because I never believed, he stole my son!' And Zulfikar: 'No, no, Doctor Sahib, you must not trouble yourself so . . .' But Aadam Aziz never forgot his vision; although the details of the particular deity he had seen grew blurred in his mind, leaving behind only a passionate, drooling desire for revenge (which lust is also common to us both) . . . at the end of the forty-day mourning period, he would refuse to go to Pakistan (as Reverend Mother had planned) because that was a country built especially for God; and in the remaining years of his life he often disgraced himself by stumbling into mosques and temples with his old man's stick, mouthing imprecations and lashing out at any worshipper or holy man within range. In Agra, he was tolerated for the sake of the man he had once been; the old ones at the Cornwallis Road paan-shop played hit-the-spittoon and reminisced with

384

compassion about the Doctor Sahib's past. Reverend Mother was obliged to yield to him for this reason if for no other – the iconoclasm of his dotage would have created a scandal in a country where he was not known.

Behind his foolishness and his rages, the cracks continued to spread; the disease munched steadily on his bones, while hatred ate the rest of him away. He did not die, however, until 1964. It happened like this: on Wednesday, December 25th, 1963 – on Christmas Day! – Reverend Mother awoke to find her husband gone. Coming out into the courtyard of her home, amid hissing geese and the pale shadows of the dawn, she called for a servant; and was told that the Doctor Sahib had gone by rickshaw to the railway station. By the time she reached the station, the train had gone; and in this way my grandfather, following some unknown impulse, began his last journey, so that he could end his story where it (and mine) began, in a city surrounded by mountains and set upon a lake.

The valley lay hidden in an eggshell of ice; the mountains had closed in, *to snarl like angry jaws around the city on the lake* . . . winter in Srinagar; winter in Kashmir. On Friday, December 27th, a man answering to my grandfather's description was seen, chugha-coated, drooling, in the vicinity of the Hazratbal Mosque. At four forty-five on Saturday morning, Haji Muhammad Khalil Ghanai noticed the theft, from the Mosque's inner sanctum, of the valley's most treasured relic: the holy hair of the Prophet Muhammad.

Did he? Didn't he? If it was him, why did he not enter the Mosque, stick in hand, to belabour the faithful as he had become accustomed to doing? If not him, then why? There were rumours of a Central Government plot to 'demoralize the Kashmiri Muslims', by stealing their sacred hair; and counter-rumours about Pakistani *agents provocateurs,* who supposedly stole the relic to foment unrest . . . did they? Or not? Was this bizarre incident truly political, or was it the penultimate attempt at revenge upon God by a father who had lost his son? For ten days, no food was cooked in any Muslim home; there were riots and burnings of cars; but my grandfather was above politics now, and is not known to have joined in any processions. He was a man with a single mission; and what is known is that on January 1st, 1964 (a Wednesday, just one week after his departure from Agra), he set his face towards the hill which Muslims erroneously called the Takht-e-Sulaiman, Solomon's seat, atop which stood a radio mast, but also the black blister of the temple of the acharya Sankara. Ignoring the distress of the city, my grandfather climbed; while the cracking sickness within him gnawed patiently through his bones. He was not recognized.

Doctor Aadam Aziz (*Heidelberg-returned*) died five days before the government announced that its massive search for the single hair of the Prophet's head had been successful. When the State's holiest saints assembled to authenticate the hair, my grandfather was unable to tell them the truth. (If they were wrong . . . but I can't answer the questions I've asked.) Arrested for the crime – and later released on grounds of ill-health – was one Abdul Rahim Bande; but perhaps my grandfather, had he lived, could have shed a stranger light on the affair . . . at midday on January 1st, Aadam Aziz arrived outside the temple of Sankara Acharya. He was seen to raise his walking-stick; inside the temple, women performing the rite of puja at the Shiva-lingam shrank back – as women had once shrunk from the wrath of another, tetrapod-obsessed doctor; and then the cracks claimed him, and his legs gave way beneath him as the bones disintegrated, and the effect of his fall was to shatter the rest of his skeleton beyond all hope of repair. He was identified by the papers in the pocket of his chugha-coat: a photograph of his son, and a half-completed (and fortunately, correctly addressed) letter to his wife. The body, too fragile to be transported, was buried in the valley of his birth.

I am watching Padma; her muscles have begun to twitch distractedly.'Consider this,' I say. 'Is what happened to my grandfather so very strange? Compare it with the mere fact of the holy fuss over the theft of a hair; because every last detail of that is true, and by comparison, an old man's death is surely perfectly normal.' Padma relaxes; her muscles give me the go-ahead. Because I've spent too long on Aadam Aziz; perhaps I'm afraid of what must be told next; but the revelation will not be denied.

One last fact: after the death of my grandfather, Prime Minister Jawaharlal Nehru fell ill and never recovered his health. This fatal sickness finally killed him on May 27th, 1964.

If I hadn't wanted to be a hero, Mr Zagallo would never have pulled out my hair. If my hair had remained intact, Glandy Keith and Fat Perce wouldn't have taunted me; Masha Miovic wouldn't have goaded me into losing my finger. And from my finger flowed blood which was neither-Alpha-nor-Omega, and sent me into exile; and in exile I was filled with the lust for revenge which led to the murder of Homi Catrack; and if Homi hadn't died, perhaps my uncle would not have strolled off a roof into the sea-breezes; and then my grandfather would not have gone to Kashmir and been broken by the effort of climbing the Sankara Acharya hill. And my grandfather was the founder of my family, and my fate was linked by my birthday to that of the nation, and the father of the nation was Nehru. Nehru's death; can I avoid the conclusion that that, too, was all my fault?

But now we're back in 1958; because on the thirty-seventh day of the mourning period, the truth, which had been creeping up on Mary Pereira – and therefore on me – for over eleven years, finally came out into the open; truth, in the shape of an old, old man, whose stench of Hell penetrated even my clogged-up nostrils, and whose body lacked fingers and toes and was littered with boils and holes, walked up our two-storey hillock and appeared through the dust-cloud to be seen by Mary Pereira, who was cleaning the chick-blinds on the verandah.

Here, then, was Mary's nightmare come true; here, visible through the pall of dust, was the ghost of Joe D'Costa, walking towards the ground-floor office of Ahmed Sinai! As if it hadn't been enough to show himself to Aadam Aziz . . . 'Arré, Joseph,' Mary screamed, dropping her duster, 'you go away now! Don't come here now! Don't be bothering the sahibs with your troubles! O God, Joseph, go, go na, you will kill me today!' But the ghost walked on down the driveway.

Mary Pereira, abandoning chick-blinds, leaving them hanging askew, rushes into the heart of the house to throw herself at the feet of my mother – small fat hands joined in supplication – 'Begum Sahiba! Begum Sahiba, forgive me!' And my mother astounded: 'What is this, Mary? What has got your goat?' But Mary is beyond dialogue, she is weeping uncontrollably, crying 'O God my hour has come, my darling Madam, only let me go peacefully, do not put me in the jailkhana!' And also, 'Eleven years, my Madam, see if I haven't loved you all, O Madam, and that boy with his face like the moon; but now I am killed, I am no-good woman, I shall burn in hell! *Funtoosh*!' cried Mary, and again, 'It's finished; *funtoosh*!'

Still I did not guess what was coming; not even when Mary threw herself upon me (I was taller than her now; her tears wet my neck): 'O baba, baba; today you must learn a thing, such a thing I have done; but come now . . .' and the little woman drew herself up with immense dignity, '. . . I will tell you all before that Joseph does. Begum, children, all you other great sirs and madams, come now to sahib's office, and I will tell.'

Public announcements have punctuated my life; Amina in a Delhi gully, and Mary in a sunless office . . . with my whole family trooping amazedly behind us, I went downstairs with Mary Pereira, who would not let go of my hand.

What was in the room with Ahmed Sinai? What had given my father a face from which djinns and money had been chased away and replaced by a look of utter desolation? What sat huddled up in the corner of the room, filling the air with a sulphurous stench? What, shaped like a man, lacked fingers and toes, whose face seemed to bubble like the hot springs of New Zealand (which I'd seen in the *Wonder Book of Wonders*)? . . . No time to explain, because Mary Pereira has begun to talk, gabbling out a secret which has been hidden for over eleven years, pulling us all out of the dream-world she invented when she changed name-tags, forcing us into the horror of the truth. And all the time she held on to me; like a mother protecting her child, she shielded me from my family. (Who were learning . . . as I was . . . that they were not . . .)

. . . It was just after midnight and in the streets there were fireworks and crowds, the many-headed monster roaring, I did it for my Joseph, sahib, but please don't send me to jail, look the boy is a good boy, sahib, I am a poor woman, sahib, one mistake, one minute in so many years, not jailkhana sahib, I will go, eleven years I gave but I will go now, sahib, only this is a good boy, sahib, you must not send him, sahib, after eleven years he is your son . . . O, you boy with your face like the sun coming out, O Saleem my piece-of-the-moon, you must know that your father was Winkie and your mother is also dead . . .

Mary Pereira ran out of the room.

Ahmed Sinai said, in a voice as faraway as a bird: 'That, in the corner, is my old servant Musa, who tried to rob me once.'

(Can any narrative stand so much so soon? I glance towards Padma; she appears to be stunned, like a fish.)

389

Once upon a time there was a servant who robbed my father; who swore he was innocent; who called down upon himself the curse of leprosy if he should prove a liar; and who was proved to be lying. He had left in disgrace; but I told you then he was a time-bomb, and he had returned to explode. Musa had, indeed, contracted leprosy; and had returned across the silence of the years to beg for my father's forgiveness, so that he could be released from his self-inflicted curse.

. . . Someone was called God who was not God; someone else was taken for a ghost, and was not a ghost; and a third person discovered that although his name was Saleem Sinai, he was not his parents' son . . .

'I forgive you,' Ahmed Sinai said to the leper. After that day, he was cured of one of his obsessions; he never tried again to discover his own (and wholly imaginary) family curse.

'I couldn't tell it any other way,' I say to Padma. 'Too painful; I had to just blurt it out, all crazy-sounding, just like that.'

'O, mister,' Padma blubbers helplessly, 'O, mister, mister!'

'Come on now,' I say, 'It's an old story.'

But her tears aren't for me; for the moment, she's forgotten about what-chews-at-bones-beneath-the-skin; she's crying over Mary Pereira, of whom, as I've said, she had become excessively fond.

'What happened to her?' she says with red eyes. 'That Mary?'

I am seized by an irrational anger. I shout: 'You ask her!'

Ask her how she went home to the city of Panjim in Goa, how she told her ancient mother the story of her shame! Ask how her mother went wild with the scandal (appropriately enough: it was a time for old folk to lose their wits)! Ask: did daughter and old mother go into the streets to seek forgiveness? Was that not the one time in each ten years when

390

the mummified corpse of St Francis Xavier (as holy a relic as the Prophet's hair) is taken from its vault in the Cathedral of Bom Jesus and carried around the town? Did Mary and old distraught Mrs Pereira find themselves pressing up against the catafalque; was the old lady beside herself with grief for her daughter's crime? Did old Mrs Pereira, shouting, 'Hai! Ai-hai! Ai-hai-hai!', clamber up on to the bier to kiss the foot of the Holy One? Amidst uncountable crowds, did Mrs Pereira enter a holy frenzy? Ask! Did she or didn't she, in the clutches of her wild spirit, place her lips around the big toe on St Francis's left foot? Ask for yourself: did Mary's mother *bite the toe right off*?

'How?' Padma wails, unnerved by my wrath. 'How, *ask*?'

... And is this also true: were the papers making it up when they wrote that the old lady had been miraculously punished; when they quoted Church sources and eyewitnesses, who described how the old woman was turned into solid stone? No? Ask her if it's true that the Church sent a stone-statue figure of an old woman around the towns and the villages of Goa, to show what happened to those who misbehave with the saints?' Ask: was this statue not seen in several villages simultaneously – and does that prove fraud, or a further miracle?

'You know I can't ask anyone,' Padma howls ... but I, feeling my fury subside, am making no more revelations tonight.

Baldly, then: Mary Pereira left us, and went to her mother in Goa. But Alice Pereira stayed; Alice remained in Ahmed Sinai's office, and typed, and fetched snacks and fizzy drinks.

As for me – at the end of the mourning period for my uncle Hanif, I entered my second exile.

Movements performed
by pepperpots

I was obliged to come to the conclusion that Shiva, my rival, my changeling brother, could no longer be admitted into the forum of my mind; for reasons which were, I admit, ignoble. I was afraid he would discover what I was sure I could not conceal from him – the secrets of our birth. Shiva, for whom the world was things, for whom history could only be explained as the continuing struggle of oneself-against-the-crowd, would certainly insist on claiming his birthright; and, aghast at the very notion of my knock-kneed antagonist replacing me in the blue room of my childhood while I, perforce, walked morosely off the two-storey hillock to enter the northern slums; refusing to accept that the prophecy of Ramram Seth had been intended for Winkie's boy, that it was to Shiva that Prime Ministers had written, and for Shiva that fishermen pointed out to sea . . . placing, in short, a far higher value on my eleven-year-old sonship than on mere blood, I resolved that my destructive, violent alter ego should never again enter the increasingly fractious councils of the Midnight Children's Conference; that I would guard my secret – which had once been Mary's – with my very life.

There were nights, at this time, when I avoided convening the Conference at all – not because of the unsatisfactory turn it had taken, but simply because I knew it would take time, and cool blood, to erect a barrier around my new knowledge which could deny it to the Children; eventually, I was confident, I would manage this . . . but I was afraid of Shiva. Most ferocious and powerful of the Children, he would penetrate where others could not go . . . At any rate, I avoided my fellow-Children; and then suddenly it was too late, because, having exiled Shiva, I found myself hurled into an exile from which I was incapable of contacting my more-than-five-hundred colleagues: I was flung across the Partition-created frontier into Pakistan.

Late in September 1958, the mourning period for my uncle Hanif Aziz came to an end; and, miraculously, the dust-cloud which had enveloped us was settled by a merciful shower of rain. When we had bathed and put on newly-washed clothes and switched on the ceiling-fans, we emerged from bath-rooms filled, briefly, with the illusory optimism of freshly-soaped cleanliness; to discover a dusty, unwashed Ahmed Sinai, whisky-bottle in his hand, his eyes rimmed with blood, swaying upstairs from his office in the manic grip of djinns. He had been wrestling, in his private world of abstraction, with the unthinkable realities which Mary's revelations had unleashed; and owing to some cockeyed functioning of the alcohol, had been seized by an indescribable rage which he directed, neither at Mary's departed back, nor at the changeling in his midst, but at my mother – at, I should say, Amina Sinai. Perhaps because he knew he should beg her forgiveness, and would not, Ahmed ranted at her for hours within the shocked hearing of her family; I will not repeat the names he called her, nor the vile courses of action he recommended she should take with her life. But in the end it was Reverend Mother who intervened.

'Once before, my daughter,' she said, ignoring Ahmed's continuing ravings, 'your father and I, whatsitsname, said there was no shame in leaving an inadequate husband. Now I say again: you have, whatsitsname, a man of unspeakable vileness. Go from him; go today, and take your children, whatsitsname, away from these oaths which he spews from his lips like an animal, whatsitsname, of the gutter. Take your children, I say, whatsitsname – *both* your children,' she said, clutching me to her bosom. Once Reverend Mother had legitimized me, there was no one to oppose her; it seems to me now, across the years, that even my cursing father was affected by her support of the eleven-year-old snotnosed child.

Reverend Mother fixed everything; my mother was like putty – like potter's clay! – in her omnipotent hands. At that time, my grandmother (I must continue to call her that) still believed that she and Aadam Aziz would shortly be emigrating to Pakistan; so she instructed my aunt Emerald to take us all with her – Amina, the Monkey, myself, even my aunty Pia – and await her coming. 'Sisters must care for sisters, whatsitsname,' Reverend Mother said, 'in times of trouble.' My aunt Emerald looked highly displeased; but both she and General Zulfikar acquiesced. And, since my father was in a lunatic temper which made us fear for our safety, and the Zulfikars had already booked themselves on a ship which was to sail that night, I left my lifelong home that very day, leaving Ahmed Sinai alone with Alice Pereira; because when my mother left her second husband, all the other servants walked out, too.

In Pakistan, my second period of hurtling growth came to an end. And, in Pakistan, I discovered that somehow the existence of a frontier 'jammed' my thought-transmissions to the more-than-five-hundred; so that, exiled once more from my home, I was also exiled from the gift which was my truest birthright: the gift of the midnight children.

We lay anchored off the Rann of Kutch on a heat-soaked afternoon. Heat buzzed in my bad left ear; but I chose to remain on deck, watching as small, vaguely ominous rowing boats and fishermen's dhows ran a ferry service between our ship and the Rann, transporting objects veiled in canvas back and forth, back and forth. Below decks, the adults were playing housie-housie; I had no idea where the Monkey was. It was the first time I had ever been on a real ship (occasional visits to American warships in Bombay harbour didn't count, being merely tourism; and there was always the embarrassment of being in the company of dozens of highly-pregnant ladies, who always came on these tour parties in the hope that they would enter labour and·give birth to children who qualified, by virtue of their seaborne birth, for American citizenship). I stared through the heat-haze at the Rann. *The Rann of Kutch* . . . I'd always thought it a magical name, and half-feared-half-longed to visit the place, that chameleon area which was land for half the year and sea for the other half, and on which, it was said, the receding ocean would abandon all manner of fabulous debris, such as treasure-chests, white ghostly jellyfish, and even the occasional gasping, freak-legendary figure of a merman. Gazing for the first time upon this amphibian terrain, this bog of nightmare, I should have felt excited; but the heat and recent events were weighing me down; my upper lip was still childishly wet with nose-goo, but I felt oppressed by a feeling of having moved directly from an overlong and dribbling childhood into a premature (though still leaky) old age. My voice had deepened; I had been forced to start shaving, and my face was spotted with blood where the razor had sliced off the heads of pimples . . . The ship's purser passed me and said, 'Better get below, son. It's the hottest time just now.' I asked about the ferrying boats. 'Just supplies,' he said and moved away, leaving me to contemplate a future in which there was little to look forward to except the grudging hospitality of General Zulfikar, the self-satisfied preening of my aunt Emerald, who would no doubt enjoy showing off her worldly success and status to her unhappy sister and bereaved sister-in-law, and the muscle-headed cockiness of their son Zafar . . . 'Pakistan,' I said aloud, 'What a complete dump!' And we hadn't even arrived

. . . I looked at the boats; they seemed to be swimming through a dizzying haze. The deck seemed to be swaying violently as well, although there was virtually no wind; and although I tried to grab the rails, the boards were too quick for me: they rushed up and hit me on the nose.

That was how I came to Pakistan, with a mild attack of sunstroke to add to the emptiness of my hands and the knowledge of my birth; and what was the name of the boat? What two sister-ships still plied between Bombay and Karachi in those days before politics ended their journeys? Our boat was the S.S. *Sabarmati*; its sister, which passed us just before we reached the Karachi harbour, was the *Sarasvati*. We steamed into exile aboard the Commander's namesake-ship, proving once again that there was no escape from recurrence.

We reached Rawalpindi by hot, dusty train. (The General and Emerald travelled in Air-Conditioned; they bought the rest of us ordinary first-class tickets.) But it was cool when we reached 'Pindi and I set foot, for the first time, in a northern city . . . I remember it as a low, anonymous town; army barracks, fruit-shops, a sports goods industry; tall military men in the streets; Jeeps; furniture carvers; polo. A town in which it was possible to be very, very cold. And in a new and expensive housing development, a vast house surrounded by a high wall which was topped by barbed wire and patrolled by sentries: General Zulfikar's home. There was a bath next to the double bed in which the General slept; there was a house catch-phrase: 'Let's get organized!'; the servants wore green military jerseys and berets; in the evenings the odours of bhang and charas floated up from their quarters. The furniture was expensive and surprisingly beautiful; Emerald could not be faulted on her taste. It was a dull, lifeless house, for all its military airs; even the goldfish in the tank set in the dining-room wall seemed to bubble listlessly; perhaps its most

396

interesting inhabitant was not even human. You will permit me, for a moment, to describe the General's dog Bonzo. Excuse me: the General's old beagle bitch.

This goitred creature of papery antiquity had been supremely indolent and useless all her life; but while I was still recovering from sunstroke she created the first furore of our stay – a sort of trailer for the 'revolution of the pepperpots'. General Zulfikar had taken her one day to a military training-camp, where he was to watch a team of mine-detectors at work in a specially-prepared minefield. (The General was anxious to mine the entire Indo-Pak border. 'Let's get organized!' he would exclaim. 'Let's give those Hindus something to worry! We'll blow their invaders into so many pieces, there'll be no damn thing left to reincarnate.' He was not, however, overly concerned about the frontiers of East Pakistan, being of the view that 'those damn blackies can look after themselves'.) . . . And now Bonzo slipped her leash, and somehow evading the frantically clutching hands of young jawans, waddled out into the minefield.

Blind panic. Mine-detecting soldiers picking their way in frenzied slow-motion through the blasting zone. General Zulfikar and other Army brass diving for shelter behind their grandstand, awaiting the explosion . . . But there was none; and when the flower of the Pakistan Army peeped out from inside dustbins or behind benches, it saw Bonzo picking her way daintily through the field of the lethal seeds, nose to ground, Bonzo-the-insouciant, quite at her ease. General Zulfikar flung his peaked cap in the air. 'Damn marvellous!' he cried in the thin voice which squeezed between his nose and chin, 'The old lady can smell the mines!' Bonzo was drafted forthwith into the armed forces as a four-legged mine-detector with the courtesy rank of sergeant-major.

I mention Bonzo's achievement because it gave the General a stick with which to beat us. We Sinais – and Pia Aziz – were helpless, non-productive members of the Zulfikar household, and the General did not wish us to forget it: 'Even a damn hundred-year-old beagle bitch can earn her damn living,' he was heard to mutter, 'but my house is full of people who can't get organized into one damn thing.' But before the end of October he would be grateful for (at least) my presence . . . and the transformation of the Monkey was not far away.

We went to school with cousin Zafar, who seemed less anxious to marry my sister now that we were children of a broken home; but his worst deed came one weekend when we were taken to the General's mountain cottage in Nathia Gali, beyond Murree. I was in a state of high excitement (my illness had just been declared cured): mountains! The possibility of panthers! Cold, biting air! – so that I thought nothing of it when the General asked me if I'd mind sharing a bed with Zafar, and didn't even guess when they spread the rubber sheet over the mattress . . . I awoke in the small hours in a large rancid pool of lukewarm liquid and began to yell blue murder. The General appeared at our bedside and began to thrash the living daylights out of his son. 'You're a big man now! Damn it to hell! Still, and still you do it! Get yourself organized! Good for nothing! Who behaves in this damn way? Cowards, that's who! Damn me if I'll have a coward for a son . . .' The enuresis of my cousin Zafar continued, however, to be the shame of his family; despite thrashings, the liquid ran down his leg; and one day it happened when he was awake. But that was after certain movements had, with my assistance, been performed by pepperpots, proving to me that although the telepathic air-waves were jammed in this country, the modes of connection still seemed to function; active-literally as well as metaphorically, I helped change the fate of the Land of the Pure.

The Brass Monkey and I were helpless observers, in those days, of my wilting mother. She, who had always been assiduous in the heat, had begun to wither in the northern cold. Deprived of two husbands, she was also deprived (in her own eyes) of meaning; and there was also a relationship to rebuild, between mother and son. She held me tightly one night and said, 'Love, my child, is a thing that every mother learns; it is not born with a baby, but made; and for eleven years, I have learned to love you as my son.' But there was a distance behind her gentleness, as though she were trying to persuade herself . . . a distance, too, in the Monkey's midnight whispers of, 'Hey, brother, why don't we go and pour water over Zafar – they'll only think he's wet his bed?' – and it was my sense of this gap which showed me that, despite their use of *son* and *brother,* their imaginations were working hard to assimilate Mary's confession; not knowing then that they would be unable to succeed in their re-imaginings of *brother* and *son,* I remained terrified of Shiva; and was accordingly driven even deeper into the illusory heart of my desire to prove myself worthy of their kinship. Despite Reverend Mother's recognition of me, I was never at my ease until, on a more-than-three-years-distant verandah, my father said, 'Come, son; come here and let me love you.' Perhaps that is why I behaved as I did on the night of October 7th, 1958.

. . . An eleven-year-old boy, Padma, knew very little about the internal affairs of Pakistan; but he could see, on that October day, that an unusual dinner-party was being planned. Saleem at eleven knew nothing about the Constitution of 1956 and its gradual erosion; but his eyes were keen enough to spot the Army security officers, the military police, who arrived that afternoon to lurk secretly behind every garden bush. Faction strife and the multiple incompetences of Mr Ghulam Mohammed were a mystery to him; but it was clear that his aunt Emerald was putting on her finest jewels. The farce of four-prime-ministers-in-two-years had never made him giggle; but he could sense, in the air of drama hanging over the General's house, that something like a final curtain was approaching. Ignorant of the emergence of the Republican party, he was nevertheless curious about the guest-list for the Zulfikar party; although he was in a country where names meant nothing – who was Chaudhuri Muhammad Ali? Or Suhrawardy? Or Chundrigar, or Noon? – the anonymity of the dinner-guests, which was carefully preserved by his uncle and aunt, was a puzzling thing. Even though he had once cut Pakistani headlines out of newspapers – FURNITURE HURLING SLAYS DEPUTY E-PAK SPEAKER – he had no idea why, at six p.m., a long line of black limousines came through the sentried walls of the Zulfikar Estate; why flags waved on their bonnets; why their occupants refused to smile; or why Emerald and Pia and my mother stood behind General Zulfikar with expressions on their faces which would have seemed more appropriate at a funeral than a social gathering. Who what was dying? Who why were the limousine arrivals? – I had no idea; but I was on my toes behind my mother, staring at the smoked-glass windows of the enigmatic cars.

Car-doors opened; equerries, adjutants, leaped out of vehicles and opened rear doors, saluted stiffly; a small muscle began to tic in my aunt Emerald's cheek. And then, who descended from the flag-waving motors? What names should be put to the fabulous array of moustaches, swagger-sticks, gimlet-eyes, medals and shoulder-pips which emerged? Saleem knew neither names nor serial numbers; ranks, however, could be discerned. Gongs and pips, proudly worn on chests and shoulders, announced the arrival of very top brass indeed. And out of the last car came a tall man with an astonishingly round head, round as a tin globe although unmarked by lines of longitude and latitude; planet-headed, he was not labelled like the orb which the Monkey had once squashed; not MADE AS ENGLAND (although certainly Sandhurst-trained) he moved through saluting gongs-and-pips; arrived at my aunt Emerald; and added his own salute to the rest.

'Mr Commander-in-Chief,' my aunt said, 'be welcome in our home.'

'Emerald, Emerald,' came from the mouth set in the earth-shaped head – the mouth positioned immediately beneath a neat moustache, 'Why such formality, such takalluf?' Whereupon she embraced him with, 'Well then, Ayub, you're looking wonderful.'

He was a General then, though Field-Marshalship was not far away . . . we followed him into the house; we watched him drink (water) and laugh (loudly); at dinner we watched him again; saw how he ate like a peasant, so that his moustache became stained with gravy . . . 'Listen, Em,' he said, 'Always such preparations when I come! But I'm only a simple soldier; dal and rice from your kitchens would be a feast for me.'

'A soldier, sir,' my aunt replied, 'but simple – never! Not once!'

Long trousers qualified me to sit at table, next to cousin Zafar, surrounded by gongs-and-pips; tender years, however, placed us both under an obligation to be silent. (General Zulfikar told me in a military hiss, 'One peep out of you and you're off to the guardhouse. If you want to stay, stay mum. Got it?' Staying mum, Zafar and I were free to look and listen. But Zafar, unlike me, was not trying to prove himself worthy of his name . . .)

What did eleven-year-olds hear at dinner? What did they understand by jocund military references to 'that Suhrawardy, who always opposed the Pakistan Idea' – or to Noon, 'who should have been called Sunset, what?' And through discussions of election-rigging and black-money, what undercurrent of danger permeated their skins, making the downy hairs on their arms stand on end? And when the Commander-in-Chief quoted the Quran, how much of its meaning was understood by eleven-year-old ears?

'It is written,' said the round-headed man, and the gongs-and-pips fell silent, '*Aad and Thamoud we also destroyed.*

401

Satan had made their foul deeds seem fair to them, keen-sighted though they were.'

It was as though a cue had been given; a wave of my aunt's hands dismissed the servants. She rose to go herself; my mother and Pia went with her. Zafar and I, too, rose from our seats; but *he,* he himself, called down the length of the sumptuous table: 'The little men should stay. It is their future, after all.' The little men, frightened but also proud, sat and stayed mum, following orders.

Just men now. A change in the roundhead's face; something darker, something mottled and desperate has occupied it . . . 'Twelve months ago,' he says, 'I spoke to all of you. Give the politicians one year – is that not what I said?' Heads nod; murmurs of assent. 'Gentlemen, we have given them a year; the situation has become intolerable, and I am not prepared to tolerate it any longer!' Gongs-and-pips assume stern, statesmanlike expressions. Jaws are set, eyes gaze keenly into the future. 'Tonight, therefore,' – yes! I was there! A few yards from him! – General Ayub and I, myself and old Ayub Khan! – 'I am assuming control of the State.'

How do eleven-year-olds react to the announcement of a coup? Hearing the words, '. . . national finances in frightening disarray . . . corruption and impurity are everywhere . . .' do their jaws stiffen, too? Do their eyes focus on brighter tomorrows? Eleven-year-olds listen as a General cries, 'The Constitution is hereby abrogated! Central and Provincial legislatures are dissolved! Political parties are forthwith abolished!' – how do you think they feel?

When General Ayub Khan said, 'Martial Law is now imposed,' both cousin Zafar and I understood that his voice – that voice filled with power and decision and the rich timbre of my aunt's finest cooking – was speaking a thing for which we knew only one word: treason. I'm proud to say I kept my head; but Zafar lost control of a more embarrassing organ. Moisture stained his trouser-fronts; the yellow moisture of

402

fear trickled down his leg to stain Persian carpets; gongs-and-pips smelled something, and turned upon him with looks of infinite distaste; and then (worst of all) came laughter.

General Zulfikar had just begun saying, 'If you permit, sir, I shall map out tonight's procedures,' when his son wet his pants. In cold fury my uncle hurled his son from the room; 'Pimp! Woman!' followed Zafar out of the dining-chamber, in his father's thin sharp voice; 'Coward! Homosexual! Hindu!' leaped from Punchinello-face to chase his son up the stairs . . . Zulfikar's eyes settled on me. There was a plea in them. *Save the honour of the family. Redeem me from the incontinence of my son.* 'You, boy!' my uncle said, 'You want to come up here and help me?'

Of course, I nodded. Proving my manhood, my fitness for sonship, I assisted my uncle as he made the revolution. And in so doing, in earning his gratitude, in stilling the sniggers of the assembled gongs-and-pips, I created a new father for myself; General Zulfikar became the latest in the line of men who have been willing to call me 'sonny', or 'sonny Jim', or even simply 'my son'.

How we made the revolution: General Zulfikar described troop movements; I moved pepperpots symbolically while he spoke. In the clutches of the active-metaphorical mode of connection, I shifted salt-cellars and bowls of chutney: This mustard-jar is Company A occupying Head Post Office; there are two pepperpots surrounding a serving-spoon, which means Company B has seized the airport. With the fate of the nation in my hands, I shifted condiments and cutlery, capturing empty biriani-dishes with water-glasses, stationing saltcellars, on guard, around water-jugs. And when General Zulfikar stopped talking, the march of the table-service also came to an end. Ayub Khan seemed to settle down in his chair; was the wink he gave me just my imagination? – at any rate, the Commander-in-Chief said, 'Very good, Zulfikar; good show.'

In the movements performed by pepperpots etcetera, one table-ornament remained uncaptured: a cream-jug in solid silver, which, in our table-top coup, represented the Head of State, President Iskander Mirza; for three weeks, Mirza remained President.

An eleven-year-old boy cannot judge whether a President is truly corrupt, even if gongs-and-pips say he is; it is not for eleven-year-olds to say whether Mirza's association with the feeble Republican Party should have disqualified him from high office under the new régime. Saleem Sinai made no political judgments; but when, inevitably at midnight, on November 1st, my uncle shook me awake and whispered, 'Come on, sonny, it's time you got a taste of the real thing!', I leaped out of bed smartly; I dressed and went out into the night, proudly aware that my uncle had preferred my company to that of his own son.

Midnight. Rawalpindi speeding past us at seventy m.p.h. Motorcycles in front of us beside us behind us. 'Where are we going Zulfy – uncle?' *Wait and see.* Black smoked-windowed limousine pausing at darkened house. Sentries guard the door with crossed rifles; which part, to let us through. I am marching at my uncle's side, in step, through half-lit corridors; until we burst into a dark room with a shaft of moonlight spotlighting a four-poster bed. A mosquito net hangs over the bed like a shroud.

There is a man waking up, startled, *what the hell is going* . . . But General Zulfikar has a long-barrelled revolver; the tip of the gun is forced mmff between the man's parted teeth. 'Shut up,' my uncle says, superfluously. 'Come with us.' Naked overweight man stumbling from his bed. His eyes, asking: *Are you going to shoot me?* Sweat rolls down ample belly, catching moonlight, dribbling on to his soo-soo; but it is bitterly cold; he is not perspiring from the heat. He looks like a white Laughing Buddha; but not laughing. Shivering. My uncle's pistol is extracted from his mouth. 'Turn. Quick march!' . . . And gun-barrel pushed between the cheeks of an overfed rump. The man cries, 'For God's sake be careful; that thing has the safety off!' Jawans giggle as naked flesh emerges into moonlight, is pushed into black limousine . . . That night, I sat with a naked man as my uncle drove him to a military airfield; I stood and watched as the waiting aircraft taxied, accelerated, flew. What began, active-metaphorically, with pepperpots, ended then; not only did I overthrow a government – I also consigned a president to exile.

Midnight has many children; the offspring of Independence were not all human. Violence, corruption, poverty, generals, chaos, greed and pepperpots . . . I had to go into exile to learn that the children of midnight were more varied than I – even I – had dreamed.

'Really truly?' Padma asks. 'You were truly there?' Really truly. 'They say that Ayub was a good man before he became bad,' Padma says; it is a question. But Saleem, at eleven, made no such judgments. The movement of pepperpots does not necessitate moral choices. What Saleem was concerned with: not public upheaval, but personal rehabilitation. You see the paradox – my most crucial foray into history up to that moment was inspired by the most parochial of motives. Anyway, it was not 'my' country – or not then. Not my country, although I stayed in it – as refugee, not citizen; entered on my mother's Indian passport, I would have come in for a good deal of suspicion, maybe even deported or arrested as a spy, had it not been for my tender years and the power of my guardian with the Punch-like features – for four long years.

Four years of nothing.

Except growing into a teenager. Except watching my mother as she fell apart. Except observing the Monkey, who was a crucial year younger than me, fall under the insidious spell of that God-ridden country; the Monkey, once so rebellious and wild, adopting expressions of demureness and submission which must, at first, have seemed false even to her; the Monkey, learning how to cook and keep house, how to buy spices in the market; the Monkey, making the final break with the legacy of her grandfather, by learning prayers in Arabic and saying them at all prescribed times; the Monkey, revealing the streak of puritan fanaticism which she had hinted at when she asked for a nun's outfit; she, who spurned all offers of worldly love, was seduced by the love of that God who had been named after a carved idol in a pagan shrine built around a giant meteorite: Al-Lah, in the Qa'aba, the shrine of the great Black Stone.

But nothing else.

Four years away from the midnight children; four years without Warden Road and Breach Candy and Scandal Point and the lures of One Yard of Chocolates; away from the Cathedral School and the equestrian statue of Sivaji and melon-sellers at the Gateway of India: away from Divali and Ganesh Chaturthi and Coconut Day; four years of separation from a father who sat alone in a house he would not sell; alone, except for Professor Schaapsteker, who stayed in his apartment and shunned the company of men.

Can nothing really happen for four years? Obviously, not quite. My cousin Zafar, who had never been forgiven by his father for wetting his pants in the presence of history, was given to understand that he would be joining the Army as soon as he was of age. 'I want to see you prove you're not a woman,' his father told him.

And Bonzo died; General Zulfikar shed manly tears.

And Mary's confession faded until, because nobody spoke of it, it came to feel like a bad dream; to everyone except me.

And (without any assistance from me) relations between India and Pakistan grew worse; entirely without my help, India conquered Goa – 'the Portuguese pimple on the face of Mother India'; I sat on the sidelines and played no part in the acquisition of large-scale U.S. aid for Pakistan, nor was I to blame for Sino-India border skirmishes in the Aksai Chin region of Ladakh; the Indian census of 1961 revealed a literacy level of 23.7 per cent, but I was not entered in its records. The untouchable problem remained acute; I did nothing to alleviate it; and in the elections of 1962, the All-India Congress won 361 out of 494 seats in the Lok Sabha, and over 61 per cent of all State Assembly seats. Not even in this could my unseen hand be said to have moved; except, perhaps, metaphorically: the *status quo* was preserved in India; in my life, nothing changed either.

Then, on September 1st, 1962, we celebrated the Monkey's fourteenth birthday. By this time (and despite my uncle's continued fondness for me) we were well-established as social inferiors, the hapless poor relations of the great Zulfikars; so the party was a skimpy affair. The Monkey, however, gave every appearance of enjoying herself. 'It's my duty, brother,' she told me. I could hardly believe my ears . . . but perhaps my sister had an intuition of her fate; perhaps she knew the transformation which lay in store for her; why should I assume that I alone have had the powers of secret knowledge?

Perhaps, then, she guessed that when the hired musicians began to play (shehnai and vina were present; sarangi and sarod had their turns; tabla and sitar performed their virtuosic cross-examinations), Emerald Zulfikar would descend on her with callous elegance, demanding, 'Come on, Jamila, don't sit there like a melon, sing us a song like any good girl would!'

And that with this sentence my emerald-icy aunt would have begun, quite unwittingly, my sister's transformation from monkey into singer; because although she protested with the sullen clumsiness of fourteen-year-olds, she was hauled unceremoniously on to the musicians' dais by my organizing aunt; and although she looked as if she wished the floor would open up beneath her feet, she clasped her hands together; seeing no escape, the Monkey began to sing.

I have not, I think, been good at describing emotions – believing my audience to be capable of *joining in;* of imagining for themselves what I have been unable to re-imagine, so that my story becomes yours as well . . . but when my sister began to sing, I was certainly assailed by an emotion of such force that I was unable to understand it until, much later, it was explained to me by the oldest whore in the world. Because, with her first note, the Brass Monkey sloughed off her nickname; she, who had talked to birds (just as, long ago in a mountain valley, her great-grandfather used to do), must have learned from songbirds the arts of song. With one good ear and one bad ear, I listened to her faultless voice, which at fourteen was the voice of a grown woman, filled with the purity of wings and the pain of exile and the flying of eagles and the lovelessness of life and the melody of bulbuls and the glorious omnipresence of God; a voice which was afterwards compared to that of Muhammed's muezzin Bilal, issuing from the lips of a somewhat scrawny girl.

What I did not understand must wait to be told; let me record here that my sister earned her name at her fourteenth birthday party, and was known after that as Jamila Singer; and that I knew, as I listened to 'My Red Dupatta Of Muslin' and 'Shahbaz Qalandar', that the process which had begun during my first exile was nearing completion in my second; that, from now on, Jamila was the child who mattered, and that I must take second place to her talent for ever.

Jamila sang – I, humbly, bowed my head. But before she could enter fully into her kingdom, something else had to happen: I had to be properly finished off.

Drainage and the desert

What-chews-on-bones refuses to pause . . . it's only a matter of time. This is what keeps me going: I hold on to Padma. Padma is what matters – Padma-muscles, Padma's hairy forearms, Padma my own pure lotus . . . who, embarrassed, commands: 'Enough. Start. Start now.'

Yes, it must start with the cable. Telepathy set me apart; telecommunications dragged me down . . .

Amina Sinai was cutting verrucas out of her feet when the telegram arrived . . . once upon a time. No, that won't do, there's no getting away from the date: my mother, right ankle on left knee, was scooping corn-tissue out of the sole of her foot with a sharp-ended nail file on September 9th, 1962. And the time? The time matters, too. Well, then: in the afternoon. No, it's important to be more . . . At the stroke of three o'clock, which, even in the north, is the hottest time of day, a bearer brought her an envelope on a silver dish. A few seconds later, far away in New Delhi, Defence Minister Krishna Menon (acting on his own initiative, during Nehru's absence at the Commonwealth Prime Ministers' Conference) took the momentous decision to use force if necessary against the Chinese army on the Himalayan frontier. 'The Chinese must be ejected from the Thag La ridge,' Mr Menon said while my mother tore open a telegram. 'No weakness will be shown.' But this decision was a mere trifle when set beside the implications of my mother's cable; because while the eviction operation, code-named LEGHORN, was doomed to fail, and eventually to turn India into that most macabre of theatres, the Theatre of War, the cable was to plunge me secretly but surely towards the crisis which would end with my final eviction from my own inner world. While the Indian XXXIII Corps were acting on instructions passed from Menon to General Thapar, I, too, had been placed in great danger; as if unseen forces had decided that I had also overstepped the boundaries of what I was permitted to do or know or be; as though history had decided to put me firmly in my place. I was left entirely without a say in the matter; my mother read the telegram, burst into tears and said, 'Children, we're going home!' . . . after which, as I began by saying in another context, it was only a matter of time.

What the telegram said: PLEASE COME QUICK SINAISAHIB SUFFERED HEARTBOOT GRAVELY ILL SALAAMS ALICE PEREIRA.

'Of course, go at once, my darling,' my aunt Emerald told her sister, 'But what, my God, can be this *heartboot*?'

It is possible, even probable, that I am only the first historian to write the story of my undeniably exceptional life-and-times. Those who follow in my footsteps will, however, inevitably come to this present work, this source-book, this Hadith or Purana or *Grundrisse,* for guidance and inspiration. I say to these future exegetes: when you come to examine the events which followed on from the 'heartboot cable', remember that at the very eye of the hurricane which was unleashed upon me – the sword, to switch metaphors, with which the *coup de grâce* was applied – there lay a single unifying force. I refer to telecommunications.

Telegrams, and after telegrams, telephones, were my undoing; generously, however, I shall accuse nobody of conspiracy; although it would be easy to believe that the controllers of communication had resolved to regain their monopoly of the nation's air-waves . . . I must return (Padma is frowning) to the banal chain of cause-and-effect: we arrived at Santa Cruz airport, by Dakota, on September 16th; but to explain the telegram, I must go further back in time.

If Alice Pereira had once sinned, by stealing Joseph D'Costa from her sister Mary, she had in these latter years gone a long way towards attaining redemption; because for four years she had been Ahmed Sinai's only human companion. Isolated on the dusty hillock which had once been Methwold's Estate, she had borne enormous demands on her accommodating good nature. He would make her sit with him until midnight while he drank djinns and ranted about the injustices of his life; he remembered, after years of forgetfulness, his old dream of translating and re-ordering the Quran, and blamed his family for emasculating him so that he didn't have the energy to begin such a task; in addition, because she was there, his anger often directed itself at her, taking the form of long tirades filled with gutter-oaths and the useless curses he had devised in the days of his deepest abstraction. She attempted to be understanding: he was a lonely man; his once-infallible relationship with the telephone had been destroyed by the economic vagaries of the times; his touch in financial matters had begun to desert him . . . he fell prey, too, to strange fears. When the Chinese road in the Aksai Chin region was discovered, he became convinced that the yellow hordes would be arriving at Methwold's Estate in a matter of days; and it was Alice who comforted him with ice-cold Coca-Cola, saying, 'No good worrying. Those Chinkies are too little to beat our jawans. Better you drink your Coke; nothing is going to change.'

In the end he wore her out; she stayed with him, finally, only because she demanded and received large pay increases, and sent much of the money to Goa, for the support of her sister Mary; but on September 1st, she, too, succumbed to the blandishments of the telephone.

By then, she spent as much time on the instrument as her employer, particularly when the Narlikar women called up.

The formidable Narlikars were, at that time, besieging my father, telephoning him twice a day, coaxing and persuading him to sell, reminding him that his position was hopeless, flapping around his head like vultures around a burning godown . . . on September 1st, like a long-ago vulture, they flung down an arm which slapped him in the face, because they bribed Alice Pereira away from him. Unable to stand him any more, she cried, 'Answer your own telephone! I'm off.'

That night, Ahmed Sinai's heart began to bulge. Overfull of hate resentment self-pity grief, it became swollen like a balloon, it beat too hard, skipped beats, and finally felled him like an ox; at the Breach Candy Hospital the doctors discovered that my father's heart had actually changed shape – a new swelling had pushed lumpily out of the lower left ventricle. It had, to use Alice's word, 'booted'.

Alice found him the next day, when, by chance, she returned to collect a forgotten umbrella; like a good secretary, she enlisted the power of telecommunications, telephoning an ambulance and telegramming us. Owing to censorship of the mails between India and Pakistan, the 'heartboot cable' took a full week to reach Amina Sinai.

'Back-to-Bom!' I yelled happily, alarming airport coolies. 'Back-to-Bom!' I cheered, despite everything, until the newly-sober Jamila said, 'Oh, Saleem, *honestly, shoo*!' Alice Pereira met us at the airport (a telegram had alerted her); and then we were in a real Bombay black-and-yellow taxi, and I was wallowing in the sounds of hot-channa-hot hawkers, the throng of camels bicycles and people people people, thinking how Mumbadevi's city made Rawalpindi look like a village, rediscovering especially the colours, the forgotten vividness of gulmohr and bougainvillaea, the livid green of the waters of the Mahalaxmi Temple 'tank', the stark black-and-white of the traffic policemen's sun umbrellas and the blue-and-yellowness of their uniforms; but most of all the blue blue

blue of the sea . . . only the grey of my father's stricken face distracted me from the rainbow riot of the city, and made me sober up.

Alice Pereira left us at the hospital and went off to work for the Narlikar women; and now a remarkable thing happened. My mother Amina Sinai, jerked out of lethargy and depression and guilt-fogs and verruca-pain by the sight of my father, seemed miraculously to regain her youth; with all her old gifts of assiduity restored, she set about the rehabilitation of Ahmed, driven by an unstoppable will. She brought him home to the first-floor bedroom in which she had nursed him through the freeze; she sat with him day and night, pouring her strength into his body. And her love had its reward, because not only did Ahmed Sinai make a recovery so complete as to astound Breach Candy's European doctors, but also an altogether more wonderful change occurred, which was that, as Ahmed came to himself under Amina's care, he returned not to the self which had practised curses and wrestled djinns, but to the self he might always have been, filled with contrition and forgiveness and laughter and generosity and the finest miracle of all, which was love. Ahmed Sinai had, at long last, fallen in love with my mother.

And I was the sacrificial lamb with which they anointed their love.

They had even begun to sleep together again; and although my sister – with a flash of her old Monkey-self – said, 'In the same bed, Allah, *chhi-chhi*, how dirty!', I was happy for them; and even, briefly, happier for myself, because I was back in the land of the Midnight Children's Conference. While newspaper headlines marched towards war, I renewed my acquaintance with my miraculous fellows, not knowing how many endings were in store for me.

On October 9th – INDIAN ARMY POISED FOR ALL-OUT EFFORT – I felt able to convene the Conference (time and my own efforts had erected the necessary barrier around Mary's secret). Back into my head they came; it was a happy night, a night for burying old disagreements, for making our own all-out effort at reunion. We repeated, over and over again, our joy at being back together; ignoring the deeper truth – that we were like all families, that family reunions are more delightful in prospect than in reality, and that the time comes when all families must go their separate ways. On October 15th – UNPROVOKED ATTACK ON INDIA – the questions I'd been dreading and trying not to provoke began: *Why is Shiva not here?* And: *Why have you closed off part of your mind?*

On October 20th, the Indian forces were defeated – thrashed – by the Chinese at Thag La ridge. An official Peking statement announced: *In self-defence, Chinese frontier guards were compelled to strike back resolutely.* But when, that same night, the children of midnight launched a concerted assault on me, I had no defence. They attacked on a broad front and from every direction, accusing me of secrecy, prevarication, high-handedness, egotism; my mind, no longer a parliament chamber, became the battleground on which they annihilated me. No longer 'big brother Saleem', I listened helplessly while they tore me apart; because, despite all their sound-and-fury, I could not unblock what I had sealed away; I could not bring myself to tell them Mary's secret. Even Parvati-the-witch, for so long my fondest supporter, lost patience with me at last. 'O, Saleem,' she said, 'God knows what that Pakistan has done to you; but you are badly changed.'

Once, long ago, the death of Mian Abdullah had destroyed another Conference, which had been held together purely by the strength of his will; now, as the midnight children lost faith in me, they also lost their belief in the thing I had made for them. Between October 20th and November 20th, I continued to convene – to attempt to convene – our nightly

414

sessions; but they fled from me, not one by one, but in tens and twenties; each night, less of them were willing to tune in; each week, over a hundred of them retreated into private life. In the high Himalayas, Gurkhas and Rajputs fled in disarray from the Chinese army; and in the upper reaches of my mind, another army was also destroyed by things – bickerings, prejudices, boredom, selfishness – which I had believed too small, too petty to have touched them.

(But optimism, like a lingering disease, refused to vanish; I continued to believe – I continue now – that what-we-had-in-common would finally have outweighed what-drove-us-apart. No: I will not accept the ultimate responsibility for the end of the Children's Conference; because what destroyed all possibility of renewal was the love of Ahmed and Amina Sinai.)

. . . And Shiva? Shiva, whom I cold-bloodedly denied his birthright? Never once, in that last month, did I send my thoughts in search of him; but his existence, somewhere in the world, nagged away at the corners of my mind. Shiva-the-destroyer, Shiva Knock-knees . . . he became, for me, first a stabbing twinge of guilt; then an obsession; and finally, as the memory of his actuality grew dull, he became a sort of principle; he came to represent, in my mind, all the vengefulness and violence and simultaneous-love-and-hate-of-Things in the world; so that even now, when I hear of drowned bodies floating like balloons on the Hooghly and exploding when nudged by passing boats; or trains set on fire, or politicians killed, or riots in Orissa or Punjab, it seems to me that the hand of Shiva lies heavily over all these things, dooming us to flounder endlessly amid murder rape greed war – that Shiva, in short, has made us who we are. (He, too, was born on the stroke of midnight; he, like me, was connected to history. The modes of connection – if I'm right in thinking they applied to me – enabled him, too, to affect the passage of the days.)

I'm talking as if I never saw him again; which isn't true. But that, of course, must get into the queue like everything else; I'm not strong enough to tell that tale just now.

The disease of optimism, in those days, once again attained epidemic proportions; I, meanwhile, was afflicted by an inflammation of the sinuses. Curiously triggered off by the defeat of Thag La ridge, public optimism about the war grew as fat (and as dangerous) as an overfilled balloon; my long-suffering nasal passages, however, which had been overfilled all their days, finally gave up the struggle against congestion. While parliamentarians poured out speeches about 'Chinese aggression' and 'the blood of our martyred jawans', my eyes began to stream with tears; while the nation puffed itself up, convincing itself that the annihilation of the little yellow men was at hand, my sinuses, too, puffed up and distorted a face which was already so startling that Ayub Khan himself had stared at it in open amazement. In the clutches of the optimism disease, students burned Mao Tse-tung and Chou En-lai in effigy; with optimism-fever on their brows, mobs attacked Chinese shoemakers, curio dealers and restaura-teurs. Burning with optimism, the Government even interned Indian citizens of Chinese descent – now 'enemy aliens' – in camps in Rajasthan. Birla Industries donated a miniature rifle range to the nation; schoolgirls began to go on military parade. But I, Saleem, felt as if I was about to die of asphyxiation. The air, thickened by optimism, refused to enter my lungs.

Ahmed and Amina Sinai were amongst the worst victims of the renewed disease of optimism; having already contracted it through the medium of their new-born love, they entered into the public enthusiasm with a will. When Morarji Desai, the urine-drinking Finance Minister, launched his 'Ornaments for Armaments' appeal, my mother handed over gold bangles and emerald ear-rings; when Morarji floated an issue of defence bonds, Ahmed Sinai bought them in bushels. War, it seemed, had brought a new dawn to India; in the *Times of India,* a cartoon captioned 'War with China' showed Nehru looking at graphs labelled 'Emotional Integration', 'Industrial Peace' and 'People's Faith in Government' and crying, 'We never had it so good!' Adrift in the sea of optimism, we – the nation, my parents, I – floated blindly towards the reefs.

As a people, we are obsessed with correspondences. Similarities between this and that, between apparently unconnected things, make us clap our hands delightedly when we find them out. It is a sort of national longing for form – or perhaps simply an expression of our deep belief that forms lie hidden within reality; that meaning reveals itself only in flashes. Hence our vulnerability to omens . . . when the Indian flag was first raised, for instance, a rainbow appeared above that Delhi field, a rainbow of saffron and green; and we felt blessed. Born amidst correspondence, I have found it continuing to hound me . . . while Indians headed blindly towards a military débâcle, I, too, was nearing (and entirely without knowing it) a catastrophe of my own.

Times of India cartoons spoke of 'Emotional Integration'; in Buckingham Villa, last remnant of Methwold's Estate, emotions had never been so integrated. Ahmed and Amina spent their days like just-courting youngsters; and while the Peking *People's Daily* complained, 'The Nehru Government has finally shed its cloak of non-alignment', neither my sister nor I were complaining, because for the first time in years we did not have to pretend we were non-aligned in the war between our parents; what war had done for India, the cessation of hostilities had achieved on our two-storey hillock. Ahmed Sinai had even given up his nightly battle with the djinns.

By November 1st – INDIANS ATTACK UNDER COVER OF ARTILLERY – my nasal passages were in a state of acute crisis. Although my mother subjected me to daily torture by Vick's

Inhaler and steaming bowls of Vick's ointment dissolved in water, which, blanket over head, I was obliged to try and inhale, my sinuses refused to respond to treatment. This was the day on which my father held out his arms to me and said, 'Come, son – come here and let me love you.' In a frenzy of happiness (maybe the optimism disease had got to me, after all) I allowed myself to be smothered in his squashy belly; but when he let me go, nose-goo had stained his bush-shirt. I think that's what finally doomed me; because that afternoon, my mother went on to the attack. Pretending to me that she was telephoning a friend, she made a certain telephone call. While Indians attacked under cover of artillery, Amina Sinai planned my downfall, protected by a lie.

Before I describe my entry into the desert of my later years, however, I must admit the possibility that I have grievously wronged my parents. Never once, to my knowledge, never once in all the time since Mary Pereira's revelations, did they set out to look for the true son of their blood; and I have, at several points in this narrative, ascribed this failure to a certain lack of imagination – I have said, more or less, that I remained their son because they could not imagine me out of the rôle. And there are worse interpretations possible, too – such as their reluctance to accept into their bosom an urchin who had spent eleven years in the gutter; but I wish to suggest a nobler motive: maybe, despite everything, despite cucumber-nose stainface chinlessness horn-temples bandy-legs finger-loss monk's-tonsure and my (admittedly unknown to them) bad left ear, despite even the midnight baby-swap of Mary Pereira . . . maybe, I say, in spite of all these provocations, my parents loved me. I withdrew from them into my secret world; fearing their hatred, I did not admit the possibility that their love was stronger than ugliness, stronger even than blood. It is certainly likely that what a telephone call arranged, what finally took place on November 21st, 1962, was done for the highest of reasons; that my parents ruined me for love.

The day of November 20th was a terrible day; the night was a terrible night . . . six days earlier, on Nehru's seventy-third birthday, the great confrontation with the Chinese forces had begun; the Indian army – JAWANS SWING INTO ACTION! – had attacked the Chinese at Walong. News of the disaster of Walong, and the rout of General Kaul and four battalions, reached Nehru on Saturday 18th; on Monday 20th, it flooded through radio and press and arrived at Methwold's Estate. ULTIMATE PANIC IN NEW DELHI! INDIAN FORCES IN TATTERS! That day – the last day of my old life – I sat huddled with my sister and parents around our Telefunken radiogram, while telecommunications struck the fear of God and China into our hearts. And my father now said a fateful thing: 'Wife,' he intoned gravely, while Jamila and I shook with fear, 'Begum Sahiba, this country is finished. Bankrupt. Funtoosh.' The evening paper proclaimed the end of the optimism disease: PUBLIC MORALE DRAINS AWAY. And after that end, there were others to come; other things would also drain away.

I went to bed with my head full of Chinese faces guns tanks . . . but at midnight, my head was empty and quiet, because the midnight Conference had drained away as well; the only one of the magic children who was willing to talk to me was Parvati-the-witch, and we, dejected utterly by what Nussie-the-duck would have called 'the end of the world', were unable to do more than simply commune in silence.

And other, more mundane drainages: a crack appeared in the mighty Bhakra Nangal Hydro-Electric Dam, and the great reservoir behind it flooded through the fissure . . . and the Narlikar women's reclamation consortium, impervious to optimism or defeat or anything except the lure of wealth, continued to draw land out of the depths of the seas . . . but the final evacuation, the one which truly gives this episode its title, took place the next morning, just when I had relaxed and thought that something, after all, might turn out all right

419

. . . because in the morning we heard the improbably joyous news that the Chinese had suddenly, without needing to, stopped advancing; having gained control of the Himalayan heights, they were apparently content; CEASEFIRE! the newspapers screamed, and my mother almost fainted in relief. (There was talk that General Kaul had been taken prisoner; the President of India, Dr Radhakrishan, commented, 'Unfortunately, this report is completely untrue.')

Despite streaming eyes and puffed-up sinuses, I was happy; despite even the end of the Children's Conference, I was basking in the new glow of happiness which permeated Buckingham Villa; so when my mother suggested, 'Let's go and celebrate! A picnic, children, you'd like that?' I naturally agreed with alacrity. It was the morning of November 21st; we helped make sandwiches and parathas; we stopped at a fizzy-drinks shop and loaded ice in a tin tub and Cokes in a crate into the boot of our Rover; parents in the front, children in the back, we set off. Jamila Singer sang for us as we drove.

Through inflamed sinuses, I asked: 'Where are we going? Juhu? Elephanta? Marvé? Where?' And my mother, smiling awkwardly: 'Surprise; wait and see.' Through streets filled with relieved, rejoicing crowds we drove . . . 'This is the wrong way,' I exclaimed; 'This isn't the way to a beach?' My parents both spoke at once, reassuringly, brightly: 'Just one stop first, and then we're off; promise.'

Telegrams recalled me; radiograms frightened me; but it was a telephone which booked the date time place of my undoing . . . and my parents lied to me.

. . . We halted in front of an unfamiliar building in Carnac Road. Exterior: crumbling. All its windows: blind. 'You coming with me, son?' Ahmed Sinai got out of the car; I, happy to be accompanying my father on his business, walked jauntily beside him. A brass plate on the doorway: *Ear Nose Throat Clinic*. And I, suddenly alarmed: 'What's this, Abba? Why have we come . . .' And my father's hand, tightening on

420

my shoulder – and then a man in a white coat – and nurses – and 'Ah yes Mr Sinai so this is young Saleem – right on time – fine, fine'; while I, 'Abba, no – what about the picnic –'; but doctors are steering me along now, my father is dropping back, the man in the coat calls to him, 'Shan't be long – damn good news about the war, no?' And the nurse, 'Please accompany me for dressing and anaesthesia.'

Tricked! Tricked, Padma! I told you: once, picnics tricked me; and then there was a hospital and a room with a hard bed and bright hanging lamps and me crying, 'No no no,' and the nurse, 'Don't be stupid now, you're almost a grown man, lie down,' and I, remembering how nasal passages had started everything in my head, how nasal fluid had been sniffed upupup into somewhere-that-nosefluid-shouldn't-go, how the connection had been made which released my voices, was kicking yelling so that they had to hold me down, 'Honestly,' the nurse said, 'such a baby, I never saw.'

And so what began in a washing-chest ended on an operating table, because I was held down hand-and-foot and a man saying 'You won't feel a thing, easier than having your tonsils out, get those sinuses fixed in no time, complete clear-out,' and me 'No please no,' but the voice continued, 'I'll put this mask on you now, just count to ten.'

Count. The numbers marching one two three.

Hiss of released gas. The numbers crushing me four five six.

Faces swimming in fog. And still the tumultuous numbers, I was crying, I think, the numbers pounding seven eight nine.

Ten.

'Good God, the boy's still conscious. Extraordinary. We'd better try another – can you hear me? Saleem, isn't it? Good chap, just give me another ten!' Can't catch me. Multitudes have teemed inside my head. The master of the numbers, me. Here they go again 'leven twelve.

But they'll never let up until . . . thirteen fourteen fifteen . . . O God O God the fog dizzy and falling back back back, sixteen, beyond war and pepperpots, back back, seventeen eighteen nineteen.

Twen

There was a washing-chest and a boy who sniffed too hard. His mother undressed and revealed a Black Mango. Voices came, which were not the voices of Archangels. A hand, deafening the left ear. And what grew best in the heat: fantasy, irrationality, lust. There was a clocktower refuge, and cheatery-in-class. And love in Bombay caused a bicycle-accident; horn-temples entered forcep-hollows, and five hundred and eighty-one children visited my head. Midnight's children: who may have been the embodiment of the hope of freedom, who may also have been freaks-who-ought-to-be-finished-off. Parvati-the-witch, most loyal of all, and Shiva, who became a principle of life. There was a question of purpose, and the debate between ideas and things. There were knees and nose and nose and knees.

Quarrels began, and the adult world infiltrated the children's; there was selfishness and snobbishness and hate. And the impossibility of a third principle; the fear of coming-to-nothing-after-all began to grow. And what nobody said: that the purpose of the five hundred and eighty-one lay in their destruction; that they had come, in order to come to nothing. Prophecies were ignored when they spoke to this effect.

And revelations, and the closing of a mind; and exile, and four-years-after return; suspicions growing, dissension breeding, departures in twenties and tens. And, at the end, just one voice left; but optimism lingered – what-we-had-in-common retained the possibility of overpowering what-forced-us-apart.

Until:

Silence outside me. A dark room (blinds down). Can't see anything (nothing there to see).

Silence inside me. A connection broken (for ever). Can't hear anything (nothing there to hear).

Silence, like a desert. And a clear, free nose (nasal passages full of air). Air, like a vandal, invading my private places.

Drained. I have been drained. The parahamsa, grounded. (For good.)

O, spell it out, spell it out: the operation whose ostensible purpose was the draining of my inflamed sinuses and the once-and-for-all clearing of my nasal passages had the effect of breaking whatever connection had been made in a washing-chest; of depriving me of nose-given telepathy; of banishing me from the possibility of midnight children.

Our names contain our fates; living as we do in a place where names have not acquired the meaninglessness of the West, and are still more than mere sounds, we are also the victims of our titles. *Sinai* contains Ibn Sina, master magician, Sufi adept; and also Sin the moon, the ancient god of Hadhramaut, with his own mode of connection, his powers of action-at-a-distance upon the tides of the world. But Sin is also the letter S, as sinuous as a snake; serpents lie coiled within the name. And there is also the accident of transliteration – Sinai, when in Roman script, though not in Nastaliq, is also the name of the place-of-revelation, of put-off-thy-shoes, of commandments and golden calves; but when all that is said and done; when Ibn Sina is forgotten and the moon has set; when snakes lie hidden and revelations end, it is the name of the desert – of barrenness, infertility, dust; the name of the end.

In Arabia – *Arabia Deserta* – at the time of the prophet Muhammad, other prophets also preached: Maslama of the tribe of the Banu Hanifa in the Yamama, the very heart of Arabia; and Hanzala ibn Safwan; and Khalid ibn Sinan. Maslama's God was ar-Rahman, 'the Merciful'; today Muslims pray to Allah, ar-Rahman. Khalid ibn Sinan was sent to the tribe of 'Abs; for a time, he was followed, but then he was lost. Prophets are not always false simply because they are overtaken, and swallowed up, by history. Men of worth have always roamed the desert.

'Wife,' Ahmed Sinai said, 'this country is finished.' After ceasefire and drainage, these words returned to haunt him; and Amina began to persuade him to emigrate to Pakistan, where her surviving sisters already were, and to which her mother would go after her father's death. 'A fresh start,' she suggested, 'Janum, it would be lovely. What is left for us on this God-forsaken hill?'

So in the end Buckingham Villa was delivered into the clutches of the Narlikar women, after all; and over fifteen years late, my family moved to Pakistan, the Land of the Pure. Ahmed Sinai left very little behind; there are ways of transmitting money with the help of multi-national companies, and my father knew those ways. And I, although sad to leave the city of my birth, was not unhappy about moving away from the city in which Shiva lurked somewhere like a carefully-concealed landmine.

We left Bombay, finally, in February 1963; and on the day of our departure I took an old tin globe down to the garden and buried it amongst the cacti. Inside it: a Prime Minister's letter, and a jumbo-sized front-page baby-snap, captioned 'Midnight's Child' . . . They may not be holy relics – I do not presume to compare the trivial memorabilia of my life with the Hazratbal hair of the Prophet, or the body of St Francis Xavier in the Cathedral of Bom Jesus – but they are all that has survived of my past: a squashed tin globe, a mildewed letter, a photograph. Nothing else, not even a silver spittoon. Apart from a Monkey-crushed planet, the only records are sealed in the closed books of heaven, Sidjeen and Illiyun, the Books of Evil and Good; at any rate, that's the story.

. . . Only when we were aboard S.S. *Sabarmati*, and

anchored off the Rann of Kutch, did I remember old Schaapsteker; and wondered, suddenly, if anyone had told him we were going. I didn't dare to ask, for fear that the answer might be *no;* so as I thought of the demolition crew getting to work, and pictured the machines of destruction smashing into my father's office and my own blue room, pulling down the servants' spiral iron staircase and the kitchen in which Mary Pereira had stirred her fears into chutneys and pickles, massacring the verandah where my mother had sat with the child in her belly like a stone, I also had an image of a mighty, swinging ball crashing into the domain of Sharpsticker sahib, and of the old crazy man himself, pale wasted flick-tongued, being exposed there on top of a crumbling house, amid falling towers and red-tiled roof, old Schaapsteker shrivelling ageing dying in the sunlight which he hadn't seen for so many years. But perhaps I'm dramatizing; I may have got all this from an old film called *Lost Horizon,* in which beautiful women shrivelled and died when they departed from Shangri-La.

For every snake, there is a ladder; for every ladder, a snake. We arrived in Karachi on February 9th – and within months, my sister Jamila had been launched on the career which would earn her the names of 'Pakistan's Angel' and 'Bulbul-of-the-Faith'; we had left Bombay, but we gained reflected glory. And one more thing: although I had been drained – although no voices spoke in my head, and never would again – there was one compensation: namely that, for the first time in my life, I was discovering the astonishing delights of possessing a sense of smell.

Jamila Singer

It turned out to be a sense so acute as to be capable of distinguishing the glutinous reek of hypocrisy behind the welcoming smile with which my spinster aunt Alia greeted us at the Karachi docks. Irremediably embittered by my father's years-ago defection into the arms of her sister, my head-mistress aunt had acquired the heavy-footed corpulence of undimmed jealousy; the thick dark hairs of her resentment sprouted through most of the pores of her skin. And perhaps she succeeded in deceiving my parents and Jamila with her spreading arms, her waddling run towards us, her cry of 'Ahmed bhai, at last! But better late than never!', her spider-like – and inevitably accepted – offers of hospitality; but I, who had spent much of my babyhood in the bitter mittens and soured pom-pom hats of her envy, who had been unknowingly infected with failure by the innocent-looking baby-things into which she had knitted her hatred, and who, moreover, could clearly remember what it was like to be possessed by revenge-lust, I, Saleem-the-drained, could smell the vengeful odours leaking out of her glands. I was, however, powerless to protest; we were swept into the Datsun of her vengeance and driven away down Bunder Road to her house at Guru Mandir – like flies, only more foolish, because we celebrated our captivity.

. . . But what a sense of smell it was! Most of us are conditioned, from the cradle onwards, into recognizing the narrowest possible spectrum of fragrances; I, however, had been incapable of smelling a thing all my life, and was accordingly ignorant of all olfactory taboos. As a result, I had a tendency not to feign innocence when someone broke wind – which landed me in a certain amount of parental trouble; more important, however, was my nasal freedom to inhale a very great deal more than the scents of purely physical origin with which the rest of the human race has chosen to be content. So, from the earliest days of my Pakistani adolescence, I began to learn the secret aromas of the world, the heady but quick-fading perfume of new love, and also the deeper, longer-lasting pungency of hate. (It was not long after my arrival in the 'Land of the Pure' that I discovered within myself the ultimate impurity of sister-love; and the slow burning fires of my aunt filled my nostrils from the start.) A nose will give you knowledge, but not power-over-events; my invasion of Pakistan, armed (if that's the right word) only with a new manifestation of my nasal inheritance, gave me the powers of sniffing-out-the-truth, of smelling-what-was-in-the-air, of following trails; but not the only power an invader needs – the strength to conquer my foes.

I won't deny it: I never forgave Karachi for not being Bombay. Set between the desert and bleakly saline creeks whose shores were littered with stunted mangroves, my new city seemed to possess an ugliness which eclipsed even my own; having grown too fast – its population had quadrupled since 1947 – it had acquired the misshapen lumpiness of a gigantic dwarf. On my sixteenth birthday, I was given a Lambretta motor-scooter; riding the city streets on my windowless vehicle, I breathed in the fatalistic hopelessness of the slum dwellers and the smug defensiveness of the rich; I was sucked along the smell-trails of dispossession and also fanaticism, lured down a long underworld corridor at whose end was the door to Tai Bibi, the oldest whore in the world . . . but I'm running away with myself. At the heart of my Karachi was Alia Aziz's house, a large old building on

Clayton Road (she must have wandered in it for years like a ghost with nobody to haunt), a place of shadows and yellowed paint, across which there fell, every afternoon, the long accusing shadow of the minaret of the local mosque. Even when, years later in the magicians' ghetto, I lived in another mosque's shade, a shade which was, at least for a time, a protective, unmenacing penumbra, I never lost my Karachi-born view of mosque-shadows, in which, it seemed to me, I could sniff the narrow, clutching, accusative odour of my aunt. Who bided her time; but whose vengeance, when it came, was crushing.

It was, in those days, a city of mirages; hewn from the desert, it had not wholly succeeded in destroying the desert's power. Oases shone in the tarmac of Elphinstone Street, caravanserais were glimpsed shimmering amongst the hovels around the black bridge, the Kala Pul. In the rainless city (whose only common factor with the city of my birth was that it, too, had started life as a fishing village), the hidden desert retained its ancient powers of apparition-mongering, with the result that Karachiites had only the slipperiest of grasps on reality, and were therefore willing to turn to their leaders for advice on what was real and what was not. Beset by illusionary sand-dunes and the ghosts of ancient kings, and also by the knowledge that the name of the faith upon which the city stood meant 'submission', my new fellow-citizens exuded the flat boiled odours of acquiescence, which were depressing to a nose which had smelt – at the very last, and however briefly – the highly-spiced nonconformity of Bombay.

Soon after our arrival – and, perhaps, oppressed by the mosque-shadowed air of the Clayton Road house – my father resolved to build us a new home. He bought a plot of land in the smartest of the 'societies', the new housing development zones; and on my sixteenth birthday, Saleem acquired more than a Lambretta – I learned the occult powers of umbilical cords.

428

What, pickled in brine, sat for sixteen years in my father's almirah, awaiting just such a day? What, floating like a water-snake in an old pickle-jar, accompanied us on our sea-journey and ended up buried in hard, barren Karachi-earth? What had once nourished life in a womb – what now infused earth with miraculous life, and gave birth to a split-level, American-style modern bungalow? . . . Eschewing these cryptic questions, I explain that, on my sixteenth birthday, my family (including Alia aunty) assembled on our plot of Korangi Road earth; watched by the eyes of a team of labourers and the beard of a mullah, Ahmed handed Saleem a pickaxe; I drove it inaugurally into the ground. 'A new beginning,' Amina said, 'Inshallah, we shall all be new people now.' Spurred on by her noble and unattainable desire, a workman rapidly enlarged my hole; and now a pickle-jar was produced. Brine was discarded on the thirsty ground; and what-was-left-inside received the mullah's blessings. After which, an umbilical cord – was it mine? Or Shiva's? – was implanted in the earth; and at once, a house began to grow. There were sweetmeats and soft drinks; the mullah, displaying remarkable hunger, consumed thirty-nine laddoos; and Ahmed Sinai did not once complain of the expense. The spirit of the buried cord inspired the workmen; but although the foundations were dug very deep, they would not prevent the house from falling down before we ever lived in it.

What I surmised about umbilical cords: although they possessed the power of growing houses, some were evidently better at the job than others. The city of Karachi proved my point; clearly constructed on top of entirely unsuitable cords, it was full of deformed houses, the stunted hunchback children of deficient lifelines, houses growing mysteriously blind, with no visible windows, houses which looked like radios or air-conditioners or jail-cells, crazy top-heavy edifices which fell over with monotonous regularity, like drunks; a wild proliferation of mad houses, whose inadequacies as living quarters were exceeded only by their quite exceptional ugliness. The city obscured the desert; but either the cords, or the infertility of the soil, made it grow into something grotesque.

Capable of smelling sadness and joy, of sniffing out intelligence and stupidity with my eyes closed, I arrived at Karachi, and adolescence – understanding, of course, that the subcontinent's new nations and I had all left childhood behind; that growing pains and strange awkward alterations of voice were in store for us all. Drainage censored my inner life; my sense of connection remained undrained.

Saleem invaded Pakistan armed only with a hypersensitive nose; but, worst of all, he invaded *from the wrong direction*! All successful conquests of that part of the world have begun in the north; all conquerors have come by land. Sailing ignorantly against the winds of history, I reached Karachi from the south-east, and by sea. What followed should not, I suppose, have surprised me.

With hindsight, the advantages of sweeping down from the north are self-evident. From the north came the Umayyad generals, Hajjaj bin Yusuf and Muhammad bin Qasim; also the Ismailis. (Honeymoon Lodge, where it is said Aly Khan sojourned with Rita Hayworth, overlooked our plot of umbilicized earth; rumour has it that the film-star created much scandal by wandering in the grounds dressed in a series of fabulous, gauzy, Hollywood négligées.) O ineluctable superiority of northernness! From which direction did Mahmud of Ghazni descend upon these Indus plains, bringing with him a language boasting no fewer than three forms of the letter S? The inescapable answer: sé, sin and swad were northern intruders. And Muhammad bin Sam Ghuri, who overthrew the Ghaznavids and established the Delhi Caliphate? Sam Ghuri's son, too, moved southwards on his progress.

430

And Tughlaq, and the Mughal Emperors . . . but I've made my point. It remains only to add that ideas, as well as armies, swept south south south from the northern heights: the legend of Sikandar But-Shikan, the Iconoclast of Kashmir, who at the end of the fourteenth century destroyed every Hindu temple in the Valley (establishing a precedent for my grandfather), travelled down from the hills to the river-plains; and five hundred years later the mujahideen movement of Syed Ahmad Barilwi followed the well-trodden trail. Barilwi's ideas: self-denial, hatred-of-Hindus, holy war . . . philosophies as well as kings (to cut this short) came from the opposite direction to me.

Saleem's parents said, 'We must all become new people'; in the land of the pure, purity became our ideal. But Saleem was forever tainted with Bombayness, his head was full of all sorts of religions apart from Allah's (like India's first Muslims, the mercantile Moplas of Malabar, I had lived in a country whose population of deities rivalled the numbers of its people, so that, in unconscious revolt against the claustrophobic throng of deities, my family had espoused the ethics of business, not faith); and his body was to show a marked preference for the impure. Mopla-like, I was doomed to be a misfit; but, in the end, purity found me out, and even I, Saleem, was cleansed of my misdeeds.

After my sixteenth birthday, I studied history at my aunt Alia's college; but not even learning could make me feel a part of this country devoid of midnight children, in which my fellow-students took out processions to demand a stricter, more Islamic society – proving that they had contrived to become the antitheses of students everywhere else on earth, by demanding more-rules-not-less. My parents, however, were determined to put down roots; although Ayub Khan and Bhutto were forging an alliance with China (which had so recently been our enemy), Ahmed and Amina would listen to no criticisms of their new home; and my father bought a towel factory.

There was a new brilliance about my parents in those days; Amina had lost her guilt-fog, her verrucas seemed not to be playing up any more; while Ahmed, although still whitened, had felt the freeze of his loins thawing under the heat of his newfound love for his wife. On some mornings, Amina had toothmarks on her neck; she giggled uncontrollably at times, like a schoolgirl. 'You two, honestly,' her sister Alia said, 'Like honeymooners or I don't know what.' But I could smell what was hidden behind Alia's teeth; what stayed inside when the friendly words came out . . . Ahmed Sinai named his towels after his wife: Amina Brand.

'Who are these multi-multis? These Dawoods, Saigols, Haroons?' he cried gaily, dismissing the richest families in the land. 'Who are Valikas or Zulfikars? I could eat them ten at a time. You wait!', he promised, 'In two years the whole world will be wiping itself on an Amina Brand cloth. The finest terry-cloth! The most modern machines! We shall make the whole world clean and dry; Dawoods and Zulfikars will beg to know my secret; and I will say, yes, the towels are high-quality; but the secret is not in the manufacturing; it was love that conquered all.' (I discerned, in my father's speech, the lingering effects of the optimism virus.)

Did Amina Brand conquer the world in the name of cleanliness (which is next to . . .)? Did Valikas and Saigols come to ask Ahmed Sinai, 'God, we're stumped, yaar, how'd you do it?' Did high-quality terry-cloth, in patterns devised by Ahmed himself – a little gaudy, but never mind, they were born of love – wipe away the moistness of Pakistanis and export-markets alike? Did Russians Englishmen Americans wrap themselves in my mother's immortalized name? . . . The story of Amina Brand must wait awhile; because the career of Jamila Singer is about to take off; the mosque-shadowed house on Clayton Road has been visited by Uncle Puffs.

*

432

His real name was Major (Retired) Alauddin Latif; he had heard about my sister's voice from 'my darn good friend General Zulfikar; use to be with him in the Border Patrol Force back in '47.' He turned up at Alia Aziz's house shortly after Jamila's fifteenth birthday, beaming and bouncing, revealing a mouth filled with solid gold teeth. 'I'm a simple fellow,' he explained, 'like our illustrious President. I keep my cash where it's safe.' Like our illustrious President, the Major's head was perfectly spherical; unlike Ayub Khan, Latif had left the Army and entered show-business. 'Pakistan's absolute number-one impresario, old man,' he told my father. 'Nothing to it but organization; old Army habit, dies darn hard.' Major Latif had a proposition: he wanted to hear Jamila sing, 'And if she's two per cent as good as I'm told, my good sir, I'll make her famous! Oh, yes, overnight, certainly! Contacts: that's all it takes; contacts and organization; and yours truly Major (Retired) Latif has the lot. *Alauddin* Latif,' he stressed, flashing goldly at Ahmed Sinai, 'Know the story? I just rub my jolly old lamp and out pops the genie bringing fame and fortune. Your girl will be in darn good hands. *Darn* good.'

It is fortunate for Jamila Singer's legion of fans that Ahmed Sinai was a man in love with his wife; mellowed by his own happiness, he failed to eject Major Latif on the spot. I also believe today that my parents had already come to the conclusion that their daughter's gift was too extraordinary to keep to themselves; the sublime magic of her angel's voice had begun to teach them the inevitable imperatives of talent. But Ahmed and Amina had one concern. 'Our daughter,' Ahmed said – he was always the more old-fashioned of the two beneath the surface – 'is from a good family; but you want to put her on a stage in front of God knows how many strange men . . .?' The Major looked affronted. 'Sir,' he said stiffly, 'you think I am not a man of sensibility? Got daughters myself, old man. Seven, thank God. Set up a little travel

433

agency business for them; strictly over the telephone, though. Wouldn't dream of sitting them in an office-window. It's the biggest telephonic travel agency in the place, actually. We send train-drivers to England, matter of fact; bus-wallahs, too. My point,' he added hastily, 'is that your daughter would be given as much respect as mine. More, actually; she's going to be a star!'

Major Latif's daughters – Safia and Rafia and five other -afias – were dubbed, collectively, 'the Puffias' by the remaining Monkey in my sister; their father was nicknamed first 'Father-Puffia' and then Uncle – a courtesy title – Puffs. He was as good as his word; in six months Jamila Singer was to have hit records, an army of admirers, everything; and all, as I'll explain in a moment, without revealing her face.

Uncle Puffs became a fixture in our lives; he visited the Clayton Road house most evenings, at what I used to think of as the cocktail hour, to sip pomegranate juice and ask Jamila to sing a little something. She, who was growing into the sweetest-natured of girls, always obliged . . . afterwards he would clear his throat as if something had got stuck in it and begin to joke heartily with me about getting married. Twenty-four-carat grins blinded me as he, 'Time you took a wife, young man. Take my advice: pick a girl with good brains and bad teeth; you'll have got a friend and a safe-deposit box rolled into one!' Uncle Puffs' daughters, he claimed, all conformed to the above description . . . I, embarrassed, smelling out that he was only half-joking, would cry, 'O, Uncle *Puffs*!' He knew his nickname; quite liked it, even. Slapping my thigh, he cried, 'Playing hard to get, eh? Darn right. O.K., my boy: you pick one of my girls, and I guarantee to have all her teeth pulled out; by the time you marry her she'll have a million-buck smile for a dowry!' Whereupon my mother usually contrived to change the subject; she wasn't keen on Uncle Puffs' idea, no matter how pricey the dentures . . . on that first night, as so often afterwards, Jamila sang to

434

Major Alauddin Latif. Her voice wafted out through the window and silenced the traffic; the birds stopped chattering and, at the hamburger shop across the street, the radio was switched off; the street was full of stationary people, and my sister's voice washed over them . . . when she finished, we noticed that Uncle Puffs was crying.

'A jewel,' he said, honking into a handkerchief, 'Sir and Madam, your daughter is a jewel. I am humbled, absolutely. Darn humbled. She has proved to me that a golden voice is preferable even to golden teeth.'

And when Jamila Singer's fame had reached the point at which she could no longer avoid giving a public concert, it was Uncle Puffs who started the rumour that she had been involved in a terrible, disfiguring car-crash; it was Major (Retired) Latif who devised her famous, all-concealing, white silk chadar, the curtain or veil, heavily embroidered in gold brocade-work and religious calligraphy, behind which she sat demurely whenever she performed in public. The chadar of Jamila Singer was held up by two tireless, muscular figures, also (but more simply) veiled from head to foot – the official story was that they were her female attendants, but their sex was impossible to determine through their burqas; and at its very centre, the Major had cut a hole. Diameter: three inches. Circumference: embroidered in finest gold thread. That was how the history of our family once again became the fate of a nation, because when Jamila sang with her lips pressed against the brocaded aperture, Pakistan fell in love with a fifteen-year-old girl whom it only ever glimpsed through a gold-and-white perforated sheet.

The accident rumour set the final seal on her popularity; her concerts packed out the Bambino theatre in Karachi and filled the Shalimar-bagh in Lahore; her records constantly topped the sales charts. And as she became public property, 'Pakistan's Angel', 'The Voice of the Nation', the 'Bulbul-e-Din' or nightingale-of-the-faith, and began to receive one

435

thousand and one firm proposals of marriage a week; as she became the whole country's favourite daughter and grew into an existence which threatened to overwhelm her place in our own family, so she fell prey to the twin viruses of fame, the first of which made her the victim of her own public image, because the accident-rumour obliged her to wear a gold-and-white burqa at all times, even in my aunt Alia's school, which she continued to attend; while the second virus subjected her to the exaggerations and simplifications of self which are the unavoidable side-effects of stardom, so that the blind and blinding devoutness and the right-or-wrong nationalism which had already begun to emerge in her now began to dominate her personality, to the exclusion of almost everything else. Publicity imprisoned her inside a gilded tent; and. being the new daughter-of-the-nation, her character began to owe more to the most strident aspects of the national persona than to the child-world of her Monkey years.

Jamila Singer's voice was on Voice-Of-Pakistan Radio constantly, so that in the villages of West and East Wings she came to seem like a superhuman being, incapable of being fatigued, an angel who sang to her people through all the days and nights; while Ahmed Sinai, whose few remaining qualms about his daughter's career had been more than allayed by her enormous earnings (although he had once been a Delhi man, he was by now a true Bombay Muslim at heart, placing cash matters above most other things), became fond of telling my sister: 'You see, daughter: decency, purity, art and good business sense can be one and the same things; your old father has been wise enough to work that out.' Jamila smiled sweetly and agreed . . . she was growing out of scrawny tomboy youth into a slender, slant-eyed, golden-skinned beauty whose hair was nearly long enough to sit on; even her nose looked good. 'In my daughter,' Ahmed Sinai told Uncle Puffs proudly, 'it is my side of the family's noble features which have prevailed.' Uncle Puffs cast a quizzical, awkward glance at me and cleared his throat. 'Darn fine-looking girl, sir,' he told my father, 'Top-hole, by gum.'

The thunder of applause was never far from my sister's ears; at her first, now-legendary Bambino recital (we sat in seats provided by Uncle Puffs – 'Best darn seats in the house!' – beside his seven Puffias, all veiled ... Uncle Puffs dug me in the ribs, 'Hey, boy – choose! Take your pick! Remember: the dowry!' and I blushed and stared hard at the stage), the cries of '*Wah! Wah!*' were sometimes louder than Jamila's voice; and after the show we found Jamila back-stage drowning in a sea of flowers, so that we had to fight our way through the blossoming camphor garden of the nation's love, to find that she was almost fainting, not from fatigue, but from the overpoweringly sweet perfume of adoration with which the blooms had filled the room. I, too, felt my head beginning to swim; until Uncle Puffs began to hurl flowers in great bushels from an open window – they were gathered by a crowd of fans – while he cried, 'Flowers are fine, darn it, but even a national heroine needs air!'

There was applause, too, on the evening Jamila Singer (and family) was invited to President House to sing for the commander of pepperpots. Ignoring reports in foreign magazines about embezzled money and Swiss bank accounts, we scrubbed ourselves until we shone; a family in the towel business is obliged to be spotlessly clean. Uncle Puffs gave his gold teeth an extra-careful polish; and in a large hall dominated by garlanded portraits of Muhammad Ali Jinnah, the founder of Pakistan, the Quaid-i-Azam, and of his assassinated friend and successor Liaquat Ali, a perforated sheet was held up and my sister sang. Jamila's voice fell silent at last; the voice of gold braid succeeded her brocade-bordered song. 'Jamila daughter,' we heard, 'your voice will be a sword for purity; it will be a weapon with which we shall cleanse men's souls.' President Ayub was, by his own admission, a simple soldier; he instilled in my sister the simple, soldierly virtues of faith-in-leaders and trust-in-God; and she, 'The President's will is the voice of my heart.' Through the hole in a perforated sheet, Jamila Singer dedicated herself to patriotism; and the diwan-i-khas, the hall of this private audience, rang with applause, polite now, not the wild wah-wahing of the Bambino crowd, but the regimented approbation of braided gongs-and-pips and the delighted clapping of weepy parents. 'I say!' Uncle Puffs whispered, 'Darn fine, eh?'

What I could smell, Jamila could sing. Truth beauty happiness pain: each had its separate fragrance, and could be distinguished by my nose; each, in Jamila's performances, could find its ideal voice. My nose, her voice: they were exactly complementary gifts; but they were growing apart. While Jamila sang patriotic songs, my nose seemed to prefer to linger on the uglier smells which invaded it: the bitterness of Aunt Alia, the hard unchanging stink of my fellow-students' closed minds; so that while she rose into the clouds, I fell into the gutter.

Looking back, however, I think I was already in love with her, long before I was told . . . is there proof of Saleem's unspeakable sister-love? There is. Jamila Singer had one passion in common with the vanished Brass Monkey; she loved bread. Chapatis, parathas, tandoori nans? Yes, but. Well then: was yeast preferred? It was; my sister – despite patriotism – hankered constantly after leavened bread. And, in all Karachi, what was the only source of quality, yeasty loaves? Not a baker's; the best bread in the city was handed out through a hatch in an otherwise blind wall, every Thursday morning, by the sisters of the hidden order of Santa Ignacia. Each week, on my Lambretta scooter, I brought my sister the warm fresh loaves of nuns. Despite long snaking queues; making light of the overspiced, hot, dung-laden odour of the narrow streets around the nunnery; ignoring all other calls upon my time, I fetched the bread. Criticism was entirely absent from my heart; never once did I ask my sister whether this last relic of her old flirtation with Christianity might not look rather bad in her new role of Bulbul of the Faith . . .

Is it possible to trace the origins of unnatural love? Did Saleem, who had yearned after a place in the centre of history, become besotted with what he saw in his sister of his own hopes for life? Did much-mutilated no-longer-Snotnose, as broken a member of the Midnight Children's Conference as the knife-scarred beggar-girl Sundari, fall in love with the new wholeness of his sibling? Once the Mubarak, the Blessed One, did I adore in my sister the fulfilment of my most private dreams? . . . I shall say only that I was unaware of what had happened to me until, with a scooter between my sixteen-year-old thighs, I began to follow the spoors of whores.

While Alia smouldered; during the early days of Amina Brand towels; amid the apotheosis of Jamila Singer; when a split-level house, rising by command of an umbilical cord, was still far from complete; in the time of the late-flowering love of my parents; surrounded by the somehow barren certitudes of the land of the pure, Saleem Sinai came to terms with himself. I will not say he was not sad; refusing to censor my past, I admit he was as sullen, often as uncooperative, certainly as spotty as most boys of his age. His dreams, denied the children of midnight, became filled with nostalgia to the point of nausea, so that he often woke up gagging with the heavy musk of regret overpowering his senses; there were nightmares of numbers marching one two three, and of a tightening, throttling pair of prehensile knees . . . but there was a new gift, and a Lambretta scooter, and (though still unconscious) a humble, submissive love of his sister . . . jerking my narrator's eyes away from the described past, I insist that Saleem, then-as-now, succeeded in turning his attention towards the as-yet-undescribed future. Escaping, whenever possible, from a residence in which the acrid fumes of his aunt's envy made life unbearable, and also from a college filled with other equally dislikeable smells, I mounted my motorized steed and explored the olfactory avenues of my new city. And after we heard of my grandfather's death in Kashmir, I became even more determined to drown the past in the thick, bubbling scent-stew of the present . . . O dizzying early days before categorization! Formlessly, before I began to shape them, the fragrances poured into me: the mournful decaying fumes of animal faeces in the gardens of the Frere Road museum, the pustular body odours of young men in loose pajamas holding hands in Sadar evenings, the knife-sharpness of expectorated betel-nut and the bitter-sweet commingling of betel and opium: 'rocket paans' were sniffed out in the hawker-crowded alleys between Elphinstone Street and Victoria Road. Camel-smells, car-smells, the gnat-like irritation of motor-rickshaw fumes, the aroma of contraband cigarettes and 'black-money', the competitive effluvia of the city's bus-drivers and the simple sweat of their sardine-crowded passengers. (One bus-driver, in those days, was so incensed at being overtaken by his rival from another company – the nauseating odour of defeat poured from his glands – that he took his bus round to his opponent's house at night, hooted until the poor fellow emerged, and ran him down beneath wheels reeking, like my aunt, of revenge.) Mosques poured over me the itr of devotion; I could smell the orotund emissions of power sent out by flag-waving Army motors; in the very hoardings of the cinemas I could discern the cheap tawdry perfumes of imported spaghetti Westerns and the most violent martial-arts films ever made. I was, for a time, like a drugged person, my head reeling beneath the complexities of smell; but then my overpowering desire for form asserted itself, and I survived.

Indo-Pakistani relations deteriorated; the borders were closed, so that we could not go to Agra to mourn my grandfather; Reverend Mother's emigration to Pakistan was also somewhat delayed. In the meantime, Saleem was working towards a general theory of smell: classification procedures had begun. I saw this scientific approach as my own, personal obeisance to the spirit of my grandfather ... to begin with, I perfected my skill at distinguishing, until I could tell apart the infinite varieties of betel-nut and (with my eyes shut) the twelve different available brands of fizzy drink. (Long before the American commentator Herbert Feldman came to Karachi to deplore the existence of a dozen aerated waters in a city which had only three suppliers of bottled milk, I could sit blindfolded and tell Pakola from Hoffman's Mission, Citra Cola from Fanta. Feldman saw these drinks as a manifestation of capitalist imperialism; I, sniffing out which was Canada Dry and which 7-Up, unerringly separating Pepsi from Coke, was more interested in passing their subtle olfactory test. Double Kola and Kola Kola, Perri Cola and Bubble Up were blindly indentified and named.) Only when I was sure of my mastery of physical scents did I move on to those other aromas which only I could smell: the perfumes of emotions and all the thousand and one drives which make us human: love and death, greed and humility, have and have-not were labelled and placed in neat compartments of my mind.

Early attempts at ordering: I tried to classify smells by colour – boiling underwear and the printer's ink of the *Daily Jang* shared a quality of blueness, while old teak and fresh farts were both dark brown. Motor-cars and graveyards I jointly classified as grey ... there was, too, classification-by-weight: flyweight smells (paper), bantam odours (soap-fresh bodies, grass), welterweights (perspiration, queen-of-the-night); shahi-korma and bicycle-oil were light-heavyweight in my system, while anger, patchouli, treachery and dung were among the heavyweight stinks of the earth. And I had a geometric system also: the roundness of joy and the angularity of ambition; I had elliptical smells, and also ovals and squares . . . a lexicographer of the nose, I travelled Bunder Road and the P.E.C.H.S.; a lepidopterist, I snared whiffs like butterflies in the net of my nasal hairs. O wondrous voyages before the birth of philosophy! . . . Because soon I understood that my work must, if it was to have any value, acquire a moral dimension; that the only important divisions were the infinitely subtle gradations of good and evil smells. Having realized the crucial nature of morality, having sniffed out that smells could be sacred or profane, I invented, in the isolation of my scooter-trips, the science of nasal ethics.

Sacred: purdah-veils, halal meat, muezzin's towers, prayer-mats; profane: Western records, pig-meat, alcohol. I understood now why mullahs (sacred) refused to enter aeroplanes (profane) on the night before Id-ul-Fitr, not even willing to enter vehicles whose secret odour was the antithesis of godliness in order to make sure of seeing the new moon. I learned the olfactory incompatibility of Islam and socialism, and the inalienable opposition existing between the after-shave of Sind Club members and the poverty-reek of the street-sleeping beggars at the Club gates . . . more and more, however, I became convinced of an ugly truth – namely that the sacred, or good, held little interest for me, even when such aromas surrounded my sister as she sang; while the pungency of the gutter seemed to possess a fatally irresistible attraction. Besides, I was sixteen; things were stirring beneath my belt, behind my duck-white pants; and no city which locks women away is ever short of whores. While Jamila sang of holiness and love-of-country, I explored profanity and lust. (I had money to burn; my father had become generous as well as loving.)

At the eternally unfinished Jinnah Mausoleum I picked up the women of the street. Other youths came here to seduce American girls away, taking them off to hotel rooms or swimming pools; I preferred to retain my independence and pay. And eventually I nosed out the whore of whores, whose gifts were a mirror for my own. Her name was Tai Bibi, and she claimed to be five hundred and twelve.

But her smell! The richest spoor he, Saleem, had ever sniffed; he felt bewitched by something in it, some air of historic majesty . . . he found himself saying to the toothless creature: 'I don't care about your age; the smell's the thing.'

('My God,' Padma interrupts, 'Such a thing – how could you?')

Though she never hinted at any connection with a Kashmiri boatman, her name exerted the strongest of pulls; although she may have been humouring Saleem when she said, 'Boy, I am five hundred and twelve,' his sense of history was nevertheless aroused. Think of me what you like; I spent one hot, humid afternoon in a tenement-room containing a flea-ridden mattress and a naked lightbulb and the oldest whore in the world.

What finally made Tai Bibi irresistible? What gift of control did she possess which put other whores to shame? What maddened the newly-sensitized nostrils of our Saleem? Padma: my ancient prostitute possessed a mastery over her glands so total that she could alter her bodily odours to match those of anyone on earth. Eccrines and apocrines obeyed the instructions of her antiquated will; and although she said, 'Don't expect me to do it standing up; you couldn't pay enough for that,' her gifts of perfume were more than he could bear.

(. . . 'Chhi-chhi,' Padma covers her ears, 'My God, such a dirty-filthy man, I never knew!' . . .)

So there he was, this peculiar hideous youth, with an old hag who said, 'I won't stand up; my corns,' and then noticed that the mention of corns seemed to arouse him; whispering the secret of her eccrine-and-apocrine facility, she asked if he'd like her to imitate anyone's smells, he could describe and she could try, and by trial-and-error they could . . . and at first he jerked away, No no no, but she coaxed him in her voice

443

like crumpled paper, until because he was alone, out of the world and out of all time, alone with this impossible mythological old harridan, he began to describe odours with all the perspicacity of his miraculous nose, and Tai Bibi began to imitate his descriptions, leaving him aghast as by trial-and-error she succeeded in reproducing the body odours of his mother his aunts, oho you like that do you little sahibzada, go on, stick your nose as close as you like, you're a funny fellow for sure . . . until suddenly, by accident, yes, I swear I didn't make her do it, suddenly during trial-and-error the most unspeakable fragrance on earth wafts out of the cracked wrinkled leather-ancient body, and now he can't hide what she sees, oho, little sahibzada, what have I hit on now, you don't have to tell who she is but this one is the one for sure.

And Saleem, 'Shut up shut up –' But Tai Bibi with the relentlessness of her cackling antiquity presses on, 'Oho yes, certainly, your lady-love, little sahibzada – who? Your cousin, maybe? Your sister . . .' Saleem's hand is tightening into a fist; the right hand, despite mutilated finger, contemplates violence . . . and now Tai Bibi, 'My God yes! Your sister! Go on, hit me, you can't hide what's sitting there in the middle of your forehead! . . .' And Saleem gathering up his clothes struggling into trousers Shut up old hag While she Yes go, go, but if you don't pay me I'll, I'll, you see what I don't do, and now rupees flying across the room floating down around five-hundred-and-twelve-year-old courtesan, Take take only shut your hideous face, while she Careful my princeling you're not so handsome yourself, dressed now and rushing from the tenement, Lambretta scooter waiting but urchins have urinated on the seat, he is driving away as fast as he can go, but the truth is going with him, and now Tai Bibi leaning out of a window shouts, 'Hey, bhaenchud! Hey, little sister-sleeper, where you running? What's true is true is true . . . !'

You may legitimately ask: Did it happen in just this . . . And surely she couldn't have been five hundred and . . . but I swore to confess everything, and I insist that I learned the unspeakable secret of my love for Jamila Singer from the mouth and scent-glands of that most exceptional of whores.

'Our Mrs Braganza is right,' Padma is scolding me, 'She says there is nothing but dirt in the heads of the mens.' I ignore her; Mrs Braganza, and her sister Mrs Fernandes, will be dealt with in due course; for the moment, the latter must be content with the factory accounts while the former looks after my son. And while I, to recapture the rapt attention of my revolted Padma Bibi, recount a fairy-tale.

Once upon a time, in the far northern princedom of Kif, there lived a prince who had two beautiful daughters, a son of equally remarkable good looks, a brand-new Rolls-Royce motor car, and excellent political contacts. This prince, or Nawab, believed passionately in progress, which was why he had arranged the engagement of his elder daughter to the son of the prosperous and well-known General Zulfikar; for his younger daughter he had high hopes of a match with the son of the President himself. As for his motor-car, the first ever seen in his mountain-ringed valley, he loved it almost as much as his children; it grieved him that his subjects, who had become used to using the roads of Kif for purposes of social intercourse, quarrels and games of hit-the-spittoon, refused to get out of its way. He issued a proclamation explaining that the car represented the future, and must be allowed to pass; the people ignored the notice, although it was pasted to shop-fronts and walls and even, it is said, to the sides of cows. The second notice was more peremptory, ordering the citizenry to clear the highways when they heard the horn of the car; the Kifis, however, continued to smoke and spit and argue in the streets. The third notice, which was adorned with a gory drawing, said that the car would henceforth run down anybody who failed to obey its horn. The Kifis added new, more scandalous pictures to the one on the poster; and then the Nawab, who was a good man but not one of infinite patience, actually did as he threatened. When the famous singer Jamila arrived with her family and impresario to sing at her cousin's engagement ceremony, the car drove her without trouble from border to palace; and the Nawab said proudly, 'No trouble; the car is respected now. Progress has occurred.'

The Nawab's son Mutasim, who had travelled abroad and wore his hair in something called a 'beetle-cut', was a source of worry to his father; because although he was so good-looking that, whenever he travelled around Kif, girls with silver nose-jewellery fainted in the heat of his beauty, he seemed to take no interest in such matters, being content with his polo-ponies and the guitar on which he picked out strange Western songs. He wore bush-shirts on which musical notation and foreign street-signs jostled against the half-clad bodies of pink-skinned girls. But when Jamila Singer, concealed within a gold-brocaded burqa, arrived at the palace, Mutasim the Handsome – who owing to his foreign travels had never heard the rumours of her disfigurement – became obsessed with the idea of seeing her face; he fell head-over-heels with the glimpses of her demure eyes he saw through her perforated sheet.

In those days, the President of Pakistan had decreed an election; it was to take place on the day after the engagement ceremony, under a form of suffrage called Basic Democracy. The hundred million people of Pakistan had been divided up into a hundred and twenty thousand approximately equal parts, and each part was represented by one Basic Democrat. The electoral college of one hundred and twenty thousand 'B.D.s' were to elect the President. In Kif, the 420 Basic Democrats included mullahs, road-sweepers, the Nawab's chauffeur, numerous men who sharecropped hashish on the Nawab's estate, and other loyal citizens; the Nawab had invited all of these to his daughter's hennaing ceremony. He had, however, also been obliged to invite two real badmashes, the returning officers of the Combined Opposition Party. These badmashes quarrelled constantly amongst themselves, but the Nawab was courteous and welcoming. 'Tonight you are my honoured friends,' he told them, 'and tomorrow is another day.' The badmashes ate and drank as if they had never seen food before, but everybody – even Mutasim the Handsome, whose patience was shorter than his father's – was told to treat them well.

The Combined Opposition Party, you will not be surprised to hear, was a collection of rogues and scoundrels of the first water, united only in their determination to unseat the President and return to the bad old days in which civilians, and not soldiers, lined their pockets from the public exchequer; but for some reason they had acquired a formidable leader. This was Mistress Fatima Jinnah, the sister of the founder of the nation, a woman of such desiccated antiquity that the Nawab suspected she had died long ago and been stuffed by a master taxidermist – a notion supported by his son, who had seen a movie called *El Cid* in which a dead man led an army into battle . . . but there she was nevertheless, goaded into electioneering by the President's failure to complete the marbling of her brother's mausoleum; a terrible foe, above slander and suspicion. It was even said that her opposition to the President had shaken the people's faith in him – was he not, after all, the reincarnation of the great Islamic heroes of yesteryear? Of Muhammad bin Sam Ghuri, of Iltutmish and the Mughals? Even in Kif itself, the Nawab had noticed C.O.P. stickers appearing in curious places; someone had even had the cheek to affix one to the boot of the Rolls. 'Bad days,' the Nawab told his son. Mutasim replied, 'That's what elections get you – latrine cleaners and cheap tailors must vote to elect a ruler?'

But today was a day for happiness; in the zenana chambers, women were patterning the Nawab's daughter's hands and feet with delicate traceries of henna; soon General Zulfikar and his son Zafar would arrive. The rulers of Kif put the election out of their heads, refusing to think of the crumbling figure of Fatima Jinnah, the mader-i-millat or mother of the nation who had so callously chosen to confuse her children's choosing.

In the quarters of Jamila Singer's party, too, happiness reigned supreme. Her father, a towel-manufacturer who could not seem to relinquish the soft hand of his wife, cried, 'You see? Whose daughter is performing here? Is it a Haroon girl? A Valika woman? Is it a Dawood or Saigol wench? Like hell!' . . . But his son Saleem, an unfortunate fellow with a face like a cartoon, seemed to be gripped by some deep malaise, perhaps overwhelmed by his presence at the scene of great historical events; he glanced towards his gifted sister with something in his eyes which looked like shame.

That afternoon, Mutasim the Handsome took Jamila's brother Saleem to one side and tried hard to make friends; he showed Saleem the peacocks imported from Rajasthan before Partition and the Nawab's precious collection of books of spells, from which he extracted such talismans and incantations as would help him rule with sagacity; and while Mutasim (who was not the most intelligent or cautious of youths) was escorting Saleem around the polo-field, he confessed that he had written out a love-charm on a piece of parchment, in the hope of pressing it against the hand of the famous Jamila Singer and making her fall in love. At this point Saleem acquired the air of a bad-tempered dog and tried to turn away; but Mutasim now begged to know what Jamila Singer really looked like. Saleem, however, kept his silence; until Mutasim, in the grip of a wild obsession, asked to be brought close enough to Jamila to press his charm against her hand. Now Saleem, whose sly look did not register on love-struck Mutasim, said, 'Give me the parchment'; and Mutasim, who, though expert in the geography of European cities, was innocent in things magical, yielded his charm to Saleem, thinking it would still work on his behalf, even if applied by another.

Evening approached at the palace; the convoy of cars bringing General and Begum Zulfikar, their son Zafar, and friends, approached, too. But now the wind changed, and began to blow from the north: a cold wind, and also an intoxicating one, because in the north of Kif were the best hashish fields in the land, and at this time of year the female plants were ripe and in heat. The air was filled with the perfume of the heady lust of the plants, and all who breathed it became doped to some extent. The vacuous beatitude of the plants affected the drivers in the convoy, which only reached the palace by great good fortune, having overturned a number of street-side barber-stalls and invaded at least one tea-shop, leaving the Kifs wondering whether the new horseless carriages, having stolen the streets, were now going to capture their homes as well.

The wind from the north entered the enormous and highly sensitive nose of Saleem, Jamila's brother, and made him so drowsy that he fell asleep in his room; so that he missed the events of an evening during which, he afterwards learned, the hashashin wind had transformed the behaviour of the guests at the engagement ceremony, making them giggle convulsively and gaze provocatively at one another through heavy-lidded eyes; braided Generals sat splay-legged on gilded chairs and dreamed of Paradise. The mehndi ceremony took place amid a sleepy contentment so profound that nobody noticed when the bridegroom relaxed so completely that he wet his pants; and even the quarrelling badmashes from the C.O.P. linked arms and sang a folk-song. And when Mutasim the Handsome, possessed by the lustiness of hashish-plants, attempted to plunge behind the great gold-and-silken sheet with its single hole, Major Alauddin Latif restrained him with beatific good humour, preventing him from seeing Jamila

Singer's face without even bloodying his nose. The evening ended when all the guests fell asleep at their tables; but Jamila Singer was escorted to her rooms by a sleepily-beaming Latif.

At midnight, Saleem awoke to find that he still clutched the magical parchment of Mutasim the Handsome in his right hand; and since the wind from the north was still blowing gently through his room, he made up his mind to creep, in chappals and dressing-gown, through the darkened passages of the lovely palace, past all the accumulated debris of a decaying world, rusting suits of armour and ancient tapestries which provided centuries of food for the palace's one billion moths, giant mahaseer trout swimming in glass seas, and a profusion of hunting trophies including a tarnished golden teetar-bird on a teak plinth which commemorated the day on which an earlier Nawab, in the company of Lord Curzon and party, had shot 111, 111 teetars in a single day; he crept past the statues of dead birds into the zenana chambers where the women of the palace slept, and then, sniffing the air, he selected one door, turned the handle and went inside.

There was a giant bed with a floating mosquito-net caught in a stream of colourless light from the maddening, midnight moon; Saleem moved towards it, and then stopped, because he had seen, at the window, the figure of a man trying to climb into the room. Mutasim the Handsome, made shameless by his infatuation and the hashashin wind, had resolved to look at Jamila's face, no matter what the cost . . . And Saleem, invisible in the shadows of the room cried out: 'Hands up! Or I shoot!' Saleem was bluffing; but Mutasim, whose hands were on the window sill, supporting his full weight, did not know that, and was placed in a quandary: to hang on and be shot, or let go and fall? He attempted to argue back, 'You shouldn't be here yourself,' he said, 'I'll tell Amina Begum.' He had recognized the voice of his oppressor; but Saleem pointed out the weakness of his position, and Mutasim, pleading, 'Okay, only don't fire,' was permitted to descend the way he'd come. After that day, Mutasim persuaded his father to make a formal proposal of marriage to Jamila's parents; but she, who had been born and raised without love, retained her old hatred of all who claimed to love her, and turned him down. He left Kif and came to Karachi, but she would not entertain his importunate proposals; and eventually he joined the Army and became a martyr in the war of 1965.

The tragedy of Mutasim the Handsome, however, is only a subplot in our story; because now Saleem and his sister were alone, and she, awakened by the exchange between the two youths, asked, 'Saleem? What is happening?'

Saleem approached his sister's bed; his hand sought hers; and parchment was pressed against skin. Only now did Saleem, his tongue loosened by the moon and the lust-drenched breeze, abandon all notions of purity and confess his own love to his open-mouthed sister.

There was a silence; then she cried, 'Oh, no, how can you –', but the magic of the parchment was doing battle with the strength of her hatred of love; so although her body grew stiff and jerky as a wrestler's, she listened to him explaining that there was no sin, he had worked it all out, and after all, they were not truly brother and sister; the blood in his veins was not the blood in hers; in the breeze of that insane night he attempted to undo all the knots which not even Mary Pereira's confession had succeeded in untying; but even as he spoke he could hear his words sounding hollow, and realized that although what he was saying was the literal truth, there were other truths which had become more important because they had been sanctified by time; and although there was no need for shame or horror, he saw both emotions on her forehead, he smelt them on her skin, and, what was worse, he could feel and smell them in and upon himself. So, in the end, not even the magic parchment of Mutasim the Handsome was powerful enough to bring Saleem Sinai and Jamila Singer together; he left her room with bowed head, followed by her deer-startled eyes; and in time the effects of the spell faded altogether, and she took a dreadful revenge. As he left the room the corridors of the palace were suddenly filled with the shriek of a newly-affianced princess, who had awoken from a dream of her wedding-night in which her marital bed had suddenly and unaccountably become awash in rancid yellow liquid; afterwards, she made inquiries, and when she learned the prophetic truth of her dream, resolved never to reach puberty while Zafar was alive, so that she could stay in her palatial bedroom and avoid the foul-smelling horror of his weakness.

The next morning, the two badmashes of the Combined Opposition Party awoke to find themselves back in their own beds; but when they had dressed, they opened the door of their chamber to find two of the biggest soldiers in Pakistan outside it, standing peacefully with crossed rifles, barring the exit. The badmashes shouted and wheedled, but the soldiers stayed in position until the polls were closed; then they quietly disappeared. The badmashes sought out the Nawab, finding him in his exceptional rose-garden; they waved their arms and raised their voices; travesty-of-justice was mentioned, and electoral-jiggery-pokery; also chicanery; but the Nawab showed them thirteen new varieties of Kifi rose, crossbred by himself. They ranted on – death-of-democracy, autocratic-tyranny – until he smiled gently, gently, and said, 'My friends, yesterday my daughter was betrothed to Zafar Zulfikar; soon, I hope, my other girl will wed our President's own dear son. Think, then – what dishonour for me, what scandal on my name, if even one vote were cast in Kif against my future relative! Friends, I am a man to whom honour is of concern; so stay in my house, eat, drink; only do not ask for what I cannot give.'

And we all lived happily . . . at any rate, even without the traditional last-sentence fiction of fairy-tales, my story does

452

indeed end in fantasy; because when Basic Democrats had done their duty, the newspapers – *Jang, Dawn, Pakistan Times* – announced a crushing victory for the President's Muslim League over the Mader-i-Millat's Combined Opposition Party; thus proving to me that I have been only the humblest of jugglers-with-facts; and that, in a country where the truth is what it is instructed to be, reality quite literally ceases to exist, so that everything becomes possible except what we are told is the case; and maybe this was the difference between my Indian childhood and Pakistani adolescence – that in the first I was beset by an infinity of alternative realities, while in the second I was adrift, disorientated, amid an equally infinite number of falsenesses, unrealities and lies.

A little bird whispers in my ear: 'Be fair! Nobody, no country, has a monopoly of untruth.' I accept the criticism; I know, I know. And, years later, the Widow knew. And Jamila: for whom what-had-been-sanctified-as-truth (by Time, by habit, by a grandmother's pronouncement, by lack of imagination, by a father's acquiescence) proved more believable than what she knew to be so.

How Saleem achieved purity

What is waiting to be told: the return of ticktock. But now time is counting down to an end, not a birth; there is, too, a weariness to be mentioned, a general fatigue so profound that the end, when it comes, will be the only solution, because human beings, like nations and fictional characters, can simply run out of steam, and then there's nothing for it but to finish with them.

How a piece fell out of the moon, and Saleem achieved purity . . . the clock is ticking now; and because all count-downs require a zero, let me state that the end came on September 22nd, 1965; and that the precise instant of the arrival-at-zero was, inevitably, the stroke of midnight. Although the old grandfather clock in my aunt Alia's house, which kept accurate time but always chimed two minutes late, never had a chance to strike.

My grandmother Naseem Aziz arrived in Pakistan in mid-1964, leaving behind an India in which Nehru's death had precipitated a bitter power struggle. Morarji Desai, the Finance Minister, and Jagjivan Ram, most powerful of the untouchables, united in their determination to prevent the establishment of a Nehru dynasty; so Indira Gandhi was denied the leadership. The new Prime Minister was Lal Bahadur Shastri, another member of that generation of politicians who seemed to have been pickled in immortality; in the case of Shastri, however, this was only maya, illusion.

454

Nehru and Shastri have both fully proved their mortality; but there are still plenty of the others left, clutching Time in their mummified fingers and refusing to let it move . . . in Pakistan, however, the clocks ticked and tocked.

Reverend Mother did not overtly approve of my sister's career; it smacked too much of film-stardom. 'My family, whatsitsname,' she sighed to Pia mumani, 'is even less controllable than the price of gas.' Secretly, however, she may have been impressed, because she respected power and position and Jamila was now so exalted as to be welcome in the most powerful and best-placed houses in the land . . . my grandmother settled in Rawalpindi; however, with a strange show of independence, she chose not to live in the house of General Zulfikar. She and my aunt Pia moved into a modest bungalow in the old part of town; and by pooling their savings, purchased a concession on the long-dreamed-of petrol pump.

Naseem never mentioned Aadam Aziz, nor would she grieve over him; it was almost as though she were relieved that my querulous grandfather, who had in his youth despised the Pakistan movement, and who in all probability blamed the Muslim League for the death of his friend Mian Abdullah, had by dying permitted her to go alone into the Land of the Pure. Setting her face against the past, Reverend Mother concentrated on gasoline and oil. The pump was on a prime site, near the Rawalpindi-Lahore grand trunk road; it did very well. Pia and Naseem took it in turns to spend the day in the manager's glass booth while attendants filled up cars and Army trucks. They proved a magical combination. Pia attracted customers with the beacon of a beauty which obstinately refused to fade; while Reverend Mother, who had been transformed by bereavement into a woman who was more interested in other people's lives than her own, took to inviting the pump's customers into her glass booth for cups of pink Kashmiri tea; they would accept with some trepidation, but when they realized that the old lady did not propose to bore them with endless reminiscences, they relaxed, loosened collars and tongues, and Reverend Mother was able to bathe in the blessed oblivion of other people's lives. The pump rapidly became famous in those parts, drivers began to go out of their way to use it – often on two consecutive days, so that they could both feast their eyes on my divine aunt and tell their woes to my eternally patient grandmother, who had developed the absorbent properties of a sponge, and always waited until her guests had completely finished before squeezing out of her own lips a few drops of simple, firm advice – while their cars were filled up with petrol and polished by pump-attendants, my grandmother would re-charge and polish their lives. She sat in her glass confessional and solved the problems of the world; her own family, however, seemed to have lost importance in her eyes.

Moustachioed, matriarchal, proud: Naseem Aziz had found her own way of coping with tragedy; but in finding it had become the first victim of that spirit of detached fatigue which made the end the only possible solution. (Tick, tock.) . . . However, on the face of it, she appeared to have not the slightest intention of following her husband into the camphor garden reserved for the righteous; she seemed to have more in common with the methuselah leaders of her abandoned India. She grew, with alarming rapidity, wider and wider; until builders were summoned to expand her glassed-in booth. 'Make it big big,' she instructed them, with a rare flash of humour, 'Maybe I'll still be here after a century, whatsits-name, and Allah knows how big I'll have become; I don't want to be troubling you every ten-twelve years.'

Pia Aziz, however, was not content with 'pumpery-shumpery'. She began a series of liaisons with colonels cricketers polo-players diplomats, which were easy to conceal from a Reverend Mother who had lost interest in the doings of everyone except strangers; but which were otherwise the talk of what was, after all, a small town. My aunt Emerald took Pia to task; she replied: 'You want me to be forever howling and pulling hair? I'm still young; young folk should gad a little.' Emerald, thin-lipped: 'But be a little respectable . . . the family name . . .' At which Pia tossed her head. 'You be respectable, sister,' she said, 'Me, I'll be alive.'

But it seems to me that there was something hollow in Pia's self-assertion; that she, too, felt her personality draining away with the years; that her feverish romancing was a last desperate attempt to behave 'in character' – in the way a woman like her was supposed to do. Her heart wasn't in it; somewhere inside, she, too, was waiting for an end . . . In my family, we have always been vulnerable to things which fall from the skies, ever since Ahmed Sinai was slapped by a vulture-dropped hand; and bolts from the blue were only a year away.

After the news of my grandfather's death and the arrival of Reverend Mother in Pakistan, I began to dream repeatedly of Kashmir; although I had never walked in Shalimar-bagh, I did so at night; I floated in shikaras and climbed Sankara Acharya's hill as my grandfather had; I saw lotus-roots and mountains like angry jaws. This, too, may be seen as an aspect of the detachment which came to afflict us all (except Jamila, who had God and country to keep her going) – a reminder of my family's separateness from both India and Pakistan. In Rawalpindi, my grandmother drank pink Kashmiri tea; in Karachi, her grandson was washed by the waters of a lake he had never seen. It would not be long before the dream of Kashmir spilled over into the minds of the rest of the population of Pakistan; connection-to-history refused to abandon me, and I found my dream becoming, in 1965, the common property of the nation, and a factor of prime importance in the coming end, when all manner of things fell from the skies, and I was purified at last.

*

Saleem could sink no lower: I could smell, on myself, the cess-pit stink of my iniquities. I had come to the Land of the Pure, and sought the company of whores – when I should have been forging a new, upright life for myself, I gave birth, instead, to an unspeakable (and also unrequited) love. Possessed by the beginnings of the great fatalism which was to overwhelm me, I rode the city streets on my Lambretta; Jamila and I avoided each other as much as possible, unable, for the first time in our lives, to say a word to one another.

Purity – that highest of ideals! – that angelic virtue for which Pakistan was named, and which dripped from every note of my sister's songs! – seemed very far away; how could I have known that history – which has the power of pardoning sinners – was at that moment counting down towards a moment in which it would manage, at one stroke, to cleanse me from head to foot?

In the meantime, other forces were spending themselves; Alia Aziz had begun to wreak her awful spinster's revenge.

Guru Mandir days: paan-smells, cooking-smells, the languor-ous odour of the shadow of the minaret, the mosque's long pointing finger: while my aunt Alia's hatred of the man who had abandoned her and of the sister who had married him grew into a tangible, visible thing, it sat on her living-room rug like a great gecko, reeking of vomit; but it seemed I was the only one to smell it, because Alia's skill at dissimulation had grown as rapidly as the hairiness of her chin and her adeptness with the plasters with which, each evening, she ripped her beard out by the roots.

My aunt Alia's contribution to the fate of nations – through her school and college – must not be minimized. Having allowed her old-maid frustrations to leak into the curricula, the bricks and also the students at her twin educational establishments, she had raised a tribe of children and young adults who felt themselves possessed by an ancient

458

vengefulness, without fully knowing why. O omnipresent aridity of maiden aunts! It soured the paintwork of her home; her furniture was made lumpy by the harsh stuffing of bitterness; old-maid repressions were sewn into curtain-seams. As once long ago into baby things of. Bitterness, issuing through the fissures of the earth.

What my aunt Alia took pleasure in: cooking. What she had, during the lonely madness of the years, raised to the level of an art-form: the impregnation of food with emotions. To whom she remained second in her achievements in this field: my old ayah, Mary Pereira. By whom, today, both old cooks have been outdone: Saleem Sinai, pickler-in-chief at the Braganza pickle works . . . nevertheless, while we lived in her Guru Mandir mansion, she fed us the birianis of dissension and the nargisi koftas of discord; and little by little, even the harmonies of my parents' autumnal love went out of tune.

But good things must also be said about my aunt. In politics, she spoke out vociferously against government-by-military-say-so; if she had not had a General for a brother-in-law, her school and college might well have been taken out of her hands. Let me not show her entirely through the dark glass of my private despondency: she had given lecture-tours in the Soviet Union and America. Also, her food tasted good. (Despite its hidden content.)

But the air and the food in that mosque-shadowed house began to take its toll . . . Saleem, under the doubly dislocating influence of his awful love and Alia's food, began to blush like a beetroot whenever his sister appeared in his thoughts; while Jamila, unconsciously seized by a longing for fresh air and food unseasoned by dark emotions, began to spend less and less time there, travelling instead up and down the country (but never to the East Wing) to give her concerts. On those increasingly rare occasions when brother and sister found themselves in the same room they would jump, startled, half an inch off the floor, and then, landing, stare furiously at the spot over which they had leaped, as if it had suddenly become as hot as a bread-oven. At other times, too, they indulged in behaviour whose meaning would have been transparently obvious, were it not for the fact that each occupant of the house had other things on his or her mind: Jamila, for instance, took to keeping on her gold-and-white travelling veil indoors until she was sure her brother was out, even if she was dizzy with heat; while Saleem – who continued, slave-fashion, to fetch leavened bread from the nunnery of Santa Ignacia – avoided handing her the loaves himself; on occasion he asked his poisonous aunt to act as intermediary. Alia looked at him with amusement and asked, 'What's wrong *with you*, boy – you haven't got an infectious disease?' Saleem blushed furiously, fearing that his aunt had guessed about his encounters with paid women; and maybe she had, but she was after bigger fish.

. . . He also developed a penchant for lapsing into long broody silences, which he interrupted by bursting out suddenly with a meaningless word: 'No!' or, 'But!' or even more arcane exclamations, such as 'Bang!' or 'Whaam!' Nonsense words amidst clouded silences: as if Saleem were conducting some inner dialogue of such intensity that fragments of it, or its pain, boiled up from time to time past the surface of his lips. This inner discord was undoubtedly worsened by the curries of disquiet which we were obliged to eat; and at the end, when Amina was reduced to talking to invisible washing-chests and Ahmed, in the desolation of his stroke, was capable of little more than dribbles and giggles, while I glowered silently in my own private withdrawal, my aunt must have been well-pleased with the effectiveness of her revenge upon the Sinai clan; unless she, too, was drained by the fulfilment of her long-nurtured ambition; in which case she, too, had run out of possibilities, and there were hollow overtones in her footsteps as she stalked through the insane asylum of her home with her chin covered in hair-plasters, while her niece jumped over suddenly-hot patches of floor and her nephew yelled 'Yaa!' out of nowhere and her erstwhile suitor sent spittle down his chin and Amina greeted the resurgent ghosts of her past: 'So it's you again; well, why not? Nothing ever seems to go away.'

Tick, tock . . . In January 1965, my mother Amina Sinai discovered that she was pregnant again, after a gap of seventeen years. When she was sure, she told her good news to her big sister Alia, giving my aunt the opportunity of perfecting her revenge. What Alia said to my mother is not known; what she stirred into her cooking must remain a matter for conjecture; but the effect on Amina was devastating. She was plagued by dreams of a monster child with a cauliflower instead of a brain; she was beset by phantoms of Ramram Seth, and the old prophecy of a child with two heads began to drive her wild all over again. My mother was forty-two years old; and the fears (both natural and Alia-induced) of bearing a child at such an age tarnished the brilliant aura which had hung around her ever since she nursed her husband into his loving autumn; under the influence of the kormas of my aunt's vengeance – spiced with forebodings as well as cardamoms – my mother became afraid of her child. As the months passed, her forty-two years began to take a terrible toll; the weight of her four decades grew daily, crushing her beneath her age. In her second month, her hair went white. By the third, her face had shrivelled like a rotting mango. In her fourth month she was already an old woman, lined and thick, plagued by verrucas once again, with the inevitability of hair sprouting all over her face; she seemed shrouded once more in a fog of shame, as though the baby were a scandal in a lady of her evident antiquity. As the child of those confused days grew within her, the contrast between its youth and her age increased; it was at this point that she collapsed into an old cane chair and received visits from the spectres of her past. The disintegration of my mother was appalling in its suddenness; Ahmed Sinai, observing helplessly, found himself, all of a sudden, unnerved, adrift, unmanned.

Even now, I find it hard to write about those days of the end of possibility, when my father found his towel factory crumbling in his hands. The effects of Alia's culinary witchcraft (which operated both through his stomach, when he ate, and his eyes, when he saw his wife) were now all too apparent in him: he became slack at factory management, and irritable with his workforce.

To sum up the ruination of Amina Brand Towels: Ahmed Sinai began treating his workers as peremptorily as once, in Bombay, he had mistreated servants, and sought to inculcate, in master weavers and assistant packers alike, the eternal verities of the master-servant relationship. As a result his workforce walked out on him in droves, explaining, for instance, 'I am not your latrine-cleaner, sahib; I am qualified Grade One weaver,' and in general refusing to show proper gratitude for his beneficence in having employed them. In the grip of the befuddling wrath of my aunt's packed lunches, he let them all go, and hired a bunch of ill-favoured slackers who pilfered cotton spools and machine parts but were willing to bow and scrape whenever required to do so; and the percentage of defective towels rocketed alarmingly, contracts were not fulfilled, re-orders shrank alarmingly. Ahmed Sinai began bringing home mountains – Himalayas! – of reject towelling, because the factory warehouse was full to overflowing of the sub-standard product of his mismanagement; he took to drink again, and by the summer of that year the house in Guru Mandir was awash in the old obscenities of his battle against the djinns, and we had to squeeze sideways past the Everests and Nanga-Parbats of badly-made terry-cloth which lined the passages and hall.

We had delivered ourselves into the lap of my fat aunt's long-simmered wrath; with the single exception of Jamila, who was least affected owing to her long absences, we all ended up with our geese well and truly cooked. It was a painful and bewildering time, in which the love of my parents disintegrated under the joint weight of their new baby and of my aunt's age-old grievances; and gradually the confusion and ruin seeped out through the windows of the house and took over the hearts and minds of the nation, so that war, when it came, was wrapped in the same fuddled haze of unreality in which we had begun to live.

My father was heading steadily towards his stroke: but before the bomb went off in his brain, another fuse was lit: in April 1965, we heard about the peculiar incidents in the Rann of Kutch.

While we thrashed like flies in the webs of my aunt's revenge, the mill of history continued to grind. President Ayub's reputation was in decline: rumours of malpractice in the 1964 election buzzed about, refusing to be swatted. There was, too, the matter of the President's son: Gauhar Ayub, whose enigmatic Gandhara Industries made him a 'multi-multi' overnight. O endless sequence of nefarious sons-of-the-great! Gauhar, with his bullyings and rantings; and later, in India, Sanjay Gandhi and his Maruti Car Company and his Congress Youth; and most recently of all, Kanti Lal Desai . . . the sons of the great unmake their parents. But I, too, have a son; Aadam Sinai, flying in the face of precedent, will reverse the trend. Sons can be better than their fathers, as well as worse . . . in April 1965, however, the air buzzed with the fallibility of sons. And whose son was it who scaled the walls of President House on April 1st – what unknown father spawned the foul-smelling fellow who ran up to the President and fired a pistol at his stomach? Some fathers remain mercifully unknown to history; at any rate, the assassin failed, because his gun miraculously jammed. Somebody's son was taken away by police to have his teeth pulled out one by one, to have his nails set on fire; burning cigarette-ends were no doubt pressed against the tip of his penis, so it would probably not be much consolation for that nameless, would-be assassin to know that he had simply been carried away by a tide of history in which sons (high and low) were frequently observed to behave exceptionally badly. (No: I do not exempt myself.)

Divorce between news and reality: newspapers quoted foreign economists – PAKISTAN A MODEL FOR EMERGING NATIONS – while peasants (unreported) cursed the so-called 'green revolution', claiming that most of the newly-drilled water-wells had been useless, poisoned, and in the wrong places anyway; while editorials praised the probity of the nation's leadership, rumours, thick as flies, mentioned Swiss bank accounts and the new American motor-cars of the President's son. The Karachi *Dawn* spoke of another dawn – GOOD INDO-PAK RELATIONS JUST AROUND THE CORNER? – but, in the Rann of Kutch, yet another inadequate son was discovering a different story.

In the cities, mirages and lies; to the north, in the high mountains, the Chinese were building roads and planning nuclear blasts; but it is time to revert from the general to the particular; or, to be more exact, to the General's son, my cousin, the enuretic Zafar Zulfikar. Who became, between April and July, the archetype of all the many disappointing sons in the land; history, working through him, was also pointing its finger at Gauhar, at future-Sanjay and Kanti-Lal-to-come; and, naturally, at me.

So – cousin Zafar. With whom I had much in common at that time . . . my heart was full of forbidden love; his trousers, despite all his efforts, filled continually with something rather more tangible, but equally forbidden. I dreamed of mythical lovers, both happy and star-crossed – Shah Jehan and Mumtaz Mahal, but also Montague-and-Capulet; he dreamed of his Kifi fiancée, whose failure to arrive at puberty even after her sixteenth birthday must have made her seem, in his thoughts, a fantasy of an unattainable future . . . in April 1965, Zafar was sent on manoeuvres to the Pakistan-controlled zone of the Rann of Kutch.

Cruelty of the continent towards the loose-bladdered: Zafar, although a Lieutenant, was the laughing-stock of the Abbottabad military base. There was a story that he had been instructed to wear a rubber undergarment like a balloon around his genitals, so that the glorious uniform of the Pak Army should not be desecrated; mere jawans, when he passed, would make a blowing movement of their cheeks, as if they were puffing up the balloon. (All this became public later, in the statement he made, in floods of tears, after his arrest for murder.) It is possible that Zafar's assignment to the Rann of Kutch was thought up by a tactful superior, who was only trying to get him out of the firing-line of Abbottabad humour . . . Incontinence doomed Zafar Zulfikar to a crime as heinous as my own. I loved my sister; while he . . . but let me tell the story the right way up.

Ever since Partition, the Rann had been 'disputed territory'; although, in practice, neither side had much heart for the dispute. On the hillocks along the 23rd parallel, the unofficial frontier, the Pakistan Government had built a string of border posts, each with its lonely garrison of six men and one beacon-light. Several of these posts were occupied on April 9th, 1965, by troops of the Indian Army; a Pakistani force, including my cousin Zafar, which had been in the area on manoeuvres, engaged in an eighty-two-day struggle for the frontier. The war in the Rann lasted until July 1st. That much is fact; but everything else lies concealed beneath the doubly hazy air of unreality and make-believe which affected all goings-on in those days, and especially all events in the phantasmagoric Rann . . . so that the story I am going to tell, which is substantially that told by my cousin Zafar, is as likely to be true as anything; as anything, that is to say, except what we were officially told.

465

. . . As the young Pakistani soldiers entered the marshy terrain of the Rann, a cold clammy perspiration broke out on their foreheads, and they were unnerved by the greeny sea-bed quality of the light; they recounted stories which frightened them even more, legends of terrible things which happened in this amphibious zone, of demonic sea-beasts with glowing eyes, of fish-women who lay with their fishy heads underwater, breathing, while their perfectly-formed and naked human lower halves lay on the shore, tempting the unwary into fatal sexual acts, because it is well known that nobody may love a fish-woman and live . . . so that by the time they reached the border posts and went to war, they were a scared rabble of seventeen-year-old boys, and would certainly have been annihilated, except that the opposing Indians had been subjected to the green air of the Rann even longer than they; so in that sorcerers' world a crazy war was fought in which each side thought it saw apparitions of devils fighting alongside its foes; but in the end the Indian forces yielded; many of them collapsed in floods of tears and wept, Thank God, it's over; they told about the great blubbery things which slithered around the border posts at night, and the floating-in-air spirits of drowned men with seaweed wreaths and seashells in their navels.

What the surrendering Indian soldiers said, within my cousin's hearing: 'Anyway, these border posts were unmanned; we just saw them empty and came inside.'

The mystery of the deserted border posts did not, at first, seem like a puzzle to the young Pakistani soldiers who were required to occupy them until new border guards were sent; my cousin Lieutenant Zafar found his bladder and bowels voiding themselves with hysterical frequency for the seven nights he spent occupying one of the posts with only five jawans for company. During nights filled with the shrieks of witches and the nameless slithery shufflings of the dark, the six youngsters were reduced to so abject a state that nobody laughed at my cousin any more, they were all too busy wetting their own pants. One of the jawans whispered in terror during the ghostly evil of their last-but-one night: 'Listen, boys, if I had to sit here for a living, I'd bloody well run away, too!'

In a state of utter jelly-like breakdown the soldiers sweated in the Rann; and then on the last night their worst fears came true, they saw an army of ghosts coming out of the darkness towards them; they were in the border post nearest the sea-shore, and in the greeny moonlight they could see the sails of ghost-ships, of phantom dhows; and the ghost-army approached, relentlessly, despite the screams of the soldiers, spectres bearing moss-covered chests and strange shrouded litters piled high with unseen things; and when the ghost-army came in through the door, my cousin Zafar fell at their feet and began to gibber horribly.

The first phantom to enter the outpost had several missing teeth and a curved knife stuck in his belt; when he saw the soldiers in the hut his eyes blazed with a vermilion fury. 'God's pity!' the ghost chieftain said, 'What are you mother-sleepers here for? Didn't you all get properly paid off?'

Not ghosts; smugglers. The six young soldiers found themselves in absurd postures of abject terror, and although they tried to redeem themselves, their shame was engulfingly complete . . . and now we come to it. In whose name were the smugglers operating? Whose name fell from the lips of the smuggler-chief, and made my cousin's eyes open in horror? Whose fortune, built originally on the miseries of fleeing Hindu families in 1947, was now augmented by these spring-and-summer smugglers' convoys through the unguarded Rann and thence into the cities of Pakistan? Which Punch-faced General, with a voice as thin as a razor-blade, commanded the phantom troops? . . . But I shall concentrate on facts. In July 1965, my cousin Zafar returned on leave to his father's house in Rawalpindi; and one morning he began to walk slowly towards his father's bedroom, bearing on his shoulders not only the memory of a thousand childhood humiliations and blows; not only the shame of his lifelong enuresis; but also the knowledge that his own father had been responsible for what-happened-at-the-Rann, when Zafar Zulfikar was reduced to gibbering on a floor. My cousin found his father in his bedside bath, and slit his throat with a long, curved smuggler's knife.

Hidden behind newspaper reports – DASTARDLY INDIAN INVASION REPELLED BY OUR GALLANT BOYS – the truth about General Zulfikar became a ghostly, uncertain thing; the paying-off of border guards became, in the papers, INNOCENT SOLDIERS MASSACRED BY INDIAN FAUJ; and who would spread the story of my uncle's vast smuggling activities? What General, what politician did not possess the transistor radios of my uncle's illegality, the air-conditioning units and the imported watches of his sins? General Zulfikar died; cousin Zafar went to prison and was spared marriage to a Kifi princess who obstinately refused to menstruate precisely in order to be spared marriage to him; and the incidents in the Rann of Kutch became the tinder, so to speak, of the larger fire that broke out in August, the fire of the end, in which Saleem finally, and in spite of himself, achieved his elusive purity.

As for my aunt Emerald: she was given permission to emigrate; she had made preparations to do so, intending to leave for Suffolk in England, where she was to stay with her husband's old commanding officer, Brigadier Dodson, who had begun, in his dotage, to spend his time in the company of equally old India hands, watching old films of the Delhi Durbar and the arrival of George V at the Gateway of India . . . she was looking forward to the empty oblivion of nostalgia and the English winter when the war came and settled all our problems.

*

468

On the first day of the 'false peace' which would last a mere thirty-seven days, the stroke hit Ahmed Sinai. It left him paralysed all the way down his left side, and restored him to the dribbles and giggles of his infancy; he, too, mouthed nonsense-words, showing a marked preference for the naughty childhood names of excreta. Giggling 'Cacca!' and 'Soo-soo!' my father came to the end of his chequered career, having once more, and for the last time, lost his way, and also his battle with the djinns. He sat, stunned and cackling, amid the faulty towels of his life; amid faulty towels, my mother, crushed beneath the weight of her monstrous pregnancy, inclined her head gravely as she was visited by Lila Sabarmati's pianola, or the ghost of her brother Hanif, or a pair of hands which danced, moths-around-a-flame, around and around her own . . . Commander Sabarmati came to see her with his curious baton in his hand, and Nussie-the-duck whispered, 'The end, Amina sister! The end of the world!' in my mother's withering ear . . . and now, having fought my way through the diseased reality of my Pakistan years, having struggled to make a little sense out of what seemed (through the mist of my aunt Alia's revenge) like a terrible, occult series of reprisals for tearing up our Bombay roots, I have reached the point at which I must tell you about ends.

Let me state this quite unequivocally: it is my firm conviction that the hidden purpose of the Indo-Pakistani war of 1965 was nothing more nor less than the elimination of my benighted family from the face of the earth. In order to understand the recent history of our times, it is only necessary to examine the bombing-pattern of that war with an analytical, unprejudiced eye.

Even ends have beginnings; everything must be told in sequence. (I have Padma, after all, squashing all my attempts to put the cart before the bullock.) By August 8th, 1965, my family history had got itself into a condition from which what-was-achieved-by-bombing-patterns provided a merciful relief. No: let me use the important word: if we were to be purified, something on the scale of what followed was probably necessary.

Alia Aziz, sated with her terrible revenge; my aunt Emerald, widowed and awaiting exile; the hollow lasciviousness of my aunt Pia and the glass-boothed withdrawal of my grandmother Naseem Aziz; my cousin Zafar, with his eternally pre-pubertal princess and his future of wetting mattresses in jail-cells; the retreat into childishness of my father and the haunted, accelerated ageing of pregnant Amina Sinai . . . all these terrible conditions were to be cured as a result of the adoption, by the Government, of my dream of visiting Kashmir. In the meantime, the flinty refusals of my sister to countenance my love had driven me into a deeply fatalistic frame of mind; in the grip of my new carelessness about my future I told Uncle Puffs that I was willing to marry any one of the Puffias he chose for me. (By doing so, I doomed them all; everyone who attempts to forge ties with our household ends up by sharing our fate.)

I am trying to stop being mystifying. Important to concentrate on good hard facts. But which facts? One week before my eighteenth birthday, on August 8th, did Pakistani troops in civilian clothing cross the ceasefire line in Kashmir and infiltrate the Indian sector, or did they not? In Delhi, Prime Minister Shastri announced 'massive infiltration . . . to subvert the state'; but here is Zulfikar Ali Bhutto, Pakistan's Foreign Minister, with his riposte: 'We categorically deny any involvement in the rising against tyranny by the indigenous people of Kashmir.'

If it happened, what were the motives? Again, a rash of possible explanations: the continuing anger which had been stirred up by the Rann of Kutch; the desire to settle, once-and-for-all, the old issue of who-should-possess-the-Perfect-Valley? . . . Or one which didn't get into the papers: the pressures of internal political troubles in Pakistan – Ayub's government was

470

tottering, and a war works wonders at such times. This reason or that or the other? To simplify matters, I present two of my own: the war happened because I dreamed Kashmir into the fantasies of our rulers; furthermore, I remained impure, and the war was to separate me from my sins.

Jehad, Padma! Holy war!

But who attacked? Who defended? On my eighteenth birthday, reality took another terrible beating. From the ramparts of the Red Fort in Delhi, an Indian prime minister (not the same one who wrote me a long-ago letter) sent me this birthday greeting: 'We promise that force will be met with force, and aggression against us will never be allowed to succeed!' While jeeps with loud-hailers saluted me in Guru Mandir, reassuring me: 'The Indian aggressors will be utterly overthrown! We are a race of warriors! One Pathan; one Punjabi Muslim is worth ten of those babus-in-arms!'

Jamila Singer was called north, to serenade our worth-ten jawans. A servant paints blackout on the windows; at night, my father, in the stupidity of his second childhood, opens the windows and turns on the lights. Bricks and stones fly through the apertures: my eighteenth-birthday presents. And still events grow more and more confused: on August 30th, did Indian troops cross the ceasefire line near Uri to 'chase out the Pakistan raiders' – or to initiate an attack? When, on September 1st, our ten-times-better soldiers crossed the line at Chhamb, were they aggressors or were they not?

Some certainties: that the voice of Jamila Singer sang Pakistani troops to their deaths; and that muezzins from their minarets – yes, even on Clayton Road – promised us that anyone who died in battle went straight to the camphor garden. The mujahid philosophy of Syed Ahmad Barilwi ruled the air; we were invited to make sacrifices 'as never before'.

And on the radio, what destruction, what mayhem! In the first five days of the war Voice of Pakistan announced the

471

destruction of more aircraft than India had ever possessed; in eight days, All-India Radio massacred the Pakistan Army down to, and considerably beyond, the last man. Utterly distracted by the double insanity of the war and my private life, I began to think desperate thoughts . . .

Great sacrifices: for instance, at the battle for Lahore? – On September 6th, Indian troops crossed the Wagah border, thus hugely broadening the front of the war, which was no longer limited to Kashmir; and did great sacrifices take place, or not? Was it true that the city was virtually defenceless, because the Pak Army and Air Force were all in the Kashmir sector? Voice of Pakistan said: O memorable day! O unarguable lesson in the fatality of delay! The Indians, confident of capturing the city, *stopped for breakfast*. All-India Radio announced the fall of Lahore; meanwhile, a private aircraft spotted the breakfasting invaders. While the B.B.C. picked up the A.I.R. story, the Lahore militia was mobilized. Hear the Voice of Pakistan! – old men, young boys, irate grandmothers fought the Indian Army; bridge by bridge they battled, with any available weapons! Lame men loaded their pockets with grenades, pulled out the pins, flung themselves beneath advancing Indian tanks; toothless old ladies disembowelled Indian babus with pitchforks! Down to the last man and child, they died: but they saved the city, holding off the Indians until air support arrived! Martyrs, Padma! Heroes, bound for the perfumed garden! Where the men would be given four beauteous houris, untouched by man or djinn; and the women, four equally virile males! *Which of your Lord's blessings would you deny?* What a thing this holy war is, in which with one supreme sacrifice men may atone for all their evils! No wonder Lahore was defended; what did the Indians have to look forward to? Only re-incarnation – as cockroaches, maybe, or scorpions, or green-medicine-wallahs – there's really no comparison.

But did it or didn't it? Was that how it happened? Or was All-India Radio – *great tank battle, huge Pak losses, 450 tanks destroyed* – telling the truth?

Nothing was real; nothing certain. Uncle Puffs came to visit the Clayton Road house, and there were no teeth in his mouth. (During India's China war, when our loyalties were different, my mother had given gold bangles and jewelled ear-rings to the 'Ornaments for Armaments' campaign; but what was that when set against the sacrifice of an entire mouthful of gold?) 'The nation,' he said indistinctly through his untoothed gums, 'must not, darn it, be short of funds on account of one man's vanity!' – But did he or didn't he? Were teeth truly sacrificed in the name of holy war, or were they sitting in a cupboard at home? 'I'm afraid,' Uncle Puffs said gummily, 'you'll have to wait for that special dowry I promised.' – Nationalism or meanness? Was his baring of gums a supreme proof of his patriotism, or a slimy ruse to avoid filling a Puffia-mouth with gold?

And were there parachutists or were there not? '. . . have been dropped on every major city,' Voice of Pakistan announced. 'All able-bodied persons are to stay up with weapons; shoot on sight after dusk curfew.' But in India, 'Despite Pakistani air-raid provocation,' the radio claimed, 'we have not responded!' Who to believe? Did Pakistani fighter-bombers truly make that 'daring raid' which caught one-third of the Indian Air Force helplessly grounded on tarmac? Did they didn't they? And those night-dances in the sky, Pakistani Mirages and Mystères against India's less romantically-titled MiGs: did Islamic mirages and mysteries do battle with Hindu invaders, or was it all some kind of astonishing illusion? Did bombs fall? Were explosions true? Could even a death be said to be the case?

And Saleem? What did he do in the war?

This: waiting to be drafted, I went in search of friendly, obliterating, sleep-giving, Paradise-bringing bombs.

The terrible fatalism which had overcome me of late had taken on an even more terrible form; drowning in the disintegration of family, of both countries to which I had belonged, of everything which can sanely be called real, lost in the sorrow of my filthy unrequited love, I sought out the oblivion of – I'm making it sound too noble; no orotund phrases must be used. Baldly, then: I rode the night-streets of the city, looking for death.

Who died in the holy war? Who, while I in bright white kurta and pajamas went Lambretta-borne into the curfewed streets, found what I was looking for? Who, martyred by war, went straight to a perfumed garden? Study the bombing pattern; learn the secrets of rifle-shots.

On the night of September 22nd, air-raids took place over every Pakistani city. (Although All-India Radio . . .) Aircraft, real or fictional, dropped actual or mythical bombs. It is, accordingly, either a matter of fact or a figment of a diseased imagination that of the only three bombs to hit Rawalpindi and explode, the first landed on the bungalow in which my grandmother Naseem Aziz and my aunty Pia were hiding under a table; the second tore a wing off the city jail, and spared my cousin Zafar a life of captivity; the third destroyed a large darkling mansion surrounded by a sentried wall; sentries were at their posts, but could not prevent Emerald Zulfikar from being carried off to a more distant place than Suffolk. She was being visited, that night, by the Nawab of Kif and his mulishly unmaturing daughter; who was also spared the necessity of becoming an adult woman. In Karachi, three bombs were also enough. The Indian planes, reluctant to come down low, bombed from a great height; the vast majority of their missiles fell harmlessly into the sea. One bomb, however, annihilated Major (Retired) Alauddin Latif and all his seven Puffias, thus releasing me from my promise for ever; and there were two last bombs. Meanwhile, at the front, Mutasim the Handsome emerged from his tent to go to

474

the toilet; a noise like a mosquito whizzed (or did not whiz) towards him, and he died with a full bladder under the impact of a sniper's bullet.

And still I must tell you about two-last-bombs.

Who survived? Jamila Singer, whom bombs were unable to find; in India, the family of my uncle Mustapha, with whom bombs could not be bothered; but my father's forgotten distant relative Zohra and her husband had moved to Amritsar, and a bomb sought them out as well.

And two-more-bombs demand to be told.

. . . While I, unaware of the intimate connection between the war and myself, went foolishly in search of bombs; after the curfew-hour I rode, but vigilant bullets failed to find their target . . . and sheets of flame rose from a Rawalpindi bungalow, perforated sheets at whose centre hung a mysterious dark hole, which grew into the smoke-image of an old wide woman with moles on her cheeks . . . and one by one the war eliminated my drained, hopeless family from the earth.

But now the countdown was at an end.

And at last I turned my Lambretta homewards, so that I was at the Guru Mandir roundabout with the roar of aircraft overhead, mirages and mysteries, while my father in the idiocy of his stroke was switching on lights and opening windows even though a Civil Defence official had just visited them to make sure the blackout was complete; and when Amina Sinai was saying to the wraith of an old white washing-chest, 'Go away now – I've seen enough of you,' I was scooting past Civil Defence jeeps from which angry fists saluted me; and before bricks and stones could extinguish the lights in my aunt Alia's house, the whining came, and I should have known there was no need to go looking elsewhere for death, but I was still in the street in the midnight shadow of the mosque when it came, plummeting towards the illuminated windows of my father's idiocy, death whining

like pie-dogs, transforming itself into falling masonry and
sheets of flame and a wave of force so great that it sent me
spinning off my Lambretta, while within the house of my
aunt's great bitterness my father mother aunt and unborn
brother or sister who was only a week away from starting life,
all of them all of them all squashed flatter than rice-pancakes,
the house crashing in on their heads like a waffle-iron, while
over on Korangi Road a last bomb, meant for the oil-refinery,
landed instead on a split-level American-style residence which
an umbilical cord had not quite managed to complete; but at
Guru Mandir many stories were coming to an end, the story
of Amina and her long-ago underworld husband and her
assiduity and public announcement and her son-who-was-
not-her-son and her luck with horses and verrucas and
dancing hands in the Pioneer Café and last defeat by her
sister, and of Ahmed who always lost his way and had a lower
lip which stuck out and a squashy belly and went white in a
freeze and succumbed to abstraction and burst dogs open in
the street and fell in love too late and died because of his
vulnerability of what-falls-out-of-the-sky; flatter than pan-
cakes now, and around them the house exploding collapsing,
an instant of destruction of such vehemence that things which
had been buried deep in forgotten tin trunks flew upward into
the air while other things people memories were buried under
rubble beyond hope of salvation; the fingers of the explosion
reaching down down to the bottom of an almirah and
unlocking a green tin trunk, the clutching hand of the explosion flinging trunk-contents into air, and now something
which has hidden unseen for many years is circling in the
night like a whirligig piece of the moon, something catching
the light of the moon and falling now falling as I pick myself
up dizzily after the blast, something twisting turning somer-
saulting down, silver as moonlight, a wondrously worked
silver spittoon inlaid with lapis lazuli, the past plummeting
towards me like a vulture-dropped hand to become what-

purifies-and-sets-me-free, because now as I look up there is a feeling at the back of my head and after that there is only a tiny but infinite moment of utter clarity while I tumble forwards to prostrate myself before my parents' funeral pyre, a minuscule but endless instant of knowing, before I am stripped of past present memory time shame and love, a fleeting, but also timeless explosion in which I bow my head yes I acquiesce yes in the necessity of the blow, and then I am empty and free, because all the Saleems go pouring out of me, from the baby who appeared in jumbo-sized frontpage baby-snaps to the eighteen-year-old with his filthy dirty love, pouring out goes shame and guilt and wanting-to-please and needing-to-be-loved and determined-to-find-a-historical-role and growing-too-fast, I am free of Snotnose and Stainface and Baldy and Sniffer and Mapface and washing-chests and Evie Burns and language marches, liberated from Kolynos Kid and the breasts of Pia mumani and Alpha-and-Omega, absolved of the multiple murders of Homi Catrack and Hanif and Aadam Aziz and Prime Minister Jawaharlal Nehru, I have shaken off five-hundred-year-old whores and confessions of love at dead of night, free now, beyond caring, crashing on to tarmac, restored to innocence and purity by a tumbling piece of the moon, wiped clean as a wooden writing-chest, brained (just as prophesied) by my mother's silver spittoon.

On the morning of September 23rd, the United Nations announced the end of hostilities between India and Pakistan. India had occupied less than 500 square miles of Pakistani soil; Pakistan had conquered just 340 square miles of its Kashmiri dream, It was said that the ceasefire came because both sides had run out of ammunition, more or less simultaneously; thus the exigencies of international diplomacy, and the politically-motivated manipulations of arms suppliers, prevented the wholesale annihilation of my family. Some of us survived, because nobody sold our

477

would-be assassins the bombs bullets aircraft necessary for the completion of our destruction. Six years later however, there was another war.

Book Three

The buddha

Obviously enough (because otherwise I should have to introduce at this point some fantastic explanation of my continued presence in this 'mortal coil'), you may number me amongst those whom the war of '65 failed to obliterate. Spittoon-brained, Saleem suffered a merely partial erasure, and was only wiped clean whilst others, less fortunate, were wiped out; unconscious in the night-shadow of a mosque, I was saved by the exhaustion of ammunition dumps.

Tears – which, in the absence of the Kashmiri cold, have absolutely no chance of hardening into diamonds – slide down the bosomy contours of Padma's cheeks. 'O, mister, this war tamasha, kills the best and leaves the rest!' Looking as though hordes of snails have recently crawled down from her reddened eyes, leaving their glutinous shiny trails upon her face, Padma mourns my bomb-flattened clan. I remain dry-eyed as usual, graciously refusing to rise to the unintentional insult implied by Padma's lachrymose exclamation.

'Mourn for the living,' I rebuke her gently, 'The dead have their camphor gardens.' Grieve for Saleem! Who, barred from celestial lawns by the continued beating of his heart, awoke once again amid the clammy metallic fragrances of a hospital ward; for whom there were no houris, untouched by man or djinn, to provide the promised consolations of eternity – I was lucky to receive the grudging, bedpan-clattering ministrations of a bulky male nurse who, while bandaging my head, muttered sourly that, war or no war, the doctor sahibs liked going to their beach shacks on Sundays. 'Better you'd stayed knocked out one more day,' he mouthed, before moving further down the ward to spread more good cheer.

Grieve for Saleem – who, orphaned and purified, deprived of the hundred daily pinpricks of family life, which alone could deflate the great ballooning fantasy of history and bring it down to a more manageably human scale, had been pulled up by his roots to be flung unceremoniously across the years, fated to plunge memoryless into an adulthood whose every aspect grew daily more grotesque.

Fresh snail-tracks on Padma's cheeks. Obliged to attempt some sort of 'There, there', I resort to movie-trailers. (How I loved them at the old Metro Cub Club! O smacking of lips at the sight of the title NEXT ATTRACTION, superimposed on undulating blue velvet! O anticipatory salivation before screens trumpeting COMING SOON! – Because the promise of exotic futures has always seemed, to my mind, the perfect antidote to the disappointments of the present.) 'Stop, stop,' I exhort my mournfully squatting audience, 'I'm not finished yet! There is to be electrocution and a rainforest; a pyramid of heads on a field impregnated by leaky marrowbones; narrow escapes are coming, and a minaret that screamed! Padma, there is still plenty worth telling: my further trials, in the basket of invisibility and in the shadow of another mosque; wait for the premonitions of Resham Bibi and the pout of Parvati-the-witch! Fatherhood and treason also, and of course that unavoidable Widow, who added to my history of drainage-above the final ignominy of voiding-below . . . in short, there are still next-attractions and coming-soons galore; a chapter ends when one's parents die, but a new kind of chapter also begins.'

Somewhat consoled by my offers of novelty, my Padma sniffs; wipes away mollusc-slime, dries eyes; breathes in deeply . . . and, for the spittoon-brained fellow we last met in

482

his hospital bed, approximately five years pass before my dung-lotus exhales.

(While Padma, to calm herself, holds her breath, I permit myself to insert a Bombay-talkie-style close-up – a calendar ruffled by a breeze, its pages flying off in rapid succession to denote the passing of the years; I superimpose turbulent long-shots of street riots, medium shots of burning buses and blazing English-language libraries owned by the British Council and the United States Information Service; through the accelerated flickering of the calendar we glimpse the fall of Ayub Khan, the assumption of the presidency by General Yahya, the promise of elections . . . but now Padma's lips are parting, and there is no time to linger on the angrily-opposed images of Mr Z. A. Bhutto and Sheikh Mujib-ur-Rahman; exhaled air begins to issue invisibly from her mouth, and the dream-faces of the leaders of the Pakistan People's Party and the Awami League shimmer and fade out; the gusting of her emptying lungs paradoxically stills the breeze blowing the pages of my calendar, which comes to rest upon a date late in 1970, before the election which split the country in two, before the war of West Wing against East Wing, P.P.P. against Awami League, Bhutto against Mujib . . . before the election of 1970, and far away from the public stage, three young soldiers are arriving at a mysterious camp in the Murree Hills.)

Padma has regained her self-control. 'Okay, okay,' she expostulates, waving an arm in dismissal of her tears, 'Why you're waiting? Begin,' the lotus instructs me loftily, 'Begin all over again.'

The camp in the hills will be found on no maps; it is too far from the Murree road for the barking of its dogs to be heard, even by the sharpest-eared of motorists. Its wire perimeter fence is heavily camouflaged; the gate bears neither symbol nor name. Yet it does, did, exist; though its existence has been hotly denied — at the fall of Dacca, for instance, when Pakistan's vanquished Tiger Niazi was quizzed on this subject by his old chum, India's victorious General Sam Manekshaw, the Tiger scoffed: 'Canine Unit for Tracking and Intelligence Activities? Never heard of it; you've been misled, old boy. Damn ridiculous idea, if you don't mind my saying.' Despite what the Tiger said to Sam, I insist: the camp was there all right . . .

. . . 'Shape up!' Brigadier Iskandar is yelling at his newest recruits, Ayooba Baloch, Farooq Rashid and Shaheed Dar. 'You're a CUTIA unit now!' Slapping swagger-stick against thigh, he turns on his heels and leaves them standing on the parade-ground, simultaneously fried by mountain sun and frozen by mountain air. Chests out, shoulders back, rigid with obedience, the three youths hear the giggling voice of the Brigadier's batman, Lala Moin: *So you're the poor suckers who get the man-dog!'*

In their bunks that night: 'Tracking and intelligence!' whispers Ayooba Baloch, proudly. 'Spies, man! O.S.S.117 types! Just let us at those Hindus — see what we don't do! Ka-dang! Ka-pow! What weaklings, yara, those Hindus! Vegetarians all! Vegetables,' Ayooba hisses, 'always lose to meat.' He is built like a tank. His crew-cut begins just above his eyebrows.

And Farooq, 'You think there'll be war?' Ayooba snorts. 'What else? How not a war? Hasn't Bhutto sahib promised every peasant one acre of land? So where it'll come from? For so much soil, we must conquer Punjab and Bengal! Just wait only; after the election, when People's Party has won — then Ka-pow! Ka-blooey!'

Farooq is troubled: 'Those Indians have Sikh troops, man. With so-long beards and hair, in the heat it pricks like crazy and they all go mad and fight like hell . . . !'

Ayooba gurgles with amusement. 'Vegetarians, I swear, yaar . . . how are they going to beat beefy types like us?' But Farooq is long and stringy.

Shaheed Dar whispers, 'But what did he mean: man-dog?'

... Morning. In a hut with a blackboard, Brigadier Iskandar polishes knuckles on lapels while one Sgt-Mjr Najmuddin briefs new recruits. Question-and-answer format; Najmuddin provides both queries and replies. No interruptions are to be tolerated. While above the blackboard the garlanded portraits of President Yahya and Mutasim the Martyr stare sternly down. And through the (closed) windows, the persistent barking of dogs ... Najmuddin's inquiries and responses are also barked. What are you here for? – Training. In what field? – Pursuit-and-capture. How will you work? – In canine units of three persons and one dog. What unusual features? – Absence of officer personnel, necessity of taking own decisions, concomitant requirement for high Islamic sense of self-discipline and responsibility. Purpose of units? – To root out undesirable elements. Nature of such elements? – Sneaky, well-disguised, could-be-anyone. Known intentions of same? – To be abhorred: destruction of family life, murder of God, expropriation of landowners, abolition of film-censorship. To what ends? – Annihilation of the State, anarchy, foreign domination. Accentuating causes of concern? – Forthcoming elections; and subsequently, civilian rule. (Political prisoners have been are being freed. All types of hooligans are abroad.) Precise duties of units? – To obey unquestioningly; to seek unflaggingly; to arrest remorselessly. Mode of procedure? – Covert; efficient; quick. Legal basis of such detentions? – Defence of Pakistan Rules, permitting the pick-up of undesirables, who may be held incommunicado for a period of six months. Footnote: a renewable period of six months. Any questions? – No. Good. You are CUTIA Unit 22. She-dog badges will be sewn to lapels. The acronym CUTIA, of course, means *bitch*. And the man-dog?

Cross-legged, blue-eyed, staring into space, he sits beneath a tree. Bodhi trees do not grow at this altitude; he makes do with a chinar, His nose: bulbous, cucumbery, tip blue with cold. And on his head a monk's tonsure where once Mr Zagallo's hand. And a mutilated finger whose missing segment fell at Masha Miovic's feet after Glandy Keith had slammed. And stains on his face like a map . . . *'Ekkkkh-thoo!'* (He spits.)

His teeth are stained; betel-juice reddens his gums. A red stream of expectorated paan-fluid leaves his lips, to hit, with commendable accuracy, a beautifully-wrought silver spittoon, which sits before him on the ground. Ayooba Shaheed Farooq are staring in amazement. 'Don't try to get it away from him,' Sgt-Mjr Najmuddin indicates the spittoon, 'It sends him wild.' Ayooba begins, 'Sir sir I thought you said three persons and a –', but Najmuddin barks, 'No questions! Obedience without queries! This is your tracker; that's that. Dismiss.'

At that time, Ayooba and Farooq were sixteen and a half years old. Shaheed (who had lied about his age) was perhaps a year younger. Because they were so young, and had not had time to acquire the type of memories which give men a firm hold on reality, such as memories of love or famine, the boy soldiers were highly susceptible to the influence of legends and gossip. Within twenty-four hours, in the course of mess-hall conversations with other CUTIA units, the man-dog had been fully mythologized . . . 'From a really important family, man!' – 'The idiot child, they put him in the Army to make a man of him!' – 'Had a war accident in '65, yaar, can't won't remember a thing about it!' – 'listen, I heard he was the brother of' – 'No, man, that's crazy, she is good, you know, so simple and holy, how would she leave her brother?' – 'Anyway he refuses to talk about it.' – 'I heard one terrible thing, she hated him, man, that's why she!' – 'No memory, not interested in people, lives like a dog!' – 'But the tracking business is true all right! You see that nose on him?' – 'Yah, man, he can follow any trail on earth!' – 'Through water,

486

baba, across rocks! Such a tracker, you never saw!' – 'And he can't feel a thing! That's right! Numb, I swear; head-to-foot numb! You touch him, he wouldn't know – only by smell he knows you're there!' – 'Must be the war wound!' – 'But that spittoon, man, who knows? Carries it everywhere like a love-token!' – 'I tell you, I'm glad it's you three; he gives me the creeps, yaar, it's those blue eyes.' – 'You know how they found out about his nose? He just wandered into a minefield, man, I swear, just picked his way through, like he could smell the damn mines!' – 'O, no, man, what are you talking, that's an old story, that was that first dog in the whole CUTIA operation, that Bonzo, man, don't mix us up!' – 'Hey, you Ayooba, you better watch your step, they say V.I.P.s are keeping their eyes on him!' – 'Yah, like I told you, Jamila Singer . . .' – 'O, keep your mouth shut, we all heard enough of your fairy-tales!'

Once Ayooba, Farooq and Shaheed had become reconciled to their strange, impassive tracker (it was after the incident at the latrines), they gave him the nickname of buddha, 'old man'; not just because he must have been seven years their senior, and had actually taken part in the six-years-ago war of '65, when the three boy soldiers weren't even in long pants, but because there hung around him an air of great antiquity. The buddha was old before his time.

O fortunate ambiguity of transliteration! The Urdu word 'buddha', meaning old man, is pronounced with the Ds hard and plosive. But there is also Buddha, with soft-tongued Ds, meaning he-who-achieved-enlightenment-under-the-bodhi-tree . . . Once upon a time, a prince, unable to bear the suffering of the world, became capable of not-living-in-the-world as well as living in it; he was present, but also absent; his body was in one place, but his spirit was elsewhere. In ancient India, Gautama the Buddha sat enlightened under a tree at Gaya; in the deer park at Sarnath he taught others to abstract themselves from worldly sorrows and achieve inner

487

peace; and centuries later, Saleem the buddha sat under a different tree, unable to remember grief, numb as ice, wiped clean as a slate . . . With some embarrassment, I am forced to admit that amnesia is the kind of gimmick regularly used by our lurid film-makers. Bowing my head slightly, I accept that my life has taken on, yet again, the tone of a Bombay talkie; but after all, leaving to one side the vexed issue of reincarnation, there is only a finite number of methods of achieving rebirth. So, apologizing for the melodrama, I must doggedly insist that I, he, had begun again; that after years of yearning for importance, he (or I) had been cleansed of the whole business; that after my vengeful abandonment by Jamila Singer, who wormed me into the Army to get me out her sight, I (or he) accepted the fate which was my repayment for love, and sat uncomplaining under a chinar tree; that, emptied of history, the buddha learned the arts of submission, and did only what was required of him. To sum up: I became a citizen of Pakistan.

It was arguably inevitable that, during the months of training, the buddha should begin to irritate Ayooba Baloch. Perhaps it was because he chose to live apart from the soldiers, in a straw-lined ascetic's stall at the far end of the kennel-barracks; or because he was so often to be found sitting cross-legged under his tree, silver spittoon clutched in hand, with unfocused eyes and a foolish smile on his lips – as if he were actually happy that he'd lost his brains! What's more, Ayooba, the apostle of meat, may have found his tracker insufficiently virile. 'Like a brinjal, man,' I permit Ayooba to complain, 'I swear – a vegetable!'

(We may also, taking the wider view, assert that irritation was in the air at the year's turn. Were not even General Yahya and Mr Bhutto getting hot and bothered about the petulant insistence of Sheikh Mujib on his right to form the new government? The wretched Bengali's Awami League had won

160 out of a possible 162 East Wing seats; Mr Bhutto's P.P.P. had merely taken 81 Western constituencies. Yes, an irritating election. It is easy to imagine how irked Yahya and Bhutto, West Wingers both, must have been! And when even the mighty wax peevish, how is one to blame the small man? The irritation of Ayooba Baloch, let us conclude, placed him in excellent, not to say exalted company.)

On training manoeuvres, when Ayooba Shaheed Farooq scrambled after the buddha as he followed the faintest of trails across bush rocks streams, the three boys were obliged to admit his skill; but still Ayooba, tank-like, demanded: 'Don't you remember really? Nothing? Allah, you don't feel *bad*? Somewhere you've maybe got mother father sister,' but the buddha interrupted him gently: 'Don't try and fill my head with that history. I am who I am, that's all there is.' His accent was so pure, 'Really classy Lucknow-type Urdu, *wah-wah*!' Farooq said admiringly, that Ayooba Baloch, who spoke coarsely, like a tribesman, fell silent; and the three boys began to believe the rumours even more fervently. They were unwillingly fascinated by this man with his nose like a cucumber and his head which rejected memories families histories, which contained absolutely nothing except smells . . . 'like a bad egg that somebody sucked dry,' Ayooba muttered to his companions, and then, returning to his central theme, added, 'Allah, even his nose looks like a vegetable.'

Their uneasiness lingered. Did they sense, in the buddha's numbed blankness, a trace of 'undesirability'? – For was not his rejection of past-and-family just the type of subversive behaviour they were dedicated to 'rooting out'? The camp's officers, however, were deaf to Ayooba's requests of 'Sir sir can't we just have a real dog sir?' . . . so that Farooq, a born follower who had already adopted Ayooba as his leader and hero, cried, 'What to do? With that guy's family contacts, some high-ups must've told the Brigadier to put up with him, that's all.'

And (although none of the trio would have been able to express the idea) I suggest that at the deep foundations of their unease lay the fear of schizophrenia, of splitting, that was buried like an umbilical cord in every Pakistani heart. In those days, the country's East and West Wings were separated by the unbridgeable land-mass of India; but past and present, too, are divided by an unbridgeable gulf. Religion was the glue of Pakistan, holding the halves together; just as consciousness, the awareness of oneself as a homogeneous entity in time, a blend of past and present, is the glue of personality, holding together our then and our now. Enough philosophizing: what I am saying is that by abandoning consciousness, seceding from history, the buddha was setting the worst of examples – and the example was followed by no less a personage than Sheikh Mujib, when he led the East Wing into secession and declared it independent as 'Bangladesh'! Yes, Ayooba Shaheed Farooq were right to feel ill-at-ease – because even in those depths of my withdrawal from responsibility, I remained responsible, through the workings of the metaphorical modes of connection, for the belligerent events of 1971.

But I must go back to my new companions, so that I can relate the incident at the latrines: there was Ayooba, tank-like, who led the unit, and Farooq, who followed contentedly. The third youth, however, was a gloomier, more private type, and as such closest to my heart. On his fifteenth birthday Shaheed Dar had lied about his age and enlisted. That day, his Punjabi sharecropper father had taken Shaheed into a field and wept all over his new uniform. Old Dar told his son the meaning of his name, which was 'martyr', and expressed the hope that he would prove worthy of it, and perhaps become the first of their family members to enter the perfumed garden, leaving behind this pitiful world in which a father could not hope to pay his debts and also feed his nineteen children. The overwhelming power of names, and the

490

resulting approach of martyrdom, had begun to prey heavily on Shaheed's mind; in his dreams, he began to see his death, which took the form of a bright pomegranate, and floated in mid-air behind him, following him everywhere, biding its time. The disturbing and somewhat unheroic vision of pomegranate death made Shaheed an inward, unsmiling fellow.

Inwardly, unsmilingly, Shaheed observed various CUTIA units being sent away from the camp, into action; and became convinced that his time, and the time of the pomegranate, was very near. From departures of three-men-and-a-dog units in camouflaged jeeps, he deduced a growing political crisis; it was February, and the irritations of the exalted were becoming daily more marked. Ayooba-the-tank, however, retained a local point of view. His irritation was also mounting, but its object was the buddha.

Ayooba had become infatuated with the only female in the camp, a skinny latrine cleaner who couldn't have been over fourteen and whose nipples were only just beginning to push against her tattered shirt: a low type, certainly, but she was all that there was, and for a latrine cleaner she had very nice teeth and a pleasant line in saucy over-the-shoulder glances . . . Ayooba began to follow her around, and that was how he spied her going into the buddha's straw-lined stall, and that was why he leaned a bicycle against the building and stood on the seat, and that was why he fell off, because he didn't like what he saw. Afterwards he spoke to the latrine girl, grabbing her roughly by the arm: 'Why do it with that crazy – why, when I, Ayooba, am, could be –?' and she replied that she liked the man-dog, he's funny, says he can't feel anything, he rubs his hosepipe inside me but can't even feel, but it's nice, and he tells that he likes my smell. The frankness of the urchin girl, the honesty of latrine cleaners, made Ayooba sick; he told her she had a soul composed of pig-droppings, and a tongue caked with excrement also; and in the throes of his

491

jealousy he devised the prank of the jump-leads, the trick of the electrified urinal. The location appealed to him; it had a certain poetic justice.

'Can't feel, huh?' Ayooba sneered to Farooq and Shaheed, 'Just wait on: I'll make him jump for sure.'

On February 10th (when Yahya, Bhutto and Mujib were refusing to engage in high-level talks), the buddha felt the call of nature. A somewhat concerned Shaheed and a gleeful Farooq loitered by the latrines; while Ayooba, who had used jump-leads to attach the metal footplates of the urinals to the battery of a jeep, stood out of sight behind the latrine hut, beside the jeep, whose motor was running. The buddha appeared, with his eyes as dilated as a charas-chewer's and his gait of walking-through-a-cloud, and as he floated into the latrine Farooq called out, 'Ohé! Ayooba, yara!' and began to giggle. The childsoldiers awaited the howl of mortified anguish which would be the sign that their vacuous tracker had begun to piss, allowing electricity to mount the golden stream and sting him in his numb and urchin-rubbing hosepipe.

But no shriek came; Farooq, feeling confused and cheated, began to frown; and as time went by Shaheed grew nervous and yelled over to Ayooba Baloch, 'You Ayooba! What you doing, man?' To which Ayooba-the-tank, 'What d'you think, yaar, I turned on the juice five minutes ago!' . . . And now Shaheed ran – FULL TILT! – into the latrine, to find the buddha urinating away with an expression of foggy pleasure, emptying a bladder which must have been filling up for a fortnight, while the current passed up into him through his nether cucumber, apparently unnoticed, so that he was filling up with electricity and there was a blue crackle playing around the end of his gargantuan nose; and Shaheed who didn't have the courage to touch this impossible being who could absorb electricity through his hosepipe screamed, 'Disconnect, man, or he'll fry like an onion here!' The buddha emerged from the latrine, unconcerned, buttoning himself with his right hand while the left hand held his silver spittoon; and the three child-soldiers understood that it was really true, Allah, numb as ice, anaesthetized against feelings as well as memories . . . For a week after the incident, the buddha could not be touched without giving an electric shock, and not even the latrine girl could visit him in his stall.

Curiously, after the jump-lead business, Ayooba Baloch stopped resenting the buddha, and even began to treat him with respect; the canine unit was forged by that bizarre moment into a real team, and was ready to venture forth against the evildoers of the earth.

Ayooba-the-tank failed to give the buddha a shock; but where the small man fails, the mighty triumph. (When Yahya and Bhutto decided to make Sheikh Mujib jump, there were no mistakes.)

On March 15th, 1971, twenty units of the CUTIA agency assembled in a hut with a blackboard. The garlanded features of the President gazed down upon sixty-one men and nineteen dogs; Yahya Khan had just offered Mujib the olive branch of immediate talks with himself and Bhutto, to resolve all irritations; but his portrait maintained an impeccable poker-face, giving no clue to his true, shocking intentions . . . while Brigadier Iskandar rubbed knuckles on lapels, Sgt-Mjr Najmuddin issued orders: sixty-one men and nineteen dogs were instructed to shed their uniforms. A tumultuous rustling in the hut: obeying without query, nineteen individuals remove identifying collars from canine necks. The dogs, excellently trained, cock eyebrows but refrain from giving voice; and the buddha, dutifully, begins to undress. Five dozen fellow humans follow his lead; five dozen stand to attention in a trice, shivering in the cold, beside neat piles of military berets pants shoes shirts and green pullovers with leather patches at the elbows. Sixty-one men, naked except for imperfect underwear, are issued (by Lala Moin the batman) with Army-approved mufti. Najmuddin barks a command; and then there they all are, some in lungis and kurtas, some in Pathan turbans. There are men in cheap rayon pants and men in striped clerks' shirts. The buddha is in dhoti and kameez; he is comfortable, but around him are soldiers squirming in ill-fitting plain clothes. This is, however, a military operation; no voice, human or canine, is raised in complaint.

On March 15th, after obeying sartorial instructions, twenty CUTIA units were flown to Dacca, via Ceylon; among them were Shaheed Dar, Farooq Rashid, Ayooba Baloch and their buddha. Also flying to the East Wing by this circuitous route were sixty thousand of the West Wing's toughest troops: sixty thousand, like sixty-one, were all in mufti. The General Officer Commanding (in a nattily blue double-breasted suit) was Tikka Khan; the officer responsible for Dacca, for its taming and eventual surrender, was called Tiger Niazi. He wore bush-shirt, slacks and a jaunty little trilby on his head.

Via Ceylon we flew, sixty thousand and sixty-one innocent airline passengers, avoiding overflying India, and thus losing our chance of watching, from twenty thousand feet, the celebrations of Indira Gandhi's New Congress Party, which had won a landslide victory – 350 out of a possible 515 seats in the Lok Sabha – in another recent election. Indira-ignorant, unable to see her campaign slogan, GARIBI HATAO, Get Rid of Poverty, blazoned on walls and banners across the great diamond of India, we landed in Dacca in the early spring, and were driven in specially-requisitioned civilian buses to a military camp. On this last stage of our journey, however, we were unable to avoid hearing a snatch of song, issuing from some unseen gramophone. The song was called 'Amar Sonar Bangla' ('Our Golden Bengal', author: R. Tagore) and ran, in part: 'During spring the fragrance of your mango-groves maddens my heart with delight.' However, none of us could understand Bengali, so we were protected against the insidious subversion of the lyric, although our feet did inadvertently tap (it must be admitted) to the tune.

At first, Ayooba Shaheed Farooq and the buddha were not told the name of the city to which they had come. Ayooba, envisaging the destruction of vegetarians, whispered: 'Didn't I tell you? Now we'll show them! Spy stuff, man! Plain clothes and all! Up and at 'em, Number 22 Unit! Ka-bang! Ka-dang! Ka-pow!'

But we were not in India; vegetarians were not our targets; and after days of cooling our heels, uniforms were issued to us once again. This second transfiguration took place on March 25th.

On March 25th, Yahya and Bhutto abruptly broke off their talks with Mujib and returned to the West Wing. Night fell; Brigadier Iskandar, followed by Najmuddin and Lala Moin, who was staggering under the weight of sixty-one uniforms and nineteen dog-collars, burst into the CUTIA barracks. Now Najmuddin: 'Snap to it! Actions not words! One-two double-quick time!' Airline passengers donned uniforms and took up arms; while Brigadier Iskandar at last announced the purpose of our trip. 'That Mujib,' he revealed, 'We'll give him what-for all right. We'll make him jump for sure!'

(It was on March 25th, after the breakdown of the talks with Bhutto and Yahya, that Sheikh Mujib-ur-Rahman proclaimed the state of Bangladesh.)

CUTIA units emerged from barracks, piled into waiting jeeps; while, over the loudspeakers of the military base, the recorded voice of Jamila Singer was raised in patriotic hymns. (And Ayooba, nudging the buddha: 'Listen, come on, don't you recognize – think, man, isn't that your own dear – Allah, this type is good for nothing but sniffing!')

At midnight – could it, after all, have been at any other time? – sixty thousand crack troops also left their barracks;

passengers-who-had-flown-as-civilians now pressed the starter buttons of tanks. Ayooba Shaheed Farooq and the buddha, however, were personally selected to accompany Brigadier Iskandar on the greatest adventure of the night. Yes, Padma: when Mujib was arrested, it was I who sniffed him out. (They had provided me with one of his old shirts; it's easy when you've got the smell.)

Padma is almost beside herself with anguish. 'But mister, you didn't, can't have, how would you do such a thing . . . ?' Padma: I did. I have sworn to tell everything; to conceal no shred of the truth. (But there are snail-tracks on her face, and she must have an explanation.)

So – believe me, don't believe, but this is what it was like! – I must reiterate that everything ended, everything began again, when a spittoon hit me on the back of the head. Saleem, with his desperation for meaning, for worthy purpose, for genius-like-a-shawl, had gone; would not return until a jungle snake – for the moment, anyway, there is was only the buddha; who recognizes no singing voice as his relative; who remembers neither fathers nor mothers; for whom midnight holds no importance; who, some time after a cleansing accident, awoke in a military hospital bed, and accepted the Army as his lot; who submits to the life in which he finds himself, and does his duty; who follows orders; who lives both in-the-world and not-in-the-world; who bows his head; who can track man or beast through streets or down rivers; who neither knows nor cares how, under whose auspices, as a favour to whom, at whose vengeful instigation he was put into uniform; who is, in short, no more and no less than the accredited tracker of CUTIA Unit 22.

But how convenient this amnesia is, how much it excuses! So permit me to criticize myself: the philosophy of acceptance to which the buddha adhered had consequences no more and no less unfortunate than his previous lust-for-centrality; and here, in Dacca, those consequences were being revealed.

'No, not true,' my Padma wails; the same denials have been made about most of what befell that night.

Midnight, March 25th, 1971: past the University, which was being shelled, the buddha led troops to Sheikh Mujib's lair. Students and lecturers came running out of hostels; they were greeted by bullets, and Mercurochrome stained the lawns. Sheikh Mujib, however, was not shot; manacled, manhandled, he was led by Ayooba Baloch to a waiting van. (As once before, after the revolution of the pepperpots . . . but Mujib was not naked; he had on a pair of green-and-yellow striped pajamas.) And while we drove through city streets, Shaheed looked out of windows and saw things that weren't-couldn't-have-been true: soldiers entering women's hostels without knocking; women, dragged into the street, were also entered, and again nobody troubled to knock. And newspaper offices, burning with the dirty yellowblack smoke of cheap gutter newsprint, and the offices of trade unions, smashed to the ground, and roadside ditches filling up with people who were not merely asleep – bare chests were seen, and the hollow pimples of bullet-holes. Ayooba Shaheed Farooq watched in silence through moving windows as our boys, our soldiers-for-Allah, our worth-ten-babus jawans held Pakistan together by turning flamethrowers machine-guns hand-grenades on the city slums. By the time we brought Sheikh Mujib to the airport, where Ayooba stuck a pistol into his rump and pushed him on to an aircraft which flew him into West Wing captivity, the buddha had closed his eyes. ('Don't fill my head with all this history,' he had once told Ayooba-the-tank, 'I am what I am and that's all there is.')

And Brigadier Iskandar, rallying his troops: 'Even now there are subversive elements to be rooted out.'

When thought becomes excessively painful, action is the finest remedy . . . dog-soldiers strain at the leash, and then, released, leap joyously to their work. O wolfhound chases of undesirables! O prolific seizings of professors and poets! O unfortunate shot-while-resisting arrests of Awami Leaguers and fashion correspondents! Dogs of war cry havoc in the city; but although tracker-dogs are tireless, soldiers are weaker: Farooq Shaheed Ayooba take turns at vomiting as their nostrils are assailed by the stench of burning slums. The buddha, in whose nose the stench spawns images of searing vividness, continues merely to do his job. Nose them out: leave the rest to the soldier-boys. CUTIA units stalk the smouldering wreck of the city. No undesirable is safe tonight; no hiding-place impregnable. Bloodhounds track the fleeing enemies of national unity; wolfhounds, not to be outdone, sink fierce teeth into their prey.

How many arrests – ten, four-hundred-and-twenty, one-thousand-and-one? – did our own Number 22 Unit make that night? How many intellectual lily-livered Daccans hid behind women's saris and had to be yanked into the streets? How often did Brigadier Iskandar – 'Smell this! That's the stink of subversion!' – unleash the war-hounds of unity? There are things which took place on the night of March 25th which must remain permanently in a state of confusion.

Futility of statistics: during 1971, ten million refugees fled across the borders of East Pakistan-Bangladesh into India – but ten million (like all numbers larger than one thousand and one) refuses to be understood. Comparisons do not help: 'the biggest migration in the history of the human race' – meaningless. Bigger than Exodus, larger than the Partition crowds, the many-headed monster poured into India. On the border, Indian soldiers trained the guerrillas known as Mukti Bahini; in Dacca, Tiger Niazi ruled the roost.

And Ayooba Shaheed Farooq? Our boys in green? How did they take to battling against fellow meat-eaters? Did they mutiny? Were officers – Iskandar, Najmuddin, even Lala

Moin – riddled with nauseated bullets? They were not. Innocence had been lost; but despite a new grimness about the eyes, despite the irrevocable loss of certainty, despite the eroding of moral absolutes, the unit went on with its work. The buddha was not the only one who did as he was told . . . while somewhere high above the struggle, the voice of Jamila Singer fought anonymous voices singing the lyrics of R. Tagore: 'My life passes in the shady village homes filled with rice from your fields; they madden my heart with delight.'

Their hearts maddened, but not with delight, Ayooba and company followed orders; the buddha followed scent-trails. Into the heart of the city, which has turned violent maddened bloodsoaked as the West Wing soldiers react badly to their knowledge-of-wrongdoing, goes Number 22 Unit; through the blackened streets, the buddha concentrates on the ground, sniffing out trails, ignoring the ground-level chaos of cigarette-packs cow-dung fallen-bicycles abandoned-shoes; and then on other assignments, out into the countryside, where entire villages are being burned owing to their collective responsibility for harbouring Mukti Bahini, the buddha and three boys track down minor Awami League officials and well-known Communist types. Past migrating villagers with bundled possessions on their heads; past torn-up railway tracks and burnt-out trees; and always, as though some invisible force were directing their footsteps, drawing them into a darker heart of madness, their missions send them south south south, always nearer to the sea, to the mouths of the Ganges and the sea.

And at last – who were they following then? Did names matter any more? – they were given a quarry whose skills must have been the equal-and-opposite of the buddha's own, otherwise why did it take so long to catch him? At last – unable to escape their training, pursue-relentlessly-arrest-remorselessly, they are in the midst of a mission without an end, pursuing a foe who endlessly eludes them, but they cannot report back to base empty-handed, and on they go, south south south, drawn by the eternally-receding scent-trail; and perhaps by something more: because, in my life, fate has never been unwilling to lend a hand.

They have commandeered a boat, because the buddha said the trail led down the river; hungry unslept exhausted in a universe of abandoned rice-paddies, they row after their unseen prey; down the great brown river they go, until the war is too far away to remember, but still the scent leads them on. The river here has a familiar name: Padma. But the name is a local deception; in reality the river is still Her, the mother-water, goddess Ganga streaming down to earth through Shiva's hair. The buddha has not spoken for days; he just points, there, that way, and on they go, south south south to the sea.

A nameless morning. Ayooba Shaheed Farooq awaking in the boat of their absurd pursuit, moored by the bank of Padma-Ganga – to find him gone. 'Allah-Allah,' Farooq yelps, 'Grab your ears and pray for pity, he's brought us to this drowned place and run off, it's all your fault, you Ayooba, that trick with the jump-leads and this is his revenge!' . . . The sun, climbing. Strange alien birds in the sky. Hunger and fear like mice in their bellies: and whatif, whatif the Mukti Bahini . . . parents are invoked. Shaheed has dreamed his pomegranate dream. Despair, lapping at the edges of the boat. And in the distance, near the horizon, an impossible endless huge green wall, stretching right and left to the ends of the earth! Unspoken fear: how can it be, how can what we are seeing be true, who builds walls across the world? . . . And then Ayooba, 'Look-look, Allah!' Because coming towards them across the rice-paddies is a bizarre slow-motion chase: first the buddha with that cucumber-nose, you could spot it a mile off, and following him, splashing through paddies, a gesticulating peasant with a

500

scythe, Father Time enraged, while running along a dyke a woman with her sari caught up between her legs, hair loose, voice pleading screaming, while the scythed avenger stumbles through drowned rice, covered from head to foot in water and mud. Ayooba roars with nervous relief: 'The old billy-goat! Couldn't keep his hands off the local women! Come on, buddha, don't let him catch you, he'll slice off both your cucumbers!' And Farooq, 'But then what? If the buddha is sliced, what then?' And now Ayooba-the-tank is pulling a pistol out of its holster. Ayooba aiming: both hands held out in front, trying not to shake, Ayooba squeezing: a scythe curves up into the air. And slowly slowly the arms of a peasant rise up as though in prayer; knees kneel in paddy-water; a face plunges below the water-level to touch its forehead to the earth. On the dyke a woman wailing. And Ayooba tells the buddha: 'Next time I'll shoot you instead.' Ayooba-the-tank shaking like a leaf. And Time lies dead in a rice-paddy.

But there is still the meaningless chase, the enemy who will never be seen, and the buddha, 'Go that way,' and the four of them row on, south south south, they have murdered the hours and forgotten the date, they no longer know if they are chasing after or running from, but whichever it is that pushes them is bringing them closer closer to the impossible green wall, 'That way,' the buddha insists, and then they are inside it, the jungle which is so thick that history has hardly ever found the way in. The Sundarbans: it swallows them up.

In the Sundarbans

I'll own up: there was no last, elusive quarry, driving us south south south. To all my readers, I should like to make this naked-breasted admission: while Ayooba Shaheed Farooq were unable to distinguish between chasing-after and running-from, the buddha knew what he was doing. Although I'm well aware that I am providing any future commentators or venom-quilled critics (to whom I say: twice before, I've been subjected to snake-poison; on both occasions, I proved stronger than venenes) with yet more ammunition – through admission-of-guilt, revelation-of-moral-turpitude, proof-of-cowardice – I'm bound to say that he, the buddha, finally incapable of continuing in the submissive performance of his duty, took to his heels and fled. Infected by the soul-chewing maggots of pessimism futility shame, he deserted, into the historyless anonymity of rainforests, dragging three children in his wake. What I hope to immortalize in pickles as well as words: that condition of the spirit in which the consequences of acceptance could not be denied, in which an overdose of reality gave birth to a miasmic longing for flight into the safety of dreams . . . But the jungle, like all refuges, was entirely other – was both less and more – than he had expected.

'I am glad,' my Padma says, 'I am happy you ran away.' But I insist: not I. He. He, the buddha. Who, until the snake, would remain not-Saleem; who, in spite of running-from, was still separated from his past; although he clutched, in his limpet fist, a certain silver spittoon.

The jungle closed behind them like a tomb, and after hours of increasingly weary but also frenzied rowing through incomprehensibly labyrinthine salt-water channels overtowered by the cathedral-arching trees, Ayooba Shaheed Farooq were hopelessly lost; they turned time and again to the buddha, who pointed, 'That way', and then, 'Down there', but although they rowed feverishly, ignoring fatigue, it seems as if the possibility of ever leaving this place receded before them like the lantern of a ghost; until at length they rounded on their supposedly infallible tracker, and perhaps saw some small light of shame or relief glowing in his habitually milky-blue eyes; and now Farooq whispered in the sepulchral greenness of the forest: 'You don't know. You're just saying anything.' The buddha remained silent, but in his silence they read their fate, and now that he was convinced that the jungle had swallowed them the way a toad gulps down a mosquito, now that he was sure he would never see the sun again, Ayooba Baloch, Ayooba-the-tank himself, broke down utterly and wept like a monsoon. The incongruous spectacle of this huge figure with a crew-cut blubbering like a baby served to detach Farooq and Shaheed from their senses; so that Farooq almost upset the boat by attacking the buddha, who mildly bore all the fist-blows which rained down on his chest shoulders arms, until Shaheed pulled Farooq down for the sake of safety. Ayooba Baloch cried without stopping for three entire hours or days or weeks, until the rain began and made his tears unnecessary; and Shaheed Dar heard himself saying, 'Now look what you started, man, with your crying,' proving that they were already beginning to succumb to the logic of the jungle, and that was only the start of it, because as the mystery of evening compounded the unreality of the trees, the Sundarbans began to grow in the rain.

At first they were so busy baling out their boat that they did not notice; also, the water-level was rising, which may have confused them; but in the last light there could be no doubt that the jungle was gaining in size, power and ferocity; the huge stilt-roots of vast ancient mangrove trees could be seen snaking about thirstily in the dusk, sucking in the rain and becoming thicker than elephants' trunks, while the mangroves themselves were getting so tall that, as Shaheed Dar said afterwards, the birds at the top must have been able to sing to God. The leaves in the heights of the great nipa palms began to spread like immense green cupped hands, swelling in the nocturnal downpour until the entire forest seemed to be thatched; and then the nipa-fruits began to fall, they were larger than any coconuts on earth and gathered speed alarmingly as they fell from dizzying heights to explode like bombs in the water. Rainwater was filling their boat; they had only their soft green caps and an old ghee tin to bale with; and as night fell and the nipa-fruits bombed them from the air, Shaheed Dar said, 'Nothing else to do – we must land,' although his thoughts were full of his pomegranate-dream and it crossed his mind that this might be where it came true, even if the fruits were different here.

While Ayooba sat in a red-eyed funk and Farooq seemed destroyed by his hero's disintegration; while the buddha remained silent and bowed his head, Shaheed alone remained capable of thought, because although he was drenched and worn out and the night-jungle screeched around him, his head became partly clear whenever he thought about the pomegranate of his death; so it was Shaheed who ordered us, them, to row our, their, sinking boat to shore.

A nipa-fruit missed the boat by an inch and a half, creating such turbulence in the water that they capsized; they struggled ashore in the dark holding guns oilskins ghee-tin above their heads, pulled the boat up after themselves, and past caring about bombarding nipa palms and snaking mangroves, fell into their sodden craft and slept. When they awoke, soaking-shivering in spite of the heat, the rain had become a heavy drizzle. They found their bodies covered in three-inch-long leeches which were almost entirely colourless owing to the absence of direct sunlight, but which had now turned bright red because they were full of blood, and which, one by one, exploded on the bodies of the four human beings, being too greedy to stop sucking when they were full. Blood trickled down legs and on to the forest floor: the jungle sucked it in, and knew what they were like.

When the falling nipa-fruits smashed on the jungle floor, they, too, exuded a liquid the colour of blood, a red milk which was immediately covered in a million insects, including giant flies as transparent as the leeches. The flies, too, reddened as they filled up with the milk of the fruit . . . all through the night, it seemed, the Sundarbans had continued to grow. Tallest of all were the sundri trees which had given their name to the jungle; trees high enough to block out even the faintest hope of sun. The four of us, them, climbed out of the boat; and only when they set foot on a hard bare soil crawling with pale pink scorpions and a seething mass of dun-coloured earthworms did they remember their hunger and thirst. Rainwater poured off leaves all around them, and they turned their mouths up to the roof of the jungle and drank; but perhaps because the water came to them by way of sundri leaves and mangrove branches and nipa fronds, it acquired on its journey something of the insanity of the jungle, so that as they drank they fell deeper and deeper into the thraldom of that livid green world where the birds had voices like creaking wood and all the snakes were blind. In the turbid, miasmic state of mind which the jungle induced, they prepared their first meal, a combination of nipa-fruits and mashed earthworms, which inflicted on them all a diarrhoea so violent that they forced themselves to examine the excrement in case their intestines had fallen out in the mess.

Farooq said, 'We're going to die.' But Shaheed was possessed by a powerful lust for survival; because, having recovered from the doubts of the night, he had become convinced that this was not how he was supposed to go.

Lost in the rainforest, and aware that the lessening of the monsoon was only a temporary respite, Shaheed decided that there was little point in attempting to find a way out when, at any moment, the returning monsoon might sink their inadequate craft; under his instructions, a shelter was constructed from oilskins and palm fronds; Shaheed said, 'As long as we stick to fruit, we can survive.' They had all long ago forgotten the purpose of their journey; the chase, which had begun far away in the real world, acquired in the altered light of the Sundarbans a quality of absurd fantasy which enabled them to dismiss it once and for all.

So it was that Ayooba Shaheed Farooq and the buddha surrendered themselves to the terrible phantasms of the dream-forest. The days passed, dissolving into each other under the force of the returning rain, and despite chills fevers diarrhoea they stayed alive, improving their shelter by pulling down the lower branches of sundris and mangroves, drinking the red milk of nipa-fruits, acquiring the skills of survival, such as the power of strangling snakes and throwing sharpened sticks so accurately that they speared multicoloured birds through their gizzards. But one night Ayooba awoke in the dark to find the translucent figure of a peasant with a bullet-hole in his heart and a scythe in his hand staring mournfully down at him, and as he struggled to get out of the boat (which they had pulled in, under the cover of their primitive shelter) the peasant leaked a colourless fluid which flowed out of the hole in his heart and on to Ayooba's gun arm. The next morning Ayooba's right arm refused to move; it hung rigidly by his side as if it had been set in plaster. Although Farooq Rashid offered help and sympathy, it was no use; the arm was held immovably in the invisible fluid of the ghost.

506

After this first apparition, they fell into a state of mind in which they would have believed the forest capable of anything; each night it sent them new punishments, the accusing eyes of the wives of men they had tracked down and seized, the screaming and monkey-gibbering of children left fatherless by their work . . . and in this first time, the time of punishment, even the impassive buddha with his citified voice was obliged to confess that he, too, had taken to waking up at night to find the forest closing in upon him like a vice, so that he felt unable to breathe.

When it had punished them enough – when they were all trembling shadows of the people they had once been – the jungle permitted them the double-edged luxury of nostalgia. One night Ayooba, who was regressing towards infancy faster than any of them, and had begun to suck his one moveable thumb, saw his mother looking down at him, offering him the delicate rice-based sweets of her love; but at the same moment as he reached out for the laddoos, she scurried away, and he saw her climb a giant sundri-tree to sit swinging from a high branch by her tail: a white wraithlike monkey with the face of his mother visited Ayooba night after night, so that after a time he was obliged to remember more about her than her sweets: how she had liked to sit among the boxes of her dowry, as though she, too, were simply some sort of thing, simply one of the gifts her father gave to her husband; in the heart of the Sundarbans, Ayooba Baloch understood his mother for the first time, and stopped sucking his thumb. Farooq Rashid, too, was given a vision. At dusk one day he thought he saw his brother running wildly through the forest, and became convinced that his father had died. He remembered a forgotten day when his peasant father had told him and his fleet-footed brother that the local landlord, who lent money at 300 per cent, had agreed to buy his soul in return for the latest loan. 'When I die,' old Rashid told Farooq's brother, 'you must open your mouth and my spirit will fly inside it; then run run run, because the zamindar will be after you!' Farooq, who had also started regressing alarmingly, found in the knowledge of his father's death and the flight of his brother the strength to give up the childish habits which the jungle had at first re-created in him; he stopped crying when he was hungry and asking Why. Shaheed Dar, too, was visited by a monkey with the face of an ancestor; but all he saw was a father who had instructed him to earn his name. This, however, also helped to restore in him the sense of responsibility which the just-following-orders requirements of war had sapped; so it seemed that the magical jungle, having tormented them with their misdeeds, was leading them by the hand towards a new adulthood. And flitting through the night-forest went the wraiths of their hopes; these, however, they were unable to see clearly, or to grasp.

The buddha, however, was not granted nostalgia at first. He had taken to sitting cross-legged under a sundri-tree; his eyes and mind seemed empty, and at night, he no longer awoke. But finally the forest found a way through to him; one afternoon, when rain pounded down on the trees and boiled off them as steam, Ayooba Shaheed Farooq saw the buddha sitting under his tree while a blind, translucent serpent bit, and poured venom into his heel. Shaheed Dar crushed the serpent's head with a stick; the buddha, who was head-to-foot numb, seemed not to have noticed. His eyes were closed. After this, the boy soldiers waited for the man-dog to die; but I was stronger than the snake-poison. For two days he became as rigid as a tree, and his eyes crossed, so that he saw the world in mirror-image, with the right side on the left; at last he relaxed, and the look of milky abstraction was no longer in his eyes. I was rejoined to the past, jolted into unity by snake-poison, and it began to pour out through the buddha's lips. As his eyes returned to normal, his words flowed so freely that they seemed to be an aspect of the monsoon. The child-soldiers listened, spellbound, to the stories issuing from his mouth, beginning with a birth at midnight, and continuing unstoppably, because he was reclaiming everything, all of it, all lost histories, all the myriad complex processes that go to make a man. Open-mouthed, unable to tear themselves away, the child-soldiers drank his life like leaf-tainted water, as he spoke of bed-wetting cousins, revolutionary pepperpots, the perfect voice of a sister . . . Ayooba Shaheed Farooq would have (once upon a time) given anything to know that those rumours had been true; but in the Sundarbans, they didn't even cry out.

And rushing on: to late-flowering love, and Jamila in a bedroom in a shaft of light. Now Shaheed did murmur, 'So that's why, when he confessed, after that she couldn't stand to be near . . .' But the buddha continues, and it becomes apparent that he is struggling to recall something particular, something which refuses to return, which obstinately eludes him, so that he gets to the end without finding it, and remains frowning and unsatisfied even after he has recounted a holy war, and revealed what fell from the sky.

There was a silence; and then Farooq Rashid said, 'So much, yaar, inside one person; so many bad things, no wonder he kept his mouth shut!'

You see, Padma: I have told this story before. But what refused to return? What, despite the liberating venene of a colourless serpent, failed to emerge from my lips? Padma: the buddha had forgotten his name. (To be precise: his first name.)

And still it went on raining. The water-level was rising daily, until it became clear that they would have to move deeper into the jungle, in search of higher ground. The rain was too heavy for the boat to be of use; so, still following Shaheed's instructions, Ayooba Farooq and the buddha pulled it far away from the encroaching bank, tied mooring-rope around sundri-trunk, and covered their craft with leaves; after which, having no option, they moved ever further into the dense uncertainty of the jungle.

Now, once again, the Sundarbans changed its nature; once again Ayooba Shaheed Farooq found their ears filled with the lamentations of families from whose bosom they had torn what once, centuries ago, they had termed 'undesirable elements'; they rushed wildly forward into the jungle to escape from the accusing, pain-filled voices of their victims; and at night the ghostly monkeys gathered in the trees and sang the words of 'Our Golden Bengal': '. . . O Mother, I am poor, but what little I have, I lay at thy feet. And it maddens my heart with delight.' Unable to escape from the unbearable torture of the unceasing voices, incapable of bearing for a moment longer the burden of shame, which was now greatly increased by their jungle-learned sense of responsibility, the three boy-soldiers were moved, at last, to take desperate measures. Shaheed Dar stooped down and picked up two handfuls of rain-heavy jungle mud; in the throes of that awful hallucination, he thrust the treacherous mud of the rainforest into his ears. And after him, Ayooba Baloch and Farooq Rashid stopped their ears also with mud. Only the buddha left his ears (one good, one already bad) unstopped; as though he alone were willing to bear the retribution of the jungle, as though he were bowing his head before the inevitability of his guilt . . . The mud of the dream-forest, which no doubt also contained the concealed translucency of jungle-insects and the devilry of bright orange bird-droppings, infected the ears of the three boy-soldiers and made them all as deaf as posts; so that although they were spared the singsong accusations of the jungle, they were now obliged to converse in a rudimentary form of sign-language. They seemed, however, to prefer their diseased deafness to the unpalatable secrets which the sundri-leaves had whispered in their ears.

510

At last, the voices stopped, though by now only the buddha (with his one good ear) could hear them; at last, when the four wanderers were near the point of panic, the jungle brought them through a curtain of tree-beards and showed them a sight so lovely that it brought lumps to their throats. Even the buddha seemed to tighten his grip on his spittoon. With one good ear between the four of them, they advanced into a glade filled with the gentle melodies of songbirds, in whose centre stood a monumental Hindu temple, carved in forgotten centuries out of a single immense crag of rock; its walls danced with friezes of men and women, who were depicted coupling in postures of unsurpassable athleticism and sometimes, of highly comic absurdity. The quartet moved towards this miracle with disbelieving steps. Inside, they found, at long last, some respite from the endless monsoon, and also the towering statue of a black dancing goddess, whom the boy-soldiers from Pakistan could not name; but the buddha knew she was Kali, fecund and awful, with the remnants of gold paint on her teeth. The four travellers lay down at her feet and fell into a rain-free sleep which ended at what could have been midnight, when they awoke simultaneously to find themselves being smiled upon by four young girls of a beauty which was beyond speech. Shaheed, who recalled the four houris awaiting him in the camphor garden, thought at first that he had died in the night; but the houris looked real enough, and their saris, under which they wore nothing at all, were torn and stained by the jungle. Now as eight eyes stared into eight, saris were unwound and placed, neatly folded, on the ground; after which the naked and identical daughters of the forest came to them, eight arms were twined with eight, eight legs were linked with eight legs more; below the statue of multi-limbed Kali, the travellers abandoned themselves to caresses which felt real enough, to kisses and love-bites which were soft and painful, to scratches which left marks, and they realized that this this this was

511

what they had needed, what they had longed for without knowing it, that having passed through the childish regressions and childlike sorrows of their earliest jungle-days, having survived the onset of memory and responsibility and the greater pains of renewed accusations, they were leaving infancy behind for ever, and then forgetting reasons and implications and deafness, forgetting everything, they gave themselves to the four identical beauties without a single thought in their heads.

After that night, they were unable to tear themselves away from the temple, except to forage for food, and every night the soft women of their most contented dreams returned in silence, never speaking, always neat and tidy with their saris, and invariably bringing the lost quartet to an incredible united peak of delight. None of them knew how long this period lasted, because in the Sundarbans time followed unknown laws, but at last the day came when they looked at each other and realized they were becoming transparent, that it was possible to see through their bodies, not clearly as yet, but cloudily, like staring through mango-juice. In their alarm they understood that this was the last and worst of the jungle's tricks, that by giving them their heart's desire it was fooling them into using up their dreams, so that as their dream-life seeped out of them they became as hollow and translucent as glass. The buddha saw now that the colourlessness of insects and leeches and snakes might have more to do with the depredations worked on their insectly, leechy, snakish imaginations than with the absence of sunlight . . . awakened as if for the first time by the shock of translucency, they looked at the temple with new eyes, seeing the great gaping cracks in the solid rock, realizing that vast segments could come detached and crash down upon them at any moment; and then, in a murky corner of the abandoned shrine, they saw the remnants of what might have been four small fires – ancient ashes, scorch-marks on stone – or perhaps four funeral pyres; and in the centre of each of the four, a small, blackened, fire-eaten heap of uncrushed bones.

How the buddha left the Sundarbans: the forest of illusions unleashed upon them, as they fled from temple towards boat, its last and most terrifying trick; they had barely reached the boat when it came towards them, at first a rumble in the far distance, then a roar which could penetrate even mud-deafened ears, they had untied the boat and leapt wildly into it when the wave came, and now they were at the mercy of the waters, which could have crushed them effortlessly against sundri or mangrove or nipa, but instead the tidal wave bore them down turbulent brown channels as the forest of their torment blurred past them like a great green wall, it seemed as if the jungle, having tired of its playthings, were ejecting them unceremoniously from its territory; waterborne, impelled forwards and still forwards by the unimaginable power of the wave, they bobbed pitifully amongst fallen branches and the sloughed-off skins of water-snakes, until finally they were hurled from the boat as the ebbing wave broke it against a tree-stump, they were left sitting in a drowned rice-paddy as the wave receded, in water up to their waists, but alive, borne out of the heart of the jungle of dreams, into which I had fled in the hope of peace and found both less and more, and back once more in the world of armies and dates.

When they emerged from the jungle, it was October 1971. And I am bound to admit (but, in my opinion, the fact only reinforces my wonder at the time-shifting sorcery of the forest) that there was no tidal wave recorded that month, although, over a year previously, floods had indeed devastated the region.

In the aftermath of the Sundarbans, my old life was waiting to reclaim me. I should have known: no escape from past acquaintance. What you were is forever who you are.

For seven months during the course of the year 1971, three soldiers and their tracker vanished off the face of the war. In October, however, when the rains ended and the guerrilla units of the Mukti Bahini began terrorizing Pakistani military outposts; when Mukti Bahini snipers picked off soldiers and petty officials alike, our quartet emerged from invisibility and, having little option, attempted to rejoin the main body of the occupying West Wing forces. Later, when questioned, the buddha would always explain his disappearance with the help of a garbled story about being lost in a jungle amid trees whose roots grabbed at you like snakes. It was perhaps fortunate for him that he was never formally interrogated by officers in the army of which he was a member. Ayooba Baloch, Farooq Rashid and Shaheed Dar were not subjected to such interrogations, either; but in their case this was because they failed to stay alive long enough for any questions to be asked.

. . . In an entirely deserted village of thatched huts with dung-plastered mud walls – in an abandoned community from which even the chickens had fled – Ayooba Shaheed Farooq bemoaned their fate. Rendered deaf by the poisonous mud of the rainforest, a disability which had begun to upset them a good deal now that the taunting voices of the jungle were no longer hanging in the air, they wailed their several wails, all talking at once, none hearing the other; the buddha, however, was obliged to listen to them all: to Ayooba, who stood facing a corner inside a naked room, his hair enmeshed in a spider's web, crying 'My ears my ears, like bees buzzing inside,' to Farooq who, petulantly, shouted, 'Whose fault, anyway? – Who, with his nose that could sniff out any bloody thing? – Who said That way, and that way? – And who, who will believe? – About jungles and temples and transparent serpents? – What a story, Allah, buddha, we should shoot you here-and-now!' While Shaheed, softly, 'I'm hungry.' Out once more in the real world, they were forgetting the lessons of the

514

jungle, and Ayooba, 'My arm! Allah, man, my withered arm! The ghost, leaking fluid . . .!' And Shaheed, 'Deserters, they'll say – empty-handed, no prisoner, after so-many months! – Allah, a court-martial, maybe, what do you think, buddha?' And Farooq, 'You bastard, see what you made us do! O God, too much, our uniforms! See, our uniforms, buddha – rags-and-tatters like a beggar-boy's! Think of what the Brigadier – and that Najmuddin – on my mother's head I swear I didn't – I'm not a coward! Not!' And Shaheed, who is killing ants and licking them off his palm, 'How to rejoin, anyway? Who knows where they are or if? And haven't we seen and heard how Mukti Bahini – *thai! thai!* they shoot from their hiding-holes, and you're dead! Dead, like an ant!' But Farooq is also talking, 'And not just the uniforms, man, the hair! Is this military hair-cut? This, so-long, falling over ears like worms? This woman's hair? Allah, they'll kill us dead – up against the wall and *thai! thai!* – you see if they don't!' But now Ayooba-the-tank is calming down; Ayooba holding his face in his hand; Ayooba saying softly to himself, 'O man, O man. I came to fight those damn vegetarian Hindus, man. And here is something too different, man. Something too bad.'

It is somewhere in November; they have been making their way slowly, north north north, past fluttering newspapers in curious curlicued script, through empty fields and abandoned settlements, occasionally passing a crone with a bundle on a stick over her shoulder, or a group of eight-year-olds with shifty starvation in their eyes and the threat of knives in their pockets, hearing how the Mukti Bahini are moving invisibly through the smoking land, how bullets come buzzing like bees-from-nowhere . . . and now a breaking-point has been reached, and Farooq, 'If it wasn't for you, buddha – Allah, you freak with your blue eyes of a foreigner, O God, yaar, how you *stink*!'

We all stink: Shaheed, who is crushing (with tatter-booted heel) a scorpion on the dirty floor of the abandoned hut;

515

Farooq, searching absurdly for a knife with which to cut his hair; Ayooba, leaning his head against a corner of the hut while a spider walks along the crown; and the buddha, too: the buddha, who stinks to heaven, clutches in his right hand a tarnished silver spittoon, and is trying to recall his name. And can summon up only nicknames: Snotnose, Stainface, Baldy, Sniffer, Piece-of-the-Moon.

. . . He sat cross-legged amid the wailing storm of his companions' fear, forcing himself to remember; but no, it would not come. And at last the buddha, hurling spittoon against earthen floor, exclaimed to stone-deaf ears: 'It's not – NOT – FAIR!'

In the midst of the rubble of war, I discovered fair-and-unfair. Unfairness smelled like onions; the sharpness of its perfume brought tears to my eyes. Seized by the bitter aroma of injustice, I remembered how Jamila Singer had leaned over a hospital bed – whose? *What name?* – how military gongs-and-pips were also present – how my sister – no, not my sister! how *she* – how she had said, 'Brother, I have to go away, to sing in service of the country; the Army will look after you now – for me, they will look after you so, so well.' She was veiled; behind white-and-gold brocade I smelled her traitress's smile; through soft veiling fabric she planted on my brow the kiss of her revenge; and then she, who always wrought a dreadful revenge upon those who loved her best, left me to the tender mercies of pips-and-gongs . . . and after Jamila's treachery I remembered the long-ago ostracism I suffered at the hands of Evie Burns; and exiles, and picnic-tricks; and all the vast mountain of unreasonable occurrences plaguing my life; and now, I lamented cucumber-nose, stain-face, bandy legs, horn-temples, monk's tonsure, finger-loss, one-bad-ear, and the numbing, braining spittoon; I wept copiously now, but still my name eluded me, and I repeated – 'Not fair; *not fair;* NOT FAIR!' And, surprisingly, Ayooba-the-tank moved away from his corner; Ayooba, perhaps recalling his own breakdown in the Sundarbans, squatted down in front of me and wrapped his one good arm around my neck. I accepted his comfortings; I cried into his shirt; but then there was a bee, buzzing towards us; while he squatted, with his back to the glassless window of the hut, something came whining through the overheated air; while he said, 'Hey, buddha – come on, buddha – hey, hey!' and while other bees, the bees of deafness, buzzed in his ears, something stung him in the neck. He made a popping noise deep in his throat and fell forwards on top of me. The sniper's bullet which killed Ayooba Baloch would, but for his presence, have speared me through the head. In dying, he saved my life.

Forgetting past humiliations; putting aside fair-and-unfair, and what-can't-be-cured-must-be-endured, I crawled out from under the corpse of Ayooba-the-tank, while Farooq, 'O God O God O!' and Shaheed, 'Allah, I don't even know if my gun will –' And Farooq, again, 'O God O! O God, who knows where the bastard is – !' But Shaheed, like soldiers in films, is flat against the wall beside the window. In these positions: I on the floor, Farooq crouched in a corner, Shaheed pressed against dung-plaster: we waited, helplessly, to see what would transpire.

There was no second shot; perhaps the sniper, not knowing the size of the force hidden inside the mud-walled hut, had simply shot and run. The three of us remained inside the hut for a night and a day, until the body of Ayooba Baloch began to demand attention. Before we left, we found pickaxes, and buried him . . . And afterwards, when the Indian Army did come, there was no Ayooba Baloch to greet them with his theories of the superiority of meat over vegetables; no Ayooba went into action, yelling, 'Ka-dang! Ka-blam! Ka-pow!!'

Perhaps it was just as well.

*

517

. . . And sometime in December the three of us, riding on stolen bicycles, arrived at a field from which the city of Dacca could be seen against the horizon; a field in which grew crops so strange, with so-nauseous an aroma, that we found ourselves incapable of remaining on our bicycles. Dismounting before we fell off, we entered the terrible field.

There was a scavenging peasant moving about, whistling as he worked, with an outsize gunny sack on his back. The whitened knuckles of the hand which gripped the sack revealed his determined frame of mind; the whistling, which was piercing but tuneful, showed that he was keeping his spirits up. The whistle echoed around the field, bouncing off fallen helmets, resounding hollowly from the barrels of mud-blocked rifles, sinking without trace into the fallen boots of the strange, strange crops, whose smell, like the smell of unfairness, was capable of bringing tears to the buddha's eyes. The crops were dead, having been hit by some unknown blight . . . and most of them, but not all, wore the uniforms of the West Pakistani Army. Apart from the whistling, the only noises to be heard were the sounds of objects dropping into the peasant's treasure-sack: leather belts, watches, gold tooth-fillings, spectacle frames, tiffin-carriers, water flasks, boots. The peasant saw them and came running towards them, smiling ingratiatingly', talking rapidly in a wheedling voice that only the buddha was obliged to hear. Farooq and Shaheed stared glassily at the field while the peasant began his explanations.

'Plenty shooting! *Thaii! Thaiii!*' He made a pistol with his right hand. He was speaking bad, stilted Hindi. 'Ho sirs! India has come, my sirs! Ho yes! *Ho* yes.' – And all over the field, the crops were leaking nourishing bone-marrow into the soil while he, 'No shoot I, my sirs. Ho no. I have news – ho, such news! India comes! Jessore is fall, my sirs; in one-four days, Dacca, also, yes-no?' The buddha listened; the buddha's eyes looked beyond the peasant to the field. 'Such a things, my sir! India! They have one mighty soldier fellow, he

518

can kill six persons at one time, break necks *khrikk-khrikk* between his knees, my sirs? Knees – is right words?' He tapped his own. 'I see, my sirs. With these eyes, ho yes! He fights with not guns, not swords. With knees, and six necks go *khrikk-khrikk*. *Ho* God.' Shaheed was vomiting in the field. Farooq Rashid had wandered to the far edge and stood staring into a copse of mango trees. 'In one-two weeks is over the war, my sirs! Everybody come back. Just now all gone, but I not, my sirs. Soldiers came looking for Bahini and killed many many, also my son. Ho yes, sirs, ho yes indeed.' The buddha's eyes had become clouded and dull. In the distance he could hear the crump of heavy artillery. Columns of smoke trailed up into the colourless December sky. The strange crops lay still, unruffled by the breeze . . . 'I stay, my sirs. Here I know names of birds and plants. Ho yes. I am Deshmukh by name; vendor of notions by trade. I sell many so-fine thing. You want? Medicine for constipation, damn good, ho yes. I have. Watch you want, glowing in the dark? I also have. And book ho yes, and joke trick, truly. I was famous in Dacca before. Ho yes, most truly. No shoot.'

The vendor of notions chattered on, offering for sale item after item, such as a magical belt which would enable the wearer to speak Hindi – 'I am wearing now, my sir, speak damn good, yes no? Many India soldier are buy, they talk so-many different tongues, the belt is godsend from God!' – and then he noticed what the buddha held in his hand. 'Ho sir! Absolute master thing! Is silver? Is precious stone? You give; I give radio, camera, almost working order, my sir! Is a damn good deals, my friend. For one spittoon only, is damn fine. Ho yes. Ho yes, my sir, life must go on; trade must go on, my sir, not true?'

'Tell me more,' the buddha said, 'about the soldier with the knees.'

But now, once again, a bee buzzes; in the distance, at the far end of the field, somebody drops to his knees; somebody's forehead touches the ground as if in prayer; and in the field, one of the crops, which had been alive enough to shoot, also becomes very still. Shaheed Dar is shouting a name:

'Farooq! Farooq, man!'

But Farooq refuses to reply.

Afterwards, when the buddha reminisced about the war to his uncle Mustapha, he recounted how he had stumbled across the field of leaking bonemarrow towards his fallen companion; and how, long before he reached Farooq's praying corpse, he was brought up short by the field's greatest secret.

There was a small pyramid in the middle of the field. Ants were crawling over it, but it was not an anthill. The pyramid had six feet and three heads and, in between, a jumbled area composed of bits of torso, scraps of uniforms, lengths of intestine and glimpses of shattered bones. The pyramid was still alive. One of its three heads had a blind left eye, the legacy of a childhood argument. Another had hair that was thickly plastered down with hair oil. The third head was the oddest: it had deep hollows where the temples should have been, hollows that could have been made by a gynaecologist's forceps which had held it too tightly at birth . . . it was this third head which spoke to the buddha:

'Hullo, man,' it said, 'What the hell are you here for?'

Shaheed Dar saw the pyramid of enemy soldiers apparently conversing with the buddha; Shaheed, suddenly seized by an irrational energy, flung himself upon me and pushed me to the ground, with, 'Who are you? – Spy? Traitor? What? – Why do they know who you – ?' While Deshmukh, the vendor of notions, flapped pitifully around us, 'Ho sirs! Enough fighting has been already. Be normal now, my sirs. I beg. Ho God.'

Even if Shaheed had been able to hear me, I could not then have told him what I later became convinced was the truth: that the purpose of that entire war had been to re-unite me with an old life, to bring me back together with my old friends. Sam Manekshaw was marching on Dacca, to meet his old friend the Tiger; and the modes of connection lingered on, because on the field of leaking bone-marrow I heard about the exploits of knees, and was greeted by a dying pyramid of heads: and in Dacca I was to meet Parvati-the-witch.

When Shaheed calmed down and got off me, the pyramid was no longer capable of speech. Later that afternoon, we resumed our journey towards the capital. Deshmukh, the vendor of notions, called cheerfully after us: 'Ho sirs! Ho my poor sirs! Who knows when a man will die? Who, my sirs, knows why?'

Sam and the Tiger

Sometimes, mountains must move before old comrades can be reunited. On December 15th, 1971, in the capital of the newly liberated state of Bangladesh, Tiger Niazi surrendered to his old chum Sam Manekshaw; while I, in my turn, surrendered to the embraces of a girl with eyes like saucers, a pony-tail like a long shiny black rope, and lips which had not at that time acquired what was to become their characteristic pout. These reunions were not achieved easily; and as a gesture of respect for all who made them possible, I shall pause briefly in my narrative to set out the whys and the wherefores.

Let me, then, be perfectly explicit: if Yahya Khan and Z. A. Bhutto had not colluded in the matter of the coup of March 25th, I would not have been flown to Dacca in civilian dress; nor, in all likelihood, would General Tiger Niazi have been in the city that December. To continue: the Indian intervention in the Bangladesh dispute was also the result of the interaction of great forces. Perhaps, if ten million had not walked across the frontiers into India, obliging the Delhi Government to spend $200,000,000 a month on refugee camps – the entire war of 1965, whose secret purpose had been the annihilation of my family, had cost them only $70,000,000! – Indian soldiers, led by General Sam, would never have crossed the frontiers in the opposite direction. But India came for other reasons, too: as I was to learn from the Communist magicians who lived in the shadow of the Delhi Friday Mosque, the

Delhi sarkar had been highly concerned by the declining influence of Mujib's Awami League, and the growing popularity of the revolutionary Mukti Bahini; Sam and the Tiger met in Dacca to prevent the Bahini from gaining power. So if it were not for the Mukti Bahini, Parvati-the-witch might never have accompanied the Indian troops on their campaign of 'liberation' . . . But even that is not a full explanation. A third reason for Indian intervention was the fear that the disturbances in Bangladesh would, if they were not quickly curtailed, spread across the frontiers into West Bengal; so Sam and the Tiger, and also Parvati and I, owe our meeting at least in part to the more turbulent elements in West Bengali politics: the Tiger's defeat was only the beginning of a campaign against the Left in Calcutta and its environs.

At any rate, India came; and for the speed of her coming – because in a mere three weeks Pakistan had lost half her navy, a third of her army, a quarter of her air force, and finally, after the Tiger surrendered, more than half her population – thanks must be given to the Mukti Bahini once more; because, perhaps naively, failing to understand that the Indian advance was as much a tactical manoeuvre against them as a battle against the occupying West Wing forces, the Bahini advised General Manekshaw on Pakistani troop movements, on the Tiger's strengths and weaknesses; thanks, too, to Mr Chou En-lai, who refused (despite Bhutto's entreaties) to give Pakistan any material aid in the war. Denied Chinese arms, Pakistan fought with American guns, American tanks and aircraft; the President of the United States, alone in the entire world, was resolved to 'tilt' towards Pakistan. While Henry A. Kissinger argued the cause of Yahya Khan, the same Yahya was secretly arranging the President's famous state visit to China . . . there were, therefore, great forces working against my reunion with Parvati and Sam's with the Tiger; but despite the tilting President, it was all over in three short weeks.

On the night of December 14th, Shaheed Dar and the buddha circled the fringes of the invested city of Dacca; but the buddha's nose (you will not have forgotten) was capable of sniffing out more than most. Following his nose, which could smell safety and danger, they found a way through the Indian lines, and entered the city under cover of night. While they moved stealthily through streets in which nobody except a few starving beggars could be seen, the Tiger was swearing to fight to the last man; but the next day, he surrendered instead. What is not known: whether the last man was grateful to be spared or peeved at missing his chance of entering the camphor garden.

And so I returned to that city in which, in those last hours before reunions, Shaheed and I saw many things which were not true, which were not possible, because our boys would not could not have behaved so badly; we saw men in spectacles with heads like eggs being shot in side-streets, we saw the intelligentsia of the city being massacred by the hundred, but it was not true because it could not have been true, the Tiger was a decent chap, after all, and our jawans were worth ten babus, we moved through the impossible hallucination of the night, hiding in doorways while fires blossomed like flowers, reminding me of the way the Brass Monkey used to set fire to shoes to attract a little attention, there were slit throats being buried in unmarked graves, and Shaheed began his, 'No, buddha – what a thing, Allah, you can't believe your eyes – no, not true, how can it – buddha, tell, what's got into my eyes?' And at last the buddha spoke, knowing Shaheed could not hear: 'O, Shaheeda,' he said, revealing the depths of his fastidiousness, 'a person must sometimes choose what he will see and what he will not; look away, look away from there now.' But Shaheed was staring at a maidan in which lady doctors were being bayoneted before they were raped, and raped again before they were shot. Above them and behind them, the cool white minaret of a mosque stared blindly down upon the scene.

As though talking to himself, the buddha said, 'It is time to think about saving our skins; God knows why we came back.' The buddha entered the doorway of a deserted house, a broken, peeling shell of an edifice which had once housed a tea-shop, a bicycle-repair shop, a whorehouse and a tiny landing on which a notary public must once have sat, because there was the low desk on which he had left behind a pair of half-rimmed spectacles, there were the abandoned seals and stamps which had once enabled him to be more than an old nobody – stamps and seals which had made him an arbiter of what was true and what was not. The notary public was absent, so I could not ask him to verify what was happening, I could not give a deposition under oath; but lying on the mat behind his desk was a loose flowing garment like a djellabah, and without waiting any longer I removed my uniform, including the she-dog badge of the CUTIA units, and became anonymous, a deserter, in a city whose language I could not speak.

Shaheed Dar, however, remained in the street; in the first light of morning he watched soldiers scurrying away from what-had-not-been-done; and then the grenade came. I, the buddha, was still inside the empty house; but Shaheed was unprotected by walls.

Who can say why how who; but the grenade was certainly thrown. In that last instant of his un-bisected life, Shaheed was suddenly seized by an irresistible urge to look up . . . afterwards, in the muezzin's roost, he told the buddha, 'So strange, Allah – the pomegranate – in my head, just like that, bigger an' brighter than ever before – you know, buddha, like a light-bulb – Allah, what could I do, I looked!' – And yes, it was there, hanging above his head, the grenade of his dreams, hanging just above his head, falling falling, exploding at waist-level, blowing his legs away to some other part of the city.

When I reached him, Shaheed was conscious, despite bisection, and pointed up, 'Take me up there, buddha, I want to I want,' so I carried what was now only half a boy (and therefore reasonably light) up narrow spiral stairs to the heights of that cool white minaret, where Shaheed babbled of light-bulbs while red ants and black ants fought over a dead cockroach, battling away along the trowel-furrows in the crudely-laid concrete floor. Down below, amid charred houses, broken glass and smoke-haze, antlike people were emerging, preparing for peace; the ants, however, ignored the antlike, and fought on. And the buddha: he stood still, gazing milkily down and around, having placed himself between the top half of Shaheed and eyrie's one piece of furniture, a low table on which stood a gramophone connected to a loud-speaker. The buddha, protecting his halved companion from the disillusioning sight of this mechanized muezzin, whose call to prayer would always be scratched in the same places, extracted from the folds of his shapeless robe a glinting object: and turned his milky gaze upon the silver spittoon. Lost in contemplation, he was taken by surprise when the screams began; and looked up to see an abandoned cockroach. (Blood had been seeping along trowel-furrows; ants, following this dark viscous trail, had arrived at the source of the leakage, and Shaheed expressed his fury at becoming the victim of not one, but two wars.)

Coming to the rescue, feet dancing on ants, the buddha bumped his elbow against a switch; the loudspeaker system was activated, and afterwards people would never forget how a mosque had screamed out the terrible agony of war.

After a few moments, silence. Shaheed's head slumped forward. And the buddha, fearing discovery, put away his spittoon and descended into the city as the Indian Army arrived; leaving Shaheed, who no longer minded, to assist at the peacemaking banquet of the ants, I went into the early morning streets to welcome General Sam.

In the minaret, I had gazed milkily at my spittoon; but the buddha's mind had not been empty. It contained three words, which Shaheed's top half had also kept repeating, until the ants: the same three which once, reeking of onions, had made me weep on the shoulder of Ayooba Baloch – until the bee, buzzing . . . 'It's not fair,' the buddha thought, and then, like a child, over and over, 'It's not fair,' and again, and again.

Shaheed, fulfilling his father's dearest wish, had finally earned his name; but the buddha could still not remember his own.

How the buddha regained his name: Once, long ago, on another independence day, the world had been saffron and green. This morning, the colours were green, red and gold. And in the cities, cries of 'Jai Bangla!' And voices of women singing 'Our Golden Bengal', maddening their hearts with delight . . . in the centre of the city, on the podium of his defeat, General Tiger Niazi awaited General Manekshaw. (Biographical details: Sam was a Parsee. He came from Bombay. Bombayites were in for happy times that day.) And amid green and red and gold, the buddha in his shapeless anonymous garment was jostled by crowds; and then India came. India, with Sam at her head.

Was it General Sam's idea? Or even Indira's? – Eschewing these fruitless questions, I record only that the Indian advance into Dacca was much more than a mere military parade; as befits a triumph, it was garlanded with side-shows. A special I.A.F. troop transport had flown to Dacca, carrying a hundred and one of the finest entertainers and conjurers India could provide. From the famous magicians' ghetto in Delhi they came, many of them dressed for the occasion in the evocative uniforms of the Indian fauj, so that many Daccans got the idea that the Indians' victory had been inevitable from the start because even their uniformed jawans were sorcerers of the highest order. The conjurers and other artistes marched

527

beside the troops, entertaining the crowds; there were acrobats forming human pyramids on moving carts drawn by white bullocks; there were extraordinary female contortionists who could swallow their legs up to their knees; there were jugglers who operated outside the laws of gravity, so that they could draw oohs and aahs from the delighted crowd as they juggled with toy grenades, keeping four hundred and twenty in the air at a time; there were card-tricksters who could pull the queen of chiriyas (the monarch of birds, the empress of clubs) out of women's ears; there was the great dancer Anarkali, whose name meant 'pomegranate-bud', doing leaps twists pirouettes on a donkey-cart while a giant piece of silver nose-jewellery jingled on her right nostril; there was Master Vikram the sitarist, whose sitar was capable of responding to, and exaggerating, the faintest emotions in the hearts of his audience, so that once (it was said) he had played before an audience so bad-tempered, and had so greatly enhanced their foul humour, that if his tabla-player hadn't made him stop his raga in mid-stream the power of his music would have had them all knifing each other and smashing up the auditorium . . . today, Master Vikram's music raised the celebratory goodwill of the people to fever-pitch; it maddened, let us say, their hearts with delight.

And there was Picture Singh himself, a seven-foot giant who weighed two hundred and forty pounds and was known as the Most Charming Man In The World because of his unsurpassable skills as a snake-charmer. Not even the legendary Tubriwallahs of Bengal could exceed his talents; he strode through the happily shrieking crowds, twined from head to foot with deadly cobras, mambas and kraits, all with their poison-sacs intact . . . Picture Singh, who would be the last in the line of men who have been willing to become my fathers . . . and immediately behind him came Parvati-the-witch.

Parvati-the-witch entertained the crowds with the help of a large wicker basket with a lid; happy volunteers entered the basket, and Parvati made them disappear so completely that they could not return until she wished them to; Parvati, to whom midnight had given the true gifts of sorcery, had placed them at the service of her humble illusionist's trade; so that she was asked, 'But how do you pull it off?' And, 'Come on, pretty missy, tell the trick, why not?' – Parvati, smiling beaming rolling her magic basket, came towards me with the liberating troops.

The Indian Army marched into town, its heroes following the magicians; among them, I learned afterwards, was that colossus of the war, the rat-faced Major with the lethal knees . . . but now there were still more illusionists, because the surviving prestidigitators of the city came out of hiding and began a wonderful contest, seeking to outdo anything and everything the visiting magicians had to offer, and the pain of the city was washed and soothed in the great glad outpouring of their magic. Then Parvati-the-witch saw me, and gave me back my name.

'Saleem! O my god Saleem, you Saleem Sinai, is it you Saleem?'

The buddha jerks, puppet-fashion. Crowd-eyes staring. Parvati pushing towards him. 'Listen, it must be you!' She is gripping his elbow. Saucer eyes searching milky blue. 'My God, that nose, I'm not being rude, but of course! Look, it's me, Parvati! O Saleem, don't be stupid now, come on come on . . . !'

'That's it,' the buddha says. 'Saleem: that was it.'

'O God, too much excitement!' she cries. 'Arré baap, Saleem, you remember – the Children, yaar, O this is too good! So why are you looking so serious when I feel like to hug you to pieces? So many years I only saw you inside here,' she taps her forehead, 'and now you're here with a face like a fish. Hey, Saleem! Come on, say one hullo at least.'

*

On December 15th, 1971, Tiger Niazi surrendered to Sam Manekshaw; the Tiger and ninety-three thousand Pakistani troops became prisoners of war. I, meanwhile, became the willing captive of the Indian magicians, because Parvati dragged me into the procession with, 'Now that I've found you I'm not letting you go.'

That night, Sam and the Tiger drank chota pegs and reminisced about the old days in the British Army. 'I say, Tiger,' Sam Manekshaw said, 'You behaved jolly decently by surrendering.' And the Tiger, 'Sam, you fought one hell of a war.' A tiny cloud passes across the face of General Sam, 'Listen, old sport: one hears such damn awful lies. Slaughters, old boy, mass graves, special units called CUTIA or some damn thing, developed for purposes of rooting out opposition . . . no truth in it, I suppose?' And the Tiger, 'Canine Unit for Tracking and Intelligence Activities? Never heard of it. Must've been misled, old man. Some damn bad intelligence-wallahs on both sides. No, ridiculous, damn ridiculous, if you don't mind me saying.' 'Thought as much,' says General Sam, 'I say, bloody fine to see you, Tiger, you old devil!' And the Tiger, 'Been years, eh, Sam? Too damn long.'

. . . While old friends sang 'Auld Lang Syne' in officers' messes, I made my escape from Bangladesh, from my Pakistani years. 'I'll get you out,' Parvati said, after I explained, 'You want it secret secret?'

I nodded. 'Secret secret.'

Elsewhere in the city, ninety-three thousand soldiers were preparing to be carted off to P.O.W. camps; but Parvati-the-witch made me climb into a wicker basket with a close-fitting lid. Sam Manekshaw was obliged to place his old friend the Tiger under protective custody; but Parvati-the-witch assured me, 'This way they'll never catch.'

Behind an army barracks where the magicians were awaiting their transport back to Delhi, Picture Singh, the Most Charming Man In The World, stood guard when, that evening, I climbed into the basket of invisibility. We loitered casually, smoking biris, waiting until there were no soldiers in sight, while Picture Singh told me about his name. Twenty years ago, an Eastman-Kodak photographer had taken his portrait – which, wreathed in smiles and snakes, afterwards appeared on half the Kodak advertisements and in-store displays in India; ever since when the snake-charmer had adopted his present cognomen. 'What do you think, captain?' he bellowed amiably. 'A fine name, isn't it so? Captain, what to do, I can't even remember what name I used to have, from before, the name my mother-father gave me! Pretty stupid, hey, captain?' But Picture Singh was not stupid; and there was much more to him than charm. Suddenly his voice lost its casual, sleepy good-nature; he whispered, 'Now! Now, captain, ek dum, double-quick time!' Parvati whipped lid away from wicker; I dived head first into her cryptic basket. The lid, returning, blocked out the day's last light.

Picture Singh whispered, 'Okay, captain – damn good!' And Parvati bent down close to me; her lips must have been against the outside of the basket. What Parvati-the-witch whispered through wickerwork:

'Hey, you Saleem: just to think! You and me, mister – midnight's children, yaar! That's something, no?'

That's something . . . Saleem, shrouded in wickerwork darkness, was reminded of years-ago midnights, of childhood wrestling bouts with purpose and meaning; overwhelmed by nostalgia, I still did not understand what that something was. Then Parvati whispered some other words, and, inside the basket of invisibility, I, Saleem Sinai, complete with my loose anonymous garment, vanished instantly into thin air. 'Vanished? How vanished, what vanished?' Padma's head jerks up; Padma's eyes stare at me in bewilderment. I, shrugging, merely reiterate; Vanished, just like that. Disappeared. Dematerialized. Like a djinn: poof, like so.

'So,' Padma presses me, 'she really-truly was a witch?'

Really-truly. I was in the basket, but also not in the basket; Picture Singh lifted it one-handed and tossed it into the back of the Army truck taking him and Parvati and ninety-nine others to the aircraft waiting at the military airfield; I was tossed with the basket, but also not tossed. Afterwards, Picture Singh said, 'No, captain. I couldn't feel your weight'; nor could I feel any bump thump bang. One hundred and one artistes had arrived, by I.A.F. troop transport, from the capital of India; one hundred and two persons returned, although one of them was both there and not there. Yes, magic spells can occasionally succeed. But also fail: my father, Ahmed Sinai, never succeeded in cursing Sherri, the mongrel bitch.

Without passport or permit, I returned, cloaked in invisibility, to the land of my birth; believe, don't believe, but even a sceptic will have to provide another explanation for my presence here. Did not the Caliph Haroun al-Rashid (in an earlier set of fabulous tales) also wander, unseen invisible anonymous, cloaked through the streets of Baghdad? What Haroun achieved in Baghdad streets, Parvati-the-witch made possible for me, as we flew through the air-lanes of the subcontinent. She did it; I was invisible; *bas. Enough.*

Memories of invisibility: in the basket, I learned what it was like, will be like, to be dead. I had acquired the characteristics of ghosts! Present, but insubstantial; actual, but without being or weight . . . I discovered, in the basket, how ghosts see the world. Dimly hazily faintly . . . it was around me, but only just; I hung in a sphere of absence at whose fringes, like faint reflections, could be seen the spectres of wickerwork. The dead die, and are gradually forgotten; time does its healing, and they fade – but in Parvati's basket I learned that the reverse is also true; that ghosts, too, begin to forget; that the dead lose their memories of the living, and at last, when they are detached from their lives, fade away – that dying, in short, continues for a long time after death.

Afterwards, Parvati said, 'I didn't want to tell you – but nobody should be kept invisible that long – it was dangerous, but what else was there to do?'

In the grip of Parvati's sorcery, I felt my hold on the world slip away – and how easy, how peaceful not to never to return! – to float in this cloudy nowhere, wafting further further further, like a seed-spore blown on the breeze – in short, I was in mortal danger.

What I held on to in that ghostly time-and-space: a silver spittoon. Which, transformed like myself by Parvati-whispered words, was nevertheless a reminder of the outside . . . clutching finely-wrought silver, which glittered even in that nameless dark, I survived. Despite head-to-toe numbness, I was saved, perhaps, by the glints of my precious souvenir.

No – there was more to it than spittoons: for, as we all know by now, our hero is greatly affected by being shut up in confined spaces. Transformations spring upon him in the enclosed dark. As a mere embryo in the secrecy of a womb (not his mother's), did he not grow into the incarnation of the new myth of August 15th, the child of ticktock – did he not emerge as the Mubarak, the Blessed Child? In a cramped wash-room, were name-tags not switched around? Alone in a washing-chest with a drawstring up one nostril, did he not glimpse a Black Mango and sniff too hard, turning himself and his upper cucumber into a kind of supernatural ham radio? Hemmed in by doctors, nurses and anaesthetic masks, did he not succumb to numbers and, having suffered drainage-above, move into a second phase, that of nasal philosopher and (later) tracker supreme? Squashed, in a small abandoned hut, beneath the body of Ayooba Baloch, did he not learn the meaning of fair-and-unfair? Well, then – trapped in the occult peril of the basket of invisibility, I was saved, not only by the glints of a spittoon, but also by another transformation: in the grip of that awful disembodied loneliness, whose smell was the smell of graveyards, I discovered anger.

Something was fading in Saleem and something was being born. Fading: an old pride in baby-snaps and framed Nehru-letter; an old determination to espouse, willingly, a prophesied historical role; and also a willingness to make allowances, to understand how parents and strangers might legitimately despise or exile him for his ugliness; mutilated fingers and monks' tonsures no longer seemed like good enough excuses for the way in which he, I, had been treated. The object of my wrath was, in fact, everything which I had, until then, blindly accepted: my parents' desire that I should repay their investment in me by becoming great; genius-like-a-shawl; the modes of connection themselves inspired in me a blind, lunging fury. Why me? Why, owing to accidents of birth prophecy etcetera, must I be responsible for language riots and after-Nehru-who, for pepperpot-revolutions and bombs which annihilated my family? Why should I, Saleem Snotnose, Sniffer, Mapface, Piece-of-the-Moon, accept the blame for what-was-not-done by Pakistani troops in Dacca? . . . *Why, alone of all the more-than-five-hundred-million, should I have to bear the burden of history?*

What my discovery of unfairness (smelling of onions) had begun, my invisible rage completed. Wrath enabled me to survive the soft siren temptations of invisibility; anger made me determined, after I was released from vanishment in the shadow of a Friday Mosque, to begin, from that moment forth, to choose my own, undestined future. And there, in the silence of graveyard-reeking isolation, I heard the long-ago voice of the virginal Mary Pereira, singing:

> Anything you want to be, you kin be,
> You kin be just what-all you want.

Tonight, as I recall my rage, I remain perfectly calm; the

Widow drained anger out of me along with everything else. Remembering my basket-born rebellion against inevitability, I even permit myself a wry, understanding smile. 'Boys,' I mutter tolerantly across the years to Saleem-at-twenty-four, 'will be boys.' In the Widows' Hostel, I was taught, harshly, once-and-for-all, the lesson of No Escape; now, seated hunched over paper in a pool of Anglepoised light, I no longer want to be anything except what who I am. Who what am I? My answer: I am the sum total of everything that went before me, of all I have been seen done, of everything done-to-me. I am everyone everything whose being-in-the-world affected was affected by mine. I am anything that happens after I've gone which would not have happened if I had not come. Nor am I particulary exceptional in this matter; each 'I', every one of the now-six-hundred-million-plus of us, contains a similar multitude. I repeat for the last time: to understand me, you'll have to swallow a world.

Although now, as the pouring-out of what-was-inside-me nears an end; as cracks widen within – I can hear and feel the rip tear crunch – I begin to grow thinner, translucent almost; there isn't much of me left, and soon there will be nothing at all. Six hundred million specks of dust, and all transparent, invisible as glass . . .

But then I was angry. Glandular hyper-activity in a wicker amphora: eccrine and apocrine glands poured forth sweat and stink, as if I were trying to shed my fate through my pores; and, in fairness to my wrath, I must record that it claimed one instant achievement – that when I tumbled out of the basket of invisibility into the shadow of the mosque, I had been rescued by rebellion from the abstraction of numbness; as I bumped out on to the dirt of the magicians' ghetto, silver spittoon in hand, I realized that I had begun, once again, to feel.

Some afflictions, at least, are capable of being conquered.

The shadow of the Mosque

No shadow of a doubt: an acceleration is taking place. Rip crunch crack – while road surfaces split in the awesome heat, I, too, am being hurried towards disintegration. What-gnaws-on-bones (which, as I have been regularly obliged to explain to the too many women around me, is far beyond the powers of medicine men to discern, much less to cure) will not be denied for long; and still so much remains to be told . . . Uncle Mustapha is growing inside me, and the pout of Parvati-the-witch; a certain lock of hero's hair is waiting in the wings; and also a labour of thirteen days, and history as an analogue of a prime minister's hair-style; there is to be treason, and fare-dodging, and the scent (wafting on breezes heavy with the ululations of widows) of something frying in an iron skillet . . . so that I, too, am forced to accelerate, to make a wild dash for the finishing line; before memory cracks beyond hope of re-assembly, I must breast the tape. (Although already, already there are fadings, and gaps; it will be necessary to improvise on occasion.)

Twenty-six pickle-jars stand gravely on a shelf; twenty-six special blends, each with its identifying label, neatly inscribed with familiar phrases: 'Movements Performed by Pepperpots', for instance, or 'Alpha and Omega', or 'Commander Sabarmati's Baton'. Twenty-six rattle eloquently when local trains go yellow-and-browning past; on my desk, five empty jars tinkle urgently, reminding me of my uncompleted task. But now I cannot linger over empty pickle-jars; the night is for words, and green chutney must wait its turn.

. . . Padma is wistful: 'O, mister, how lovely Kashmir must be in August, when here it is hot like a chilli!' I am obliged to reprove my plump-yet-muscled companion, whose attention has been wandering; and to observe that our Padma Bibi, long-suffering tolerant consoling, is beginning to behave exactly like a traditional Indian wife. (And I, with my distances and self-absorption, like a husband?) Of late, in spite of my stoic fatalism about the spreading cracks, I have smelled, on Padma's breath, the dream of an alternative (but impossible) future; ignoring the implacable finalities of inner fissures, she has begun to exude the bitter-sweet fragrance of hope-for-marriage. My dung-lotus, who remained impervious for so long to the sneer-lipped barbs hurled by our workforce of downy-forearmed women; who placed her cohabitation with me outside and above all codes of social propriety, has seemingly succumbed to a desire for legitimacy . . . in short, although she has not said a word on the subject, she is waiting for me to make an honest woman of her. The perfume of her sad hopefulness permeates her most innocently solicitous remarks – even at this very moment, as she, 'Hey, mister, why not – finish your writery and then take rest; go to Kashmir, sit quietly for some time – and maybe you will take your Padma also, and she can look after . . . ?' Behind this burgeoning dream of a Kashmiri holiday (which was once also the dream of Jehangir, the Mughal Emperor; of poor forgotten Ilse Lubin; and, perhaps, of Christ himself), I nose out the presence of another dream; but neither this nor that can be fulfilled. Because now the cracks, the cracks and always the cracks are narrowing my future towards its single inescapable full point; and even Padma must take a back seat if I'm to finish my tales.

*

Today, the papers are talking about the supposed political rebirth of Mrs Indira Gandhi; but when I returned to India, concealed in a wicker basket, 'The Madam' was basking in the fullness of her glory. Today, perhaps, we are already forgetting, sinking willingly into the insidious clouds of amnesia; but I remember, and will set down, how I – how she – how it happened that – no, I can't say it, I must tell it in the proper order, until there is no option but to reveal . . . On December 16th, 1971, I tumbled out of a basket into an India in which Mrs Gandhi's New Congress Party held a more-than-two-thirds majority in the National Assembly.

In the basket of invisibility, a sense of unfairness turned into anger; and something else besides – transformed by rage, I had also been overwhelmed by an agonizing feeling of sympathy for the country which was not only my twin-in-birth but also joined to me (so to speak) at the hip, so that what happened to either of us, happened to us both. If I, snot-nosed stain-faced etcetera, had had a hard time of it, then so had she, my subcontinental twin sister; and now that I had given myself the right to choose a better future, I was resolved that the nation should share it, too. I think that when I tumbled out into dust, shadow and amused cheers, I had already decided to save the country.

(But there are cracks and gaps . . . had I, by then, begun to see that my love for Jamila Singer had been, in a sense, a mistake? Had I already understood how I had simply transferred on to her shoulders the adoration which I now perceived to be a vaulting, all-encompassing love of country? When was it that I realized that my truly-incestuous feelings were for my true birth-sister, India herself, and not for that trollop of a crooner who had so callously shed me, like a used snake-skin, and dropped me into the metaphorical waste-basket of Army life? When when when? . . . Admitting defeat, I am forced to record that I cannot remember for sure.)

. . . Saleem sat blinking in the dust in the shadow of the mosque. A giant was standing over him, grinning hugely, asking, 'Achha, captain, have a good trip?' And Parvati, with huge excited eyes, pouring water from a lotah into his cracked, salty mouth . . . Feeling! The icy touch of water kept cool in earthenware surahis, the cracked soreness of parched-raw lips, silver-and-lapis clenched in a fist . . . 'I can feel!' Saleem cried to the good-natured crowd.

It was the time of afternoon called the chaya, when the shadow of the tall red-brick-and-marble Friday Mosque fell across the higgledy shacks of the slum clustered at its feet, that slum whose ramshackle tin roofs created such a swelter of heat that it was insupportable to be inside the fragile shacks except during the chaya and at night . . . but now conjurers and contortionists and jugglers and fakirs had gathered in the shade around the solitary stand-pipe to greet the new arrival. 'I can feel!' I cried, and then Picture Singh, 'Okay, captain – tell us, how it feels? – to be born again, falling like baby out of Parvati's basket?' I could smell amazement on Picture Singh; he was clearly astounded by Parvati's trick, but, like a true professional, would not dream of asking her how she had achieved it. In this way Parvati-the-witch, who had used her limitless powers to spirit me to safety, escaped discovery; and also because, as I later discovered, the ghetto of the magicians disbelieved, with the absolute certainty of illusionists-by-trade, in the possibility of magic. So Picture Singh told me, with amazement, 'I swear, captain – you were so light in there, like a baby!' – But he never dreamed that my weightlessness had been anything more than a trick.

'Listen, baby sahib,' Picture Singh was crying, 'What do you say, baby-captain? Must I put you over my shoulder and make you belch?' – And now Parvati, tolerantly: 'That one, baba, always making joke shoke.' She was smiling radiantly at everyone in sight . . . but there followed an inauspicious event. A woman's voice began to wail at the back of the cluster of magicians: 'Ai-o-ai-o! Ai-o-o!' The crowd parted in surprise and an old woman burst through it and rushed at Saleem; I was required to defend myself against a brandished frying pan, until Picture Singh, alarmed, seized her by pan-waving arm and bellowed, 'Hey, capteena, why so much noise?' And the old woman, obstinately: 'Ai-o-ai-o!'

'Resham Bibi,' Parvati said, crossly, 'You got ants in your brain?' And Picture Singh, 'We got a guest, capteena – what'll he do with your shouting? Arré, be quiet, Resham, this captain is known to our Parvati personal! Don't be coming crying in front of him!'

'Ai-o-ai-o! Bad luck is come! You go to foreign places and bring it here! Ai-oooo!'

Disturbed visages of magicians stared from Resham Bibi to me – because although they were a people who denied the supernatural, they were artistes, and like all performers had an implicit faith in luck, good-luck-and-bad-luck, luck . . . 'Yourself you said,' Resham Bibi wailed, 'this man is born twice, and not even from woman! Now comes desolation, pestilence and death. I am old and so I know. Arré baba,' she turned plaintively to face me, 'Have pity only; go now – go go quick!' There was a murmur – 'It is true, Resham Bibi knows the old stories' – but then Picture Singh became angry. 'The captain is my honoured guest,' he said, 'He stays in my hut as long as he wishes, for short or for long. What are you all talking? This is no place for fables.'

Saleem Sinai's first sojourn at the magicians' ghetto lasted only a matter of days; but during that short time, a number of things happened to allay the fears which had been raised by ai-o-ai-o. The plain, unadorned truth is that, in those days, the ghetto illusionists and other artistes began to hit new peaks of achievement – jugglers managed to keep one thousand and one balls in the air at a time, and a fakir's as-yet-untrained protégée strayed on to a bed of hot coals, only

540

to stroll across it unconcerned, as though she had acquired her mentor's gifts by osmosis; I was told that the rope-trick had been successfully performed. Also, the police failed to make their monthly raid on the ghetto, which had not happened within living memory; and the camp received a constant stream of visitors, the servants of the rich, requesting the professional services of one or more of the colony at this or that gala evening's entertainment . . . it seemed, in fact, as though Resham Bibi had got things the wrong way round, and I rapidly became very popular in the ghetto. I was dubbed Saleem Kismeti, Lucky Saleem; Parvati was congratulated on having brought me to the slum. And finally Picture Singh brought Resham Bibi to apologize.

'Pol'gize,' Resham said toothlessly and fled; Picture Singh added, 'It is hard for the old ones; their brains go raw and remember upside down. Captain, here everyone is saying you are our luck; but will you go from us soon?' – And Parvati, staring dumbly with saucer eyes which begged no no no; but I was obliged to answer in the affirmative.

Saleem, today, is certain that he answered, 'Yes'; that on the selfsame morning, still dressed in shapeless robe, still inseparable from a silver spittoon, he walked away, without looking back at a girl who followed him with eyes moistened with accusations; that, strolling hastily past practising jugglers and sweetmeat-stalls which filled his nostrils with the temptations of rasgullas, past barbers offering shaves for ten paisa, past the derelict maunderings of crones and the American-accented caterwauls of shoe-shine boys who importuned bus-loads of Japanese tourists in identical blue suits and incongruous saffron turbans which had been tied around their heads by obsequiously mischievous guides, past the towering flight of stairs to the Friday Mosque, past vendors of notions and itr-essences and plaster-of-Paris replicas of the Qutb Minar and painted toy horses and fluttering unslaughtered chickens, past invitations to cockfights and empty-eyed games

541

of cards, he emerged from the ghetto of the illusionists and found himself on Faiz Bazar, facing the infinitely-extending walls of a Red Fort from whose ramparts a prime minister had once announced independence, and in whose shadow a woman had been met by a peepshow-merchant, a Dilli-dekho man who had taken her into narrowing lanes to hear her son's future foretold amongst mongeese and vultures and broken men with leaves bandaged around their arms; that, to be brief, he turned to his right and walked away from the Old City towards the roseate palaces built by pink-skinned conquerors long ago: abandoning my saviours, I went into New Delhi on foot.

Why? Why, ungratefully spurning the nostalgic grief of Parvati-the-witch, did I set my face against the old and journey into newness? Why, when for so many years I had found her my staunchest ally in the nocturnal congresses of my mind, did I leave her so lightly in the morning? Fighting past fissured blanks, I am able to remember two reasons; but am unable to say which was paramount, or if a third . . . firstly, at any rate, I had been taking stock. Saleem, analysing his prospects, had had no option but to admit to himself that they were not good. I was passport-less; in law an illegal immigrant (having once been a legal emigrant); P.O.W. camps were waiting for me everywhere. And even after setting aside my status as defeated-soldier-on-the-run, the list of my disadvantages remained formidable: I had neither funds nor a change of clothes; nor qualifications – having neither completed my education nor distinguished myself in that part of it which I had undergone; how was I to embark on my ambitious project of nation-saving without a roof over my head or a family to protect support assist . . . it struck me like a thunderclap that I was wrong; that here, in this very city, I had relatives – and not only relatives, but influential ones! My uncle Mustapha Aziz, a senior Civil Servant, who when last heard of had been number two in his Department;

what better patron than he for my Messianic ambitions? Under his roof, I could acquire contacts as well as new clothes; under his auspices, I would seek preferment in the Administration, and, as I studied the realities of government, would certainly find the keys of national salvation; and I would have the ears of Ministers, I would perhaps be on first-name terms with the great . . . ! It was in the clutches of this magnificent fantasy that I told Parvati-the-witch, 'I must be off; great matters are afoot!' And, seeing the hurt in her suddenly-inflamed cheeks, consoled her: 'I will come and see you often. Often often.' But she was not consoled . . . high-mindedness, then, was one motive for abandoning those who had helped me; but was there not something meaner, lowlier, more personal? There was. Parvati had drawn me secretly aside behind a tin-and-cratewood shack; where cockroaches spawned, where rats made love, where flies gorged themselves on pie-dog dung, she clutched me by the wrist and became incandescent of eye and sibilant of tongue; hidden in the putrid underbelly of the ghetto, she confessed that I was not the first of the midnight children to have crossed her path! And now there was a story of a Dacca procession, and magicians marching alongside heroes; there was Parvati looking up at a tank, and there were Parvati-eyes alighting on a pair of gigantic, prehensile knees . . . knees bulging proudly through starched-pressed uniform; there was Parvati crying, 'O you! O you . . .' and then the unspeakable name, the name of my guilt, of someone who should have led my life but for a crime in a nursing home; Parvati and Shiva, Shiva and Parvati, fated to meet by the divine destiny of their names, were united in the moment of victory. 'A hero, man!' she hissed proudly behind the shack. 'They will make him a big officer and all!' And now what was produced from a fold of her ragged attire? What once grew proudly on a hero's head and now nestled against a sorceress's breasts? 'I asked and he gave,' said Parvati-the-witch, and showed me a lock of his hair.

Did I run from that lock of fateful hair? Did Saleem, fearing a reunion with his alter ego, whom he had so-long-ago banned from the councils of the night, flee back into the bosom of that family whose comforts had been denied the war-hero? Was it high-mindedness or guilt? I can no longer say; I set down only what I remember, namely that Parvati-the-witch whispered, 'Maybe he will come when he has time; and then we will be three!' And another, repeated phrase: 'Midnight's children, yaar . . . that's something, no?' Parvati-the-witch reminded me of things I had tried to put out of my mind; and I walked away from her, to the home of Mustapha Aziz.

Of my last miserable contact with the brutal intimacies of family life, only fragments remain; however, since it must all be set down and subsequently pickled, I shall attempt to piece together an account . . . to begin with, then, let me report that my Uncle Mustapha lived in a commodiously anonymous Civil Service bungalow set in a tidy Civil Service garden just off Rajpath in the heart of Lutyens's city; I walked along what-had-once-been-Kingsway, breathing in the numberless perfumes of the street, which blew out of State Handicraft Emporia and the exhaust-pipes of auto-rickshaws; the aromas of banyan and deodar mingled with the ghostly scents of long-gone viceroys and memsahibs in gloves, and also with the rather more strident bodily odours of gaudy rich begums and tramps. Here was the giant election Scoreboard around which (during the first battle-for-power between Indira and Morarji Desai) crowds had thronged, awaiting the results, asking eagerly: 'Is it a boy or a girl?' . . . amid ancient and modern, between India Gate and the Secretariat buildings, my thoughts teeming with vanished (Mughal and British) empires and also with my own history – because this was the city of the public announcement, of many-headed monsters and a hand, falling from the sky – I marched resolutely onwards, smelling, like everything else in sight, to high heaven. And at last, having turned left towards Dupleix Road, I arrived at an anonymous garden with a low wall and a hedge; in a corner of which I saw a signboard waving in the breeze, just as once signboards had flowered in the gardens of Methwold's Estate; but this echo of the past told a different story. NOT FOR SALE, with its three ominous vowels and four fateful consonants; the wooden flower of my uncle's garden proclaimed strangely: *Mr Mustapha Aziz and Fly.*

Not knowing that the last word was my uncle's habitual, desiccated abbreviation of the throbbingly emotional noun 'family', I was thrown into confusion by the nodding signboard; after I had stayed in his household for a very short time, however, it began to seem entirely fitting, because the family of Mustapha Aziz was indeed as crushed, as insect-like, as insignificant as that mythically truncated Fly.

With what words was I greeted when, a little nervously, I rang a doorbell, filled with hopes of beginning a new career? What face appeared behind the wire-netted outer door and scowled in angry surprise? Padma: I was greeted by Uncle Mustapha's wife, by my mad aunt Sonia, with the exclamation; '*Ptui!* Allah! How the fellow stinks!'

And although I, ingratiatingly, 'Hullo, Sonia Aunty darling,' grinned sheepishly at this wire-netting-shaded vision of my aunt's wrinkling Irani beauty, she went on, 'Saleem, is it? Yes, I remember you. Nasty little brat you were. Always thought you were growing up to be God or what. And why? Some stupid letter the P.M.'s fifteenth assistant under-secretary must have sent you.' In that first meeting I should have been able to foresee the destruction of my plans; I should have smelled, on my mad aunt, the implacable odours of Civil Service jealousy, which would thwart all my attempts to gain a place in the world. I had been sent a letter, and she never had; it made us enemies for life. But there was a door, opening; there were whiffs of clean clothes and shower-baths;

and I, grateful for small mercies, failed to examine the deadly perfumes of my aunt.

My uncle Mustapha Aziz, whose once-proudly-waxed moustache had never recovered from the paralysing dust-storm of the destruction of Methwold's Estate, had been passed over for the headship of his Department no less than forty-seven times, and had at last found consolation for his inadequacies in thrashing his children, in ranting nightly about how he was clearly the victim of anti-Muslim prejudice, in a contradictory but absolute loyalty to the government of the day, and in an obsession with genealogies which was his only hobby and whose intensity was greater even than my father Ahmed Sinai's long-ago desire to prove himself descended from Mughal emperors. In the first of these consolations he was willingly joined by his wife, the half-Irani would-be-socialite Sonia (née Khosrovani), who had been driven certifiably insane by a life in which she had been required to begin 'being a chamcha' (literally a spoon, but idiomatically a flatterer) to forty-seven separate and succes-sive wives of number-ones whom she had previously alienated by her manner of colossal condescension when they had been the wives of number-threes; under the joint batterings of my uncle and aunt, my cousins had by now been beaten into so thorough a pulp that I am unable to recall their number, sexes, proportions or features; their personalities, of course, had long since ceased to exist. In the home of Uncle Mustapha, I sat silently amongst my pulverized cousins listening to his nightly soliloquies which contradicted themselves constantly, veering wildly between his resentment of not having been promoted and his blind lapdog devotion to every one of the Prime Minister's acts. If Indira Gandhi had asked him to commit suicide, Mustapha Aziz would have ascribed it to anti-Muslim bigotry but also defended the statesmanship of the request, and, naturally, performed the task without daring (or even wishing) to demur.

546

As for genealogies: Uncle Mustapha spent all his spare time filling giant logbooks with spider-like family trees, eternally researching into and immortalizing the bizarre lineages of the greatest families in the land; but one day during my stay my aunt Sonia heard about a rishi from Hardwar who was reputedly three hundred and ninety-five years old and had memorized the genealogies of every single Brahmin clan in the country. 'Even in that,' she screeched at my uncle, 'you end up being number two!' The existence of the Hardwar rishi completed her descent into insanity, so that her violence towards her children increased to the point at which we lived in daily expectation of murder, and in the end my uncle Mustapha was forced to have her locked away, because her excesses were embarrassing him in his work.

This, then, was the family to which I had come. Their presence in Delhi came to seem, in my eyes, like a desecration of my own past; in a city which, for me, was forever possessed by the ghosts of the young Ahmed and Amina, this terrible Fly was crawling upon sacred soil.

But what can never be proved for certain is that, in the years ahead, my uncle's genealogical obsession would be placed at the service of a government which was falling increasingly beneath the twin spells of power and astrology; so that what happened at the Widows' Hostel might never have happened without his help . . . but no, I have been a traitor, too; I do not condemn; all I am saying is that I once saw, amongst his genealogical logbooks, a black leather folder labelled TOP SECRET, and titled PROJECT M.C.C.

The end is near, and cannot be escaped much longer; but while the Indira sarkar, like her father's administration, consults daily with purveyors of occult lore; while Benarsi seers help to shape the history of India, I must digress into painful, personal recollections; because it was at Uncle Mustapha's that I learned, for certain, about the deaths of my family in the war of '65; and also about the disappearance, just a few days before my arrival, of the famous Pakistani singer Jamila Singer.

. . . When mad aunt Sonia heard that I had fought on the wrong side in the war, she refused to feed me (we were at dinner), and screeched, 'God, you have a cheek, you know that? Don't you have a brain to think with? You come to a Senior Civil Servant's house – an escaped war criminal, Allah! You want to lose your uncle his job? You want to put us all out on the street? Catch your ears for shame, boy! Go – go, get out, or better, we should call the police and hand you over just now! Go, be a prisoner of war, why should we care, you are not even our departed sister's true-born son . . .'

Thunderbolts, one after the other: Saleem fears for his safety, and simultaneously learns the inescapable truth about his mother's death, and also that his position is weaker than he thought, because in this part of his family the act of acceptance has not been made; Sonia, knowing what Mary Pereira confessed, is capable of anything! . . . And I, feebly, 'My mother? Departed?' And now Uncle Mustapha, perhaps feeling that his wife has gone too far, says reluctantly, 'Never mind, Saleem, of course you must stay – he must, wife, what else to do? – and poor fellow doesn't even know . . .'

Then they told me.

It occurred to me, in the heart of that crazy Fly, that I owed the dead a number of mourning periods; after I learned of the demise of my mother and father and aunts Alia and Pia and Emerald, of cousin Zafar and his Kifi princess, of Reverend Mother and my distant relative Zohra and her husband, I resolved to spend the next four hundred days in mourning, as was right and proper: ten mourning periods, of forty days each. And then, and then, there was the matter of Jamila Singer . . .

She had heard about my disappearance in the turmoil of the war in Bangladesh; she, who always showed her love when it was too late, had perhaps been driven a little crazy by the news. Jamila, the Voice of Pakistan, Bulbul-of-the-Faith, had spoken out against the new rulers of truncated, moth-eaten, war-divided Pakistan; while Mr Bhutto was telling the U.N. Security Council, 'We will build a new Pakistan! A better Pakistan! My country hearkens for me!', my sister was reviling him in public; she, purest of the pure, most patriotic of patriots, turned rebel when she heard about my death. (That, at least, is how I see it; all I heard from my uncle were the bald facts; he had heard them through diplomatic channels, which do not go in for psychological theorizing.) Two days after her tirade against the perpetrators of the war, my sister had vanished off the face of the earth. Uncle Mustapha tried to speak gently: 'Very bad things are happening over there, Saleem; people disappearing all the time; we must fear the worst.'

No! No no no! Padma: he was wrong! Jamila did not disappear into the clutches of the State; because that same night, I dreamed that she, in the shadows of darkness and the secrecy of a simple veil, not the instantly recognizable gold-brocade tent of Uncle Puffs but a common black burqa, fled by air from the capital city; and here she is, arriving in Karachi, unquestioned unarrested free, she is taking a taxi into the depths of the city, and now there is a high wall with bolted doors and a hatch through which, once, long ago, I received bread, the leavened bread of my sister's weakness, she is asking to be let in, nuns are opening doors as she cries sanctuary, yes, there she is, safely inside, doors being bolted behind her, exchanging one kind of invisibility for another, there is another Reverend Mother now, as Jamila Singer who once, as the Brass Monkey, flirted with Christianity, finds safety shelter peace in the midst of the hidden order of Santa Ignacia . . . yes, she is there, safe, not vanished, not in the grip of police who kick beat starve, but at rest, not in an unmarked grave by the side of the Indus, but alive, baking bread, singing sweetly to the secret nuns; I know, I know, I know. How do I know? A brother knows; that's all.

Responsibility, assaulting me yet again: because there is no way out of it – Jamila's fall was, as usual, all my fault.

I lived in the home of Mr Mustapha Aziz for four hundred and twenty days . . . Saleem was in belated mourning for his dead; but do not think for one moment that my ears were closed! Don't assume I didn't hear what was being said around me, the repeated quarrels between uncle and aunt (which may have helped him decide to consign her to the insane asylum): Sonia Aziz yelling, 'That bhangi – that dirty-filthy fellow, not even your nephew, I don't know what's got into you, we should throw him out on his ear!' And Mustapha, quietly, replying: 'Poor chap is stricken with grief, so how can we, you just have to look to see, he is not quite right in the head, has suffered many bad things.' Not quite right in the head! That was tremendous, coming from them – from that family beside which a tribe of gibbering cannibals would have seemed calm and civilized! Why did I put up with it? Because I was a man with a dream. But for four hundred and twenty days, it was a dream which failed to come true.

Droopy-moustachioed, tall-but-stooped, an eternal number-two: my Uncle Mustapha was not my Uncle Hanif. He was the head of the family now, the only one of his generation to survive the holocaust of 1965; but he gave me no help at all . . . I bearded him in his genealogy-filled study one bitter evening and explained – with proper solemnity and humble but resolute gestures – my historic mission to rescue the nation from her fate; but he sighed deeply and said, 'Listen, Saleem, what would you have me do? I keep you in my house; you eat my bread and do nothing – but that is all right, you are from my dead sister's house, and I must look after – so stay, rest, get well in yourself; then let us see. You want a clerkship or so, maybe it can be fixed; but leave these dreams of God-knows-what. Our country is in safe hands. Already Indiraji is making radical reforms – land reforms, tax structures, education, birth control – you can leave it to her and her sarkar.' Patronizing me, Padma! As if I were a foolish child! O the shame of it, the humiliating shame of being condescended to by dolts!

At every turn I am thwarted; a prophet in the wilderness, like Maslama, like ibn Sinan! No matter how I try, the desert is my lot. O vile unhelpfulness of lickspittle uncles! O fettering of ambitions by second-best toadying relatives! My uncle's rejection of my pleas for preferment had one grave effect: the more he praised his Indira, the more deeply I detested her. He was, in fact, preparing me for my return to the magicians' ghetto, and for . . . for *her* . . . the Widow.

Jealousy: that was it. The great jealousy of my mad aunt Sonia, dripping like poison into my uncle's ears, prevented him from doing a single thing to get me started on my chosen career. The great are eternally at the mercy of tiny men. And also: tiny madwomen.

On the four hundred and eighteenth day of my stay, there was a change in the atmosphere of the madhouse. Someone came to dinner: someone with a plump stomach, a tapering head covered with oily curls and a mouth as fleshy as a woman's labia. I thought I recognized him from newspaper photographs. Turning to one of my sexless ageless faceless cousins, I inquired with interest, 'Isn't it, you know, Sanjay Gandhi?' But the pulverized creature was too annihilated to be capable of replying . . . was it wasn't it? I did not, at that time, know what I now set down: that certain high-ups in that extraordinary government (and also certain unelected sons of prime ministers) had acquired the power of replicating themselves . . . a few years later, there would be gangs of Sanjays all over India! No wonder that incredible dynasty wanted to impose birth control on the rest of us . . . so maybe it was, maybe it wasn't; but someone disappeared into my uncle's study with Mustapha Aziz; and that night – I sneaked a look – there was a locked black leather folder saying TOP SECRET and also PROJECT M.C.C; and the next morning my uncle was looking at me differently, with fear almost, or with that special look of loathing which Civil Servants reserve for those who fall into official disfavour. I should have known then what was in store for me; but everything is simple with hindsight. Hindsight comes to me now, too late, now that I am finally consigned to the peripheries of history, now that the connections between my life and the nation's have broken for good and all . . . to avoid my uncle's inexplicable gaze, I went out into the garden; and saw Parvati-the-witch.

She was squatting on the pavement with the basket of invisibility by her side; when she saw me her eyes brightened with reproach. 'You said you'd come, but you never, so I,' she stuttered. I bowed my head, 'I have been in mourning,' I said, lamely, and she, 'But still you could have – my God, Saleem, you don't know, in our colony I can't tell anyone about my real magic, never, not even Picture Singh who is like a father, I must bottle it and bottle it, because they don't believe in such things, and I thought, Here is Saleem come, now at last I will have one friend, we can talk, we can be together, we have both been, and known, and arré how to say it, Saleem, you don't care, you got what you wanted and went off just like that, I am nothing to you, I know . . .'

That night my mad aunt Sonia, herself only days away from confinement in a straitjacket (it got into the papers, a small piece on an inside page; my uncle's Department must have been annoyed), had one of the fierce inspirations of the profoundly insane and burst into the bedroom into which, half an hour earlier, someone-with-saucer-eyes had climbed through a ground-floor window; she found me in bed with Parvati-the-witch, and after that my Uncle Mustapha lost interest in sheltering me, saying, 'You were born from bhangis, you will remain a dirty type all your life'; on the four hundred and twentieth day after my arrival, I left my uncle's house, deprived of family ties, returned at last to that true inheritance of poverty and destitution of which I had been cheated for so long by the crime of Mary Pereira. Parvati-the-witch was waiting for me on the pavement; I did not tell her that there was a sense in which I'd been glad of the interruption, because as I kissed her in the dark of that illicit midnight I had seen her face changing, becoming the face of a forbidden love; the ghostly features of Jamila Singer replaced those of the witch-girl; Jamila who was (I know it!) safely hidden in a Karachi nunnery was suddenly also here, except that she had undergone a dark transformation. She had begun to rot, the dreadful pustules and cankers of forbidden love were spreading across her face; just as once the ghost of Joe D'Costa had rotted in the grip of the occult leprosy of guilt, so now the rancid flowers of incest blossomed on my sister's phantasmal features, and I couldn't do it, couldn't kiss touch look upon that intolerable spectral face, I had been on the verge of jerking away with a cry of desperate nostalgia and shame when Sonia Aziz burst in upon us with electric light and screams.

And as for Mustapha, well, my indiscretion with Parvati may also have been, in his eyes, no more than a useful pretext for getting rid of me; but that must remain in doubt, because the black folder was locked – all I have to go on is a look in his eye, a smell of fear, three initials on a label – because afterwards, when everything was finished, a fallen lady and her labia-lipped son spent two days behind locked doors, burning files; and how can we know whether-or-not one of them was labelled M.C.C.?

I didn't want to stay, anyway. Family: an overrated idea. Don't think I was sad! Never for a moment imagine that lumps arose in my throat at my expulsion from the last gracious home open to me! I tell you – I was in fine spirits when I left . . . maybe there is something unnatural about me, some fundamental lack of emotional response; but my thoughts have always aspired to higher things. Hence my resilience. Hit me: I bounce back. (But no resistance is of any use against the cracks.)

To sum up: forsaking my earlier, naive hopes of preferment in public service, I returned to the magicians' slum and the chaya of the Friday Mosque. Like Gautama, the first and true Buddha, I left my life and comfort and went like a beggar into the world. The date was February 23rd, 1973; coal-mines and the wheat market were being nationalized, the price of oil had begun to spiral up up up, would quadruple in a year, and in the Communist Party of India, the split between Dange's Moscow faction and Namboodiripad's C.P.I.(M.) had become unbridgeable; and I, Saleem Sinai, like India, was twenty-five years, six months and eight days old.

The magicians were Communists, almost to a man. That's right: reds! Insurrectionists, public menaces, the scum of the earth – a community of the godless living blasphemously in the very shadow of the house of God! Shameless, what's more; innocently scarlet; born with the bloody taint upon their souls! And let me say at once that no sooner had I discovered this than I, who had been raised in India's other true faith, which we may term Businessism, and who had abandoned-been-abandoned-by its practitioners, felt instantly and comfortingly at home. A renegade Businessist, I began zealously to turn red and then redder, as surely and completely as my father had once turned white, so that now my mission of saving-the-country could be seen in a new light; more revolutionary methodologies suggested themselves. Down with the rule of unco-operative box-wallah uncles and their beloved leaders! Full of thoughts of direct-communication-with-the-masses, I settled into the magicians' colony, scraping a living by amusing foreign and native tourists with the marvellous perspicacities of my nose, which enabled me to smell out their simple, touristy secrets. Picture Singh asked me to share his shack. I slept on tattered sackcloth amongst baskets sibilant with snakes; but I did not mind, just as I found myself capable of tolerating hunger thirst mosquitoes and (in the beginning) the bitter cold of a Delhi winter. This Picture Singh, the Most Charming Man In The World, was also the ghetto's unquestioned chieftain; squabbles and problems were resolved beneath the shade of his ubiquitous and enormous black umbrella; and I, who could read and write as well as smell, became a sort of aide-de-camp to this monumental man who invariably added a lecture on socialism to his serpentine performances, and who was famous in the main streets and alleys of the city for more than his snake-charmer's skills. I can say, with utter certainty, that Picture Singh was the greatest man I ever met.

One afternoon during the chaya, the ghetto was visited by another copy of that labia-lipped youth whom I'd seen at my Uncle Mustapha's. Standing on the steps of the mosque, he unfurled a banner which was then held up by two assistants. It read: ABOLISH POVERTY, and bore the cow-suckling-calf symbol of the Indira Congress. His face looked remarkably like a plump calf's face, and he unleashed a typhoon of halitosis when he spoke. 'Brothers-O! Sisters-O! What does Congress say to you? This: that all men are created equal!' He got no further; the crowd recoiled from his breath of bullock dung under a hot sun, and Picture Singh began to guffaw. 'O ha ha, captain, too good, sir!' And labia-lips, foolishly: 'Okay, you, brother, won't you share the joke?' Picture Singh shook his head, clutched his sides: 'O speech, captain! Absolute master speech!' His laughter rolled out from beneath his umbrella to infect the crowd until all of us were rolling on the ground, laughing, crushing ants, getting covered in dust, and the Congress mooncalf's voice rose in panic: 'What is this? This fellow doesn't think we are equals?

What a low impression he must have –' but now Picture
Singh, umbrella-over-head, was striding away towards his
hut. Labia-lips, in relief, continued his speech . . . but not for
long, because Picture returned, carrying under his left arm a
small circular lidded basket and under his right armpit a
wooden flute. He placed the basket on the step beside the
Congress-wallah's feet; removed the lid; raised flute to lips.
Amid renewed laughter, the young politico leaped nineteen
inches into the air as a king cobra swayed sleepily up from its
home . . . Labia-lips is crying: 'What are you doing? Trying to
kill me to death?' And Picture Singh, ignoring him, his
umbrella furled now, plays on, more and more furiously, and
the snake uncoils, faster faster Picture Singh plays until the
flute's music fills every cranny of the slum and threatens to
scale the walls of the mosque, and at last the great snake,
hanging in the air, supported only by the enchantment of the
tune, stands nine feet long out of the basket and dances on its
tail . . . Picture Singh relents. Nagaraj subsides into coils. The
Most Charming Man In The World offers the flute to the
Congress youth: 'Okay, captain,' Picture Singh says agree-
ably, 'you give it a try.' But labia-lips: 'Man, you know I
couldn't do it!' Whereupon Picture Singh seizes the cobra just
below the head, opens his own mouth wide wide wide,
displaying an heroic wreckage of teeth and gums; winking
left-eyed at the Congress youth, he inserts the snake's tongue-
flicking head into his hideously yawning orifice! A full minute
passes before Picture Singh returns the cobra to its basket.
Very kindly, he tells the youth: 'You see, captain, here is the
truth of the business: some persons are better, others are less.
But it may be nice for you to think otherwise.'

  Watching this scene, Saleem Sinai learned that Picture
Singh and the magicians were people whose hold on reality
was absolute; they gripped it so powerfully that they could
bend it every which way in the service of their arts, but they
never forgot what it was.

The problems of the magicians' ghetto were the problems of the Communist movement in India; within the confines of the colony could be found, in miniature, the many divisions and dissensions which racked the Party in the country. Picture Singh, I hasten to add, was above it all; the patriarch of the ghetto, he was the possessor of an umbrella whose shade could restore harmony to the squabbling factions; but the disputes which were brought into the shelter of the snake-charmer's umbrella were becoming more and more bitter, as the prestidigitators, the pullers of rabbits from hats, aligned themselves firmly behind Mr Dange's Moscow-line official C.P.I., which supported Mrs Gandhi throughout the Emergency; the contortionists, however, began to lean more towards the left and the slanting intricacies of the Chinese-oriented wing. Fire-eaters and sword-swallowers applauded the guerrilla tactics of the Naxalite movement; while mesmerists and walkers-on-hot-coals espoused Namboodiripad's manifesto (neither Muscovite nor Pekinese) and deplored the Naxalites' violence. There were Trotskyist tendencies amongst card-sharpers, and even a Communism-through-the-ballot-box movement amongst the moderate members of the ventriloquist section. I had entered a milieu in which, while religious and regionalist bigotry were wholly absent, our ancient national gift for fissiparousness had found new outlets. Picture Singh told me, sorrowfully, that during the 1971 general election a bizarre murder had resulted from the quarrel between a Naxalite fire-eater and a Moscow-line conjurer who, incensed by the former's views, had attempted to draw a pistol from his magic hat; but no sooner had the weapon been produced than the supporter of Ho Chi Minh had scorched his opponent to death in a burst of terrifying flame.

Under his umbrella, Picture Singh spoke of a socialism which owed nothing to foreign influences. 'Listen, captains,' he told warring ventriloquists and puppeteers, 'will you go to your villages and talk about Stalins and Maos? Will Bihari or Tamil peasants care about the killing of Trotsky?' The chaya of his magical umbrella cooled the most intemperate of the wizards; and had the effect, on me, of convincing me that one day soon the snake-charmer Picture Singh would follow in the footsteps of Mian Abdullah so many years ago; that, like the legendary Hummingbird, he would leave the ghetto to shape the future by the sheer force of his will; and that, unlike my grandfather's hero, he would not be stopped until he, and his cause, had won the day . . . but, but. Always a but but. What happened, happened. We all know that.

Before I return to telling the story of my private life, I should like it to be known that it was Picture Singh who revealed to me that the country's corrupt, 'black' economy had grown as large as the official, 'white' variety, which he did by showing me a newspaper photograph of Mrs Gandhi. Her hair, parted in the centre, was snow-white on one side and blackasnight on the other, so that, depending on which profile she presented, she resembled either a stoat or an ermine. Recurrence of the centre-parting in history; and also, economy as an analogue of a Prime Ministerial hairstyle . . . I owe these important perceptions to the Most Charming Man In The World. Picture Singh it was who told me that Mishra, the railway minister, was also the officially-appointed minister for bribery, through whom the biggest deals in the black economy were cleared, and who arranged for pay-offs to appropriate ministers and officials; without Picture Singh, I might never have known about the poll-fixing in the state elections in Kashmir. He was no lover of democracy, however: 'God damn this election business, captain,' he told me, 'Whenever they come, something bad happens; and our countrymen behave like clowns.' I, in the grip of my fever-for-revolution, failed to take issue with my mentor.

*

558

There were, of course, a few exceptions to the ghetto's rules: one or two conjurers retained their Hindu faith and, in politics, espoused the Hindusectarian Jana Sangh party or the notorious Ananda Marg extremists; there were even Swatantra voters amongst the jugglers. Non-politically speaking, the old lady Resham Bibi was one of the few members of the community who remained an incurable fantasist, believing (for instance) in the superstition which forbade women to climb mango trees, because a mango tree which had once borne the weight of a woman would bear sour fruit for ever more . . . and there was the strange fakir named Chishti Khan, whose face was so smooth and lustrous that nobody knew whether he was nineteen or ninety, and who had surrounded his shack with a fabulous creation of bamboo-sticks and scraps of brightly-coloured paper, so that his home looked like a miniature, multi-coloured replica of the nearby Red Fort. Only when you passed through its castellated gateway did you realize that behind the meticulously hyperbolic façade of bamboo-and-paper crenellations and ravelins hid a tin-and-cardboard hovel like all the rest. Chishti Khan had committed the ultimate solecism of permitting his illusionist expertise to infect his real life; he was not popular in the ghetto. The magicians kept their distance, lest they become diseased by his dreams.

So you will understand why Parvati-the-witch, the possessor of truly wondrous powers, had kept them secret all her life; the secret of her midnight-given gifts would not have been easily forgiven by a community which had constantly denied such possibilities.

On the blind side of the Friday Mosque, where the magicians were out of sight, and the only danger was from scavengers-after-scrap, from searchers-for-abandoned crates or hunters-for-corrugated-tin . . . that was where Parvati-the-witch, eager as mustard, showed me what she could do. In a humbie shalwar-kameez constructed from the ruins of a dozen others, midnight's sorceress performed for me with the verve and enthusiasm of a child. Saucer-eye, rope-like pony-tail, fine full red lips . . . I would never have resisted her for so long if not for the face, the sick decaying eyes nose lips of . . . There seemed at first to be no limits to Parvati's abilities. (But there were.) Well, then: were demons conjured? Did djinns appear, offering riches and overseas travel on levitating rugs? Were frogs turned into princes, and did stones metamorphose into jewels? Was there selling-of-souls, and raising of the dead? Not a bit of it; the magic which Parvati-the-witch performed for me – the only magic she was ever willing to perform – was of the type known as 'white'. It was as though the Brahmins' 'Secret Book', the Atharva-Veda, had revealed all its secrets to her; she could cure disease and counter poisons (to prove this, she permitted snakes to bite her, and fought the venom with a strange ritual, involving praying to the snake-god Takshasa, drinking water infused with the goodness of the Krimuka tree and the powers of old, boiled garments, and reciting a spell: *Garudamand, the eagle, drank of poison, but it was powerless; in a like manner have I deflected its power, as an arrow is deflected*) – she could cure sores and consecrate talismans – she knew the sraktya charm and the Rite of the Tree. And all this, in a series of extraordinary night-time displays, she revealed to me beneath the walls of the Mosque – but still she was not happy.

As ever, I am obliged to accept responsibility; the scent of mournfulness which hung around Parvati-the-witch was my creation. Because she was twenty-five years old, and wanted more from me than my willingness to be her audience; God knows why, but she wanted me in her bed – or, to be precise, to lie with her on the length of sackcloth which served her for a bed in the hovel she shared with a family of contortionist triplets from Kerala, three girls who were orphans just like her – just like myself.

What she did for me: under the power of her magic, hair began to grow where none had grown since Mr Zagallo pulled too hard; her wizardry caused the birthmarks on my face to fade under the healing applications of herbal poultices; it seemed that even the bandiness of my legs was diminishing under her care. (She could do nothing, however, for my one bad ear; there is no magic on earth strong enough to wipe out the legacies of one's parents.) But no matter how much she did for me, I was unable to do for her the thing she desired most; because although we lay down together beneath the walls on the blind side of the Mosque, the moonlight showed me her night-time face turning, always turning into that of my distant, vanished sister . . . no, not my sister . . . into the putrid, vilely disfigured face of Jamila Singer. Parvati anointed her body with unguent oils imbued with erotic charm; she combed her hair a thousand times with a comb made from aphrodisiac deer-bones; and (I do not doubt it) in my absence she must have tried all manner of lovers' sorceries; but I was in the grip of an older bewitchment, and could not, it seemed, be released; I was doomed to find the faces of women who loved me turning into the features of . . . but you know whose crumbling features appeared, filling my nostrils with their unholy stench.

'Poor girl,' Padma sighs, and I agree; but until the Widow drained me of past present future, I remained under the Monkey's spell.

When Parvati-the-witch finally admitted failure, her face developed, overnight, an alarming and pronounced pout. She fell asleep in the hut of the contortionist orphans and awoke with her full lips stuck in a protruding attitude of unutterably sensuous pique. Orphaned triplets told her, giggling worriedly, what had happened to her face; she tried spiritedly to pull her features back into position, but neither muscles nor wizardry managed to restore her to her former self; at last, resigning herself to her tragedy, Parvati gave in, so that Resham Bibi told anyone who would listen: 'That poor girl – a god must have blown on her when she was making a face.'

(That year, incidentally, the chic ladies of the cities were all wearing just such an expression with erotic deliberation; the haughty mannequins in the Eleganza-'73 fashion show all pouted as they walked their catwalks. In the awful poverty of the magicians' slum, pouting Parvati-the-witch was in the height of facial fashion.)

The magicians devoted much of their energies to the problem of making Parvati smile again. Taking time off from their work, and also from the more mundane chores of reconstructing tin-and-cardboard huts which had fallen down in a high wind, or killing rats, they performed their most difficult tricks for her pleasure; but the pout remained in place. Resham Bibi made a green tea which smelled of camphor and forced it down Parvati's gullet. The tea had the effect of constipating her so thoroughly that she was not seen defecating behind her hovel for nine weeks. Two young jugglers conceived the notion that she might have begun grieving for her deceased father all over again, and applied themselves to the task of drawing his portrait on a shred of old tarpaulin, which they hung above her sackcloth mat. Triplets made jokes, and Picture Singh, greatly distressed, made cobras tie themselves in knots; but none of it worked, because if Parvati's thwarted love was beyond her own powers to cure, what hope could the others have had? The power of Parvati's pout created, in the ghetto, a nameless sense of unease, which all the magicians' animosity towards the unknown could not entirely dispel.

And then Resham Bibi hit upon an idea. 'Fools that we are,' she told Picture Singh, 'we don't see what is under our noses. The poor girl is twenty-five, baba – almost an old woman! She is pining for a husband!' Picture Singh was impressed. 'Resham Bibi,' he told her approvingly, 'your brain is not yet dead.'

After that, Picture Singh applied himself to the task of finding Parvati a suitable young man; many of the younger men in the ghetto were coaxed bullied threatened. A number of candidates were produced; but Parvati rejected them all. On the night when she told Bismillah Khan, the most promising fire-eater in the colony, to go somewhere else with his breath of hot chillies, even Picture Singh despaired. That night, he said to me, 'Captain, that girl is a trial and a grief to me; she is your good friend, you got any ideas?' Then an idea occurred to him, an idea which had had to wait until he became desperate because even Picture Singh was affected by considerations of class – automatically thinking of me as 'too good' for Parvati, because of my supposedly 'higher' birth, the ageing Communist had not thought until now that I might be . . . 'Tell me one thing, captain,' Picture Singh asked shyly, 'you are planning to be married some day?'

Saleem Sinai felt panic rising up inside himself.

'Hey, listen, captain, you like the girl, hey?' – And I, unable to deny it, 'Of course.' And now Picture Singh, grinning from ear to ear, while snakes hissed in baskets: 'Like her a lot, captain? A *lot* lot?' But I was thinking of Jamila's face in the night; and made a desperate decision: 'Pictureji, I can't marry her.' And now he, frowning: 'Are you maybe married already, captain? Got wife-children waiting somewhere?' Nothing for it now; I, quietly, shamefully, said: 'I can't marry anyone, Pictureji. I can't have children.'

The silence in the shack was punctuated by sibilant snakes and the calls of wild dogs in the night.

'You're telling truth, captain? Is a medical fact?'

'Yes.'

'Because one must not lie about such things, captain. To lie about one's manhood is bad, bad luck. Anything could happen, captain.'

And I, wishing upon myself the curse of Nadir Khan, which was also the curse of my uncle Hanif Aziz and, during the freeze and its long aftermath, of my father Ahmed Sinai, was goaded into lying even more angrily: 'I tell you,' Saleem cried, 'it is true, and that's that!'

'Then, captain,' Pictureji said tragically, smacking wrist against forehead, 'God knows what to do with that poor girl.'

A wedding

I married Parvati-the-witch on February 23rd, 1975, the second anniversary of my outcast's return to the magicians' ghetto.

Stiffening of Padma: taut as a washing-line, my dung-lotus inquires: 'Married? But last night only you said you wouldn't – and why you haven't told me all these days, weeks, months . . . ?' I look at her sadly, and remind her that I have already mentioned the death of my poor Parvati, which was not a natural death . . . slowly Padma uncoils, as I continue: 'Women have made me; and also unmade. From Reverend Mother to the Widow, and even beyond, I have been at the mercy of the so-called (erroneously, in my opinion!) gentler sex. It is, perhaps, a matter of connection: is not Mother India, Bharat-Mata, commonly thought of as female? And, as you know, there's no escape from her.'

There have been thirty-two years, in this story, during which I remained unborn; soon, I may complete thirty-one years of my own. For sixty-three years, before and after midnight, women have done their best; and also, I'm bound to say, their worst.

In a blind landowner's house on the shores of a Kashmiri lake, Naseem Aziz doomed me to the inevitability of perforated sheets; and in the waters of that same lake, Ilse Lubin leaked into history, and I have not forgotten her deathwish;

Before Nadir Khan hid in his underworld, my grandmother had, by becoming Reverend Mother, begun a sequence of women who changed their names, a sequence which continues even today – and which even leaked into Nadir, who became Qasim, and sat with dancing hands in the Pioneer Café; and after Nadir's departure, my mother Mumtaz Aziz became Amina Sinai;

And Alia, with the bitterness of ages, who clothed me in the baby-things impregnated with her old-maid fury; and Emerald, who laid a table on which I made pepperpots march;

There was the Rani of Cooch Naheen, whose money, placed at the disposal of a humming man, gave birth to the optimism disease, which has recurred, at intervals, ever since; and, in the Muslim quarter of Old Delhi, a distant relative called Zohra whose flirtations gave birth, in my father, to that later weakness for Fernandas and Florys;

So to Bombay. Where Winkie's Vanita could not resist the centre-parting of William Methwold, and Nussie-the-duck lost a baby-race; while Mary Pereira, in the name of love, changed the baby-tags of history and became a second mother to me . . .

Women and women and women: Toxy Catrack, nudging open the door which would later let in the children of midnight; the terrors of her nurse Bi-Appah; the competitive love of Amina and Mary, and what my mother showed me while I lay concealed in a washing-chest: yes, the Black Mango, which forced me to sniff, and unleashed what-were-not-Archangels! . . . And Evelyn Lilith Burns, cause of a bicycle-accident, who pushed me down a two-storey hillock into the midst of history.

And the Monkey. I mustn't forget the Monkey.

But also, also, there was Masha Miovic, goading me into finger-loss, and my aunty Pia, filling my heart with revenge-lust, and Lila Sabarmati, whose indiscretions made possible my terrible, manipulating, newspaper-cut-out revenge;

And Mrs Dubash, who found my gift of a Superman comic and built it, with the help of her son, into Lord Khusro Khusrovand;

And Mary, seeing a ghost.

In Pakistan, the land of submission, the home of purity, I watched the transformation of Monkey-into-Singer, and fetched bread, and fell in love; it was a woman, Tai Bibi, who told me the truth about myself. And in the heart of my inner darkness, I turned to the Puffias, and was only narrowly saved from the threat of a golden-dentured bride.

Beginning again, as the buddha, I lay with a latrine-cleaner and was subjected to electrified urinals as a result; in the East, a farmer's wife tempted me, and Time was assassinated in consequence; and there were houris in a temple, and we only just escaped in time.

In the shadow of a mosque, Resham Bibi issued a warning.

And I married Parvati-the-witch.

'Oof, mister,' Padma exclaims, 'that's too much women!'

I do not disagree; because I have *not* even included her, whose dreams of marriage and Kashmir have inevitably been leaking into me, making me wish, if-only, if-only, so that, having once resigned myself to the cracks, I am now assailed by pangs of discontent, anger, fear and regret.

But above all, the Widow.

'I swear!' Padma slaps her knee, 'Too much, mister; too much.'

How are we to understand my too-many women? As the multiple faces of Bharat-Mata? Or as even more . . . as the dynamic aspect of maya, as cosmic energy, which is represented as the female organ?

Maya, in its dynamic aspect, is called Shakti; perhaps it is no accident that, in the Hindu pantheon, the active power of a deity is contained within his queen! Maya-Shakti mothers, but also 'muffles consciousness in its dream-web'. Too-many-women: are they all aspects of Devi, the goddess – who is

Shakti, who slew the buffalo-demon, who defeated the ogre Mahisha, who is Kali Durga Chandi Chamunda Uma Sati and Parvati . . . and who, when active, is coloured red?

'I don't know about that,' Padma brings me down to earth, 'They are just women, that's all.'

Descending from my flight of fancy, I am reminded of the importance of speed; driven on by the imperatives of rip tear crack, I abandon reflections; and begin.

This is how it came about: how Parvati took her destiny into her own hands; how a lie, issuing from my lips, brought her to the desperate condition in which, one night, she extracted from her shabby garments a lock of hero's hair, and began to speak sonorous words.

Spurned by Saleem, Parvati remembered who had once been his arch-enemy; and, taking a bamboo stick with seven knots in it, and an improvised metal hook attached to one end, she squatted in her shack and recited; with the Hook of Indra in her right hand, and a lock of hair in her left, she summoned him to her. Parvati called to Shiva; believe don't believe, but Shiva came.

From the beginning there were knees and a nose, a nose and knees; but throughout this narrative I've been pushing him, the other, into the background (just as once, I banned him from the councils of the Children). He can be concealed no longer, however; because one morning in May 1974 – is it just my cracking memory, or am I right in thinking it was the 18th, perhaps at the very moment at which the deserts of Rajasthan were being shaken by India's first nuclear explosion? Was Shiva's explosion into my life truly synchronous with India's arrival, without prior warning, at the nuclear age? – he came to the magicians' slum. Uniformed, gonged-and-pipped, and a Major now, Shiva alighted from an Army motorcycle; and even through the modest khaki of his Army pants it was easy to make out the phenomenal twin bulges of his lethal knees . . . India's most decorated war hero, but once he led a gang of apaches in the back-streets of Bombay; once, before he discovered the legitimized violence of war, prostitutes were found throttled in gutters (I know, I know – no proof); Major Shiva now, but also Wee Willie Winkie's boy, who still remembered the words of long-silenced songs: 'Good Night, Ladies' still echoed on occasion in his ears.

There are ironies here, which must not pass unnoticed; for had not Shiva risen as Saleem fell? Who was the slum-dweller now, and who looked down from commanding heights? There is nothing like a war for the re-invention of lives . . . On what may well have been May 18th, at any rate, Major Shiva came to the magicians' ghetto, and strode through the cruel streets of the slum with a strange expression on his face, which combined the infinite disdain for poverty of the recently-exalted with something more mysterious: because Major Shiva, drawn to our humble abode by the incantations of Parvati-the-witch, cannot have known what force impelled him to come.

What follows is a reconstruction of the recent career of Major Shiva; I pieced the story together from Parvati's accounts, which I got out of her after our marriage. It seems my arch-rival was fond of boasting to her about his exploits, so you may wish to make allowances for the distortions of truth which such chest-beating creates; however, there seems no reason to believe that what he told Parvati and she repeated to me was very far removed from what-was-the-case.

At the end of the war in the East, the legends of Shiva's awful exploits buzzed through the streets of the cities, leaped on to newspaper and into magazines, and thus insinuated themselves into the salons of the well-to-do, settling in clouds as thick as flies upon the eardrums of the country's hostesses, so that Shiva found himself elevated in social status as well as military rank, and was invited to a thousand and one different gatherings – banquets, musical soirées, bridge parties, diplomatic receptions, party political conferences, great melas and also smaller, local fêtes, school sports days and fashionable balls – to be applauded and monopolized by the noblest and fairest in the land, to all of whom the legends of his exploits clung like flies, walking over their eyeballs so that they saw the young man through the mist of his legend, coating their fingertips so that they touched him through the magical film of his myth, settling on their tongues so that they could not speak to him as they would to an ordinary human being. The Indian Army, which was at that time fighting a political battle against proposed expenditure cuts, understood the value of so charismatic an ambassador, and permitted the hero to circulate amongst his influential admirers; Shiva espoused his new life with a will.

He grew a luxuriant moustache to which his personal batman applied a daily pomade of linseed oil spiced with coriander; always elegantly turned out in the drawing-rooms of the mighty, he engaged in political chit-chat, and declared himself a firm admirer of Mrs Gandhi, largely because of his hatred for her opponent Morarji Desai, who was intolerably ancient, drank his own urine, had skin which rustled like rice-paper, and, as Chief Minister of Bombay, had once been responsible for the banning of alcohol and the persecution of young goondas, that is to say hooligans or apaches, or in other words, of the child Shiva himself . . . but such idle chatter occupied a mere fraction of his thoughts, the rest of which were entirely taken up with the ladies. Shiva, too, was besotted by too-much-women, and in those heady days after the military victory acquired a secret reputation which (he boasted to Parvati) rapidly grew to rival his official, public fame – a 'black' legend to set beside the 'white' one. What was whispered at the hen-parties and canasta-evenings of the land? What was hissed through giggles wherever two or three glittering ladies got together? This: Major Shiva was becoming a notorious seducer; a ladies'-man; a cuckolder of the rich; in short, a stud.

There were women – he told Parvati – wherever he went: their curving bird-soft bodies quaking beneath the weight of their jewellery and lust, their eyes misted over by his legend; it would have been difficult to refuse them even had he wanted to. But Major Shiva had no intention of refusing. He listened sympathetically to their little tragedies – impotent husbands, beatings, lack-of-attention – to whatever excuses the lovely creatures wished to offer. Like my grandmother at her petrol pump (but with more sinister motives) he gave patient audience to their woes; sipping whisky in the chandeliered splendour of ballrooms, he watched them batting their eyelids and breathing suggestively while they moaned; and always, at last, they contrived to drop a handbag, or spill a drink, or knock his swagger-stick from his grasp, so that he would have to stoop to the floor to retrieve whatever-had-fallen, and then he would see the notes tucked into their sandals, sticking daintily out from under painted toes. In those days (if the Major is to be believed) the lovely scandalous begums of India became awfully clumsy, and their chappals spoke of rendezvous-at-midnight, of trellises of bougainvillaea outside bedroom windows, of husbands conveniently away launching ships or exporting tea or buying ball-bearings from Swedes. While these unfortunates were away, the Major visited their homes to steal their most prized possessions: their women fell into his arms. It is possible (I have divided by half the Major's own figures) that at the height of his philanderings there were no less than ten thousand women in love with him.

And certainly there were children. The spawn of illicit midnights. Beautiful bouncing infants secure in the cradles of the rich. Strewing bastards across the map of India, the war hero went his way; but (and this, too, is what he told Parvati) he suffered from the curious fault of losing interest in anyone who became pregnant; no matter how beautiful sensuous loving they were, he deserted the bedrooms of all who bore his children; and lovely ladies with red-rimmed eyes were obliged to persuade their cuckolded husbands that yes, of course it's your baby, darling, life-of-mine, doesn't it look just like you, and of course I'm not sad, why should I be, these are tears of joy.

One such deserted mother was Roshanara, the child-wife of the steel magnate S. P. Shetty; and at the Mahalaxmi Racecourse in Bombay, she punctured the mighty balloon of his pride. He had been promenading about the paddock, stooping every few yards to return ladies' shawls and parasols, which seemed to acquire a life of their own and spring out of their owners' hands as he passed; Roshanara Shetty confronted him here, standing squarely in his path and refusing to budge, her seventeen-year-old eyes filled with the ferocious pique of childhood. He greeted her coolly, touching his Army cap, and attempted to pass; but she dug her needle-sharp nails into his arm, smiling dangerously as ice, and strolled along beside him. As they walked she poured her infantile poison into his ear, and her hatred and resentment of her former lover gave her the skill to make him believe her. Callously she whispered that it was so funny, my God, the way he strutted around in high society like some kind of rooster, while all the time the ladies were laughing at him behind his back, O yes, Major Sahib, don't fool yourself, high-class women have always enjoyed sleeping with animals peasants brutes, but that's how we think of you, my God it's disgusting just to watch you eat, gravy down your chin, don't you think we see how you never hold teacups by their handles, do you imagine we can't hear your belches and breakings of wind, you're just our pet ape, Major Sahib, very useful, but basically a clown.

After the onslaught of Roshanara Shetty, the young war hero began to see his world differently. Now he seemed to see women giggling behind fans wherever he went; he noticed strange amused sidelong glances which he'd never noticed before; and although he tried to improve his behaviour, it was no use, he seemed to become clumsier the harder he tried, so that food flew off his plate on to priceless Kelim rugs and belches broke from his throat with the roar of a train emerging from a tunnel and he broke wind with the rage of typhoons. His glittering new life became, for him, a daily humiliation; and now he reinterpreted the advances of the beautiful ladies, understanding that by placing their love-notes beneath their toes they were obliging him to kneel demeaningly at their feet ... as he learned that a man may possess every manly attribute and still be despised for not knowing how to hold a spoon, he felt an old violence being renewed in him, a hatred for these high-ups and their power, which is why I am sure – why I *know* – that when the Emergency offered Shiva-of-the-knees the chance of grabbing some power for himself, he did not wait to be asked a second time.

On May 15th, 1974, Major Shiva returned to his regiment in Delhi; he claimed that, three days later, he was suddenly seized by a desire to see once more the saucer-eyed beauty whom he had first encountered long ago in the conference of the Midnight Children; the pony-tailed temptress who had asked him, in Dacca, for a single lock of his hair. Major Shiva declared to Parvati that his arrival at the magicians' ghetto had been motivated by a desire to be done with the rich bitches of Indian high society; that he had been besotted by her pouting lips the moment he laid eyes on them; and that these were the only reasons for asking her to go away with him. But I have already been overgenerous to Major Shiva – in this, my own personal version of history, I have allowed his account too much space; so I insist that, whatever the knock-kneed Major might have thought, the thing that drew him into the ghetto was quite simply and straightforwardly the magic of Parvati-the-witch.

Saleem was not in the ghetto when Major Shiva arrived by motorcycle; while nuclear explosions rocked the Rajasthani wastes, out of sight, beneath the desert's surface, the explosion which changed my life also took place out of my sight. When Shiva grasped Parvati by the wrist, I was with Picture Singh at an emergency conference of the city's many red cells, discussing the ins and outs of the national railway strike; when Parvati, without demurring, took her place on the pillion of a hero's Honda, I was busily denouncing the government's arrests of union leaders. In short, while I was preoccupied with politics and my dream of national salvation, the powers of Parvati's witchcraft had set in motion the scheme which would end with hennaed palms, and songs, and the signing of a contract.

. . . I am obliged, perforce, to reply on the accounts of others; only Shiva could tell what had befallen him; it was Resham Bibi who described Parvati's departure to me on my return, saying, 'Poor girl, let her go, so sad she has been for so long, what is to blame?'; and only Parvati could recount to me what befell her while she was away.

Because of the Major's national status as a war hero, he was permitted to take certain liberties with military regulations; so nobody took him to task for importing a woman into what were not, after all, married men's quarters; and he, not knowing what had brought about this remarkable alteration in his life, sat down as requested in a cane chair, while she took off his boots, pressed his feet, brought him water flavoured with freshly-squeezed limes, dismissed his batman, oiled his moustache, caressed his knees and after all that produced a dinner of biriani so exquisite that he stopped wondering what was happening to him and began to enjoy it instead. Parvati-the-witch turned those simple Army quarters into a palace, a Kailasa fit for Shiva-the-god; and Major Shiva, lost in the haunted pools of her eyes, aroused beyond endurance by the erotic protrusion of her lips, devoted his undivided attentions to her for four whole months: or, to be precise, for one hundred and seventeen nights. On September

12th, however, things changed: because Parvati, kneeling at his feet, fully aware of his views on the subject, told him that she was going to have his child.

The liaison of Shiva and Parvati now became a tempestuous business, filled with blows and broken plates: an earthly echo of that eternal marital battle-of-the-gods which their namesakes are said to perform atop Mount Kailasa in the great Himalayas . . . Major Shiva, at this time, began to drink; also to whore. The whoring trails of the war hero around the capital of India bore a strong resemblance to the Lambretta-travels of Saleem Sinai along the spoors of Karachi streets; Major Shiva, unmanned in the company of the rich by the revelations of Roshanara Shetty, had taken to paying for his pleasures. And such was his phenomenal fecundity (he assured Parvati while beating her) that he ruined the careers of many a loose woman by giving them babies whom they would love too much to expose; he sired around the capital an army of street-urchins to mirror the regiment of bastards he had fathered on the begums of the chandeliered salons.

Dark clouds were gathering in political skies as well: in Bihar, where corruption inflation hunger illiteracy landlessness ruled the roost, Jaya-Prakash Narayan led a coalition of students and workers against the governing Indira Congress; in Gujarat, there were riots, railway trains were burned, and Morarji Desai went on a fast-unto-death to bring down the corrupt government of the Congress (under Chimanbhai Patel) in that drought-ridden state . . . it goes without saying that he succeeded without being obliged to die; in short, while anger seethed in Shiva's mind, the country was getting angry, too; and what was being born while something grew in Parvati's belly? You know the answer: in late 1974, J. P. Narayan and Morarji Desai formed the opposition party known as the Janata Morcha: the people's front. While Major Shiva reeled from whore to whore, the Indira Congress was reeling too.

And at last, Parvati released him from her spell. (No other explanation will do; if he was not bewitched, why did he not cast her off the instant he heard of her pregnancy? And if the spell had not been lifted, how could he have done it at all?) Shaking his head as though awaking from a dream, Major Shiva found himself in the company of a balloon-fronted slum girl, who now seemed to him to represent everything he most feared – she became the personification of the slums of his childhood, from which he had escaped, and which now, through her, through her damnable child, were trying to drag him down down down again . . . dragging her by the hair, he hurled her on to his motorcycle, and in a very short time she stood, abandoned, on the fringes of the magicians' ghetto, having been returned whence she came, bringing with her only one thing which she had not owned when she left: the thing hidden inside her like an invisible man in a wicker basket, the thing which was growing growing growing, just as she had planned.

Why do I say that? – Because it must be true; because what followed, followed; because it is my belief that Parvati-the-witch became pregnant in order to invalidate my only defence against marrying her. But I shall only describe, and leave analysis to posterity.

On a cold day in January, when the muezzin's cries from the highest minaret of the Friday Mosque froze as they left his lips and fell upon the city as sacred snow, Parvati returned. She had waited until there could be no possible doubt about her condition; her inner basket bulged through the clean new garments of Shiva's now-defunct infatuation. Her lips, sure of their coming triumph, had lost their fashionable pout; in her saucer-eyes, as she stood on the steps of the Friday Mosque to ensure that as many people as possible saw her changed appearance, there lurked a silvered gleam of contentment. That was how I found her when I returned to the chaya of the mosque with Picture Singh. I was feeling disconsolate, and the sight of Parvati-the-witch on the steps, hands folded calmly over her swollen belly, long rope-of-hair blowing gently in the crystal air, did nothing to cheer me up.

Pictureji and I had gone into the tapering tenement streets behind the General Post Office, where memories of fortune-tellers peepshow-men healers hung in the breeze; and here Picture Singh had performed an act which was growing more political by the day. His legendary artistry drew large good-natured crowds; and he made his snakes enact his message under the influence of his weaving flute music. While I, in my role of apprentice, read out a prepared harangue, serpents dramatized my speech. I spoke of the gross inequities of wealth distribution; two cobras performed, in dumbshow, the mime of a rich man refusing to give alms to a beggar. Police harassment, hunger disease illiteracy, were spoken of and also danced by serpents; and then Picture Singh, concluding his act, began to talk about the nature of red revolution, and promises began to fill the air, so that even before the police materialized out of the back-doors of the post office to break up the meeting with lathi-charges and tear-gas, certain wags in our audience had begun to heckle the Most Charming Man In The World. Unconvinced, perhaps, by the ambiguous mimes of the snakes, whose dramatic content was admittedly a little obscure, a youth shouted out: 'Ohé, Pictureji, you should be in the Government, man, not even Indiramata makes promises as nice as yours!'

Then the tear-gas came and we had to flee, coughing spluttering blind, from riot police, like criminals, crying falsely as we ran. (Just as once, in Jallianwalabagh – but at least there were no bullets on this occasion.) But although the tears were the tears of gas, Picture Singh was indeed cast down into an awesome gloom by the heckler's gibe, which had questioned the hold on reality which was his greatest pride; and in the aftermath of gas and sticks, I, too, was dejected, having suddenly identified a moth of unease in my stomach, and realized that something in me objected to

Picture's portrayal in snake-dance of the unrelieved vilenesses of the rich; I found myself thinking, 'There is good and bad in all – and they brought me up, they looked after me, Pictureji!' After which I began to see that the crime of Mary Pereira had detached me from two worlds, not one; that having been expelled from my uncle's house I could never fully enter the world-according-to-Picture-Singh; that, in fact, my dream of saving the country was a thing of mirrors and smoke; insubstantial, the maunderings of a fool.

And then there was Parvati, with her altered profile, in the harsh clarity of the winter day.

It was – or am I wrong? I must rush on; things are slipping from me all the time – a day of horrors. It was then – unless it was another day – that we found old Resham Bibi dead of cold, lying in her hut which she had built out of Dalda Vanaspati packing-cases. She had turned bright blue, Krishna-blue, blue as Jesus, the blue of Kashmiri sky, which sometimes leaks into eyes; we burned her on the banks of the Jamuna amongst mud-flats and buffalo, and she missed my wedding as a result, which was sad, because like all old women she loved weddings, and had in the past joined in the preliminary henna-ceremonies with energetic glee, leading the formal singing in which the bride's friends insulted the groom and his family. On one occasion her insults had been so brilliant and finely calculated that the groom took umbrage and cancelled the wedding; but Resham had been undaunted, saying that it wasn't her fault if young men nowadays were as faint-hearted and inconstant as chickens.

I was absent when Parvati went away; I was not present when she returned; and there was one more curious fact . . . unless I have forgotten, unless it was on another day . . . it seems to me, at any rate, that on the day of Parvati's return, an Indian Cabinet Minister was in his railway carriage, at Samastipur, when an explosion blew him into the history books; that Parvati, who had departed amid the explosions of atom bombs, returned to us when Mr L. N. Mishra, minister for railways and bribery, departed this world for good. Omens and more omens . . . perhaps, in Bombay, dead pomfrets were floating belly-side-up to shore.

January 26th, Republic Day, is a good time for illusionists. When the huge crowds gather to watch elephants and fireworks, the city's tricksters go out to earn their living. For me, however, the day holds another meaning; it was on Republic Day that my conjugal fate was sealed.

In the days after Parvati's return, the old women of the ghetto formed the habit of holding their ears for shame whenever they passed her; she, who bore her illegitimate child without any appearance of guilt, would smile innocently and walk on. But on the morning of Republic Day, she awoke to find a rope hung with tattered shoes strung up above her door, and began to weep inconsolably, her poise disintegrating under the force of this greatest of insults. Picture Singh and I, leaving our shack laden with baskets of snakes, came across her in her (calculated? genuine?) misery, and Picture Singh set his jaw in an attitude of determination. 'Come back to the hut, captain,' the Most Charming Man instructed me, 'We must talk.'

And in the hut, 'Forgive me, captain, but I must speak. I am thinking it is a terrible thing for a man to go through life without children. To have no son, captain: how sad for you, is it not?' And I, trapped by the lie of impotence, remained silent while Pictureji suggested the marriage which would preserve Parvati's honour and simultaneously solve the problem of my self-confessed sterility; and despite my fears of the face of Jamila Singer, which, superimposed on Parvati's, had the power of driving me to distraction, I could not find it in myself to refuse.

Parvati – just as she had planned, I'm sure – accepted me at once, said yes as easily and as often as she had said no in the past; and after that the Republic Day celebrations acquired the air of having been staged especially for our benefit, but what was in my mind was that once again destiny, inevitability, the antithesis of choice had come to rule my life, once again a child was to be born to a father who was not his father, although by a terrible irony the child would be the true grandchild of his father's parents; trapped in the web of these interweaving genealogies, it may even have occurred to me to wonder what was beginning, what was ending, and whether another secret countdown was in progress, and what would be born with my child.

Despite the absence of Resham Bibi, the wedding went off well enough. Parvati's formal conversion to Islam (which irritated Picture Singh, but on which I found myself insisting, in another throwback to an earlier life) was performed by a red-bearded Haji who looked ill-at-ease in the presence of so many teasing, provocative members of the ungodly; under the shifting gaze of this fellow who resembled a large and bearded onion she intoned her belief that there was no God but God and that Muhammad was his prophet; she took a name which I chose for her out of the repository of my dreams, becoming Laylah, night, so that she too was caught up in the repetitive cycles of my history, becoming an echo of all the other people who have been obliged to change their names . . . like my own mother Amina Sinai, Parvati-the-witch became a new person in order to have a child.

At the henna ceremony, half the magicians adopted me, performing the functions of my 'family'; the other half took Parvati's side, and happy insults were sung late into the night while intricate traceries of henna dried into the palms of her hands and the soles of her feet; and if the absence of Resham Bibi deprived the insults of a certain cutting edge, we were not overly sorry about the fact. During the nikah, the wedding proper, the happy couple were seated on a dais hastily constructed out of the Dalda-boxes of Resham's demolished shack, and the magicians filed solemnly past us, dropping coins of small denominations into our laps; and when the new Laylah Sinai fainted everyone smiled contentedly, because every good bride should faint at her wedding, and nobody mentioned the embarrassing possibility that she might have passed out because of the nausea or perhaps the kicking-pains caused by the child inside her basket. That evening the magicians put on a show so wonderful that rumours of it spread throughout the Old City, and crowds gathered to watch, Muslim businessmen from a nearby muhalla in which once a public announcement had been made and silversmiths and milk-shake vendors from Chandni Chowk, evening strollers and Japanese tourists who all (on this occasion) wore surgical face-masks out of politeness, so as not to infect us with their exhaled germs; and there were pink Europeans discussing camera lenses with the Japanese, there were shutters clicking and flash bulbs popping, and I was told by one of the tourists that India was indeed a truly wonderful country with many remarkable traditions, and would be just fine and perfect if one did not constantly have to eat Indian food. And at the valima, the consummation ceremony (at which, on this occasion, no bloodstained sheets were held up, with or without perforations, since I had spent our nuptial night with my eyes shut tight and my body averted from my wife's, lest the unbearable features of Jamila Singer come to haunt me in the bewilderment of the dark), the magicians surpassed their efforts of the wedding-night.

But when all the excitement had died down, I heard (with one good and one bad ear) the inexorable sound of the future stealing up upon us: tick, tock, louder and louder, until the birth of Saleem Sinai – and also of the baby's father – found a mirror in the events of the night of the 25th of June.

*

While mysterious assassins killed government officials, and narrowly failed to get rid of Mrs Gandhi's personally-chosen Chief Justice, A. N. Ray, the magicians' ghetto concentrated on another mystery: the ballooning basket of Parvati-the-witch.

While the Janata Morcha grew in all kinds of bizarre directions, until it embraced Maoist Communists (such as our very own contortionists, including the rubber-limbed triplets with whom Parvati had lived before our marriage – since the nuptials, we had moved into a hut of our own, which the ghetto had built for us as a wedding present on the site of Resham's hovel) and extreme right-wing members of the Ananda Marg; until Left-Socialists and conservative Swatantra members joined its ranks . . . while the people's front expanded in this grotesque manner, I, Saleem, wondered incessantly about what might be growing behind the expanding frontage of my wife.

While public discontent with the Indira Congress threatened to crush the government like a fly, the brand-new Laylah Sinai, whose eyes had grown wider than ever, sat as still as a stone while the weight of the baby increased until it threatened to crush her bones to powder; and Picture Singh, in an innocent echo of an ancient remark, said, 'Hey, captain! It's going to be big big: a real ten-chip whopper for sure!'

And then it was the twelfth of June.

History-books newspapers radio-programmes tell us that at two p.m. on June 12th, Prime Minister Indira Gandhi was found guilty, by Judge Jag Mohan Lal Sinha of the Allahabad High Court, of two counts of campaign malpractice during the election campaign of 1971; what has never previously been revealed is that it was at precisely two p.m. that Parvati-the-witch (now Laylah Sinai) became sure she had entered labour.

The labour of Parvati-Laylah lasted for thirteen days. On the first day, while the Prime Minister was refusing to resign, although her convictions carried with them a mandatory penalty barring her from public office for six years, the cervix of Parvati-the-witch, despite contractions as painful as mule-kicks, obstinately refused to dilate; Saleem Sinai and Picture Singh, barred from the hut of her torment by the contortionist triplets who had taken on the duties of midwives, were obliged to listen to her useless shrieks until a steady stream of fire-eaters card-sharpers coal-walkers came up and slapped them on the back and made dirty jokes; and it was only in my ears that the ticking could be heard . . . a countdown to God-knows what, until I became possessed by fear, and told Picture Singh, 'I don't know what's going to come out of her, but it isn't going to be good . . .' And Pictureji, reassuringly: 'Don't you worry, captain! Everything will be fine! A ten-chip whopper, I swear!' And Parvati, screaming screaming, and night fading into day, and on the second day, when in Gujarat Mrs Gandhi's electoral candidates were routed by the Janata Morcha, my Parvati was in the grip of pains so intense that they made her as stiff as steel, and I refused to eat until the baby was born or whatever happened happened, I sat cross-legged outside the hovel of her agony, shaking with terror in the heat, begging don't let her die don't let her die, although I had never made love to her during all the months of our marriage; in spite of my fear of the spectre of Jamila Singer, I prayed and fasted, although Picture Singh, 'For pity's sake, captain,' I refused, and by the ninth day the ghetto had fallen into a terrible hush, a silence so absolute that not even the calls of the muezzin of the mosque could penetrate it, a soundlessness of such immense powers that it shut out the roars of the Janata Morcha demonstrations outside Rashtrapati Bhavan, the President's house, a horror-struck muteness of the same awful enveloping magic as the great silence which had once hung over my grandparents' house in Agra, so that on the ninth day we could not hear Morarji Desai calling on President Ahmad to sack the disgraced Prime

Minister, and the only sounds in the entire world were the ruined whimperings of Parvati-Laylah, as the contractions piled upon her like mountains, and she sounded as though she were calling to us down a long hollow tunnel of pain, while I sat cross-legged being dismembered by her agony with the soundless sound of ticktock in my brain, and inside the hut there were the contortionist triplets pouring water over Parvati's body to replenish the moisture which was pouring out of her in fountains, forcing a stick between her teeth to prevent her from biting out her tongue, and trying to force down her eyelids over eyes which were bulging so frighteningly that the triplets were afraid they would fall out and get dirty on the floor, and then it was the twelfth day and I was half dead of starvation while elsewhere in the city the Supreme Court was informing Mrs Gandhi that she need not resign until her appeal, but must neither vote in the Lok Sabha nor draw a salary, and while the Prime Minister in her exultation at this partial victory began to abuse her opponents in language of which a Koli fishwife would have been proud, my Parvati's labour entered a phase in which despite her utter exhaustion she found the energy to issue a string of foul-smelling oaths from her colour-drained lips, so that the cesspit stink of her obscenities filled our nostrils and made us retch, and the three contortionists fled from the hut crying that she had become so stretched, so colourless that you could almost see through her, and she would surely die if the baby did not come now, and in my ears tick tock the pounding tick tock until I was sure, yes, soon soon soon, and when the triplets returned to her bedside in the evening of the thirteenth day they screamed Yes yes she has begun to push, come on Parvati, push push push, and while Parvati pushed in the ghetto, J. P. Narayan and Morarji Desai were also goading Indira Gandhi, while triplets yelled push push push the leaders of the Janata Morcha urged the police and Army to disobey the illegal orders of the disqualified Prime

Minister, so in a sense they were forcing Mrs Gandhi to push, and as the night darkened towards the midnight hour, because nothing ever happens at any other time, triplets began to screech it's coming coming coming, and elsewhere the Prime Minister was giving birth to a child of her own . . . in the ghetto, in the hut beside which I sat cross-legged and starving to death, my son was coming coming coming, the head is out, the triplets screeched, while members of the Central Reserve Police arrested the heads of the Janata Morcha, including the impossibly ancient and almost mythological figures of Morarji Desai and J. P. Narayan, push push push, and in the heart of that terrible midnight while ticktock pounded in my ears a child was born, a ten-chip whopper all right, popping out so easily in the end that it was impossible to understand what all the trouble had been. Parvati gave a final pitiable little yelp and out he popped, while all over India policemen were arresting people, all opposition leaders except members of the pro-Moscow Communists, and also schoolteachers lawyers poets news-papermen trade-unionists, in fact anyone who had ever made the mistake of sneezing during the Madam's speeches, and when the three contortionists had washed the baby and wrapped it in an old sari and brought it out for its father to see, at exactly the same moment, the word Emergency was being heard for the first time, and suspension-of-civil rights, and censorship-of-the-press, and armoured-units-on-special-alert, and arrest-of-subversive-elements; something was ending, something was being born, and at the precise instant of the birth of the new India and the beginning of a con-tinuous midnight which would not end for two long years, my son, the child of the renewed ticktock, came out into the world.

And there is more: because when, in the murky half-light of that endlessly prolonged midnight, Saleem Sinai saw his son for the first time, he began to laugh helplessly, his brain

585

ravaged by hunger, yes, but also by the knowledge that his relentless destiny had played yet another of its grotesque little jokes, and although Picture Singh, scandalized by my laughter which in my weakness was like the giggling of a schoolgirl, cried repeatedly, 'Come on, captain! Don't behave mad now! It is a son, captain, be happy!', Saleem Sinai continued to acknowledge the birth by tittering hysterically at fate, because the boy, the baby boy, the-boy-my-son Aadam, Aadam Sinai was perfectly formed – except, that is, for his ears. On either side of his head flapped audient protuberances like sails, ears so colossally huge that the triplets afterwards revealed that when his head popped out they had thought, for one bad moment, that it was the head of a tiny elephant.

. . . 'Captain, Saleem captain,' Picture Singh was begging, 'be nice now! Ears are not anything to go crazy for!'

He was born in Old Delhi . . . once upon a time. No, that won't do, there's no getting away from the date: Aadam Sinai arrived at a night-shadowed slum on June 25th, 1975. And the time? The time matters, too. As I said: at night. No, it's important to be more . . . On the stroke of midnight, as a matter of fact. Clock-hands joined palms. Oh, spell it out, spell it out: at the precise instant of India's arrival at Emergency, he emerged. There were gasps; and, across the country, silences and fears. And owing to the occult tyrannies of that benighted hour, he was mysteriously handcuffed to history, his destinies indissolubly chained to those of his country. Unprophesied, uncelebrated, he came; no prime ministers wrote him letters; but, just the same, as my time of connection neared its end, his began. He, of course, was left entirely without a say in the matter; after all, he couldn't even wipe his own nose at the time.

He was the child of a father who was not his father; but also the child of a time which damaged reality so badly that nobody ever managed to put it together again;

He was the true great-grandson of his great-grandfather, but elephantiasis attacked him in the ears instead of the nose – because he was also the true son of Shiva-and-Parvati; he was elephant-headed Ganesh;

He was born with ears which flapped so high and wide that they must have heard the shootings in Bihar and the screams of lathi-charged dock-workers in Bombay . . . a child who heard too much, and as a result never spoke, rendered dumb by a surfeit of sound, so that between then-and-now, from *slum* to pickle factory, I have never heard him utter a single word;

He was the possessor of a navel which chose to stick out instead of in, so that Picture Singh, aghast, cried, 'His bimbi, captain! His bimbi, look!', and he became, from the first days, the gracious recipient of our awe;

A child of such grave good nature that his absolute refusal to cry or whimper utterly won over his adoptive father, who gave up laughing hysterically at the grotesque ears and began to rock the silent infant gently in his arms;

A child who heard a song as he rocked in arms, a song sung in the historical accents of a disgraced ayah: 'Anything you want to be, you kin be; you kin be just what-all you want.'

But now that I've given birth to my flap-eared, silent son – there are questions to be answered about that other, synchronous birth. Unpalatable, awkward queries: did Saleem's dream of saving the nation leak, through the osmotic tissues of history, into the thoughts of the Prime Minister herself? Was my lifelong belief in the equation between the State and myself transmuted, in 'the Madam's' mind, into that in-those-days-famous phrase: *India is Indira and Indira is India?* Were we competitors for centrality – was she gripped by a lust for meaning as profound as my own – and was that, was that why . . . ?

Influence of hairstyles on the course of history: there's another ticklish business. If William Methwold had lacked a centre-parting, I might not have been here today; and if the Mother of the Nation had had a coiffure of uniform pigment, the Emergency she spawned might easily have lacked a darker side. But she had white hair on one side and black on the other; the Emergency, too, had a white part – public, visible, documented, a matter for historians – and a black part which, being secret macabre untold, must be a matter for us.

Mrs Indira Gandhi was born in November 1917 to Kamala and Jawaharlal Nehru. Her middle name was Priyadarshini. She was not related to 'Mahatma' M. K. Gandhi; her surname was the legacy of her marriage, in 1942, to one Feroze Gandhi, who became known as 'the nation's son-in-law'. They had two sons, Rajiv and Sanjay, but in 1949 she moved back into her father's home and became his 'official hostess'. Feroze made one attempt to live there, too, but it was not a success. He became a ferocious critic of the Nehru Government, exposing the Mundhra scandal and forcing the resignation of the then Finance Minister, T. T. Krishnamachari – 'T.T.K.' himself. Mr Feroze Gandhi died of a heart seizure in 1960, aged forty-seven. Sanjay Gandhi, and his ex-model wife Menaka, were prominent during the Emergency. The Sanjay Youth Movement was particularly effective in the sterilization campaign.

I have included this somewhat elementary summary just in case you had failed to realize that the Prime Minister of India was, in 1975, fifteen years a widow. Or (because the capital letter may be of use): a Widow.

Yes, Padma: Mother Indira really had it in for me.

Midnight

No! – But I must.

I don't want to tell it! – But I swore to tell it all. – No, I renounce, not that, surely some things are better left . . .? – That won't wash; what can't be cured, must be endured! – But surely not the whispering walls, and treason, and snip snip, and the women with the bruised chests? – Especially those things. – But how can I, look at me, I'm tearing-myself apart, can't even agree with myself, talking arguing like a wild fellow, cracking up, memory going, yes, memory plunging into chasms and being swallowed by the dark, only fragments remain, none of it makes sense any more! – But I mustn't presume to judge; must simply continue (having once begun) until the end; sense-and-nonsense is no longer (perhaps never was) for me to evaluate. – But the horror of it, I can't won't mustn't won't can't no! – Stop this; begin. – No! – Yes.

About the dream, then? I might be able to tell it as a dream. Yes, perhaps a nightmare: green and black the Widow's hair and clutching hand and children mmff and little balls and one-by-one and torn-in-half and little balls go flying flying green and black her hand is green her nails are black as black. – No dreams. Neither the time nor the place for. Facts, as remembered. To the best of one's ability. The way it was: Begin. – No choice? – None; when was there ever? There are imperatives, and logical-consequences, and inevitabilities, and recurrences; there are things-done-to, and accidents, and

589

bludgeonings-of-fate; when was there ever a choice? When options? When a decision freely-made, to be this or that or the other? No choice; begin. – Yes.

Listen:

Endless night, days weeks months without the sun, or rather (because it's important to be precise) beneath a sun as cold as a stream-rinsed plate, a sun washing us in lunatic midnight light; I'm talking about the winter of 1975–6. In the winter, darkness; and also tuberculosis.

Once, in a blue room overlooking the sea, beneath the pointing finger of a fisherman, I fought typhoid and was rescued by snake-poison; now, trapped in the dynastic webs of recurrence by my recognition of his sonship, our Aadam Sinai was also obliged to spend his early months battling the invisible snakes of a disease. The serpents of tuberculosis wound themselves around his neck and made him gasp for air . . . but he was a child of ears and silence, and when he spluttered, there were no sounds; when he wheezed, no raspings issued from his throat. In short, my son fell ill, and although his mother, Parvati or Laylah, went in search of the herbs of her magical gift – although infusions of herbs in well-boiled water were constantly administered, the wraith-like worms of tuberculosis refused to be driven away. I suspected, from the first, something darkly metaphorical in this illness – believing that, in those midnight months when the age of my connection-to-history overlapped with his, our private emergency was not unconnected with the larger, macrocosmic disease, under whose influence the sun had become as pallid and diseased as our son. Parvati-then (like Padma-now) dismissed these abstract ruminations, attacking as mere folly my growing obsession with light, in whose grip I began lighting little dia-lamps in the shack of my son's illness, filling our hut with candle-flames at noon . . . but I insist on the accuracy of my diagnosis; 'I tell you,' I insisted then, 'while the Emergency lasts, he will never become well.'

Driven to distraction by her failure to cure that grave child who never cried, my Parvati-Laylah refused to believe my pessimistic theories; but she became vulnerable to every other cockeyed notion. When one of the older women in the colony of the magicians told her – as Resham Bibi might have – that the illness could not come out while the child remained dumb, Parvati seemed to find that plausible. 'Sickness is a grief of the body,' she lectured me, 'It must be shaken off in tears and groans.' That night, she returned to the hut clutching a little bundle of green powder, wrapped in newspaper and tied up with pale pink string, and told me that this was a preparation of such power that it would oblige even a stone to shriek. When she administered the medicine the child's cheeks began to bulge, as though his mouth were full of food; the long-suppressed sounds of his babyhood flooded up behind his lips, and he jammed his mouth shut in fury. It became clear that the infant was close to choking as he tried to swallow back the torrential vomit of pent-up sound which the green powder had stirred up; and this was when we realized that we were in the presence of one of the earth's most implacable wills. At the end of an hour during which my son turned first saffron, then saffron-and-green, and finally the colour of grass, I could not stand it any more and bellowed, 'Woman, if the little fellow wants so much to stay quiet, we mustn't kill him for it!' I picked up Aadam to rock him, and felt his little body becoming rigid, his knee-joints elbows neck were filling up with the held-back tumult of unexpressed sounds, and at last Parvati relented and prepared an antidote by mashing arrowroot and camomile in a tin bowl while muttering strange imprecations under her breath. After that, nobody ever tried to make Aadam Sinai do anything he did not wish to do; we watched him battling against tuberculosis and tried to find reassurance in the idea that a will so steely would surely refuse to be defeated by any mere disease.

In those last days my wife Laylah or Parvati was also being gnawed by the interior moths of despair, because when she came towards me for comfort or warmth in the isolation of our sleeping hours, I still saw superimposed upon her features the horribly eroded physiognomy of Jamila Singer; and although I confessed to Parvati the secret of the spectre, consoling her by pointing out that at its present rate of decay it would have crumbled away entirely before long, she told me dolorously that spittoons and war had softened my brain, and despaired of her marriage which would, as it transpired, never be consummated; slowly, slowly there appeared on her lips the ominous pout of her grief . . . but what could I do? What solace could I offer – I, Saleem Snotnose, who had been reduced to poverty by the withdrawal of my family's protection, who had chosen (if it was a choice) to live by my olfactory gifts, earning a few paisa a day by sniffing out what people had eaten for dinner the previous day and which of them were in love; what consolation could I bring her, when I was already in the clutches of the cold hand of that lingering midnight, and could sniff finality in the air?

Saleem's nose (you can't have forgotten) could smell stranger things than horse-dung. The perfumes of emotions and ideas, the odour of how-things-were: all these were and are nosed out by me with ease. When the Constitution was altered to give the Prime Minister well-nigh-absolute powers, I smelled the ghosts of ancient empires in the air . . . in that city which was littered with the phantoms of Slave Kings and Mughals, of Aurangzeb the merciless and the last, pink conquerors, I inhaled once again the sharp aroma of despotism. It smelled like burning oily rags.

But even the nasally incompetent could have worked out that, during the winter of 1975–6, something smelled rotten in the capital; what alarmed me was a stranger, more personal stink: the whiff of personal danger, in which I discerned the presence of a pair of treacherous, retributive knees . . . my first intimation that an ancient conflict, which began when a love-crazed virgin switched name-tags, was shortly to end in a frenzy of treason and snippings.

Perhaps, with such a warning pricking at my nostrils, I should have fled – tipped off by a nose, I could have taken to my heels. But there were practical objections: where would I have gone? And, burdened by wife and son, how fast could I have moved? Nor must it be forgotten that I did flee once, and look where I ended up: in the Sundarbans, the jungle of phantasms and retribution, from which I only escaped by the skin of my teeth! . . . At any rate, I did not run.

It probably didn't matter; Shiva – implacable, traitorous, my enemy from our birth – would have found me in the end. Because although a nose is uniquely equipped for the purpose of sniffing-things-out, when it comes to action there's no denying the advantages of a pair of grasping, choking knees.

I shall permit myself one last, paradoxical observation on this subject: if, as I believe, it was at the house of the wailing women that I learned the answer to the question of purpose which had plagued me all my life, then by saving myself from that palace of annihilations I would also have denied myself this most precious of discoveries. To put it rather more philosophically: every cloud has a silver lining.

Saleem-and-Shiva, nose-and-knees . . . we shared just three things: the moment (and its consequences) of our birth; the guilt of treachery; and our son, Aadam, our synthesis, unsmiling, grave, with omni-audient ears. Aadam Sinai was in many respects the exact opposite of Saleem. I, at my beginning, grew with vertiginous speed; Aadam, wrestling with the serpents of disease, scarcely grew at all. Saleem wore an ingratiating smile from the start; Aadam had more dignity, and kept his grins to himself. Whereas Saleem had subjugated his will to the joint tyrannies of family and fate, Aadam fought ferociously, refusing to yield even to the coercion of green powder. And while Saleem had been so determined to absorb the universe that he had been, for a time, unable to blink, Aadam preferred to keep his eyes firmly closed . . . although when, every so often, he deigned to open them, I observed their colour, which was blue. Ice-blue, the blue of recurrence, the fateful blue of Kashmiri sky . . . but there is no need to elaborate further.

We, the children of Independence, rushed wildly and too fast into our future; he, Emergency-born, will be is already more cautious, biding his time; but when he acts, he will be impossible to resist. Already, he is stronger, harder, more resolute than I: when he sleeps, his eyeballs are immobile beneath their lids. Aadam Sinai, child of knees-and-nose, does not (as far as I can tell) surrender to dreams.

How much was heard by those flapping ears which seemed, on occasion, to be burning with the heat of their knowledge? If he could have talked, would he have cautioned me against treason and bulldozers? In a country dominated by the twin multitudes of noises and smells, we could have been the perfect team; but my baby son rejected speech, and I failed to obey the dictates of my nose.

'Arré baap,' Padma cries, 'Just tell what happened, mister! What is so surprising if a baby does not make conversations?'

And again the rifts inside me: I can't. – You must. – Yes.

April 1976 found me still living in the colony or ghetto of the magicians; my son Aadam was still in the grip of a slow tuberculosis that seemed unresponsive to any form of treatment. I was full of forebodings (and thoughts of flight); but if any one man was the reason for my remaining in the ghetto, that man was Picture Singh.

Padma; Saleem threw in his lot with the magicians of Delhi partly out of a sense of fitness – a self-flagellant belief in the rectitude of his belated descent into poverty (I took with me, from my uncle's house, no more than two shirts, white, two pairs trousers, also white, one tee-shirt, decorated with pink guitars, and shoes, one pair, black); partly, I came out of loyalty, having been bound by knots of gratitude to my rescuer, Parvati-the-witch; but I stayed – when, as a literate young man, I might at the very least have been a bank clerk or a night-school teacher of reading and writing – because, all my life, consciously or unconsciously, I have sought out fathers, Ahmed Sinai, Hanif Aziz, Sharpsticker sahib, General Zulfikar have all been pressed into service in the absence of William Methwold; Picture Singh was the last of this noble line. And perhaps, in my dual lust for fathers and saving-the-country, I exaggerated Picture Singh; the horrifying possibility exists that I distorted him (and have distorted him again in these pages) into a dream-figment of my own imagination . . . it is certainly true that whenever I inquired, 'When are you going to lead us, Pictureji – when will the great day come?', he, shuffling awkwardly, replied, 'Get such things out from your head, captain; I am a poor man from Rajasthan, and also the Most Charming Man In The World; don't make me anything else.' But I, urging him on, 'There is a precedent – there was Mian Abdullah, the Hummingbird . . .' to which Picture, 'Captain, you got some crazy notions.'

During the early months of the Emergency, Picture Singh remained in the clutches of a gloomy silence reminiscent (once again!) of the great soundlessness of Reverend Mother (which had also leaked into my son . . .), and neglected to lecture his audiences in the highways and back-streets of the Old and New cities as, in the past, he had insisted on doing; but although he, 'This is a time for silence, captain', I remained convinced that one day, one millennial dawn at midnight's end, somehow, at the head of a great jooloos or procession of the dispossessed, perhaps playing his flute and wreathed in deadly snakes, it would be Picture Singh who led us towards the light . . . but maybe he was never more than a snake-charmer; I do not deny the possibility. I say only that to me my last father, tall gaunt bearded, his hair swept back into a knot behind his neck, seemed the very avatar of Mian Abdullah; but perhaps it was all an illusion, born of my attempt to bind him to the threads of my history by an effort of sheer will. There have been illusions in my life; don't think I'm unaware of the fact. We are coming, however, to a time beyond illusions; having no option, I must at last set down, in black and white, the climax I have avoided all evening.

Scraps of memory: this is not how a climax should be written. A climax should surge towards its Himalayan peak; but I am left with shreds, and must jerk towards my crisis like a puppet with broken strings. This is not what I had planned; but perhaps the story you finish is never the one you begin. (Once, in a blue room, Ahmed Sinai improvised endings for fairy-tales whose original conclusions he had long ago forgotten; the Brass Monkey and I heard, down the years, all kinds of different versions of the journey of Sinbad, and of the adventures of Hatim Tai . . . if I began again, would I, too, end in a different place?) Well then: I must content myself with shreds and scraps: as I wrote centuries ago, the trick is to fill in the gaps, guided by the few clues one is given. Most of what matters in our lives takes place in our absence; I must be guided by the memory of a once-glimpsed file with tell-tale initials; and by the other, remaining shards of the past, lingering in my ransacked memory-vaults like broken bottles on a beach . . . Like scraps of memory, sheets of newsprint used to bowl through the magicians' colony in the silent midnight wind.

Wind-blown newspapers visited my shack to inform me that my uncle, Mustapha Aziz, had been the victim of unknown assassins; I neglected to shed a tear. But there were other pieces of information; and from these, I must build reality.

On one sheet of paper (smelling of turnips) I read that the Prime Minister of India went nowhere without her personal astrologer. In this fragment, I discerned more than turnip-whiffs; mysteriously, my nose recognized, once again, the scent of personal danger. What I am obliged to deduce from this warning aroma: soothsayers prophesied me; might not soothsayers have undone me at the end? Might not a Widow, obsessed with the stars, have learned from astrologers the secret potential of any children born at that long-ago midnight hour? And was that why a Civil Servant, expert in genealogies, was asked to trace . . . and why he looked at me strangely in the morning? Yes, you see, the scraps begin to fit together! Padma, does it not become clear? *Indira is India and India is Indira* . . . but might she not have read her own father's letter to a midnight child, in which her own, sloganized centrality was denied; in which the role of mirror-of-the-nation was bestowed upon me? You see? You *see*? . . . And there is more, there is even clearer proof, because here is another scrap of the *Times of India*, in which the Widow's own news agency Samachar quotes her when she speaks of her 'determination to combat the deep and widespread conspiracy which has been growing'. I tell you: she did not mean the Janata Morcha! No, the Emergency had a black part as well as a white, and here is the secret which has lain concealed for too long beneath the mask of those stifled days: the truest, deepest motive behind the declaration of a State of Emergency was the smashing, the pulverizing, the irreversible discombobulation of the children of midnight. (Whose Conference had, of course, been disbanded years before; but the mere possibility of our re-unification was enough to trigger off the red alert.)

Astrologers – I have no doubt – sounded the alarums; in a black folder labelled M.C.C., names were gathered from extant records; but there was more to it than that. There were also betrayals and confessions; there were knees and a nose – a nose, and also knees.

*

Scraps, shreds, fragments: it seems to me that, immediately before I awoke with the scent of danger in my nostrils, I had dreamed that I was sleeping. I awoke, in this most unnerving of dreams, to find a stranger in my shack: a poetic-looking fellow with lank hair that wormed over his ears (but who was very thin on top). Yes: during my last sleep before what-has-to-be-described, I was visited by the shade of Nadir Khan, who was staring perplexedly at a silver spittoon, inlaid with lapis lazuli, asking absurdly, 'Did you steal this? – Because otherwise, you must be – is it possible? – my Mumtaz's little boy?' And when I confirmed, 'Yes, none other, I am he –,' the dream-spectre of Nadir-Qasim issued a warning: 'Hide. There is little time. Hide while you can.'

Nadir, who had hidden under my grandfather's carpet, came to advise me to do likewise; but too late, too late, because now I came properly awake, and smelled the scent of danger blaring like trumpets in my nose . . . afraid without knowing why, I got to my feet; and is it my imagination or did Aadam Sinai open blue eyes to stare gravely into mine? Were my son's eyes also filled with alarm? Had flap-ears heard what a nose had sniffed out? Did father and son commune wordlessly in that instant before it all began? I must leave the question-marks hanging, unanswered; but what is certain is that Parvati, my Laylah Sinai, awoke also and asked, 'What's up, mister? What's got your goat?' – And I, without fully knowing the reason: 'Hide; stay in here and don't come out.'

Then I went outside.

It must have been morning, although the gloom of the endless midnight hung over the ghetto like a fog . . . through the murky light of the Emergency, I saw children playing seven-tiles, and Picture Singh, with his umbrella folded under his left armpit, urinating against the walls of the Friday Mosque; a tiny bald illusionist was practising driving knives through the neck of his ten-year-old apprentice, and already a conjurer had found an audience, and was persuading large woollen balls to drop from the armpits of strangers; while in another corner of the ghetto, Chand Sahib the musician was practising his trumpet-playing, placing the ancient mouthpiece of a battered horn against his neck and playing it simply by exercising his throat-muscles . . . there, over there, were the three contortionist triplets, balancing surahis of water on their heads as they returned to their huts from the colony's single stand-pipe . . . in short, everything seemed in order. I began to chide myself for my dreams and nasal alarums; but then it started.

The vans and bulldozers came first, rumbling along the main road; they stopped opposite the ghetto of the magicians. A loudspeaker began to blare: 'Civic beautification programme . . . authorized operation of Sanjay Youth Central Committee . . . prepare instantly for evacuation to new site . . . this slum is a public eyesore, can no longer be tolerated . . . all persons will follow orders without dissent.' And while a loudspeaker blared, there were figures descending from vans: a brightly-coloured tent was being hastily erected, and there were camp beds and surgical equipment . . . and now from the vans there poured a stream of finely-dressed young ladies of high birth and foreign education, and then a second river of equally-well-dressed young men: volunteers, Sanjay Youth volunteers, doing their bit for society . . . but then I realized no, not volunteers, because all *the* men had the same curly hair and lips-like-women's-labia, and the elegant ladies were all identical, too, their features corresponding precisely to those of Sanjay's Menaka, whom news-scraps had described as a 'lanky beauty', and who had once modelled nighties for a mattress company . . . standing in the chaos of the slum clearance programme, I was shown once again that the ruling dynasty of India had learned how to replicate itself; but then there was no time to think, the numberless labia-lips and lanky-beauties were seizing magicians and old beggars, people were being dragged towards the vans, and now a

599

rumour spread through the colony of magicians: 'They are doing nasbandi – sterilization is being performed!' – And a second cry. 'Save your women and children!' – And a riot is beginning, children who were just now playing seven-tiles are hurling stones at the elegant invaders, and here is Picture Singh rallying the magicians to his side, waving a furious umbrella, which had once been a creator of harmony but was now transmuted into a weapon, a flapping quixotic lance, and the magicians have become a defending army, Molotov cocktails are magically produced and hurled, bricks are drawn out of conjurers' bags, the air is thick with yells and missiles and the elegant labia-lips and lanky-beauties are retreating before the harsh fury of the illusionists; and there goes Picture Singh, leading the assault against the tent of vasectomy . . . Parvati or Laylah, disobeying orders, is at my side now, saying, 'My God, what are they –', and at this moment a new and more formidable assault is unleashed upon the slum: troops are sent in against magicians, women and children.

Once, conjurers card-tricksters puppeteers and mesmerists marched triumphantly beside a conquering army; but all that is forgotten now, and Russian guns are trained on the inhabitants of the ghetto. What chance do Communist wizards have against socialist rifles? They, we, are running now, every which way, Parvati and I are separated as the soldiers charge, I lose sight of Picture Singh, there are rifle-butts beating pounding, I see one of the contortionist triplets fall beneath the fury of the guns, people are being pulled by the hair towards the waiting yawning vans; and I, too, am running, too late, looking over my shoulder, stumbling on Dalda-cans empty crates and the abandoned sacks of the terrified illusionists, and over my shoulder through the murky night of the Emergency I see that all of this has been a smoke-screen, a side-issue, because hurtling through the confusion of the riot comes a mythical figure, an incarnation of destiny and destruction: Major Shiva has joined the fray, and he is looking only for me. Behind me, as I run, come the pumping knees of my doom . . .

. . . The picture of a hovel comes into my mind: my son! And not only my son: a silver spittoon, inlaid with lapis lazuli! Somewhere in the confusion of the ghetto a child has been left alone . . . somewhere a talisman, guarded for so long, has been abandoned. The Friday Mosque watches impassively as I swerve duck run between the tilting shacks, my feet leading me towards flap-eared son and spittoon . . . but what chance did I have against those knees? The knees of the war hero are coming closer closer as I flee, the joints of my nemesis thundering towards me, and he leaps, the legs of the war hero fly through the air, closing like jaws around my neck, knees squeezing the breath out of my throat, I am falling twisting but the knees hold tight, and now a voice – the voice of treachery betrayal hate! – is saying, as knees rest on my chest and pin me down in the thick dust of the slum: 'So, little rich boy: we meet again. Salaam.' I spluttered; Shiva smiled.

O shiny buttons on a traitor's uniform! Winking blinking like silver . . . why did he do it? Why did he, who had once led anarchistic apaches through the slums of Bombay, become the warlord of tyranny? Why did midnight's child betray the children of midnight, and take me to my fate? For love of violence, and the legitimizing glitter of buttons on uniforms? For the sake of his ancient antipathy towards me? Or – I find this most plausible – in exchange for immunity from the penalties imposed on the rest of us . . . yes, that must be it; O birthright-denying war hero! O mess-of-pottage-corrupted rival . . . But no, I must stop all this, and tell the story as simply as possible: while troops chased arrested dragged magicians from their ghetto, Major Shiva concentrated on me. I, too, was pulled roughly towards a van; while bulldozers moved forwards into the slum, a door was slammed shut . . . in the darkness I screamed, 'But my son! – And Parvati, where is she, my Laylah? – Picture Singh! Save me, Pictureji!' – But there were bulldozers now, and nobody heard me yelling.

Parvati-the-witch, by marrying me, fell victim to the curse of violent death that hangs over all my people . . . I do not know whether Shiva, having locked me in a blind dark van, went in search of her, or whether he left her to the bulldozers . . . because now the machines of destruction were in their element, and the little hovels of the shanty-town were slipping sliding crazily beneath the force of the irresistible creatures, huts snapping like twigs, the little paper parcels of the puppeteers and the magic baskets of the illusionists were being crushed into a pulp; the city was being beautified, and if there were a few deaths, if a girl with eyes like saucers and a pout of grief upon her lips fell beneath the advancing juggernauts, well, what of it, an eyesore was being removed from the face of the ancient capital . . . and rumour has it that, during the death-throes of the ghetto of the magicians, a bearded giant wreathed in snakes (but this may be an exaggeration) ran – FULL-TILT! – through the wreckage, ran wildly before the advancing bulldozers, clutching in his hand the handle of an irreparably-shattered umbrella, searching searching, as though his life depended on the search.

By the end of that day, the slum which clustered in the shadow of the Friday Mosque had vanished from the face of the earth; but not all the magicians were captured; not all of them were carted off to the barbed-wire camp called Khichripur, hotch-potch-town, on the far side of the Jamuna River; they never caught Picture Singh, and it is said that the day after the bulldozing of the magicians' ghetto, a new slum was reported in the heart of the city, hard by the New Delhi railway station. Bulldozers were rushed to the scene of the reported hovels; they found nothing. After that the existence of the moving slum of the escaped illusionists became a fact known to all the inhabitants of the city, but the wreckers never found it. It was reported at Mehrauli; but when vasectomists and troops went there, they found the Qutb Minar unbesmirched by the hovels of poverty. Informers said it had appeared in the gardens of the Jantar Mantar, Jai Singh's Mughal observatory; but the machines of destruction, rushing to the scene, found only parrots and sun-dials. Only after the end of the Emergency did the moving slum come to a standstill; but that must wait for later, because it is time to talk, at long last, and without losing control, about my captivity in the Widows' Hostel in Benares.

Once Resham Bibi had wailed, 'Ai-o-ai-o!' – and she was right: I brought destruction down upon the ghetto of my saviours; Major Shiva, acting no doubt upon the explicit instructions of the Widow, came to the colony to seize me; while the Widow's son arranged for his civic-beautification and vasectomy programmes to carry out a diversionary manoeuvre. Yes, of course it was all planned that way; and (if I may say so) most efficiently. What was achieved during the riot of the magicians: no less a feat than the unnoticed capture of the one person on earth who held the key to the location of every single one of the children of midnight – for had I not, night after night, tuned in to each and every one of them? Did I not carry, for all time, their names addresses faces in my mind? I will answer that question: I did. And I was captured.

Yes, of course it was all planned that way. Parvati-the-witch had told me all about my rival; is it likely that she would not have mentioned me to him? I will answer that question, too: it is not likely at all. So our war hero knew where, in the capital, lurked the one person his masters wanted most (not even my uncle Mustapha knew where I went after I left him; but Shiva knew!) – and, once he had turned traitor, bribed, I have no doubt, by everything from promises of preferment to guarantees of personal safety, it

603

was easy for him to deliver me into the hands of his mistress, the Madam, the Widow with the particoloured hair.

Shiva and Saleem, victor and victim; understand our rivalry, and you will gain an understanding of the age in which you live. (The reverse of this statement is also true.)

I lost something else that day, besides my freedom: bulldozers swallowed a silver spittoon. Deprived of the last object connecting me to my more tangible, historically-verifiable past, I was taken to Benares to face the consequences of my inner, midnight-given life.

Yes, that was where it happened, in the palace of the widows on the shores of the Ganges in the oldest living city in the world, the city which was already old when the Buddha was young, Kasi Benares Varanasi, City of Divine Light, home of the Prophetic Book, the horoscope of horoscopes, in which every life, past present future, is already recorded. The goddess Ganga streamed down to earth through Shiva's hair . . . Benares, the shrine to Shiva-the-god, was where I was brought by hero-Shiva to face my fate. In the home of horoscopes, I reached the moment prophesied in a rooftop room by Ramram Seth: 'soldiers will try him . . . tyrants will fry him!' the fortune-teller had chanted; well, there was no formal trial – Shiva-knees wrapped around my neck, and that was that – but I did smell, one winter's day, the odours of something frying in an iron skillet . . .

Follow the river, past Scindia-ghat on which young gymnasts in white loincloths perform one-armed push-ups, past Manikarnika-ghat, the place of funerals, at which holy fire can be purchased from the keepers of the flame, past floating carcasses of dogs and cows – unfortunates for whom no fire was bought, past Brahmins under straw umbrellas at Dasashwamedh-ghat, dressed in saffron, dispensing blessings . . . and now it becomes audible, a strange sound, like the baying of distant hounds . . . follow follow follow the sound, and it takes shape, you understand that it is a mighty, ceaseless wailing, emanating from the blinded windows of a riverside palace: the Widows' Hostel! Once upon a time, it was a maharajah's residence; but India today is a modern country, and such places have been expropriated by the State. The palace is a home for bereaved women now; they, understanding that their true lives ended with the death of their husbands, but no longer permitted to seek the release of sati, come to the holy city to pass their worthless days in heartfelt ululations. In the palace of the widows lives a tribe of women whose chests are irremediably bruised by the power of their continual pummellings, whose hair is torn beyond repair, and whose voices are shredded by the constant, keening expressions of their grief. It is a vast building, a labyrinth of tiny rooms on the upper storeys giving way to the great halls of lamentation below; and yes, that was where it happened, the Widow sucked me into the private heart of her terrible empire, I was locked away in a tiny upper room and the bereaved women brought me prison food. But I also had other visitors: the war hero invited two of his colleagues along, for purposes of conversation. In other words: I was encouraged to talk. By an ill-matched duo, one fat, one thin, whom I named Abbott-and-Costello because they never succeeded in making me laugh.

Here I record a merciful blank in my memory. Nothing can induce me to remember the conversational techniques of that humourless, uniformed pair; there is no chutney or pickle capable of unlocking the doors behind which I have locked those days! No, I have forgotten, I cannot will not say how they made me spill the beans – but I cannot escape the shameful heart of the matter, which is that despite absence-of-jokes and the generally unsympathetic manner of my two-headed inquisitor, I did most certainly talk. And more than talk: under the influence of their unnameable – forgotten – pressures, I became loquacious in the extreme. What poured, blubbering, from my lips (and will not do so now): names addresses physical descriptions. Yes, I told them everything, I named all five hundred and seventy-eight (because Parvati, they informed me courteously, was dead, and Shiva gone over to the enemy, and the five-hundred-and-eighty-first was doing the talking . . .) – forced into treachery by the treason of another, I betrayed the children of midnight. I, the Founder of the Conference, presided over its end, while Abbott-and-Costello, unsmilingly, interjected from time to time: 'Aha! Very good! Didn't know about her!' or, 'You are being most co-operative; this fellow is a new one on us!'

Such things happen. Statistics may set my arrest in context; although there is considerable disagreement about the number of 'political' prisoners taken during the Emergency, either thirty thousand or a quarter of a million persons certainly lost their freedom. The Widow said: 'It is only a small percentage of the population of India.' All sorts of things happen during an Emergency: trains run on time, black-money hoarders are frightened into paying taxes, even the weather is brought to heel, and bumper harvests are reaped; there is, I repeat, a white part as well as a black. But in the black part, I sat bar-fettered in a tiny room, on a straw palliasse which was the only article of furniture I was permitted, sharing my daily bowl of rice with cockroaches and ants. And as for the children of midnight – that fearsome conspiracy which had to be broken at all costs – that gang of cut-throat desperadoes before whom an astrology-ridden Prime Minister trembled in terror – the grotesque aberrational monsters of independence, for whom a modern nation-state could have neither time nor compassion – twenty-nine years old now, give or take a month or two, they were brought to the Widows' Hostel, between April and December they were rounded up, and their whispers began to fill the walls. The walls of my cell (paper-thin, peeling-plastered, bare) began to whisper, into one bad ear and one good ear, the consequences of my shameful confessions. A cucumber-nosed prisoner, festooned with iron rods and rings which made various natural functions impossible – walking, using the tin chamber-pot, squatting, sleeping – lay huddled against peeling plaster and whispered to a wall.

It was the end; Saleem gave way to his grief. All my life, and through the greater part of these reminiscences, I have tried to keep my sorrows under lock and key, to prevent them from staining my sentences with their salty, maudlin fluidities; but no more. I was given no reason (until the Widow's Hand . . .) for my incarceration: but who, of all the thirty thousand or quarter of a million, was told why or wherefore? Who needed to be told? In the walls, I heard the muted voices of the midnight children: needing no further footnotes, I blubbered over peeling plaster.

What Saleem whispered to the wall between April and December 1976:

. . . Dear Children. How can I say this? What is there to say? My guilt my shame. Although excuses are possible: I wasn't to blame about Shiva. And all manner of folk are being locked up, so why not us? And guilt is a complex matter, for are we not all, each of us in some sense responsible for – do we not get the leaders we deserve? But no such excuses are offered. I did it, I. Dear children: and my Parvati is dead. And my Jarnila, vanished. And everyone. Vanishing seems to be yet another of those characteristics which recur throughout my history: Nadir Khan vanished from an underworld, leaving a note behind; Aadam Aziz vanished, too, before my grandmother got up to feed the geese; and where is Mary Pereira? I, in a basket, disappeared; but Laylah or Parvati went phutt without the assistance of spells. And now here we are, disappeared-off-the-face-of-the-earth. The curse of vanishment, dear children, has evidently leaked into you. No, as to the question of guilt, I refuse absolutely to take the larger view; we are too close to what-is-happening, perspective is impossible, later perhaps analysts will say why and wherefore, will adduce underlying economic trends and political developments, but right now we're too close to the cinemascreen, the picture is breaking up into dots, only subjective judgments are possible. Subjectively, then, I hang my head in shame. Dear children: forgive. No, I do not expect you to forgive.

Politics, children: at the best of times a bad dirty business. We should have avoided it, I should never have dreamed of purpose, I am coming to the conclusion that privacy, the small individual lives of men, are preferable to all this inflated macrocosmic activity. But too late. Can't be helped. What can't be cured must be endured.

Good question, children: what must be endured? Why are we being amassed here like this, one by one, why are rods and rings hanging from our necks? And stranger confinements (if a whispering wall is to be believed): who-has-the-gift-of-levitation has been tied by the ankles to rings set in the floor, and a werewolf is obliged to wear a muzzle; who-can-escape-through-mirrors must drink water through a hole in a lidded can, so that he cannot vanish through the reflective surface of the drink; and she-whose-looks-can-kill has her head in a sack, and the bewitching beauties of Baud are likewise bagheaded. One of us can eat metal; his head is jammed in a brace, unlocked only at mealtimes . . . what is being prepared for us? Something bad, children. I don't know what as yet, but it's coming. Children: we, too, must prepare.

Pass it on: some of us have escaped. I sniff absences through the walls. Good news, children! They cannot get us all. Soumitra, the time-traveller, for instance – O youthful folly! O stupid we, to disbelieve him so! – is not here; wandering, perhaps, in some happier time of his life, he has eluded search-parties for ever. No, do not envy him; although I, too, long on occasion to escape backwards, perhaps to the time when I, the apple of the universal eye, made a triumphant tour as a baby of the palaces of William Methwold – O insidious nostalgia for times of greater possibility, before history, like a street behind the General Post Office in Delhi, narrowed down to this final full point! – but we are here now; such retrospection saps the spirit; rejoice, simply, that some of us are free!

And some of us are dead. They told me about my Parvati. Across whose features, to the last, there fell the crumbling ghost-face of. No, we are no longer five hundred and eighty-one. Shivering in the December cold, how many of us sit walled-in and waiting? I ask my nose; it replies, four hundred and twenty, the number of trickery and fraud. Four hundred and twenty, imprisoned by widows; and there is one more, who struts booted around the Hostel – I smell his stink approaching receding, the spoor of treachery! – Major Shiva, war hero, Shiva-of-the-knees, supervises our captivity. Will they be content with four hundred and twenty? Children: I don't know how long they'll wait.

. . . No, you're making fun of me, stop, do not joke. Why whence how-on-earth this good nature, this bonhomie in your passed-on whisperings? No, you must condemn me, out of hand and without appeal – do not torture me with your cheery greetings as one-by-one you are locked in cells; what kind of time or place is this for salaams, namaskars, how-you-beens? – Children, don't you understand, they could do anything to us, anything – no, how can you say that, what do you mean with your what-could-they-do? Let me tell you, my friends, steel rods are painful when applied to the ankles; rifle-butts leave bruises on foreheads. What could they do? Live electric wires up your anuses, children; and that's not the only possibility, there is also hanging-by-the-feet, and a candle – ah, the sweet romantic glow of candlelight! – is less, than comfortable when applied, lit, to the skin! Stop it now, cease all this friendship, aren't you afraid! Don't you want to kick stamp trample me to smithereens? Why these constant whispered reminiscences, this nostalgia for old quarrels, for the war of ideas and things, why are you taunting me with your calmness, your normality, your powers of rising-above-the-crisis? Frankly, I'm puzzled, children: how can you, aged twenty-nine, sit whispering flirtatiously to each other in your cells? Goddamnit, this is not a social reunion!

Children, children, I'm sorry. I admit openly I have not been myself of late. I have been a buddha, and a basketed ghost, and a would-be-saviour of the nation . . . Saleem has been rushing down blind alleys, has had considerable problems with reality, ever since a spittoon fell like a piece-of-the- . . . pity me: I've even lost my spittoon. But I'm going wrong again, I wasn't intending to ask for pity, I was going to say that perhaps I see – it was I, not you, who failed to understand what is happening. Incredible, children: we, who could not talk for five minutes without disagreeing: we, who as children quarrelled fought divided distrusted broke apart, are suddenly together, united, as one! O wondrous irony: the Widow, by bringing us here, to break us, has in fact brought us together! O self-fulfilling paranoia of tyrants . . . because what can they do to us, now that we're all on the same side, no language-rivalries, no religious prejudices: after all, we are twenty-nine now, I should not be calling you children . . . ! Yes, here is optimism, like a disease: one day she'll have to let us out and then, and then, wait and see, maybe we should form, I don't know, a new political party, yes, the Midnight Party, what chance do politics have against people who can multiply fishes and turn base metals into gold? Children, something is being born here, in this dark time of our captivity; let Widows do their worst; unity is invincibility! *Children: we've won!*

Too painful. Optimism, growing like a rose in a dung-heap: it hurts me to recall it. Enough: I forget the rest. – No! – No, very well, I remember . . . What is worse than rods bar-fetters candles-against-the-skin? What beats nail-tearing and starvation? I reveal the Widow's finest, most delicate joke: instead of torturing us, she gave us hope. Which meant she had something – no, more than something: the finest thing of all! – to take away. And now, very soon now, I shall have to describe how she cut it off.

Ectomy (from, I suppose, the Greek): a cutting out. To which medical science adds a number of prefixes: appendectomy tonsillectomy mastectomy tubectomy vasectomy testectomy hysterectomy. Saleem would like to donate one further item, free gratis and for nothing, to this catalogue of excisions; it is, however, a term which properly belongs to history, although medical science is, was involved:

Sperectomy: the draining-out of hope.

On New Year's Day, I had a visitor. Creak of door, rustle of expensive chiffon. The pattern: green and black. Her glasses, green, her shoes were black as black . . . In newspaper articles this woman has been called 'a gorgeous girl with big, rolling hips . . . she had run a jewellery boutique before she took up social work . . . during the Emergency she was, semi-officially, in charge of sterilization'. But I have my own name for her: she was the Widow's Hand. Which one by one and children mmff and tearing tearing little balls go . . . greenly-blackly, she sailed into my cell. Children: it begins. Prepare, children. United we stand. Let Widow's Hand do Widow's work but after, after . . . think of then. Now does not bear thinking about . . . and she, sweetly, reasonably, 'Basically, you see, it is all a question of God.'

(Are you listening, children? Pass it on.)

'The people of India,' the Widow's Hand explained, 'worship our Lady like a god. Indians are only capable of worshipping one God.'

But I was brought up in Bombay, where Shiva Vishnu Ganesh Ahuramazda Allah and countless others had their flocks . . . 'What about the pantheon,' I argued, 'the three hundred and thirty million gods of Hinduism alone? And Islam, and Bodhisattvas . . . ?' And now the answer: 'Oh yes! My God, *millions* of gods, you are right! But all manifestations of the same OM. YOU are Muslim: you know what is OM? Very well. For the masses, our Lady is a manifestation of the OM.'

There are four hundred and twenty of us; a mere 0.00007 per cent of the six-hundred-million strong population of India. Statistically insignificant; even if we were considered as a percentage of the arrested thirty (or two hundred and fifty) thousand, we formed a mere 1.4 (or 0.168) per cent! But what I learned from the Widow's Hand is that those who would be gods fear no one so much as other potential deities; and that, that and that only, is why we, the magical children of midnight, were hated feared destroyed by the Widow, who was not only Prime Minister of India but also aspired to be Devi, the Mother-goddess in her most terrible aspect, possessor of the shakti of the gods, a multi-limbed divinity with a centre-parting and schizophrenic hair . . . And that was how I learned my meaning in the crumbling palace of the bruised-breasted women.

Who am I? Who were we? We were are shall be the gods you never had. But also something else; and to explain that, I must tell the difficult part at last.

All in a rush, then, because otherwise it will never come out, I tell you that on New Year's Day, 1977, I was told by a gorgeous girl with rolling hips that yes, they would be satisfied with four hundred and twenty, they had verified one hundred and thirty-nine dead, only a handful had escaped, so now it would begin, snip snip, there would be anaesthetic and count-to-ten, the numbers marching one two three, and I, whispering to the wall, Let them let them, while we live and stay together who can stand against us? . . . And who led us, one-by-one, to the chamber in the cellar where, because we are not savages, sir, air-conditioning units had been installed, and a table with a hanging lamp, and doctors nurses green and black, their robes were green their eyes were black . . . who, with knobbly irresistible knees, escorted me to the chamber of my undoing? But you know, you can guess, there is only one war hero in this story, unable to argue with the venom of his knees I walked wherever he ordered . . . and then I was there, and a gorgeous girl with big rolling hips saying, 'After all, you can't complain, you won't deny that you once made assertions of Prophethood?', because they knew everything, Padma, everything everything, they put me down on the table and the mask coming down over my face and count-to-ten and numbers pounding seven eight nine . . .

Ten.

And Good God he's still conscious, be a good fellow, go on to twenty . . .'

. . . Eighteen nineteen twen

They were good doctors: they left nothing to chance. Not for us the simple vas- and tubectomies performed on the teeming masses; because there was a chance, just a chance that such operations could be reversed . . . ectomies were performed, but irreversibly: testicles were removed from sacs, and wombs vanished for ever.

Test- and hysterectomized, the children of midnight were denied the possibility of reproducing themselves . . . but that was only a side-effect, because they were truly extraordinary doctors, and they drained us of more than that: hope, too, was excised, and I don't know how it was done, because the numbers had marched over me, I was out for the count, and all I can tell you is that at the end of eighteen days on which the stupefying operations were carried out at a mean rate of 23.33 per day, we were not only missing little balls and inner sacs, but other things as well: in this respect, I came off better than most, because drainage-above had robbed me of my midnight-given telepathy, I had nothing to lose, the sensitivity of a nose cannot be drained away . . . but as for the rest of them, for all those who had come to the palace of the wailing widows with their magical gifts intact, the awakening from anaesthesia was cruel indeed, and whispering through the wall came the tale of their undoing, the tormented cry of children who had lost their magic: she had cut it out of us, gorgeously with wide rolling hips she had devised the operation of our annihilation, and now we were nothing, who were we, a mere 0.00007 per cent, now fishes could not be multiplied nor base metals transmuted; gone forever, the possibilities of flight and lycanthropy and the originally-one-thousand-and-one marvellous promises of a numinous midnight.

Drainage below: it was not a reversible operation.

Who were we? Broken promises; made to be broken.

And now I must tell you about the smell.

Yes, you must have all of it: however overblown, however Bombay-talkie-melodramatic, you must let it sink in, you must *see*! What Saleem smelled in the evening of January 18th, 1977: something frying in an iron skillet, soft unspeakable somethings spiced with turmeric coriander cumin and fenugreek . . . the pungent inescapable fumes of what-had-been-excised, cooking over a low, slow fire.

When four-hundred-and-twenty suffered ectomies, an avenging Goddess ensured that certain ectomized parts were curried with onions and green chillies, and fed to the pie-dogs of Benares. (There were four hundred and twenty-one ectomies performed: because one of us, whom we called Narada or Markandaya, had the ability of changing sex; he, or she, had to be operated on twice.)

No, I can't prove it, not any of it. Evidence went up in smoke: some was fed to pie-dogs; and later, on March 20th, files were

614

burned by a mother with particoloured hair and her beloved son.

But Padma knows what I can no longer do; Padma, who once, in her anger, cried out: 'But what use are *you*, my God, as a *lover*?' That part, at least, can be verified: in the hovel of Picture Singh, I cursed myself with the lie of impotence; I cannot say I was not warned, because he told me: 'Anything could happen, captain.' It did.

Sometimes I feel a thousand years old: or (because I cannot, even now, abandon form), to be exact, a thousand and one.

The Widow's Hand had rolling hips and once owned a jewellery boutique. I began among jewels: in Kashmir, in 1915, there were rubies and diamonds. My great-grandparents ran a gemstone store. Form – once again, recurrence and shape! – no escape from it.

In the walls, the hopeless whispers of the stunned four-hundred-and-nineteen; while the four-hundred-and-twentieth gives vent – just once; one moment of ranting is permissible – to the following petulant question . . . at the top of my voice, I shriek: 'What about him? Major Shiva, the traitor? Don't you care about him?' And the reply, from gorgeous-with-big-rolling-hips: 'The Major has undergone voluntary vasectomy.'

And now, in his sightless cell, Saleem begins to laugh, wholeheartedly, without stinting: no, I was not laughing cruelly at my arch-rival, nor was I cynically translating the word 'voluntary' into another word; no, I was remembering stories told me by Parvati or Laylah, the legendary tales of the war hero's philandering, of the legions of bastards swelling in the unectomied bellies of great ladies and whores; I laughed because Shiva, destroyer of the midnight children, had also fulfilled the other role lurking in his name, the function of Shiva-lingam, of Shiva-the-procreator, so that at this very moment, in the boudoirs and hovels of the nation, a new generation of children, begotten by midnight's darkest child, was being raised towards the future. Every Widow manages to forget something important.

Late in March 1977, I was unexpectedly released from the palace of the howling widows, and stood blinking like an owl in the sunlight, not knowing how what why. Afterwards, when I had remembered how to ask questions, I discovered that on January 18th (the very day of the end of snip-snip, and of substances fried in an iron skillet: what further proof would you like that we, the four hundred and twenty, were what the Widow feared most of all?) the Prime Minister had, to the astonishment of all, called a general election. (But now that you know about us, you may find it easier to understand her over-confidence.) But on that day, I knew nothing about her crushing defeat, nor about burning files; it was only later that I learned how the tattered hopes of the nation had been placed in the custody of an ancient dotard who ate pistachios and cashews and daily took a glass of 'his own water'. Urine-drinkers had come to power. The Janata Party, with one of its leaders trapped in a kidney-machine, did not seem to me (when I heard about it) to represent a new dawn; but maybe I'd managed to cure myself of the optimism virus at last – maybe others, with the disease still in their blood, felt otherwise. At any rate, I've had – I had had, on that March day – enough, more than enough of politics.

Four hundred and twenty stood blinking in the sunlight and tumult of the gullies of Benares; four hundred and twenty looked at one another and saw in each other's eyes the memory of their gelding, and then, unable to bear the sight, mumbled farewells and dispersed, for the last time, into the healing privacy of the crowds.

What of Shiva? Major Shiva was placed under military detention by the new régime; but he did not remain there long, because he was permitted to receive one visit: Roshanara Shetty bribed coquetted wormed her way into his cell, the same Roshanara who had poured poison into his ears at Mahalaxmi Racecourse and who had since been driven crazy by a bastard son who refused to speak and did nothing he did not wish to do. The steel magnate's wife drew from her handbag the enormous German pistol owned by her husband, and shot the war hero through the heart. Death, as they say, was instantaneous.

The Major died without knowing that once, in a saffron-and-green nursing home amid the mythological chaos of an unforgettable midnight, a tiny distraught woman had changed baby-tags and denied him his birthright, which was that hillock-top world cocooned in money and starched white clothes and things things things – a world he would dearly have loved to possess.

And Saleem? No longer connected to history, drained above-and-below, I made my way back to the capital, conscious that an age, which had begun on that long-ago midnight, had come to a sort of end. How I travelled: I waited beyond the platform at Benares or Varanasi station with nothing but a platform-ticket in my hand, and leaped on to the step of a first-class compartment as the mail-train pulled out, heading west. And now, at last, I knew how it felt to clutch on for dear life, while particles of soot dust ash gritted in your eyes, and you were obliged to bang on the door and yell, 'Ohé, maharaj! Open up! Let me in, great sir, maharaj!' While inside, a voice uttered familiar words: 'On no account is anyone to open. Just fare-dodgers, that's all.'

In Delhi: Saleem asks questions. Have you seen where? Do you know if the magicians? Are you acquainted with Picture Singh? A postman with the memory of snake-charmers fading in his eyes points north. And, later, a black-tongued paan-wallah sends me back the way I came. Then, at last, the trail ceases meandering; street-entertainers put me on the scent. A Dilli-dekho man with a peepshow machine, a mongoose-and-cobra trainer wearing a paper hat like a child's sailboat, a girl in a cinema box-office who retains her nostalgia for her childhood as a sorcerer's apprentice . . . like fishermen, they point with fingers. West west west, until at last Saleem arrives at the Shadipur bus depot on the western outskirts of the city. Hungry thirsty enfeebled sick, skipping weakly out of the paths of buses roaring in and out of the depot – gaily-painted buses, bearing inscriptions on their bonnets such as *God Willing!* and other mottoes, for instance *Thank God!* on their backsides – he comes to a huddle of ragged tents clustered under a concrete railway bridge, and sees, in the shadow of concrete, a snake-charming giant breaking into an enormous rotten-toothed smile, and, in his arms, wearing a tee-shirt decorated with pink guitars, a small boy of some twenty-one months, whose ears are the ears of elephants, whose eyes are wide as saucers and whose face is as serious as the grave.

Abracadabra

To tell the truth, I lied about Shiva's death. My first out-and-out lie – although my presentation of the Emergency in the guise of a six-hundred-and-thirty-five-day-long midnight was perhaps excessively romantic, and certainly contradicted by the available meteorological data. Still and all, whatever anyone may think, lying doesn't come easily to Saleem, and I'm hanging my head in shame as I confess . . . Why, then, this single barefaced lie? (Because, in actuality, I've no idea where my changeling-rival went after the Widows' Hostel; he could be in hell or the brothel down the road and I wouldn't know the difference.) Padma, try and understand: I'm still terrified of him. There is unfinished business between us, and I spend my days quivering at the thought that the war hero might somehow have discovered the secret of his birth – was he ever shown a file bearing three telltale initials? – and that, roused to wrath by the irrecoverable loss of his past, he might come looking for me to exact a stifling revenge . . . is that how it will end, with the life being crushed out of me by a pair of superhuman, merciless knees?

That's why I fibbed, anyway; for the first time, I fell victim to the temptation of every autobiographer, to the illusion that since the past exists only in one's memories and the words which strive vainly to encapsulate them, it is possible to create past events simply by saying they occurred. My present fear put a gun into Roshanara Shetty's hand; with the ghost of Commander Sabarmati looking over my shoulder, I enabled her to bribe coquette worm her way into his cell . . . in short, the memory of one of my earliest crimes created the (fictitious) circumstances of my last.

End of confession: and now I'm getting perilously close to the end of my reminiscences. It's night; Padma is in position; on the wall above my head, a lizard has just gobbled up a fly; the festering heat of August, which is enough to pickle one's brains, bubbles merrily between my ears; and five minutes ago the last local train yellow-and-browned its way south to Churchgate Station, so that I did not hear what Padma said with a shyness cloaking a determination as powerful as oil. I had to ask her to repeat herself, and the muscles of disbelief began to nictate in her calves. I must at once record that our dung-lotus has proposed marriage, 'so that I can look after you without going to shame in the eyes of the world'.

Just as I feared! But it's out in the open now, and Padma (I can tell) will not take no for an answer. I have been protesting like a blushing virgin: 'So unexpected! – and what about ectomy, and what was fed to pie-dogs: don't you mind? – and Padma, Padma, there is still what-chews-on-bones, it will turn you into a widow! – and just think one moment, there is the curse of violent death, think of Parvati – are you sure, are you sure you're sure . . . ?' But Padma, her jaw set in the concrete of a majestically unshakeable resolve, replied: 'You listen to me, mister – but me no buts! Never mind all that fancy talk any more. There is the future to think of.' The honeymoon is to be in Kashmir.

In the burning heat of Padma's determination, I am assailed by the demented notion that it might be possible, after all, that she may be capable of altering the ending of my story by the phenomenal force of her will, that cracks – and death itself – might yield to the power of her unquenchable solicitude . . . 'There is the future to think of,' she warned me – and maybe (I permit myself to think for the first time since I began this narrative) – maybe there is! An infinity of new endings

620

clusters around my head, buzzing like heat-insects . . . 'Let us be married, mister,' she proposed, and moths of excitement stirred in my guts, as if she had spoken some cabbalistic formula, some awesome abracadabra, and released me from my fate – but reality is nagging at me. Love does not conquer all, except in the Bombay talkies; rip tear crunch will not be defeated by a mere ceremony; and optimism is a disease.

'On your birthday, how about?' she is suggesting. 'At thirty-one, a man is a man, and is supposed to have a wife.'

How am I to tell her? How can I say, there are other plans for that day, I am have always been in the grip of a form-crazy destiny which enjoys wreaking its havoc on numinous days . . . in short, how am I to tell her about death? I cannot; instead, meekly and with every appearance of gratitude, I accept her proposal. I am, this evening, a man newly affianced; let no one think harshly of me for permitting myself – and my betrothed lotus – this last, vain, inconsequential pleasure.

Padma, by proposing a marriage, revealed her willingness to dismiss everything I've told her about my past as just so much 'fancy talk'; and when I returned to find Picture Singh beaming in the shadow of a railway bridge, it rapidly became clear that the magicians, too, were losing their memories. Somewhere in the many moves of the peripatetic slum, they had mislaid their powers of retention, so that now they had become incapable of judgment, having forgotten everything to which they could compare anything that happened. Even the Emergency was rapidly being consigned to the oblivion of the past, and the magicians concentrated upon the present with the monomania of snails. Nor did they notice that they had changed; they had forgotten that they had ever been otherwise, Communism had seeped out of them and been gulped down by the thirsty, lizard-quick earth; they were beginning to forget their skills in the confusion of hunger, disease, thirst and police harassment which constituted (as usual) the present. To me, however, this change in my old companions seemed nothing short of obscene. Saleem had come through amnesia and been shown the extent of its immorality; in his mind, the past grew daily more vivid while the present (from which knives had disconnected him for ever) seemed colourless, confused, a thing of no consequence; I, who could remember every hair on the heads of jailers and surgeons, was deeply shocked by the magicians' unwillingness to look behind them. 'People are like cats,' I told my son, 'you can't teach them anything.' He looked suitably grave, but held his tongue.

My son Aadam Sinai had, when I rediscovered the phantom colony of the illusionists, lost all traces of the tuberculosis which had afflicted his earliest days. I, naturally, was certain that the disease had vanished with the fall of the Widow; Picture Singh, however, told me that credit for the cure must be given to a certain washerwoman, Durga by name, who had wet-nursed him through his sickness, giving him the daily benefit of her inexhaustibly colossal breasts. 'That Durga, captain,' the old snake-charmer said, his voice betraying the fact that, in his old age, he had fallen victim to the dhoban's serpentine charms, 'What a woman!'

She was a woman whose biceps bulged; whose preternatural breasts unleashed a torrent of milk capable of nourishing regiments; and who, it was rumoured darkly (although I suspect the rumour of being started by herself) had two wombs. She was as full of gossip and tittle-tattle as she was of milk: every day a dozen new stories gushed from her lips. She possessed the boundless energy common to all practitioners of her trade; as she thrashed the life out of shirts and saris on her stone, she seemed to grow in power, as if she were sucking the vigour out of the clothes, which ended up flat, buttonless and beaten to death. She was a monster who forgot each day the moment it ended. It was with the greatest reluctance that I agreed to make her acquaintance; it is with the greatest reluctance that I admit her into these pages. Her name, even before I met her, had the smell of new things; she represented novelty, beginnings, the advent of new stories events complexities, and I was no longer interested in anything new. However, once Pictureji informed me that he intended to marry her, I had no option; I shall deal with her, however, as briefly as accuracy permits.

Briefly, then: Durga the washerwoman was a succubus! A bloodsucker lizard in human form! And her effect on Picture Singh was comparable only to her power over her stone-smashed shirts: in a word, she flattened him. Having once met her, I understood why Picture Singh looked old and forlorn; deprived now of the umbrella of harmony beneath which men and women would gather for advice and shade, he seemed to be shrinking daily; the possibility of his becoming a second Hummingbird was vanishing before my very eyes. Durga, however, flourished: her gossip grew more scatological, her voice louder and more raucous, until at last she reminded me of Reverend Mother in her later years, when she expanded and my grandfather shrank. This nostalgic echo of my grandparents was the only thing of interest to me in the personality of the hoydenish washerwoman.

But there is no denying the bounty of her mammary glands: Aadam, at twenty-one months, was still suckling contentedly at her nipples. At first I thought of insisting that he be weaned, but then remembered that my son did exactly and only what he wished, and decided not to press the point. (And, as it transpired, I was right not to do so.) As for her supposed double womb, I had no desire to know the truth or otherwise of the story, and made no inquiries.

I mention Durga the dhoban chiefly because it was she who, one evening when we were eating a meal composed of twenty-seven grains of rice apiece, first foretold my death. I, exasperated by her constant stream of news and chit-chat, had exclaimed, 'Durga Bibi, nobody is interested in your stories!' To which she, unperturbed, 'Saleem Baba, I have been good with you because Pictureji says you must be in many pieces after your arrest; but, to speak frankly, you do not appear to be concerned with anything except lounging about nowadays. You should understand that when a man loses interest in new matters, he is opening the door for the Black Angel.'

And although Picture Singh said, mildly, 'Come now, capteena, don't be rough on the boy,' the arrow of Durga the dhoban found its mark.

In the exhaustion of my drained return, I felt the emptiness of the days coating me in a thick gelatinous film; and although Durga offered, the next morning, and perhaps in a spirit of genuine remorse for her harsh words, to restore my strength by letting me suckle her left breast while my son pulled on the right, 'and afterwards maybe you'll start thinking straight again', intimations of mortality began to occupy most of my thoughts; and then I discovered the mirror of humility at the Shadipur bus depot, and became convinced of my approaching demise.

It was an angled mirror above the entrance to the bus garage; I, wandering aimlessly in the forecourt of the depot, found my attention caught by its winking reflections of the sun. I realized that I had not seen myself in a mirror for months, perhaps years, and walked across to stand beneath it. Looking upwards into the mirror, I saw myself transformed into a big-headed, top-heavy dwarf; in the humblingly foreshortened reflection of myself I saw that the hair on my head was now as grey as rainclouds; the dwarf in the mirror, with his lined face and tired eyes, reminded me vividly of my grandfather Aadam Aziz on the day he told us about seeing God. In those days the afflictions cured by Parvati-the-witch had all (in the aftermath of drainage) returned to plague me; nine-fingered, horn-templed, monk's-tonsured, stain-faced, bow-legged, cucumber-nosed, castrated, and now prematurely aged, I saw in the mirror of humility a human being to whom history could do no more, a grotesque creature who had been released from the pre-ordained destiny which had battered him until he was half-senseless; with one good ear and one bad ear I heard the soft footfalls of the Black Angel of death.

The young-old face of the dwarf in the mirror wore an expression of profound relief.

I'm becoming gloomy; let's change the subject . . . Exactly twenty-four hours before a paan-wallah's taunt provoked Picture Singh into travelling to Bombay, my son Aadam Sinai made the decision which permitted us to accompany the snake-charmer on his journey: overnight, without any warning, and to the consternation of his washerwoman wet-nurse, who was obliged to decant her remaining milk into five-litre vanaspati drums, flat-eared Aadam weaned himself, soundlessly refusing the nipple and demanding (without words) a diet of solid foods: pulped rice overboiled lentils biscuits. It was as though he had decided to permit me to reach my private, and now-very-near, finishing line.

Mute autocracy of a less-than-two-year-old infant: Aadam did not tell us when he was hungry or sleepy or anxious to perform his natural functions. He expected us to know. The perpetual attention he required may be one of the reasons why I managed, in spite of all indications to the contrary, to stay alive . . . incapable of anything else in those days after my release from captivity, I concentrated on watching my son. 'I tell you, captain, it's lucky you came back,' Picture Singh joked, 'otherwise this one would have turned us all into ayahs.' I understood once again that Aadam was a member of a second generation of magical children who would grow up far tougher than the first, not looking for their fate in prophecy or the stars, but forging it in the implacable furnaces of their wills. Looking into the eyes of the child who was simultaneously not-my-son and also more my heir than any child of my flesh could have been, I found in his empty, limpid pupils a second mirror of humility, which showed me that, from now on, mine would be as peripheral a role as that of any redundant oldster: the traditional function, perhaps, of reminiscer, of teller-of-tales . . . I wondered if all over the country the bastard sons of Shiva were exerting similar tyrannies upon hapless adults, and envisaged for the second time that tribe of fearsomely potent kiddies, growing waiting listening, rehearsing the moment when the world would become their plaything. (How these children may, in the future, be identified: their bimbis stick out instead of in.)

But it's time to get things moving: a taunt, a last railway-train heading south south south, a final battle . . . on the day following the weaning of Aadam, Saleem accompanied Picture Singh to Connaught Place, to assist him in his snake-charming. Durga the dhoban agreed to take my son with her to the dhobi-ghat: Aadam spent the day observing how power was thrashed out of the clothes of the well-to-do and absorbed by the succubus-woman. On that fateful day, when the warm weather was returning to the city like a swarm of bees, I was consumed by nostalgia for my bulldozed silver spittoon. Picture Singh had provided me with a spittoon-surrogate, an empty Dalda Vanaspati can, but although I used this to entertain my son with my expertise in the gentle art of spittoon-hittery, sending long jets of betel-juice across the grimy air of the magicians' colony, I was not consoled. A question: why such grief over a mere receptacle of juices? My reply is that you should never underestimate a spittoon. Elegant in the salon of the Rani of Cooch Naheen, it permitted intellectuals to practise the art-forms of the masses; gleaming in a cellar, it transformed Nadir Khan's underworld into a second Taj Mahal; gathering dust in an old tin trunk, it was nevertheless present throughout my history, covertly assimilating incidents in washing-chests, ghost-visions, freeze-unfreeze, drainage, exiles; falling from the sky like a piece of the moon, it perpetrated a transformation. O talismanic spittoon! O beauteous lost receptacle of memories as well as spittle-juice! What sensitive person could fail to sympathize with me in my nostalgic agony at its loss?

. . . Beside me at the back of a bus bulging with humanity, Picture Singh sat with snake-baskets coiled innocently on his lap. As we rattled and banged through that city which was also filled with the resurgent ghosts of earlier, mythological Delhis, the Most Charming Man In The World wore an air of faded despondency, as if a battle in a distant darkroom were already over . . . until my return, nobody had understood that Pictureji's real and unvoiced fear was that he was growing old, that his powers were dimming, that he would soon be adrift and incompetent in a world he did not understand: like me, Picture Singh clung to the presence of Baby Aadam as if the child were a torch in a long dark tunnel. 'A fine child, captain,' he told me, 'a child of dignity: you hardly notice his ears.'

That day, however, my son was not with us.

New Delhi smells assailed me in Connaught Place – the biscuity perfume of the J. B. Mangharam advertisement, the mournful chalkiness of crumbling plaster; and there was also the tragic spoor of the auto-rickshaw drivers, starved into fatalism by rising petrol costs; and green-grass-smells from the circular park in the middle of the whirling traffic, mingled with the fragrance of con-men persuading foreigners to change money on the black market in shadowy archways. From the India Coffee House, under whose marquees could be heard the endless babbling of gossips, there came the less pleasant aroma of new stories beginning: intrigues marriages quarrels, whose smells were all mixed up with those of tea and chilli-pakoras. What I smelled in Connaught Place: the begging nearby presence of a scar-faced girl who had once been Sundari-the-too-beautiful; and loss-of-memory, and turning-towards-the-future, and nothing-really-changes . . .

turning away from these olfactory intimations, I concentrated on the all-pervasive and simpler odours of (human) urine and animal dung.

Underneath the colonnade of Block F in Connaught Place, next to a pavement bookstall, a paan-wallah had his little niche. He sat cross-legged behind a green glass counter like a minor deity of the place: I admit him into these last pages because, although he gave off the aromas of poverty, he was, in fact, a person of substance, the owner of a Lincoln Continental motor-car, which he parked out of sight in Connaught Circus, and which he had paid for by the fortunes he earned through his sales of contraband imported cigarettes and transistor radios; for two weeks each year he went to jail for a holiday, and the rest of the time paid several policemen a handsome salary. In jail he was treated like a king, but behind his green glass counter he looked inoffensive, ordinary, so that it was not easy (without the benefit of a nose as sensitive as Saleem's) to tell that this was a man who knew everything about everything, a man whose infinite network of contacts made him privy to secret knowledge . . . to me he provided an additional and not unpleasant echo of a similar character I had known in Karachi during the time of my Lambretta voyages; I was so busy inhaling the familiar perfumes of nostalgia that, when he spoke, he took me by surprise.

We had set up our act next to his niche; while Pictureji busied himself polishing flutes and donning an enormous saffron turban, I performed the function of barker. 'Roll up roll up – once in a lifetime an opportunity such as this – ladees, ladahs, come see come see come see! Who is here? No common bhangi; no street-sleeping fraud; this, citizens, ladies and gents, is the Most Charming Man In The World! Yes, come see come see: his photo has been taken by Eastman-Kodak Limited! Come close and have no fear – PICTURE SINGH is here!' . . . And other such garbage; but then the paan-wallah spoke:

'I know of a better act. This fellow is not number-one; oh, no, certainly not. In Bombay there is a better man.'

That was how Picture Singh learned of the existence of his rival; and why, abandoning all plans of giving a performance, he marched over to the blandly smiling paan-wallah, reaching into his depths for his old voice of command, and said, 'You will tell me the truth about this faker, captain, or I will send your teeth down your gullet until they bite up your stomach.' And the paan-wallah, unafraid, aware of the three lurking policemen who would move in swiftly to protect their salaries if the need arose, whispered to us the secrets of his omniscience, telling us who when where, until Picture Singh said in a voice whose firmness concealed his fear: 'I will go and show this Bombay fellow who is best. In one world, captains, there is no room for two Most Charming Men.'

The vendor of betel-nut delicacies, shrugging delicately, expectorated at our feet.

Like a magic spell, the taunts of a paan-wallah opened the door through which Saleem returned to the city of his birth, the abode of his deepest nostalgia. Yes, it was an open-sesame, and when we returned to the ragged tents beneath the railway bridge, Picture Singh scrabbled in the earth and dug up the knotted handkerchief of his security, the dirt-discoloured cloth in which he had hoarded pennies for his old age; and when Durga the washerwoman refused to accompany him, saying, 'What do you think, Pictureji, I am a crorepati rich woman that I can take holidays and what-all?', he turned to me with something very like supplication in his eyes and asked me to accompany him, so that he did not have to go into his worst battle, the test of his old age, without a friend . . . yes, and Aadam heard it too, with his flapping ears he heard the rhythm of the magic, I saw his eyes light up as I accepted, and then we were in a third-class railway carriage heading south south south, and in the quinquesyllabic monotony of the wheels I heard the secret word: abracadabra abracadabra abracadabra sang the wheels as they bore us back-to-Bom.

Yes, I had left the colony of the magicians behind me for ever, I was heading abracadabra abracadabra into the heart of a nostalgia which would keep me alive long enough to write these pages (and to create a corresponding number of pickles); Aadam and Saleem and Picture Singh squeezed into a third-class carriage, taking with us a number of baskets tied up with string, baskets which alarmed the jam-packed humanity in the carriage by hissing continually, so that the crowds pushed back back back, away from the menace of the snakes, and allowed us a measure of comfort and space; while the wheels sang their abracadabras to Aadam's flapping ears.

As we travelled to Bombay, the pessimism of Picture Singh expanded until it seemed that it had become a physical entity which merely looked like the old snake-charmer. At Mathura an American youth with pustular chin and a head shaved bald as an egg got into our carriage amid the cacophony of hawkers selling earthen animals and cups of chaloo-chai; he was fanning himself with a peacock-feather fan, and the bad luck of peacock feathers depressed Picture Singh beyond imagining. While the infinite flatness of the Indo-Gangetic plain unfolded outside the window, sending the hot insanity of the afternoon loo-wind to torment us, the shaven American lectured to occupants of the carriage on the intricacies of Hinduism and began to teach them mantras while extending a walnut begging bowl; Picture Singh was blind to this remarkable spectacle and also deaf to the abracadabra of the wheels. 'It is no good, captain,' he confided mournfully, 'this Bombay fellow will be young and strong, and I am doomed to be only the second most charming man from now on.' By the time we reached Kotah Station, the odours of misfortune exuded by the peacock-feather fan had possessed Pictureji utterly, had eroded him so alarmingly that although everyone in the carriage was getting out on the side farthest from the platform to urinate against the side of the train, he showed no sign of needing to go. By Ratlam Junction, while my excitement was mounting, he had fallen into a trance which was not sleep but the rising paralysis of the pessimism. 'At this rate,' I thought, 'he won't even be able to challenge this rival.' Baroda passed: no change. At Surat, the old John Company depot, I realized I'd have to do something soon, because abracadabra was bringing us closer to Bombay Central by the minute, and so at last I picked up Picture Singh's old wooden flute, and by playing it with such terrible ineptitude that all the snakes writhed in agony and petrified the American youth into silence, by producing a noise so hellish that nobody noticed the passing of Bassein Road, Kurla, Mahim, I overcame the miasma of the peacock-feathers; at last Picture Singh shook himself out of his despondency with a faint grin and said, 'Better you stop, captain, and let me play that thing; otherwise some people are sure to die of pain.'

Serpents subsided in their baskets; and then the wheels stopped singing, and we were there:

Bombay! I hugged Aadam fiercely, and was unable to resist uttering an ancient cry: 'Back-to-Bom!' I cheered, to the bewilderment of the American youth, who had never heard this mantra: and again, and again, and again: 'Back! Back-to-Bom!'

By bus down Bellasis Road, towards the Tardeo round-about, we travelled past Parsees with sunken eyes, past bicycle-repair shops and Irani cafés; and then Hornby Vellard was on our right – where promenaders watched as Sherri the mongrel bitch was left to spill her guts! Where cardboard effigies of wrestlers still towered above the entrances to Vallabhbhai Patel Stadium! – and we were rattling and banging past traffic-cops with sun-umbrellas, past Mahalaxmi temple – and then Warden Road! The Breach

Candy Swimming Baths! And there, look, the shops . . . but the names had changed: where was Reader's Paradise with its stacks of Superman comics? Where, the Band Box Laundry and Bombelli's, with their One Yard Of Chocolates? And, my God, look, atop a two-storey hillock where once the palaces of William Methwold stood wreathed in bougainvillaea and stared proudly out to sea . . . look at it, a great pink monster of a building, the roseate skyscraper obelisk of the Narlikar women, standing over and obliterating the circus-ring of childhood . . . yes, it was my Bombay, but also not-mine, because we reached Kemp's Corner to find the hoardings of Air-India's little rajah and of the Kolynos Kid gone, gone for good, and Thomas Kemp and Co. itself had vanished into thin air . . . flyovers crisscrossed where, once upon a time, medicines were dispensed and a pixie in a chlorophyll cap beamed down upon the traffic. Elegiacally, I murmured under my breath: 'Keep Teeth Kleen and Keep Teeth Brite! Keep Teeth Kolynos Super White!' But despite my incantation, the past failed to reappear; we rattled on down Gibbs Road and dismounted near Chowpatty Beach.

Chowpatty, at least, was much the same: a dirty strip of sand aswarm with pickpockets, and strollers, and vendors of hot-channa-channa-hot, of kulfi and bhel-puri and chutter-mutter; but further down Marine Drive I saw what tetrapods had achieved. On land reclaimed by the Narlikar consortium from the sea, vast monsters soared upwards to the sky, bearing strange alien names: OBEROI-SHERATON screamed at me from afar. And where was the neon Jeep sign? . . . 'Come on, Pictureji,' I said at length, hugging Aadam to my chest, 'Let's go where we're going and be done with it; the city has been changed.'

What can I say about the Midnite-Confidential Club? That its location is underground, secret (although known to omniscient paan-wallahs); its door, unmarked; its clientèle,

632

the cream of Bombay society. What else? Ah, yes: managed by one Anand 'Andy' Shroff, businessman-playboy, who is to be found on most days tanning himself at the Sun 'n' Sand Hotel on Juhu Beach, amid film-stars and disenfranchised princesses. I ask you: an Indian, sun-bathing? But apparently it's quite normal, the international rules of playboydom must be obeyed to the letter, including, I suppose, the one stipulating daily worshipping of the sun.

How innocent I am (and I used to think that Sonny, forceped-dented, was the simple one!) – I never suspected that places like the Midnite-Confidential existed! But of course they do; and clutching flutes and snake-baskets, the three of us knocked on its doors.

Movements visible through a small iron eye-level grille: a low mellifluous female voice asked us to state our business. Picture Singh announced: 'I am the Most Charming Man In The World. You are employing here one other snake-charmer as cabaret; I will challenge him and prove my superiority. For this I do not ask to be paid. It is, capteena, a question of honour.'

It was evening; Mr Anand 'Andy' Shroff was, by good fortune, on the premises. And, to cut a long story short, Picture Singh's challenge was accepted, and we entered that place whose name had already unnerved me somewhat, because it contained the word *midnight,* and because its initials had once concealed my own, secret world: M.C.C., which stands for Metro Cub Club, once also stood for the Midnight Children's Conference, and had now been usurped by the secret nightspot. In a word: I felt invaded.

Twin problems of the city's sophisticated, cosmopolitan youth: how to consume alcohol in a dry state; and how to romance girls in the best Western tradition, by taking them out to paint the town red, while at the same time preserving total secrecy, to avoid the very Oriental shame of a scandal? The Midnite-Confidential was Mr Shroff's solution to the agonizing difficulties of the city's gilded youth. In that underground of licentiousness, he had created a world of Stygian darkness, black as hell; in the secrecy of midnight darkness, the city's lovers met, drank imported liquor, and romanced; cocooned in the isolating, artificial night, they canoodled with impunity. Hell is other people's fantasies: every saga requires at least one descent into Jahannum, and I followed Picture Singh into the inky negritude of the Club, holding an infant son in my arms.

We were led down a lush black carpet – midnight-black, black as lies, crow-black, anger-black, the black of 'hai-yo, black man!'; in short, a dark rug – by a female attendant of ravishing sexual charms, who wore her sari erotically low on her hips, with a jasmine in her navel; but as we descended into the darkness, she turned towards us with a reassuring smile, and I saw that her eyes were closed; unearthly luminous eyes had been painted on her lids. I could not help but ask, 'Why . . .' To which she, simply: 'I am blind; and besides, nobody who comes here wants to be seen. Here you are in a world without faces or names; here people have no memories, families or past; here is for *now*, for nothing except right now.'

And the darkness engulfed us; she guided us through that nightmare pit in which light was kept in shackles and bar-fetters, that place outside time, that negation of history . . . 'Sit here,' she said, 'The other snake-man will come soon. When it is time, one light will shine on you; then begin your contest.'

We sat there for – what? minutes, hours, weeks? – and there were the glowing eyes of blind women leading invisible guests to their seats; and gradually, in the dark, I became aware of being surrounded by soft, amorous susurrations, like the couplings of velvet mice; I heard the chink of glasses held by twined arms, and gentle brushings of lips; with one good ear and one bad ear, I heard the sound of illicit sexuality filling the midnight air . . . but no, I did not want to know what was happening; although my nose was able to smell, in the susurrating silence of the Club, all manner of new stories and beginnings, of exotic and forbidden loves, and little invisible contretemps and who-was-going-too-far, in fact all sorts of juicy titbits, I chose to ignore them all, because this was a new world in which I had no place. My son, Aadam, however, sat beside me with ears burning with fascination; his eyes shone in the darkness as he listened, and memorized, and learned . . . and then there was light.

A single shaft of light spilled into a pool on the floor of the Midnight-Confidential Club. From the shadows beyond the fringe of the illuminated area, Aadam and I saw Picture Singh sitting stiffly, cross-legged, next to a handsome Brylcreemed youth; each of them was surrounded by musical instruments and the closed baskets of their art. A loudspeaker announced the beginning of that legendary contest for the title of Most Charming Man In The World; but who was listening? Did anyone even pay attention, or were they too busy with lips tongues hands? This was the name of Pictureji's opponent: the Maharaja of Cooch Naheen.

(I don't know: it's easy to assume a title. But perhaps, perhaps he really was the grandson of that old Rani who had once, long ago, been a friend of Doctor Aziz; perhaps the heir to the supporter-of-the-Hummingbird was pitted, ironically, against the man who might have been the second Mian Abdullah! It's always possible; many maharajas have been poor since the Widow revoked their civil-list salaries.)

How long, in that sunless cavern, did they struggle? Months, years, centuries? I cannot say: I watched, mesmerized, as they strove to outdo one another, charming every kind of snake imaginable, asking for rare varieties to be sent from the Bombay snake-farm (where once Doctor Schaapsteker . . .); and the Maharaja matched Picture Singh snake for snake, succeeding even in charming constrictors, which only Pictureji had previously managed to do. In that infernal Club whose darkness was another aspect of its proprietor's obsession with the colour black (under whose influence he tanned his skin darker darker every day at the Sun 'n' Sand), the two virtuosi goaded snakes into impossible feats, making them tie themselves in knots, or bows, or persuading them to drink water from wine-glasses, and to jump through fiery hoops . . . defying fatigue, hunger and age, Picture Singh was putting on the show of his life (but was anyone looking? Anyone at all?) – and at last it became clear that the younger man was tiring first; his snakes ceased to dance in time to his flute; and finally, through a piece of sleight-of-hand so fast that I did not see what happened, Picture Singh managed to knot a king cobra around the Maharaja's neck.

What Picture said: 'Give me best, captain, or I'll tell it to bite.'

That was the end of the contest. The humiliated princeling left the Club and was later reported to have shot himself in a taxi. And on the floor of his last great battle, Picture Singh collapsed like a falling banyan tree . . . blind attendants (to one of whom I entrusted Aadam) helped me carry him from the field.

But the Midnight-Confidential had one trick left up its sleeve. Once a night – just to add a little spice – a roving spotlight searched out one of the illicit couples, and revealed them to the hidden eyes of their fellows: a touch of luminary Russian roulette which, no doubt, made life more thrilling for the city's young cosmopolitans . . . and who was the chosen victim that night? Who, horn-templed stain-faced cucumber-nosed, was drowned in scandalous light? Who, made as blind as female attendants by the voyeurism of light-bulbs, almost dropped the legs of his unconscious friend?

Saleem returned to the city of his birth to stand illuminated in a cellar while Bombayites tittered at him from the dark.

Quickly now, because we have come to the end of incidents, I record that, in a back room in which light was permitted, Picture Singh recovered from his fainting fit; and while Aadam slept soundly, one of the blind waitresses brought us a congratulatory, reviving meal. On the thali of victory: samosas, pakoras, rice, dal, puris; and green chutney. Yes, a little aluminium bowl of chutney, green, my God, green as grasshoppers . . . and before long a puri was in my hand; and chutney was on the puri; and then I had tasted it, and almost imitated the fainting act of Picture Singh, because it carried me back to a day when I emerged nine-fingered from a hospital and went into exile at the home of Hanif Aziz, and was given the best chutney in the world . . . the taste of the chutney was more than just an echo of that long-ago taste – it was the old taste itself, the very same, with the power of bringing back the past as if it had never been away . . . in frenzy of excitement, I grabbed the blind waitress by the arm; scarcely able to contain myself, I blurted out: 'The chutney! Who made it?' I must have shouted, because Picture, 'Quiet, captain, you'll wake the boy . . . and what's the matter? You look like you saw your worst enemy's ghost!' And the blind waitress, a little coldly: 'You don't like the chutney?' I had to hold back an almighty bellow. 'I like it,' I said in a voice caged in bars of steel, 'I *like* it – now will you tell me where it's from?' And she, alarmed, anxious to get away: 'It's Braganza Pickle; best in Bombay, everyone knows.'

I made her bring me the jar; and there, on the label, was the address: of a building with a winking, saffron-and-green neon goddess over the gate, a factory watched over by neon Mumbadevi, while local trains went yellow-and-browning past: Braganza Pickles (Private) Ltd, in the sprawling north of the town.

Once again an abracadabra, an open-sesame: words printed on a chutney-jar, opening the last door of my life . . .

I was seized by an irresistible determination to track down the maker of that impossible chutney of memory, and said, 'Pictureji, I must go . . .'

I do not know the end of the story of Picture Singh; he refused to accompany me on my quest, and I saw in his eyes that the efforts of his struggle had broken something inside him, that his victory was, in fact, a defeat; but whether he is still in Bombay (perhaps working for Mr Shroff), or back with his washer-woman; whether he is still alive or not, I am not able to say . . . 'How can I leave you?' I asked, desperately, but he replied, 'Don't be a fool, captain; you have something you must do, then there is nothing to do but do it. Go, go, what do I want with you? Like old Resham told you: go, go quickly, go!' Taking Aadam with me, I went.

Journey's end: from the underworld of the blind waitresses, I walked north north north, holding my son in my arms; and came at last to where flies are gobbled by lizards, and vats bubble, and strong-armed women tell bawdy jokes; to this world of sharp-lipped overseers with conical breasts, and the all-pervasive clank of pickle-jars from the bottling-plant . . . and who, at the end of my road, planted herself in front of me, arms akimbo, hair glistening with perspiration on the forearms? Who, direct as ever, demanded, 'You, mister: what you want?'

'Me!' Padma is yelling, excited and a little embarrassed by the memory. 'Of course, who else? Me me me!'

'Good afternoon, Begum,' I said. (Padma interjects: 'O you – always so polite and all!') 'Good afternoon; may I speak to the manager?'

O grim, defensive, obstinate Padma! 'Not possible, Manager Begum is busy. You must make appointment, come back later, so please go away just now.'

Listen: I would have stayed, persuaded, bullied, even used force to get past my Padma's arms; but there was a cry from

638

the catwalk – this catwalk, Padma, outside the offices! – the catwalk from which someone whom I have not been willing to name until now was looking down, across gigantic pickle-vats and simmering chutneys – someone rushing down clattering metal steps, shrieking at the top of her voice:

'O my God, O my God, O Jesus sweet Jesus, baba, my son, look who's come here, arré baba, don't you see me, look how thin you got, come, come, let me kiss you, let me give you cake!'

Just as I had guessed, the Manager Begum of Braganza Pickles (Private) Ltd, who called herself Mrs Braganza, was of course my erstwhile ayah, the criminal of midnight, Miss Mary Pereira, the only mother I had left in the world.

Midnight, or thereabouts. A man carrying a folded (and intact) black umbrella walks towards my window from the direction of the railway tracks, stops, squats, shits. Then sees me silhouetted against light and, instead of taking offence at my voyeurism, calls: 'Watch this!' and proceeds to extrude the longest turd I have ever seen. 'Fifteen inches!' he calls, 'How long can you make yours?' Once, when I was more energetic, I would have wanted to tell his life-story; the hour, and his possession of an umbrella, would have been all the connections I needed to begin the process of weaving him into my life, and I have no doubt that I'd have finished by proving his indispensability to anyone who wishes to understand my life and benighted times; but now I'm disconnected, unplugged, with only epitaphs left to write. So, waving at the champion defecator, I call back: 'Seven on a good day,' and forget him.

Tomorrow. Or the day after. The cracks will be waiting for August 15th. There is still a little time: I'll finish tomorrow.

Today I gave myself the day off and visited Mary. A long hot dusty bus-ride through streets beginning to bubble with the excitement of the coming Independence Day, although I can smell other, more tarnished perfumes: disillusion, venality, cynicism . . . the nearly-thirty-one-year-old myth of freedom is no longer what it was. New myths are needed; but that's none of my business.

Mary Pereira, who now calls herself Mrs Braganza, lives with her sister Alice, now Mrs Fernandes, in an apartment in the pink obelisk of the Narlikar women on the two-storey hillock where once, in a demolished palace, she slept on a servant's mat. Her bedroom occupies more or less the same cube of air in which a fisherman's pointing finger led a pair of boyish eyes out towards the horizon; in a teak rocking-chair, Mary rocks my son, singing 'Red Sails In The Sunset'. Red dhow-sails spread against the distant sky.

A pleasant enough day, on which old days are recalled. The day when I realized that an old cactus-bed had survived the revolution of the Narlikar women, and borrowing a spade from the mali, dug up a long-buried world: a tin globe containing yellowed ant-eaten jumbo-size baby-snap, credited to Kalidas Gupta, and a Prime Minister's letter. And days further off: for the dozenth time we chatter about the change in Mary Pereira's fortunes. How she owed it all to her dear Alice. Whose poor Mr Fernandes died of colour-blindness, having become confused, in his old Ford Prefect, at one of the city's then-few traffic lights. How Alice visited her in Goa with the news that her employers, the fearsome and enterprising Narlikar women, were willing to put some of their tetrapod-money into a pickle firm. 'I told them, nobody makes achar-chutney like our Mary,' Alice had said, with perfect accuracy, 'because she puts her feelings inside them.' So Alice turned out to be a good girl in the end. And baba, what do you think, how could I believe the whole world would want to eat my poor pickles, even in England they eat. And now, just think, I sit here where your dear house used to be, while God-knows what-all has happened to you, living like a beggar so long, what a world, baapu-ré!

And bitter-sweet lamentations; O, your poor mummy-daddy! That fine madam, dead! And the poor man, never knowing who loved him or how to love! And even the Monkey . . . but I interrupt, no, not dead: no, not true, not dead. Secretly, in a nunnery, eating bread.

Mary, who has stolen the name of poor Queen Catharine who gave these islands to the British, taught me the secrets of the pickling process. (Finishing an education which began in this very air-space when I stood in a kitchen as she stirred guilt into green chutney.) Now she sits at home, retired in her white-haired old-age, once more happy as an ayah with a baby to raise. 'Now you finished your writing-writing, baba, you should take more time for your son.' But Mary, I did it for him. And she, switching the subject, because her mind makes all sorts of flea-jumps these days: 'O baba, baba, look at you, how old you got already!'

Rich Mary, who never-dreamed she would be rich, is still unable to sleep on beds. But drinks sixteen Coca-Colas a day, unworried about teeth, which have all fallen out anyway. A flea-jump: 'Why you getting married so sudden sudden?' Because Padma wants. No, she is not in trouble, how could she, in my condition? 'Okay, baba, I only asked.'

And the day would have wound down peacefully, a twilight day near the end of time, except that now, at last, at the age of three years, one month and two weeks. Aadam Sinai uttered a sound.

'Ab . . .' Arré, O my God, listen, baba, the boy is saying something! And Aadam, very carefully: 'Abba . . .' Father. He is calling me father. But no, he has not finished, there is strain on his face, and finally my son, who will have to be a magician to cope with the world I'm leaving him, completes his awesome first word: '. . . cadabba.'

Abracadabra! But nothing happens, we do not turn into toads, angels do not fly in through the window: the lad is just

641

flexing his muscles. I shall not see his miracles . . . Amid Mary's celebrations of Aadam's achievement, I go back to Padma, and the factory; my son's enigmatic first incursion into language has left a worrying fragrance in my nostrils.

Abracadabra: not an Indian word at all, a cabbalistic formula derived from the name of the supreme god of the Basilidan gnostics, containing the number 365, the number of the days of the year, and of the heavens, and of the spirits emanating from the god Abraxas. 'Who,' I am wondering, not for the first time, 'does the boy imagine he *is*?'

My special blends: I've been saving them up. Symbolic value of the pickling process: all the six hundred million eggs which gave birth to the population of India could fit inside a single, standard-sized pickle-jar; six hundred million spermatozoa could be lifted on a single spoon. Every pickle-jar (you will forgive me if I become florid for a moment) contains, therefore, the most exalted of possibilities: the feasibility of the chutnification of history; the grand hope of the pickling of time! I, however, have pickled chapters. Tonight, by screwing the lid firmly on to a jar bearing the legend *Special Formula No. 30: 'Abracadabra'*, I reach the end of my long-winded autobiography; in words and pickles, I have immortalized my memories, although distortions are inevitable in both methods. We must live, I'm afraid, with the shadows of imperfection.

These days, I manage the factory for Mary. Alice – 'Mrs Fernandes' – controls the finances; my responsibility is for the creative aspects of our work. (Of course I have forgiven Mary her crime; I need mothers as well as fathers, and a mother is beyond blame.) Amid the wholly-female workforce of Braganza Pickles, beneath the saffron-and-green winking of neon Mumbadevi, I choose mangoes tomatoes limes from the women who come at dawn with baskets on their heads. Mary, with her ancient hatred of 'the mens', admits no males

642

except myself into her new, comfortable universe . . . myself, and of course my son. Alice, I suspect, still has her little liaisons; and Padma fell for me from the first, seeing in me an outlet for her vast reservoir of pent-up solicitude; I cannot answer for the rest of them, but the formidable competence of the Narlikar females is reflected, on this factory floor, in the strong-armed dedication of the vat-stirrers.

What is required for chutnification? Raw materials, obviously – fruit, vegetables, fish, vinegar, spices. Daily visits from Koli women with their saris hitched up between their legs. Cucumbers aubergines mint. But also: eyes, blue as ice, which are undeceived by the superficial blandishments of fruit – which can see corruption beneath citrus-skin; fingers which, with featheriest touch, can probe the secret inconstant hearts of green tomatoes: and above all a nose capable of discerning the hidden languages of what-must-be-pickled, its humours and messages and emotions . . . at Braganza Pickles, I supervise the production of Mary's legendary recipes; but there are also my special blends, in which, thanks to the powers of my drained nasal passages, I am able to include memories, dreams, ideas, so that once they enter mass-production all who consume them will know what pepper-pots achieved in Pakistan, or how it felt to be in the Sundarbans . . . believe don't believe but it's true. Thirty jars stand upon a shelf, waiting to be unleashed upon the amnesiac nation.

(And beside them, one jar stands empty.)

The process of revision should be constant and endless; don't think I'm satisfied with what I've done! Among my unhappinesses: an overly-harsh taste from those jars containing memories of my father; a certain ambiguity in the love-flavour of 'Jamila Singer' (Special Formula No. 22), which might lead the unperceptive to conclude that I've invented the whole story of the baby-swap to justify an incestuous love; vague implausibilities in the jar labelled

'Accident in a washing-chest' – the pickle raises questions which are not fully answered, such as: Why did Saleem need an accident to acquire his powers? Most of the other children didn't . . . Or again, in 'All-India radio' and others, a discordant note in the orchestrated flavours: would Mary's confession have come as a shock to a true telepath? Sometimes, in the pickles' version of history, Saleem appears to have known too little; at other times, too much . . . yes, I should revise and revise, improve and improve; but there is neither the time nor the energy. I am obliged to offer no more than this stubborn sentence: It happened that way because that's how it happened.

There is also the matter of the spice bases. The intricacies of turmeric and cumin, the subtlety of fenugreek, when to use large (and when small) cardamoms; the myriad possible effects of garlic, garam masala, stick cinnamon, coriander, ginger . . . not to mention the flavourful contributions of the occasional speck of dirt. (Saleem is no longer obsessed with purity.) In the spice bases, I reconcile myself to the inevitable distortions of the pickling process. To pickle is to give immortality, after all: fish, vegetables, fruit hang embalmed in spice-and-vinegar; a certain alteration, a slight intensification of taste, is a small matter, surely? The art is to change the flavour in degree, but not in kind; and above all (in my thirty jars and a jar) to give it shape and form – that is to say, meaning. (I have mentioned my fear of absurdity.)

One day, perhaps, the world may taste the pickles of history. They may be too strong for some palates, their smell may be overpowering, tears may rise to eyes; I hope nevertheless that it will be possible to say of them that they possess the authentic taste of truth . . . that they are, despite everything, acts of love.

One empty jar . . . how to end? Happily, with Mary in her teak rocking-chair and a son who has begun to speak? Amid recipes, and thirty jars with chapter-headings for names? In melancholy, drowning in memories of Jamila and Parvati and even of Evie Burns? Or with the magic children . . . but then, should I be glad that some escaped, or end in the tragedy of the disintegrating effects of drainage? (Because in drainage lie the origins of the cracks: my hapless, pulverized body, drained above and below, began to crack because it was dried out. Parched, it yielded at last to the effects of a lifetime's battering. And now there is rip tear crunch, and a stench issuing through the fissures, which must be the smell of death. Control: I must retain control as long as possible.)

Or with questions: now that I can, I swear, see the cracks on the backs of my hands, cracks along my hairline and between my toes, why do I not bleed? Am I already so emptied desiccated pickled? Am I already the mummy of myself?

Or dreams: because last night the ghost of Reverend Mother appeared to me, staring down through the hole in a perforated cloud, waiting for my death so that she could weep a monsoon for forty days . . . and I, floating outside my body, looked down on the foreshortened image of myself, and saw a grey-haired dwarf who once, in a mirror, looked relieved.

No, that won't do, I shall have to write the future as I have written the past, to set it down with the absolute certainty of a prophet. But the future cannot be preserved in a jar; one jar must remain empty . . . What cannot be pickled, because it has not taken place, is that I shall reach my birthday, thirty-one today, and no doubt a marriage will take place, and Padma will have henna-tracery on her palms and soles, and also a new name, perhaps Naseem in honour of Reverend Mother's watching ghost, and outside the window there will be fireworks and crowds, because it will be Independence Day and the many-headed multitudes will be in the streets, and Kashmir will be waiting. I will have train-tickets in my pocket, there will be a taxi-cab driven by a country boy who once dreamed, at the Pioneer Café, of film-stardom, we will drive south south south into the heart of the tumultuous crowds, who will be throwing balloons of paint at each other, at the wound-up windows of the cab, as if it were the day of the paint-festival of Holi; and along Hornby Vellard, where a dog was left to die, the crowd, the dense crowd, the crowd without boundaries, growing until it fills the world, will make progress impossible, we will abandon our taxi-cab and the dreams of its driver, on our feet in the thronging crowd, and yes, I will be separated from Padma, my dung-lotus extending an arm towards me across the turbulent sea, until she drowns in the crowd and I am alone in the vastness of the numbers, the numbers marching one two three, I am being buffeted right and left while rip tear crunch reaches its climax, and my body is screaming, it cannot take this kind of treatment any more, but now I see familiar faces in the crowd, they are all here, my grandfather Aadam and his wife Naseem, and Alia and Mustapha and Hanif and Emerald, and Amina who was Mumtaz, and Nadir who became Qasim, and Pia and Zafar who wet his bed and also General Zulfikar, they throng around me pushing shoving crushing, and the cracks are widening, pieces of my body are falling off, there is Jamila who has left her nunnery to be present on this last day, night is falling has fallen, there is a countdown ticktocking to midnight, fireworks and stars, the cardboard cut-outs of wrestlers, and I see that I shall never reach Kashmir, like Jehangir the Mughal Emperor I shall die with Kashmir on my lips, unable to see the valley of delights to which men go to enjoy life or to end it, or both; because now I see other figures in the crowd, the terrifying figure of a war hero with lethal knees, who has found out how I cheated him of his birthright, he is pushing towards me through the crowd which is now wholly composed of familiar faces, there is Rashid the rickshaw boy arm-in-arm with the Rani of Cooch Naheen, and Ayooba Shaheed Farooq with Mutasim the Handsome, and from another direction, the direction of Haji Ali's island tomb, I see a mythological apparition approaching, the Black Angel, except that as it nears me its face is green its eyes are black, a centre-parting in its hair, on the left green and on the right black, its eyes the eyes of Widows; Shiva and the Angel are closing closing, I hear lies being spoken in the night, anything you want to be you kin be, the greatest lie of all, cracking now, fission of Saleem, I am the bomb in Bombay, watch me explode, bones splitting breaking beneath the awful pressure of the crowd, bag of bones falling down down down, just as once at Jallianwala, but Dyer seems not to be present today, no Mercurochrome, only a broken creature spilling pieces of itself into the street, because I have been so-many too-many persons, life unlike syntax allows one more than three, and at last somewhere the striking of a clock, twelve chimes, release.

Yes, they will trample me underfoot, the numbers marching one two three, four hundred million five hundred six, reducing me to specks of voiceless dust, just as, all in good time, they will trample my son who is not my son, and his son who will not be his, and his who will not be his, until the thousand and first generation, until a thousand and one midnights have bestowed their terrible gifts and a thousand and one children have died, because it is the privilege and the curse of midnight's children to be both masters and victims of their times, to forsake privacy and be sucked into the annihilating whirlpool of the multitudes, and to be unable to live or die in peace.

www.vintage-books.co.uk